MW01201976

THE KEEPER CHRONICLES

Morgan,
Enjoy this
otter-worldly
adventure!

COMPLETE TRILOGY
BEN MEEKS

—Ben Meeks

THE KEEPER CHRONICLES: COMPLETE TRILOGY
Copyright © 2022 by Ben Meeks

PETRIFIED, 2nd Edition, Copyright © 2020 by Ben Meeks
BETRAYAL, Copyright © 2020 by Ben Meeks
TORCH'S FATE, Copyright © 2021 by Ben Meeks
TAKEN, Copyright © 2022 by Ben Meeks

All rights reserved.
Sidestreet Publishing, LLC
www.authorbenmeeks.com
ISBN: 978-1-951107-09-3

Cover art © 2020 by Monica Maschke.
All rights reserved.
monicamaschke44@gmail.com

Interior by JW Manus

Torch's Fate
First Publication, *Summer Slasher Horror Anthology,* Vol 1, Springer
Mountain Press, 2021

This collection is a work of fiction. Names, places, and incidents are
either products of the author's imagination or are used fictitiously.

CONTENTS

PETRIFIED

"WHERE'D YOU GET this old beater anyway? It sounds like it's about to fall apart," Holt said.

"That's called character," I said.

"Don't get me wrong, Obie, I'm sure it was a nice truck at some point but it's a little past its prime," he said.

The old Ford groaned and puttered through the curves of the mountain roads, creaking at the joints like an old man straining to get up from his rocking chair. It was true it had seen better days. The paint had faded from a vibrant blue into a more pallid shade accentuated with rusted spots and lines. It still had a kind of style with large rounded wheel wells and a triangular hood that formed an aggressive edge at the front. From the right angle it reminded me of a parrot's face.

"I bought it new in forty-one, they don't make them like this anymore." I patted the dash to let the old girl know Holt was full of it. "Don't listen to him, old girl."

"It's a good thing, too. This thing's a death trap. I mean, did it come with these lap belts or did you put them in yourself? It doesn't even have AC. The high is what, ninety-eight today? We're going to die of a heatstroke before we get there. I'm sweating bullets over here and don't get me started on the choke. You know what else has a choke? A lawnmower. You're driving around an oversized lawnmower that don't even cut grass."

"You'll get used to the heat. You've only been here a few months, it takes time, and show some respect, this truck is older than you are," I said, crossing the center line to cut the curve.

"Exactly. That's my point, and can you keep it in your own lane or does this hunk o' junk just not drive straight?"

"Everyone up here crosses the line at some point or other," I said, returning to my lane.

Holt ran a hand through his black hair, pulling it out of his face. He stared out the window, shaking his head. He must have decided it was a lost cause because when he spoke again it was all business.

"So, what's the plan? We go in and rough him up a bit?" he asked.

"I was planning on talking to him."

A confused expression crossed his face. "What do you mean?"

"You know, spoken words put together into sentences to convey ideas or emotions," I said.

"You think you're just going to show up and say, 'Hey bub, would you please tell me where the demon you've been talking to is hiding', and he's just going to tell you?"

"Why not? It's worth a shot," I said.

"It's stupid."

"What would you do?"

"I don't know." He looked out the window again at the passing trees. "Break some fingers maybe? Whatever I need to do to get what we need to know."

"You can always be mean later, Holt. If I need to break his fingers then I will, but if I can just talk to him then that's better for everyone," I said.

"I guess."

He didn't sound convinced, but he would come around. We hadn't been working together that long, after all. Still it's odd. I am sure Cedric didn't operate like that. I didn't know where this *break fingers first and ask questions later* attitude was coming from. I flipped on the blinker and pulled into the gravel parking lot of the Inclusive Assembly of Christ. The church was a plain, single-story brick building, wholly unremarkable other than the large cross on the outside wall. The parking lot had two cars parked up front. I pulled in line with them, giving me a front row seat to the cross.

"Just stay in the truck. This shouldn't take more than a couple minutes," I said, killing the engine. I gave the outside of the building a quick scan for security cameras, an occupational habit.

"Why don't you stay here, and I'll go. I bet I could have him spilling his guts in two minutes."

"That's what I'm afraid of, another mess to clean up," I said. "That reminds me, maybe you could do some dishes when we get back? Think about it."

I got out, giving the area one last look, while Holt scowled in the passenger seat.

"Hey, why don't you leave it running so I can use the AC," he mocked.

I ignored him and walked inside through a pair of plain glass doors. The entryway was more elaborate than the plain exterior suggested. It had tile floor with fake flowers, pictures, and crosses covering every available surface. I sniffed the air, specifically looking for the sulfuric smell of demons. Instead of the demon stink, it smelled like a library, full of old knowledge.

An open door to my right had a sign that read Steve Heck, Pastor. Inside, a man thumbed through papers at a large wooden desk. I knocked on the doorframe to get his attention. He was short and pudgy around the edges, sporting a button-up shirt and graying hair.

"Hey, I'm Obie. I talked to you on the phone," I said, leaning into the room.

"Sure, come on in," the man said, sparing only a glance up before returning to his papers.

I walked in, closing the door behind me. The room was a large rectangle and the desk's position on the far side left a good twenty-five feet between us and only accentuated how much wasted space there was. Bookcases, pictures, and Christian paraphernalia covered the room, with a spare pew resting against the left wall beside another door. He stayed focused on his papers as I approached.

He looked up when I arrived, eyeballing my Han Shot First shirt, and extending his hand without getting up. "Steve Heck, Pastor."

"Nice to meet you." His hand was limp and clammy, like shaking a dead squid. He smelled like spearmint gum and old cheese, with a hint of rotting garbage underneath.

This meeting was probably a waste of time, like Holt thought, but still I had to try. I sat in a chair in front of his desk, taking a moment to scratch the stubble on my face. My hair and nails grew quickly, quickly enough to make any kind of style more trouble than it was worth. My look could vary anywhere from clean shaven to full beard with a dirty blond mop on top of my head. Judging from the length of growth it was getting closer to the mop persuasion and time to cut it all off. The chair was a plain, boxy thing with lopsided padding that made me squirm to get comfortable. Not the first time that being in church had made me squirm.

"What can I do for you, Obie?"

"I've been following what you have been posting about demons," I said.

He leaned back in his chair, focusing on me instead of the paperwork. The light coming through the window to my right reflected off his head. A shadow passed in front of the window and all I could think was Holt had gotten out of the truck.

"It has been attracting a lot of attention lately," he said. "Let me guess, you are here to tell me that demons don't exist and I've lost my marbles. Well, Obie, putting the biblical support for them aside for a minute, I have seen them, and I assure you they are quite real."

"Yeah, I know."

He perked up at my validation. "So, you believe me?"

"Of course, Steve," I said, shaking my head. "I've had the pleasure of their company on multiple occasions."

"If you are familiar with them then you understand how misunderstood they are," he said.

"Yes, people have all kinds of misconceptions about them." I hoped the subtlety of my statement wasn't lost on him.

"That's great! I would love to meet some of them that you know. Do you think they would be interested in a personal relationship with Jesus Christ?"

"I don't think so," I said, shifting my weight to the other side of the chair. It wasn't any better. "From what I have been reading from your blog, it sounds like we have had very different experiences. In fact, I would suggest that you reconsider trying to convert them."

Steve tapped his fingers on the arm of his chair. "God loves all His children and as He created all of us, what people call demons included, they deserve a chance at salvation."

"I'm not here to question your conviction," I said.

"Then why are you here?"

I shifted my weight back to my left side. "You've mentioned a specific demon you refer to as P.V.T. and I was hoping you would tell me how I can find him."

"Her," he said.

"What?"

"P.V.T. is a her, not a him. She explained to me how once word got out people would come looking for her and that they would hurt or kill me to get what they want. You understand if I'm cautious."

"I'd be suspicious if you weren't," I said.

"So why do you want to find her?"

"It's my job," I said.

"Your job? Are you with the two guys that came by last week?" he asked.

"I'm not sure what you're talking about. I have another person that helps me out, but that's it," I said, wondering what trouble Holt was getting into.

"Then who do you work for?" he asked.

The clicking of high heels on the tile outside caught my attention. I started to wonder if this P.V.T. could be in the building. He did say it was a she. But I would have smelled it and demons don't generally wear heels. Probably just a secretary. Steve was oblivious to the sound of course, as the clicking would be out of earshot for a human. I wasn't your average human. Hell, I wasn't human at all, not anymore.

"An interested third party," I answered.

"What would you do if you find her?" he asked.

"I just need to make sure that she isn't a threat," I said. Telling him that I already knew she was a threat and I planned on jumping ahead to the eliminating the threat part of things wasn't going to get me what I wanted.

He thought about it for a minute before answering. "I can talk to her about it and see if she would meet with you."

"Why don't you tell me how to find her and I'll save you the trouble," I said. "You clearly have a lot of important work to do here."

"I can't do that. I am responsible for protecting my congregation so I'd have to be sure you wouldn't hurt her. You understand how people have judged them because of the way they look. I admit they can be hard to get used to but . . ."

"It's not safe for you to be playing with demons. You don't know them like I do," I said.

He paused, stunned at the abruptness of my statement, and then continued. "'Go ye therefore, and teach all nations, baptizing them in the name of the Father, and of the Son, and of the Holy Ghost.' Matthew 28:19."

Why is it whenever people start quoting scripture I feel like my face is melting into my shoes? "I understand what you're trying to do, but the path you are on will get you killed. If there's one thing I know, it's demons. There's plenty to do for your own kind, this world is sick enough. Why not spend a long meaningful life making it a better place for the people around you?"

"Are you threatening me?" he asked.

"I'm trying to save you," I said.

"And if you can't save me?"

"Then I have to stop you."

He clearly took this personally, leaning forward with a sneer. "How would you stop me? Would you kill me?"

"I'd rather not, but even if I don't, someone or something else will. Your days are numbered on the road you're on," I said. "That's not a threat, it's just a fact."

He pointed toward the ceiling. "I have to stick to my conviction and trust in Him."

This was pointless. "Listen, Steve—"

"Pastor Heck."

"Sure, Steve, if you don't want to tell me that's your business, but if you don't let me help this is going to end real bad for you. It may not seem like it but I'm the only friend you've got in all this," I said.

"I appreciate your concern, but I'm afraid I have another appointment in a few minutes that I need to prepare for," he said, picking up his pen and returning to his papers. "I trust you can find the way out on your own."

I sat there for a few seconds trying to think of what I could say to change his mind. I couldn't come up with anything and I didn't want to start breaking fingers so I stood up to leave. "Thanks for your time. I'll be in touch."

"With all due respect, I would rather you didn't come by again," he said, not looking up.

I turned and headed for the door. I had to get to the bottom of this and nothing was going to come from Steve right now. I would just have to pay him a visit at home to get some answers. We could have a more private conversation there. A sigh of frustration escaped my lips when I made it outside and found the truck empty. Tracking on gravel can be tough but Holt's scent was still strong. I picked up another familiar scent underneath his: noxious sulfur. There was a demon about. I followed the scents into the woods to the right of the church, into an overgrown graveyard. Holt stood close to the center, looking around the tombstones.

I walked cautiously to where a wooden fence had once enclosed the graveyard. It had long since fallen down, with only a hint of the decaying wood left behind. "What is it?" I whispered.

"Not sure. I didn't get a good look at it, something small and fast. What happened to these graves? I think the bodies are gone," he said moving from one grave to the next.

I stepped over the remains of the fence for a closer look. The ground in front of each headstone was an open crater, they had all been dug up. The tombstone closest to me was dated 1979. Some of them dated much farther back. The people in the older graves would have been buried in a shroud or a wooden box, nothing that would still be around. This grave was more modern with a large metal casket lying open. The skeleton had been disturbed. I could see pieces of bones, some fragments and some whole, tossed haphazardly around the grave. Whatever did this definitely removed a few choice bones.

"Over here," Holt said from the far side of the graveyard. "You've got to see this."

I walked over to find the answer to the mystery of the missing bones. They had been arranged in a central pile about three feet in diameter with three rows on each side of varying lengths pointing off in different directions. The end of each row came to a point with a bone that had been cut sharp. I knelt for a closer inspection.

"It looks like a weird compass, like you see on old maps," Holt said over my shoulder. "What do you think it is?"

"I don't know, maybe some kind of marker or cantrip? Whatever it is, it's not good," I said. The breeze shifted, blowing against my back, bringing with it a smell akin to rotten eggs. "You smell that?"

"Yep."

I stood and turned to see a small grey face peeking up over a headstone. The imp crawled up on the headstone, giving us a clear view of it. It stood almost two feet tall with four arms, grey skin, and long claws on its hands and feet. Its long arms and pallid complexion made it look like a miniature resurrected gorilla, with a Cheshire cat smile. A line of black barbed quills ran down its back. By far my least favorite thing about imps was catching them.

"What's it doing?" Holt asked.

He was right, this was strange behavior. Imps are small and not inherently powerful. They use their speed and size to evade; they never go toe-to-toe or expose themselves like this.

"Something's wrong," I said, trying to put the puzzle together.

It clicked just as pressure, followed by severe pain, shot through my calf. I looked down to see one of the sharpened bones sticking out of the front of my leg. The bone pile behind us had stabbed me with the row closest to where I was standing. Holt jumped to the side, avoiding a similar strike meant for him.

"Get the imp," I said through gritted teeth.

The five rows of bone that didn't have me impaled moved underneath the center pile, lifting it off the ground like a spider. The orientation of the bones suddenly made more sense: they were legs. I bent forward to support myself with my hands and donkey-kicked its center mass with my good leg, sending it flying back into the woods. The bone piercing my leg was ripped free, leaving a gushing wound that was quickly filling up my shoe.

Holt was busy chasing the imp around the graveyard and not having much luck catching it. I wasn't going to be much help until my leg healed. The skeleton monster came shambling out of the woods like a Model T with loose wheels. My kick didn't seem to have done any real damage. I was going to need a weapon. With nothing but tombstones and rotten sticks on the ground to choose from, I hobbled over to the closest headstone and pulled it out of the ground. I lifted it into my right hand and hurled it like a discus. It spun vertically before hitting the ground and rolling. It collided with the legs on the right side of the bone spider, severing them. They flailed on the ground like fish out of water as the monster crashed to the ground.

My sense of accomplishment was short lived. The legs that remained churned rhythmically like a tiller, pulling the body across the ground. I liked it better with all its legs attached. I pulled up another large headstone and lifted it over my head, waiting for the spider to claw itself into range. When it was a few feet away, I slammed the stone on top of it. Bones crunched from the impact of the stone. It lay still for a moment before the legs started clawing the ground again, leaving long gouges with their sharp points.

Luckily the weight of the stone held the monster in place. I took a third tombstone and slammed it down on each leg individually to sever them. When that was done, I flipped the other stone off and the round pile shook like boney Jell-O, unable to propel itself in any direction. I drove the stone down on it repeatedly until whatever dark magic was holding it together released its grip, letting the bones fall into a loose pile.

I turned to find myself alone in the graveyard. Holt must have chased the imp into the woods. My leg had already stopped bleeding but there was still a large wound that would take a bit to heal. It would be done soon but in the meantime it still hurt like hell.

I pulled off my shoe and poured out the blood. Taking off my sock, I wrung it out before putting the bloody sock in the shoe. Opting to walk back barefoot, I started limping my way back to the truck.

"It got away," Holt said, coming out of the woods a minute later. "I almost had it."

He had a few of the barbed quills in his hand.

I waved him over. "I see that, let me help you with those."

He held up his hand for inspection as he reached me. There were three barbs but they weren't in too deep. I grabbed them and yanked them clean without any warning.

He jerked his hand back with a yelp. "You couldn't have done that a little gentler?"

"What's the fun in that? It's better to get them out sooner rather than later. Besides, you'll be healed up in a minute," I said, continuing to limp back to the truck.

"How's your leg? Want me to jab a stick in it?" he yelled from behind me.

"Let's go," I said. "We've got somewhere to be."

He jogged up beside me. "Where are we headed?"

"Steve's house. It's time for plan B."

CHAPTER · 2

THERE'S A POINT where people don't come back. From what he had posted online, it sounded like Steve was close to learning how to open a portal. I have to get to him before he goes that far. It's not that practicing some minor magic, or a single summoning, is going to corrupt him, but once people get a taste for the power behind it, they can have a hard time giving it up. If he didn't fall victim to the power, he would to whatever came through the first portal he opened.

Finding Steve had been easy, I read an article in the paper about a local preacher touting salvation for otherworldly creatures. From there all it took was a quick trip to the library for some internet research and I found everything I needed. Most people thought he was crazy, but the details he wrote about told me it was for real. What worried me the most was a book he described. A grimoire of ancient knowledge and rituals. If this P.V.T. really had one I had to get it. A book like that wasn't something you want to be unaccounted for. Books have a way of spreading ideas and these ideas have to be contained.

His house was on the edge of a subdivision backed by some woods and a small creek. This was a nice setup for me because it gave me an easy way in. I parked my truck a couple miles away on the side of highway 575 and pulled my knife out of the glovebox. It was carved out of solid mahogany with an eight-inch blade and a leather-wrapped handle. Symbols carved into the blade instilled it with magical energy. While it was wood, with the enchantments it was as sharp and strong as anything forged, and it didn't set off metal detectors.

"Nice hardware. You got one of those for me?" Holt asked.

"Nope." I tucked the knife into the belt of my shorts and got out of the truck.

Holt followed me as we walked into the woods on the side of the highway. "So, Obie, I know it's our first real job together but how about you let me take point on this one? Let me show you what I can do."

"I'm sure Cedric trained you well and I appreciate the enthusiasm, but I would prefer you see how I handle things before you start doing things on your own. You guys were only together for what, thirty years at most? It may seem like a long time, but you're still new at this," I said. I didn't get the impression he liked that answer but he didn't argue, which was a pleasant change.

Steve's backyard was surrounded by a wooden fence that backed up to the tree line. It gave us plenty of cover to check things out without worrying about being seen. The grass needed a trim, it was up to knee height. A small patio had a table with a few chairs, one of which was flipped over on its side. I stood behind the fence, watching and listening. I could hear some kids playing out on the street, a random car passing, and Holt's impatient shuffling in the leaves. The neighbor's houses were quiet and there was no sign of anyone home. It was late afternoon, sometime between when kids got home from school and adults got home from work. It looked clear.

"Let's go," I said and jumped the fence. We crossed the yard to the sliding glass door on the back of the house. The lights were off, making it hard to see in. Holt stepped up to the glass, cupping his hands around his eyes to see inside.

"Nothing. Want me to bust the door in?" he asked a little too eagerly.

I pushed the handle and it slid open freely. "I think we're okay."

The smell of rotting food drifted through the open door. I held my nose as I stepped in to a small dining area, kitchen adjacent, open to the living room to my left. It looked like what you would expect for a pastor's home. The décor wasn't fancy. It largely religious themed, with a picture of Jesus on the wall in the dining area with blood dripping from open wounds on his head and hands. Not my choice of a picture to hang where you eat, but to each his own I guess. The open floor plan didn't do much to contain the mess or smell. The table in front of me was covered in empty soda bottles, fast food wrappers, and other debris that might have had a chance to make it into the garbage can, if it wasn't already overflowing onto the floor. I opened a pizza box on top of the pile, half-eaten pepperoni. A large stack of mail, most of it unopened with PAST DUE stamped on the front, sat in a pile on the kitchen counter. Shuffling though the stack I found a plain envelope with "Steve" written on it by hand at the bottom. Curious guy that I am, I had to check it out.

> Steve,
>
>   I don't understand what is happening to you. What you are doing isn't right. I will always love you, but I can't stay and watch you do this to yourself. I will be staying at Belleview, apartment 1703. Please get help.
>
>   Candice

A lump in the envelope turned out to be a wedding and engagement ring. At least I didn't have to worry about the wife coming home.

The sound of splintering wood caught my attention. I turned to see Holt ripping a large flat screen off the wall.

"What the hell are you doing?"

"I'm going to stick this in the truck. My games would look awesome on this baby," he said.

"We're not here to loot the place."

"What? You said I could take things," he said.

"Don't you think a guy walking out of the woods with a TV might draw some attention? That's the last thing we need. If you're going take things, take small things, things you need."

"I can handle a cop, I'm not worried about them," he said.

"Sure, you can take a cop," I said. "The thing about cops is they don't fight you one-on-one. If you take on that one, you'll have ten more chasing you down. Next thing you know you're getting run over by a tank or locked up in a lab getting anal probed. So, for all our sakes, just put the TV down."

He tossed it into the fireplace, cracking the screen. "Fine, what can I take then?"

"Nothing with a serial number," I said, looking around. I spotted a few crumpled up bills on the counter beside some Chinese containers that maggots were going to town on. "Here, here's four dollars." I threw the bills over the couch into the living room.

"Four dollars won't buy a TV," he mumbled as he picked up them up.

"You could just go buy one. Hell, you can afford a nicer one than that. There's plenty of money from dust coming in," I said.

He shrugged. "Maybe for you. I didn't have anything when I came here and since this is our first hunt together the money isn't exactly rolling in."

"Just be patient, you should have something to work with real soon," I said.

"Soon? It takes months to turn a demon into dust, and after that wait I'm only getting a portion of it between your cut and Hob's cut. There may not be enough left to get something nice."

"I'll buy you a TV if you shut the hell up, how about that?" Why did Cedric have to die and stick me with this guy? I could deal with him later, right now I had more important things to think about. "Come on, let's get to work."

I put the letter back in the envelope with the rings and shoved it into one of the pockets of my cargo shorts before heading upstairs. I found an office that appeared to be where Steve spent most of his time. The walls had summoning circles framed like artwork. On the desk, I found a small plastic container about half full of a light grey powder. Under it were copies from a grimoire he had scribbled notes on during his sessions with the mysterious P.V.T. It was basic stuff: demon descriptions, summoning incantations written out phonetically. I popped the top off the container and gave it a sniff, it smelled like minerals.

"What is it?" Holt asked.

"Pixie Dust." I took a tiny pinch and placed it in my palm and focused my intention. The dust burst into a clear gray flame that novaed in a few seconds. "What did that tell us?" I said turning to Holt.

"Gray is on the lower end of the demon spectrum, so the dust was made from a demon without a lot of inherent magic. The flame burned clear and at least from here the powder looks uniform in consistency so it is well refined, a passable lower grade powder," Holt said.

"Good job, here's your TV," I said putting the top on and tossing him the container.

He deposited it in the cargo pocket on his leg, leaving an obvious bulge. "Sweet."

It left no doubt that this was the real thing. Not a good sign for Steve. More concerning than the dust and demon literature—where did it come from? P.V.T. probably supplied it to him. If she had access to dust it might complicate things. Hopefully she didn't have a large supply sitting around.

"All right, let's change to krasis. Steve should be home soon," I said, kicking off the flip flops I kept in the truck for when something happens to my shoes.

"Hell yeah!" Holt closed his eyes and concentrated, starting his change.

I reached back and opened the Velcro I had sewn into the back of all my pants, loosened my belt, and started to change into my real form, one of part man, part otter. My body contorted and elongated. My feet turned to paws, claws grew from my fingers and toes, a long muscular tail grew out of my back, and my head rounded out, growing long teeth and whiskers. Light brown fur covered everything from head to claws, finishing my transformation in a matter of seconds into the half-man half-animal form known as krasis.

Holt's body, being much newer to this than mine, made the change slower. After centuries or even decades of changing between forms, a kind of muscle memory eases the transition. It took maybe thirty seconds for his body to take its new shape. He was something new in our world. Thera, the Earth Mother, had always linked her Keepers to predators. Holt was the first to be bonded with a domesticated animal, a Doberman. It was a curiosity why Thera chose to stray from her normal routine, but I guess one advantage to being the boss is that you get to do what you want. Holt groaned his way through the change, panting when it was finally done. His loose clothing now stretched tight by his muscles, with black fur sticking out from underneath.

"Still getting used to it, huh?" I asked.

"Yeah, it's a lot better than it was," he said. "The first time took a couple minutes. It was like getting run over by a steamroller, covered in salt, and scraped back into a pile with a shovel. You remember your first change?"

"I remember my first time in krasis but the pain of the change I forgot a long time ago. It doesn't last forever." I could see Holt smirking. "What?"

"Don't get me wrong, you change fast, but you look like a stuffed animal, not exactly scary. You sure you don't want me to handle Steve?" he asked.

"I'm sure. I can be plenty scary if I need to. See?" I raised a lip and put my finger on a canine. "I've got big teeth, too."

"You have a couple big ones but not like this," he said giving me a low rumbling growl and revealing a face full of pointy teeth.

"You're very scary," I said casually so as not to give away that he really was rather intimidating. "Let's bust up these circles."

He got excited about that and started smashing them with his claws, mutilating not only the pictures and frames but the wall behind them as well. They were cheap frames with a plastic cover instead of glass. The one I did I just put a claw in through the plastic and dragged it down through the circle. Not even noticeable compared to Holt's work. When I was done he smashed mine anyway, for good measure.

"So, what's with the Velcro on the pants?" Holt asked catching his breath.

"Just a little modification for my tail. It's necessary unless I want to wear a kilt everywhere."

"Is that what you did before Velcro, wore skirts? The first thing Cedric did was dock my tail. No problem with pants for me," he said, turning to show a slight bulge at the base of his back.

"For a while I had a version with buttons, but it got all droopy in the back, so it wasn't the best."

He chuckled. "Yeah, anything that makes you look like you crapped yourself is probably a bad idea."

"How were things with Cedric?" I asked to change the subject.

"It was great. He really got me. I really felt like I had a place there. Ever since he was killed it hasn't been the same."

"We all miss him. Cedric was one hell of a Keeper. Give it some time. I'm sure you will come to like it here. How long were you with him for?"

He looked up in thought. "About twenty years, not long enough."

"I was with Cearbhall, my teacher, for about a hundred as an apprentice, and we worked together for almost another fifty after that," I said. "Just focus on the work and I'm sure you'll feel right at home before you know it."

"Focus on the work? I can do this in my sleep," he said.

"You haven't been at it that long, you some kind of expert now?"

With a smug look he said, "What can I say, poopy pants, some people are more talented than others."

That remark wasn't going to fly. "Don't call me that."

"What are you going to do, otter boy, cuddle me to death?"

I squared up to him. "You're out of line."

"Cedric never got all bent out of shape over nothing. Why do you overreact to everything?"

It was clear I was going to have to teach him a lesson in manners. That was no problem, hell, it would be fun. Before class got officially under way, the front door opened. Steve was home. The lesson would have to wait.

CHAPTER · 3

THE DOOR CLOSED and footsteps stomped their way up the stairs. I was glad too; if he had gone into the living room and seen the mess Holt had made with the TV, we may not have been able to get the jump on him. I gave a nod toward the corner of the room and Holt moved to it without argument. I ducked into the next room down the hallway and peeked around the doorframe. When Steve walked passed, carrying a briefcase in one hand and a bag of fast food in the other, I followed behind him quickly and quietly. He went in the office but didn't turn on the light. He plopped down in the office chair in the dark, put his briefcase on the desk, and fumbled with the bag of fast food.

Trying to lean against the doorframe with an air of nonchalance, I flipped the light switch. "That smells like a bacon cheeseburger. I've never had one but I have to admit sometimes I am tempted to swing through the drive-thru to pick one up. Are they everything they're cracked up to be?"

He swiveled around slowly, wide-eyed and clutching the bag to his chest like he was trying to protect it from the Hamburglar. Holt stepped into the center of the room, staring him down with bared teeth and fierce eyes. It didn't seem necessary. Steve didn't appear to have any real fight in him.

"Are you from the other world?" Steve stammered.

"Nope. I'm a red-blooded American, just like you," I said.

He looked at me with a puzzled expression, then realization dawned over his face. "It's you, from earlier today, that stupid shirt."

"There's no reason to get nasty," I said.

"You're here to kill me then," he said, more to himself than to me.

"I'm just here to talk, Steve. There doesn't have to be any killing tonight."

He motioned with his chin toward Holt. "What about him?"

Holt bent forward and snarled. "Yeah, I'll kill you. First you're going to tell me what I want to know."

So dramatic. Before I could tell him to chill out, chanting started from one of the other rooms. The voice was scratchy and deep. Holt and I swapped a look while Steve, unable to hear it, sat oblivious in his chair, clinging to his dinner.

"I got it," I said, moving into in the hallway. "Be nice."

I followed the chanting to a spare bedroom, but the source wasn't visible, it seemed to be coming from the entire room at once. The demon must be using some kind of magic to hide its location. Giving the room a quick once over turned up nothing but an open window with a few claw marks on the sill. What concerned me most is what I could smell. Even over the rotting garbage from downstairs I could smell the stink of this demon.

I sniffed around the room. The smell seemed slightly stronger from the closet and the chanting stopped abruptly when I stepped in front of the door. I drew the mahogany dagger from my belt and reached for the door handle. No sooner had I turned it than the door burst open on me. Something small and fast shot out, little more than a blur scurrying under the bed. The chanting started again where it left off. If I could find the circle and destroy it, the demon could chant for the rest of its life and it wouldn't make a difference. Peeking in the closet, I found a circle scratched roughly into the wall over a nest of torn up paper and cardboard, with bones of what looked to be dogs and cats scattered around it. No doubt missing pets from around the neighborhood. A swipe of my knife rendered the circle harmless.

Some talking in the other room caught my attention. Holt laughed and said, "Go for it." A gunshot followed by a heavy thud made my heart sink, especially since it was followed a few seconds later by Steve beginning a summoning of his own. I left the room, closing the door behind me, hopefully trapping the demon for the time being.

In the office I found Holt lying face down, bleeding into the carpet. Steve was leaning back against the desk, holding a revolver in one hand and his summoning notes in the other. Everything on the desk had been knocked off, except the monitor that was sitting face down beside the container of dust Steve had retrieved from Holt's pocket. He had a cut on the side of his face; Holt must have started the interrogation without me. Steve whipped the gun in my direction when I stepped into the doorway. He motioned toward the ground with the gun but continued his chanting.

I raised my hands, dropped my cheeks, and opened my eyes wide. In this case I wanted to prove Holt right, I'm not threatening, just a cute oversized otter. It's not always a bad thing to be adorable. If he got me with a head shot, I would be out for a while before my body could heal itself. It looked like Holt had avoided a direct hit, but it was enough to take him out of commission for a bit. I couldn't afford to lose that time, with a demon loose and potentially more on the way. I knew Steve's incantation, I had a minute, maybe more, the way he was reciting it. I would have to talk him down.

"I'll put it away," I said, moving the knife slowly down and tucking it back in my shorts. "There Steve, everything's okay but I need you to listen to me. I know it doesn't seem like it but I'm here to help you. He's not dead, by the way. He's going to wake up in a few minutes and he's going to be pissed. I don't blame you for shooting him. I've wanted to shoot him more than once. But that's not your only problem, you have a demon in the other room. They don't care about you or your beliefs. I don't know why but they are using you. I don't care about the gun, keep it, just stop the chanting and let's get you somewhere safe until we can get this figured out."

He didn't stop.

"You know you need a circle for that, right? We destroyed them all. It's not going to work," I said.

Just as he finished chanting, Steve reached over and lifted the monitor revealing a summoning circle wallpaper on his desktop.

"That's new," I said.

I wasn't even sure a digital circle would work, never heard of anyone trying it before. We stood looking at each other, waiting for something to happen. Uncertainty crept over his face and just when I decided that his incantation was a dud, a pinpoint of orange materialized in the ceiling. The air began to churn around the room as the light became a circle steadily increasing in diameter. As the circle grew, the air picked up speed, sending loose papers, dust, and debris flying around in an office-themed maelstrom. Heat began to spill out of the expanding portal.

The air pressure must be higher in the demon world because whenever a portal is opened, a giant vortex of stank comes billowing out of it. Maybe one day I will get used to it, but it's awful every time. That may be due in part to my hyper-sensitive otter nose. I think it was a combination of the smell and the heat, but when I was new at this it wasn't uncommon for me to lose my lunch when portals opened. It wasn't a problem for me anymore. Steve, on the other hand, was clearly not as acclimated, and wasted no time retching all over the wall of his office.

I broke into a sweat from the intense heat pouring into the room. Since the portal opened on the ceiling, I expected to see the demon sky, but instead it was like someone took a painting of a landscape and hung it on the ceiling. A red and barren scene stretched off in the distance. It was a rookie mistake; the worlds hadn't been aligned properly, Steve probably messed up the incantation just a bit. I moved back out into the hallway to escape the heat and stench, and if something came tumbling through the portal I didn't want it to fall on me. Holt was on his own. I say "if" but I knew something would come though, something always comes through. The question was, what?

As if on cue, the floor shook with a loud thud—we had company. It made a sound somewhere between a shriek and a squawk, and I recognized it immediately: a hellhound. The orange light and wind told me the portal was still open. Steve was so new at this he may not know how to close it, assuming he wanted to. There was enough dust in that container to keep it operational for a few minutes. There could be dozens of demons here in that time. I had to shut it down before anything else came through. I turned to go back in the room when it felt like I had been punched in the back of the head. I had forgotten all about my little friend under the bed. It stunned me at first, but the clawing on my head and neck snapped me out of it. It felt like it was trying to burrow into my skull. I reached back and grabbed whatever I could get hold of to pull it away.

I could feel the blood running down my back as I pulled an imp, glistening with my blood in the orange light, off my neck. I had it by its back, which is a very inconvenient way to hold an imp. The barbed spines common on many of the smaller demons were already working their way into my hand. We sized each other up for a second before it went full-on honey badger, hands, feet, and tail flailing wildly, its little jaws snapping wildly trying to get ahold of me. The blood made it hard to hold onto and the movement pushed the barbs deeper into my palm. It was only a matter of time before it got away, time I didn't have. I clenched my teeth and then my hand. The barbs sank in deep, sending shooting pain up my arm. The resistance suddenly gave way as the demon's bones shifted with a loud pop. It howled and writhed in pain. I reared back and pitched it into the wall, sending it straight through the sheetrock, disappearing into a newly minted imp-sized hole.

My hand was thoroughly pin-cushioned by more barbs than I could count, with more running up my arm from the imp's thrashing tail. Another shot boomed from Steve's office. It was probably too soon for Holt to be awake, so Steve was most likely coming to the difficult realization that he was going to need my help. Instinctively, I reached for my dagger with my right hand, but I couldn't really grab anything with all the barbs in my palm, so my left would have to do. From the doorway, I saw the hound. It looked like a six-legged hairless dog the size of a Saint Bernard, with big red Chihuahua eyes bugging out of its head. It was standing over Holt's still lifeless body and had Steve backed into a corner. The shot had gone into its shoulder, pissing it off more than anything.

Before I could intervene, it lunged for Steve, sinking its shark-like rows of teeth into his abdomen. He screamed as it lifted him off the ground and shook violently side to side. Steve's body wasn't up to the strain and the part of him in demon's mouth ripped free, sending the rest skidding across the floor, leaving a red streak behind him. He came to a rest close to where I was standing. His intestines, still attached to both pieces, unraveled across the room like a Slinky stretched to its limits. The scene gave me pause for one reason. The portal was still open, swirling papers and gushing stink into the room. I guess it's possible that someone could maintain a portal while having a large piece of themselves ripped off, but I have never seen it. It would take someone accomplished, well beyond Steve's ability, or anyone else I have known for that matter. He was still conscious, screaming, crying, and pulling the loose pieces of himself back like a rope.

Movement on the ceiling caught my attention. Another hound was investigating the portal. When it saw what a tasty treat Steve was, it would no doubt come through. This was getting out of hand quickly. The demon scarfed down the chunk of Steve, thrusting its head forward repeatedly to catch the dangling pieces. It turned to get another morsel and spotted me in the doorway. Charging the room, I slashed my knife across its face, sending it reeling back, and spun, whipping the monitor with my tail, then turned to face the hound. The monitor exploded and the portal on the ceiling slammed shut with a loud crack. The wind abruptly stopped. Papers in the office drifted gently to the floor. Without the orange light coming through the portal, the room returned to the more earthly glow of the overhead light. A hard thud shook the floor behind me. Something else must have made it through before the portal closed.

The hound screeched through its bloody teeth and charged. I jumped back and slammed the heel of my right hand down on it, sending its head into the floor. My hand exploded in pain from the barbs still stuck in it. Throwing myself on top of the hound, I wrapped my right arm around its neck, pushing my weight down to keep it pinned to the floor, being careful to keep my legs away from the snapping jaws. This left my other hand free to drive my knife repeatedly into the beast's underbelly. I held on until its strength drained away enough to let it go. As soon as it was safe, I pushed off the floor and spun to face the room, ready for another hound. Instead I found half a hound lying dead on top of Holt. It had gotten caught halfway through when the portal closed. Fine with me. Without the portal pushing rotten air into the room, thick smoke began coming in from the hallway. I could hear fire crackling downstairs.

A whimpering from the doorway caught my attention. Steve was still with me, barely. Tears ran down his cheeks and he was looking at me quiet and unmoving. I could have tried to heal him but he was scattered all over the room, and probably wouldn't have survived anyway.

"I'm sorry I couldn't help you," I said. I wasn't going to let him spend his last minutes on earth burning alive, assuming he lived that long. One strategic stab later and he was pain-free. I wiped the knife off on his shirt and tucked it back into my belt.

Moving to the stairs to check out the fire, I found the entire bottom floor engulfed, and fire was already crawling its way up the stairs. The imp stood in the flames on the bottom step, leaning against the wall with a grin and one leg hanging limp. The flames were moving fast and while they circled the imp, it didn't seem to mind. This was pretty much its natural environment after all.

"Burn," it said in a deep burping voice.

I wasn't expecting it to know any English. That told me it had either been here for a long time or had been working with something that has. Demons don't hop out of the portal reciting Shakespeare. There's no way I was going to tangle with a demon, even a small one, in the middle of a house fire. This one got a pass tonight.

"Rain check," I said.

Back in the office Holt was just pulling himself out from under the partial hound. "What happened?"

"Grab that half a hound and head out the window. The house is coming down," I said.

"What?"

I didn't wait to explain. I grabbed the whole hellhound and heaved it through the window. The glass exploded as its body tumbled onto the roof and off into the yard. I hopped out the window and jumped down to the grass. The backyard was lit up like Christmas from the fire and was too warm for my liking. I dragged the hound to the back fence and tossed it over before jumping myself. There I waited, watching the upstairs window for Holt. I thought I saw a dark figure perched on the edge of the roof. I blinked and it was gone, I wasn't sure it was there at all. I stood still, watching and listening when he finally came out, lugging the other hell hound on his back.

"What is it?" he asked when he finally made it over the fence and saw how on guard I was.

"Nothing, what took you so long?" I asked.

"The dust was spilled everywhere. I couldn't save any of it. I did get my shoes though," he said.

It wasn't until then I remembered my flip flops burning up in the house. I lose a lot of good shoes that way. We changed back to human form before making our way through the woods back to the truck. We were battered and bloody, so even though we looked human again, we weren't in any shape to be seen in public. We waited on the side of the road for a break in the cars before moving out and tossing the hounds in the back. I grabbed a tarp and some bungees from behind the seat to cover things up. In a few minutes we were pulling out. Firetrucks screamed down the interstate in the opposite direction.

"I have to admit, Obie, I was wrong about you. I thought you were kind of a pussy. One of those guys that talks a good game but is afraid to get their hands dirty. What you did back there, though. Killing two hounds, ripping that asshole's guts out, and burning his house down—damn, that's cold blooded. Oh, and you have to tell me what you did to the other half of that hound," he said.

"Maybe, one day." I wasn't about to correct him. If his conclusions bought me a little peace, then that's all right by me.

"Where to now?" he asked.

"I'm going to get rid of these hounds, drop you off at the house, and then I have to do something about this," I said, showing the barbs in my hand.

"Wait, those are imp barbs. You killed another demon . . . That's what I'm talking about!"

CHAPTER·4

"WHAT ARE WE doing here?" Holt asked, looking down rows of corn as we drove by.

"This is Hob's farm," I said.

"Wait, Hob, that's the duster," he said, excitement in his voice.

"Sure is. I don't know if you will meet him this trip though, we're just dropping off today. We will be coming here a lot. If you don't meet him today I'm sure you will soon." We drove past the farmhouse toward the back of the property where Hob conducted his other business. "Actually, there he is now," I said, pointing to an overall-clad figure sitting in a swing on the porch. He wore a baseball cap that kept his hair mostly contained, which did nothing to hide his pointy ears.

"Kinda bold to have his ears out like that," Holt observed.

"He's a bold fella, but no one comes back here, and if they did he has people for that," I said giving him a wave as we passed.

He gave us a wave back, not breaking the rhythmic swaying of his leisure.

"Should we stop and say hi?" Holt asked.

"We'd be here all day. I just want to drop these demons off and get out of here. Trust me, you will do more than enough chatting with Hob," I said. "He's a talker."

Most dusters are magical experts and Hob was no exception. Some people think the amount of dust he has access to at any given time makes him a threat, and they might be right. He left his elvin kin in Germany, coming here for a quiet life of farming. He made a good living from it until we approached him about supplementing his income with some knowledge from the Old World. He was reluctant but saw the good in establishing a steady dust trade. His condition was that his involvement remained secret. The secret probably wasn't as well kept as it should have been—Holt makes one more—what could it hurt?

Past a few more fields, we pulled up to a two-story red barn tucked away by the tree line. I backed the truck up to the doors and we got out.

"Give the door three good knocks," I said as I started untying the tarp.

Holt walked up to the large double doors and tapped on it with his knuckles three times.

"They aren't going to hear that, really go for it," I said.

He looked a little uncertain but delivered three strikes to the door in slow succession. Nothing happened. I went around the truck to untie the other side.

Holt turned to me, placing his hands on his hips. "Well?"

"Give them a minute, they don't move so quick," I said.

After another thirty seconds, I had the tarp off the hounds in the back of the truck when a speakeasy style viewing slit slid open ten feet up the wall. A large gray face looked down on us.

"Come back here and let them get a look at you," I said to Holt who had remained close to the door.

He moved back and after a short inspection the opening slid shut. *Ka-Chunk*, a heavy lock was opened. *Ka-Chunk, ka-chunk*, two more followed suit before the large doors were swung open, revealing an ogre, roughly twelve feet tall with stone gray skin and a blank expression lumbering over us. He came outside, grabbed a demon in each hand and took them into the barn. Hob hired ogres because they are huge, loyal, and they lack the imagination to use dust, intentionally or accidentally, but most importantly, they don't mind the smell. The perfect worker for a duster.

"Hey, buddy, wait up," Holt said.

"His name's Eric."

"Eric? Really?" he questioned. "Hey, Eric, hold up a second."

Eric ignored him, disappearing inside. Holt followed in protest. The inside of the building looked more like the industrial processing facility that it was. All the equipment was steel, the floors were a dark red tile, and everything was spotless. The machines were custom builds Hob made to refine Pixie Dust. Eric put the demons on a massive scale to the left of the door.

Holt walked up in front of him. "How long is it going to take to get the dust from these?"

Eric gave him a blank stare and said nothing, continuing with his work.

"Earth to Eric, anybody home?" Holt said waving a hand as close to Eric's face as he could reach.

"You really shouldn't antagonize ogres," I said.

Holt spun to face me. "He's antagonizing me. I'm just trying to get a couple questions answered."

While all this was going on, Tailypo Wilix, the foreman of the facility, had made his way behind Holt. A rather pudgy goblin with dark green skin and long pointy ears, bald on top with grey hair on the sides, he wore black plastic-framed glasses and barely came up to Holt's knees. He held a clipboard in one hand and a pencil in the other that he promptly stabbed into the back of Holt's calf and withdrew. Holt yelped and stepped forward, running into Eric, who didn't seem to notice.

"What's the big idea?" Holt shouted when he put together what had happened.

"You're in the way and you're bothering Eric," Wilix said. "Obie, you do know what a secret is, don't you? As in this is supposed to be a secret facility, hmm?"

"Actually, this is Holt, my new apprentice. I expect he will be making plenty of drop-offs in the future so I'm just showing him the ropes," I said.

"Mm hmm, let's see then, 387 pounds," he said, cocking his head back to peer at the scale's readout through the glasses resting on the end of his nose. He climbed a ladder to get a closer look at the demons. "One-and-a-half hellhounds." He shot me a look of disapproval.

I smiled and shrugged. He went to make some notes on his clipboard when he noticed the end of his pencil had Holt's blood all over it. He stuck it in his mouth, swirling his tongue around until it was clean, and made his notations.

"So how long will it take to get dust?" Holt asked.

Wilix tapped his pencil against the clipboard in thought before climbing down and replying. "About three months. Eric, go ahead and move them to the freezer, please."

"Three months? Can I get an advance or something?"

"Come on, let's get out of here," I said, before Holt could embarrass us further. "Thanks, Wilix and Eric, appreciate ya." Eric gave me a nod as I directed Holt outside. "Get in the truck, let's get out of here."

"We didn't talk percentages or anything," Holt said when we were back in the truck.

I cranked the engine. "Percentages of what?"

"You know, the dust, how everything is getting split up."

I put the truck in reverse and started backing out. "What were you thinking?"

"I figure you've been doing this long enough where you have a nice bit saved up. Since I'm just getting started I should probably get a little more. Maybe a seventy-thirty split? That should get me up to speed pretty quickly," he said.

"It's not a cash operation. You have to have an account set up before you can do anything, remember? Did you get your account set up?" I asked, already knowing the answer.

"Nah, I haven't had time. I'll get around to it," he said.

"Let's wait till you do before we start talking business," I said.

Hob wasn't on the porch anymore when we drove by the farm house. Maybe if he was I could have dropped Holt off and subjected him to hours of Southern hospitality as punishment. I never thought having an apprentice would be this hard. I could really use a vacation.

"I'm going to drop you off at the house and get some help with these quills. I'll swing by the church on the way back and see if Steve left us any clues there.

Just take tomorrow off. If you feel like it you can go get your account set up and we'll figure out how we're going to split everything," I said.

We were going to split everything fifty-fifty, he just didn't know it yet, and I wasn't in the mood for another argument. That was actually generous for how much of his slack I had to pick up.

CHAPTER · 5

NAYLET LIVED DEEP in the mountains close to Suches, Georgia, the modern equivalent of a one-horse town. The house was small, one room and a loft; I had helped her build it decades ago. In typical nymph fashion, she loved plants and she had a perfectly maintained lawn and garden. It was after dark when I pulled into my normal parking space, gravel hissing a protest under the tires. The light shining through the front window told me she was still awake and I couldn't help but smile. I shut off the truck, got out, and headed for the front door.

A nymph's garden is distilled life, concentrated like Thera's essence. Being one of her servants, I was particularly sensitive to it. The area felt more alive than the surrounding woods, the sound of running water coming from behind the house increased that perception. Lightning bugs danced in the yard, crickets chirped in the woods. The katydids' rhythmic chanting always seemed like the heartbeat of the forest to me. The night was hot and muggy, as only a Georgia night in the heart of summer could be. This place was special and I loved it here. I gave the door a courtesy knock as I let myself in.

"Anybody home?" I said, dropping my keys on the table.

The house had a studio layout, with the kitchen and bathroom on the far side, and a combined dining and living area we called the lounge by the front door. The walls were covered with storage and shelving. There wasn't much open wall space and what little there was had been covered by pictures of people and places, many of them Naylet drew herself. I was featured in a couple of them, which is quite a compliment considering the amount of real estate and the long history competing for it. A ladder led up to a small loft sleeping area. Naylet popped her head over the edge, cascading her golden curls down, concealing her face.

"You're late," she said. "I was starting to think you weren't coming."

"Sorry. I had a little trouble at work today."

"Nothing too serious?"

I held up my hand with the barbs protruding and wiggled my fingers, making the barbs wave. "I lost another pair of shoes and this."

"That's gross," she said.

"Can you help me out?"

She tumbled off the loft, landing gracefully on her feet, and held out her palm. I put my hand on hers and she looked closely at my injuries.

"Yep, you healed up nicely. We're going to have to cut them out," she said, sounding a little too happy about it.

"I think there's a few more in my back," I said, giving her a sheepish grin.

She pulled out a spare blanket and pillow and laid it out on the floor. "Take your shirt off and lay down."

I tried to remove my shirt but it was caught on the barbs imbedded in my back. She stopped rummaging in the kitchen for a minute and returned to help.

"I think this shirt's had it. It's full of holes back here. We're going to have to cut it."

"I am going to kill the hell out of that imp when I get my hands on him. This is one of my favorite shirts," I said.

"It's ratty. You should have thrown it out already," she said.

I lay down while she went back to the kitchen. She returned a minute later with a scalpel, scissors, a plate, and a newspaper.

She handed me the paper. "Remember when we didn't spend our nights doing minor surgery?"

"I remember when I did my best without you," I said. "This is a lot better."

"Mm hmm. Stay still."

I spread the paper on the floor as she cut the shirt revealing the barbs. It had become our routine that I read something to her while she patched me up. It started as a way to distract me from the pain but turned into something nice that I did, even if I wasn't being cut on. Reading to her had become one of my favorite pastimes.

"So, what's going on in the world today?" she asked. That was code for *This is going to hurt*. Before I could answer I felt the pinch of the scalpel.

I looked at the front page and read the headline: "Baby Stephanie missing ten days. Police say no new leads. Deborah Olson says her newborn daughter was taken from a second story window around 10:30 P.M. while she was downstairs. Police investigate all possibilities. Continued on page—Ow! Damn Naylet."

"Don't be such a wimp," she said with the distant tone that comes with focus. "I hate that kind of news."

"Yeah, I would think you would be used to the terrible things humans do to each other by now."

"Unless it wasn't human. The baby was taken from a second-story window and the police have no leads? From what I have read there aren't any witnesses or any evidence at all. Nothing they are sharing anyway. That's why the baby's picture has been plastered everywhere. They are hoping to get lucky with a sighting."

"So what, a ghost decides it's lonely so it floats into a random house and takes a baby? Hate to break it to you but a ghost wouldn't need to open a window," I said.

"It would to get the baby out, genius, but I never said it was a ghost."

She had me there. "I don't think so, this has 'inside job' written all over it. The mother did it. Had to be," I said. "She probably tossed the kid into a dumpster or off a bridge. Humans are crazy like that. I heard a story about a guy in Atlanta that threw a baby out of a car on the interstate."

"That's horrible," she exclaimed, giving me a poke with the scalpel that I am pretty sure had nothing to do with getting barbs out of my back.

"Hey, I didn't do it. Just calling it like I see it," I said.

"Well, when I saw her pleading on the TV to have her baby returned I could tell she didn't do it. A woman can tell these kind of things," she replied.

"A nymph can tell those kinds of things maybe," I said. "And when did you see her on the TV? You don't even have one."

"When I was out with the girls last week. Don't think my life revolves around you, Obie."

"I wouldn't dream of it."

"So . . ." she said.

"So, what?"

"Are you going to look into it?" she inquired.

"Look, if you don't want me around so much you can just say so. You don't have to make more work for me," I replied, turning to look at her.

"You know that's not what I'm doing. That baby needs help, and if you can help her then I would like you to do whatever you can to make sure she gets home to her mother safely."

"I tell ya what. I'll stop by first thing in the morning before I follow up on my other lead," I said.

"You promise?"

"I give you my word as a gentleman."

She pushed my head back to the paper with the dull side of the scalpel. "If that's the best you can do I guess I'll take it. Now find me something happy in there. This stuff is depressing."

"You know this is a newspaper, right?"

"Ok, that's all of them from your back," she said. "Let's move to the table for your hand. Don't bleed on the couch."

I got up off the floor, taking the plate of bloody quills and moving it to the table. There had been six in my back but my hand had that beat easily, not to mention my arm.

"What would you think about taking a trip? Maybe to the beach?"

She stopped working on my hand and looked me right in the eyes. "What's the matter?"

"Nothing. I just thought it would be nice to get away, that's all." I looked down at the paper.

"What are you trying to get away from?"

"Nothing . . . Everything . . . I don't know. Things with Holt haven't gotten any better. He got himself shot tonight and I had to handle everything by myself. Then he tells me he should get a bigger cut of the dust than me. It's like he's living in some fantasy world where he is actually contributing something."

"What would you think about having kids?" she asked out of left field.

"I think that's the opposite of a vacation. Where did that come from?"

"Just something I've been thinking about," she said. "We've been together a long time and we would be good parents."

"I'm not disputing that. I'm just not sure Georgia is ready for a bunch of little wereotters running around. You know that's what they would be right?"

"I think the world could use more of them actually," she said.

"We don't live together, what about that?"

She turned my hand over in hers deciding where to start. "We can fix that."

"And Holt?" I asked.

"We can figure all that out later. I'm just asking if it's something you would be interested in."

"Yeah, I'm interested," I said. "How about this: we get away for a week and when we get back we'll figure all that out."

"When did you want to go?" she asked.

"As soon as I take care of this P.V.T. situation. I should have a little free time after that."

"I need a couple days to take care of the Japanese beetles eating the peach trees, so that will be perfect. Don't worry about a thing. I'm going to plan the whole trip," she said.

We chatted for most of the hour it took to remove all the quills, about places to go and things to do. Seeing a sea turtle was on the top of her list. I didn't really care as long as I got away. When she was finished, I tied up the quills into a bundle. I would drop them off at Hob's next time I was over there.

"I'm going to get a shower. I still have a change of clothes here, right?"

"Yeah, go ahead. I'll get them for you," she said.

The water felt great and it was nice to wash off the dried blood and grime. The only sign of my injuries was a little discoloration in the skin. By morning there would be no trace.

"Let me get your back," Naylet said, sliding into the shower with me.

I had no objection, of course, it felt great. I turned around to face her and she kissed me.

"What's that for," I asked.

"Be careful, okay?"

"Hey, there's nothing to worry about. This time next week we are going to have the sand in our toes and drinks in our hands."

I TOSSED MY CLOTHES off the loft onto the floor and kissed her on the cheek before climbing out of bed as quietly as I could. I had been laying there staring at the ceiling and listening to Naylet's gentle breathing for hours. Having a personal connection to Thera was good in a lot of ways, the rapid healing was a plus, and learning to channel her energy to heal others came in handy. Being hooked into a power that great also meant that Keepers didn't sleep; we never get tired since we live in a state of constant regeneration. It also means we don't have to eat. We *can* eat, but most choose not to. When you don't sleep, nights can be tough. If you don't stay busy they drag on for what seems like forever, even with the best of company next to you. You find ways to pass the time, get some reading done, learn a language or three, maybe pick up a ukulele every now and again. I became a Keeper when I was just into double digits, it's been so long now I don't remember what sleep is like, probably like being knocked unconscious but without the headache when you wake up.

I got dressed, filled the coffee pot, and set the delay for an hour, she should be getting up around then. Leaning against the counter, I thought about what Naylet had said about having kids. I imagined taking them down to the creek to teach them how to catch crawfish or watching them play in the yard. Having kids wasn't something I had thought would ever happen but now that it was a possibility, I was starting to look forward to it. First things first, I had to find P.V.T. and get the grimoire. If I could arrange a little revenge on that imp for messing up my shirt, all the better. I let myself out and crossed the yard to my truck. The sun would be up in a few minutes and I had a lot to do.

CHAPTER · 6

ABOUT AN HOUR south in Alpharetta, I pulled up to what was more of a mansion than a house. It seemed like another world compared to the modest means I was used to. A massive white building with Roman-style pillars and an immaculately kept yard made me feel out of place in my cargo shorts and tee shirt. Being around expensive things has always made me uncomfortable. Through no fault of my own, things tend to get smashed up when I'm around and it's a lot of liability, if it can be traced back to you. The sun was just coming up when I parked in the driveway. I wondered if anyone was up yet. I got out and walked up the stone steps to the front door. I hesitated, feeling a little self-conscious about my casual attire.

"Too late now," I said, ringing the doorbell.

There were no sounds from inside the house. I couldn't see a car in the driveway, maybe no one was home? If so I could break in and have a look around. A place like this was bound to have a security system. Even better, if no one answered I could just tell Naylet I tried but no one was home. She would probably bring it up again, but it would get me off the hook for now. Just when I had given up and turned to leave, I heard footsteps inside. A woman opened the door. It was evident she was fresh out of bed, sporting a bathrobe, messy hair, and puffy red eyes.

"Hello, Ms. Olson? My name is Obie. I was asked to look into the disappearance of your daughter Stephanie," I said. "I'm sorry to show up unannounced but I was hoping you could spare a few minutes to talk to me."

She rubbed her eyes. "You don't look like a detective."

"No, ma'am, I'm not."

"Do the police know you are here?"

"No, I work independently of the police, kind of like a private investigator."

"Do you have any credentials, like a badge or something?" she asked.

I shrugged. "No, ma'am, I'm afraid not."

"Are you some kind of scam artist? Oh I know, you work for a tabloid, right? Trying to get some pictures or some front page quote to make me look like I did something to my little girl. Why don't you crawl back to whatever sewer you came out of and leave me alone."

"I'd be happy to. I just made a promise I would see if I could help you. Sorry to bother you." I turned around, happy to have gotten out of this so easily.

"Hey, what could you do that the police can't?" she called after me.

Crap, I must have been too eager to leave. I should have pushed a little more until she slammed the door in my face. "I handle . . . special cases. I may not even be able to help you. To be honest, my girlfriend has been following your story. She heard the police didn't have any leads and asked me to check it out. I would just need a few minutes to look around, if you're interested. Ten minutes and I can tell you. If you don't want my help, I will be happy to tell her I tried and you weren't interested. I have a lot of other things going on today."

She paused for a moment, looking from me, to the stairs behind her, and finally rested her gaze on the ground. "What would you need?"

"I need to see where Stephanie was taken from, and answers to any questions that come up."

"Give me your driver's license. Anything fishy and I'm calling the cops."

I took out my license and placed it in her hand. She pulled her phone out of a pocket of the bathrobe and took a picture before she handed it back.

"Top of the stairs, first door on the left," she said, stepping aside and opening the door wide.

The room was painted light pink and had all the expected trappings of a newborn girl's room. A crib sat in the corner beside a changing table. Two windows were juxtaposed on the wall to the right of the crib. I stepped into the center of the room, taking stock of everything.

"Tell me what happened," I said.

"I had put the baby to bed and was downstairs cleaning up. I heard the alarm beep from a door or window being opened. We were here alone, her father was working late again, so I started looking around. I couldn't find anything open downstairs. Stephanie had started crying upstairs and I was about to go up and check on her when I heard a voice whisper on the monitor and it sounded like someone whipped a sheet, like when you make the bed and hold one end and shake it up and down. I ran up here as fast as I could, but by the time I got here Stephanie was gone."

I stepped over to inspect the window. "And you found the window open?"

"Yes. The first thing I did was look out but I didn't see anything. I couldn't have been more than a few seconds behind whoever took her. It's like they just disappeared."

"Tell me about the voice. What did it say? Male or female?"

"It was a woman's voice but I couldn't make it out," she said. "It was just a whisper."

"Where's her father now?"

"I don't know. He accused me of doing something to her. He left and hasn't been back since." She folded her arms across her chest like she was giving herself a hug. "The police took me in and questioned me for hours. They should have been out looking for her."

I looked out the pair of windows into the back yard. The tree line was about thirty feet behind the house. "Which window was open?"

"The right one," she said.

Unlocking the window, I opened it to look out. While the baby's room was located on the second story of the house, the back yard was dug out for basement access making it more of a three-story drop. Definitely not something that a ladder could be taken down from quickly or that a normal human could jump without sustaining injuries.

"Were the windows locked?" I asked.

"Yes ... No ... I'm not sure," she replied. "I think they were, but I have gone over it in my head and second guessed myself so many times, I just can't be sure anymore. If they were unlocked, they shouldn't have been."

I noticed a notch on the window sill. It looked like a knife had been stuck in the wood. I put my finger on the mark and had an idea. In my other forms I have non-retractable claws. Sometimes they leave marks on things. If I grabbed this window sill I could leave a claw mark from my thumb on top like this and ... Sure enough, under the sill there were four similar marks. I lined my fingers up to the marks. The hand that left these marks was smaller than mine but whatever had come here had claws and had grabbed the sill, leaving indentations in the wood.

I grunted an acknowledgement and closed the window. Ms. Olson was leaning against the door with her arms still holding herself. I walked over to the crib but it wasn't much to look at, just a bare mattress.

"The police took the bedding," she offered from the doorway.

"Is there anything here that Stephanie had with her that night?"

"No, the police took everything. Wait, there is one thing. I had forgotten all about it. Her bunny. She wouldn't sleep without her bunny. Hang on." She disappeared from the room and returned a moment later with a stuffed animal. "It was in the middle of the floor. I picked it up that night before I looked out the window and carried it into the bedroom when I called the police. It has been there ever since."

I took it and turned the small stuffed animal over in my hands. I saw a spot on the side where the fur was matted and greasy. It had a faint smell of rose and spices, but there was something else there I couldn't recognize.

I held it out for her to inspect. "There's a spot on the rabbit here, do you know what it is?"

She looked it over with a confused expression, "No idea. I hadn't noticed it."

"Do you recognize the scent?"

She gave it a sniff. "Not sure, some kind of perfume maybe? I haven't smelled anything like that before. What does it mean?"

It meant that she was never going to see her kid again. I wasn't sure if it was a good thing the child wasn't devoured on the spot, at least then she would have some closure, even if she would have been blamed for it. The flapping of the sheet she described had to be wings. Something came in, took the baby, and flew away, leaving marks on the windowsill on the way out. The baby wouldn't have been taken unless there was a plan for it, and a demon with a plan is a terrible thing.

"Well?" she asked, snapping me out of thought.

"I'm going to do my best to help you. From what I have seen, I believe this case falls under my area of expertise. I will do my best to find Stephanie," I said. "I want to stress that we are already ten days past the time she was taken and the chances of a positive outcome at this point are pretty slim."

"So you believe me?" she asked.

"Mrs. Olson, I am one hundred percent certain you are telling the truth."

She touched her mouth as her eyes began to tear up, and she hugged me.

"I said I would only take ten minutes and I'm already a couple over. May I borrow the bunny? It could help me locate her."

"Yes, thank you."

"Thanks, I will let myself out," I said, moving toward the door.

"Wait, how do I get in touch with you?" she asked.

"If you need me or have any kind of trouble, there's a motorcycle club in Dawsonville beside Rock Creek Park. They are called the Tortured Occult, they know how to find me. Tell them that Obie sent you and they will keep you safe and get in touch with me. They look rough but they're just a bunch of teddy bears. I'll let you know if I find anything."

She followed me out into the hallway. "Okay, please let me know as soon as you find anything."

"I will, I promise."

She showed me out. Naylet would be happy to hear she was right. The bad news is the trip to the beach would have to wait. It's always something.

CHAPTER·7

I PARKED THE TRUCK by the graveyard where we had the run in with the imp. I hadn't noticed it the day before, but an old road, overgrown with weeds and trees, led up to it from the front of the parking lot. From the growth I guessed it probably hadn't been used in ten years or more, a perfect place to keep the truck out of sight while I worked. I never liked to park out in the open. Maybe it's a habit that comes from having a vehicle that stands out, or maybe I am just paranoid.

After getting ambushed by the imp yesterday, I was going to be good and sure it didn't happen a second time. A quick pass around the graveyard checking for fresh scents reassured me that I didn't have any surprises in store. Nothing stood out, the bones were still sitting crushed under the tombstone. They fell further out of spider shape when I nudged them with my foot. I walked over to get a look at the church. The parking lot was empty, as expected. I shouldn't have any company considering that Steve would be tied up in the morgue, and with the boss gone the secretary didn't have a reason to come in. When word got out, the church would become a center of activity. I had a day or two tops before memorial services and arrangements for new leadership would make it impossible to find any clues. I needed to get in and out now while things were still quiet.

The church was right beside a road, anyone could drive by and see me poking around. The fact that I didn't see any cameras yesterday probably meant there weren't any; a small town church like this wouldn't have much of a security budget. Worse than cameras, though, were nosy locals, word might already be out about Steve burning up last night. Anyone driving by that knew about it might find a stranger at the church suspicious. I found some bushes to stash my clothes in and took the form of an otter. That would be the best way to get in under the radar. I circled the building first and found two entrances, the glass double doors in the front I had used yesterday and a metal door in the back. There were a few windows, most with the blinds drawn. I would have to go in the front. A key would be nice, but I hadn't thought to get one off Steve when I had the chance, so a rock would have to do. I looked around until I found the right rock for the job. It was the size of a tennis ball and would definitely break the glass. I picked it up and walked on my hind legs to the door. A couple good whacks cracked the glass. Holt can make fun of me if he wants, but having thumbs in all three of my forms is a real advantage. Let's see him smash a window when he's taken the form of a Doberman. Maybe if he used his thick head.

One more solid hit and the glass broke, a little more than I wanted. It shattered into large sharp pieces, raining down jagged shards that could seriously hurt me if I didn't move. I scurried away just in time to avoid the glass that shattered on impact with the concrete. My first thought was how I would have been remembered. Cedric was ambushed and ripped apart. He killed many of his attackers and bought enough time for his apprentice to get away. A noble death. Oh, and then there was Obie who was beheaded by a plate glass window, just shameful. My second thought was that it was a much bigger hole than I intended. I was going for something smaller than a human could get through. Too late now, better get to work. I put the rock on the inside of the door to make it look like it was thrown through and jumped in, being careful not to hit the door and risk dislodging more glass.

I did another sweep for unearthly scents. Two hallways lead off in opposite directions. I took the left hallway, passing activity and classrooms. A set of double wood doors at the end of the hall were labeled as the sanctuary. I went back to the other hallway, following it around in a large circle to a second sanctuary entrance. Nothing looked or smelled out of place. I went back to the entryway and Steve's office.

I had no choice but to change back into human form. Having otter thumbs is great, but they don't do any good if you can't reach the door handle. It wouldn't have mattered anyway; after the change was complete, I found the door locked. A small matter really. I slammed my bare foot into it, splintering the frame and throwing the door wide open. Starting with the desk, I sat down, rubbing my naked bum in the soft leather. After visiting his home, I thought the garbage I smelled on him yesterday had been from his house. Sitting behind his desk I had a different vantage point. The garbage can under the desk was overflowing onto the floor. The mess was concealed, so unless you were sitting behind the desk or had heightened senses, you wouldn't know it was there. I wondered if anyone knew that his wife had left him. He was probably keeping up appearances, hiding the stinky stuff out of sight to keep his image intact. Another reason why going public about demons didn't make sense. There had to be something here to shed some light on his strange behavior.

Rifling through the drawers turned up nothing but office supplies. The large desk calendar had a couple notes on it but nothing that looked important. I found the page of the calendar for last month in the garbage with some ketchup stains on it. I unfolded it on the desk, noticing right away that Steve's schedule had freed up a lot since last month. The first two weeks of this calendar had

something on almost every day then tapering off for weeks three and four. That's
when I saw it:

P.V.T.
MOCA GA
3 PM

The handwriting looked like the note I'd found at Steve's house. If his wife
made the appointment she might have some insight to who P.V.T. is. The other
mystery was Moca, GA. I had never heard of that town before. Maybe it was in
south Georgia somewhere. I didn't get down there often.

My thoughts were interrupted by the familiar sound of tires on gravel, someone was coming. Looking out the window I saw a patrol car rolling up to the
church. There may have been more clues here but I was out of time. I ripped the
note out of the calendar and shoved the rest back in the garbage can, being careful to cover it back up with some of what was on the floor. Didn't want to leave
any clues as to what I was looking for. Time for a strategic exit out the back. I
tried the side door, hoping it wasn't a closet. I was in luck, it opened into a class-
room. From there I made it back to the hallway, out of sight of the lobby. The
metal door I had seen outside had to be in the sanctuary. It was my best chance
to get away unseen.

There were no windows, not even the fancy stained glass ones, so the room
was dark except for an emergency light mounted on the left wall. Rows of pews
stretched out in front of me, facing a pulpit with a pew on each side and a large
cross on the back wall. I found the door I had seen from the outside hidden behind a curtain. I moved the curtain and pressed the handle stepping out into the
bright summer sun. I squinted as my eyes struggled to adjust to the light.

"Police, don't move," a voice shouted.

Without hesitation, I grabbed the handle and retreated back into the building. The door slammed behind me and locked. Why did I do that? I should have
run for it. I could have easily outpaced him in the woods and changed forms,
effectively disappearing. While they were out chasing me it would have been
no problem to circle around to the truck and roll it out quietly before more
cops showed up. Now they would be calling for backup and have their guns out.
Making a run for it now could get me shot. I needed another plan.

The best way to get past cops that are looking for you is to be someone else,
in this case something else. I moved back through the hallway toward the front

door, stopping just out of sight of it. I crumpled up my clue and shoved it in my mouth, tasting the paper and stale ketchup, and changed back into an otter. Moving down the hallway I didn't see anyone outside but I knew someone was there—they wouldn't leave the front unguarded. Being careful around the broken glass on the floor, I hopped through the hole in the door and walked into the sunlight. A police cruiser sat caddy-corner to the building.

"Police, let me see . . . What the hell," a voice said from the direction of the car to my right.

I turned to see an officer with something between surprise and confusion plastered on his face, pointing a pistol in my direction. He must have reacted to my movement before putting the pieces together of exactly what was happening. I stopped and stood on my back paws, raising my front paws in the air, I couldn't resist. I could make out the scents of two people. I am sure his partner had already told him he had spotted someone inside which explained why his attention was split between me and the door. He kept looking over like someone was going to jump out of the door at any second. I couldn't help but laugh, which sounded like a lot like a human laughing after breathing helium with a few squeaks thrown in for good measure. Lowering myself down on all fours I headed off toward the hill and the safety of the brush. I spotted the other officer at the side of the building with his gun trained on the door I had tried to come out of a minute before.

I made my way up the embankment, disappearing from sight into the bushes. I found a hidden spot where I could see the parking lot. I couldn't risk driving away with cops around; it would attract too much attention. I would have to wait them out. A few more patrol cars showed up, followed by a black Explorer. A man sporting a righteous mustache and wearing a polo shirt and khakis got out of the Explorer. He adjusted his pants around his portly belly and draped a badge on a lanyard around his neck. They all took strategic positions around the building but didn't go in. Shortly after, a woman in a sedan drove up and parked in the back. She didn't get out of the car but the mustached man went over, chatted for a few minutes, and took a key from her. Must be the secretary. That's when things got exciting. A few stayed in the front but most went to the side door where I had been spotted. They unlocked it and poured in, shouting commands at the empty church. It was kind of funny, really. Part of me wanted to be there to see their faces when they figured out no one was there.

The shouting died down and a few officers trickled out here and there. They would no doubt do an extensive search to find me. The man that showed up in the Explorer was talking to the first two on the scene. I could tell from his hand motions and body language that he was talking about the otter that came out and went up the hill. He gave the hill a questioning glance before walking over and appeared to be looking for tracks though I doubted he was an expert tracker. It's not hard to follow tracks in eroded dirt. When he found them, he stood looking at the hill in thought. After a minute, he walked off in the opposite direction toward the road. When he got to the entrance to the parking lot he stopped and examined the ground again. I wasn't worried about that. After so many cars coming in there was no way he could pick my truck tires out.

I hadn't thought about the tracks my truck had left in the grass. He turned around, examining the parking lot, and must have noticed the grass pushed down from where I had driven up to the graveyard. Before I knew it, he was walking up the trail and on the way to discovering my truck. That I didn't expect—well played, mustached man. The wind shifted and I got a scent of him: Old Spice and dog, terrier maybe. I could try to distract him, but I couldn't keep him away forever, and couldn't move the truck while they were around. Talking to him wouldn't help because I couldn't give him any real answers. He would probably try to arrest me and I couldn't let that happen. I could always kill him. Sooner or later someone would figure out he was missing and come looking. By the end of it I would have to kill them all. I could see the headlines: Police force murdered, otter taken into custody for questioning. Pass. The thing that made the most sense was to do nothing and wait.

He walked into the clearing and spotted the truck. He drew his gun and moved forward, checking the cab first before moving on to the bed. Finding it empty, he holstered his gun and walked around to the back of the truck, pulled out a notepad, and jotted down my tag before going back to the cab to peer in through the window. I knew he wasn't going to see anything; I keep my truck clean. He looked around, making sure the coast was clear, and pulled some latex gloves out of his back pocket. He put them on and tried the passenger door—I guess Mister Mustache sees a little leeway with the law. I wasn't in the habit of locking my doors but there wasn't anything for him to find except my license, the wooden knife in the glovebox, and my gear bag behind the seat. None of it was illegal. Strange, absolutely, but not illegal.

He rummaged around for a minute before getting into the glovebox. He paused before holding up my wooden knife between two fingers, eyeballing it. That was a problem. If he held it by the handle, I could have a dead cop on my hands. If I changed to human form it would just lead to more questions, why

I was in the area and naked to boot. It's possible the guy that got a glimpse of me at the door could identify me. If so, they would try to arrest me. *Just put it back asshole.* I scraped the ground with my back legs, sending leaves flying and making some noise to get his attention. He whipped his head up, looking in my direction. I sank down into the leaves. Sitting still, I'm sure he couldn't see me. After a few seconds without finding the cause of the sound, he put the knife back and closed the door. He put the gloves back in his pocket and stood, facing my direction, watching and listening for what had made the noise. When he was satisfied he wasn't going to find anything, he gave up and headed back down the trail.

I was stuck there for most of the day before they had finished processing the scene and cleared out. I was itching to get out of there but I waited another thirty minutes after the last car left just to make sure I wouldn't be followed. I had a new lead and needed to get back to Naylet to report in. I would never have admitted it to her but I was looking forward to seeing her reaction to the news. I would get a thorough round of *I told you so's* and she would be a little too smug about it but she would be happy. When I was satisfied the coast was clear, I changed back into human form, got dressed, and headed back to Naylet's house.

CHAPTER·8

THERE WEREN'T ANY lights on when I pulled up to the house. That seemed a little strange, it wasn't Naylet's night out with the girls, she didn't say she was going anywhere, and it was much too early for her to be in bed. Maybe she went out; she does love to point out how much of a life she has outside of me. That might not be a bad thing, between this missing baby and the recent demon issues. A couple days to focus on work might be good, it would get us on that vacation a lot quicker. Still, I had to check in, just to make sure everything was okay.

Leaving the truck running, I got out and headed for the front door. As soon as my foot hit the grass I knew something was wrong. I couldn't tell what it was. I stood frozen in my tracks looking for something out of place. The lightning bugs were flashing, the katydids chirped, a bobwhite sang in the woods off to my right. I could smell the leaves and earth of the woods. Everything looked the same but it felt differently, it felt empty. The vitality Naylet had cultivated in the area seemed to have drained away. Covering the yard and steps leading to the front door in a few strides I turned the knob and let myself in.

"Naylet, are you here?" I asked the empty room.

I had to question if my nose was playing tricks on me. A faint scent of spices lingered in the house, the same scent that was on the bunny in the truck. A half-finished cup of coffee sat on the counter beside a few sweet potatoes, peeled but not chopped, as well as a few other ingredients, hinting at the dish that was being made. Pecans, brown sugar, banana, chia seed—I knew this. It was a casserole Naylet makes for breakfast sometimes. It was closer to dinnertime now. That wasn't the only strange thing. Pictures that normally hung on the walls were in a pile on the table beside the newspaper I had read the night before. Turning the light on, I checked the loft to find it empty. Flipping through the pictures I noticed a couple had been taken out of the frames. One was from about forty years ago, the last time we took a trip to the beach. It was the only physical evidence that I had ever worn bell bottoms, and one of the happiest times of my life.

Maybe whatever had taken Baby Stephanie had come after Naylet; that would explain the smell, but it didn't explain the pictures. Still, none of this made any sense. Sitting down at the table, I pondered my next move. Nymphs weren't known for being fighters but if she got away she could disappear in the woods. She probably had some trouble, ran out, and was staying hidden until she knew it's safe. If she was laying low, she would come out when she heard me. I had to check the woods.

Heading back to the truck, I grabbed a flashlight out of the bag I kept behind the seat and turned to start my search. Stopping dead in my tracks I paused for a second before going into the glovebox to get my knife. I tucked it in my shorts, better safe than sorry, and headed for the storage shed. I didn't think she would be there, but it was close and I might as well check. It was neat and tidy; she likes to keep things in order like that. Some people might call her O.C.D.; I don't. Gardening tools hung on the walls, and bags of soil were stacked neatly beside a wheelbarrow in the corner. I made my way around the house. It all looked normal but I found a set of tracks heading off into the woods behind the house. Naylet had made a reading garden by a stream that flowed at the bottom of the hill. The tracks led off in that direction, and from the small tufts of dirt thrown behind the track it looked like she was running. The path wove its way through the woods and down a hill for about two hundred feet, which I covered at full speed. It opened into a mossy area beside the creek, with flower beds scattered around the edges. A bench sat off on the right side. She was nowhere to be found.

"Naylet," I called. There was no answer.

I held the flashlight low, sending the beam across the ground and discovered a pair of tracks in the grass. It looked like Naylet's and another set I didn't recognize. The new set looked humanoid with distinct claw marks around the toes. I didn't recognize them. Being that they appeared on the ground out of nowhere, whatever it was could probably fly.

There was a chase. I followed Naylet's tracks, telling the story of how she evaded her pursuer around the entire clearing in large circles. The clawed set took a much more direct approach. Wherever Naylet had gone, this creature followed her, leaving straight lines of tracks with scrapes in the ground from its claws. Keeping up with Naylet was tough, even for me; whatever this thing was, it was quick.

Naylet's tracks escaped into the creek. It was four feet wide and barely a foot deep. The clawed tracks skidded to a stop, avoiding the water. That was a hint—demons hated water. The stranger's tracks disappeared, the demon must have taken flight again. That left me with nothing to go on. I was a good tracker, but no one was good enough to track in moving water or through the air. I stepped into the stream, the cold water biting at my feet, and shone the light downstream looking for clues. Coming up with nothing, I turned upstream, revealing a figure hunched low in the water, almost completely submerged. I stepped forward, cautiously moving to the side to get a better look. It was Naylet. Only her head and one arm was raised out of the water, shielding her face.

"Naylet, are you alright?" I asked, taking a cautious step forward.

There was no response, not so much as a flinch. She had a stillness with the absoluteness of death. I moved forward a few more steps and could see she was wearing shorts and a red tee shirt, no shoes. Her skin looked to be a light grey color. I was hoping it was a trick of the light, but the closer I got the more I was sure it wasn't. I didn't know if it was just in my head, but the whole area took on a feeling of heaviness, like the woods before a hard rain. When I was close enough, I reached out and touched her hand. It was solid and cool to the touch, not living, but as if she had been carved from a piece of stone.

I moved around and knelt beside her, my breath catching in my throat. It was definitely Naylet but I had no explanation for what had happened to her. Although I had only seen it a couple times in all the years we had been together, I recognized the expression on her face: fear. That was it for me, the tears started to pool in my eyes. I wiped them away and took a breath. There's no time for that.

"Hang on, Naylet, I'll get you to Livy. She can fix this," I said, trying to convince myself as much as her.

I've been around a while and thought I had seen just about everything, but this one was new. Naylet may not look that tough, but she was mean as a snake in a pinch, it was one of her many endearing qualities. The tracks told me she couldn't get away from her pursuer but there was no evidence that she put up a fight either. I only knew one thing about whatever did this to her: it was dangerous. A breeze drifted through the woods from behind me and I was sure I could smell the perfume I had found at the Olson house. It was faint but it was there. I was about to shift into krasis and track down where it was coming from when I was distracted by the sound of a car pulling up to the house. New lights, combined with my truck's lights, shone over the crest of the hill and through the trees, making it look like a scene from the *X-Files*.

"Were you expecting company?" I asked Naylet's lifeless form.

I couldn't very well go up the hill in krasis without knowing who was up there, but I didn't want to stay in human form if I had to face whatever was lurking out of sight in the woods. Deciding to keep my human form, at least until I knew who had come knocking, I lifted Naylet out of the water. With one arm under her legs and the other across her back, I carried her out of the stream. In the past I have never had trouble picking her up, she couldn't have been more than a buck twenty-five, tops. This transformation, however, added the weight of stone and not just the look. It actually took some effort to lift her. Walking toward the hill, I thought of the wheelbarrow I had seen in the shed. I didn't want to leave her alone in the dark with whatever was out there. It didn't feel right. I could make it, I just might have Jell-O legs by the time I got there.

Halfway up the hill I heard the slow and deliberate crunching of leaves in the woods behind me, footsteps. I dropped Naylet's legs, spinning quickly with my light. The beam found something that leapt straight up and disappeared into the night sky with only the flapping of wings and rustled leaves to give away that it had been there at all. I had only caught a glimpse of something, a shadowy figure in the darkness, but not enough to tell what it was. I was right, though, there was something out here.

"Which one of us do you think it's after?" I asked. Naylet didn't answer.

Whatever it was, it was gone for the moment. It would be back, though, they always come back. Retrieving Naylet's legs, I continued up toward the headlights. Maybe that would deter it—I doubt it, but here's to hoping. Coming over the crest of the hill and into the headlights, I couldn't see anything but the house illuminated to my left and two sets of headlights shining in my direction. I had to get Naylet into my truck, that was a given, I just needed to figure out who was there and how in the way they were going to get. With no time to beat around the bush, I started walking straight across the yard. Halfway there I caught a whiff of Old Spice and dog, now with a hint of B.O. I knew who it was before I stepped past the beams to find the mustached officer from the church.

He must have had me followed, something I should have noticed, another slipup I guess. It's not like he couldn't look up who I was and my home address from my tag if he wanted to. Regardless, I wasn't in the mood to deal with this. He got out of his Explorer with the kind of smirk on his face I instinctively wanted to wipe off with light violence. He had to have seen me as soon as I came over the crest of the hill. I could have easily gotten away from him but that meant leaving Naylet behind. I would play along for a bit, disposing of a cop and his car is one more thing that I really didn't want to deal with. I'd get Naylet in the truck and see how far this encounter would go.

"Evening. Detective Farwell," he said when I stepped past the headlights. He tapped a badge hanging from a lanyard around his neck as he spoke. "Does the owner of this place know you are hauling off their statue?"

"Yes, officer, I assure you she would be pleased to know that I am taking care of it," I said.

"She would be, you say? So she doesn't know you are taking it?" Right then I knew this guy wanted to bust me for something, par for the course. Unfortunately for him that's not going to happen tonight.

"Yeah, I'm afraid she's not here at the moment. I hope she will be back soon. She had mentioned that she wanted it taken care of and I wasn't busy so I thought I would do a favor for a friend. You know how it goes," I replied.

"Oh sure," he agreed. "It's awful Christian of you. Do you attend church regular? I go to Inclusive Assembly of Christ, over by Canton. Have you ever been there before?"

I set Naylet down by the truck and opened the tailgate. "I might have been by there once or twice."

"I was hoping to talk to you about something that happened there today," he said, squinting at me.

"Of course, officer, I would be happy to come down to the station and talk to you. Does tomorrow afternoon work for you?" I knew it wasn't going to be this easy.

"I'm a 'rip the bandage off' kind of guy. We could straighten it out right now," he said.

I had just finished heaving Naylet into the back of the truck and closed the gate when, for the second time, I heard shuffling in the woods. Again they came from behind me. I turned and put my arms up on the tailgate with a foot up on the bumper. I was going for a casual look but really, I was preparing to launch myself at whatever would come out of the woods.

"Sir, can you step over here, please," Farwell said.

I didn't have time for this. I could tell from the look on his face that he was about to stop beating around the bush and get down to business. Something was out there and if I didn't get him out of here he could be killed—or worse, he could live, and that would be a real mess. Maybe Thera would consider an exception to the "protect life" rule if she knew how inconvenient it was for me. On second thought, probably not. I walked away from the truck, to get between him and the footsteps. Standing with my back to him I looked into the woods for a few seconds and smelled the air. It was out there.

"Sir . . ." Farwell said, trying to redirect my attention from the trees.

I was about to turn around to tell him that I didn't have anything to discuss tonight when I was interrupted.

"Is there a problem, officer?" a woman's voice said from the trees.

I didn't recognize it or the young woman it was attached to. She was in skinny jeans and a form-fitting black tank top. Her dark clothing, combined with her dark complexion, made her seem to appear out of nowhere as she stepped out of the trees. She had long thick dreadlocks reaching almost to her waist and wasn't wearing shoes. I already figured she was up to no good, but the lack of shoes sealed the deal. You have to be careful around people that don't wear shoes. They are either going to be the salt of the earth or some monster that will try to eat your face; there's not a lot of in between. I moved back to my truck to put myself between Naylet and the new visitor.

Farwell's hand had instinctively gone to his gun. It lingered there as he spoke: "And you are?"

"I'm Naylet Kirtane. I live here. I overheard your conversation and I can clear up this little misunderstanding. You see, I did ask him to move the statue for me. I'm afraid I have been thinking some more about it and have decided to keep it. I'm sorry to put you through all this trouble, Obie. Be a dear and set it over by the shed please. I will find the perfect place for it tomorrow morning. I promise you I won't bother you with it again."

My lip curled, I couldn't help it. "Not going to happen."

I had squared up with her, put a hand on the tailgate to emphasize my point.

"Obie," she exclaimed. "What has gotten into you? I assure you, officer, he's not normally like this. What's the matter, hun?"

"Don't call me that."

Farwell had moved away during this process. He was speaking softly and trying to be discreet while we were distracting each other. It almost worked. "Hey, it's Ryan. I'm okay but need a couple marked units at my location," he said and started walking back in our direction. "Ma'am, this is getting a little heated. Could you go inside and let's take a few minutes to calm down, then we can get this figured out."

"Marked units . . . he is referring to police cars?" she asked.

It might have been a rhetorical question but I answered it anyway. "Yep, he's got backup on the way. Guess you better scurry back to whatever shithole you crawled out of."

"Don't be crass, Obie, it's beneath you. Officer Farwell, I wish you hadn't done that," she said stepping backward into the woods the way she came and disappeared into the shadows, her eyes locked on me as she went.

CHAPTER · 9

"DETECTIVE, YOU SHOULD call off that backup, leave, and forget you ever saw me," I said without turning around.

"We aren't done with our conversation," he said.

He's going to get himself killed. "Like I said, I will happily come speak to you tomorrow. There's business here that doesn't concern you. For your own safety, you need to leave."

He put his hands on his hips. "That doesn't work for me."

"Suit yourself."

I circled around the cars trying to locate where the imposter had gone. Neither the crunching of leaves nor the flapping of wings gave away her location in the woods. Either she was staying perfectly still or she had vanished. If she wasn't here she couldn't stop me. Farwell would, he would try at least, but I wasn't going to be arrested today. I could kill him but that just didn't seem very gentlemanly. Instead, I turned to face him and realized he was speaking, I hadn't been paying attention. Looking him directly in the eyes, I made the change into krasis. That shut him up. The blood drained from his face and he pulled his pistol from its holster but didn't start shooting, yet.

"I am going to get in my truck and I'm going to leave," I said. "We can meet so you can make sense of all this later but now isn't the time. If you try to stop me, I will have to hurt you. I don't want to hurt you, but I will, and that pea shooter isn't going to protect you."

With that, I moved to the driver side of my truck, keeping an eye on him to make sure he didn't get any funny ideas. I didn't get the impression he was going to try to take me down to the station. Placing a hand on the door handle, I was just starting to think this was going to turn out all right when something hit me like a sledgehammer. I didn't hear a gunshot so it wasn't Farwell, but before I knew what happened I was airborne. The only distraction from sharp pain in my shoulder was the beating of large wings right above me. I couldn't orient myself fast enough to make sense of what was happening. I found myself tumbling through the air into the yard. I landed hard on my back and was left gasping for breath. I raised up on my elbows to get my bearings. I had been thrown about thirty feet into the yard away from the truck. The beast touched down in front of Farwell's Explorer. The headlights concealed any distinct features and cast a long shadow across the ground in my direction. I raised a hand for a better look. The webbing between my fingers kept the light from my eyes, but the figure advancing was still a mystery.

It was unmistakably female, with large bat-like wings. Her skin looked a little shiny around the edges as if it was reflecting the light or wet, not unlike the silver lining of a cloud, but nothing good was going to come from this. There was something moving around her head and shoulders that I couldn't make out. It might be some kind of magic at work. I was recovering quickly, the injury to my shoulder almost closed. In a couple minutes it should be back to normal. Already the bleeding had stopped and nothing seemed broken. I reached back with my good arm to get my knife but it wasn't there. It must have fallen out while I was airborne. I spotted where it had dropped about fifteen feet in front of me. I couldn't get to it at the moment, it was too close to this demon. Luckily, I have claws and teeth, and they have never let me down in the past. It's a lot more work that way, but as they say, if you like what you do you never work a day in your immortal life.

"You don't know who you're fucking with, lady," I said, getting to my feet.

She laughed. "Oh, Obie, I know all about you, how your parents died, your experiences at the orphanage, when you became a Keeper, the problems with Cearbhall, when you fell in love—I know exactly who I'm fucking with, and I have to admit I have been looking forward to it for quite a while."

There's no way she could know all that. No one knows that much about me, except maybe Cearbhall and Naylet, so how did this thing? She took a couple steps forward, only a few feet from my knife now. It didn't look like she realized it was there. I started circling slowly to the left. With any luck she would play along.

"So what, you did a little research? You get all that from Naylet before you . . ." I trailed off not knowing exactly what she had done or wanting to vocalize it.

She circled to my right into the light and letting me get a good look at her for the first time. That's when I realized what the mass on her head was. Snakes, big black ones. *Why did it have to be snakes?* There was a noise behind her, it must have been Farwell but I couldn't see what he was doing with the lights in my eyes. She heard it as well and turned her back to me to face him, bad move. I didn't waste the opportunity to run for my knife. She didn't seem interested in stopping me. I grabbed it off the ground and dashed a few paces away in anticipation of an attack that never came.

Moving around the back of Farwell's Explorer, I found her standing in front of him. He was standing perfectly still by the open car door. The snakes had spread out on her head and I could see all their eyes, as well as hers, glowing yellow. She was working some kind of magic. He had her distracted and I had no intention of missing an opportunity to finish her off. That's when I saw his hands, they were turning grey, grey like Naylet. He was being turned to stone. She was not going to have another victim tonight, not on my watch. Coming up behind Farwell, I stepped between them, blocking her sight. The hair all over my body immediately stood on end and my skin tingled like I had electricity running all over me. I wasn't worried about it affecting me. Thera shields her Keepers from magical attacks, the tingling told me it was working. At least something was going my way. I lunged forward, delivering three quick jabs with my knife. One hit her jaw and the other two landed solidly on her neck, too solidly in fact. It hadn't penetrated, there was no blood or visible sign of damage. The snakes, along with her gaze, redirected their focus to me. The tingling increased to an almost painful level.

I needed to put an end to this before it got any more out of hand, and before she realized her spell wasn't working. I reared back and landed a solid punch right in her nose. Her head whipped back with a satisfying crack. The snakes flailed uncontrollably and for a second their glowing yellow eyes went out like I had flipped a light switch. She stumbled back a step, clearly stunned. I wasn't sure how much of it was from the blow and how much was from the shock that her magic wasn't working. Farwell moaned behind me and fell to the ground; better than being stone, buddy. I glanced back to see the grayness in his hands slowly receding. Picking him up, I tried to put him in his car, but the demon had recovered enough to come after me, black blood running out of her nose and hatred pouring out of her eyes.

Throwing Farwell over my shoulder I retreated around the back of the Explorer and dumped him in the back of my truck with Naylet as I passed it. She closed on me fast, screeching as she came. As soon as my arms were free from tossing Farwell in the truck I spun with the dagger, delivering a slash across the chest that would have killed her if she were any kind of decent creature. She stumbled back, grabbing her chest, and hunched forward. The snakes moved around to protect her and blocked my view of the gore that was undoubtedly starting to spill out. It would kill the grass but it's a small price to pay, if you've seen one pile of demon guts you've seen them all. The snakes moved back revealing a fanged grin. There was no visible sign of the cut except that the shirt had a large slash mark through it showing scaled breasts underneath. It hung loosely from her shoulders now, being mostly open in the front and not so form fitting. She ripped it away and tossed it to the ground.

She smirked. "Are you really so desperate to get me undressed?"

"I'll have you skinned by the time this is done."

If my blade wouldn't penetrate her scales then I would have to hit her somewhere it would penetrate, her eyes looked like prime candidates. We circled, sizing each other up for a second before moving in simultaneously. She slashed with clawed fingers, while snakes struck from all directions. I countered with quick footwork and aggressive parries, hitting away the snakes that couldn't be avoided. It was not a winning strategy, and she knew it. Between the snakes and her claws, I couldn't get through to land an attack. It became clear to me that I didn't have any real options; it was only a matter of time before I was overcome. If I wanted to take her out I was going to have to take the hits and count on my ability to heal to get me through it. I waited for as clear an opening as I was going to get, and thrust my blade hard at her face. The knife made contact but my attacking arm was struck repeatedly as snakes buried their teeth into my flesh. I dropped the knife and grabbed a snake. I gave it a sharp pull and simultaneously sent a foot into her belly with everything I had. The snake tore free in my hand as she sprawled out on the ground from the impact. Point Obie. The snake writhed for a few seconds and then went still.

She didn't appear to be in any hurry to get up so I took advantage and walked backward toward my truck, as not to turn my back on her. My happiness at the success was short lived. I could feel numbness starting to creep into my arm. She rose, leisurely and grinning like she knew something I didn't, not the best feeling. Blood ran down from her head over her shoulder from where the snake had been. She looked too happy for someone who had just had a piece of themselves ripped off.

"I have to say I'm surprised, Obie. You have always been so gentle in the past. It will all be over soon now though," she said. "The venom will make quick work of you."

"You might be getting a little ahead of yourself. I'm not dead yet."

"Yes, not dead yet. I'll give you that. You are quite resilient. I'm surprised that you've lasted this long if I'm being honest. You know you have a reputation for being a little soft? Naylet thinks so too, but she actually likes it. Look at you now, you even managed to kill one of my serpents, the part of me that is her is impressed I think. No one has given me this much trouble in a very long time."

I was getting really tired of the talking in riddles and speaking to me like she actually knew something about my relationship. "I'll celebrate later."

The numbness continued to spread. Slow enough, at first, for me to question if it was spreading at all. The fact that I had to question it told me it was spreading faster than my body could recover from it. I had a resistance to her magic; the venom on the other hand, wasn't magic. It was just everyday venom, but being from a demon and from another place meant my normal protections against everything from Thera didn't apply. Without a natural resistance, only relying on my healing ability, there was no telling how bad it would be. I needed to get Naylet and Farwell out of here now. The best place I could take them was Livy's house. It was well hidden and I had a feeling I was going to need her help soon. The longer this fight took the less likely it would turn out in my favor.

My dagger was on the ground a couple feet away from her although my fists seemed to do a better job on her than the blade. Naylet had a sledgehammer in the shed. I pondered for a moment. If I could get to it that might do the trick. Still the blade might be able to help me if I could get her to pick it up.

"You got a name?" I asked.

"I already told you, Naylet," she said.

"I'm not going to call you that. Quit fucking around, tell me your name."

She smiled again, revealing fangs. "I have many names. Petra, Laelius, Vibiana, Colleen, Afia . . . I have more if one of those doesn't suit you."

"Why so many? You have a collection or something?" I asked.

"I collect lives, not names."

"What does that mean, collect lives?" I knew I wasn't going to like the answer as soon as I asked the question.

"It means that sometimes I require an infusion to sustain myself. I assure you, it's a painless process. The subject is absorbed, becoming part of me, leaving behind an empty shell. I gain their experiences and potential in the process. Many people are hesitant at first, but they come around. Take Naylet," she raised a hand to the statue in my truck. "She fought hard at first before I wore her down, but look at her now! She's stunning, a work of art, she will be beautiful forever and no doubt she is thrilled with the arrangement. I can almost hear her, 'thank you Petra' and 'you've saved me' she says, and I will tell you, Obie, I am honored to be able to help her. We do have one little problem though."

"What's that," I asked.

"I'm afraid I just can't let you take her from me. She's part of my family now," she said, her tone changing from joy to menace.

"That is a problem, because I'm not going to leave without her." I shifted my eyes to the blade on the ground and made sure to move my head a little to accentuate my intention.

"Sweetie, you're not leaving either way," she said following my eyes to the knife. "It is a remarkable blade, useless against me of course but the craftsmanship is very nice. Did you want it? Here, take it." She bent over and picked it up.

She held it out to me, opening her mouth to speak again, when the enchantment triggered. The air charged, building quickly, and then burst, sending electricity coursing through Petra's body. She convulsed under its effect before collapsing to the ground, steam rising from her body. The smell of charred flesh filled the air. I moved forward and nudged her with my foot to see if that had finished her off. She let out a moan, but neither she nor the snakes moved. She was tough, I'll give her that. The dagger had been destroyed in the explosion. The pieces that remained were on fire, scattered across the ground.

Having a second to breathe, the first thing I noticed was the numbness moving into my right leg. I needed to get help soon. If anyone was going to be able to counteract the venom it would be Livy. Farwell had come to and climbed out of the back of the truck. He leaned against the truck bed with his gun out but not pointed at anything, a confused look on his face.

"Get in," I said, limping toward the truck. He obliged without an argument.

It was hard to ignore how weak my grip had become when I shifted the truck into first. My hand was swollen and its sensations felt foreign. Driving straight out into the yard, the truck lurched to the right as the front tire rolled over Petra. Putting it in reverse and cranking the wheel, I backed out, running over her a second time. The dirt road leading to my rescue stretched out in front of me but I stopped. Putting it into reverse again, I backed up over Petra a third time and rolled forward until the tires came to rest against her body. Pressing the gas, the engine rattled and then burst to life in a roar. I popped the clutch, sending the tires spinning with centrifugal fury.

There was a loud thud as the tires grabbed her limp body, slamming it against the underside of the truck before she ricocheted off into the yard. I hit the brakes and looked in the rearview, the engine retuning to a steady rumble. Naylet's once impeccable yard, now gouged by my tires, with Petra's twisted and broken body littering the grounds, and small flaming pieces of my knife looked right out of a nightmare when bathed in the red glow of the tail lights.

Focusing my attention ahead instead of behind, I roared down the driveway, sending gravel flying into the woods in waves as I spun around the curves. It occurred to me it might have been better to take Farwell's car, the lights might have come in handy, but it was too late now. Livy lived deep in the mountains. The good news is that she and Naylet were practically neighbors, by country standards. Livy only lived twenty minutes away, give or take. The bad news is that the venom was working its way through my system and I wasn't sure if I had that long.

"You need to call off the backup," I said once we made it back on the pavement.

Farwell seemed not entirely aware of what was going on.

I waved my hand in front of his face. "Hey . . . Snap out of it." I tried snapping a few times to get his attention but my thumb wouldn't cooperate. "If she's still alive she's going to kill your backup, call them off."

"Ok, I'll call," he said.

He took out the phone and stared at it but didn't hit any buttons. That's when the dizziness set in. I concentrated on the road, putting my entire force of will into staying awake and delivering us in one piece. I heard a voice that sounded distant and fuzzy, it was Farwell. I didn't know what he was saying but I hoped no cops showed up. They would find a demon body and a missing detective. As the minutes passed, my right arm became completely useless, preventing me from shifting gears. I would have to finish the drive in whatever gear I was in. My vision started to blur and it was getting harder to keep the truck in one lane. There wasn't any traffic on these roads at this hour but there were steep drop-offs on the right side of the road. Since I couldn't change gears, the only logical thing to do was to keep my speed up as much as I could.

There weren't any traffic lights and only a couple stop signs that I ignored. I turned onto the forest service road Livy's house was off of and followed the well-manicured gravel road before whipping the truck off the road onto what most people wouldn't even consider a deer trail. The truck skidded down the path, gaining speed from the hill. Farwell's hand reached over and grabbed the

wheel. I passed through the camouflage barrier concealing the house from outsiders. We were closing on the house much too quickly. I let go of the wheel,
reached down, pulled the parking brake, and passed out.

CHAPTER • 10

I FELT THE WARM sun and a gentle steady breeze on my fur that I have only
felt at high altitude. Opening my eyes, I found a clear blue sky with a single turkey vulture gliding in lazy circles overhead. The ground was hard, it felt like a
solid stone; not entirely uncomfortable to lay on, at least there weren't rocks to
make things lumpy. I heard some children playing and a train whistle in the distance. Putting all of this together I knew where I was before I sat up. I had never
been anywhere else like this.

"You shouldn't lie there all day. The vultures will make a meal out of you
if you don't get up soon," Thera said. I turned my head to my right to see dark
brown feet. The feet were attached to bountiful legs that disappeared into a
thick mixture off summer grass and wildflowers that grew from her head and
cascaded around her body.

She never appeared with clothes, and her appearance changed with the seasons and areas where she appeared. While she appeared like this in summer, in
winter she would have almost snow white skin with deep evergreen boughs. Regardless of how she looked, if you were in the presence of the Earth Mother you
knew it. She brought with her an essence of power and vitality unmatched by
anything else. In any case, now it made sense how I could be close to death, with
my truck careening out of control one second, and basking in the sun on the top
of Stone Mountain the next.

Stone Mountain is a solid rock that reaches twenty-three hundred feet above
a relatively flat landscape. I always thought it seemed out of place—the locals
had turned it into a park complete with Confederate generals carved on the
front of it. Pain shot through my right side as I sat up; my arm and leg were stiff
and not responding. I sat on a slope a few feet away from the edge. A landscape
of green stretched out in front of me with the Atlanta skyline off in the distance. Thera sat down beside me, her elbows on her knees, barely able to touch
around her large fertile belly. She stared off into the distance. The wind pushed
the grasses back from her face.

I doubted any of this was real, of course. When she appears to me in the real
world, wind and rain can't touch her because she isn't actually there. Her appearance is just a visual representation of her spirit. So that meant I wasn't actu-

ally there; it felt real enough just the same. I wondered if I had died and this was what the afterlife was like: a tourist trap. I think I would prefer nothingness, but looking into Thera's scowling face, I decided being left alone would be enough. It was quite possible I was bleeding out in the cab of my truck right now. The least she could do is let me bleed in peace.

"Something has happened," she said, not looking away from the horizon.

"You could say that," I replied. I relayed the story of finding Naylet and the encounter with the demon calling herself Petra, complete with the snakes, poison, and running her over with the truck.

"So you let her escape," she said.

"I ran her over four times," I said. "And that's after she took a lightning strike from my knife. I really don't think . . ."

"That's right, you don't think. You should have made sure. What if she's not dead? She was incapacitated, helpless, and you did nothing."

"Now just hold on. I was trying to save Naylet, not to mention that pain in the ass detective. Plus, I am seriously injured. I almost died. I barely made it to Livy's . . ." I paused realizing I still didn't know what had happened. "Did I make it to Livy's?"

She stared off into the distance like I wasn't there.

"Hey, talk to me. What's going on?"

"Holt is in trouble," she said.

"Isn't he always?"

She looked me in the eyes. "This isn't a joke, he's in pain."

"Do you know where he is?" I asked, not feeling quite as jovial as I did a moment before.

"He was attacked and taken somewhere. Not long after, he was in pain. Now I have lost sight of him completely and I feel my connections to others stretching thin," she said. "Whatever this is, it is affecting me directly. That can't stand."

"Do you know what's doing it?"

"It could be some demon or magic maybe. I have never experienced this before. I think whatever it is, it's centered around Holt."

"Did you get a look at what attacked him?" I asked.

Thera didn't respond. Worry swept across her face, an unfamiliar look for her to say the least. I had never seen that expression on her before and I didn't like it. Nothing shakes Thera, she is solid as the earth. She stood up and looked around.

"What is it?" I asked.

She looked around. "Obie?"

That's when I realized, she couldn't see me. I reached out to touch her leg, my hand passed through like she was an illusion. I wasn't sure if that would be normal or not since we weren't physically here. There was nothing for me to do so I sat and watched. She closed her eyes and concentrated, vanishing to leave me sitting alone. I wondered exactly how I was going to get out of the dream, or whatever it was. Maybe I would wake up whenever my body recovered. What if I didn't? Physical contact maybe? Livy was seventy miles or so north, I didn't feel good about my chances as a spirit hitchhiker.

"There you are, right where I left you," Thera said from behind me.

I twisted around to see her standing over me. I reached out and touched her leg; it was solid.

"I lost you. You need to find what is doing this and put an end to it," she said.

"It has to be Petra," I said, standing to face her. "She has a grimoire and I think she was following me. She seems to have some kind of sick obsession with me. I just need some time to heal and I'll take care of it."

"You already let her escape once. If you can't handle this I will take care of it myself. She will not get away again," she said.

I wasn't sure about what she meant by "take care of it herself." In the two hundred plus years I have been a Keeper she has never handled a demon personally. She's never even mentioned it. "If you can handle it yourself then why did you tell me to look into it? I am doing my best to handle this up to your standard, preserving life and all that."

Her tone softened slightly at this. "Obie, do you think I am powerful?"

This caught me off guard. I was suspicious of why she would ask that question. She could create life, she created the Keepers and we are pretty powerful, as things go.

"Terrifyingly so," I conceded.

"Before the Keepers I had to handle these kinds of things myself. I could bring in a storm strong enough to level this entire landscape. I bet this Petra can't swim, maybe a flood is in order. I could submerge everything as far as the eye can see—it wouldn't be the first time. Just to be sure, I could do both of them together. Maybe a few volcanoes to make the air unbreathable. Nothing would survive but I would be rid of one demon. I can handle it myself but attrition has to be considered. I made the Keepers to be surgical instruments. I don't want to have to decimate entire populations to handle a relatively small threat. Normally these demons kill and eat. It's inconvenient but little more than a nuisance. This is different, this is affecting me directly, and it can't continue, no matter the cost. For me to handle it means destruction on a massive scale. I need you to take care of it and I need to know right now if you are incapable for any reason."

I looked out at the Atlanta skyline ahead of me and imagined what it would look like underwater. "I see. I will handle it, I just need a little time. You really used to fight demons?"

"You should see what I have tucked away in here," she said patting the mountain with her foot. Again her face dropped. "I've lost you again. If you can hear me I'll give you three days and then I'll handle it myself."

Clouds formed in the sky out of nowhere, white at first but quickly turning dark and heavy. The wind picked up, bending the trees and throwing leaves. Lightning streaked across the sky as rain started to fall. I could see and hear it all but none of it touched me. The rain and wind passed through me. I stood and hobbled over to Thera. I reached out a hand but didn't see the unevenness in the rock before I stepped on it. My already weakened ankle twisted, sending me off balance. Since the leg I needed to take a step with wasn't working at the moment. I fell backward onto the slope and started sliding. I clawed at the rock but it was smooth and slick, I couldn't get a grip. I looked up and reached out for Thera just as I slid over the edge. She probably couldn't see me, but if she could she didn't put any effort into helping me. I flipped, falling face first, wind rushing over me with the ground coming up fast. A large boulder barreled towards me, or I at it as the case may be, at an alarming rate with no way to stop. Panic set in and I scrambled for any way out. I flapped my arms and tried to grab a tree growing out of the cliff face but nothing came except the boulder. I had never fallen from this height before; I wasn't sure I could live through it. I closed my eyes tight and waited for the impact.

CHAPTER·11

THE WIND STOPPED. I didn't feel any impact, no bone crushing injuries. I opened my eyes to find a boulder a few feet from my face. Without thinking, I brought my hands up to shield myself from the impact. Pain coursed through my body. Not a "pancaking into a boulder" kind of pain, but pain like soreness after a workout where the trainer's trying to make you cry. I lowered my arms back onto the cot I was lying on and looked again at the rock above me. I knew this rock, it was part of the ceiling in Livy's house. I had spent many nights staring up at it. She had built her home into a hillside using some protruding rock as walls and ceiling. The gaps were filled in with logs and sealed with a mud mixture, the same way it was done in the old days. To be fair it was still the old days when she built it. I still felt like death warmed up and I couldn't help but wonder if this boulder would fall free any second and finish the job. It wouldn't be entirely unwelcome.

What Thera said came back to me: something was affecting her directly and she was ready to incite mass destruction to stop it. "Why are all the women in my life lunatics?" I said, trying to stretch some of the soreness out of my neck. I was still in krasis, which didn't surprise me. The change takes a force of will. It's hard to do that and be unconscious at the same time.

"We choose who we spend time with, Obie. Maybe you just need to pick better company," Livy said from somewhere off to my left.

I turned my head and saw her sitting in a rocking chair, knitting. "I've got you, so I must be doing something right."

She smiled, put the knitting in her lap, and laid her hands, misshapen from years of use, on top of it. She wasn't much younger than me, definitely one of the oldest humans living. It's probably one reason we got along so well. While she was weathered with age in the winter of her years, I hadn't changed. I felt bad about it, watching her grow old and her body fail a little at a time.

"How are you feeling?" she asked.

I had to ponder the question. So much had happened it took me a minute to figure out exactly how I was feeling. I moved a little and discovered I was sore all over, especially my right side. My body was stiff and I felt cold. Definitely not like a badass Keeper. My right arm and leg were clearly swollen and I could feel some bruising under my fur. And that was just physically. There was a whole emotional cesspool I wasn't even going to touch at the moment.

"Like roadkill," I said, grunting my way into an upright position.

The house was one large room with a natural stone ceiling. Being mostly underground, the inside stayed comfortable, if not a little cool, year round. The mud-sand mixture used to fill in the spaces between the logs did a good job insulating. A wood burning stove that Livy did all her cooking on sat opposite the door. She burned wood or coal depending on what she could get her hands on. I had spent many days splitting wood to fuel that stove and I hoped to spend many more.

To the left of the stove was a small kitchen area that wasn't more than a prep station with some storage and an old-timey ice box. The Coolerator didn't actually take ice anymore; she had worked some magic that kept it nice and chilly.

Who needs electricity when you've got magic? A small stream that ran just outside had some of its water diverted into the house through one wall, down a trough, and out another wall back to the stream. Her bed sat against the right wall, with a chest of drawers and armoire placed beside it. It was a nice set I helped her move in about a hundred and twenty years ago, and it had held up well all that time. She had a divider she could put up for some privacy if she needed it but it was in its normal spot folded up against the wall, covered with a thick layer of dust. Farwell was lying in her bed and looked to be asleep.

"How is he?" I asked.

"Not too well. He wasn't wearing a seatbelt and got all tore up in the crash. I did what I could for him but he needs more help than I can give him. We need to talk about your parking skills, Obie. You came barreling down that hill and plowed right into my house. It's a good thing it's mostly stone or you might have run me down. You did knock loose a couple of the logs on that side." She extended a crooked finger to the wall by where Farwell was lying.

"I'm sorry, Livy, I'll fix it. Where's Naylet?" I said, giving the house another look. "Were you able to help her?"

"I'm sorry, hun. I tried a few things but I think it's beyond me. You came barreling in half dead yourself, between you and him I haven't had a lot of spare time. I just about threw my back out getting the two of you in here," she said. "And lord, that snake head. What have you gotten yourself into? If I hadn't found it in the truck I might not have been able to save you. I tried everything I knew and talked to the spirits but they weren't able to help any."

I wanted to tell her that wasn't good enough, that she should journey in the spirit world until she got the answer, but I knew she was doing her best. She loved Naylet as much as I did. "Please keep trying," I said.

"I will, hun, I promise. Besides looking for answers I also was looking for her spirit. Obie, I couldn't find it. We may be able to fix this, and I hope we can, but you should be open to the possibility that she might be gone."

"I'm going to fix this," I said.

"Well, I will do anything I can to help," she said. "In the meantime, I was just about to take my medicine. Can I get you some tea, maybe a little something to eat?"

"No thanks. I just need to stretch a little," I said, pushing through the pain to raise my arms over my head.

"Are you still not eating?" she asked. "Let me make you something. You're nothing but skin and hair."

"I'm not eating because I don't need to eat, you know this."

"Just because you don't need to doesn't mean you shouldn't. Life's short, Obie, enjoy yourself a little. How about a sandwich?"

"Okay, you win. I'll have some tea," I said.

I wasn't going to argue with her about it. She would keep badgering me until I had something, so a concession was good for both of us. She eased out of her chair and walked to the stove where she put in a couple pieces of wood. She took an old coffee tin from above the stove and opened it, taking a pinch of Pixie Dust between her fingers.

Opening the stove, she threw the dust in and whispered, "Fire."

The wood burst into flames. It was an expensive way to start fires but a lot easier than matches. Closing the stove, she put some water into a kettle from the trough and placed it on top. She walked back to her chair and took a seat. Sticking her finger through the loop on top of a jug beside her chair she spun and lifted it so it rested in the top of her arm and took a long swig. What she called "medicine" was a blend of plants she collected from the forest steeped in alcohol with a touch of magic. She took three shots a day religiously to keep her young, as she would say.

A few minutes later, the tea was ready. Livy was kind enough to let me sit for a few minutes with my tea to process. I didn't drink it but the warmth coming through the cup felt oddly reassuring. It was the first time I had to think since I found Naylet. What if I couldn't get her back? What would that even be like? We had been together so long just the idea of her not being around left a big question mark over my entire future. Now wasn't the time to get caught up in my head; I still had a job to do. Besides, just because Livy couldn't do anything for Naylet doesn't mean she was beyond help, only that we didn't have the answer yet. It was out there somewhere, I just had to find it.

"How long have I been here?" I asked.

"You came in last night. What did this to you anyway?"

I relayed the story for the second time, in full detail. Livy listened patiently for me to finish and when I did, I asked her if she had ever heard of anything like Petra before.

"It sounds like a demon from the Old World, but I've never run across anything like that," she said.

"I think I'm going to get Cearbhall to help out with this one."

She paused at this. "Cearbhall? Are you sure you want to do that? You made a pretty big deal about getting out on your own. Is it that bad?"

"I don't feel like I have much of a choice. There's a lot going on here and I'm going to need some help. Thera's not playing around and the stakes are too high not to," I said. "Besides, this is bigger than me."

"How long has it been since you have seen him?" she asked.

I had to stop and think about it. "We were hunting a Siren who was working her way through free love hippies like they were going out of style. Mid-sixties sometime." I said.

"That's been a while, a lot could've changed since then."

"And a lot can stay the same. I guess I better take a look at Farwell here," I said to change the subject.

I set my tea on the floor and stood up, ignoring my body's protest. Moving hurt, but it's exactly what I needed to do to get the soreness out. Farwell wasn't tucked in, more like tossed on the bed. He was lying face up with a dried, greenish crust on his forehead that covered a bloody gash—a salve Livy uses for injuries. I looked over his body to make sure everything was in place. His limbs seemed to be on straight, that was a good sign. There was some bruising on his face and no doubt more I couldn't see.

"Let's get this show on the road," I said.

I held my hands out over him and concentrated. I could feel the energy moving, slowly at first, funneling through my body, down my arms, out through my hands, and into Farwell. This essence of life, the same power that nourishes my body and lets me get away without eating and sleeping, poured into Farwell, repairing his body. At the same time, the defects and contaminants in his system flowed into mine. A person's hurt doesn't just disappear, it has to be dealt with. In healing him, I took responsibility for it. It wasn't a big deal, my system can recover from it much more efficiently than his can. What's another hour of aching joints when I'm already beat to hell? As the energy grew a light, blue like the sky, began to emanate from my hands and eyes. Farwell groaned and began to stir. As the healing took hold, his eyes opened slowly. Confusion turned into realization, followed by horror. He jumped away from me across the bed and almost made it before the injuries that hadn't been healed yet got the best of him, sending him tumbling onto the floor. I walked around the bed to where he was lying in a battered lump on his back, holding his chest, his legs propped up against the bed.

"I think my ribs are broken," he said.

"It wouldn't surprise me. You weren't wearing a seatbelt when we crashed."

"What are you?" he said giving me a sideways glance.

"Me?" I questioned. "I'm just a guy trying to get by like everybody else."

He didn't look reassured, it was probably the whiskers. I took my human form. Watching the transformation didn't appear to give him any comfort. "If you will hold still for a second, I can fix you right up."

He didn't say anything but gave a quick nod. He didn't really have a choice. I knelt beside him and continued. Again the energy flowed with the blue light.

"It's warm," he said.

I nodded. "That means it's working."

After a minute the bruising and all outward signs of damage had vanished. The energy that had flowed into him now poured over him like a stream flowing around a stone telling me the process was complete.

"How do you feel?" I asked.

"I feel..." He took a minute to assess his situation, look of surprise spreading across his face. "Great! Like a teenager. Nothing hurts, not even my elbow and that's bothered me for years." He moved his arm back and forth to test it out.

"I'm sure you have a lot of questions and I'll be happy to answer them but first, it's morning. I don't know what your schedule is, but if you're supposed to be working today maybe you could call in sick while we get this worked out? I don't want them to think you're missing," I said.

He gave me a sideways glance, sizing me up. "All right, and then I get some answers."

"All the answers you want," I agreed.

"Just need my phone. Do you have it?"

I looked at Livy and she shook her head no.

"It's probably still in the truck. I'll help you look," I said.

We made it outside and my heart sank when I saw the truck smashed against the side of Livy's house. I could tell it was done for. The entire front end was pancaked into the stone, the glass busted out. It didn't even sit straight anymore but lurched off to the right, maybe a broken axle. Farwell wasted no time looking in the cab, not thinking twice about the truck, as I surveyed the damage.

My inspection led me to the back of the truck where I found Naylet, still frozen in stone but tipped over, lying face down from the impact. I hopped into the bed and pulled her back into an upright position. She was cold and lifeless as the stone she had become, more so even, because I knew exactly how much life was missing. Even the rocks are infused with Thera's essence, but not Naylet, not now. There was no energy at all coming from her, she was like a void, the same way demons feel.

"I'm going to fix this," I whispered.

The impact from hopping back onto solid ground sent a shock of pain through my muscles, reminding me that I still had a good bit of healing to do. Farwell had found the phone and was doing his best to sound sick to whoever was on the other end.

After a few fake coughs he hung up and turned toward me. "How about those answers?"

"Sure, just let me borrow your phone for a sec, I need to get us a ride."

He held it out without protest. I took it and dialed my home number. From what Thera said, Holt had been taken so he wouldn't answer but it's worth trying. It didn't ring but gave me a busy signal. Probably knocked off the hook from whatever had happened. I dialed the only other number I knew by heart. A voice grunted on the other end.

"Hey, Tico, it's Obie. Is Hank around?"

"Hang on," he said.

The gentle hum of conversation and the clanking of glasses drifted through the phone. It sounded like a busy day at the clubhouse.

After a minute Hank picked up the phone. "Obie, are you okay? We've been looking for you."

"I've been better. Ran into some trouble yesterday. Everything okay?"

"We need you, Hob got hit. You weren't answering your phone so I drove over to your place. It's trashed and there are a couple dead demons laying around," he said. "We've been looking for you all night."

"I'm at Livy's. I need a ride. The truck's broke."

"All right, don't go anywhere. I'm on my way," he said.

I hung up and turned around to Farwell. "Our ride's coming. Let's talk inside."

Farwell sat down in Livy's rocking chair while I went back to the cot. He stared at me intently with a neutral expression, his eyes following my every movement. If I didn't know better, I would think my human form freaked him out more than krasis.

"You alright there, Detective?"

"Fine," he said, continuing to stare.

"You know you're safe here, right? Relax a little."

"I know, if you wanted to hurt me you could have. I'm just coming to terms with things," he said.

"Is there something on my face?"

"Sorry, no, I am looking for a tell. Something to give away that you aren't human. I want to be able to spot your kind."

"And? What do you think? Have you figured out how the secrets to spotting ultranaturals?" I asked.

He looked down at the tea Livy had made him. "No."

"It's going to be tough, my kind don't survive by sticking out," I said.

He relaxed back into the seat and took a sip of the tea. "What's an ultranatural?"

"An assortment of people that keep their existence hidden from humans," I said. "You've heard of my kind referred to as 'supernatural' in the movies, but we haven't removed ourselves from the earth the way humans have so that label didn't doesn't fit."

"Why stay hidden? What do you think would happen?"

"I think we would be pursued and treated in ways that would make Nazi Germany look tame in comparison," I said.

"I don't think you understand humans too well," he said with a dismissive chuckle.

"Actually, I used to be human and after a few hundred years of personal experience I think I have a better understanding than you think."

He leaned forward in his chair. "So what happened?"

"I was just a kid. My parents had died of consumption, and I—"

"Wait, what's consumption?" Farwell asked.

"Tuberculosis," Livy said from the kitchen.

"Right, so after they passed I was sent to Bethesda. It's an orphanage down close to Savannah. Mr. Whitefield ran it and, well, we never quite saw eye to eye. I liked to run and swim and he liked the Bible and making sure all of us kids knew it and stuck to it. Whatever means it took, that's what he would do. One night I had snuck out, I did that a lot, and heard some screaming in the woods. I followed the sound and found some people torn to pieces by what I thought was the devil. It looked like a man with grey skin, wings, and these hands with extremely long clawed fingers, a real knuckle dragger. I watched as it started eating the bodies and before I knew it, it spotted me. I must have made some noise or something and got its attention. I wasn't going to wait and see what it wanted so I took off running, but it caught me. I pulled my pocket knife, all the boys had knives back then. I guess I just decided, if that was going to be it for me, I was going to go down fighting. Next thing I know this wolf man comes out of the bushes and jumps on the demon. It only took him maybe fifteen seconds to kill the thing. I'd never seen anything like either one of them. He turns to me and in this deep voice says, 'run home, little boy.' I didn't run though, maybe because the orphanage never really felt like home to me, or maybe I was just afraid to move. I couldn't really tell you. He didn't seem like he was going to hurt me, and I've always been more curious than reasonable. When he started cleaning everything up, the bodies and the demon, I helped. The only thing I had waiting at the orphanage was another punishment anyway. After we were done, he changed into man right before me. I found a new family that night. Eventually I became like him, I was given abilities, and a mission, and I've been doing it ever since."

"But you're not a wolf," he said. "You some kind of weasel or something?"

"My kind are connected to predators. He was joined to the wolf, I'm bound to the otter."

"What mission?" he asked.

"I keep the earth and everything living on it safe, mostly from outside threats. We aren't that different," I said. "I'm kind of like a cop, in my own way."

"But you have been breaking the law," he said.

"Human law, yes, on occasion. I answer to a higher purpose than what your politicians decide should be against the rules. I will tell you I only break them if I need to. It's not something I do for fun."

He considered this but didn't argue, deciding to change the subject instead. "There are multiple cases of otters being spotted at crime scenes. Every few years it happens. Is that you? Are you putting otters in these places for some reason?"

I couldn't help but laugh. "No, those are all one otter, and it's me. Just like I can take the form you saw, that we call krasis, I can take the form of an otter. Cops don't shoot otters."

He nodded. "Okay, what happens to me now?"

"Well, when our ride shows up we'll drop you off at your car."

He looked skeptical. "That's it?"

"That's it. The only thing I ask is that now, and in the future, if you think I might be involved with something you're working on, just steer clear, unless you want to get involved in all this," I said.

"Look, Obie, I don't want you to think I'm not grateful for saving me back there, I am. If I'm being honest, this is all a little too much for me. I just want to go back to things the way they were, the sooner the better," he said.

"I understand. Our ride will be here soon. We will drop you off at your car and you can go back to your normal life if that's what you want to do," I replied.

I was glad to hear him saying this. I really don't want him to be involved, or to try to become some kind of hunter like they show on TV. That's a good way to get killed. If he wanted to pretend this all never happened and bury his head back in the sand, then I would be right there with a shovel to help him dig.

"I need to talk to Livy. Would you mind giving us a minute?"

"Sure, I'll be outside," he said, standing up.

Livy came and sat in the rocking chair. "That's an interesting story, why didn't you tell him the truth?" she said once he had left.

"It was true, mostly. I just left a couple things out," I said.

She crossed her arms with disapproval. "Like that you were the one that summoned that demon and Cearbhall almost killed you for it? Don't you think that's a big thing to leave out?"

"It doesn't really matter to Farwell, besides that as a long time ago and I'm not that person anymore. We can't hold onto the past and we're all entitled to our secrets. What kind of world would we have if we knew everything about each other?"

"Still, sometimes secrets can come back to bite you," she said.

"Speaking of biting, the snake venom—Do you have any ideas about how we can get around that one?" I asked.

"Sure, hun, it's not a problem at all. All I need is some more venom and I can make you a little immunity potion. You don't think Petra would mind giving us a sample, do you?" she asked.

"I'll have to find her and ask," I said with a grin. "How long do you think it would take to make the potion?"

"Less than a day," she said. "Making it's the easy part, the materials are the challenge. I used all the venom in the head I found. You're going to have to get another, more than one would be better."

"So all I have to do is find Petra, get a sample of the venom without getting bitten or killed, and figure out some way to kill her. Maybe instead of a truck I can find a tank to run her over with. That might do it. You know anyone that has a tank?"

"Nobody that would let you borrow it," she said.

"Then I'll just have to do this one step at a time," I said.

CHAPTER 12

THE SOUND OF an engine rumbling up to the house caught my attention. A slamming car door confirmed it was time to go.

"Sounds like my ride is here. Thanks, Livy, you never let me down."

I gave her a hug, grabbed the remains of the snake from the fridge, and went outside. A large pickup was parked beside my truck. It had Morrison Salvage and Repair in cursive on the side. Farwell shot me a glance as soon as I had both feet out the door. He pulled me to the side for a private word.

"What's going on here?"

I had a feeling I knew what the issue was before I asked. "That's our ride, what's the problem?"

"I'm not going anywhere with *him*," he said, giving a disdainful nod in the direction of the truck.

"Is it because he's black?" I knew it wasn't, but it can be fun to watch middle-aged white men squirm when accused of racism.

"What? No, he's a gang member," he said in a hushed tone.

"Not all black folks are in gangs?"

"Will you shut the hell up, it's not like that" he snapped. "He's in a biker gang, the Tortured Occult. That one percent patch he's wearing means something."

I held my hands up, palms out to him in the international symbol of non-aggression. "I'm just messing with you. I know all about the T.O."

"Not an hour ago you told me you didn't break the law if you can help it, and now you're telling me you have gang affiliations? What's the truth?"

"The truth is that the T.O. is a motorcycle club whose main focus is community outreach," I said.

"Bullshit, there are active investigations for drug trafficking, murder, kidnapping, you name it. If they are such a charitable group, how come no one knows about it?" He crossed his arms, defying me to give him an explanation.

"Because they don't serve your community," I said.

"What do you mean 'my community'? They live in my community, and believe me, they aren't providing any services that are legal," he said.

"Farwell, not an hour ago you told me that you didn't want to know these kinds of things and now you're Johnny-on-the-spot with the questions. Have you changed your mind? Are you ready to hear about all the nice things the local werebear motorcycle club does to help other ultranaturals in the area?"

His face dropped. "Werebear?"

"Well, not all of them, to be fair. They do take outsiders as members sometimes, but the bears formed the group and lead it," I said.

"Let's just get this over with," he said and stomped over to the truck.

Hank, my mechanic and friend, had left the wrecker idling to inspect the damage to my truck. He had done all of the work on it since I bought it and I am sure it hurt him as much as me to see it smashed up. He was down on all fours looking underneath it when I walked up behind him. The back of his kutte displayed Tom C's colors; a pentacle with oak leaves and acorns in its center that formed a snarling bear face. The words Tortured Occult lined the top, with North Georgia underneath in bold lettering.

He stood up and brushed off some dirt that had collected on his vice-president patch. "What happened here?" he asked pointing to Naylet.

I shrugged. "Demon attack. It's not like anything I've seen before. It has these snakes for hair, some nasty poison, and it used some kind of magic to turn her to stone."

"Sounds like Medusa," he said.

"Yeah, if you believe in that kind of thing," I said, running a hand through my hair. "I've never known anyone who has run into anything like that. I thought it was just a story."

He reached out and touched her extended hand. "That mythology had to come from somewhere. Humans aren't that creative," he said. "Are you able to turn her back?"

"I don't know. I am going to try everything I can," I said. "I hope so."

"I hope you get your lady back. That being said, you've done a real number on my lady here," he said, patting the bed of the truck.

"Think you can fix her?"

He paused, thinking it over before nodding. "You can do anything if you throw enough money at it. It's just a question of how much it's going to cost and how long it's going to take."

I didn't like the sound of that. I had a good bit stashed away for a rainy day. I was able to keep that stash by avoiding the rain as much as possible. Most of it had come from what I collected during the gold rush. There were quite a few prospectors that tried to evoke dark magic to strike it rich. It worked well for them until they caught my attention, then it worked well for me. "Maybe it's time to retire the old girl," I said. "Put her out to pasture."

"That would be a shame. It's a great truck," he replied.

"Be sure to tell that to Holt next time you see him. Let me know what it would take to fix and we'll go from there. In the meantime, I'm going to need a ride to the house, and Officer Farwell left his car at Naylet's, if you don't mind." I pointed to Farwell standing by the wrecker, looking like a sourpuss.

"I went by Naylet's earlier looking for you. The yard's all tore up but there's no cars," he said. "Hey, where is Holt anyway? Is he all right?"

"He's missing. I was hoping he was at the house but if you didn't find him then I have no idea. You said something happened with Hob?"

"The factory was attacked, some of his workers were killed. Whoever did it made off with almost all the dust he had. We're calling a council meeting to figure out what we're going to do," he said.

"Give me a couple days. I am going to get Cearbhall to help out. Something is really wrong with all this," I said. "First, we need to get Farwell back to his normal life before he goes into conniptions."

"Whatever you need, Obie. Just do me a favor and get back as soon as you can. A lot of people are worried," he said. "The world's going to shit and we need a plan."

We loaded Naylet onto the back of the wrecker and secured her with some straps and a tarp. Farwell sat between us in the cab, looking more than a little uncomfortable as we left. I was trying to decide to tell him that his cruiser had been stolen, but since it was a short trip I opted to let him discover it organically. The ride was already awkward enough.

HANK PULLED THE WRECKER into the gravel driveway leading to Naylet's house. I didn't want to say it with Farwell there, but exchanging a glance with Hank, I could tell we were thinking the same thing: Petra could still be around. Getting Farwell back to his life in one piece was the first priority, one less person to babysit. When we rounded the corner to the house, the most noticeable thing was the absence of Farwell's Explorer. Hank parked where it should have been and we piled out of the truck. The signs of last night's fight with Petra were clearly visible. Large lines of torn up earth, looking like a bad plow job, ran the length of the yard where I had run over Petra. They stood in stark contrast to the beauty of the rest of the grounds. The brown lines on the lush green lawn were reminiscent of open wounds. Cuts not yet healed into scars.

"No, *NO*," Farwell said in disbelief. "Where the hell is my cruiser?"

"The demon must have taken it," I said. "I think we broke at least one of its wings last night. It must have used your car to get away."

Farwell stood staring where his car should be. "I have to report it. I'm responsible for the car," he said reaching for his phone.

I put my hand on his arm to stop him. "Just hold on a minute. We can find it before anyone misses it."

"I already miss it. Besides, there's a shotgun in it. What if someone gets hurt with it? That's on me," he said.

"That demon doesn't care about your shotgun, trust me. She only took the car to get away. She's running. We will find it and get it back to you," I said. "Give me a day."

He looked uncertain at my request but reluctantly agreed. "One day," he said holding up an index finger.

"Thanks," I said. "Just hang out here for a minute and we'll get you home. I need to take a quick look around."

Hank and I walked out into the yard where I could immediately see the brown spot where Petra's body had come to rest. The large oval of dead grass was easy to pick out against the lush green. Demon blood is toxic, like an oil spill but worse. The ground was effectively dead where she had bled into it, nothing would grow there now. I could fix it, of course, when things calmed down, or it would eventually return to normal on a long enough timeframe. I would add it to the to-do list.

The spot of brown grass stank of rotten eggs and death, but I found it encouraging. If Petra bleeds then I can kill her, even if I had to do it with heavy machinery. I was debating the merits of getting a chainsaw to go *Army of Darkness* on her when Hank pointed out some smaller patches of dead grass leading off toward the shed. I found corresponding claw marks, making it clear she had dragged herself away.

"Looks like she crawled to the shed," I said.

"Krasis?" Hank asked.

I nodded, kicked off my shoes, and pulled the Velcro on my pants before making the change. Hank completed his change a few seconds after me. We were about six feet tall in human form, but in krasis the black bear biker had a good six inches on me. Where I retained my slender physique, Hank's already stocky build widened even further to accommodate the extra bulk. I would be lying if I said I wasn't glad to have some backup.

"Jesus Christ," Farwell said from behind us.

I turned around to see him walking to the back of the wrecker, shaking his head.

"I don't think he likes us," Hank said, watching him go.

"He doesn't know us, how could he not like us," I countered. "Let's get this over with."

Following the claw marks and spots of dead grass up to the shed, we found the door cracked. I took the left door while Hank took the right. I gestured a count and on three we pulled them open, ready to pounce on whatever we found.

Inside we didn't find a demon, but the shed wasn't in the same condition as the last time I saw it. A couple of the tools were scattered on the floor and the bags of soil that had been neatly stacked in the corner had been torn apart. The dirt from them formed into a mound with a depression in the center with what looked like crumpled paper piled up in the bottom of it. It reminded me of how Livy made biscuits, by using a mound of flour as a bowl and mixing directly in it. This wasn't an attempt at the world's largest mud pie, though; gun to my head, it looked like a nest. The dirt in the center had been compacted where Petra had been lying. I could smell the traces of her blood fouling the dirt. The question was, what was all the white stuff?

"Have you seen anything like this before?" I said, taking a step into the shed.

Hank looked in without setting foot inside. "It's new to me."

I took a rake off the wall and dug at the white stuff at the bottom of the mound. I hooked what turned out to be a leg on the rake and raised it to reveal a Petra-shaped skin suit, wings and all. She was injured in our fight, crawled here, and shed her skin. It must be part of her healing process. Regardless, I didn't think she would still be in the area. That's when I noticed the black mass in the bottom of the nest. I dragged the skins away for a better look. Snakes, a whole pile of them, big and black and still. I changed my grip on the rake to drive it down on the snake pile. The impact sent a shockwave through the snakes, but they appeared lifeless. Tossing the skin off the rake, I prodded the snake pile. Still nothing moved, confirming my suspicion.

"What's all that?" Hank asked, keeping a comfortable distance by the door.

"Looks like the snakes from her head. They must have been killed between the lightning and getting run over," I said.

After hearing they were dead, Hank came in for a closer look. "Big sons of bitches."

I scooped one up with the rake for a closer inspection. It was about four feet long and wasn't a whole snake, just a head and body. It was missing the tail, looking like it had been cut in half. That must have been where it had been attached to her head.

"Maybe Livy can make some more antivenom now," I said. "I am going to have to take them."

"As long as they ride in the back," Hank said. "I'd rather not have them in the cab."

Rifling through the soil bags, I found the most intact one and held it out to Hank. "Can you hold this for me?"

He didn't take it. "Why do I got to hold the bag?"

"Come on," I said giving the bag a little shake. "You're not afraid of a few snakes are you, Hank?"

"Not afraid, but I don't want to get bit either," he said.

"Ok, I'll hold the bag and you scoop," I said holding out the rake.

He took it, and once I had the bag open, carefully lifted and deposited the snakes into it, one by one. None of them were alive but I can't blame him for being cautious. Spinning the bag to seal it I walked outside and looked for tracks, footprints specifically. A set led off toward the house.

"What do you think?" Hank asked.

"Looks like she went to the house," I said. "I don't think she's still here. Let me check it out and we'll get out of here."

"Should I come too?" he asked.

"No. If you don't mind keeping an eye on Farwell I would appreciate it," I said. "He's not taking this well."

Hank changed back to human form and went back to the truck while I crossed the yard to the house with the snake bag. Inside it looked the same as before except the food that had been on the counter had been cleaned up and the pictures that were on the table had been put back on the walls. After Petra was healed did she come inside and clean up the mess? That didn't make sense. Some of the pictures were missing and empty frames hung in their place. The bed in the loft looked like it had been slept in since last time I saw it. I climbed up and smelled the sheets. I could make out the stench of demon blood and that same perfume but the bed was neatly made, the way Naylet kept it. I guess after Petra shed, she made herself at home.

CHAPTER 13

THE TRUCK LURCHED onto a dirt path that didn't deserve to be called a road. It was the back entrance to Morrison Salvage and the Tortured Occult's clubhouse. The clubhouse, garage adjacent, stood in the middle of a large field. Old and wrecked cars surrounded the buildings like a metal horde laying siege to the garage. I thought of my Ford joining the ranks of this ramshackle legion and it just didn't seem right. It had been with me through too much for it to become just another anonymous occupant in this mechanical graveyard. The truth was, it would never make it out here. These vehicles were slowly and surly being parted out, the auto equivalent of decomposing. Once everything of worth was taken, they were crushed and sold for scrap. That would be the fate of my truck. It didn't make sense to repair it and keep driving it. While I would never admit it to him, Holt was right, the truck was outdated.

Hank parked in front of the garage. We got out and he went up to one of the mechanics working under a car on the lift before coming back to talk to us, notepad and pen in hand.

"He's going to take you home. Write down your number and we will give you a call when we find your car," he said, holding out the pad to Farwell.

He took it and jotted down a number. A couple minutes later he was on his way home, finally leaving Hank and I alone so we could speak freely.

"If it's all right I'd like to leave Naylet here, until I can figure out this Petra situation. She seems to know a lot about me and if she knows where I live, taking Naylet back there wouldn't be safe," I said, not looking away from the junkyard. "I think she took Holt and may be responsible for the attack on Hob as well."

"We'll have to call a vote, but after seeing what I have seen, you have my support," Hank said. "But how could that demon do all that if you almost killed her just yesterday?"

"I don't know, but I am going to find out."

We walked over to the clubhouse, a two-story building that doubled as the premier social destination for all non-humans in North Georgia, and made our way inside through a heavy wood door with a dog door installed on the bottom. This was a safe haven for ultranaturals and inside there was no need for disguises—in fact they were discouraged. Wearing a false face was unnecessary, unless you had something to hide. We walked through the front door into the changing room. The walls of the rectangular room were lined with coat racks and cubbies. Assorted items of clothing hung on the hooks or lay in piles around the room; shoes of all kinds filled the cubbies.

A pile of dirt in the corner caught my attention. I walked over to see a hole in the floor. Peering inside I saw a pair of yellow, glowing eyes attached to a small shadowy figure that scurried farther down when it spotted me.

"What was that?" I said taking a knee to get a better angle to look down the hole.

"A hunter chased some tommy knockers out of a mine. They are holed up at the clubhouse and refusing to leave until they have a 'safe' place to go. They're burrowing all over the clubhouse, coming up though the floor in random places. They're making a huge mess of things. I need to figure out how to get them out of here before they bring the whole building down," he said.

Knockers were a kind of fairy that lived underground and in mines. They were nice enough but not ideal houseguests. Hank and I added our shoes to an empty spot and shifted to krasis. A door on each end of the room exited to the bar. Hank and I walked out separate doors into the bar. A large room taking up most of the first story that opened to a loft on the second floor with additional tables. The bar ran across the wall underneath the loft, almost the length of the room, with a pool table and dart board on the right with the rest of the room dedicated to tables. Adan, the wererat emissary, was losing a game of billiards to a forest troll. While it wasn't as busy as it would have been at night, there was still an assortment of regulars scattered around the room that would have sent Farwell into a coma. Cotton, an artic werewolf and Torch, one of Hank's sons, both club members, leaned against the balcony, staring down at the festivities. The white of Cotton's fur next the black of Torch's reminded me of a shifter Yin Yang.

"Give me a minute to get everyone together," Hank said.

He walked over and whispered something to Hornet, a grey fox shifter sitting at one of the tables. She wore a kutte with PROSPECT across the back, showing she was applying for membership in the club. She got up and went outside, while Hank stuck his index finger up in the air, waved it around in a circle, and disappeared into the rooms behind the bar reserved for club business. Everyone wearing the T.O.'s colors started migrating into the back rooms. It would have almost been discreet if I didn't know a meeting had been called.

Now I would just have to wait. It shouldn't take more than ten or fifteen minutes; the T.O. was a lot of things but indecisive wasn't one of them. I took a seat at the bar in front of the phone kept behind the counter. Leaning forward, I reached behind the counter feeling around for it. When I located it I picked it up and placed it front of me. Holding the receiver to my ear, I dialed Hob. It rang a few times with no answer. The bartender, a wereraccoon everyone called Tico, gave me a nod from the opposite end of the bar.

"Come on, pick up," I said, listening to the metered ringing.

Tico crossed the bar to greet me. "What'll ya have?"

"The usual," I said, not paying him much attention.

He placed a napkin with an empty cup on top of it on the bar in front of me.

"You don't have to be a smartass," I said, as he moved to help another patron.

After a couple more rings a man with a heavy German accent answered. "*Guten Tag.*"

"Hey, Hob, it's Obie. I heard you had some trouble. Everyone okay?"

"Oh, *nein*, Eric was killed. The attack was late at night. He was working alone and was taken by surprise," he said.

"I'm sorry to hear that," I said. "I'm coming over in a couple days. We're going to make this right."

"Obie, the dust was taken," he said not bothering to hide the concern in his voice. "We will have serious trouble stopping anyone with that much power."

"I'm not worried about the dust. I'm just glad you're okay. Stay safe and I'll be over soon," I said.

"Mind if I join you?" a yapping voice said from my left.

I turned to see the eyes and ears of a coyote peering over the edge of the chair next to me.

"Listen I got to go," I said into the phone.

"Thanks, Obie. Come see me soon," Hob said.

"I promise I will."

"Hambone, what a surprise," I said, hanging up the phone, not feeling even the slightest bit of astonishment. I gestured toward an empty chair beside me for him to have a seat.

He slid the chair back from the bar a little and a moment later the very overweight kobold was doing his best to heave himself into the seat. After a short struggle, that I wasn't sure he was going to win, he sat beside me, panting with his tongue hanging out of the side of his mouth. He was about three feet tall and looked like a mix between a very short fat man and a coyote. American kobolds all resembled coyotes, but where other shifters could turn into humans, kobolds only had two forms: coyote and krasis. As a result, they kept their distance from humans, and since they don't blend in very well, that was probably for the best.

After a couple minutes to catch his breath he said, "Just mingling with my constituents. There's an election coming up you know. Competition looks to be tough this year. The fairies got some looker showboating around like she's already won. They just want to get one of their own elected, and I tell you, I don't know why. I've always done right by them, the ungrateful flower bugs. That's beside the point, I'm glad I caught you."

Here it comes . . . "What do you want, Hambone?"

"Your support, of course. If I had the backing of a Keeper, I don't see how I could lose," he said, giving me a hopeful look.

"I don't really get involved in politics," I said.

"Oh, I know, I know. I'm not asking for much, just your permission to let people know you support me, and if anyone asks you, just tell them that you think I'm the best candidate. Oh, I almost forgot, if you could wear this button while you're at the clubhouse it would be really helpful." He slid a neon yellow button across the bar that said HAMBONE FOR THE PEOPLE in big black letters.

I put the button into my pocket. "I'll think about it."

"Please do, Obie. We all have to work together, you know. There was one other thing I wanted to talk to you about. I couldn't help but overhear you say you weren't worried about the dust."

I knew there had to be more to it. "So?"

"Well, surely you understand how important it is to keep the dust flowing," he said, making a swooshing motion with his hands. "We would be thrust into chaos without it, hunted like dogs. It's in everyone's best interest that we find it and find it fast."

"Is it in everyone's interest or is it in your interest?" I asked.

"Obie, I am a servant of the people, that's all. I am just trying to keep everyone safe. I'm just asking you to keep the greater good in mind. You're one of our top producers, but even at your best you can't replace all that dust quickly enough. There's a lot of families in need, not just of food and shelter but peace of mind most of all."

I turned to look at him directly. "You don't think I know what's at stake here?"

"Of course you do. I'm just voicing my concern about how nonchalant you are about the dust being stolen," he said. "It hasn't even been announced yet. If we move quickly we might be able to recover it before it's missed, that's all. We need to avoid a panic."

Otis, Hank's father and president of the Tortured Occult, came out of the back room and waved me over. He was as large and imposing as Hank in krasis. They looked almost identical, except Otis was a little squarer around the shoulders and had grey on his chin. He had been around a long time and was starting to show his age.

"Maybe we shouldn't be talking about it at the bar, if it's such a big deal," I said. "Listen, I'm working on it. That's all I can tell you right now."

I didn't wait for him to excuse me or even to see his reaction. Hambone seems to forget sometimes that I don't work for him; I only answer to Thera. I crossed the room to where Otis was waiting.

"Well?" I asked.

He raised his hands, palms facing me, like he was already telling me to calm down. I knew it wasn't good news. "The vote passed but you can't keep Naylet in the clubhouse. You will have to hide her outside in the junkyard. There are a few vans out there that you can put her in. We will keep an eye on her for a few days until you can make other arrangements."

"Outside? Why can't I put her in one of the rooms in the back? Petra isn't going to bust into the clubhouse to get her." I looked around the room to see many other people absorbed in their own lives, unaware and unconcerned with my situation. "A van isn't going to offer any protection."

"It was discussed and that's what was agreed to. This is the best I can do, take it or leave it," he said.

"Sure, sorry, Otis. It's been a rough couple days. I appreciate the help."

"No problem. I'll have Hank help you find a safe hideaway," he said.

Hank came out a few minutes later. We went back into the changing room and made the shift to human form before going to look around the junkyard. Hank pointed out a couple potential hiding places and I picked an old Ford Econoline van on blocks close to the clubhouse. All its glass was intact and the doors still closed and locked although the key was long gone. That didn't bother me. If it was a pain for me to get her out, it would be a pain for Petra as well. I found a wrecked hood and bent it so it would fit in the van in front of Naylet to prevent anyone from seeing her from the windows. Once she was in place we locked the doors and closed it up.

"I need one more favor," I said. "I need some transportation until I can arrange something. You still have that loaner?"

"Yeah, no problem. I'll grab the keys while you get those snakes out of my truck. They give me the heebie jeebies."

CHAPTER · 14

THE LOANER WASN'T a nice truck. Anything that identified it as a specific brand had rusted or been knocked off years ago. It was brown, but I couldn't tell how much of it was rust and how much was paint. Despite its appearance it ran like new. Hank was a master of his craft and I knew any vehicle he got his hands on would be mechanically solid. It took a little over five hours to get to Jekyll, including stopping for gas.

I had been to the island a few times over the years, so I did a lap around the island to get my bearings. I hadn't been here in a long time and it had changed a lot. At the same time, it seemed like the same old place. No longer in the prime of the hunting club days, when the rich Yankees migrated for the winter, now it resembled a quaint seaside community. A small shopping mall on the east side of the island was new. What was left of the original buildings, some looking the worse for wear, took up most of the developed area on the south side of the island. A golf course, some hotels, and a few rows of ranch style houses made up the difference. That's not to say that the island was crowded, far from it. Large portions of the island were left undeveloped on principle. It's my kind of place.

A part of me hoped to see Cearbhall walking down the street but I wasn't that lucky. It would take some work to find him, but I knew where to start. I parked in the historical district and after a few minutes of walking found a booklet with a map of the island that helped refresh my memory. I found what I was looking for just north of Crane Cottage. An oak tree somewhere around 375 years old. The branches stretched out, reaching all the way into the ground and back up again with limbs large enough to be trees in their own right if they hadn't been attached. Resurrection fern sat atop the uppermost branches, brown and shriveled waiting for rain to be restored to its lush green, accompanied by Spanish moss wafting lazily in the sea breeze.

I couldn't help but smile when I saw it. The tree had grown noticeably since the last time I was here but I recognized it immediately. I ran my fingers over the branches, appreciating the twists and bumps of the limbs. It's the imperfections that make it beautiful. Many of the lower branches stretched out around chest height and one in particular was flat enough on top to make a seat. I hopped up, leaving my legs dangling, and was sent back to my childhood in the orphanage. Every so often I would run off into the woods to explore on my own. I would get the speech of how it wasn't safe, receive a personalized sermon on the danger my everlasting soul was in, and then be beaten with a belt, or a paddle, or whatever was handy, for my transgressions. It had been worth it. My time among the trees is one of my oldest and most treasured memories.

"It's good to see you again, my friend. It's been too long," I said.

There was no response. That didn't bother me. In life you can't expect everyone to operate at your pace. Sometimes you have to sit and wait for them to catch up and, if you're lucky, those ahead of you will help you along.

"How have you been? It looks like you are doing well. You have gotten a lot wider since I saw you last. Your branches are really sturdy. It's really beautiful," I said.

"You always were a sweet talker," said a voice that seemed to manifest from inside the trunk.

The tree spirit manifested as a curvy woman with light brown skin with grey stripes reminiscent of a tiger or zebra, but less structured. Her hair was green and brown reaching almost to her knees, like the fern and moss on her branches.

"Let me have a look at you," she said, walking over to me.

I couldn't help but grin at seeing her. She looked more mature since I had seen her last. I hopped down off the limb and held out my hands, putting myself on display.

"No, Obie, I want to see the real you," she said.

"I thought what's inside is what matters," I replied.

She tilted her head with an expression suggesting she didn't approve. "What's the point of having something beautiful inside if you don't let it out?"

It wasn't the kind of place I was comfortable shifting. A public area in the middle of the day. I was only about forty feet off the sidewalk, with some bushes and branches between me and one of the largest buildings on the island. Anyone that happened by or looked out the window would get an eyeful of something that could make the front page of a tabloid. I gave the area a once over. There were a few people around but no one was too close or looking in my direction. I stepped closer to the trunk and shifted to krasis.

"Wonderful, you haven't changed a bit," she said, eyeballing me up and down.

I didn't want to give the impression I was uncomfortable by changing back right away. The truth is I enjoyed being in krasis; I would do it all the time if I could. Maybe that's why I liked hanging out at the clubhouse, no need for pretense. In the middle of the day, out in the open, is a different story. Secrets must be kept and cameras are everywhere now. The risk of being recorded is just too great for this kind of thing. I held this form for a couple minutes, without feeling particularly comfortable, before making the change back to human.

"I see you updated your pants," she said as I fastened the Velcro. "These are much better. The buttons weren't flattering."

"I wish I had stuck to the kilt," I said, my heart sinking into my feet. There were so many things I could have been known for in the past three hundred years, but the only thing anyone seems to remember are some ugly pants.

"We all do, Obie," she replied, not bothering to hide her smirk.

"So listen, I was hoping you could help me out. I need to find Cearbhall. Last I heard he was on the island, but we haven't kept in touch. Any idea where he is running these days?" I asked, glad to be changing the subject.

"He's still around, but he hasn't come by to visit in a while. I heard through the rustle and the roots that he fishes a lot on the pier. You might find him there. He made friends with some dogs he runs with from time to time, nothing serious, mind you, just some local pets longing for pack life. The last I heard he was spending a lot of nights by the old cemetery. There's been some shady characters sneaking around up there, at least that's what they say," she said. "Maybe he is keeping an eye on them."

"Sounds like he is staying busy," I replied, not thinking much about the "shady characters" comment. "Shady" to a plant could mean a vegetarian pulling carrots from the garden or the grounds keepers trimming the trees. "Thanks for your help. I'll come see you again soon, okay?"

"Sure, Obie, please do, and tell Cearbhall to come see me too," she said.

I promised that I would, and made my way back to the truck. I sat in the truck, pondering my next move. My best chance to run into him would be on the pier, assuming he didn't have a more private spot he liked to fish at. I could have a stakeout at the pier and move over to the cemetery tonight if he didn't show up.

I drove over and parked in a largely vacant lot by the Jekyll Fishing Center. The pier, in the shape of an anchor, was cast out into the water as if its sole purpose was to keep the island from floating away. I walked out onto the pier under the pretense of a casual stroll. People were fishing from all over it, but Cearbhall wasn't among them. It was only a few hours before sundown and there were worse places to wait. At least here I'd have a nice ocean breeze and would get to see the sunset over the water. I went back to the truck and moved it to a position to give me a good view of the pier and the sunset, and waited. I didn't have a book and the fishing center was really only good for one visit. That left me with almost three hours with nothing to do but think. I thought about Holt and wondered what Petra could be doing to him. The sooner I could find him, the better, but I needed help. He would have to hold on until Cearbhall and I could make it back.

I thought about Cearbhall, and what I would say to him when I found him. We hadn't parted on the best terms the last time I saw him. I was more principled back then, hung up on right and wrong. Cearbhall operates in a grey area that I understand much better now. We'd been bound to have it out at some point, but I never thought it would result in us going our separate ways. I decided it would be best not to bring up the past, unless I had to. We needed to focus on the future, and nothing positive would come from reincarnating old arguments.

When I had run out of everything else, my thoughts turned to Naylet. Before I let myself get too far into it I decided it was a perfect time to check out the fishing center. I got out of the truck and walked inside. Despite having a grandiose name, the fishing center was just a small building that rented rods and sold bait, food, and tourist stuff. The distraction didn't last long and by the time I had done two laps around the small store it wasn't nearly as late as I had hoped. Going back to the truck, I gave the pier one more look before climbing in and cranking the engine. The graveyard wasn't far away, but I decided to drive the long way around the island and soak up the scenery.

The sun had just gone down when I parked in front of Horton House, or what was left of it. The building had been a large rectangle, like an enormous Lego block long before Lego was a thing. Now, it was little more than a shell of a building. The walls were made of tabby, a mixture of sand, lime, oyster shell, and water used in costal construction in days past. They were partially degraded from time and weather, not to mention assholes scratching their initials or attempts at witticisms into them. Each side of the building had nine windows and a door in the center. The balcony was gone, hell: everything was gone. It used to be a real nice place. I crossed the road, walking to a tiny graveyard with a knee-high brick wall marking its boundaries. I stood in the entry looking at the graves and sniffed the air—nothing. The gravel path in front ran beside the road through the trees. I decided to take a stroll and see if I could pick up Cearbhall's scent. After walking for about ten minutes and coming up with nothing, I turned around and headed back.

A faint yellow light coming from Horton House caught my attention. It was probably just someone on their phone having a look around. From outside, it looked like someone waving around a weak flashlight. I crossed the road for a closer look. It was probably nothing, but I had nothing else going on. This whole trip was turning into a giant waste of time. I rounded the corner of the empty doorway into the main room to find a normal looking guy in jeans and a black tee shirt. A backpack was slung over one shoulder. He had his back to me and was looking up at the walls. When he turned to the side I saw he didn't have a phone, it was a pendant on a necklace he wore emitting the yellow light. I couldn't tell what the design was, but it formed a circle. He held it up to one eye and looked through it, scanning the walls meticulously. He must have heard me come in. He turned in my direction and when he saw me his head jerked back like he had been hit in the face. He jerked the pendant away and rubbed his eye with the heel of his hand.

That was a little strange, I'll admit, but by itself wasn't something I needed to get involved with. Some people use magic; it's what they do with it that's important. Magic alone wasn't a problem. "Sorry to give you a start there, thought you were someone else."

"Hey, no problem," he said. When I turned to leave he followed up with, "Who were you looking for? Maybe I could help you look?"

I heard the scuff of a shoe from behind the wall to my right. Someone else was in the house with him.

"No thanks," I said.

Halfway to the truck I was hit in the back so hard I almost didn't register the gunshot. I collapsed to the ground as the pain surged through my back and out into my limbs. It took a second for my mind to get up to speed on the fact I had been shot. My back was burning intensely and a warm wet feeling started running down my back and legs. This was bad and I knew I had to get out of here. I ran for cover behind the truck, at least I tried to; I couldn't stand up. I looked back to see my shorts were saturated with blood and clinging to my legs. I tried to move them but they weren't responding, being dragged lifelessly behind me as I crawled. The man with the looking glass, followed by a punk looking chick with piercings and pink hair, were advancing on me, guns drawn. He was again looking through the monocle and that must be how he saw me. There's no way he could make a shot like that without some kind of night vision helping him out.

"The rumors are true," he said walking up to me.

"What is it?" the woman asked, keeping her gun on me. She had a silver dagger drawn in the hand supporting the gun.

I had unwittingly stumbled on a pair of hunters. People who supply the black market with dust by tracking down and killing ultranaturals. There was no way I was going to get away. The bleeding had stopped, the healing was underway with a tingling already returning to my toes, but all this guy had to do was keep popping rounds into me, assuming they didn't try to kill me outright. I only had one chance to make a move before they figured it out.

"Let me see," the woman said.

Her companion held the monocle to her eye so she didn't have to free a hand from her weaponry. "We hit the jackpot, look how he glows. Hey, he looks like he's healing up pretty fast, we should get him secured quick."

"Let's do a couple more, just to be safe," the man said before firing three more rounds into my chest.

The impact slammed into me as the bullets tore through my body. I fell back, not even able to scream, only gasping as my lungs filled with blood. They actually laughed at seeing my body fail. That's when I saw it behind him, a single eye glowing yellow, bounding up and down in a charge. The world disappeared into a tunnel as distant gun fire and screaming echoed in my ears. Then all was quiet.

CHAPTER • 15

I WOKE UP FACE down in a bathtub, the cold porcelain chilling my cheeks. It felt good, but took a second for my mind to come around to what had happened. Getting shot once wasn't one of my favorite things, let alone four times. I was glad to have been unconscious for the healing process—you miss a lot of pain when you're unconscious, small blessings. I wasn't sure where I was in the healing process. I didn't have any pain but I hadn't moved yet either. I took a minute to move every piece of my body, just a little wiggle, starting with my fingers and toes, moving through my arms and into my back. Nothing hurt, so I pulled myself into a seated position in the tub. I was still wearing my clothes and they, along with the white porcelain of the tub, were covered with blood, some pooled and dried into a rusty brown around the edges. A few pieces of mushroomed metal, the bullets expelled by my body during the healing process, rested in the blood.

Through the open door of the bathroom I could see a small studio apartment. A kitchen was directly beside the bathroom, with a bed and a couple of chairs facing a TV against the far wall. A playground and palms illuminated by streetlights were visible through the sliding glass door. Some folded clothes had been placed on top of a towel on the toilet. A note covered the pile that read: *Out, clean up the blood.* It was a familiar scribble; I could recognize Cearbhall's handwriting anywhere.

My skin had a crusty feeling as I climbed out of the tub for a quick look around. I was alone, as I expected. I wish Cearbhall had waited around for me to wake up, but at least now I had found him, even if I had to wait for him to get back. I returned to the bathroom for a shower and got in with my clothes on. I stuck my fingers through the holes in my shirt where the bullets penetrated. I'm going to have to go shopping. I pulled the shirt off and rinsed as much of the blood out of it as I could. I was throwing it out but like so many things in my life, bloody bullet-ridden clothes tended to attract attention, even in the garbage. After rinsing my clothes, I started on my body, working on the tub last. When I had finished, and was double-checking the tub to make sure I didn't miss anything, I heard the door open.

"Hurry up in there. I need to get cleaned up," Cearbhall shouted from the other room. "We've got work to do."

"Good to see you, Obie, glad you're okay, Obie, it's been too long, Obie, we should catch up," I mumbled to myself as I turned off the water. I pulled open the curtain, grabbed my soggy clothes out of the tub, and stepped out. "All yours."

He stepped around the corner in human form wearing a red shirt and a black leather kilt. The shirt looked wet in places, and it wasn't until I smelled the iron that I realized it was blood. He wasn't wearing his eye patch, not something I was used to seeing. The skin healed over the eye socket gave his face a hollow look, like a painting with a blank spot in the canvas.

"Lose your eye patch?" I asked, grabbing the towel from under the clothes.

"Quit wearing it actually," he said, stepping past me into the shower. "It got hard to keep up with and I just asked myself one day who I was covering up for. I don't care who sees it, and I don't care what anyone thinks about it, so why bother?"

"Sure. I'm just not used to it, that's all," I said. I dropped my wet clothes in the sink and began wringing the water out of them. "Have you heard from Thera lately?"

"Not in a while. She doesn't talk to me much anymore. I kinda just do my own thing now," he said.

"What is your thing exactly? Does it have something to do with the couple I met at Horton House?" I asked.

"Yeah," he chuckled, stepping inside the shower. "I sent all the ultras off the island and started a rumor that Bigfoot is wandering around. Hunters come and I make them see the error of their ways. The gators are fat and happy, even if the hunters aren't."

Having wrung out all the water I could, I put my clothes in the trash and put on what Cearbhall had left out for me. They were loose but got the job done. "What do you do with all their stuff?"

He swished the curtain open and stepped out of the shower naked. "There's a little chop shop on the mainland that takes the cars," he said, grabbing a towel and drying off. "I know a guy that will buy all the guns he can get. Not sure if he collects them or sells them. Whatever he does with them, having the serial numbers scratched off doesn't bother him. Everything else gets cleaned up and donated to Goodwill. You wouldn't believe the tax deductions I'm getting." He dropped the towel and went into the kitchen. "Things like this on the other hand," he held up the pendant recovered from the man who shot me in the back. "Haven't decided what to do with them yet, just keep them in the junk drawer for now." He slid open a drawer and added the item to a pile of trinkets.

"Quite a collection," I said.

He contemplated the pile before slamming the drawer shut. "Yeah, I've been doing this a while. Let me get dressed and we'll go."

"Where are we going?"

"A little side project," he said grabbing some clothes out of the closet. "Last week I was out for a run with a few strays in the area. It was the middle of the night and we had come out of the woods beside the road, just jogging, minding our own business. Out of nowhere this big car swerved off the road to hit us. It wasn't an accident, he wasn't drunk, just some guy wanting to hurt something."

"Did he hit anyone?"

"Just me. It took me a few days to track him down but I found him," he said.

"So, what, you want to kill this guy or something?"

Revenge killings by Keepers aren't by the book, but they have been known to happen. It would be a little naïve to think a people whose existence centers around violence don't have the tools within easy reach at all times.

"I'm not going to kill him. He's not going to get off that easy, and besides, he shouldn't even be home right now. This douche likes his toys but if he can't be responsible with them then I will take them away in the most painful way possible," he said. "I hired some gremlins to make sure he has car problems for the rest of his life. Of course, I want to get the first shot in myself. Sugar in the gas tank, drain the oil, you get the idea."

"You take up your free time with vandalism now? This is what retirement looks like," I said, crossing my arms.

"Who said I was retired?" he said.

"What do you call this then?" I asked.

"Justice," he replied. "This guy deserves it."

"No doubt, but it's going to have to wait." I looked him in the eye. "I came here for something more important."

"The guy ran me over, tried to kill me and others just for the joy of it. Making him pay is a top priority," he said.

"Something's wrong with Thera. Holt was taken and I think he is being used to get to her. She came to me yesterday and said she was being cut off from us. I don't know how exactly. Hob's place was attacked, a bunch of dust was stolen. I'm not sure what's going on."

"Who's Holt?" he asked.

"My apprentice. He was working with Cedric before, well, you know."

"Your first apprentice. Well aren't you something?"

I couldn't tell if he was mocking me or not, but I had a feeling he was.

"Can you not? There are more important things going on right now." I was afraid my visit would bring up some old hurts on both sides, looked like I was right.

"Fine. So what did she say exactly?" he asked.

I relayed the encounter on Stone Mountain. "I think I know what's doing it," I said when I had finished. "Is the truck outside? I want to show you something."

"It's out front."

He led me outside to where my truck had been parked. We were surrounded by what looked like single story seaside condominiums. The area was well maintained, with palm trees planted in strategic locations around the property. My truck was parked across the street beside the dumpster.

"Take a look at that," I said, pointing to the bag in the back.

He looked a little puzzled but reached over and started opening it. "What is it?"

I didn't answer, figuring it would explain itself once he got it open. When the knot was undone he recoiled a bit at the stench coming out of the bag. I could smell it from the other side of the truck as well. He rolled the bag so as not to get his hands dirty as he explored to find out what the source was.

"That's what I wanted to talk to you about. I think that's what's doing this," I replied.

When the snake head met the light his face fell into a blank expression. He stood still, not saying anything for a moment. Then, not worrying about touching the rotting head anymore, he grabbed it. He starred at it for a few seconds before squeezing it. Gasses bubbled from its nostrils and juices ran from the stump where it had previously been attached. The skull cracked and collapsed under the pressure. His face had changed from blankness to hate, lips curled in a snarl and eye burning into the carrion. When it was as crushed as he could make it, he threw it into the dumpster. It ricocheted off the wall with a splat, and he spit on the ground after it disappeared inside.

"I've fought these demons before. They're bad for sure, but they aren't strong enough to mess with Thera," he said, not looking away from the dumpster. "What makes you think this is the demon causing problems?"

"She had a grimoire, and Hob was attacked. Someone stole all the dust he had, Holt was taken, and now Thera is being attacked directly. I suppose the timing could be a coincidence, but I doubt it."

He thought this over for a few seconds. "The question is how did this 'Petra' know how to find Hob? These demons can turn people to stone, like in the old myths, but they kind of take the memories the people they've turned. They know what those people knew. We need to find who she turned. Then we will know what kind of trouble we can expect. She shouldn't have been able to turn Holt. She got her hands on someone that knows you, when we find out who we will know how much trouble we are in."

I looked at the ground and shuffled my feet. "Actually, it was Naylet."

He stood frozen, seeming to process the news before responding. "Well that's unfortunate."

"My cupita was turned to stone and all you can say is 'that's unfortunate'?"

"We have bigger problems than your love life," he said. "We've got to get back now. You check with Hob to see what he can tell us and I'll check on Livy. We'll meet back at your place."

CHAPTER·16

THE SUN WAS just coming up when I pulled the truck onto the dirt road that ran between the fields to the main house. I drove slowly, not because of the condition of the road but because they didn't know this truck, and I wasn't expected. I came looking to prevent trouble, not start it. I didn't really like showing up unannounced but, everything considered, it would be okay. Stopping short of the house, I rolled down the window, looked out into the cornfield, and waited. After a minute, I was pretty sure someone was there. No scent or sound hinted at a presence in the corn but I had a prickly feeling at the base of my neck like I was being watched.

"I need to see Hob, it's important. Where can I find him?" I asked the stalks.

A figure seemed to materialize out of the corn, taking a couple steps out of the field. It looked to be more plant than man: skin that looked dry, the tan color of old husks, with yellow hair fading into brown like corn silk. The face was smooth and looked like a tree that has had the bark scraped off, with two slits where eyes should be but lacking a nose or mouth. A large hound with similar characteristics walked out beside him. These were known as corn demons, although they weren't demons like Petra. They came from another place that I am told is completely plant, but I'd never seen it. A strange but pleasant race, they don't talk much, not having a mouth, but more importantly, they don't cause problems. Hob brought them from Germany to help with the farm. The plant man raised a finger pointing to the barn opposite the house. I gave him a wave and drove over. The two disappeared back into the field in the rearview.

The barn door was open, light spilling out into a picturesque scene of country nightlife. I parked in the light, no doubt spoiling the scene but making my presence known at the same time. Inside Hob was elbows deep in a tractor. He stood up and walked toward the truck when he saw me, wiping the oil off his hands with a rag.

"Who is this stranger that shows up at my door? It can't be my old friend Obie, ja," he said when I got out of the truck.

"Sorry, Hob, I would have stopped by sooner but I've had a lot of trouble over the past couple days," I said. "I'm glad I didn't wake you."

"I am out of bed at four-thirty every morning, working by five. You have missed all the excitement," he said, rubbing the grease from his fingers.

"So, what happened?" I asked.

"As I have said on the phone, Eric was killed. He was finishing up the processing for the day when we were attacked by many demons. It was over only a few seconds after it started. Some of the corn demons responded but they were overwhelmed." He smiled, putting an arm around my shoulder. "What is it the children do, showing and telling? Come, I will show you the damage and you can then tell me about your trouble."

We hopped into the truck and headed to the barn on the back of the property behind the fields, the processing center for his operation.

I didn't feel like going into all the details, so I kept it short and sweet, "There's a demon that . . . well . . . it's new to me. Closest as I can tell it is like the old Gorgon myth. Snakes on its head, wings, some nasty poison."

"It turns people to the stone with the glowing yellow eyes and black snakes on the head?" he asked, placing his hands on his head and waving his fingers in a decent Petra impression.

I nodded as I parked in front of the barn. "Yeah, pretty much exactly. Cearbhall said they take people's memories?"

"Not exactly," he said. "They don't take the memories, they take the people, the entire life, past and future."

"What does that mean, how do they take a future?"

"As far as I can tell, this demon is a kind of parasite. It takes in the memories, ja, but it also prolongs its own life from the life force of the victim. Do you know of children going missing? The little babies?" he asked.

"Actually, for the past year, human infants have been disappearing. Naylet had me look into the most recent case a couple days ago."

"Come, let me show you something," he said, getting out of the truck.

I got out as Hob slid the door of the barn open. It looked the same as it did a few days ago except the back door had been busted in. It was boarded up as a temporary fix. There was broken wood on the ground and claw marks on some of the posts. In the center of the floor a dried grey pool of ogre blood marked the spot where Eric had fallen, surrounded by darker pools of demon blood. Hopefully, he took a few with him.

"They came in through the back," he said, holding a hand out toward the smashed up door. "It seems at least six demons attacked together but the gorgon wasn't with them. Eric never stood a chance. They carried off the dust that was ready to go out, ten crates in all. I am told they were mainly hounds and athols. They were led by an imp with a bad leg. Once they secured the dust the athol flew off with the imp, leaving the hounds to keep us busy."

He led me to an industrial style freezer and opened the door. I was hit with a blast of cold much stronger than I expected. Walking inside was like stepping into a blizzard. Multiple fans moved the frigid air so forcefully it seemed to cut straight to my bones. Demons hung upside down, including the hound and a half I had brought him a few days before. They were covered with ice and frost.

"These are the demons we were able to kill from the attack," Hob said, pointing to a row of three hounds and one athol. The athol looked a lot like an imp but was man sized with wings instead of a second set of arms. People called them flying monkeys because they looked so much like winged gorillas with crazy eyes and big teeth. "This demon isn't working alone. It is organized and with that much pixie dust it will be very dangerous."

He was right about that. Ten crates were enough to do just about anything. Petra had to have a plan for it, and that plan seemed to involve Holt.

"They knew where to find you because of Naylet? Because Petra knows everything she knows," I asked.

"This Petra doesn't know what Naylet knew, she is Naylet. At least a part of her is," he said.

"So Naylet is still alive then?"

"No, Obie, she was sucked up," he said. "She may still exist, but only as part of Petra."

"Right, but they could be separated? You're the one that says magic can do anything. I would just have to restore Naylet's body and put her mind back into it. What would I have to do to do that?"

"The body you can do. If you kill the demon and put its blood on one who was turned, they will be restored, but they will not be the same person. I've seen it before," he said. "You should find another way."

"When you say not the same person?" I questioned.

"It's like they have amnesia, there is nothing in them," he said. "I would help you with anything, except for this. I will have no part of it."

That seemed easy enough. I just had to kill Petra, which I had to do anyway. "That shouldn't be a problem."

"Oh no, but the problem will come later. The blood brings the darkness. The few that have been restored all became murderers and such," he said. "You should not use the blood. Good things do not come from it."

That wasn't reassuring. It's possible that if the body was restored without the mind that was what happened. If the person's mind was restored they couldn't be corrupted like that. They would know who they were and have the same values as before. That was the key for successfully restoring Naylet.

"Ok, what about getting her mind back. Is there a trick to that?" I asked.

"As far as I know it can't be done."

A corn demon appeared in the door to the barn. It raised a hand to its head, its long leafy fingers positioned from its ear to where its mouth would be if it had one. Then it pointed in my direction.

"You have a call," Hob said.

We drove to the main house where I found a rotary phone with a fifteen foot cord off the hook. "This is Obie," I said, pressing the phone to my ear.

"Glad I found you," Hank said. "We found the car. It's parked in the Belleview apartment complex. I'm looking at it right now."

"That sounds familiar." I reached in my pocket and pulled out the letter from Steve's wife I had found on the counter at Steve's house. She wrote her address as 1703 Belleview. "Let me guess, it's in front of building seventeen?" I asked.

"Yeah, how'd you know?"

"I have to make a stop by my house to get Cearbhall and then we will be on the way. Just hang tight and keep an eye on things," I said. "We'll handle it together when we get there."

CHAPTER 17

"LOOKS LIKE SOMEONE'S here," I said to myself, spotting a Subaru in the driveway beside Holt's Honda. I pulled the truck in line and got out. Halfway up the steps, I noticed the door was cracked. I stopped before going inside and listened. I could hear a motor running somewhere inside but nothing else. No movement or footsteps. If Cearbhall was inside he was staying perfectly still. Then again, maybe there were still some demons hanging around. Petra seemed to have a lot of friends from what Hob said.

I made the change to krasis and pushed the door open with my foot. Stepping inside, I found the living room trashed. The couch was the only thing in the right place. Everything else had been tipped over, tossed, or lost. That's when I smelled it, demon stink. Not fresh stink either, the kind of stink after they have been dead for a couple days, like the snakes outside in the truck. No doubt if any live demons were still around they already knew I was here, so there was no point in being quiet.

"Cearbhall, you here?" I called.

There was no response, no movement, no sounds at all except the strained hum of the motor coming from the kitchen. I followed it to find the kitchen in the same state of disrepair as the living room. The refrigerator had been tipped and was leaning against the counter with the door open. Luckily there wasn't anything in it but some ketchup and a bottle of pickles, both of which had been dumped out on the floor. Its motor strained impotently, trying to maintain the proper temperature. Broken dishes crunched and cut my feet as I crossed to the fridge. I leaned forward over the busted condiments grabbing the shelf in the fridge door. I pulled it up to close it and revealed a hell hound on the floor behind it. Startled, I let go of the door and fell back into the rubble. The door swung open, hitting the beast in the head. From my new vantage point on the floor I could see that the hound hadn't moved. I got up and stepped forward gingerly, peering under the door.

The demon was clearly dead. Its body had claw marks but Holt had finished it off by ripping its throat out. I reoriented the fridge and closed the door, muffling the noise. Stepping over the hound, I continued my search of the kitchen. The only thing intact I could see was the sink of dirty dishes Holt had still not bothered to clean. I wondered if Petra knew they were a sore spot from Naylet's memories and left them on purpose, or just missed them somehow. I did my best to step around the chairs and broken flatware littering the kitchen floor as I moved to the hallway leading back to Holt's room. It was relatively clear, as there had been nothing in it to begin with. I moved slowly, on guard, listening for anything.

I could smell the sweet copper of Keeper blood from the hallway. I took a breath to prepare and moved into the room. I half expected to find him in his chair facing the TV like I had seen him many times before. A couple steps in and I could see the writing on the wall. Scrawled in Holt's blood was written: RETURN HER. I touched the H and pressed it between my finger and thumb. It was dry.

I was about to head to my room when I heard footsteps coming up the front steps and inside. I moved as quickly and quietly as I could around the random debris, stopping at the corner just out of sight of my mystery guest. I popped out, intending to use the element of surprise, but instead found a fist speeding toward my face. Too late to block, my only recourse was to move with the fist to reduce its impact. As it contacted, I used the momentum of the spin to whip my tail toward the intruder and felt it impact. A second later a stabbing pain shot through my tail. I looked back to see Cearbhall with my tail in his mouth. He was in krasis, his large wolf jaws easily wrapped around my tail.

"How did you beat me here?" I asked.

He spit my tail out. "I guess you still drive like an old lady. Besides, I know some shortcuts."

Bound to the gray wolf, he was as imposing as I remember. I had forgotten how intense his stare was in krasis, missing an eye seemed to amplify its intensity more than two-fold. He'd sustained that injury long before me and had always refused to talk about it. I couldn't help but wonder, why couldn't I have been joined to an animal with a little more street cred? Otters just don't demand respect the same way some other predators do. Even Holt, bound with the Doberman, while not traditional, demanded a certain respect.

Cearbhall stretched and rubbed his jaw. I couldn't help but feel a little proud that the strike had bothered him that much—he wasn't one to acknowledge pain openly. "I followed a demon trail into the woods and turned around when I heard someone pull up. This is definitely where your apprentice was taken from. He killed at least one before they got him," he said. "He was your responsibility. You were supposed to be looking after him."

"I guess I'm still a disappointment. Good to know some things never change. They found the detective's car, so if you don't mind I'm going to go help him," I said.

I didn't wait to see if he minded and went into my room for a change of clothes and a new pair of shoes. I changed back to human form, picked something to wear that I didn't care if it got ripped up, and grabbed a change of clothes just in case. I found Cearbhall, also in human form, waiting by the door. I heaved the hound from the kitchen over my shoulder and went outside, leaving him alone in the house.

"Hold on, I'm coming with you. In fact, why don't you let me drive? We'll have more room than in your Honda," he said.

"You know that's not my Honda," I said without turning around. "You really want these demons in your car?"

"It's not mine, it belonged to those hunters from last night."

"I'll take the truck. You can do whatever you want," I said.

I wasn't thrilled about driving around in what was essentially a stolen car, especially with a demon in the back. I put the hound in the back with the bag of snakes and covered it all up with a tarp. Cearbhall joined me in the truck and we headed to the apartment complex.

"So what's with the message on the wall of your house?" he asked.

"As far as I can tell, Petra feels some kind of connection with Naylet. She tried to get her from me the other night when we fought. She doesn't know where I've hidden her. I guess she wants to get her back," I said.

"That's good," he said. "It gives us something we can use against her."

I didn't like the idea of using Naylet as bait or some kind of bargaining chip, but he was right, if leverage was needed, she could provide it. I would save that for a last resort.

"I just need a little time to figure out how to get her back to normal. There has to be some way to do it," I said.

"What did Hob say?" he asked.

I paused before I answered. "Nothing promising."

"You need to remember the bigger picture. Petra is going to be hunting, and since she knows everything Naylet knew, anyone close to you could be in danger, not to mention the humans. There's potential for a lot of people to get hurt here, and that's without Thera nuking the region. You might want to come to terms with the idea that she's gone and focus on what you can do to stop Petra," he said.

"I'll stop Petra and get Naylet back. Wait and see," I said. "Was Livy okay?"

"She was fine. I moved her to DeSoto Falls. It's a safe place," he said. "I hope you're right about Naylet, I just don't see it. Try not to worry, Obie, we'll get it straightened out."

I looked out the window. "Who said I was worried? I know you find it hard to believe but I have the situation under control."

"If that were true then I wouldn't be here."

What could I say to that? He's right. I didn't have to tell him though. Better to say nothing than swell his ego any further. With any luck Petra would be at the apartment and we could put an end to this, but then again, if I killed Petra today, would that mean Naylet would be lost? I might need to find a way to pull her out of Petra before I killed her. I needed more time, time I might not have.

CHAPTER·18

"YOU DON'T REALLY notice how clean the air is up here until you've been away," Cearbhall said, breaking the silence.

"Yeah, must be nice to be back," I said.

"So, what do we know?"

"Not much, really. Petra took a baby in Alpharetta a few weeks ago and attacked Naylet yesterday. I found a stuffed bunny at the kid's house with some weird perfume on it." I pointed absently toward his feet. "It's rolling around in the floorboard there."

He retrieved it, stuck a finger on the discolored spot and gave it a whiff. "People used to do this in the old days. They made perfume out of oil and spices. I haven't seen this for a long time. This demon has been around for a while if she knows how to do this."

"We don't know about her whereabouts except that she was meeting with a pastor, Steve Heck, who wouldn't give her up and died in a house fire. She has a grimoire that she was copying pages out of to give to him. He was being trained to summon. I found a note in his office that said P.V.T. Moca, GA. Steve referenced P.V.T. in his blog as well. I'm guessing the 'P' stands for Petra so that should be the initials of the name she is going by, at least for now. The only clue as to her location is 'Moca', have you heard of it before?"

"Never. If neither one of us has heard of it it's probably not a city. Could be a code for Starbucks for all we know," he said.

"Steve's widow probably knew but I found this note at his house," I said, fishing the letter and scrap of calendar out of my pocket to hand it to him. "I think she is the one who wrote it on the calendar judging by the handwriting. See? Same handwriting. The kicker is, the Tortured Occult found Farwell's car in front of her building. That's the apartment complex we are headed to right now."

We followed what seemed to be an unnecessarily winding road leading to the apartment complex, only to be stopped short by a gate.

"Humans love their false sense of security," Cearbhall said. "Park and walk in?"

I spotted a car coming up behind us in the mirror. "We'll scoot in behind this car." I pulled into the guest entrance and started hitting the buttons like I was looking for someone.

The car pulled up and the young woman driving scanned a card. When the gate opened I pulled up quickly behind her and we drove in before the gate could close. The complex was made up of two-story buildings set in large rectangles, with parking and green space in the center. We found building seventeen on the lower level, tucked away to the side. Hank, Fisheye, and Razor had their motorcycles parked on the opposite side of the parking lot. They lounged on the bikes watching the building. Hornet, wearing a vest with *Prospect* on the back, leaned against the club's black van. I pulled into an open space, biker adjacent, and killed the engine.

"What's the word?" I asked through the open window.

"It's been quiet," Hank said. "No movement, the car is right there in front of the building. Haven't gotten close enough to check it out, but it looks empty and undamaged from here."

"Wait here, I'm going to get a closer look," I said, getting out of the truck.

I crossed the parking lot to Farwell's car and looked in through the windows. Nothing looked out of place and there was no visible damage to the interior. I tried the door, it was unlocked. I found a few spots of dried demon blood on the headrest, and the entire thing smelled like Petra's perfume. The keys were in the ignition. I grabbed them and went back to where everyone was waiting.

"She's here, or at least she was. First priority, let's get Farwell his car. Hank, can you have someone detail it and return it to him as quick as they can, please?" I asked. "I'll cover the cost."

"Prospect," Hank shouted.

Hornet held out a hand for the keys. "I got it."

I tossed her the keys with a nod. She walked over to the Explorer, got in, and drove away.

"It's your territory. What's our play?" Cearbhall asked.

"We don't know what we're dealing with. We'll keep someone in the front and send one to watch the back, the rest of us will go in. If anyone wants out now is the time," I said.

"Fisheye, head around back, Razor will stay up front. We're ready when you are," Hank said.

"All right," I said. "Then let's go."

Cearbhall, Hank, and I crossed the parking lot as the two bikers took position. Approaching the door to apartment 1703 I put a finger over my mouth, signaling to my companions, and put my ear to the door.

Inside a rhythmic *tick-tick* repeated over and over. I couldn't place what it was coming from; if it was a clock it would have to be the loudest in existence.

The knob turned freely and I opened the door slowly, the ticking becoming much clearer. The smell of blood and the spices of Petra's perfume filled the air. I moved in quietly, not wanting to announce our presence, just in case. The door opened to a kitchen on the right, with a dining area to the left that spilled over to the living room. The ceiling fan was broken, and hanging lopsided from the ceiling, throwing it out of alignment, making it tick with every rotation. Cearbhall and Hank came in, closing the door behind them. We gave each other a nod and made the transformation to krasis.

I couldn't have picked two finer people for backup; Cearbhall with centuries of experience and Hank, huge, fearless, and strong as, well, the bear that he was. I couldn't say if we were heard coming in or if it was the sound of the Velcro on my pants I pulled apart before the change that alerted them, but no sooner had I finished my change than two large hounds burst into the kitchen and attacked. Being the first in, I was knocked down with one on top of me, sinking its teeth deep into my arm and shaking violently like a dog with a toy. Pain shot up my arm as I tried to position myself to gain the advantage.

A loud clap rang out. The hound let go of my arm and was lifted off of me. Hank had sunk his claws into its sides and lifted it effortlessly over his head. It screeched and squirmed, scratching the ceiling and sending drywall and blood cascading down around me.

"You okay?" he asked.

"Yep," I said, rolling out of the way and getting to my feet.

When I was clear, he slammed the beast down onto the linoleum. The building shook from the impact but the hound was still. Cearbhall had dealt the other hound a mortal wound and had it pinned to keep it from biting anyone as it bled out.

"Go ahead, I'm right behind you," he said.

I rounded the corner into the living room to see Petra exiting through a back door onto a patio. She clutched a book to her chest and had the imp with a gimpy leg on her shoulder. She slammed the door behind her when she saw me.

"Find Holt," I shouted as I chased after her.

I pulled the door open and ran out into a small screened-in porch just as Petra jumped through the screen and over the railing. The apartment backed up to the woods with a two-story drop. She flew off, weaving around the trees, carrying the book and imp away. Below, Fisheye had taken off after her. Not content to be left out, I leapt off the balcony through the hole in the screen, landing hard on the ground below.

When I caught up to Fisheye he was busy stomping out a fire on the forest floor under a large oak tree. Petra had landed on one of the upper branches out of reach. The imp had busied himself throwing little fireballs. They weren't large enough to do any real damage beyond starting a small brushfire. Petra stood with her wings stretched out, the significant wingspan making her look much larger than she was. The bald head was replaced with bulbous scabs where the snakes had been the day before. One of her wings looked to be a little crooked.

"Where is she, Obie?" she asked.

"Who, Candice Heck? How should I know, we just got here," I said, looking up at her.

She scowled. "Not that incessant do-gooder. Naylet."

"Somewhere safe," I said.

"I will find her," she said, looking down her nose at me. "It's just a question of how many of our friends get hurt before I do."

Calling people she's about to kill "our friends", and the way she spoke to me last time, told me she thinks of people the same way Naylet did. Maybe she even considers me her cupitus. The difference is this demon clearly lacks Naylet's compassionate nature. Petra will hurt anyone that gets in her way. The imp tossed down another fireball that landed a couple feet to my left, and Fisheye went to work on it right away.

"You want Naylet back. I want your grimoire, and there's no reason for anyone else to get in the middle of it. Let's make a deal," I said.

"Are you proposing a trade? I don't have any reason to bargain. I will get what I want either way," she said.

"Maybe, but how long will it take? You've lost the advantage. I didn't fully understand this situation before, but I do now. As soon as I leave here, Naylet will be gone. You won't be looking for her anymore, you'll be looking for someone that knows where she is hidden, and I'm not even going to know myself," I said. "I'll arrange someone to make arrangements with others I don't know to make other arrangements. It will take decades, even centuries, for you to track her through a labyrinth of acquaintances—if you can do it at all. To be sure, you'll have to absorb them all. Are you up for that?"

"I won't trade the book for her," she said. "And I can live forever. It will be an inconvenience, yes, but I will have her if I choose."

"If not a trade, then how about a duel. We fight to the death, winner takes all," I said.

She glared at me through slanted eyes. "How do I know I can trust you?"

"Have I ever lied to you before?" I asked.

She paused to think about this which is exactly what I was hoping for. I never needed to lie to Naylet, she knew who and what I was and our relationship wasn't the sort where secrets needed to be kept.

"An intriguing offer . . . The two of us together, like old times," she said.

I held up three fingers. "The three of us. I want Cearbhall in on this."

"I will need a day or two to prepare."

"What do you need to prepare? I could tell you where Naylet is and just finish it now."

"I have to fix my hair," she said. "Two on one isn't a fair fight without my snakes."

"Two days then, I'll come up with a private location for our meeting. In the meantime, don't mess with my friends, don't look for Naylet, you lay low," I said. "No more trouble."

"That's fine, Obie, but you haven't seen the preacher's wife, so please don't be mad at me about that." She grinned in a way that made me think she wasn't looking for absolution.

"We have an agreement then?"

"It's a date," she said leaping into the air.

"Wait, how do I find you?" I shouted after her.

She hovered overhead for a moment before saying, "I'll be at the Museum of Contemporary Art of Georgia. No surprises."

She didn't stick around for anymore conversation before she flew away.

"You're really taking that 'love thy enemy' thing seriously, huh," Fisheye said.

CHAPTER·19

I WALKED IN SILENCE with Fisheye back to the porch of the apartment. Keeping an eye out for nosey neighbors, I jumped up, grabbed the porch, and pulled myself up. Fisheye followed behind me. The apartment was quiet when we came back in, minus the ticking of the broken fan. I had missed a large blood stain on the carpet below the fan, with a drag mark flowing down the hallway like some kind of twisted brush stroke. I flipped a few light switches before I found the one to turn it off. A small sofa sat on one side of the room with the TV mounted above a fireplace. Candice hadn't made herself at home yet. Maybe she was hoping Steve would come to his senses and she would be back home soon. That wasn't going to happen now, assuming she was still alive to worry about it.

"Come take a look at this," I heard Cearbhall say from the other room.

We followed his voice, and the blood trail, into a spare bedroom. I rounded the corner to find the stolen dust crates and Holt laying on his back in the middle of a large circle drawn in dust. It looked similar to the summoning circles I was familiar with, but not the same. I didn't recognize all the demonic runes and the ones I knew weren't in the correct places. Cearbhall, Hank, and Razor had changed back to human form. Fisheye and I followed suit.

"What is it?" Hank asked.

"It's a binding circle. I haven't seen one of these in a long time," Cearbhall said, kneeling for a closer look. "It's used to hold someone inside it. Until the circle is broken the person trapped is held in a kind of stasis."

I looked at Holt lying unconscious in the circle. The dust that made the circle was rising a grain at a time, evaporating on the way up to fuel the binding. There looked to be enough dust in the lines to keep it going for days at the rate it was being consumed.

"So, is there a process here or do we just scoop it up?" I asked.

"Nothing special to it," he answered. "Grab that open crate and we'll shovel what we can back in."

I picked up the crate and placed it on the floor beside the circle. Cearbhall scooped up a handful of dust and dropped it in the crate. A piercing shriek that I didn't recognize as a scream at first assaulted my ears. Clasping a hand over each ear, I collapsed to my knees, involuntarily squeezing my eyes and mouth shut as if they could help block out the sound. It was over as abruptly as it started. I took a breath and opened my eyes to see Cearbhall in a similar position and the T.O. looking like they were practicing surfing. That's when I realized the ground was shaking. Thera appeared in front of me looking generally pissed off.

"Tomorrow at midnight or I finish it myself," she said before disappearing.

Cearbhall and I got to our feet as the rumble of the earth died down. He had seen and heard her just like I had but the bikers lacked the necessary gift.

"What was that?" Hank said after the rumbling had subsided.

"Thera's not happy," I answered, moving over to check out Holt.

He didn't appear to be hurt but had a pale complexion with sweat dotting his forehead. His shirt was soaked in blood around his stomach and running down from his clearly swollen shoulder that was. I pulled his shirt back for a closer look. It was shredded around his stomach but there was no sign of injuries underneath. I spread his shirt above his shoulder and found four uniform holes in it—fang marks. Petra, sans snakes, appears to have bitten him. She must have the same poison that the snakes did. She had done a number on him for sure. The injuries to his belly had probably been sustained during the original attack. Instead of dying he had healed, but looked to be losing the fight with the poison. Regardless, there wasn't much I could do for him, but with the snakes I found, Livy could help him. I had to get him back to her fast.

"Mrs. Heck I presume," Razor said, from behind me. "Come take a look at this. That demon did a number on her."

I turned to see a woman hanging in the closet. She wore a white sundress with a blue floral pattern. The poker from the fireplace had been used to suspend her from the shelf in the closet. It had been bent into a hook shape and shoved into her head. The pointy end wedged close enough to her left eye to make it bulge in its socket. While she wasn't a large woman by any standards, the shelf bent, barely holding onto the wall under the load. Her body hung limp with her legs touching the floor and bent awkwardly at the knees, reminding me of a marionette. She was covered in blood that had run down her neck, soaked her dress, and pooled on the floor around her feet. A cross on a chain was tangled in the fingers of her right hand.

"What do you think? Take her down?" I asked, not taking my eyes off the woman dangling in the closet.

"We have to clean up a lot of stuff here the cops shouldn't see," Cearbhall said. "She's not one of them."

I thought about it but I didn't want to leave her hanging. "Let's take her down and I'll call it in. Doesn't seem right to leave her like this. Hell, the cops are probably already on the way from all that racket we made. Can you all get the dust and demons loaded and I'll take care of this?"

I reached out to take her down. When I touched her, she let out a gurgling sob that bubbled blood out of her nose. I recoiled a step from the surprise. My heart dropped in my chest followed by an uneasiness in my stomach. It had never occurred to me that she could still be alive.

"Fuck, hold her up," Cearbhall said.

I stepped forward and wrapped one arm around her waist and put my other hand on her neck for support. I lifted as Cearbhall unhooked her as carefully as he could from the shelf. Muffled sobs escaped her pinned jaw and tears rolled out of her one good eye. As a Keeper I was used to death, I was baptized in it and forged by it. I had become an efficient killer early on, of both man and beast. I won't apologize for it. If Candice had been killed and strung up for whatever reason, I would chalk it up to normal demon shit and move on. This was something else. The infliction of pain and suffering for its own sake is a sickness with no place in the world. It highlighted why we needed to put an end to Petra and I couldn't help think that Thera was right; I should have finished her there in the yard, even if it meant I died doing it. This was my fault. We laid her on the floor as gently as we could.

"End her suffering," Cearbhall said, the disgust in his voice revealing he shared my view.

"You're going to kill her? Can't you do that healing voodoo on her?" Razor protested.

"With a fire poker jammed in her skull? We would have to take it out and that would kill her anyway," I said.

"It just don't seem right," he said. "There has to be something we can do."

"There is. You can get the dust and demons loaded. I'll take care of this," I said.

The bikers and Cearbhall grabbed the crates and made their way out of the room. I raised a hand to her throat and she grabbed it with both hands. She clutched it against her chest as she sobbed. Maybe Razor was right, there was another way.

"Candice, I'm here to help you. If you hear me squeeze my hand," I said, trying to sound as soothing as I could.

I felt a squeeze.

"I can end this for you or I can call an ambulance. Give me one squeeze if you want to be finished or two for the ambulance," I said.

There was no response at first. I can imagine what she must have been going through. In the course of my work I have experienced extreme pain. The difference is that it's temporary for me. I heal so fast, the worst is over in minutes. When pain is so short-lived, it's an easy thing to look past. I could feel the hesitation in her answer when I received it, two squeezes.

"Hold on," I said, "Help is on the way."

I went to look for a landline but there wasn't one. I found her purse on the kitchen table and dumped it. Her phone toppled onto the floor in a pile of gum, tissues, and tampons.

"What are you doing?" Cearbhall asked when he came back in and found me rummaging through the purse's contents.

"She wants to live," I said.

He put his hands on his hips. "Since when did we start giving anyone a choice?"

"Since now."

Hank came in a second later. "Fisheye is pulling the van around. Doesn't appear to be anyone around so we should be able to get everything loaded," he said. "What's he doing?"

"Calling for help," Cearbhall said. "The lady wants to live."

"Good for her," Hank said. "That means we have to move."

I went back into the room with Candice, knelt beside her, and dialed the number.

"911, what is your emergency?" the woman on the other end said.

"Candice Heck has been attacked in her apartment at 1703 Belleview Way. She needs an ambulance," I said.

"Did you attack her, sir?" the woman said as I put the phone down on the floor beside Candice.

"Help is on the way. Be well, Candice," I said.

I picked up Holt in a fireman's carry and headed for the door. I stopped short before going outside, waiting for Hank to give me the all-clear. He did a scan of the area and waved me out, opening the truck door for a quick entry. I sat Holt into the passenger seat and closed the door.

"Livy should be able to work with the snakes in the back to help Holt. I have to get Naylet and I'll meet you up there," I said. Cearbhall nodded and pulled out as I turned to Hank. "I'll drive the van."

CHAPTER·20

DESOTO FALLS WASN'T much more than a campground, a hiking trail, and a trickle of water pouring over a rock. What it lacked in extravagance it made up for with seclusion. Located inside the Elvin Nation, right off of GA 19, it wasn't much to look at. Parking in a small gravel lot by the road was mandatory. Access to the falls and campground was by foot only. I didn't know why Cearbhall brought Livy here. It meant nothing to me, I hadn't spent any real time here, and maybe that was the point. There would be no reason for Petra to think it's where we would be hiding out. If everything went according to plan, she would lay low and stick to our agreement, which would make this precaution a moot point. Fingers crossed.

After we dropped the demons off at Hob's and picked up Naylet from the clubhouse, Hank drove me up. I tried to talk him out of it, as he wasn't exactly welcome this far into the Elvin Nation unannounced. But a quick trip in and out would most likely go unnoticed. We found the truck parked on the edge of the gravel parking lot. The truck was empty and I figured Cearbhall had Livy set up at one of the campsites. I gave Hank my thanks and he left Naylet and me alone by the truck, not wanting to spend any more time here than he had to. I knelt and found their scent leading down a gravel path in the direction of the camping area. Heaving Naylet onto my shoulders, I started after them. It was hard going with the extra weight she had put on; hopefully Livy wasn't too far away. I followed Cearbhall's scent down the path, past some picnic tables, but instead of leading right to the camping area, it went left to the hiking trail.

"Where are they going?" I asked myself absently.

I followed his scent up the trail, stopping every few minutes to squat and make sure I was still on track. Cearbhall's scent led off the trail to the north, through the woods. I knelt, wondering if he was playing some kind of joke on me. Lead me on some roundabout way through the woods, hauling Naylet's now cumbersome form. Normally I'm on board for a nice nature hike, but not today. While I pondered, some hikers had come up on me from the trail to my right. I would have slipped into the woods if I had been aware of them a minute sooner. Better to stay out of sight than have to explain why I was carrying a statue into the woods. I stood up, already smiling and ready for the cordial hellos that strangers around here exchange for casual meetings. The hikers, a man and a woman looking mostly miserable, kept their eyes on the ground and walked by without acknowledging my presence.

Deciding to follow Cearbhall's scent, I ducked into the woods as soon as they were out of sight. After about ten minutes of walking I could smell a campfire, and found Livy's camp set up in a holler, shielded by mountains on all sides. I set Naylet beside the tent and stretched my back, glad we had made it. Cearbhall was sitting by the fire, poking at it with a stick. Livy and Holt must be in the tent.

"What took you so long?" Cearbhall said as soon as I finished my stretching.

"Nothing. Just dropped the demons off and got Naylet. How's Holt?" I asked.

"Don't know yet." He tossed his stick into the flames. "Livy's working on him in the tent. There's someone I want you to meet."

I looked around but didn't notice anyone with us. "Are they in the tent, too?" I asked.

"No, he's right here," he said. "Quiet your mind and listen. You will hear him."

I stood still and listened. I heard the birds, the rustle and pop of the fire, the wind moving through the trees. That was all at first, and then it wasn't.

More company. Alone for so long and now five, but two are not well. The voice, deep and groaning, seemed to come from inside my head rather than outside.

"What was that?" I asked. "Did you hear it, too?"

"Yeah, he's talking to both of us. That's Walasi, an Old One," he said.

I had heard stories about Old Ones throughout the years. Thera's original Keepers. Forces of nature stronger than anything I had ever come across. I always thought the Old Ones were long gone and the stories were embellished. I guess I was about to find out.

"Where is he?" I asked, my excitement evident. I looked all around but still didn't see anything unusual or particularly old looking. "The stories say Walasi was a frog the size of a house. So either they are wrong or I'm just not looking at the right place."

"He's right here," Cearbhall said throwing a thumb over his shoulder. "Why don't you show him?"

A tremor ran through the earth as the trees on the hillside directly behind him began to shake. It seemed to be an earthquake or landslide at first, until the earth itself began to rise. I didn't put together what was happening until two round eyes the size of large tractor tires opened about fifteen feet apart on the hill. Two large legs lifted the body from the ground, revealing an enormous toad protruding from the hillside. Its head cocked to one side, putting an eye in position to give me a thorough inspection. The eye itself had a horizontal, oval pupil with a light green iris. Black streaks ran through the iris and I could see they moved like the electricity in a plasma globe. Just a hint of the power this Old One contained, I deduced.

"Bigger than a house," I said, staring up at the megatoad.

You fought a snake head. It did not go well. Walasi eyeballed the statue of Naylet behind me.

"It's still not going well," I said. "It's still out there."

"Hey, Walasi, see that poplar over there," Cearbhall said, pointing to a tree on the opposite hillside. "Pretend that was a snake head and show Obie how you would handle it."

Walasi's head shifted toward the tree and Cearbhall lay flat on the ground. I opened my mouth to ask him if I should take cover as well but before I could get a word out Walasi sent his tongue shooting across the holler. It slammed into the tree, shearing it from its roots and, having a solid hold on the tree, brought it back with terrifying intensity. I dove to the ground to avoid the arboreal missile. Walasi caught the tree in his mouth, spit it out on the ground in front of him, and raised a giant foot, sending it crashing down, splintering the tree to pieces and forming a toad-print crater at the same time. The ground shook from the impact, toppling Naylet. I looked at Cearbhall in shock.

"And now we have firewood," he said, grinning.

Livy's head popped out of the tent. "It's bad enough you bring me rotten snake heads and Holt on death's door but now you're making all that racket and shaking the whole world. Keep it down. I'm trying to work!" she yelled before disappearing back inside. "I swanie!"

Walasi sank back down into the hillside while Cearbhall and I said at the same time, "Sorry, Livy."

It was probably best to leave Livy alone for a bit, so I helped Cearbhall gather the wood. Cearbhall jumped into the crater, standing waist deep and tossed the splintered wood out for me to stack by the fire. I thought about trying to lure Petra up here to have Walasi deal with her. After all, it looked like he would have no trouble handling her. That would be taking the easy way out. This was all happening because I didn't finish Petra off that night in the yard. I could use Walasi as a backup plan, but I needed to see this through myself. Plus, if there was any hope for getting Naylet back, I had to get Petra's blood and figure out how to separate the two of them. Walasi smashing Petra into dust wouldn't leave me much to work with.

Walasi's voice popped in my head. *I sense uncertainty.*

I looked over at Cearbhall who didn't seem to get the same message. Walasi must just be speaking to me now. I walked closer in a futile attempt for a little privacy. "I fought the demon once and didn't kill it. I am trying to figure out how to kill the demon and undo the damage she caused," I said, motioning toward Naylet. "You are so powerful and I'm struggling. It would be easy if I had the kind of power you do."

The giant toad lowered his head, putting one of his electrically charged eyes in front of me. *Focus on the gifts you have, not the gifts you don't. My gifts are my prison. I stay hidden here.*

That was a good point. He couldn't exactly go anywhere or even move around that much without risking busting the veil wide open. It must be a miserable existence. "Any other tips for me?"

Trust Thera, she is life.

The blind faith in Thera didn't surprise me but I wasn't sure putting trust in someone who was prepared to kill all of us to suit her own needs was wise. I started to compile a list of the things I was good at. I was a great swimmer but demons avoid water like the plague so I probably wouldn't talk Petra into an eight hundred meter freestyle to settle this. My claws had already proved to be useless. With Otis's help I'd managed to arrange some form of cooperation between almost everyone in the region but I couldn't cooperate Petra to death, or could I?

"I'm going to go fight the demon again. If I lose, she will come for Naylet," I said. "Will you protect her for me?"

She is safe here.

"Thanks, Walasi. I need to check on Holt. I will talk to you again soon," I said.

I stuck my head in the tent to test the waters before diving in. Holt lay on the cot from Livy's house and she sat on a stool beside him, putting a reddish liquid into his mouth one drop at a time.

"In or out," she said, still annoyed. "You're going to let the bugs in."

It seemed safe enough so I stepped into the tent and closed the flap behind me. "How's he doing?"

"Too early to tell. He's a tough one, that's for sure, but those snakes you brought me had started to turn," she said, motioning with her head to the bag in the corner. "They're stinking up the place good and I don't think the antivenom is quite as strong as it could be."

"I'll get rid of those," I said, picking up the bag to dispose of later.

"I've got a couple vials sitting on top of my kit there in the corner. Two doses of antivenom. It's better to take it right before you get bit, but we won't know how well it will work until we see how Holt responds, so it's probably best to not get bit at all if you can help it."

"That is the idea," I said. "Do you need anything before I head out?"

"You just got here. Where are you running off to so soon?"

"I got to get back to work," I said. "No rest for the wicked, right?"

"Be careful out there," she said, methodically administering the antivenom.

"I will, I promise," I said.

When I made it back outside Walasi had disappeared into the mountainside. He blended in completely, his rock skin the perfect camouflage.

Cearbhall looked up from the fire when I came out of the tent. "Ready to go?"

"I was planning to go alone. Did you want to come?" I asked.

"There's nothing for me to do here and you might need my help. When was the last time we visited a museum anyway?" he asked, getting up from his seat.

"First time for everything."

CHAPTER · 21

"I'M NOT INTERESTED in meeting on her terms," Cearbhall said, eyeballing the area. "We need to find out where she's staying now and catch her off guard. Put an end to this before it gets any more out of hand. I don't like this."

The Museum of Contemporary Art of Georgia was tucked down a side street on the north side of Atlanta behind a collection of shops and an electrical substation. It wasn't a high traffic area and it was easy to see why Cearbhall was concerned. For a city, it was about as secluded as a place could get. The empty parking lot gave away that they must not get a lot of business in the middle of the day, heightening the sense of seclusion.

"It will be okay," I said, turning off the engine. "I don't think she will try anything."

"What makes you so sure?" he asked.

"I'm not sure at all," I said. "Petra is unpredictable at best. There's no telling how many people she has rattling around in her head. The thing is, one of those people is Naylet. I don't know if she is actively conscious in there or if it's more that they merged, but either way she's in there and I have to believe that counts for something. I don't think Petra will try anything here."

He shot me a look from the passenger seat. "Am I talking to myself here? It's a bad idea."

"I hear you. I have no intention of meeting on her terms, but I gave my word and I intend to honor it," I said. "Besides, our best chance of finding her is to play along for now."

He chuckled to himself at my statement. "You gave your word to a demon, and you intend to honor it?"

"Doesn't matter who I gave it to, my word is good," I said, getting out of the truck.

"That's very principled. What idiot taught you that?" he asked.

I leaned against the door and spoke to him through the window. "You did," I said.

He cocked his head to the side in fake contemplation. "Hmm, doesn't sound like me."

"It was a long time ago," I said. "You coming?"

"No, art isn't my thing."

The building was unremarkable from the outside, it looked like an industrial building, except for the large triangular awning over the steps leading up to the front door. Well-kept bushes planted on either side of the steps, combined with the awning, went a long way to give it a classy feel otherwise absent in the surrounding area.

Part of me was glad Cearbhall decided to wait in the car. If he went inside there's a good chance things would devolve quickly—he's not always good with tact. I had spent a lot of time thinking on the way down on how to handle this. I thought about both of us going in and taking our chances. Maybe we could kill her right here and be done with it. Then again, she could have a building full of demons waiting to eat us alive. Petra seemed to be sincere in her invitation, so maybe it would turn out all right.

Going through the glass doors at the top of the steps, I followed the signs in the hallway around to the entrance to the museum. I found the entrance to my left and went in. A young lady behind a counter, seeming bored, stopped typing to greet me. I paid the admission fee and listened to the spiel about the different exhibits. The last one she described caught my attention.

"In the back is our most recent addition, a selection of sculptures by Petra Von Thelan," she said. "The artist is on site today."

"That's what I came to see," I said. "Tell me the truth, what do you think about it?"

She looked past me to make sure the coast was clear. She whispered, "Honestly, it gives me the creeps. It's a little too real for my taste, but it's very well done."

I thanked her and headed to the back. It was an open floorplan; most of the building was empty space. The floors were concrete painted in a splotchy brown. The walls were beige with pieces hanging every few feet with little tags describing the work. The ceiling was unfinished with pipes and beams visible but everything painted white, giving it a sophisticated industrial vibe. I heard the clicking of heels echoing from the other room. As I rounded the corner I found its source: Petra walking in my direction. She looked human again, no doubt an illusion. She smiled as she walked over to me, her head wrapped in the scarf like a cancer patient, and looking genuinely happy to see me.

"I thought I heard you, I'm so glad you could make it. I'm excited to show you my work. I think you'll like it," she said, opening her arms as if she was going to hug me.

I held my hand out to stop her and said, "I found Candice."

"You knew she wasn't going to get out of this alive. Don't be mad at me about that, Obie, it will make me think you aren't happy to see me. Besides, I have kept my end, haven't I? That Candice business was before our agreement."

I would have to play along. If I didn't I couldn't get her where I wanted her. "Actually, she survived. Definitely worse for the wear, but still with us."

"You didn't kill her? Wouldn't that have been the humane thing to do? I mean, the way her eye popped out I doubt she will ever look right again." She laughed. "She's tougher than she looks, I'll give her that."

Bitch.

"Are you going to show me around?" I asked, extending my arm and smiling through the disgust.

She beamed and wrapped her arm around mine. We walked to her exhibit arm in arm, which made my stomach turn. The exhibit consisted of four adults with six babies in front of them. The layout reminded me of an apocalyptic nativity scene, with five too many baby Jesuses. A closer look of the horror on their faces and I understood why the receptionist didn't care for the exhibit. I wondered how she would feel if she knew these used to be living people, locked forever in their last moment of agony.

"They are all wonderful, Obie, but this is the one I really want you to meet. His name is Titus Ovidius Malleolus. He was a sculptor outside of Rome many years ago. So skilled and so passionate, and very attractive, don't you think?" she said. She paused for my input.

His face was frozen in a scream, with his hands gripping at his chest as if he were still alive in the stone and was trying to tear himself out of it. I cocked my head to one side, inspecting his tormented features. "He's all right, I guess."

"Yes, quite all right indeed. I couldn't resist having him. He is one of my favorite companions. I've used his passion ever since, all the way to my current masterpieces like baby Stephanie here," she said, running a hand over the baby on the far right. "I used that passion in creating my most recent work, Naylet, who I hold as important to me as Titus. She is just as remarkable and has shown me so much. Having her away from me has forced me to use my passion in other ways, like the message I made out of sweet Candice Heck." Her voice took on a decidedly darker tone. "I hope that you are receiving that message, Obie, because the truth is, all this is to say that you shouldn't fuck with me."

This was becoming more confrontational than I was hoping for. I thought for a moment, what would I say to Naylet in this situation? I couldn't quite come up with it so I went for sarcasm instead. "Ladies and their drama. Is all that necessary? We were getting along so well."

She glared at me through squinted eyes. Her gaze softened and she smiled before saying, "Obie, I wish things had worked out differently between us. I just hate that I have to kill you."

"And I hate to have to die," I said. Looked like the honeymoon was over already. "Are you ready to talk business?'

"I'm listening," she said.

"It simple really, you fight Cearbhall and I, to the death. Winner take all. You win, and you get Naylet, we win, and we get your grimoire," I said.

She considered it for a moment. "And where would this fight take place?"

"Browns Bridge outside of Gainesville. Meet us on the bridge at ten PM sharp," I said.

"Why a bridge?" she said suspiciously.

"I know some people that can shut down the road. It will give us a nice private place to resolve our problem."

She smiled. "And no weapons?"

"No weapons. Just the three of us fighting until someone wins," I replied.

As she pondered my offer, she walked back to her statues. She moved among them, putting her hand on the shoulder of one, touching the face of another. I guessed that she was drawing on their experiences. Again I wondered if the people she absorbed were trapped in her, still conscious but disembodied. Was she actually speaking to them in there, or just running through lifetimes of memories to come to the best conclusion?

"How do I know I can trust you, Obie? What assurance do I have that this isn't a trick?" she asked, turning to face me.

"I give you my word as a gentleman," I replied using the same words I used with Naylet in hopes that it jogged some sentiment inside her. "If you agree and can beat Cearbhall and I, you will get what you're looking for."

"If that's the best you can do . . ." She trailed off with a distant look as if she was trying to remember something, before coming back to the present and saying, "Agreed."

"All right, then I will see you tomorrow at ten," I said, turning for the door.

"Obie," she called after me.

I turned around to see what she wanted. "Yeah?"

"It's a date," she said with a smile and a wink.

Back at the truck, Cearbhall was sitting on the tailgate. "Well," he said when I came outside.

"It's on, tomorrow night at ten," I said.

We got in the truck. Before I could start it he said, "What's the plan?"

"First we need some help. I'll drop you off at the clubhouse. I need you to get Hank and have him meet me at ground zero, bottom level. I will explain everything when I get there," I said.

"Where are you going?" he asked.

"I have some other friends to talk to," I said.

CHAPTER·22

IT'S NOT HARD to find elves, if elves are all you're looking for. All you have to do is take a drive into the Elvin Nation, the area covering northernmost Georgia and part of Tennessee sharing a border almost exactly with the Chattahoochee National Forest. The royal court, on the other hand, can be hard to track down. I'm not sure if it's paranoia from the strained relations with the T.O., or if the Queen just prefers a more mobile lifestyle. Whatever the cause, the court was never in the same place for more than a few days and there was no way to tell where it would be at any given time. The only way to find her highness was to go through an elf with connections. Luckily for me, there are outposts set up on the edges of their territory to accommodate these kinds of requests. The southernmost outpost sat in the mountains just north of Dahlonega.

I pulled up a winding mountain road, barely more than a horse trail, that snaked around the mountain to the outpost on top. I drove slowly, the truck lurching into the potholes and over the occasional root. I think they kept the road in such poor shape to deter visitors, as if their general dispositions didn't do an adequate job already. A little over halfway up I came to a small security building that looked wholly out of place in the middle of the woods. A barricade with a stop sign blocked the road. It was undoubtedly excessive, one of those things I thought the Queen did more for show than anything else. The elves didn't get many visitors as far as I knew, and someone would have to be plumb crazy to attack them outright.

An elf stepped out of the building, taking a tactical position as I rolled to a stop in front of the barricade. Her sleeves rolled up, hands resting on the rifle attached to the harness on her vest. Her golden hair pulled back, proudly showing her pointed ears. She stood sleek and muscular, form filling the camouflage uniform exquisitely. I could see the silhouette of another elf behind the tinted glass of the security building, probably watching the feed from the camera focused on me from the roof. A window slid open, revealing the second elf, looking very much like the first except for her hair hanging lazily about her face.

She addressed me without looking up from whatever had her attention. "What's your business?"

"I am Obie, Keeper of Thera. I need to speak with the Queen regarding a threat to the Elvin Nation," I said.

The elf looked up, brushing her hair aside to see me clearly. Her eyes went wide, and she slammed the glass closed. The first elf stared at me as I sat there with the truck idling, not moving a muscle. I gave her a friendly nod and smile; she didn't return the gesture. I was just starting to think I should have brought a book or some Sudoku when the elf stepped out of the building and up to my window.

"We need to search the car. Please step out," she said.

"Do we really have to go through all that?" I asked.

She gave me a grin. "Only if you want to get in."

I did in fact want to get in, so I got out. I was frisked, and a pretty thorough job was done searching the car, even going so far as to take a mirror and looked underneath for explosives. They confiscated my kit from behind the seat but otherwise I made it through unscathed.

"We will keep this at the checkpoint. You'll get it back when you leave," she said, walking my bag into the building.

I nodded and got back in the truck. They slid the barricade open allowing me to continue to the compound. The road corkscrewed around the mountain, ending at a huge octagon shaped house. Three stories tall with the entire top story being mostly windows. Three large wraparound porches encircled each story, giving quick access to any side of the house. There were a few vehicles in a paved parking area in front. I put my car in line with the rest and got out to see Harlan coming down the stairs to meet me. He wore black fatigues instead of the camo like the ladies at the checkpoint, with a loose fitting beanie covering his head. His blond hair, also as long as the ladies, stuck out in places making him look like a military hipster. He was the Queen's son but, being male, was forbidden from serving in the Nations Army. Being that the Elvin males were smaller and weaker in stature, the Queen deemed them insufficient. Many were put to work as servants. Harlan, due to his birthright, achieved as much as an Elvin male could hope for.

"Obie, it's good to see you. What have you been up to?" he said, extending a hand.

I shook it. "Oh, you know, life of a Keeper, it's all glamour and women. What are you doing here?"

"I run the outpost now. It's nothing to be excited about, just something to keep me away from my mother's ears. Wouldn't want my presence to remind her of what a constant embarrassment I am," he said.

"She must think highly of you to put you in charge here, protecting the border with the T.O.? That's a big job," I said.

"I wouldn't call protecting a border from a conflict that only lives in the minds of the elders a big job. Nothing ever happens here and even if it did, the guard could handle it without me. Hell, they already do it without me. I'm just here to greet guests and make them feel special to be greeted by the Queen's son. So I hope you feel important or I've failed in my duties."

"I'm just tickled," I said.

He held an arm out to direct me toward the stairs. "Come on up and get comfortable. The Queen will be here soon to talk to you."

I started walking and stopped abruptly as I passed him when a scent caught my nose. I knew it immediately, sweet and delicate with a slight metallic undertone, not unlike an Elf in general. It was blood—Elvin blood specifically.

I stopped walking and looked at him. "Are you injured?"

"No, it's nothing," he said, clearly not wanting to engage in the subject.

"Hello? Keeper here, mystical healer with the nose of a basset hound. I can smell the blood on you. Let me take a look, it will just take a second," I said.

He looked worried at this and glanced around to see who was watching. A sentry on the middle level was making her rounds. She was out of earshot and didn't take any interest in us or our conversation.

"Come over here," Harlan said, pulling me under the porch in a corner. "I . . . uh . . . Well, I'm leaving." He lifted the side of his beanie to show me his ear. It was bandaged on the top and I could see red soaking through.

I took a step closer to whisper, "Harlan, what did you do?"

"Just something to make fitting in easier where I am going," he said.

"But no elf kingdom will accept you with trimmed ears. You'll be an outcast," I said. "Where are you going to go?"

"You can't be an outcast from something you're not a part of, Obie. I don't fit in here, I'm not happy. I'm going to go somewhere and start fresh. Just find a place for myself with the humans," he said.

"Hold still," I said, raising a hand up on either side of his head. The blue light emanating from my hands was largely drowned out in the daylight, only illuminating his cheeks and reflecting in his eyes. The wounds on his ears closed quickly. A slight ache worked its way into my arms and was gone a moment later.

If he was willing to trim his ears there would be nothing I could do to change his mind. "You know when the Queen finds out about this—"

He didn't let me finish my sentence. "She doesn't have to find out. Just don't say anything, okay? I will be gone tomorrow night."

If the Queen finds out I knew she would probably refuse to help me, not to mention what she would do to him. On the other hand, it's none of my business and I did have plausible deniability. "Okay, I won't say anything. I hope you know what you're doing."

He thanked me and escorted me into the top floor of the compound. It held a kitchen on one side with the rest of the floor a single open room. It had a few couches, tables and chairs, a pool table, and a large fireplace opposite the kitchen. A couple of sentries patrolled outside on the second and third floor with rifles. I doubt there was much to see but the Queen was ever vigilant with the security of the Elvin Nation.

"I can have the kitchen boy make you something," Harlan said. "Something to eat or drink, tea maybe?"

"No thanks, I'm fine," I said.

I changed to krasis in preparation for my meeting with the Queen. After a short wait, two vehicles pulled up to the compound. The first was a truck with two people in the cab and an elf in the back. From above I could see what looked to be an empty bracket welded to the center of the bed with a pole rising up from it. The elf sat on a large lockbox mounted against the cab. No doubt the heavy firepower. The second vehicle was an SUV with blacked out windows. The vehicles didn't bother parking neatly, instead they just stopped caddy-corner in front of the compound. The Queen was followed by the royal guard, a seven elf strong, well-armed, and very well trained security force made up entirely of women. Her personal attendant, a thin male in plain clothes who looked unimpressive by comparison to the rest of the entourage, brought up the rear. Not a group I would want to tangle with, personally, although the attendant wouldn't be so bad. As the Queen ascended to the third level, the security force broke off, taking positions to secure the area. By the time they reached the top it was just the Queen, her attendant and two guards. The guards took position on opposite sides of the room while the Queen came to greet me, ignoring Harlan completely as she passed him.

She was tall and slender, standing almost six feet, a full seven inches taller than Harlan and her attendant. Her long blonde hair was pulled back showing her pointed ears like a badge. She wore combat boots, jeans, and a black spaghetti strap top. The most noticeable part of her outfit was the Old West style six-shooters hanging from a belt that sat lopsided off of her hips, which accentuated their sway as she walked.

"Obie, I hear you have a warning for me. Are you here to deliver the warning or is this a courtesy?" she asked.

Say what you want about the Queen, but she was sharp. She understood my position on a level that few did and knew I could be here as a friend or as Thera's representative. "It's a courtesy, Your Highness," I replied. She wasn't my Queen and I really had no obligation to address her that way but I have found stroking egos tends to make things go easier.

"Then please have a seat and give me your message," she said.

I sat down at the closest table. She took a seat opposite me. "I am hunting a demon on Thera's orders. I have a plan in the works but if I fail, Thera is prepared to destroy the region to eliminate it. If this happens, you and your people will most likely be killed along with everybody else. I wanted to warn you and ask for your help to ensure my success. It would be minimal risk to your people but there are a few things we would need to discuss."

"I appreciate the information, Obie. You are again showing your intention to be a friend of the elves. What are you asking of me?"

"This creature can fly. To make sure she can't escape I need to keep it on the ground. I was hoping you could provide some air support."

"That's simple enough," she said. "What's the catch?"

"Well . . ." I pulled out my most charming smile. "This demon is a gorgon and, like the old legends say, can turn people to stone. I don't know the specifics of how it works but your elves could be in serious danger. I have a plan to prevent this but I am afraid you won't like it."

"Let's have it then," she said.

"The Tortured Occult have a natural resistance to her magic. If you can keep her grounded, they can shield you from her magic. That way your elves will be safe and I can focus on killing her, instead of worrying about if your people are in danger."

She leaned back in her chair in thought. I was hoping she was considering my proposal rather than deciding how to tactfully banish me from the kingdom.

"I would like to help you, Obie, but they are not trustworthy. They would pose as much of a threat to us as this demon, if not more. We will help you, but not with the Tortured Occult," she replied.

"I know you have a strained relationship with the T.O., but this threat affects both of you, and you know what they say about the enemy of my enemy. This could be an opportunity to start mending fences with them. Surely you could both benefit from a better relationship," I said.

"It's true that there could be benefit," she agreed, "but it doesn't change the fact that they can't be trusted."

"What if I take responsibility for them?" I said.

She squinted at this turn. "Meaning if they turn on us, you will make it right?"

"Yes, whatever it takes," I said. "Will you at least meet with them to see if we can work something out?"

"If you take responsibility for them, then yes," she said. "We will meet, but I promise nothing else."

I couldn't help but let out a sigh of relief. Just getting her to agree to show up was a giant step. We might actually be able to pull this off. "Thank you. The meeting is set for tonight at ground zero. I can escort you there whenever you are ready."

The Queen turned to the member of her security force closest to us. "Stock up on silver bullets. Harlan, you will attend our meeting as well."

"Do you need me there? Wouldn't it be better if I stayed behind?" Harlan answered.

Her response had an air of disdain. "I don't need you but you are in charge of the southern border. Any agreements reached will impact your responsibilities. So do us a favor, quit whining and go get in the truck."

CHAPTER·23

DAWSON FOREST, A ten-thousand-acre nuclear test site turned wildlife management area, was known as the Dead Forest to ultras. It still housed several concrete structures that had been too expensive to tear down when they were abandoned. The largest of these buildings was three stories tall and fenced off to the public with No Trespassing signs. We referred to it as ground zero and used it as a meeting place when the more public venue of the clubhouse wouldn't work. The general public was largely unaware of the place and the only people that might be around were high schoolers looking for a private place to get into trouble. We parked our three-car caravan off one of the side roads close by and walked over to ground zero.

The building was completely obscured by the trees and undergrowth. It didn't become visible until we were almost to the fence. Cotton and Razor were standing by the hole that had been cut as an entrance. Razor held the fence open for us as we approached. We ducked under it one by one and proceeded inside. One of the security force followed the Queen, her attendant, Harlan, and me into the building. Inside it was dilapidated and dark. We made our way through the skeleton of a building, consisting of a steel reinforced concrete frame and garbage. No doors or windows, only empty spaces where they used to be. Pipes coming out of the floor and walls had been cut off, leaving hints as to what had been there. The ground was covered with debris: pieces of concrete that had broken free from the walls and ceilings, and garbage that had been brought in and left. Graffiti lined the walls, partially covered by vines growing in through the empty window slits. The free flowing air combined with the concrete gave the area an old smell, stone and nature combining into something that I think buildings of long abandoned civilizations would smell like.

I led the Queen's procession down the stairs to the lowest level; The attendant stepped aside and waited at the top of the stairs. He would be able to hear everything from there but it was far enough away to not be considered a part of the meeting. The large room below ground level was nothing but trash and rubble. Hank waited with Cearbhall and Otis on the far side of the room. A lantern was placed in the center of the room, providing enough light for our meeting but casting long shadows across the floor and walls. I could feel the tension in the air as soon as we stepped into the room.

"What the hell's this?" Otis said.

"An opportunity. If you all will just bear with me for a few minutes," I said. "Pun intended." One day Otis is going to find the humor in bear puns, until then I'll just have to keep trying.

It's customary to conduct business unveiled, the idea being that pacts made behind disguises can't be trusted. I kicked off my shoes and changed into krasis. Cearbhall, Otis, and Hank did the same. The Queen had come with her ears showing; her guard took off her cap and pulled her hair back revealing her ears. Harlan stood against the wall behind the Queen in the dark and kept his hat on. It hadn't occurred to me until now, but if he took his hat off there's no keeping his secret. No wonder he didn't want to come. The Queen and her guard had her back turned to him. I decided to ignore him and with any luck Otis wouldn't make a big deal about it.

"Let's get started," I said. "First, thank you all for showing up. As you have heard already we face a threat that is putting not just your families in jeopardy but the entire region. I believe that by meeting and speaking we can come to an under—"

"Hold on, Obie," Otis said, stepping forward. "That one in the back is still veiled."

The room turned to look at Harlan, who had deer-in-headlights down pat.

"I'm sorry, sir, no disrespect intended. I'll just go wait outside. Please don't let my mistake affect your negotiations," he said, moving for the stairs.

"Stop," the Queen said. "This is my son, Harlan. He runs the Southern Outpost and if something were going to come from this, you would be his responsibility. Take off your hat and step forward."

He looked at me over her shoulder. I would have loved to help him out but there was nothing I could do. I shrugged.

"Now," she commanded when he didn't respond immediately.

He met his mother's eyes and pulled the beanie from his head with one hand. He pulled his hair back showing his cropped ears. No one said anything at first—there was a fair amount of shock to go around—but the Queen never looked away from her son or showed any emotion.

"Take him to the truck," she said and turned her back to him. She stood quietly facing Otis until the guard had escorted him out leaving her without any backup. If she was upset, she wasn't showing it.

"Please excuse my son, he is . . . Let's just get this over with," she said.

"Right," I said, glad to get back to business, "So, I believe that the two of you would benefit from a better relationship. We are in a bad situation with this demon, but we can turn it into something positive by using it as an opportunity to mend fences."

"As I have said, Obie, if the Tortured Occult shows itself to be trustworthy, you will have Elvin support," the Queen said.

"Tom C's word is good. The organization is run by honor above all," Otis said.

"Yes, I am well aware of the honor among your kind," she said.

"You are the one that brought silver to a peaceful negotiation. I can smell it on you." Otis took a step forward.

"I leave the silver when you pull your fangs," she said stepping forward to meet him.

"I'll pull my fangs when you cut your ears," Otis snarled back.

Admittedly, that was a low blow considering what she had just seen with Harlan. They stood face to face, or as close as face to face as they could get with Otis in krasis looming a good two feet over the Queen. Otis's breath hit the Queen in strong bursts, pushing her hair back with each breath. Her hand drifted lazily down to her pistol. If she was intimidated, she didn't show it. Even with the difference in size and strength between the two, it would be foolish to underestimate her, and Otis was no fool. Bullets hurt and even without silver the Queen's reflexes, speed, and skill made her a dangerous adversary.

"Friends, let's step back and focus on what's important. We don't have much time to pull this off and I really need your help. Please," I said, motioning for a tactful retreat.

Otis was the first to step back but their gazes didn't unlock until they both moved back a few feet. The mood in the room lightened somewhat.

"Excellent, thank you. The plan is simple. This demon can fly. The elves keep her pinned down so Cearbhall and I can deal with her. The T.O. keeps her off the elves. Neither one of your groups should be in any real danger. You are not there to get involved. You're there to make sure the demon doesn't get away when things start going bad for her," I said.

"So we are only there to keep elves safe," Otis asked.

"Yes, exactly," I replied.

"The T.O. will help. In return for protecting the elves, I want access to ride and run inside Elvin lands. There's not a lot of forest secluded enough in our territory for a full pack run," Otis answered. "Additionally, if we are going to be friends again, then the elves need to come to the meetings."

The Queen didn't have to think about her answer, "There will be no shifter packs running freely on Elvin lands. You may schedule a preapproved quarterly run, so long as you stay within a designated area. At the first sign of aggression, the agreement is void, and you and your kind will be expelled from our lands—the ones that survive anyway."

"Agreed," he said.

"I will send a representative to attend the council meetings, but I want the meetings moved to the Southern Outpost. Additionally, there will be no restrictions on the materials, silver included, that the Elvin Nation can import," she said.

"Those are decisions the council would have to vote on," Otis said.

"Yes, but there are five seats and three of them are in this room. We can pass the resolution without the support of the rats or that fat Tailypo Wilix. That is, if we all agree," she said, looking at me.

This is exactly the kind of back door dealings that I try to avoid but I needed her help. Besides, moving the meeting place was not a big deal and she could get any materials she wanted as it was. She was probably just testing us. If Thera floods the region, we will have bigger problems than where we have social hour.

"Actually, Wilix lost a lot of weight and was replaced a few years ago by a fat Kobold, Hambone. Regardless, I will vote yes if it gets this done," I said.

"You'll have my vote, too," Otis said. The Queen smiled at getting her way, until he followed up with, "On the condition that your son, the one that was here earlier, holds the seat for the elves."

"It's my right to appoint whomever I choose to the position," she said.

"I'm not challenging your authority. Politics is about give and take, I'm just asking for a little consideration. You said he is already running the outpost, so he'll already be there. You don't have to change anything."

She wasn't smiling now. "Fine. When is it taking place, Obie?"

"Tomorrow night, Browns Bridge on 53, just outside Gainesville at ten sharp. You should get there early to have everything set up and concealed," I said.

"We will be there," she said and turned to head back up the stairs.

"We are also calling a meeting tonight to update everyone on the situation," I said. "We can take your votes tonight and make everything official, but you will need your representative for it to pass."

"You may take Harlan and bring him back tonight. If he doesn't return, the deal's off," she said.

"Highness," Otis said after her.

She stopped but didn't look back.

"My youngest is six and has watched nearly every Disney movie made, about five hundred times. Drives me crazy. She is now telling me she doesn't want to hunt. She doesn't want to hurt the innocent animals. A bear that won't hunt, it's terrifying," Otis said.

"And what did you do?" she asked without turning around.

"I remember that she is going to grow into her own person and hope she comes back to reality. Forcing a hunt on her would only make her hate it that much more. I also remind myself that even if she never hunts, she can still be a valuable member of the pack and do great things. Being different isn't a bad thing, unless we make it that way," he said.

The Queen turned around to meet his gaze, "If I wanted two-bit advice from a flea bitten mongrel, I would find a stray bitch in the woods to ask council of." With that, she turned and headed up the stairs.

I looked at Otis, ready to jump in the way if he lunged after her but he was smiling. Not a happy smile but a smile nonetheless.

"I'm starting to think she doesn't like me," he said.

"I'm sorry, guys. I didn't expect that level of vitriol. She always seemed more reasonable to me," I said.

"She is stuck in the past. We will keep our word, but I'm afraid we won't have peace as long as people sacrifice the future for old grudges," he said.

"I have one more favor," I said. "Tomorrow night I need the bridge closed.

We don't need any traffic happening by. What will it cost me to have you make some calls and make sure the bridge is under construction?"

"I am tired of bargaining. We will do it for friendship and mutual benefit. Just remember who your friends are, Obie," Otis replied.

"Thank you. If I'm still alive in two days I will never forget it," I said.

I changed back into human form and headed up the stairs. The Queen's reaction surprised me. I had never seen her lash out like that. I'd seen her lash out with her pistols, but she was still calm while doing it. She lost her cool down there. Harlan must have really gotten to her. I caught up to her just outside the fence.

"Highness, there was one more thing I wanted to talk to you about. I heard about a magical device called a soul stone. It supposed to contain a person in it. Kind of pulling a person out of their body and keeping them in storage, so to speak. Do you know of it?"

She gave me a sideways glance. "I am familiar with it. Why do you ask?"

"This demon has taken someone very dear to me. I believe I can restore her but to do it I will need a soul stone. I was hoping you could get me one. I know it's a lot to ask," I said.

She spun to face me, obviously still upset. "Have I not been imposed on enough with those curs? You know I banned magic in my kingdom. Why do you think I would be willing or able to supply magical artifacts?"

She didn't worry about the bikers standing within earshot by the fence. They took note of the disrespect and took a few steps in our direction. The Queen didn't appear concerned, but her guards made ready with their guns. We continued toward the cars as we talked, the guards following behind keeping an eye on Tom C.

"Rumor has it that when you banned magic, you collected everything in the kingdom and locked it up. If that's true you might have what I need. Look, I'm desperate here," I said.

"I apologize, Obie, these negotiations have brought up some old feelings I thought had dissipated, and that's on top of what my idiot son did. You have always been a friend to us, but soul stones are hard to come by. I'm not saying it's impossible, but if I can, what are you willing to give for it?" she asked.

"I've got money, name your price" I said.

She gave me a dismissive smile. "I don't need money, Obie."

"What do you need then?" I asked.

"Security. I'm afraid this bargain will be short-lived. When it falls through, there's a good chance it's going to be bad. If that happens the Elvin Nation will need friends, and a Keeper is a good friend to have. I'll get you a soul stone and as payment, some point in the future, I'll call on you for a favor. You come when I call and do what you are asked. No questions," she said. "Also, if hostilities break out you will side with me."

This kind of offer was something I was obligated to pass on. My loyalties had to be to Thera first, but what are the chances the Queen would call in a favor that would interfere with my obligations to Thera? I knew Otis wasn't going to do anything to break the peace so having either one of them to side with shouldn't be an issue. It had to be slim to none, besides, with only a day to spare, I didn't have any other options. Without a soul stone, there was no other way to get Naylet back. We made it to the cars and the attendant opened the door to the SUV for the Queen to get in. I was out of time to think about it.

"Agreed," I said, extending my hand.

She shook it and got into the car. Harlan sat in the back, looking at the floor. I didn't envy him.

"Give us a minute, Obie," she said, closing the door.

I could hear the Queens muffled voice from inside the car—she was clearly not pleased. While I waited, I thought about my plan and all the moving pieces that had to come together to make it work. The best I could do was show up and hope everyone came through. If they do then we just might pull it off. If just one thing fell through, then the plan for killing Petra probably wouldn't work and getting Naylet back would be impossible. The sound of an opening door brought me back to the present. Harlan got out of the SUV while the Queen rolled down the window.

"I will be expecting you tonight," she said.

CHAPTER·24

"IT'S NOT AT ALL like I pictured it," Harlan said when he spotted the clubhouse on top of the hill surrounded by the junkyard.

Otis had it built in the Forties, around the time Harlan was born. They made the transition from the local werebear pack to what would become the modern Tortured Occult. By that time, the Shifter and Elvin cold war was well under way, so Harlan would have never had the chance to see the headquarters of the Elvin Nation's most hated enemy.

"Not as nice as what you're used to?" I asked.

"I've never seen anything like it. It's magnificent," he said. "The stories I've heard make it sound—"

I knew why he stopped talking; he was about to say something he shouldn't. "How could you hear stories about it if the elves stay within the Nation? The Queen wouldn't have spies running around would she?"

"Would it surprise you to hear that she did?" he asked.

"I would be disappointed if she didn't," I said.

I parked in my usual spot beside the clubhouse. We went in through the front, stepped into the changing room and closed the door behind us.

"You should probably leave the hat. You can stick it on any of those pegs," I said, pointing to a row of open pegs behind him as I slid my shoes off.

Harlan was reluctant but removed the beanie from his head. Completely understandable considering what he had just been through. "How does this work?"

"It's very informal. The only people here will be the five council members and Cearbhall. The meetings are closed to the public but we do have others attend if they have a reason to be here. All you have to do is make the proposals the Queen instructed and vote on anything that comes up."

An overweight coyote squeezed its way into the changing room through the dog door. It sat down and looked at us with its tongue out panting.

"Does he bite?" Harlan said, eyeballing the creature.

"Not unless you're made of nougat," I said. "This is Hambone. He represents the masses. This is Harlan, prince of the Elvin Nation."

The coyote shifted into a panting kobold. "A pleasure."

"Nice to meet you." Harlan extended his hand.

Hambone shook it with all the enthusiasm he could muster. "Wow, an elf, here and royalty no less. I can see why you called a meeting. It's very nice to meet you," he said. "I'll see you back there, okay?"

Hambone exited into the bar. Chatter flooded into the changing room when he opened the door.

"What's this?" Harlan asked, showing me one of Hambone's buttons.

"Oh, it's close to election time. He loves passing out those buttons," I said. "Just throw it out."

"This should be interesting," Harlan said, taking a breath.

"Nothing to it," I said, shifting to krasis. "Let's get back there."

The chatter died off almost completely in the packed clubhouse when we stepped through the door. Most people here hadn't seen an elf in a century or more and some never had, much less part of the royal family, even if it was just one of the males. I spotted Cearbhall, Otis, and Adan in the corner and gave them a nod. Hambone was busy buttering up some constituents at a nearby ta-ble. Harlan followed me to the back room for our meeting. Inside was a large pentagonal table with five chairs. We each took our normal seats, with Cear-bhall leaning against the wall by the door. Harlan hesitated before moving to the only vacant chair, between Hambone and me.

He pulled the chair out, picked up a doughnut box off of it, and peeked in-side. "What about the moldy doughnuts?"

"Oh, sorry about that. Your seat has been vacant so long, I was using it," Hambone said.

"Should I throw these out?" Harlan asked.

Hambone fell back in his seat like he had been struck. "Throw them out? There's nothing wrong with them!"

Harlan gave the doughnuts a second look. "Ugh, they're fuzzy."

Hambone patted the table in front of him. "Doughnuts are like wine, they get better with age. Just set them here."

Harlan complied, brushed some crumbs off the chair, and took his seat.

"Let's get this meeting started. Harlan, you have met Otis, and Hambone. The last member of the council is Adan, the emissary for the wererats in At-lanta."

They nodded a greeting to each other.

"Thanks, everyone, for showing up on such short notice. I called the meeting because we have a serious situation that I wanted to make you aware of. There is a demon on the loose that's caught Thera's attention. I won't go into the specif-ics, but Thera is prepared to bring down floods, tornadoes, the whole nine if we can't kill this demon quick. The result would be death and devastation on a mas-sive scale of both humans and ultras. I have a plan in place to deal with the de-mon. The elves and the T.O. are both helping, so if everything goes according to plan, tomorrow night we will kill the demon and things will be back to normal."

"And if it doesn't go according to plan?" Adan asked.

"Then I feel sorry for anyone living in North Georgia," I said.

"Maybe we should evacuate," Hambone said.

"What about the humans?" Otis asked.

Hambone rifled through the doughnuts and began chewing one, his ca-nid jaws sending crumbs falling all over himself and the floor and muffling his words. "The humans aren't our responsibility, besides, how would we warn them? Call in a bomb threat for the state?"

"I think it might be wise not to tell anyone," I said. "Any kind of mass exodus could scare the demon off, ensuring what we're trying to avoid. We need everything to look normal."

"And if you fail, we let everyone die," Hambone said.

I leaned forward to accentuate my point. "We won't fail."

Adan stroked his muzzle. "What about the elves?"

Everyone looked at Harlan. "The Queen is moving all nonessential personnel to the northern border."

"Why do the elves get to evacuate but no one else can?" Hambone said. "That's not right."

"I went to the Queen to get her help, so she was aware of the threat ahead of time. Elves move around all the time, and with the way relations have been, no one is even looking at them. It won't change anything," I said.

"That's not the point. We are talking about keeping a secret that could cost the lives of our friends and neighbors, unless it's the elves, which aren't really our friends. No offense, Harlan, you're wonderful," Hambone said. "You know Adan is going to report back to Atlanta and they will do something, too. If the T.O. is helping in this fight then they are already aware. The only people left out are the ones that are going to die ugly."

"I don't like it any more than you do but it is what it is. We can't risk a panic messing things up," I said.

"Vote then," Otis said. "All in favor of keeping it secret."

Everyone except Hambone raised their hand.

"Opposed."

Hambone held the opposition alone with a scowl.

"It passes. We don't make an announcement. Do we have any other business?"

Harlan took the cue and opened his mouth to speak. Before he could get a word out Hambone cut in. "I want to talk about the dust. While a lot of the dust was recovered from the recent theft, we lost four crates. That's a big problem both in potential threat, and the hit we are going to take to our supply. Assuming we're all still alive in a few days, we need to address the issue. Word has already gotten out that Hob was attacked. People are worried."

"I agree. It will take months to recover and with the supply down, prices will rise. Trouble is inevitable if the dust runs out or people can't afford it. Some people will stop practicing magic but some will go to the black market to get dust and that's bad for all of us," Adan said.

"I've been looking at the numbers and there's another problem. Base supply is down about twenty-five percent," Hambone said.

"Sorry, what's base supply?" Harlan asked.

"It's materials taken from the ultras that are produced in daily life, fingernail clippings, shed scales, lost teeth, and hair from haircuts for example. Things that can be dusted without harming the donor. When someone dies they have the option to donate their body as well," I said.

Harlan nodded and Hambone continued. "That by itself is within the normal ranges but it's just going to exacerbate the problem if it doesn't turn around."

"There's nothing we can do about base supply. It is what it is," Otis said.

"We have to do something," Hambone said, starting on his second doughnut.

"Could we recover the missing dust?" Adan asked.

"I think it was used. Hank and Cearbhall saw it as well. This demon had a magic like I had never seen before. It looked like it was burning the dust pretty quick. The good news is it's not out there to cause trouble," I said.

"Yeah, but we can't get it back either," Adan said.

"A couple of days isn't going to make a difference. Why don't we table this until we settle the bigger problem of this demon?" I said.

"Anyone opposed?" Otis asked.

The table was silent.

"Any more business?" Otis said, looking directly at Harlan.

"Yeah, I have a couple things. The Queen is willing to participate in the council again. I have been appointed as her representative. There are changes she would like. First, she would like to move the meetings from the clubhouse to the Southern Outpost," Harlan said.

"That's pretty far away," Adan said.

Hambone wasted no time in voicing his disapproval. "That's not going to work! I don't want to move into the Elvin Nation. There's no way I can run that far for a meeting."

"I can give everyone a ride to the meetings, it's not that big of a deal. Less than an hour away," Otis said. "My only concern is that we have our privacy. We need a place to talk freely."

"That's not a problem, there's a room on the second floor we can use. It's private and can be designated as our meeting room," Harlan said.

"A snack table," Hambone said.

"What?" Harlan asked.

"If I'm going all that way there's going to be a snack table, since I don't have an empty chair anymore, and you provide the doughnuts."

"Sure, no problem," Harlan said.

"And candy bars."

"Candy bars too," Harlan conceded.

"Maybe some chocolate covered slugs?" Hambone's eyes widened in anticipation.

"Don't push your luck," Harlan said.

"Vote," Otis said. "In favor of moving the meetings to the outpost?" Everyone but Adan raised their hand. "It passes, we will have the table moved and starting with our next meeting will be at the Southern Outpost. What's next?"

Harlan continued, "The Nation is used to a certain level of freedom. The Queen is looking for a promise that there won't be any restrictions placed on the Nation."

"So that would mean nothing would change really," Otis said.

"Do we need to discuss it or can we vote?" I said.

"Vote," Adan said. "In favor."

Everyone raised their hands.

"Excellent. Well, if you will excuse me, I have a lot to prepare for," I said, standing up from the table.

"One second, Obie, I have one more thing," Harlan said. "The Queen would like the use of magic to be banned from the region, both its use and the production and distribution of dust."

"Outrageous!" Hambone said, his mouth falling open, spilling half chewed doughnut on the table.

I sat back down and shot a look to Otis. He didn't appear to have any more answers than I did. This wasn't agreed to. Did she expect that we would back this? She couldn't think that we would.

"You can't be serious," Adan said. "The rats will never agree."

"Oh, I don't expect it to pass. I was told to bring it to vote and that's what I'm doing," Harlan said.

"Ok, vote then," I said. "In favor."

Harlan raised his hand.

"Opposed?"

The rest of the table voted as expected.

"Motion denied," I said. "Anything else?"

Harlan smiled and shook his head.

"Let's get out of here," I said, getting up from the table.

We all stood up and made our way to the door, except for Hambone who remained in his seat.

"Well, wasn't that an exciting meeting," he said. "It sure is nice to have the elves cooperating again. I'm just so happy that I got to meet you, Harlan, it was a pleasure. Obie, could I bother you for just a minute, please?"

The others left and I sat back down. This better not be about dust again. "What's up?"

"Snack table aside, I'm really not happy about this," he said.

I listened to Hambone complain for a good fifteen minutes before I could make it out. When I finally did, I found Harlan sitting at the bar alone. Hank and Cearbhall were at a table close by.

I walked up to the table. "I need to get Harlan back to the Queen. You coming?" I asked.

"I'm going to hang out here tonight. I'll catch up with you tomorrow," Cearbhall said.

"Suit yourself. I'll see you on the bridge," I said.

I turned to see Harlan walking over from the bar. I motioned toward the door with my head and we crossed into the changing room. Harlan grabbed his hat and I assumed a more suitable appearance for the outside world before leaving. We got back into the truck.

"Where to?" I said, cranking it up.

"Any chance you'll let me go?" he asked. "I'll just disappear. You can say I got away from you."

"If you want to disappear in two days, then great. I need the Queen's help tomorrow and the only way I get it is if I take you back. I know you're in a bad spot but there's nothing I can do. If I let you go, she will blame me. She's not the most forgiving person," I said.

"I understand. Let's get it over with," he said.

I followed his directions to a place deep inside the Elvin Nation. Turn after turn of backroads, winding through dense woods. Finally, we pulled up to a couple RVs with the Queen's SUV and escort truck parked beside them. The Queen was sitting at a picnic table with a grill set up beside it. Her guard patrolled the area, on the lookout for any threat. The scene looked like a normal campsite except with armed guards around the perimeter. I parked beside the Queen's SUV. Harlan and I got out and went to the table where the Queen was sitting.

"Delivered, as promised," I said.

"Have a seat," she said. "We have one more order of business."

"Okay, what's going on?" I asked, sitting at the table beside her, hoping she was going to say she found a soul stone.

"Harlan told me you healed his ears earlier today. It wasn't your place to intervene in my affairs," she said.

"I'm sorry if I overstepped, Your Highness. I only saw someone in pain that I could help. There wasn't anything malicious in it. Is this going to cause a problem for our plans tomorrow night?" I asked.

"I'll honor our agreement but I need you to know where the lines are. If you are aware of a situation with my family, especially one that would disgrace my house, I expect that you will bring it to my attention. I also expect that you would consider my wishes before getting involved," she said.

"I understand," I said.

"Good, then there's just one more thing. Take him," she said to the guards. Two of them stepped forward and grabbed Harlan by the arms. "Would you like a snack or some refreshment? I can have my boy make you something."

"What are you doing?" I asked as they dragged him over to the back of the RV.

His arms were tied to a ladder on the back. The head of her security force, Harlan's sister Patsy, looked back at their mother for confirmation. The Queen nodded. Patsy pulled out a pair of scissors and cut Harlan's hair. When he was as close to bald as she could get, she cut off his shirt.

"Harlan is being punished for his transgression," the Queen replied.

Patsy retrieved a coiled leather whip from the truck and took position behind him. Harlan kept his eyes straight ahead and his body still, as if he knew what was coming. Patsy again looked over at us.

"Ten," the Queen said.

Patsy released the whip and gave it a wiggle, unfurling it out onto the ground behind her. From the way she took a ready stance and gave her arm a few shakes to loosen it up, it was clear she had no intention of going easy on him. I wonder if that was ordered from the Queen or if she decided to do as much damage as she could—neither would surprise me. She drove the whip forward into his back. It made a ripping sound that reminded me of a zipper as it came into contact, tearing his skin with a splash of blood. Harlan was silent other than a sharp gasp. I wasn't as composed. Having lived through the tail end of slavery and the following years of Jim Crow, I've seen a few lashings and lynchings. I've never cared for either. Something was different about this from the other lashings I had seen, there was too much blood. That when I spotted the glimmer of metal on the end of the whip. Small pieces, barely sticking out at all but enough to add a bite that did some real damage. I put my hands on the table and pushed up to stand, not really sure what I was going to do, just knowing something had to be done. Before I was halfway out of my seat, the guards had guns drawn and pointed in my direction. I froze in place.

"Obie, you aren't planning on interfering with my family business, are you? I thought we had an understanding," the Queen said.

"We do, I still have some things to do tonight and I've seen floggings before. Thought I would head out," I said.

"I would prefer you stay," she said. "We have more business to discuss once this is done."

For the first time I thought maybe my plan wasn't such a good idea. The only thing keeping me from stopping this was that I was sticking to an idea that I needed the elves. There had to be another option. The Tortured Occult had guns, just not as big, but they aren't nearly as good with them.

"Obie?" the Queen questioned.

I lowered myself slowly back to my seat. Patsy struck him again and again. By the fourth, his legs were giving out and he could no longer stifle the sounds of his pain. By ten, he hung limply from his wrists, quiet and bloody, his back shredded. Patsy wound the whip and placed it on the table in front of me, the lamp light reflected in the blood covering its end.

I wasn't going to give the Queen the pleasure of knowing how much this bothered me. "What's the other business you mentioned?" I said.

The Queen motioned to one of her guards, who placed a plain wooden box in the center of the whip.

"If you take this then I will hold you to our agreement. You come when I call and do what you're asked," she said. "And if hostilities should erupt you will help us."

I opened the box to see what looked to be a baseball-sized diamond. It was perfectly clear but had no sparkle. It felt empty, as if it had its own gravity trying to pull me in. I closed the box and considered my options. I didn't want to be indebted to the Queen, especially considering the demonstration I just witnessed, but this was my only option if I wanted to get Naylet back. If there was a chance, I had to try it.

"It's a deal. What's going to happen to him?" I said, nodding to Harlan's limp form suspended from the RV.

"He will represent the Elvin Nation at your meetings as promised. We can discuss any final details later. I know you have a lot to do to get ready for tomorrow night, and I would hate to keep you," she said.

I smiled and nodded. I wasn't going to ask about healing Harlan. She wouldn't go for it and might actually make things worse for him. I took the box, getting a little blood on my hand as I did, and headed for the truck. I wiped it on my shirt as I got in. I couldn't wait to get out of there. As I pulled out, the headlights illuminated Harlan, his blood and pain. He was still hanging there when I pulled away and they didn't seem to be in any hurry to help him.

CHAPTER·25

IF I WAS BEING honest with myself, Petra could probably kill Cearbhall and me at the same time on an even playing field. The poison tipped the scales in her favor and she knew it. I promised no weapons, but that didn't mean I had to fight fair. Walasi was right; I could get the advantage back by fighting her my way, on my terms, and taking advantage of Livy's alchemical skills. If everything went according to plan, the demon would be dead and Naylet would be back to normal in a few days.

I pulled into Northside Cherokee Hospital, found a parking spot, and picked up a passing shuttle to the front entrance. Inside I found the receptionist playing with her cell phone behind the desk.

When she saw me approaching she put it down and smiled. "Can I help you sir?"

"Hi, could you tell me if Rebecca Lin is working tonight," I said.

She typed away on the keys of an undisclosed keyboard behind the counter. "Is she expecting you?"

"No, I'm an old friend, just stopping by. It's really important," I said.

"What's your name?" she asked, picking up the phone.

"Obie."

"Have a seat," she said, stabbing the keypad with a pin. "I'll page her."

I found a large cushy couch by an enormous window in the corner to wait. Putting my feet up on the table, I leaned back and rubbed my eyes.

I was suddenly aware of a presence to my left. I knew it was Thera before she spoke. "Holt is awake."

"I guess Livy's antivenom works then. That's good news."

She sat beside me on the white upholstery, grass and wildflowers cascading down to the floor.

"Have you decided if you can work with him?"

"Haven't really had time to think about it. I've been too busy trying to keep you from killing everyone," I said. "What happens if I can't? Can you make him human again?"

"Once the link is established it can't be undone, but it can be broken," she said.

"And breaking it would kill him wouldn't it?" I asked.

"Yes."

I didn't like the sound of that. "I don't want him to die but I don't want things to be the same either."

"Things never stay the same for long. Tell me and I will cut the link. Then you will pick someone new to take his place," she said.

"I pick? I thought you did the picking," I said.

"No, Obie, you choose who you want to work with, just like Cearbhall chose you and Cedric chose Holt," she said.

"Wait, Cearbhall chose me?" How have I gone this long without knowing Thera didn't choose new Keepers? "I thought he resented me."

"He always had positive things to say," she said.

I had spent my roughly two hundred years working with Cearbhall thinking I was a burden. It put all the times he tortured me in a new light. He wasn't trying to make me fail but pushing me to be my best. It changed everything I thought I knew. I searched myself, trying to make sense of our relationship. The times he was hard on me and what seemed to me now to be my childish responses.

"I can work with him," I said. "If Cedric chose him then there must be more to him than I am seeing."

"As opposed to if I chose him?" she questioned.

"Let's be honest, you don't really get people," I said.

She changed the subject instead of arguing. "I know why you're here. You're wasting time."

"No, I'm waiting. There's a difference," I said. "Besides, this is important."

She leaned back in the couch in feigned relaxation. "You've made progress then?"

"It ends tonight," I said.

"And the grimoire?"

"Will be recovered," I said. "The situation is under control. Even if Cearbhall and I die tonight, the demon wants Naylet. Walasi is watching her. If the demon shows up there, she will be killed for sure. It's a solid plan. I've seen how important the demon's victims are to it."

"You sound confident," she said.

"I am, this will work. By this time tomorrow things are going to be back to normal. I hope this means you have changed your mind about the whole mass destruction thing?"

"Do you talk to yourself a lot?" Rebecca had walked up without me seeing her.

Rebecca Lin was a surgeon I helped a couple of years ago. She was short, even by Chinese standards, and couldn't have weighed more than a buck ten soaking wet. She wore her white coat over jeans and a nice blouse rather than her usual blue scrubs. Bright white shoes that looked brand new finished the ensemble.

I stood up and gave her a hug. "I am an excellent conversationalist." Spotting the new title on her name tag, I said, "Administrator . . . you got a promotion?"

I looked back to the couch to find Thera had vanished.

"Obie, what are you doing here?" she asked, obviously not feeling like small talk.

Right to the point then. "I need a favor. A woman was brought in yesterday, she was attacked in her apartment. Candice Heck."

"Yes, she's upstairs, that poor woman. You wouldn't believe what some sick bastard did to her," she said.

"I'd believe it. I'm the one that found her," I said.

"So what do you want with her then?" she asked.

I smiled. "Just to help. You know me, always lending a helping hand."

She looked over her shoulder as if she was afraid someone was watching. "Help her the way you helped me?"

I nodded. "I just need a couple minutes."

"You could have done that at her apartment. Why wait until she's here?"

"She had a fire poker shoved in her head," I said, making a jabbing motion with my finger under my jaw. "I'm good at a lot of things, but removing giant hooks from someone's face isn't one of them."

She crossed her arms and put a hand over her mouth. "I don't know, she just got out of surgery an hour ago, they wired her jaw shut and have experts coming in in the morning. How would I explain it?"

"You don't have to, miracles happen every day. Two minutes, please."

She groaned with frustration. "Come on. We'll go the back way, but this better not come back on me."

She took me up a stairwell and through a few hallways before we came to the room. Inside Candice was lying with her head bandaged—everything except her right eye, which was closed.

"I don't think she's woken up yet," Rebecca said.

I gave the machines she was connected to a once over. I didn't know what anything on the screens meant except for the steady beep of the heart rate monitor. "Do you want to wait outside?"

She closed the door. "I think I'll stay. I'm curious how you do it."

I placed a hand over Candice's head and concentrated. The room took on a blue hue from my eyes and hands as the energy began to flow.

"Jesus, your eyes. I didn't see that last time. Do they always glow like that?"

"Only when I'm working," I said without looking up.

Rebecca stepped up to the bed. "That's it? I thought there would be more chanting and arm waving."

"You watch too much TV."

Candice began to moan and shift around in her bed as the healing took hold. The beeping of her heartrate monitor sped up with the little line on the screen bouncing around like a game of Pong on steroids.

Rebecca reached out a hand to intervene but stopped just before she touched me. "Obie, her heart, you need to stop."

I could feel the energy pouring into her, swirling and pulsing. I could feel some resistance coming from her stomach, maybe some kind of cancer, couldn't be sure. Might as well take care of that since I was already warmed up. I focused on the obstruction and it melted away in a matter of a few seconds. I could tell when she was healed because instead of going in, the energy flowed over her like water spilling out of a cup—she was full. I took my hand back and her heart went from racing to normal in an instant. Rebecca looked at the monitor, giving it a tap to figure out if it was malfunctioning. Candice opened her unbandaged eye and looked around.

"Candice, you're in the hospital. Don't try to speak, your jaw was wired shut," Rebecca said, leaning over her bed.

"You're safe now. Try to take it easy. It will take them a few days to figure out you've been healed, remove the wires, and let you go," I said, resting a hand on the side if the bed. "Oh, and I took care of that stomach issue, too."

Candice nodded, tears welling up in her eye. When Rebecca stepped back Candice saw me and reached out to hold the hand I had on the railing of the bed. She raised the other hand and made a scribbling gesture in the air. Rebecca got a pad and pen and handed it to her. She wrote one word and turned the pad over for me to see. *Angel?* it said. I took the letter she had written Steve with her rings in it and placed it her hand. Rebecca was still busy when I left. I wanted to get out discreetly. I was barely out of the room when I heard Rebecca calling after me. She caught up to me just as I opened the door to the stairwell.

"Obie, wait. Listen, I was thinking maybe you could take a look at a couple other people while you're here," she said.

I was afraid of this. "I can't, sorry."

She crossed her arms. "You can't or you won't?"

"I won't."

"You could help so many people with your gift and you just won't? I thought you were better than that," she said.

"We all make mistakes," I said, starting down the stairs.

"At least tell me why," she said.

"One is a miracle. Any more than that and people dig for an explanation, and they won't let it go until they find one. They will find the surveillance video of us and they will come asking questions we can't answer. Maybe they give up eventually or maybe word gets out that I'm some kind of faith healer. People will come from far and wide looking for their own miracle and then I won't be able to do my job. See, healing people isn't why I'm here, it's just a bonus I get to help some people sometimes. I wish I could do more but it's not possible," I said. "If you know someone that needs help and they aren't admitted in a hospital or have extensive medical records give me a call."

She didn't say anything but stood there processing. After a few seconds without a response, I headed for the truck.

CHAPTER · 26

IT WAS A LITTLE after nine in the morning when I left the hospital, giving me about half a day before my battle with Petra. With nothing to do but wait, I headed to the clubhouse. It was mostly empty inside. Besides the goblin at the bar looking like he already had a few too many, the only other person was Adan, sitting at his normal table in the corner by the pool table. He had a plate of bacon and eggs with a beer, looking over papers spread all over the table. The rats in Atlanta handled not only the broad distribution network for the dust but also the necessities for modern life like driver's licenses and bank accounts. As the representative of Atlanta, he handled all those things for the ultras in the area. I joined him at his table.

"What are you doing here? Don't you have a demon to get ready for," he asked.

"I'm as ready as I am going to be. Just wasting time," I said. "I do have some business I wanted to talk to you about."

"Oh yeah, what's that?" he asked, taking off his reading glasses to give the full attention that business requires.

"Holt told me he hadn't set up his accounts yet. I wanted to get that in order for him," I said.

"He was in bad shape last I heard. Rumor has it he isn't going to make it," he said.

"Well, I know he's awake. He's strong, he'll be okay," I said. "I just need the usual, bank account, debit card, he already has a license but it's for Tennessee, so we need to have that updated to Georgia. Go ahead and transfer ten thousand from my account to get him started, and fifty percent of the take from the dust going forward."

"Are you sure? That's pretty generous," he said.

"Yeah, just make it happen," I answered.

"It's your money," he mumbled jotting down notes on a scrap piece of paper. "You must be feeling pretty confident about tonight if you're making plans for the future."

"Of course he's confident. Keepers always win," Otis said from behind me, putting his hands on my shoulders.

"While I appreciate the vote of confidence we both know that's not true," I said.

He sat down in a chair to my right. "It's true enough. Listen, Obie, we have about ten hours until we have to be at the bridge, and I know you don't drink, but we're going to have a few today."

"What's the occasion?" I asked.

"The world as we know it could be ending," he said, getting up and heading to the bar.

"How is that different from any other day?" I shouted after him.

Otis returned a few minutes later carrying six large mugs and having to step around a knocker that scurried across the floor in front of him. He put them down on the table, getting beer rings on Adan's papers, who didn't seem to mind in the least.

"Any luck finding a home for the knockers?" I asked when he sat down.

"Not in the least. They won't go back to the mine and no one wants to take them in. Imagine that," he said.

Tico called over from the bar. "Travis is snooping around the shop."

"Travis? What's that about," Otis said. "I got to check this out."

"I'll come with you," I said, getting up from the table. "Adan?"

Adan reached for a beer. "I'm good here. You fellas go ahead."

We changed back into human form and walked over to Morrison Salvage and Repair, the more legitimate business of the Tortured Occult. We walked into the shop through one of the open garage doors. The mechanics always kept the doors open with giant fans running in the middle of summer, not that it did much to stifle the heat. The building had a small waiting room with a window to the shop where people could watch their cars being repaired. Travis stood by the window with a magazine, trying to discreetly watch one of the mechanics. He fancied himself as a hunter, and he did in fact hunt, he just never caught anything, which made him mostly harmless. Otis and I joined him in the waiting room.

"Something wrong with the car?" Otis asked when he opened the door.

"Just getting an oil change," he said.

"Weren't you in here a couple weeks ago for an oil change? Unless I'm mistaken," Otis said. "There has to be something other than that. You're holding your magazine upside down."

He wasn't, but since he wasn't paying any attention to it he did a double take before he figured out Otis was testing him.

"All right, you got me," Travis said. "You know how I look into strange things sometimes. Well . . . I've got a story for you."

He put the magazine on the table and took a seat on the couch. Otis and I took chairs across from him.

"First, tell me about that feller working on the Buick," he said. "How long's he been 'round here?"

Now that Travis mentioned it, I hadn't seen the guy around before. He looked Japanese, wore navy coveralls, and was focused on his work.

Otis turned to verify who Travis was talking about before responding. "Five or six weeks. He was passing through, looking for work. I don't know if he's planning on staying or not. We call him Panda," he said, giving me a look to let me know the name was more literal than he was letting on. "Is there a problem?"

"Well, now that's what I'm trying to figure out," Travis said. "Have you noticed any funny looking scars on him? Maybe something looking like a penny-gram?"

"A pentagram?" Otis asked. "No, he stays covered up most of the time. What's this about?"

"Couple days ago I was checking out an old house in Dahlonega, behind the Dairy Queen. It's been abandoned for a while and all overgrown. It just looks like a place you could find a ghost or spook or something. Well, I was there poking around and I run across this light coming out from under the door in one of the rooms upstairs. It was kinda shimmering and I didn't know what to make of it. So I pop the door open, ready for anything, and there's a tiny little person with wings flying around, like Tinkerbell or something. It's got this little rock that's giving off all the light. I didn't waste any time grabbing it up. So then I'm thinking what do I do with it now?"

"What did you do with it?" I asked.

"This is the good part," Travis said leaning forwarded in the couch. "So this little thing starts talking. Stuff like 'please let me go' and all that. I'm thinking no way I'm letting it go! Then it says how it's harmless and never hurt nobody and if I let it go it can tell me where a real, honest to God, werewolf is. I says, 'baloney, you're just trying to get away'. Then it says it will tell me where there's a werewolf and these little things called tommy knockers, both. I didn't know what they were until it told me. It told me where there's this mine close by with these little yellow-eyed critters in it. I checked it out and sure enough there was. I didn't catch any but they were there. That checked out so I thought there might be something to the werewolf. It says there's one working right here. I know if you had some kinda maneater working in yer shop you want to know, so I come a looking. Now I've seen y'all around and I know you good people, the only feller I don't know is that one. It has to be him," he said pointing discreetly in Panda's direction.

"So let me get this straight. You're telling me that you caught some kind of fairy that told you there was a monster working in my shop? Do you hear what you're saying?" Otis asked.

Travis looked a little hurt by the lack of confidence. "I know how it sounds but as sure as the day's long there's some funny stuff going on around here. I just want to make sure folks are safe, that's all."

"Why did you ask about a scar?" I asked.

"I don't reckon I know anything about werewolves other than that what ya see in movies and whatnot, so I looked in the Google. I found all kinds of stuff I never heard of. One of them was that werewolves have a scar in the shape of a penny-gram."

"I see," Otis said. "While I appreciate you looking out for us I can say with one hundred percent certainty that he is not a werewolf, okay? I like you, Travis. You're a good guy but please don't come around here snooping around for some kind of monster or something. It's bad for business and people are going to think you're nuttier than a squirrel turd."

"Well, I don't mean to cause you no trouble, that's for sure," Travis said, looking a little hurt.

Otis stood up and shook hands with Travis. "Don't worry about it. It's always good to see you, and that oil change is on the house, okay?"

We said our goodbyes and went back to the clubhouse. It was a strange story, one I felt we needed to figure out. We made it back to the table where Adan had finished off four of the six beers.

"Really?" Otis questioned, when he saw the work Adan had done on the beer. "We were gone for five minutes."

Adan was just putting down his fourth empty mug. "What's that saying? A fool and his beer are soon parted?"

"You're getting the next round," Otis said, sitting down and claiming the remaining two beers. He put one in front of me and kept the other for himself. "Drink."

"What do you think about Travis? It sounded like he was talking about a pixie to me, and we both know a real pixie would have evaded or killed him rather than be captured," I said.

"I think someone's playing games. Maybe sending a message," he said, taking a drink.

"What message is that?" Adan asked, holding up three fingers to Tico for another round.

"That they aren't afraid to cause problems," he said.

I picked up the beer. "Who do you think is responsible?"

"There's only one person that has any kind of beef with Tom C: the Queen," he said.

"Assuming we make it through the night, what are you going to do about her?" I asked.

"What can I do? Sometimes you just have to wait for the old to die and take their ideas with them," he said taking another swig. "Maybe whoever replaces her will be more interested in getting along."

Adan took a long swig from the beer. "You know how long elves live, especially paranoid ones with armed guards?"

"We can address that at the next meeting. Let's not let it spoil our good time," he said. "Obie, drink up, we have another on the way."

The first gulp gave me a strange sensation in my throat. It was the first thing I had to drink in a long time, and I had forgotten what carbonation felt like in my throat. There was a good chance this was going to be my last day, even if I wouldn't admit it to anyone else. Sharing a few cold ones with friends was a good way to spend it.

CHAPTER·27

TRAFFIC BACKED UP about a mile away from the bridge, to be expected with the detours in place. I waited in the line of cars approaching the bridge, where a cop parked in the road was waving traffic onto a side street. Behind him, some assorted machinery, I had no idea what any of it was, was sitting in the road. I recognized Razor and Cotton dressed up as construction workers, milling around the machines, not really doing anything—they were pulling off the disguise of your average road worker to a tee. When the officer saw me, he waved me into the construction site. I pulled slowly around the police car, giving him a nod as I went by. I arrived at the bridge a few minutes behind schedule, but still with time to spare for the final arrangements. I found the elves and T.O. parked on opposite sides of the road, like boys and girls at a middle school dance. I pulled up close to where Cearbhall and Otis were sitting on a tailgate, and got out.

"You smell like beer," Cearbhall said when I had walked over to them.

"I'm fine," I said. "I was wasting some time with Otis today."

"He needed to loosen up a bit," Otis said.

"You do look a little more relaxed," Cearbhall said with a smile. "I'm sorry I missed it."

"Let's get ready, we don't have long," I said, stepping out toward the center of the road and waving everyone in. "Thanks for coming, folks. Let's get everyone together and go over the plan one more time to make sure we're all on the same page."

Looking over the crowd I saw the Queen hadn't attended our little soiree, but I spotted Harlan with a weird looking hat in one of the trucks. She had held up her end of the bargain and sent him to handle business with Tom C as promised. A small group of eight elves represented the Elvin Nation with what looked to be ten from the T.O. in attendance, on top of what I already saw manning the construction equipment. Harlan still sat in the truck by himself and didn't seem to notice we were getting underway, so I walked over to see if he was okay.

When I got close he got out of the truck, slowly and deliberately, clearly in pain. That's when I noticed he wasn't wearing a hat, he had bandages on his ears again. This time, they were covered completely with the cloth wrapped all the way around his head, so only his face and the back of his head were uncovered. His head had been shaven clean, and blood was soaking through on each side of the bandages where his ears were.

"What happened, Harlan?"

"My dear mother has punished me for embarrassing her. I couldn't be banished because of the agreement with the Tortured Occult, but I don't really think she would have banished me anyway. I imagine I would have just disappeared and been forgotten like so many others. Since that wasn't an option, she said if I wasn't proud of my ears then I shouldn't have them. So she had Patsy cut them off," he said. "I'm not allowed to hide my shame, with a hat or hair."

"She cut off your ears?" I said, not really believing what I was hearing. "Let me help."

"Just stay the hell away from me. She wants me to suffer, you're just going to make it worse," he said, shooting me a look that actually gave me pause.

"We aren't in the Elvin Nation and she isn't my Queen. Show me," I said.

His expression softened. "If you wanted to help you would have let me go. If you heal me she'll just hurt me again. There's nothing you can do. The best thing you can do now is leave me alone."

"I'm sorry, Harlan. I hope you believe that," I said.

"Let's get down to business. Why don't I show you what your loyalty bought?" he said.

He walked slowly, almost shambling, but with his head up. He was in pain, a lot of it, but he didn't let it show or make apologies. He ignored the sneers of the elves and the concerned looks from the T.O. as he approached the trucks. Each had a large bulge covered by a heavy tarp in the back. He waved a hand and a couple of elves pulled the tarp back, revealing the largest gun I had ever seen.

"We have two trucks mounted with M134D Gatling guns. These will take down anything we run into tonight, flying or not. We would normally have tracers, but since we are trying to stay low profile we aren't using them. The upside is there won't be streaks of light to attract unwanted attention, the downside is it will take an extra second or two to acquire the target once we open up. Each truck has a crew of four with additional small arms if needed."

I stepped forward to get a closer look at the machine. "I am going to be honest, I don't know what that means, but it sounds good. Like I said, I am hoping they won't be needed. It's just insurance. If you do shoot them, I am guessing it's going to attract a lot of attention, right? Even without the tracers? Are we going to be on the clock to wrap this up and get out of here before the National Guard shows up?"

"I think we will be okay. Yes, they are loud but you have to understand that these fire three thousand rounds a minute. Shooting that fast the gun doesn't go bang-bang, it hums. If anyone around is familiar with it they might be able to tell what it is, but we are working under the pretense that there is construction going on tonight. It would be easy for the layperson to confuse it for machinery and not give it a second thought. As long as we position the trucks where the muzzle flash can't be seen from passing boats, then it should largely blend in. We're going to have two or three feet of fire coming out of the barrels when we let go, so placement is important."

The members of the T.O. standing around began to mumble among themselves. They hadn't had any real dealings with the Elvin Nation in over a hundred years. Weapons had come a long way in that time and I don't think they realized the resources that their historical adversaries had access to. A bit of a wakeup call, to say the least.

Harlan waved again and the tarp was placed back over the gun. "We should be able to find a good position in the tree line that will serve our purpose."

"Okay, great, that sounds good. Otis, can we have the machines making as much noise as possible to conceal any sounds from the fight or gunfire?"

"Sure, not a problem," he said.

"Ok, don't open fire unless she tries to fly away. Just hang back and let Cearbhall and I finish her off. The T.O. will keep her away from the elves in case she gets away from us. That's it," I said.

"What if she kills the both of you?" Harlan asked.

"Then you all can do whatever you like. It won't matter to me," I said. "All we have to do now is get into position and wait. Please don't kill each other in the next hour or so. I'll catch up to you when it's done."

Cearbhall and I got in the truck while the T.O. and elves split into two groups. One group went into the trees on the close side of the bridge; the second group took position on the opposite side. We drove to the center and parked. The machinery started up a few minutes later, flooding the area with the rumbling and clanging of construction. With an hour to wait, we got out of the car and made the change to krasis. I put the box with the soul stone and the two vials of antivenom on the hood and we took a seat on either side.

"Thera told me something interesting today. She said that you chose me to be a Keeper. Since our fight, I spent all this time under the impression that you resented me," I said.

"What fight?" he asked.

"You know, the one where we had it out and started working separately."

He scratched his neck, his face wrinkled in contemplation. "I really don't remember any fight. We split up because you were ready to get out on your own. Don't get me wrong, you still do stupid stuff, like making that little club, but you're a good Keeper. I wouldn't have left if you weren't ready."

All that time, I had been carrying around hostility and hurt over something that he didn't remember. What a waste.

"Livy said the antivenom might not be at full strength, so let's take it right before and try to avoid the snakes as much as we can," I said, handing him one of the vials.

"What's in the box?" Cearbhall asked.

I opened it to show him the stone. I held it up to the moon, expecting to see right through it but while the stone looked clear, no light passed through it.

"It's a soul stone. Once we have Petra beaten down, I am going to use it to take her soul to hold until I find a way to extract Naylet from her. I know how to restore her body but this is the last piece of the puzzle. It should buy me the time I need," I said.

"Can I see?" he said, holding out his hand.

I passed the stone to him without thinking about it. He held it up to inspect it while I looked at the paper to decipher the procedures to trap a soul; it looked pretty straightforward.

"Yeah, this is the real thing," he said. "Do you think it's a good idea to keep a demon soul, especially one like Petra's, locked up for later use?"

"I don't like it any more than you do but it's my only option to get Naylet back. It's what I have to do," I said.

"You know Thera isn't going to let that stand," he said, bouncing the stone in his hand, feeling its heft. "If you trap it, the demon wouldn't be completely dead. You're not thinking this through. Where'd you get it from anyway?"

"I got it from the Queen, we made a deal," I said absently.

"Must have been pricy," he said. "Why don't you send it back with Harlan and call the deal off. It's not too late. She may not like it, but I doubt she would refuse."

"I know it's stupid, but I love Naylet. If there's any chance, I have to take it, regardless of the consequences," I said.

He looked over at me and said, "Then I'm sorry about this," and threw the stone down into the pavement.

I couldn't see where it hit, the truck was blocking my view. The shattering sound made the bottom immediately fall out of my stomach and nausea set in. I jumped off the hood and moved around, half in shock, to get a look at the damage. Maybe it wasn't so bad. What had been a solid object just seconds before had disintegrated into a small pile of powder on the asphalt. I couldn't stop staring at it, trying to make sense out of what had just happened. My body started trembling and my eyes began to water. I had been through so much getting to this point and the one person I was supposed to be able to count on had sabotaged my plan. Without the soul stone there was no hope to restore Naylet. It was too late to come up with another plan. At that moment I might have actually been crazy.

Cearbhall didn't look happy about what he had done. He started to say, "I'm sorry," but I cut him off with a fist to the throat, reducing his apology to a rasping gurgle. He didn't fight back or try to stop me and I didn't stop hitting him until he collapsed off the side of the hood. He landed motionless beside what had been the soul stone. Looking up I could tell that had caused some commotion with the elves and the T.O., no doubt they were wondering what was going on. A stiff breeze ran across my face, tingling my whiskers and bringing the smell of rain. I noticed the stars were gone, a storm was moving in. We still had a few hours before the deadline Thera set, she was being impatient. I looked down at Cearbhall as the trembling in my body subsided and I came back to my senses.

"Shit," I said, realizing what I had done.

I needed him one hundred percent before Petra arrived. He would come to soon, I just hoped it would be soon enough. If we made it through this, we were going to have to settle up, and I wasn't sure what that would look like. I sat down on the bridge beside him and the hopelessness of it all came crashing in. I had been a fool. All the effort I had put in trying to hold onto something that I never really had a chance to get back. Cearbhall was right. Thera wouldn't stand for the demon to live in any form, even trapped in a stone. I had lost Naylet when she was turned and I was never going to get her back. I had been clinging onto a fantasy and things kept getting worse because of it. No more fairy tales, there is no happily ever after for my kind. I've had it drilled into me since the day I became a Keeper.

I heard flapping overhead and looked up to see Petra landing on the bridge twenty feet in front of the truck. She wore no disguise, or clothes. The curves of her unmistakably feminine form were only covered by her black scales. She had a leather bag slung across her back, secured by a strap running over each shoulder. She looked different than she had at Naylet's house. Before, her scales had looked scuffed and dull, now they were smooth and shiny all over. The snakes that had lay flat during flight were now rising up over her. They were much smaller now and looked to be just over a foot long. That should be much more manageable, at least I had that going for me. I looked back to check on Cearbhall, he was still unconscious. I needed him to wake up soon. I would have to stall her if I could.

"Why is it every time the two of you get together you fight," she said. "I mean, I know about that business with the siren, and I still agree he was out of line, but you two should really leave your problems in the past."

I just smiled. "I love what you've done with your hair, it suits you."

"Why do you show me such animosity?" she asked. "There's no reason to be so hostile."

"I have to admit, I am going to miss our back and forth after I have killed you," I said.

"Is there a line I should wait in? You seem to be killing everyone around you tonight," she said, looking at Cearbhall, still lying on the ground. "Perhaps you want to do me a favor and take care of those men on the trucks? That wasn't part of the agreement, Obie. You weren't supposed to bring help."

"They are just here to make sure you live up to your part of the deal," I said.

She laughed. "And you thought a few men with rifles would do the job? You underestimate me."

"Those are soldiers from the Elvin Nation. That makes them women with rifles but they brought a little more than that," I said, sticking a thumb out at the truck behind me. "That's not to mention the T.O. backing them up. As long as you stay on the bridge until the fight is over, then they stay out of it."

"This isn't what we agreed to," she said. Her disposition was growing increasingly sour by the second. At this rate we would be fighting before Cearbhall woke up.

"This is exactly what we agreed to," I countered.

"We agreed that if I win I would get Naylet, you don't appear to have brought her. Where is she?" she asked stretching her arms wide.

"Naylet is at DeSoto Park, just north of the campground in the woods. Livy is camped there, keeping an eye on her. You won't have any trouble finding the place," I said.

She gave her wings a couple of agitated flaps. "How do I know you're telling the truth?"

I shrugged. "I've never lied to you before, besides, it's not like you have a choice. What about the grimoire? Did you bring it?"

She took the bag off her back and opened the top, revealing a plain leather-bound book. She placed it, still in the bag, on the bridge behind her. "Are you ready then?"

"Answer one question for me first," I said. "Why Naylet? You were living off babies under the radar for who knows how long. Why go out of your way to kill the woman I love?"

"I didn't kill her, Obie. I told you, she lives in me now. But to answer your question, I have been here since these humans were beating each other with rocks and cowering in caves. I have always been on the run, hiding from the mighty Keepers. I'm not doing it anymore. I came to Georgia for a start fresh and I decided instead of waiting for one of you to find me, I would strike first. Of course that meant finding you, but that was easy enough. That idiot Steve was easy to manipulate into getting your attention. After you showed up at the church, I followed you until I found someone that could tell me everything I needed to know about you. I didn't realize you were a couple at the time, or I wouldn't have done it. Feelings can be such sticky things. Your kindness and generosity, it's sickeningly endearing."

"I led you to her." The realization that I was the one that was responsible for Naylet really stung. Petra seemed to take my statement as a question.

"I had an imp at the church and Steve's house. Once he told me you paid Steve a visit I went to his house and waited. I followed you from there," she said. "So yes, you made our bonding possible."

"And Thera?" I asked. "Was the plan to kill her, too?"

"Even if I could, I wouldn't want to. That would ruin this rich buffet of a world," she said. "No, I needed her trapped, not killed. Her Keepers are her weakness as well as her strength. I was trying to bind her to Holt. Then she would be trapped in a vessel that doesn't have to eat and can't die. I could keep her in that prison for centuries before Holt's inevitable death freed her, and with his arms and legs removed it would be no trouble keeping him under control. The rest of you would have been easy enough to handle without her. You ruined that for me though."

I heard Cearbhall moving behind me. I turned to see him pulling himself to his feet.

"We're going to have a long talk when this is over with," he said.

"Fair enough. You ready to do this?" I said, walking back to the truck to get my vial of antivenom.

"Let's get it over with," he said, downing the other one.

I drank my vial. "Well, Petra, I wish I could say it's been a pleasure, but I'm afraid your time is up."

"I feel there is one more thing I should tell you," she said. A grin spread across her face, exposing her fangs and giving me a general feeling of uneasiness. "I didn't come alone either." She spread her wings and gave three flaps. Almost immediately commotion broke out at the truck on the bank behind her. Dark figures moved all around, with muzzle flashes accentuating the scene like a strobe light. I turned to see the same thing happening at the truck behind us. There was nothing I could do to help them, not until after Petra was dead. They should be able to hold their own, as long as they worked together.

"We can't help them. Let's handle what's in front of us and then see what we can do for them," Cearbhall said.

I nodded in agreement as rain began to fall.

CHAPTER·28

HE WENT RIGHT while I went left, positioning ourselves at opposite sides of Petra. We circled for a few seconds, looking for an opening but none presented itself. The snakes on her head shifted around, monitoring our positions—she had too many eyes. I lunged forward, dodging and swatting snakes. She turned to face me, bringing the full fury of her rage. Putting most of my attention into dealing with the snakes left me vulnerable to her claws, which dug in repeatedly on my arms and chest. This gave Cearbhall the opening he needed to close in from behind. I could see his arms popping up and down behind her as he landed multiple blows to her back. Even though her scales were shiny and new, they were still tough. If his strikes had any affect I couldn't tell, but I was too busy trying not to get bit to know what was going on.

Suddenly, she yelped and jumped to the side, retreating a few steps to put some distance between us. Cearbhall stood with a snake in one hand and black demon blood covering the claws of his other.

"Strike upwards under the scales," he said, gesturing upwards with his bloodied claws. "They aren't so tough if you can get under them."

I nodded. "Are you bit?"

"Yep, you?"

"Not sure, scratched up pretty good," I said.

The shirt I was wearing was in tatters and blood soaked. Couldn't tell the extent of my injuries, but my shoulders and chest were on fire.

"Got an idea, see if you can knock her down," he said.

We split up again for our second attack. She didn't appear much worse for wear so far, besides a little blood trickling down where Cearbhall had removed the snake and a couple of bloody footprints on the pavement. Her face contorted in anger as she gingerly touched the place on her head where the snake had been. Cearbhall threw his prize on the pavement between them.

"You're losing your cool, Petra. Feeling a little outmatched?" I asked.

"This is the end for you, Obie. I have tried to be reasonable and you have given me nothing but contempt. You don't worry about the snakes. My venom isn't going to kill you. I am going to eat you alive."

"Then I will have to kill you with indigestion," I said.

Again I closed in, pressing the attack. This time giving two high strikes before dropping suddenly and spinning, sending my tail out to sweep her legs. She collapsed to the ground, landing hard but recovering almost instantly, or would have if Cearbhall gave her the chance. He was on her in an instant, grabbing one of her wings and using it as a shield to protect him from the snakes. Throwing the full weight of his body on her head, he had her pinned for the moment.

"Now!" he yelled.

I jumped forward, being careful to avoid the couple of snakes that had worked their way free from under her wing. She squirmed, unable to escape, her exposed belly prime real estate where I wasted no time moving in. Strike after strike sent my claws digging under her scales into the soft flesh underneath. She shrieked and writhed under Cearbhall's weight. The more blows I landed, the more enraged she became. She thrashed wildly and rolled Cearbhall off onto the bridge beside her. She spun and jumped on top of him, digging her claws deep into his shoulder. He bared his teeth and snarled in defiance as he grabbed her hand and pulled it out. I tried to get her off but her snakes turned, hissing and striking, keeping me just out of reach.

Petra's position made it nearly impossible for Cearbhall to get the angle needed to get under her scales. He wouldn't stand a chance if I couldn't get her off him. I moved around behind her as she drove her fist into his head. He deflected a few strikes at first, with the amount of blows Petra was able to land cascading into a wave of punishment. After a few seconds his defense was shot. She landed a few blows with his head trapped between her fist and the concrete; he lost consciousness. Her wings stuck back far enough to be out of reach of the snakes. I grabbed them and spun, slamming her into the side of the bridge. She collapsed to the concrete, lying still. I knelt for a moment to take a look at Cearbhall. I needed to know about how long he would be out for. His head was intact with blood running out of his mouth, nose, and ears, so maybe a couple minutes.

The sprinkling rain turned into a light shower pattering on the bridge. Lightning flashed and thunder rolled, rumbling the bridge under my feet. The storm was making enough noise to keep me from hearing Petra get up. I wasn't aware she was moving again until she was almost on top of me. I tried to jump clear but slipped in the water. She leapt on my back, sending me face first onto the water.

"A promise is a promise, love," she said, and drove her teeth into my shoulder.

I kicked and screamed my way out of her bite, not entirely sure I was still in one piece. My shoulder revolted and stung; blood poured down my back. I managed to crawl a few feet before she grabbed me from behind, lifted me above her head, and threw me into the front of the truck. The collision, along with all the other injuries I had sustained, had taken their toll. I hurt all over and was glad to have at least a few seconds to rest. I slowly lifted myself into a seated position and waited for her to come to me. Petra composed herself and walked slowly in my direction, my blood running down either side of her mouth. I saw her jaw moving but couldn't hear what she was saying. It took me a second to realize she wasn't speaking, she was chewing.

She swallowed and said, "I have to hand it to you, Obie, you are a tasty dish. I bet you will go right to my hips, but what the hell. We'll call it a cheat day."

I reached back to where she had bit me to find a gaping wound, it stung when my fingers touched the exposed flesh. There's no way I was going to win this one on one in my current condition. I needed to buy time for Cearbhall to recover. I tried to think of something to say but it was too hard to concentrate with the burning in my shoulder. I looked around, desperate for anything I could use against her. The truck would be no use. The glass vial that had held the antivenom had found its way onto the ground beside me, probably knocked off when I collided with the truck. I grabbed it without having in mind what good it could be. Something was better than nothing. I threw it at her and then got the other vial out of my pocket and threw that one too. The first one missed and she didn't bother dodging the second. It bounced harmlessly off her chest and shattered when it contacted the concrete. I shuffled backward around the side of the truck as she closed in on me. My hand landed in something that made it tingle on contact. I looked back to see the powder of the soul stone Cearbhall had smashed. The rain had turned it into a kind of soul paste. I stopped backing away and waited, taking as much of the goop in my hand as I could. The tingling changed into a burning sensation as I scooped it up. I wish I had taken a few minutes to finish reading the instructions that came with the stone. Regardless, this had to work.

She straddled my legs, grabbed my ripped shirt in one hand, and pulled me close to her. "You're going to have to do better than that," she whispered almost seductively.

"How's this?" I said, smearing the paste into her eyes and face.

She fell back off of me, screaming and clutching her eyes. Liquid goo ran down from underneath her hands as she clawed at her eyes. Using the truck for support, I got to my feet. As Petra suffered and thrashed, I took a minute to catch my breath. I felt my shoulder and the crater in it again. That would take a while to heal. I looked up to where the elves and T.O. should be. The commotion had died down, no more muzzle flashes, but the rain kept me from seeing how they were doing. With her hands over her eyes, Petra spread her wings and crouched as if she was about to take off. Hopefully there were still some elves alive to work the guns.

"You sure that's a good idea? You can't see it but the elves are back on the guns. What do you think the odds are you can outfly bullets?" I said.

She paused and stood erect again. She didn't make a sound, standing as still as one of her statues. I was starting to feel a little better. My back felt like it had stopped bleeding. I took a step forward. "I believe the agreement was to the death. What do you say we finish this?"

The snakes turned toward me. "You've taken my eyes but I'm not blind." The calmness of her voice bothered me more than any anger I had seen from her so far. "Yes, we will finish it and I won't underestimate you again." She spread her wings, not to fly but to make herself as large and imposing as possible.

Cearbhall lifted his head off the concrete behind Petra. He rose slowly and quietly off the ground and crouched. Before she knew what happened he was on top of her. He wrapped his arms under her wings, pinning her arms to her body. He winced as the snakes bit him repeatedly, he didn't try to defend. This was my chance.

"Jump!" I yelled, and rushed in.

He did, lifting them both off the ground. I charged into them, grabbing them around the waist, pushing with everything I had to drive us into the side of the bridge. Their higher center of gravity was enough to send us toppling over toward the water. Petra spread her wings, flapping as hard as she could. She was able to slow, but not stop, our descent. Cearbhall shifted his grip and grabbed a wing. The result sent us spiraling out of control as the other wing flapped helplessly. Pushing off, I turned head first into a dive and glided smoothly into the water. The cool water was refreshing on my fur and my shoulder. With only a second to enjoy myself, my moment was interrupted by Cearbhall and Petra's collision with the water. I picked up the vibrations in my whiskers telling me the direction and distance of their impact. In contrast to the gentle pattering of the rain on the surface, the initial shock felt like a violent wave, immediately followed by smaller but frequent tremors running through the water from their movement. Glad to be in my own element, I rose to the surface.

It was hard to see anything. The storm had made the lake choppy and the rain didn't help. I caught glimpses of a dark figure I thought to be Petra splashing on the surface about ten feet away. There was no sign of Cearbhall. Two spotlights came on from the trucks, flooding the area with blinding light. I squinted as my eyes adjusted and considered diving just to get away from it when Petra surprised me. I wouldn't have thought it possible, but she started to lift out of the water. She floated face down, her large wings sticking out of the water and catching just enough air to take flight. By the time I realized it, it was too late to catch her. She was going to get away.

The water's already tumultuous surface exploded in a large circle off to my left like the rain had intensified tenfold in a finite circle. I had never seen anything like this before. It wasn't until I noticed the humming a split second later that I realized the elves had let loose with the big guns. I looked to the top of the hill to see a line of fire coming out of the end of the gun, illuminating the truck as well as the elves and shifters watching. The bullets slamming into the water were redirected onto the fleeing demon. Some ricocheted into the water off her scales, while others tore her leathery wings to pieces and hammered her back into the water.

The fire ceased when she had disappeared back into the lake. Now it was my turn. Taking a breath, I disappeared under the water. I could feel the vibrations of her movement in my whiskers, indicating her direction before I spotted her. The spotlight penetrated the water revealed her, or what was left, I should say. The light surrounded her, casting a long shadow into the darkness below, looking almost like the darkness was reaching up to claim her. Her wings looked to be intact structurally, but the leathery skin that ran between them had been shredded.

I came up underneath, grabbed her foot, and pulled her under. At first she struggled to return to the surface but when that didn't work, she turned down to try and attack me. I let her go and swam out of reach before she could get me. She again tried to get to the surface but the extra drag created by her ripped wings combined with the inability to swim made it impossible for her make any progress before I pulled her even deeper. We repeated this dance a few more times until she was still. I stayed under with her a few minutes extra, just to be sure.

CHAPTER·29

THE SPOTLIGHTS WERE still on, scanning the water in lazy circles, when I pulled Petra's now lifeless body to the surface. It didn't take long for them to find me when I appeared, but the lights only stayed on me for a moment before being redirected into the sky. I looked up to see an athol with what looked like Petra's leather satchel dangling from one of its feet, circling toward the bridge. The elves on the bank closest to me opened fire. The creature lacked the protective scales Petra had, and after a violent jarring that seemed to suspend it midflight, it fell lifelessly into the water twenty feet to my right. I made a quick detour to retrieve it and pulled the two demons to shore.

Cearbhall was waiting on the bank when I finally made it to shore with Petra. He sat on a large rock under the bridge with his head between his knees.

"It's done," I said. "You going to make it?"

"Aye, feeling dizzy. The antivenom works but not all the way," he said. "I got bit a lot."

"Hang out here until you feel better," I said. "I better check on everyone."

I hauled Petra's body up the steep incline, opting to retrieve the athol later, stepping over large rocks and using trees to pull myself to the top. Coming over the crest of the hill, I found multiple demons lying dead, strewn around the truck. Two elves sat wounded but conscious against the truck while a third tended to them. Harlan stood by himself but was in one piece, as far as I could tell. Otis laid lay in the road with Hank and a werewolf named Chisel crouched over him.

Hank stood and turned to the elves with a fire in his eyes I knew from past experience to be wary of. "You killed him."

If Otis was dead Hank was next in line for leadership. Chisel followed Hank's lead and took a threatening posture but waited for Hank to start the attack. They both bared their teeth and emitted low rumbling growls as they started to stalk forward.

The elf tending to her comrades rose and spun, raising a pistol in their direction. I threw Petra's body on a collision course that made impact just as she was in position to fire, sending her sprawling defenseless onto the ground. The pack charged, but I was already on my way to intercept. I leapt in front of the snarling group before they could tear the elves to pieces. I wasn't sure they would stop, they could plow right over me and there wouldn't be anything I could do about it. Hank put the brakes on with only inches to spare. The T.O. jumped to the side but didn't attack—they wouldn't go against him. If Otis was in fact dead, Hank was in line to be the new club leader.

"Let me take a look, maybe I can help," I said.

"Can you raise the dead?" he asked, spittle flying out of his mouth onto my face.

I wiped his anger from my nose and whiskers. "No, just let me take a look." I moved around him, holding palms out. Otis lay on his back. His stomach had some large gashes, probably from the claws of the demon that lay a few feet away. That shouldn't be life-threatening but he didn't appear to be healing. I knelt beside him and found a bloody spot on the side of his head. Moving his hair back I found an entry wound. I turned his head and found the much larger exit wound, still something he should be able to heal through, unless . . . I held my hand out and concentrated. The energy didn't flow, there was nowhere for it to go. Otis was, in fact, dead.

"Who shot him?" I said, turning back to Hank.

He pointed a finger at the elf that had just made it out from under Petra. Again, she raised the pistol, this time as much in my direction as Hank's.

I walked past him directly into her firing line, moving up to where her gun was three inches from my face. "What happened?"

Her voice was stern but I could see the uncertainty in her eyes. "He had a demon on him. I tried to help, it was an accident."

"Elves don't miss," Hank yelled from behind me.

He was right about that. I reached up and put my hand on the pistol. She let me take it without a fight. I released the clip and looked at the cartridges. As I suspected, silver bullets. Otis didn't stand a chance after a headshot with these.

I slid the clip back in and handed the gun back to her. "Let me see your AK."

She slid it off her shoulder and handed it to me. Again I released the magazine, no silver here, but there were rounds left. She wouldn't have needed to draw the pistol as long as the rifle still had rounds. I looked up at her and she knew she was busted. I replaced the magazine and put the gun in the back of the truck.

"Load your wounded and get out of here," I said.

"Now just hold on a damn minute!" Hank screamed.

I turned, holding my hands out again to put myself between them. "She's empty, Hank. She must have pulled the pistol trying to help and a shot got away from her."

"They don't miss, those guns are their lives. No way it was a mistake," he said.

"Maybe she's just not that good of a shot." I turned to see if I had hit my mark.

She was helping the second wounded elf into the back of the truck and paused from my comment. Elves are too proud. I could see her contemplating her next move. She could admit she killed Otis on purpose and start a war, or take the shame of one of the worst insults you can give to an elf. She clenched her jaw and loaded her comrades into the truck before quietly getting in herself and starting the engine.

Harlan had gotten in his truck and pulled up, followed closely by the elves and T.O. from the other side of the bridge. "What happened?"

I moved over to the truck so I could speak a little more privately. "Otis is dead. Y'all should get out of here. Tell the Queen I will be by to see her soon."

He pulled out without another word. I waved the other two trucks of elves off and they followed Harlan out. The first stopped just long enough to let the shifters jump out of the back. We had at least avoided a war tonight. Maybe Hank could cool off for a couple days and things could calm down. The Tortured Occult surrounded Otis's body, beginning to come to grips with their pack leader being dead. There was a lot of anger, but more uncertainty. It was going to be a hard few weeks for the T. O. to move forward from this. I found Hank standing off by himself by Petra's body, while the pack stood vigil over Otis.

"Have you given any thought to joining the T.O.?" he said. "With Otis dead we're going to need new leadership. They would follow you."

"You know I can't. My loyalty has to stay with Thera first. That's something I haven't been as good about as I should have, but I'm going to do better. You don't want to lead?"

"I always figured I would lead one day, somewhere off in the distant future," he said. "I'm not ready. I don't know what I'm doing."

"I think you're more ready than you realize. Otis already relied on you for a lot of the management of the T.O. You're a strong and competent leader. I know you are going to get through this just fine," I said.

"What about them?" He looked over at the club.

"They'll be fine, they have you," I said.

He looked uncertain. "Maybe you're right, but I don't feel ready."

"If everyone waited until they were ready to do things, then nothing would get done," I said. "I'll load the truck and take the demons to Hob. The pack should stay together tonight."

"That's a good idea. Thanks, Obie. One more thing, her eyes are gone. Looks like they melted out. What did you do to her?"

There were black charred holes where Petra's eyes used to be. "Old Keeper trick," I said. "Cearbhall is down by the water, he should be up soon. He got a lot of poison in his system. I need to get some things done. Can he stay at the clubhouse tonight?"

"No problem," he said.

I helped Cearbhall get back up to the bridge and in a car, and put the athol in the back of the truck with the rest of the demons. After fifteen minutes of searching, I found the remains of the leather satchel. It was little more than a strap and a few scraps of leather. The book had either been shredded by the guns or was somewhere in the lake. Otis was put into the back of a truck and we all pulled out together.

CHAPTER · 30

I SPLIT OFF FROM the T.O. and headed to Hob's to drop off the demons. It was the largest haul that I ever remembered delivering at one time, maybe the largest we had ever had. It might even have been large enough to keep Hambone from complaining, but I doubt it.

"Is it finished?" Thera asked, from what had been an empty passenger seat a moment before.

"Yes, the demon that was causing you problems is dead. I am taking her to the duster right now," I said.

"And the grimoire?"

I was hoping she would have forgotten about it, not that that was a real possibility. "Well, it's either destroyed or somewhere in Lake Lanier."

"Which is it, destroyed or in the lake?" she asked.

"Same thing. I got a look at it, it's an old book. Even an hour floating will severely damage it, if not completely destroy it. Just because I don't have it in hand doesn't mean it's going to cause any more trouble," I said. "Even if it is still out there somewhere, which it isn't, then whoever finds it won't know what to do with it. They will think it's worth something and try to sell it and get it translated and then I will find out about it. There's no scenario where that book shows up again without me finding out about it."

"I would rather you have found it," she said.

"Well, me, too," I replied.

I didn't get the impression that she was happy about the grimoire being unaccounted for, but she must have accepted it because she vanished from the truck and the rain seemed to lighten just a bit. By the time I got to Hob's farm it had stopped completely. I pulled in slowly, not so worried about alerting my presence since they had seen me in this truck the day before. The lights were still on in the house so I parked there instead of going around to the barn. Hob was sitting out on the porch, enjoying the night air. I got out of the truck and joined him in a vacant rocking chair.

"I have always enjoyed the rain," he said when I took a seat. "Does this mean the battle is over then?"

"Yes, it's finished," I said.

"I'm glad to see you have lived," he said.

We sat quietly for a few minutes, listening to the katydids. My mind wandered to the Queen and Otis's assassination.

"What are elves like in other places?" I asked.

Hob looked a little confused by the question. "Elves are people like all other people. What do you mean?"

"I'm pretty sure the Queen had Otis killed tonight," I said. "I'm just trying to wrap my head around why. As you know I've never lived anywhere else so the Queen's rule is all I've ever known. It seems normal to me. Are there places where elves aren't so . . . you know, authoritarian and murdery?"

"In my homeland we had a Queen *and* a King. They worked together for the good of their people. Magic wasn't shunned like it is here. It was seen as a valuable tool to be used for the good. When I came here I was surprised to see how the Queen behaved. I knew right away I wouldn't be living with my kind anymore, and that was okay. I worry if she has done this then she might be making plans for a larger attack. If I am lucky, she has forgotten about me."

I shook my head. "She doesn't forget anything. I'm going to pay her a visit and see what I can find out. I should probably get going before she moves her camp again. Is Wilix in the barn for me to unload?" I asked, getting up from the rocking chair.

"*Ja*, he is there. What about Naylet? Have you made up your mind about the blood?"

"I wanted to talk to you about that. Have you actually seen someone that was restored that way?"

"I knew of a human child in the Fatherland many years ago, I think in his sixth year. His family had a small farm close to where I lived. He was a good boy. One day, he was made to stone from a gorgon. There were rumors going around that I was a witch and his father came to me to ask for help. To make the long story shorter, I help him. I got the blood and the boy was restored. His father was so happy but the boy wasn't the same. Where he had been so full of life before he had become quiet, like he was empty. There was no more playing for him and he would just stare off blankly into nothing. A few months after, I went to check in on him. I was curious, you see because I had heard stories, but it was the first time to see it in person. The boy had killed his family with the sickle. When I found him he had cut his sister open and was eating the insides." He leaned back in his rocking chair and put his feet up on the railing. "I left my homeland for America a few weeks after."

There was no way I would bring her back to have her change like that. She wouldn't have wanted it, and neither did I. "No, I won't be needing the blood," I said. "If I had some way to bring back her memories then maybe, but I've come up empty on that."

"It is for the best," he said. "Come. It is not good to dwell on the past. Let us get your truck cleaned out."

We had the truck empty in twenty minutes flat and I was on my way. It was a long drive to the Queen's camp, made longer by a couple of wrong turns on the unfamiliar backroads. By the time I arrived, the Queen's RV was just pulling out, with a guard truck on either side. I pulled up in front of the convoy, blocking the road, got out, and waited. They rolled to a stop in front of me, headlights illuminating my truck and hurting my eyes. They didn't try to drive around but no one came out to talk to me either. I leaned against the truck and waited for a good two minutes before the door to the RV opened and the elf that had shot Otis stepped out. She held the door open and stood to the side so I could enter.

"Took you long enough," I said, stepping past her into the RV.

Two of her guards sat up front, driver and shotgun, literally. The other elf followed me in, and went to stand by the back of the RV. I found the Queen at the table and sat down. We stared at each other for a few seconds, both waiting for the other to start.

"I wanted to give you the opportunity to explain yourself," I said, tired of the game.

"Obie, we have done some business and you have shown yourself to be a friend to the Nation," she said, leaning forward and pointing one of her revolvers at me. "Don't make the mistake of thinking that that grants you the right to question or detain me. We are not equals."

"Is that supposed to scare me? You think I haven't been shot more times than I can count already," I asked.

"You don't think I know how to kill a Keeper?" she replied.

I leaned forward into the gun. "Then do it, but if you do, my kind will take everything from you."

That wasn't an empty threat and she knew it. The response to murdering a Keeper is both immediate and absolute. She sat still for a few seconds before returning the six-shooter to its holster.

"Why are you here?" she asked.

"Did you have Otis killed? I want the truth," I said.

She relaxed back in her seat. "Do you know what the most admirable thing about a dog is? It doesn't know it's going to die. It lives in the moment because the moment is all it knows. It can't contemplate the future. Occasionally, it can be beneficial to remind a dog of its mortality."

"Why don't you cut the crap and just give it to me straight," I asked.

"Yes, I had him killed. Are you happy?" she said.

"Not even a little bit," I said. "Why would you do that? We were finally, after years of tension and hostilities, starting to work together. Is peace not important to you at all?" I asked.

"Peace." She laughed. "What kind of peace could we ever have with those beasts? They aren't capable of it."

"You don't think Otis was serious about the agreement?"

"I have no doubt he meant it when he said it, but he would break his word eventually. He couldn't help it, his nature would get the better of him."

"What nature is that exactly?" I asked.

"Shifters have violent tendencies, I don't need to tell you that. It's not their fault, they just can't control themselves. Combine their violent nature with the primitive male mind and throw in an entire pack that blindly follows, the threat was just too great. It had to be eliminated for the good of the Nation."

"I see," I said. I knew she felt some hostility toward males and shifters but I didn't realize the extent of her prejudice until then. I didn't think I was going to change her mind, at least not right then, and with everything that had happened, I wasn't up for trying. "One more thing and I'll go. I can't owe you a favor. It could conflict with my obligations to Thera and I can't be indebted to someone like that. It was wrong of me to make that agreement. I will be happy to pay for the soul stone, just let me know what you want."

"See, you're proving my point, not twenty-four hours into our agreement and you're already backing out. It's not your fault, males are dishonest by nature. Just return the stone and we will pretend it never happened. I would rather not have something that powerful unaccounted for anyway," she said.

"Well, that's a problem," I said. "It was destroyed."

"In that case I will hold you accountable to our original agreement."

"I can't do that," I said.

"Maybe you should spend some time thinking about it. You're smart for what you are, you could make the right decision. I will come to you to fulfill our agreement and if you refuse you will have to face the consequences. Either way, you are going to pay for that stone," she said.

"I'm trying to pay for it," I said.

"You've held us up too long already," she said. "You're dismissed."

There was no point trying to reason with her. We would have to settle it later. I slid out of the seat and went back to the truck without another word.

CHAPTER·31

I PULLED INTO DeSoto Falls a little after three in the morning. Besides the fact that the park was supposed to be closed, it was an excellent time for discretion. I found an open spot to park the truck and made my way down the trail beside the campground. Most of the campers were asleep, a few adding gentle snores to the ambience of the forest. The few that were awake huddled beside dying fires. Most of the time people built fires for novelty, and not just the tourists. The easiest way to spot a tourist wasn't by the campfire on a sweltering night; it was that they wouldn't look at or speak to you. Afraid to make eye contact, no friendly greeting in passing. I just have to remind myself that they don't mean to be rude, they just aren't from around here. A moot point when they're all unconscious.

I followed the trail to where I cut into the woods toward Livy's camp. When I arrived, I found a few glowing embers of what was a campfire. That, combined with the gentle breathing I heard coming from the tent, lead me to believe Livy had gone to sleep hours ago. Thera had said Holt was awake but that didn't mean he's mobile yet. Deciding to let them rest, I got a couple of the tree shards and rekindled the fire.

Walasi's voice entered my mind. *Is it finished?*

"Yes, the demon is dead. Everything is back to normal, sort of," I said, looking at Naylet's figure in the moonlight.

A crack opened in the hillside as Walasi peeked out, the electric green of his eye illuminated the campsite. *Will you be leaving soon?*

"We will pack up in the morning and get Livy and Holt home. It's time to get on with things," I said.

No need to hurry. You could stay and rest.

He wasn't wrong. A few days in the woods might be a nice break. I would miss Otis's funeral if I stayed and I needed to be there. "I would like to but there are some things I have to take care of."

He settled, sending a shudder through the ground and little bits of dirt and rock cascading down the hill. I got the feeling he was disappointed.

"You okay?" I asked.

Always alone.

It hadn't occurred to me until now, but there was no telling how old Walasi was, and he had to be in hiding here for three or four hundred years at least for me to have not known about him. It would be a horribly lonely existence. Could there be a time when I wouldn't be able to blend in anymore and would be in a similar boat? I wouldn't want to be out in the woods on my own like that.

"I'm sorry. I'll try to get back up here soon," I said.

"I thought I heard someone out here," Holt said with his head sticking out of the tent.

"Good to see you're awake. How are you feeling?" I asked.

He came over to join me by the fire. He moved deliberately, obviously still recovering from the venom. "Like I was hit by a train. I'm sore but I'll be okay. Did you take care of the demon?"

"She is on a date with Hob as we speak," I said, poking the fire with a branch from the tree. "We need to talk. Since you showed up we haven't been much of a team. We need to fix that if we are going to work together. I don't want to keep doing things the way we have been."

"It hasn't seemed like you want to work together. You've just been on my case about everything," he said.

I nodded in agreement. "You're right. I wish I had a good excuse but the truth is I just don't know what I'm doing. You're my first apprentice and I have been treating you the way Cearbhall treated me. I learned some things recently that changed things for me. I'll just say, I don't want the same kind of relationship with you that Cearbhall and I have."

"I was excited when I found out we were going to be working together. One of Cedric's favorite stories was when the two of you shut down those hunters in

Chattanooga. Then I got here and things weren't what I expected. If I'm being honest, I don't know what I'm doing anymore," he said. "With Cedric it was easy. Then he died and ever since I've been lost. I don't feel like I belong here, or anywhere for that matter."

"I've heard losing a mentor can be really tough. It can be disorienting to have such an important figure disappear overnight. Let's start over together. Everyone should have the right to reinvent themselves. We will take it a day at a time and it will get better," I said.

"It sounds good, but I don't know how to do it," he said.

"You haven't met most of the people here so there's still time to make those first impressions. The people you have met don't know you well so they will come to know the person you become instead of the person you were. In the spirit of our new partnership, I spoke to Adan and set up a split for our dusting profits. You should have enough for your TV and anything else you want in a few weeks."

He stretched his back, cringing at the stiffness. "Right now, all I want is to not feel like death."

"As soon as Livy is awake we can get packed up, and get you somewhere comfortable to recover," I said.

"Oh, she's not asleep. She was meditating or something, sitting there staring off into nothing for hours. It's kinda creeping me out," he said. "What is she doing?"

"She's a shaman, it's called journeying. She sends her consciousness to the spirit world looking for answers or help. I don't really understand it that well myself."

"Aren't they supposed to beat on drums and stuff?" he asked.

"She quit using the drum a long time ago. I don't think she needs it anymore," I said. "I'll go wait on her to come back in the tent. We will get packed up and go as soon as she does."

I got up and moved to the tent where I found Livy sitting cross-legged on the ground, eyes open, staring off into the infinite. If she saw me come in, she didn't show it. I took a seat on the cot and waited.

After a few minutes of silence, she turned to me and said, "Obie, I am glad to see you safe."

I smiled. "You ready to go home?"

"I'm sorry, Obie. I have been searching for Naylet, asking the spirits for guidance but I couldn't find her. I tried my best." Tears started to well up in her eyes and she covered her mouth with a hand.

"Oh, hey, don't do that," I said moving down to give her a hug. "It's really okay. I'm coming to terms with . . . everything. You know what, let's get both of you back home before we start worrying about anything else," I said. "I'll get the camp packed up."

"What about Naylet?" Livy asked.

"I'm going to leave her here with Walasi for a bit. I'm not ready to deal with that yet," I said.

In an hour we had the truck loaded. Everyone piled in and we headed to Livy's. I unloaded the truck and got her settled before we left. Holt waited in the car. It wasn't long before we said our goodbyes and I was on my way, glad for things to start to resemble normal again. We couldn't go home. It would take some work before it would be livable again after what Petra had done to it. It was no place for Holt to recover. I had him up to speed on what the Queen had done by the time we got to the clubhouse. The junkyard was busier than normal. All the space not taken up by junked cars, waiting to be stripped and crushed, was being used for parking. A few of the T.O. were outside greeting people as they came in. I pulled up to Fisheye and rolled down the window.

"What's going on?" I asked.

"Service for Otis. There's still a little parking left on the south side," he said, pointing to the far side of the property.

I gave him a nod and drove slowly, maneuvering around the cars and people making their way into the clubhouse, to an open patch of dirt large enough to park the truck on.

"The Queen really had Otis killed," Holt said more to himself than me, still trying to wrap his head around it.

"Listen, before we go in there, I need to make sure we're on the same page. I lied about it to Hank and said it was an accident. I would appreciate it if you keep that between us. I don't want a war to break out over this. It would desta-bilize the region and cost a lot of lives. I'm going to tell him when things calm down and we will figure out how to handle it then."

"I get it, but what about the Queen? She just gets away with it?" he asked.

It's a fair question, there should be some consequences for her. "I'd like to think it will come back around."

"Maybe we should make sure it does," he said.

"Justice isn't really our mission," I said. "Come on, let's go inside."

"Kind of fast to hold services isn't it?" he asked, getting out of the truck.

"They don't embalm, so things have to move quickly before the body decays,"

I said. "It's an abomination to preserve a body and prevent it from rejoining the earth. We did the same thing with Cedric, remember?"

Hank was halfway to the truck by the time we got out. Deciding to wait on him so we could speak without a crowd around, I lowered the tailgate to sit on. I was hesitant, knowing that only a few hours ago it was filled with demon bodies, but Hob had sprayed it out before I left and there wasn't a trace of what had been there hours before. I hopped on the tailgate and waited. Holt eased his way from the passenger seat to join me at the back of the truck.

"Holt, good to see you up and about," Hank said.

"Thanks, I hope to be one hundred percent in a few days," he said.

"We're having a little get together to honor Otis. We're taking him to Hob tonight so if you want to pay your respects sooner would be better than later."

"He's not getting buried?" I asked.

He shook his head. "He wanted to be dusted. I guess he really believed in what the two of you put together here."

That stung a little considering I was keeping a secret about his death.

"I'll go in and pay my respects, but after that, I have a couple things to take care of, not least of which is finding a place for us to stay."

"What do you mean?" Hank asked.

"Petra trashed the house. It's pretty much destroyed." I said. "It's going to take a while to get everything cleaned up and fixed."

"You'll stay at the clubhouse and the T.O. will help you fix it up," Hank said.

"I appreciate the offer but I can't. I will figure something out," I replied, probably out of guilt more than anything.

"You can and you will. You saved a lot people on both sides of the veil tonight. It's only fair that your life be put back as close to normal as we can get it. Luckily the Tortured Occult specializes in helping ultranaturals down on their luck," he said.

"All right, I appreciate it."

"I haven't had a chance until now to say it, but I'm sorry about Naylet. Any chance of getting her back to normal?" Hank asked.

"I've been giving it a lot of thought," I said. "Do you still have that moving truck?"

"Yeah, it's parked around back," he said.

"I need to borrow it for a while," I said. "Let's go pay our respects first though."

I went back to the truck and picked up the pink bunny that had rolled under the seat and stuffed it into the pocket of my cargo shorts.

CHAPTER·32

I WATCHED CAROLINA wrens chasing each other through the trees. Diving and banking, the aerial maneuvers were enough to make a Blue Angel jealous. Their rusty brown wings fluttered as they jumped from branch to branch, only stopping their games to sing their songs. They blended in well with the trees beside the little path leading back to where I had everything set up. I had arranged this little rendezvous on some private land where I knew we wouldn't be disturbed. With everything in place, I just had to wait. I was feeling anxious and was glad to have the distraction the birds offered.

Farwell pulled his black SUV up beside the moving truck and rolled down the window. "Could you have picked a spot that's harder to find? I got turned around twice already. You want to tell me what we're doing here?"

"I'm about to make you famous," I said, getting out of the truck.

"Make somebody else famous and leave me alone," he said, looking generally sour.

"I'm afraid you're my only option," I said. "I don't have a lot of contacts in the police department. If you want to introduce me to someone else, I'll be happy to bother them—if you want to explain all this to them that is."

"So what do you want?" he questioned.

"You know all those missing babies over the past year? I think we found them. If everything goes according to plan, they will be here for you to return to their families soon," I said. "I'm just waiting on a few more people to show up and we can see."

"Let me get this straight, you don't know if you found them, but you think you might have, and I'm here just in case it turns out that you did, in fact, find them?" he asked.

I gave him a smile. "Exactly."

"How can you not know if you found them or not? That doesn't make any sense," he said.

"Do you really want to know?"

"Not really," he said. "So, how am I supposed to explain finding a bunch of missing kids? Assuming you did find them, that is."

I pulled a piece of paper from my pocket and handed it to him. It was a note giving directions to where we were and explaining that the missing children could be found here. I had cut the letters out of magazines and pasted them to a sheet of paper; it looked like fun on TV, turns out it's a lot of work. "Now you have an anonymous tip."

"Goodie," he said, looking at the note.

The rumble of motorcycles down the road foretold the T.O.'s arrival. Hank pulled off the road a minute later, followed by eight motorcycles and a van. The bikes parked in a line facing the road with the van to the side. Hank was the first off his bike and came over to where I was standing beside Farwell's car.

He leaned with an arm against the roof. "Hey, Farwell, good to see you again."

Farwell looked Hank in the eye and rolled the window up without breaking his stare.

"He definitely doesn't like us," Hank said.

"I don't know what you're talking about. He was chatting my ear off before you showed up," I said. "Did you bring everything?"

"In the van, come on." Hank led me to the back of the van and opened it. Inside were stacks of blankets, some clothes, and bottles of water. "Want me to help you out?"

"Nah, I need to go alone. We will know if it works soon enough," I said. "Before I forget, are you still having problems with those knockers?"

Hank put his hands on his hips and shook his head. "Yeah, they burrowed passageways to just about every room in the clubhouse. I have to get them out of there soon."

"I have a friend that could use some company. I think they would be a perfect fit," I said. "I can swing by and pick them up tomorrow, if you don't have any objections."

"By all means," he said. "I'll have them ready to go."

I grabbed a stack of blankets and headed down the trail about thirty feet to a clearing where I had arranged Petra's statues in a semi-circle. After Petra disappeared the museum was glad to be rid of the statues. I think they freaked out more than the receptionist. Naylet was on the left, with the babies in the front, not unlike Petra had set it up at the museum. I put each baby in a blanket and draped one over every adult, except for Naylet, who still had her clothes from when she was turned. I pulled the pink bunny out of my pocket and put it in the blanket with Stephanie. Stepping back to survey the scene, I decided it looked as good as it was going to get.

"Thera," I said to the open air, "I need to talk to you."

I waited. The birds chirped, a gentle breeze rustled the leaves, but no Thera. Calling her was a little unorthodox for sure. Normally she just popped in when she wanted something and that was that.

I had decided she wasn't going to show, and opened my mouth to try again, when she spoke from behind me. "Why are you calling me, Obie?"

"I need your help," I said.

She looked a little confused at my statement. "You aren't injured."

"I need your help with something," I clarified. "I was talking to Walasi and he told me that you were life. I thought he was saying I should focus on my duties to you and he was right, but the more I thought about it, I realized that he was also speaking literally. You are the essence of life. These statues used to be living people. The demon that was attacking you attacked them as well. I called you here to ask you to put them back to normal, return them to life."

"I can do this," she said. "But why would I? We are surrounded by life already and it would take more to restore them than I would get from them."

Thera was too removed to feel any kind of attachment or responsibility for a single life, or a small group of them for that matter. She was more of a big picture kind of gal. I knew a heartfelt plea about humanity and how everyone was special wouldn't mean anything.

I said the only thing I could think of that might have a chance of working: "Because I'm asking you to."

"What right do you have to ask me for anything, especially considering how we came to know each other?" she said.

She was referring to how I had gotten Cearbhall's attention by summoning that demon when I was a boy.

"That was a long time ago. I've done a good job for you for well over three hundred years," I said.

She scoffed. "Do you know how long three hundred years is for me? Imagine three hundred breaths and then convince me that I owe you something."

"It's not about you owing me something. You don't owe me anything, I know that. They didn't deserve this," I said, waving a hand at the statues. "They are victims of that demon, the same as you. I'm asking you, not out of expectation or entitlement, but simply a desire to help them."

"It won't bring her back. Her mind is gone," she said.

"I know."

"And you would still want her restored, even if it means you could never be together again?"

I shrugged. "It's not about me,"

"I'll ask Cearbhall. If he agrees then I will restore them."

She vanished from in front of me. Cearbhall was resting at the clubhouse.

His wounds weren't as serious as Holt's. I didn't expect Thera to get a second opinion. After smashing the soul stone on the bridge, could I really count on him to back me up on this? I waited, trying to figure out what the chances were that Cearbhall would support me. After a few minutes, Thera returned.

She looked past me to the statues. "I'll need your help. I told you I have trouble with precision on this level."

"What do you need me to do?" I asked, relieved.

"Put your hand on each one," she said. "I can use that to focus on them."

I went to Naylet and touched her face. It felt cold and gritty, no longer smooth and warm like I remembered. Thera raised her hands, making vines and brush grow rapidly to cover Naylet's stone form. We repeated the process for each person. The vegetation engulfed the statues, forming cocoon like shapes that closed in tight around them. A light, pure and white, shone through the cracks as Thera's magic went to work. When we finished with the last statue, I could start to hear muffled cries coming from inside some of the cocoons. I turned to see Naylet pulling her way free, looking confused and scared. I wanted to run over and help her, but when she saw me she ducked back behind the brush in fear. I knew I wouldn't be the one to help her.

"Thank you," I said to Thera, who had already vanished, before going back up the trail to where Farwell and the T.O. were waiting.

Hank met me on the trail when he saw me coming. "Well?"

"It worked. They are ready for you," I said.

He waved to the rest of Tom C. that was standing around and they went down the trail to help everyone. Hank arranged for all of the adults to get the help they would need to have some kind of normal life again. The babies were returned to their families, since the lack of a memory wasn't an issue for them.

"Thanks, Hank. I'll be by tomorrow to get the knockers out of your hair," I said.

"You're not going to stay? You don't want to talk to her?" he asked.

I shook my head. "I've thought about it a lot and the thing is, she doesn't know me. That's not the Naylet I knew. She's going to need some time to figure out who she is. I'm not going to drop a bomb on her like that. It wouldn't be fair for me to be hanging around with these expectations." "Anything she needs, have Adan put it on my account."

"I will," he said. "We're going to take real good care of her."

I gave Farwell a thumbs up. He was still in the car with the windows up with no sign of coming out. I got back in the truck and drove away. Maybe one day

Naylet and I would end up back together. She would need time to figure herself out. It would happen if it was meant to, but in the meantime, I had work to do. I was going to be busy training Holt, dealing with the mess the Queen started, and that imp was still out there somewhere. He would show up again, and when he did, I would be ready.

Betrayal.

"DIBS," HOLT SAID, eyeballing Martina.

She was a gray fox shifter and member of the Tortured Occult, a shifter-out-law motorcycle club. In her human form she was a small but strong Latina. She wore boots, jeans, and a T-shirt. Her leather kutte proudly displayed her allegiance. Though she was young, her hair was silver. Today, like most days, she had it pulled back in a ponytail. It would be a mistake to assume that her small stature or gray hair was an indication of frailty. All members of the T.O. were held to certain standards and there were no concessions made for anyone. Weakness wasn't tolerated.

"She might be more woman than you can handle," I said.

"I hope so." He grinned. "Hey, before I forget, I got you this." He pulled a large black rectangle out of his pocket. "It's a smartphone."

"Pass," I said. "I tried one of those things about twenty years ago. It didn't last a week."

"This is different, it's waterproof. I got this protective case for it, you'll love it. It's called an Otter Box, and look, it's got a little otter floating on the back. See? Isn't he cute?" He held the phone up for me to inspect. "And I can connect it to the Bluetooth on your truck, so you can take calls while you're driving."

I did like it, but I wasn't going to let him know. "All right, I'll try it out. I give it two weeks before it's broke and I get to give out some 'I told you so's.'"

He placed it on the seat beside me. I looked out the windshield at the two other club members standing with Martina. The first was Big Ticket, a wolverine shifter, and the muscle of the Tortured Occult. The second was Chisel. Chisel was all right, but I preferred my bikers a little more refined. He was large and rough around the edges with a perpetually sour disposition. Three bikes and the club's black van were parked in front of a small thatched-roof house. It was a modest home, as most of them are in this area. Straight ahead, a second building sat on the edge of the yard. It looked like a shop. It had a large brick chimney and plain gray walls. It was part of a subdivision, of sorts, for those who can't easily blend into human society. This was one of a few more traditional houses for people too large for the trees or lacking the temperament for underground living. The rest of the homes were camouflaged into the landscape to keep things low-key.

Chisel was leaning against his bike. He had a short scruffy beard and unkempt hair. A streak of grease that he either didn't know or care about on his right cheek stood out in stark contrast to his pale complexion. I pulled my truck up in front of them. Chisel chugged the rest of a beer and tossed the can over his shoulder into the yard. I rolled the window down as he walked over. I saw he had gotten a promotion since I had seen him last. He had a Vice President patch sewn onto his kutte.

"What do we have?" I asked.

Chisel let out a loud belch and blew it in my face. It smelled like cheap beer and unbrushed teeth. "Hank's inside with him. Some weird shit going on."

I pulled the truck in line with the van and put it into park. I decided to leave the window down to let the burp air out.

"Why don't you wait out here and keep an eye out," I said to Holt.

He was my apprentice. A Keeper in training. We had been working together three and a half months. If this call turned out to be something demon related, it would be our second job together. He still had a long way to go.

"I'll keep an eye on Martina," he said with a wink.

"If I need you, I'll holler," I said, getting out of the truck.

I crossed the yard toward the house, stopping to pick up Chisel's beer can along the way.

I looked at the bikers and saw Big Ticket looking at me. He was short and stocky, built like a tractor, with the nonchalant bearing of a professional fighter. I lifted my head in a nod. He put an index finger on his temple and pointed it at me in a kind of salute. I pulled the front door open and stepped inside. The room had a kitchen to the left and a large table on the right. A couple of doors led to what I assumed were bedrooms. Hank, leader of the T.O., sat at the table. He was in krasis, the half animal-half human form shifters could take. Werebears were some of the largest of all shifters and Hank was no exception. Black fur added to his bulky frame, stretching his jeans and gray T-shirt to their limits. Over his shirt he wore his cut: A black leather vest with the club's colors and the President patch declaring him its leader.

The orc opposite him was muscular with grayish skin, wearing cutoff jean shorts, a plain green T-shirt, and no shoes. The skin of his face drooped loosely, with two large teeth sticking up from his bottom jaw making him look like a bulldog. He seemed to be in a daze or under a spell, completely unaware of his surroundings. He was bruised and bloody with one eye swollen shut. His clothes were ripped and stained with blood. He wore a silver pendant around his neck. It was a circle with an eye in the center. An arrow was affixed to the circle so that it could be moved to rest above the eye or cross it. A pretty standard magical device used to disguise ultranaturals in public. When the arrow was placed across the eye, it would make him look like a human.

"This is Yarwor," Hank said. "He came into the clubhouse with a hammer and tried to kill one of the patrons. Some of the boys roughed him up pretty good. He put up a fight at first, but after we restrained him it was like the lights turned off and he's been like this ever since."

"You really did a number on him. You sure it's not just that you beat him silly?" I asked, moving over, and waving a hand in front of Yarwor's face.

Hank shook his head. "In our defense, a lotta that blood was already there, but I don't think so. He looked kinda loopy when he came in. All he would say is that he's hungry. His family's missing. We started checking around with the neighbors, but they're all gone too. I think this might be more up your alley."

While the Tortured Occult had done a lot for the ultranatural community, my expertise was in creatures invading from other planes. Humans know them as demons, the ones that make trouble anyway.

I put the beer can on the table and knelt in front of Yarwor. "Can you hear me?"

"Hungry," he mumbled.

"You're hungry?" I asked.

"Always hungry."

"Has he said anything else?" I asked Hank.

Hank shook his head.

"Where's your family?" I continued.

"On the pile," he said.

"And your neighbors?" I asked.

"Always hungry," he replied again as a long ribbon of drool ran out of his mouth and onto his bloody shirt.

I gave the house a quick once over; it appeared to be in order. The only thing that really looked out of place was a large bloodstain on the pillow in the master bedroom. I wouldn't put money on the donor being alive.

"Did you find anything at the neighbors' houses?" I asked Hank, returning from the bedroom.

"Blood, no bodies," Hank said, looking out the door. "I think he killed them all. Regardless, he came into the clubhouse starting trouble. We're going to have to do something about that."

"Let's figure out what happened before we start making plans for justice," I said. "I don't think he ate them. There would be a hell of a mess if he butchered them and the place is pretty clean, considering."

Hank leaned back in his chair. "Unless we haven't found where he did it."

"Hungry," Yarwor mumbled from the bed. "Grubby."

I stood in front of him. "Where are the bodies?"

"The mine," Yarwor said without looking at me. "Grubby."

"The copper mines are a couple miles east through the woods," Hank said. "That could be what he's talking about."

I headed for the door. "I'll check it out."

"Want some help?" Hank asked.

"I have Holt. If there's anything in there, we can handle it. Just keep an eye on things here."

Outside, Holt looked downright chummy with the Tortured Occult. With a beer in his hand, the only thing that made him look out of place was that he wasn't wearing a kutte. They laughed and cut up until I had made it across the yard to the truck. I waved him over as I opened the door and pulled out my gear bag.

"Well, is it true?" Holt asked placing his beer on the hood of my truck.

I pulled a couple flashlights out of the bag. "Is what true?"

"They say he went crazy and killed a bunch of people. What do you think?"

I shrugged. "Looks like the cheese slid off his cracker. We're gonna check the mine."

I handed Holt a flashlight. On the far side of the yard we found a trail leading off in the direction of the mine and followed it.

When we were out of earshot of the bikers Holt asked, "Isn't Hank the leader of the Tortured Occult?"

"You know he is," I said, pushing a low hanging branch out of the trail. "Why are you asking?"

Holt stuck his hand out to keep the branch from whipping him in the face as we passed. "Big Ticket has a patch on his vest that says Pack Leader."

"In the T.O. anyone who's killed for the club gets a Wolfpack patch. B.T. is the pack leader of the wolfpack. He's pretty much the club enforcer."

We walked in silence a couple more minutes before Holt asked, "What do ya think's in the mine?"

"If I had to guess," I said, "a pile of bodies."

I stopped walking when we were in sight of the mine.

"What are you doing?" Holt asked. "We're here."

"Let's just watch for a few minutes. No reason to rush in."

We knelt in the brush. I didn't really expect to see anyone, but if someone, or something, was in there, the sooner we knew about it the better. It's too cold and damp in the mine to be fun for any length of time. It dated back to the early 1900s and until recently was open to the public. Now it's fenced off from the road, discouraging visitors. After a few minutes, I was satisfied, and we moved closer.

It'd been years since I'd been here, but it hadn't changed much. The mine shaft was about thirty feet in diameter and two hundred feet deep. It disappeared into a hillside on the edge of the Chestatee River. A large puddle, taking up almost the entrance, blocked the way. There was a small path on the left just big enough for one person to walk at a time and keep their feet dry. The only sound from the mine was steady dripping. I flipped on my flashlight. It was woefully underpowered for the job. Here the darkness was absolute. Holt clicked on his flashlight and we walked single file into the mine. The light looked out of place, like an intruder the darkness was fighting to push out. The mine's chill, a good twenty degrees cooler than the autumn air, sent goosebumps across my arms.

"Krasis?" Holt whispered from behind me.

I nodded. When we cleared the puddle, we made the change to krasis. After a few centuries, my body had become acclimated to the change. Being bound to the otter, I grew a long tail, light brown fur, sharp claws, and teeth. Holt was much newer at this and his body took longer to make the transformation. He twitched and grunted through the thirty seconds it took for him to make the change. He took on the aspect of a Doberman with short black fur and a long snout and teeth. Both of our bodies grew and added muscle.

"How long till it doesn't hurt anymore?" Holt asked when he had finished.

I shrugged. "Hard to say. I think I stopped noticing any pain around eighty years in."

He scowled, apparently unsatisfied with that answer. I understood why. He had been a Keeper about thirty years. Fifty years of the pain from shifting was nothing to shake a stick at. No doubt, by now, the worst of it was over for him.

"Let's split up. I'll follow the right wall and you take the left," I said.

We continued into the mine. My fur did a good job insulating against the cold and I was glad to have it. Even though I couldn't see anything but darkness around me, I could feel the openness of the cavern in my whiskers. It stretched out all around me. Holt moved off to the left, quickly disappearing except for the beam of his flashlight. It bobbed and shook as he made his way over the rocky floor of the mine. I ran my fingers along the wall as I went. It was slow going over cantaloupe-sized rocks littering the floor of the mine. I passed a refrigerator someone had dumped. I couldn't help but wonder if all the effort to get it this far into the mine was better than disposing of it properly. Either way, it probably had something to do with the fence going up. It's been a theme in the area for a while. Some really wonderful places where people would go to take a dip in a river or explore nature are now blocked and signed off. People afraid of being on the receiving end of a lawsuit, or having their property destroyed, tell everyone to stay away. Rites of passage and pieces of the culture die as a result. It's a shame really.

I followed the wall until I came to a large canvas sack sitting on the ground beside a pick. The sack had some rocks in it. I ran my fingers over some fresh gashes on the wall. It looked like someone had been doing a little mining recently. I shined my flashlight around to find I had hit a dead end. I was in a smaller section of the mine near the back wall with nowhere else to go. There was no sign of any bodies or demons. Maybe Holt was having better luck. As if on cue, he gasped from somewhere on the other side of the mine. His voice echoed, making it hard to tell exactly where he was.

"You okay?" I shouted.

I waited for a reply as the sound of my voice bouncing from the walls died down. No response came. He must have found something, or maybe something found him. I could hear movement from somewhere in the mine. I worked my way back along the opposite wall as quickly as I could manage over the rough terrain.

The sound had stopped by the time I got to the other tunnel. I scanned the area for Holt, bodies, or anything unusual. Nothing turned up. As I moved into the other side of the mine, I began to make out a light about fifty feet in front of me, just a pinprick in the distance. I killed my flashlight, stopped, and listened. The only sound was the steady dripping of the forming stalactites. I approached cautiously, moving slowly over the cold, jagged rocks littering the floor. I couldn't help but think that at any second something would jump out from a shadow or from behind a rock.

CHAPTER · 2

I COULD BARELY MAKE out a boulder beside where Holt had dropped his light. As I moved down the tunnel it became clear it wasn't a rock at all. Holt's flashlight was in front of a pile of bodies. I turned my flashlight off and slipped it into my back pocket, retrieving Holt's to use instead. It was newer and more powerful than mine. Now that I had more lumens to work with, I inspected the pile of bodies. On the bottom were an orc woman and child. That must be Yarwor's family. Covering them were a variety of ultranaturals I assumed to be the missing neighbors. They all looked to have died hard. Some had stab wounds, others blunt force trauma. It looked like Yarwor had been busy. The bodies on the bottom of the pile had pieces missing with strange circular bite marks. Something had been munching on them. It was hard to tell how long the bodies had been there. The coolness of the cave slowed the decay and muted the stench. A trail of blood led into a hole on the left wall. Something had been coming in and out long enough to leave a smooth trail streaked with dried blood. Holt was nowhere to be found.

I inspected the hole. It looked slimy around the edges. I really didn't want to climb down there. I eyeballed it, trying to come up with any other explanation for where Holt had gone. I just couldn't reason my way out of it. The mouth of the hole was just wide enough to fit though. I opted to go in face first. At least that way I wouldn't be sucked in by some unseen monster like a scene in a horror flick. I got down on my hands and knees and shined the light in the hole. It went down for a couple feet and opened to the left. I crawled in. It was a tight fit squeezing around a rock jutting out from the side. I got to the bottom and quickly rolled to pull my legs through. The opening looked to reach back about fifteen feet with lots of irregular formations. It was about four feet tall and smelled like a demon kennel. A few partially eaten body parts and feces were strewn randomly around the cave.

I leaned forward to look around a stalactite and stuck my hand in a pile of crap I hadn't noticed. It was cold and wet, I picked my hand out, stretching strings of slime between my hand and the floor. I shook my hand, sending much of what had stuck onto the nearby wall with a splat. The rest I wiped off onto the rocks. Moving carefully to avoid any more surprises, I made my way around the cave, searching inch by inch, floor to ceiling. When I got to the back wall without finding anything I stopped and turned around. Where was Holt? I climbed out into the main section of the mine.

None of this made any sense. If he had found the demon or if he left for some reason, then why didn't he let me know? And why didn't he take his flashlight? Maybe he did find the demon and that's what that yelp was. He could be anywhere in the mine; it was large and would take an hour or more to go over in detail. I would need help. With the Tortured Occult I could do it in a fraction of the time. Reluctantly, I made my way back to the mouth of the mine.

The air felt warm when I made it outside. I changed back to human form and spotted Holt's tracks in the mud at the mouth of the mine. He had walked through the puddle, instead of around it, on his way out. He was still in krasis. He knew better than to run around like that in the open—maybe he was chasing something. The tracks went in the direction of Yarwor's house. I followed at a jog. I came out of the trail to see the three bikers chatting the way they had when we left for the mine.

"Where is he?" I asked.

"Where's who?" Chisel said, turning toward me.

"Holt. Did he not come back?"

They looked at each other, confused.

"You're the only person we've seen," Martina replied.

"Obie," Hank called from the doorway of the house. "You're going to want to hear this."

"Keep an eye out," I said, jogging past the bikers. "Something's wrong."

Inside the house I found Yarwor no longer had the glazed over expression. He wrung his hands with worry and paced around the room. I shot Hank a questioning glance.

"This is Obie," Hank said. "He's looking into what happened to you."

"Don't go in the mine," Yarwor said, taking a few steps toward me.

I held my hand out to keep some distance between us. "Too late, we've already been there and back again."

"Did you find it?" he asked.

"I found signs of demon activity and some chewed up bodies," I said. "Holt was with me but left for some reason. I followed his tracks back this way, but no one's seen him."

Yarwor took a seat at the table. "It has him then. That must be why it let me go."

"You wanna catch me up on what we're talking about?" I asked.

"I'd been doing a little digging in the mine, for copper mostly. A couple weeks ago I was attacked. It came out of nowhere and was on me before I knew what was happening. It looked like an overgrown slug with tentacles. It attached to my head and sort of . . . took over. I knew what was going on around me, but couldn't control myself. Even after it got off my head I was still under its control. I could hear it in my mind . . . and this insatiable hunger. That first night when I came back . . . my family." He choked up as he spoke. "I watched as they were killed, by my own hands. I was used as a weapon against them and there's nothing I could do."

Yarwor buried his face in his hands and began to sob quietly. Hank looked skeptical about the claims of being mind controlled. I couldn't blame him, it was unorthodox. Not impossible though. I gave Hank a shrug to let him know the jury was still out.

"That wasn't enough for it," Yarwor continued with tears streaming down his cheeks. "Then it made me start hunting my neighbors. There was already more than it could eat, but it wanted more, always more."

"So, you're not under its control now?" Hank asked.

"About fifteen minutes ago it just went away, like waking up from a bad dream. If two of you went into the mine and now one's missing then it has to have him."

"And what does it want?" I asked.

"To eat," he said grimly, "That's all."

I heard a commotion outside. Hank looked out the window as I moved to the front door. I saw Holt fighting all three of the T.O. and doing pretty well. Chisel was down and not getting up, Martina had stumbled back, holding her face while blood ran through her fingers, and Big Ticket stood toe to toe swapping punches with Holt. The T.O. were still in their human form, apparently taken by surprise. In krasis Holt had a clear advantage. Humans blend in well but are decidedly lacking in natural weaponry. Despite that fact, Big Ticket seemed to be enjoying the exchange. He had a big grin on his face Holt wasn't wiping off, no matter how many times he was hit.

I changed back into krasis and charged outside. While Big Ticket had him distracted, I ran up behind Holt and spun, delivering a whip with my tail. I heard ribs pop when my tail made contact. The impact sprawled Holt out on the ground. With Big Ticket's help, we pinned him to the ground. I wanted to resolve this with as little damage to him as possible. B.T. didn't seem to feel the same way and took a couple shots while Holt was pinned. Holt struggled, but when he couldn't break free, he lay still. His head was covered in an ooze that matted his fur and had run down his shoulders in strings. I didn't see the demon anywhere.

"Everybody okay?" I shouted.

I turned my head to see Martina had changed to krasis. The gray fur and canid features of the fox shifter did little to hide the fresh claw marks running across her face. It would heal completely, but the scars would linger for a bit. I doubt that helped Holt's chances with her any.

"There it is!" Yarwor shouted.

We all looked up to see what appeared to be the back end of a Chihuahua-sized slug disappearing into the side building.

"I'll get it," Yarwor said, running after it.

Holt thrashed without warning, with an unusual strength, even for him. It caught Big Ticket and me by surprise, and Holt was able to wrestle free. He dashed after Yarwor, both of them disappearing into the building, one after the other.

"Check on Chisel," I said to B.T., running after them.

The building turned out to be a smithy. A large anvil mounted to a stump sat in the middle of the room with a coal forge to the right. The walls were lined with tools and tables with plenty of places for the little demon to hide. Yarwor had managed to catch it. He was doing his best to squeeze the life out of it. It screeched and writhed, tentacles flailing wildly. Yarwor wasn't prepared to defend himself. Holt closed in and punched him in the side of the head with enough force to send Yarwor toppling over the anvil. Yarwor dropped the demon and disappeared behind the anvil. The demon scurried under a table. Holt turned slowly toward me. He had the glazed over expression I had seen on Yarwor earlier.

"Snap out of it already," I said.

Holt walked casually over to the wall of tools and picked up a sling blade. "Grubby's hungry."

"Holt, you can fight this," I said. "That demon can't be stronger than you are."

He took a step toward me, then cringed and rubbed the heel of his hand on his temple. "But it's hungry, Obie", he groaned. "It's so hungry,"

It looked like he was starting to come out of it. If he could hang on just long enough to stay out of the way, I could find and kill the demon. It must have realized that it was losing control of Holt because it came scurrying out from under the table, giving me a good look at it for the first time. Yarwor's description was right. The demon had a white, slug-like body about a foot long with tentacles surrounding a circular ring of teeth. It pulled itself with the tentacles and crawled with its segmented body. It moved surprisingly quick for what could best be described as a land squid. It scurried and climbed up Holt, latching onto his head with a stomach-turning slurping sound. With its tentacles hanging and the demon's body on top, Holt looked like a Rastafarian wannabe.

Physical contact must have reinforced the demon's connection; Holt's eyes glazed over again. He raised the sling blade. I jumped back, avoiding his first swing but tripped over some scrap metal, falling backward. I grabbed a piece of pipe and used it as a shield, blocking blow after blow. There's no way I could get to my feet without taking a hit from the blade. The pipe was bending. It wouldn't last much longer, I had to do something quick before the pipe broke. I raised a leg to kick Holt's knee. He went rigid and stopped swinging. He dropped the blade and fell forward on top of me. I got a face full of tentacles and was suddenly overcome by the fear that the demon would try to make a Rastafarian out of me, too. I pushed Holt off to see Yarwor standing there with a rather menacing looking hammer and determination on his face.

The demon thrashed in pain from the blow, but it wasn't dead. It crawled off Holt's head, dragging its way toward some wood stacked in the corner. It appeared to be crippled. It pulled itself with its tentacles and wasn't making good time. Yarwor screamed with the rage and sorrow only a man who watched his family die can understand. He drove the hammer down on the demon. The first strike sent its thick black blood splattering into my face. Yarwor pummeled the demon into the dirt. When it was over, there was little more than paste in a hole with some tentacles beside it. I ran a hand over my face wiping the blood away. Yarwor looked down at the demon puddle, dropped the hammer, and walked quietly out of the smithy.

CHAPTER · 3

"HE'S GOTTA ANSWER for it," Chisel yelled. "Hell, they both do."

I wiped some spittle from my cheek. "First thing, Yarwor's already even. You kicked the crap out of him remember? Second, Holt's a Keeper of Thera, and you're not gonna touch him."

"Oh yeah?" Chisel sneered. "And what if I do?"

I smiled at him. "Then you'll have to answer for it."

We stared each other in the eye for what seemed like ten minutes before Big Ticket chimed in. "I don't see what the big deal is. It's just a little scrap."

"It's not up to you," Chisel snapped.

"You're right. It's up to me," Hank said. "Chisel's right. We have to send a message if somebody comes into the clubhouse causing trouble."

"How about this," I said. "I won't heal him. You already hurt him and that way he has to live with it. Message sent."

Hank ran his tongue over his teeth and looked off into the woods as he contemplated my proposal. "All right. Let's roll."

"Hold up," Chisel said. "What about Holt?"

Hank stepped up, getting in Chisel's face. "Let's roll," he repeated.

They glared at each other. Chisel turned and headed for his bike with the rest of the T.O.

"You good here?" Hank asked.

"Yeah, I'm gonna load the bodies and get them to Hob," I said.

"Sounds good," Hank said.

Hank, Chisel, and Big Ticket climbed on their motorcycles and cranked the engines. Martina had been looking at her face in the van mirror. The scratches Holt gave her had closed into three noticeable scars running from her forehead, across her nose, and down her cheek. On Hank's order, she got in the van and followed them.

I watched them drive away. When they were gone, Holt and I retrieved all the bodies from the mine. Any ultranatural without immediate family would be taken to the duster. I had organized an agreement between local factions years ago to keep the peace. The agreement established borders between the Tortured Occult and the Elven Nation and put rules in place for the manufacture of pixie dust. Dust, used to power magic, was made from the processed corpses of ultranaturals. Dust was dangerous to manufacture. It took specialized knowledge and equipment to produce. Beyond that, the producer had to have a mastery of magic or be close to mindless. If not, the dust could accidentally be ignited by any hint of anger or frustration. To say it would be an explosive situation would be an understatement.

We had Hob to work as our duster and the Tortured Occult handled local distribution. Any surplus went to the rats in Atlanta. Most of the dust came from demons that I supplied. Unfortunately, this time I had a truck full of innocents. I left Yarwor's wife and daughter behind for him to bury and covered the rest under a tarp in the back of my truck.

"WHAT ARE WE EVEN doing here?" Holt asked. "Shouldn't we be getting these corpses to Hob?"

"Just making a little stop. I've been hearing rumors about this place and I wanted to check it out. I won't be long." I opened the door to the truck and got out.

"What if someone comes along and starts poking around? About . . . You know," he said, pointing a thumb toward the back of the truck.

"No one's going to mess around in the back of a truck if someone's in it," I said. "Just wait here. Shouldn't take but ten minutes at most."

I closed the truck door and walked down the street to the Bear Book Market. Dahlonega had been without a bookstore for years before this one opened up. It was in a tiny space just off the square. I had been hearing rumors that it was more than just a bookstore, but hadn't had the chance to look into it yet. The storefront had a large glass window and a single door. The shop looked unattended. A rocking chair was placed beside the window with a desk beside it. The walls were lined with bookshelves packed neatly to the gills. Slips of paper were taped to the front of the shelves, designating the sections. I pulled the door open and stepped inside.

The store smelled like old paper. I caught a whiff of cologne and faint scents of humans and ultras that had come through the store. No one greeted me, so I took a minute to look through the books. I pulled a book off the shelves, *Henderson the Rain King*. It had a lion on the cover and I was just flipping it over the read the blurb when the back door opened, and two people walked out.

The first was wearing dirty jeans and a dingy red flannel. He looked tired. He was rolling his right sleeve down and raised his eyebrows when he saw me. I felt as if I had walked into the middle of something that was supposed to be private. The man headed for the door and walked out without saying a word. He smelled like iodine and sweat.

"Hello, I'm Clay. Welcome to the Bear Book Market," the other man said, walking over to the desk and sitting down.

He was wearing khakis, a blue button-up shirt, and a newsboy cap. He had a few days of scruff and gave off an air of sophistication that was unusual for the area. It was clear he wasn't from around here.

"Thanks," I said. "It's my first time in the shop."

"Well, we deal mostly in used books, except for the section there for local authors," he said, pointing to a shelf across the room. "I have more books in the back. If you're looking for something special, I can probably get it for you."

I had heard rumors that a bat shifter was working out of the Bear Book Market. I couldn't tell if it was true yet. The cologne covered his natural scent. If the rumors were true it could be problematic. The myth of vampires was based on werebats: They drank blood and changed into bats. They didn't *need* to drink blood; they had a special ability to draw power from the blood of those they drank from. The more powerful the victim, the more power werebats gained. They had also figured out how to manufacture Ichor from their blood. It was a highly addictive drug that was responsible for ruining countless lives. Not something to take lightly.

The werebats tended to stay in cities. If one had come to Dahlonega it might bring trouble, such as Ichor, with it. It technically wasn't my responsibility, but I live around here, and I didn't want the town going to hell. First thing to do was figure out if the rumors were true. From the guy smelling of iodine and pulling his sleeve down, I had reason to think they were.

"When you say, 'something special,' what do you mean?" I asked, wishing I was more street savvy.

"I have some first edition, autographed Stephen Kings, if that's your thing," he said.

I looked at the book I was holding. "What about Ichor?"

"I'm not familiar with it," he said. "Who wrote it?"

He had the hint of a smirk, barely perceptible.

My phone rang. I pulled it out and looked at the screen. It was Holt. I hit the button on the side of the phone to silence it. I was almost done, and the truck was a two-minute walk away. He was probably just bored. What kind of trouble could he be getting into in town?

"Come on, you know what I'm talking about," I said.

His nose flexed slightly as he subtly sniffed the air. No doubt he was figuring out who and what I was. My phone rang again. This time it came up as Harlan. I swiped the green phone icon to answer and raised it to my ear.

"Hello?" I said.

There was a lot of background noise. It sounded like Harlan had butt-dialed me. I stepped toward the door, thinking I might have a bad connection. I heard a distinctive screech. I immediately recognized it as a hellhound.

"Harlan?" I shouted into the phone.

Automatic gunfire roared over the phone, drowning out the other sounds. I waited and listened, there was nothing else to I could do.

"Demons at the Southern Outpost," Harlan shouted over gunfire and screams. "They're everywhere!"

I ran out the door toward the truck. It was empty. Holt was nowhere to be found. I didn't have time to wait on him. If the elves were being attacked by demons, I had to get there quick with or without him. I jumped behind the driver's seat and realized I still had the book in my hand. I tossed it onto the seat beside me and turned the key in the ignition. The truck roared to life. I slammed it into gear. The tires screamed as I pulled out.

CHAPTER·4

THE SOUTHERN OUTPOST was only a fifteen-minute drive from Dahlonega. I made it in twelve. The outpost sat on top of a mountain in North Georgia with the only access being a poorly maintained road that wound lazily to the top. I went up as fast as I could, swerving to avoid potholes and ruts, sparing my suspension from the worst of it. I stopped at the checkpoint halfway up the mountain. The checkpoint was a small concrete building just big enough for the two guards normally on duty. On any other day one of the guards would come outside as soon as they saw my truck. No one greeted me today. I left the truck idling and got out to see if I could lower the barricade blocking the road. Nothing looked out of place. There were no dead elves, blood pools, or bullet holes to hint at what had happened. The autumn air smelled crisp. I didn't detect the scent of gunpowder or the sulfuric stink of demons.

I had never been inside the checkpoint before. It was just a counter, a couple of chairs, and a few monitors. A small fridge and space heater sat in the far corner. A back window had an air conditioning unit mounted to it. All the necessities and none of the comfort. A large red button, the kind you imagine launches nuclear missiles, was mounted to the wall by the counter. That had to be what lowered the barricade. The building seemed to have lost power. The light on the ceiling and the monitors were off. I flipped the light switch a few times. I tried the button, giving it a few slaps, but nothing happened. The place was dead.

I'd have to run the rest of the way. I had just stepped outside when I saw a shadowy reflection in my truck window. An athol, a demon resembling a hairless gorilla with wings and a lot of pointy teeth, hit me. The force of the impact sent me flying back into the building. I crashed to the floor with the athol on top of me.

Covering my head and neck with my arms, I made the change to krasis as the demon bit and scratched me. I pulled the demon close and bit into its throat. Its thick, black blood spilled into my mouth. It tasted bitter, like motor oil. I pulled it over on the ground in front of me. I pinned it on the ground with one hand on its chest and the other on its face. I pushed with my hands, pulled with my neck, and ripped its throat out.

The demon writhed and flapped like a fatally wounded chicken, fruitlessly struggling to cling to life. I spit the flesh and as much of the bitter, viscous blood out of my mouth as I could. I spotted a bottle of water on the counter that had been knocked over in the skirmish and used it to wash out my mouth, spitting onto the floor beside the carcass. I had added Velcro to the back of all my pants to make room for my muscular tail in krasis. I hadn't had time to open it and my tail had ripped the left leg of my shorts.

Bursts of gunfire coming from the top of the mountain got my attention. I ran uphill, weaving my way through the trees and rocks jutting out of the mountainside. The leaves on the forest floor were dry and brittle, crunching with every step; they made enough noise to alert whatever was up there that I was coming. I stopped my charge before the crest of the hill. I moved up the last few feet as slowly and quietly as I could to get an idea of the situation before I went charging out into the open.

A moving truck was parked in front of the compound. It looked to be about half-full of crates. Bodies of elves and demons littered the ground around it. The demons lay, more or less, in lines where the waves of their attack broke against the elven defenses. The elves were scattered, picked off one by one while trying to get to the safety of the outpost. I couldn't remember the last time I had seen so many demons at one time. A few months ago there had been an incident on the bridge outside Gainesville that I don't like to talk about. There were more than a few demons there, but this . . . there had to be at least thirty demons, and that's just what I could see. The air was thick with the scent of demon blood and the acidic burn of gunpowder. Spent brass littered the ground among the bodies. If there was a winner in this battle, it wasn't clear which side it was.

The only living thing I could see was a hellhound on the far side of the compound. A shadow passed overhead. Another athol was banking hard. It swooped down to where the hound was chewing on an elf carcass. There was plenty of fresh meat scattered around the area, but the athol decided it wanted to eat the only elf that was already being chewed on. It was testament to the nature of these beasts. The athol landed and flapped its wings in the hound's face. The hound jumped away, letting the athol move in. The hellhound circled as the athol took a bite from the elf's abdomen. The body jostled and shook as pieces were bitten away. The hound screeched at the athol, revealing rows of teeth. The athol didn't mind the noise as long as it was getting to eat.

With both of them distracting each other, it gave me the perfect opportunity for a surprise attack. I moved as quietly as I could to the remains of an elven guard, her body mutilated beyond recognition. Her rifle, however, complete with a grenade launcher, was intact. I detached the sling, which still held the weapon to what was left of the body. I took aim at the demons. Pulling the trigger, a baseball-sized explosive flew toward the unaware demons with a loud metallic *pung*. It passed directly between them, exploding harmlessly on the hillside. The detonation showered the area with dirt and disappointment.

The demons spotted me and charged, ready for some fresh meat. The athol took flight and closed the distance faster than the hellhound, even with all six of its legs pushing as hard as they could.

While I had missed with the grenade it meant I now had an opportunity that doesn't come around often: I could unload with one of these elven guns. I don't have anything against guns, they just aren't my tool of choice. When I get the opportunity to use one, I thoroughly enjoy it. I kept the gun at my hip and took a wide stance. My tail waved back and forth with excitement and I found myself laughing a little more maniacally than I care to admit.

"Eat hot lead, stinkbugs!" I shouted, pulling the trigger while visions of Rambo danced in my head.

The rifle sprang to action but only fired a couple rounds, neither of which found the target. I looked down to find the bolt open and the magazine empty. The athol would be on me in a second. I had no time to reload and nothing to reload with. I flipped the gun around, and held it by the barrel. I sidestepped the athol, using the rifle as a club to strike the demon's left wing. It spun out of control and crashed to the ground behind me.

The hound leapt, but I was ready. I thrust the gun into its mouth and rolled back, pushing my feet into its belly. The hound flipped over me, landing on its back. I got to my feet first, twisting the rifle free of the demon's jaws. I brought it down, striking the creature in the head repeatedly as it tried to get to its feet. By the third hit it wasn't fighting anymore.

The athol lumbered over, one wing sticking out awkwardly, broken. It wasn't as agile on the ground as in the air and it was easy to keep out of the way of its claws. After it over-committed with a swipe of its claws, I struck it in the leg with the rifle. It collapsed and I was able to finish it off quickly.

After a quick check to make sure there weren't any more demons about to attack me, I walked around the dead toward the outpost. Surveying the carnage, I couldn't help but wonder if anyone had survived at all. There had to be at least one: Harlan, the Queen's son, who called me. Of course, that call was about twenty minutes ago. By now everyone could be killed. If there were any survivors, they would be inside the outpost.

I had only made it a few steps when a sound caught my attention. A hellhound lying on the ground to my left was still alive. It had been shot at least four times, and something had nearly blown off its front leg. It didn't appear to have any fight left in it. It just lay there with its belly rising and falling, each labored breath a kind of groaning wheeze. I approached it slowly, ready for it to spring to life and attack.

The rule for Keepers has always been to keep suffering to a minimum. It was never mandated that it applied to demons, as well, but I always figured the way you treat your enemies says more about you than the way you treat your friends. I drove the rifle barrel into the creature's head, giving it as quick a death as I could. I left the gun sticking out of the creature's skull like a flag claiming foreign soil.

I spotted something that made me stop in my tracks. Two of the Queen's three daughters lay dead. Their bodies weren't in good shape, but there was no question that it was them. Patsy, the oldest daughter, had been ripped open from throat to abdomen. What was left of her guts had spilled on the ground; most were missing. Shelly, the middle daughter, was missing her right leg and left arm. It looked like someone, or something, had played tug of war with her. I looked around the courtyard again to see if anyone was watching. My first instinct was to run. Head to the truck, start driving, and never look back. There was going to be hell to pay when the Queen found out, and I didn't want to be anywhere in the vicinity when that happened. If I did run and she found out, she would probably take that as proof I had something to do with the attack. Besides that, there could still be people here that needed my help. I didn't see Harlan among the dead. He had to be here somewhere.

If he was still alive, he had to be in the compound. The Southern Outpost was a huge three-story octagon with porches encircling each level. It looked normal enough from the outside, once you got past the unusual structure and size. What couldn't be seen were reinforced concrete walls over a foot thick and the ballistic-glass windows. It was a fortress. On the lower level I found a door ajar, being held open by a dead elf. Her legs stuck out into the sunshine with torn pants and claw marks visible underneath.

I approached the door cautiously, not wanting any surprises, and peeked inside. The air was hazy and heavy with the smell of demon stench and gunpowder. Bodies of demons and elves littered the floor, but nothing moved. I carefully worked my way down the hallway, stepping over bodies and looking for survivors. There were multiple doors in the hallway, all closed except one on the far end. Light spilled into the hallway and I could make out whispering coming from inside. I had almost made it to the door when a shuffling noise behind me caught my attention. A hellhound had come in behind me and was sniffing around the bodies, apparently unaware of my presence. It must have been in the area and the noise of the fighting brought it back.

I turned as quietly as I could and made my way toward it. The demon began chewing on the elf stuck in the doorway. It pulled the elf inside, the door swinging shut behind them. I was feeling good about my chances of killing this hound before it knew I was there when a loud crash came from the room behind me. It was enough to get the attention of the hound. It spotted me and charged.

I was ready for it. It lunged at me, and I took a step back, intending to jump on top of it. I wanted to control its head and, by extension, its teeth. I slipped in some blood, going down on a knee. This put me at eye level with the demon, the exact vantage point I was trying to avoid. I put my hands on its neck and pushed. I was able to stay out of the demon's mouth, but lost any chance of gaining an advantage.

It lunged again. I had no choice, but to drop to the floor. It wasn't expecting this and it ended up over me. I wrapped my arms around the hound's neck before it could reorient itself to my position. Its six legs pumped powerfully, dragging me down the hallway and through the blood and gore lining the floor. The hound jerked its head erratically and slammed up against the walls, trying to get me loose.

It stopped its charge long enough for me to get my feet under me. I pressed up, lifting its front four legs off the ground, and evening the odds. I swept its back legs, threw it to the ground, and fell on top. Things were finally starting to go my way.

We landed on the ground in front of the open door. Inside I saw Harlan and two soldiers. Their rifles were pointed in our direction. I held my left hand out to them, using my right arm to keep the demon under control.

"Don't—"

Their rifles burst to life with automatic fire.

CHAPTER·5

I OPENED MY EYES to a white light. For a moment I thought I might be dead, but if I was, then I wouldn't feel the tingling in my chest that comes from rapid healing. My body had cooled in the fall air and felt stiff. My eyes adjusted to the light and I became aware of a texture in the light. It was a sheet. I took a deep breath and sat up. The sheet clung to me, refusing to concede that I was alive. I pulled it off my face. I found myself lying in a line of elves that had been killed in the attack.

We had been laid in neat rows with bloodstained sheets covering the bodies. The dead elves numbered twelve in all. Blood soaked in the sheets giving hints to what killed them. Some had red stains and empty spaces where limbs should be; many others had head and chest wounds. While the air had a slight chill, it was still too warm for bodies to be outside for any amount of time; the smell of death was creeping in. My shirt had a number of holes in the front, mostly in a central circle at my heart. I ran a hand over my chest and felt a lump. I pulled up my shirt for a look and found the end of a bullet embedded in my skin under my fur. Whenever I got shot, my body would push out the foreign material. I pried at it with my fingers and was rewarded by a stinging pain and a trickle of blood as I pulled the mushroomed piece of metal free. I was covered in blood, not all of it my own. I had a change of clothes in the truck—I always carried extra clothes for situations like this.

I was suddenly aware of the elf lying beside me. I had inadvertently uncovered her. I couldn't tell what killed her. Much of her abdomen was missing, leaving exposed ribs and an empty cavity. She had been chewed on after she died—at least, I hope she died first. Her head was untouched. Her blank eyes stared at me accusingly. She was pretty; her face held the long and deceivingly soft features of elven kind.

"Sorry," I said, standing up.

I restored the sheet and her dignity. A thud from the direction of the compound got my attention and I looked up to see the two elves who had shot me.

They had been carrying a demon corpse, and had dropped it and grabbed their guns when they saw me.

"If you shoot me again, we're going to have a problem," I yelled, pointing a finger in their direction. "Go tell Harlan I'm awake."

They squinted and glared at me with distrust. They walked toward the outpost without relaxing the grip on their rifles. I took the opportunity to look around.

In contrast to the care shown the elves, the demons were piled together. The demon stack was about eight feet in diameter and growing. Wings and legs stuck out haphazardly in all directions. There had to be at least twenty in the pile, with more around the grounds waiting to be stacked. Two bodies had been laid on a table close to the building and covered with sheets. I knew those would be the princesses.

Harlan came out to meet me while I surveyed the corpses. A guard followed behind him. They were back on duty, this time watching me. Harlan's head was shaved and his ears had been removed, his punishment for embarrassing the Queen. As always, he wore a plain black shirt, black pants, and combat boots. His left hand was bandaged and he had blood on his hands and face. He had run this outpost, up until an incident almost three months ago, when he was replaced by his sister, Patsy. Due to a promise by the Queen, he was kept around as a representative of the Elven Nation, but I never got the feeling he was particularly welcome here after his sister took over.

"What the hell, Harlan?" I asked.

"Sorry about that," he said. "Would you believe it was an accident?"

I shook my head. "Not even a little bit."

"I'd like to tell you I could reprimand them or something, but we both know I'm a figurehead here. I'd also like to tell you that I'll make it up to you but . . ." He shrugged.

"There must be thirty demons out here, practically an army. How did this happen?"

Harlan glanced at the guards, and pulled me by the elbow in the other direction, so we could speak privately.

"Nobody's asking my opinion, but I'm telling you, there's something really wrong with this," he said. "The attack was timed perfectly."

"What do you mean?"

"The attack happened when both my sisters were together outside. Patsy was running the outpost and Shelly was overseeing the delivery. It's the only time they could be caught together."

"You think they were the targets?" I asked.

He shrugged. "It makes sense."

"What about you? You're the son of the Queen and here for the attack. Do you think you were a target, too?"

"No one cares about me."

I ran a hand over the scruff on my face. "I understand having a problem with the Queen, but using demons like this . . . Why would someone do that?"

"I'm sure I couldn't say," he answered. "I'm just glad some of us made it out alive."

"How many survivors are there?"

"Me, those two," he said, pointing to the two guards watching us, "and a few more wounded inside. They could use your help."

"That's it? What about the guards from the checkpoint?"

He pointed to a pair of bodies. "It took them a few minutes to get up here. By that time, the attack was well underway. They never stood a chance out in the open like that. Easy pickin's."

"Take me to 'em. I'll see what I can do."

I followed Harlan back through the door on the lower level of the Southern Outpost. The hallway had been cleared of most of the bodies, but the blood remained. Harlan did his best to avoid puddles of demon and elf blood as we went. Since I had already been dragged through it, I didn't see the point.

We stepped around the hound I had been shot with and into the room. Judging by the rows of weapons and ammunition lining the walls, this had to be the armory. This was where they'd made their last stand. The room was littered with bodies, mostly elves, but a few demons, still lay just inside the door. Three elven women rested on the far side of the room, two lying unconscious and one standing guard. The guard reached for the pistol at her hip when she saw us walk in.

"I can forgive one," I said, waving my tail with irritation. "But only one, so think about it before you draw."

Harlan moved to stand between us. "Everybody relax. We're all friends here."

She lowered her hand, but didn't relax. I paused momentarily at the sight of the compound's staff, the cook and cleaning crew, all male and all dead. It looked as if they fell at the edge of the demon line. They had bite marks and bullet holes, obviously sacrificed, shoved out front as a wall to protect the guards. They had taken the females out and covered them, they were taking out the demons, which I understood, the smell wasn't pleasant. Apparently, these poor men weren't worth picking up. I passed over them, moving on to someone I might be able to help.

I stepped around the guard to the two unconscious elves. I held my hand over the first and concentrated. The energy started flowing through me, but there was nowhere for it to go; she was dead. I moved to the next elf in line. She had a half-moon shape in blood soaked into one of her pant legs. It looked like a hellhound had gotten a nibble in on her, a good bite could have removed the leg completely. I had seen injuries like this many times before.

"Just the leg," I said, giving her a once over for other injuries.

The guard scowled at me. "Is that not enough? I think it's broken."

I hate it when patients are bitchy. I placed one hand on either side of her leg and concentrated. The blue light synonymous with my abilities began to glow from my eyes and hands. I could feel her wounds closing and the bone mending.

I stopped when it was done, but before the energy could spill over to any other injuries or ailments. I only wanted to bring them back to the condition they were in before the attack, though maybe a little worse for wear.

I turned back to the first guard. She looked to have some minor scratches, making out far better than anyone else here, except for Harlan.

"I'm fine," she said, holding a hand out before I could even ask.

"Okay," I said, turning to Harlan. "What about you? Need me to look at that hand?"

"It's just a cut. I don't even know how it happened, but it's not bad. Besides, I don't think the Queen would like you healing me. I'm not sure she got over the last time," he said over the rumble of vehicles. "Speaking of the Queen, that should be her now."

We walked out just as the Queen's SUV and two guard trucks pulled up to the outpost. The Royal Guard, the Queen's personal protection force, poured out of the three vehicles, taking positions to secure the area. After everyone was in place, the back door of the SUV opened. The Queen exited, pausing in front of the door to survey damage. Her long blonde hair was pulled back, revealing her long ears. She wore black jeans over combat boots and a flannel shirt. A pair of Old West-style six-shooters hung lazily from her hips. She spotted the surviving elves with Harlan and me standing by the door and walked toward us. Her youngest daughter, Princess Isabelle, climbed out of the car and followed.

The Queen walked in the direction of the elf and demon bodies with Isabelle close behind. Isabelle looked like a ten-year-old human, but she was probably closer to fifty or sixty. She wore a tiara of flowers and a long, silky, blue dress. It was a different style of dress than the other women of the royal family, but she was young. She hadn't started training for the military yet. She had already received her first gun, a bolt action rifle she wore slung over her shoulder. Weapons in the Nation were a status symbol as much as a tool, and a daughter of the Queen would be expected to carry one and be proficient with it early on. I had no doubt she could already outshoot me.

The Queen and Isabelle passed Harlan and me without acknowledging us. Harlan did a quick check to be sure no one was looking, and stuck his tongue out at Isabelle as she passed. She wasted no time in returning the gesture.

"Isn't that kinda dangerous?" I whispered. "I can't imagine the Queen would approve."

"It's worth it," Harlan replied.

It was the first time I had seen him smile in months. The Queen had the sheet removed to properly review the carnage. When she was done, she walked back to where we were standing.

"Where are Patsy and Shelly?" the Queen demanded.

Harlan motioned toward the table. The lead truck had parked in front of the table and blocked her view of them. She walked over and whipped the sheet off, staring at the mangled bodies for a few seconds. She turned to face us. She didn't appear upset, but when she spoke there was a coldness in her voice akin to rage.

"Report," the Queen commanded.

The elf I had healed spoke up: "It was a surprise attack. I've never even heard of anything like it before. We didn't see any portals; all these demons just came out of the woods. They attacked just as Patsy had come out to inspect the monthly delivery. I think she was the target of the attack. She and Shelly were swarmed. The door was propped open with half the soldiers unloading, so we weren't able to save her."

"Why was the door propped open and why were half the soldiers unloading the truck? They should have been standing guard. These are serious security breaches."

"Patsy ordered the guards to help unload the shipment," the guard said. "I can't speak as to who propped the door open."

The Queen nodded, taking in the information. "Survivors?"

"Just the four of us. Oh and him," the elf said, throwing Harlan a contemptuous look. "We lost fourteen and the help."

"Our sisters will be missed," the Queen said.

The four elves nodded in agreement as the Queen turned and approached Harlan and me. She stopped in front of us, taking stock. "Obie, what are you doing here?"

"I called him," Harlan said. "When it looked like we—"

"You will speak when spoken to," the Queen snapped.

Harlan lowered his head.

After giving him a few seconds for the message to sink in, she turned back to me.

"Harlan called and said the outpost was under attack. I was in Dahlonega at the time, so I wasn't far away," I said.

"Were you injured?" she asked, eyeballing my blood-soaked clothing.

"After I fought my way inside to the survivors, they shot me."

I didn't get the impression she was bothered by her soldiers' actions.

She looked me in the eye. "Did you have a hand in this attack?"

"A demon attack?" I scoffed. "You know I didn't."

"Your truck was blocking the road. Perhaps you left it there on purpose to keep help from responding?"

I'd like to tell her that she was being paranoid and asinine, but in my experience, royalty doesn't take to criticism. "The barricade was raised and there wasn't power to lower it. I had to leave the truck and run."

"The barricade can be lowered in the case of emergencies," the Queen said.

"I believe you," I said. "But I don't know how to do it."

"I assure you, I will find whoever is responsible for this attack and make them pay. If you know anything, it's in your interest to speak up now."

I rested my hands on my hips and tried not to let frustration come through as I spoke. "Hunting demons is kind of my whole reason to exist. I want whoever's responsible found as much as you do."

"Your truck was pushed clear," she said. "In the future, I expect the road to be kept open. Take Harlan to the clubhouse to arrange for the next council meeting to be held there. The situation is under control now, you may go."

I smiled to hide my aggravation at being dismissed like one of her servants.

"A question, my Queen," Harlan asked, without looking up.

"Speak."

"The Tortured Occult will want to know if this incident will affect the upcoming run. What should I tell them?"

The Queen thought it over. "Against my better judgement, the run may proceed."

Harlan bowed, and we walked down the hill toward my truck. When we were out of sight of the outpost, I picked up the pace to a jog. When my old truck had been wrecked, I'd driven a loaner for a while before settling on a Nissan Frontier. After I bought it, it spent two months in the shop getting a number of upgrades that would be helpful for the rough life it would lead. Aesthetically, the only changes were a heavy-duty grill guard and some metal cages to protect the lights. Anything to reduce the chances of a run-in with the law was worth it. Underneath, there were a number of improvements, including a nice sturdy suspension, armor around the engine and cab, and bulletproof glass. Things have been tense for the past few months and I can't afford to be unprepared.

We found the truck, still idling and resting against a tree off the road below the checkpoint. Harlan waited by the checkpoint while I inspected the truck. The grill guard seemed to have done its job and prevented any damage. The bodies in the back were still secure. I put on a change of clothes and deposited my old clothes into the bed of the truck to get rid of later. I found the book I had in-advertently stolen and put it in the glovebox. Then I got in, put it in four-wheel drive, and backed up the hill onto the road.

It wasn't until Harlan was getting in the truck that I noticed two new guards already manning the checkpoint, watching our progress. The door hung off broken hinges and a dead demon lay on the floor, but security first, I suppose. I gave them a wave and pulled out.

CHAPTER · 6

THE CLUBHOUSE OF the Tortured Occult Motorcycle Club sat in the middle of a junkyard. The property belonged to Hank, president of the T.O., and owner of the club's legitimate business, by human standards: Morrison Salvage and Repair. The clubhouse served not only as the headquarters for the motorcycle club but also as a social hotspot for ultranaturals in the area. I found an open spot to park among the wrecked and rusted vehicles.

"Go on in," I said to Harlan. "I need a minute."

Harlan got out and headed for the door. I waited a few seconds to have some privacy before I pulled out my phone and called Holt. The phone rang a few times and went to voicemail.

After the beep, I said, "I'm at the clubhouse. I have to take the bodies to Hob as soon as I'm done here. If you haven't got a ride yet, let me know where you are, and I'll pick you up."

I didn't get the impression he was in any kind of trouble, probably just got bored and wandered off. It wouldn't be the first time.

I put the phone back in my pocket, got out of the truck, and went inside. I stepped through the front door into the changing room, a rectangular room with a door on either end that exited into the bar. Harlan was waiting for me there.

"Everything okay?" I asked.

He nodded. "Yeah, I just figured I'd wait on you."

The walls were lined with coat and shoe racks. The clubhouse was a place where people didn't wear disguises. The changing room was the place where pretense was shed. I pulled my shoes off and added them to the row of shoes already lining the wall. As not to lose another pair of pants today, I pulled open the Velcro stitched in the back to make room for my tail and made the change to krasis.

Elves in this situation would normally have made sure their ears were showing. Harlan, having no ears or hair to hide them with, lived unveiled. When I finished the change, we exited through the door on the left into the clubhouse. While relations were better between the Elven Nation and the T.O., the Queen still forbade elves from leaving the Nation. When we walked in, the few people that were there took notice of Harlan. Everyone had heard what the Queen had done to him. I was the only one outside of the elves to witness it firsthand. If he was self-conscious about his appearance, he didn't show it as the curious patrons turned to get their first look at the Queen's brand of justice.

In many respects, the clubhouse was a typical bar. A pool table and dart board claimed the right side of the room with tables spread around the rest. The bar itself took up most of the back wall with a door to the right that lead to the back. There were only two things that made it stand out from a normal bar. The first was the filing cabinet and a single table tucked into the corner to the right of the pool table. It was a de facto office for Adan, the wererat emissary. The second was the fact that there weren't any humans here. An assortment of different shifters lounged around the tables, as well as a group of goblins and kobolds playing a rather spirited game of darts.

I spotted Hank at the bar, sitting with my wayward apprentice. I led Harlan straight to the conference room. It was devoid of decoration, with a plain round table in its center. I thought it would be more comfortable for him to wait there rather than in the bar being eyeballed by everyone.

"Give me a few minutes to get everyone together," I said.

Harlan took a seat at the table. I went back to the bar.

"What's he doing here?" Hank asked.

"Need an emergency meeting," I said. "We got a problem."

Hank downed the rest of his beer and got up. "All right, I'll get folks together."

I sat down in the newly vacant seat beside Holt. I really wasn't pleased with him at the moment and I took a minute to keep from jumping all over his case.

"You were supposed to stay with the truck," I said.

"I just ran over to the Fudge Factory," he said. "I needed a little something."

"You didn't *need* something. We are sustained by Thera. You don't have to eat or drink."

He took a swig from his beer. "Maybe *you* don't need to eat, but I get hungry. I can't go a day without putting something in my stomach."

"You can if you try," I said. "And I need you to try. I needed you in the truck."

"You're the one that said no one would mess with it."

I was trying to be more patient with him than I had been in the past. He was still learning, after all, and it was my job to teach him. I wouldn't have complained if he were a little less pig-headed at times.

"I said no one would mess with it if someone was in it. You were supposed to be that someone. Look, the long and short of it is, I asked you to do something and you didn't. I need you to do better going forward."

"All right," he said. "I hear what you're sayin."

That was about as good a reaction as I could hope for from him. At least he wasn't arguing with everything I said anymore. Hank stuck his head through the door and gave me a nod; we were ready for the meeting. I followed Hank into the conference room and we took our seats.

Hank began. "Harlan, I'm more than a little surprised to see you here, not that you aren't welcome, of course. What's so important we had to call an emergency meeting?"

Hambone cleared his throat and stood on his chair. The kobold was about three feet tall with the head and fur of a coyote on a humanoid body. Unlike normal shifters, kobolds could only take two forms, a coyote or krasis. He was the member of the council elected to represent the masses and had gotten fat from the benefit of his position. He wheezed from the effort of standing up and began to speak. "Actually, before we get started with that, I have something to say. This will be our first meeting since the election and I am sure you are all as happy as I am that I was reelected."

Adan cut in. "I think Harlan has something important to talk about."

"Yes, yes," Hambone continued. "This will just take a second. I just wanted to say that I appreciate your support in the election."

"You're welcome, Hambone," I said, giving Harlan a nod to start.

"I mean, there was a lot of competition this year," Hambone continued.

Hank put a hand to his head and rubbed his temples.

"I had two opponents and I won by a very slim margin. I know I have a couple years before the next election, but—"

"Hambone, we have something we really need to talk about," I said. "It's important."

"And this isn't?" he asked. "Elections matter and come to think of it, all of you could have been more supportive through it. I mean, not one of you wore the buttons I gave you."

"The Southern Outpost was attacked!" Harlan blurted out.

Hank removed the hand from his head at this revelation. "What do you mean, attacked?"

"It was attacked by demons," Harlan answered.

"A lot of demons," I added.

"Almost everyone at the outpost was killed," Harlan said.

"If you have something like that to talk about then why are we discussing the elections? Really, Harlan, sometimes I wonder about your priorities," Hambone said, sitting back down.

"Sorry, Hambone," Harlan said. "I'll try to stay on topic better in the future."

"It's okay. You're still new at this. Please tell us about the attack," he said.

"Like I said, pretty much everyone was killed, including Patsy and Shelly," Harlan continued. "I don't know how many demons attacked or how many were killed. They were still pulling the bodies out by the time we left."

Hank tapped a finger on the table as he thought about the news. "What the hell's going on? First that thing at the bridge a few months ago and now this? The world's going to shit. I'm guessing the Queen closed the border, right?"

"No, actually, and the run's still on," Harlan said.

"That doesn't sound like her," Adan said.

Harlan shrugged. "I asked specifically about the run and she said it was still on."

Hank and Adan seemed skeptical and looked at me for confirmation.

I nodded. "It's true. I heard her say it."

They were right to be concerned. I couldn't think of a scenario where the Queen's suspicion and paranoia would allow the run to continue. Then again, maybe these past few months since the elves rejoined the council had had some positive impact. Maybe she was starting to come around to the idea that the Tortured Occult wasn't trying to undermine her at every turn.

"If she's up to something, she didn't tell me," Harlan said. "Not that *that* should surprise anyone. She may think you aren't involved because of the attack. The fact that it was a demon attack means magic is involved. It wasn't a normal demon attack either, it was organized. They attacked at a time when the outpost was most vulnerable. It had to be someone with knowledge of the inner workings of the Southern Outpost."

"How do you think she will handle something like that?" I asked.

"Let's just say it would be a good time for her subjects to keep their heads down and not draw attention. She's going to find someone responsible and punish them. Time will tell if she finds the person who actually did it or not," Harlan said.

"It sounds like we need to find who did it before she comes after us," Hambone said. "The last thing we want is a war."

Adan nodded in agreement. "Who could've done it though?"

"The most likely suspect is a resistance group that wants to restore magic to the Elven Nation. The Queen views them as terrorists and let's just say she doesn't negotiate with terrorists," Harlan said. "You know that's why she distrusts you, right?"

"She thinks I'm an elven terrorist?" Hank asked.

Harlan shook his head. "No, she thinks your dust operation is supplying them, intentionally or not."

"It's not just his operation. We set it up together, with the other groups, too. Everyone here is benefiting from it. Does she think we are all out to get her?" Adan asked.

"She did accuse me of being involved in the attack," I said.

Hambone let out a high-pitched cackle that reminded me of a hyena. "Obie involved in a demon attack, that's a good one."

"I think she mostly blames the T.O. for it," Harlan said.

"The Queen has a resistance group." Hank chuckled. "That's what happens when a dictator rules by fear; people start fighting back. She can't be surprised people want her out."

"She's not surprised; she's resentful and bitter," Harlan said.

"Out of control, is more like it," I added. "Which brings us back to why the run wasn't canceled. Do you think it's smart to still go?"

"I'm glad I won't be there," Adan said.

Hank scratched behind his ear as he thought it over. "I don't know if it's smart, but everyone's been looking forward to it. The T.O. needs this and if we don't show up it might look suspicious. Do you think she would do something at the run?"

"I have learned, when trying to predict the Queen's behavior, to err on the side of cruelty and paranoia. You attend that run at your own risk," Harlan said.

"Regardless of what the Queen believes, if someone's summoning demon hordes, that's something I need to look into. Assuming it isn't that resistance group, who do we know that could pull something like this off?" I asked.

Whoever was doing it had to be skilled magically and have access to a large amount of dust. There were very few people around that could meet that criteria, so few I couldn't really think of any.

"Well," Hank said. "Hob could do it."

"Hob? Really? You can't be serious," I said.

"I didn't say I thought he did do it, just that he *could*. I don't know if you've seen him in action, but Hob is scary good with magic," Hank said.

Adan leaned forward, resting an elbow on the table. "Come to think of it, he never sells his cut of the dust. In the years we've been doing this, he could have more than enough stockpiled by now."

"Fair enough. Who else?" I asked.

The five of us looked at each other for a minute. No one could think of another lead.

CHAPTER · 7

WITH THE MEETING over, everyone walked out into the bar. I found Holt still sitting at the counter, drinking a beer. Harlan and I joined him.

"Obie, one sec," Hank said, coming out of the back room behind us. "Before I forget, we're getting an early start on the run with a party next Thursday night. You should stop by."

"Who all'll be there?" Holt asked.

"The T.O. and friends of the club," Hank said.

"Asking about anyone specific?" I asked. "Martina, maybe?"

"Nope," Holt answered. "But we should go."

I tapped my fingers on the bar, in thought. "We should be able to make it."

"All right," Hank said. "See you then."

"What are you doing here, anyway?" Holt asked when Hank had walked away.

"Trouble at the Southern Outpost," I said, sitting beside him. "I'll fill you in when we have a little more privacy."

Harlan sat down beside me. Tico, the wereraccoon bartender, came up after a minute with a rag over one shoulder. He leaned an elbow on the bar in front of us.

"What can I get you," he asked.

"Nitro Milk Stout," Harlan said before he leaned over and whispered, "The Queen doesn't allow me to drink, so let's keep this between us."

Tico looked at me, even though he knew I wasn't going to get anything.

"I'm good, thanks," I said.

Tico got a pint glass and filled it from the tap with a dark beer with a frothy head, put it on the counter in front of Harlan, and started wiping down the counter with the rag from his shoulder.

"Aren't you worried about the Queen's spies seeing you drink that beer?" I asked as Harlan took his first swig.

"I think she has more important things to worry about, with what just happened and the run coming up," he said.

"Just be careful. I don't need to tell you how seriously she takes disobedience."

"Did you see who else showed up tonight?" Holt asked, motioning to a table by the door.

"Is that Naylet?" Harlan asked. "Who's the guy?"

Naylet and I were together for a long time until about three months ago when she lost her memory from a demon attack. I was able to save her, and the other victims, but I hadn't spoken to her since. I wanted to give her the space to rediscover who she was without pressure and expectations from me. I looked over to discover she was sitting with a man and appeared to be having a good time. I recognized him, too. His name was Titus, another one of the demon's victims. They chatted and laughed and I found myself focusing on the ambient noise to avoid hearing any part of it. Naylet smiled and brushed her hair back behind her ear. She looked in our direction and caught me looking at her. Our eyes met and I looked back to the bar a little too quickly to be played off as casual.

"A victim of the gorgon, like Naylet. He was a sculptor in ancient Rome, I think," I said.

"You know what they say about those Eye-talians," Harlan said, taking a drink from his beer.

"What do they say?" I asked.

"Hell if I know. I don't think I've ever met one," Harlan said. "Why's she sitting with him and not with you? Have you still not talked to her?"

Holt chuckled. "Not only has he not talked to her, he's still paying all her bills."

"I've been giving her time. I've been told she's been having a rough time," I said.

"Yeah, she looks real torn up with all that laughing and smiling," Holt said. "Looks to me like she doesn't know you exist."

"She's got her diary and pictures of me on the wall, so she has to know who I am," I said. "She'll talk to me when she's ready."

"Looks like she's ready now," Tico said. "She's headed this way."

The three of us turned around to see her walking toward us.

"We'll give you some privacy," Harlan said.

The two of them got up and walked off. Tico, on the other hand, continued to wipe the same spot on the bar in front of me.

"You mind?"

"Oh, I wouldn't miss this for the world," he said with a smile.

Naylet eased up to the bar and leaned against it. She stood, arms crossed, with her long blond curls cascading around her shoulders. I knew the pose, assuming it held the same meaning since before she lost her memories. It was the one she used when she wanted to look confident but wasn't. I waited a few seconds and then looked over at her. We stared at each other without speaking. Seconds seemed like an eternity. My mind raced as I tried to think of what the right thing to say in this situation was; nothing came to mind.

"Hey," she said.

My heart pumped a little faster. "Hey babe, I've been looking forward to spending some quality time with you."

Her face contorted into a scowl. "Never mind."

She turned and walked back the way she came.

"That was real smooth," Tico said.

"Shut up." I scowled, getting up to follow her. "Sorry, I didn't mean that the way it sounded."

She stopped walking and turned around.

"You came over because you wanted to talk, right? I'd like to talk to you if you still want to," I said, motioning toward an empty table. "Why don't you tell me what you wanted?"

She moved to the table slowly, as if she hadn't made her mind up on what to do, before she pulled a chair out and sat down. I sat across from her. After putting my foot in my mouth like that, I wasn't going to risk scaring her off again.

Awkward silence filled up most of a minute before I decided I better say something. "You know, autumn's my favorite season. After all the warm weather I really enjoy things cooling off. I haven't told many people this, but while some people are getting ready to hibernate this time of year, the cooler weather always makes me want to travel. It's like the cool breeze is an invitation from somewhere far away."

I watched her face as I said it, looking for any kind of recognition. She was the only person who knew that about me. If it rang any bells for her, she didn't show it.

"I saw you that day," she said. "When I woke up. You were the first one there. I've seen you at the house a few times, too, when you stopped by to talk to Zaria. I found out about everyone else I met that day except for you. I've been getting vague answers about what happened to me and who you are, so I thought I would ask you while I had the chance."

"What do you mean, 'while you had the chance'?" I asked.

"Zaria says I should stay away from you," she said.

"Does she now?" I was speaking more to myself than Naylet.

Zaria and Naylet had been friends a long time. When Naylet was attacked she needed help. Zaria was my first choice. I arranged for Zaria to move in and I took care of all of Naylet's expenses. Naylet was right that I had been to the house. I stopped by a few times early on to check in on her. Zaria always met me in the yard and said Naylet wasn't having a good day. I didn't know why she would tell Naylet to stay away from me, but it sounded like she had been doing a good job keeping her in the dark.

"What do you know about me?" I asked.

"I'm told you're a Keeper and that you're trouble."

"I see." I said resting my elbow on the table. "Anything else?"

"I don't even know your name," she said.

Zaria definitely had some explaining to do.

"My name is Obie," I said. "I'm really a nice guy, I just don't have any references. They're all dead or in jail." I waited for a reaction to my joke. She just sat across from me looking unsure. "So, you don't recognize me from anywhere? Maybe a picture? Wait, the pictures are of my human form." I changed to my human form, hoping she recognized it. "Ringing any bells?"

She shook her head.

"Where's Zaria at now?" I asked after I changed back to krasis.

"She'll be here soon."

"She may be right, I might be trouble," I said. "But what do you think?"

"I think there's more to it. She's not telling me something. I have good instincts and you don't seem that bad to me. Did I know you?" She cocked her head to one side.

I found myself just looking at her, wondering how to answer that question. Her expression softened and she lowered her arms. I was suddenly aware my answer was taking too long and I wasn't sure what my face was saying, so I looked over at the bar trying to appear casual.

"You did," I said. "I hoped you would remember."

She crossed her arms and looked at the floor. "I wish I could."

"Can I get you a drink?"

I got Tico's attention with a wave and motioned toward Naylet. He gave me a nod. We had done that so many times before it was almost unconscious.

"So, you're Obie?" she asked. "Is that short for something?"

"It was a long time ago, but not anymore," I said. "How have you been?"

Naylet shrugged. "It's been hard. Everyone is acting nice, but it's all fake. I'm tired of being coddled."

Tico put a sangria on the table in front of her. The red beverage with apple and orange slices floating in it had been one of Naylet's favorite afternoon drinks before the attack. She took a sip and stared at the concoction, moving it around in her hands.

"This is what I'm talking about," she said, eyeballing her drink.

"You don't like it?" I asked.

Naylet pushed the drink away from her. "I do like it. That's the problem."

"I'm not following."

"Somebody puts a drink in front of me and tells me I'll like it and I do, or I'm going to order something for myself and I'm told I won't like it. I get it anyway and they were right. Did you know everything I do is paid for?" she asked. "I could make an offer on this bar and the money would just show up. Where's it all coming from?"

I guess she wasn't told I was the one paying her expenses. It wasn't a burden; I had the money with nothing to spend it on and she had simple tastes, although apparently, she didn't know it.

"You don't want this place. Some knockers dug a bunch of tunnels under it a while ago. I say fifty-fifty chance, it falls into a sinkhole," I said.

"Everyone else seems to know what I want more than I do, that's the problem," she said. "It's driving me crazy. Sometimes I just want to run away."

"Where would you go?" I asked.

"I don't know. I don't even know what's out there," she replied.

I didn't like the idea of her leaving, but she didn't seem to be happy where she was. It had to be hard to have lost all your memories, to feel that you had been put in someone else's life.

"Maybe you should go," I said.

She scoffed. "I can't do that."

"Why not? What do you really have keeping you here?" I asked. "If getting away is what you need, then I think you should. It's better than buying this dump."

"I can't afford something like that," she said.

"You don't have to worry about that. If you want to travel the money will be there."

Naylet narrowed her eyes. "Are you the one that's been paying for me?"

I nodded. "It's not a problem."

"Why would you do that?" Naylet asked.

"Have you not read your diary?"

Naylet shook her head. "I don't have a diary."

"Sorry I'm late," Zaria said, walking up to table.

Zaria was a nymph, like Naylet, and shared the slender build and delicate features. They could have passed for sisters; the biggest difference between them was Zaria had long brown hair compared to Naylet's blonde curls.

"I need to borrow Zaria for one second," I said, pushing my chair back and standing up.

I led her by the elbow to the far side of the bar where we could speak privately.

"Well?" I asked.

She jerked her arm out of my hand. "Well what?"

"Why doesn't she know who I am?"

"I'm not going to let you hurt her again. You need to stay away, or I'll make you sorry," she said jabbing a finger into my chest.

"First, I have never hurt her. Second, I'll support whatever she decides," I said. "So you go ahead and make me sorry, if you have it in you, because I'm not going to let you manipulate her. You're going to give her the diary and pictures and answer any questions she has. Honestly."

Zaria crossed her arms and looked away. "Are you done?"

"Yep."

She turned around and headed back to the table where Naylet was sitting.

"Tonight," I called after her.

I met Naylet's gaze from across the room and gave her a half-hearted smile. I was pretty sure Zaria would do the right thing, but I would have to double-check in a few days, just to be safe. I found Adan at his usual table in the corner and sat down.

"I need a woman," I said.

"Obie, I didn't know you had it in you." Adan grinned. "What'd you have in mind?"

CHAPTER · 8

THE CHECKPOINT DOOR at the Southern Outpost had been boarded up with plywood, making it functional, if not visually appealing. I pulled up to the barricade, intending to drive Harlan all the way to the top of the mountain. A guard stepped out and walked over to the driver's side window.

"No one can enter, on orders of the Queen. He'll have to walk," she said.

"Is the outpost closed or the Nation itself," I asked.

She stared at me, but didn't answer. I guess I didn't have the proper clearance or something.

Harlan and I shared a look. He got out of the truck.

"Let me know if anything's changed," I said.

"I'll be in touch," he said and started walking up the road to the outpost.

Having dropped Harlan off, Holt and I headed to meet Hob. It didn't take us long to get to the farm. We pulled off highway twenty onto the dirt road running between the cornfields that led to the main house. The farmhouse sat in the middle of the property. There was a chicken coop, and a few barns, the largest of which housed the dust facility. It was tucked away on the back of the property beside the Etowah River. I saw Hob sitting on his front porch, enjoying the evening air. I needed to talk to him, but I needed to get rid of the bodies in the back of the truck more. We exchanged a wave as I passed him on the way to the dust barn. When I got there, I backed the truck up to the door. Holt pounded on the door while I removed the tarp from the bodies. The barn door opened, revealing an interior of polished steel and machinery. A large ogre wearing an apron, hairnet, and booties came out and began unloading the truck.

"Hey, Eric, good to see you," I said.

The ogre grunted in recognition, about as warm a greeting you could expect. Tallypo Wilix, the goblin foreman, came out with his clipboard and climbed on the bumper of the truck to get a look.

"Hmmm . . ." Wilix said, looking over the carnage. "I hope this wasn't your handiwork?"

"I'm just delivering it. The demon that's responsible is in there somewhere," I said. "What's left of it anyway."

Wilix jumped down from the truck. "All right, it'll take us about ten minutes to weigh everything and get the numbers for you."

"We're not going to stick around for all that. Just put it on our accounts," I said. "I trust you."

"That's bad business," Wilix said, shaking his pencil in my general direction.

I shrugged. "Yeah, it really is."

Wilix shook his head and sighed. "We'll have you on your way in a minute."

Holt came over and whispered, "Just had an idea. What if they're skimming dust, considering everything that's going on?"

I shook my head. "If Hob or Wilix wanted to rip us off, we would never know it. They're both a lot smarter than either of us. But they keep records that track the whole process. We could run the numbers. Hob already gets a cut of the dust. I don't see why he would need to skim a little more. Either way, I trust 'em."

WITH THE BODIES unloaded and the bed of the truck sprayed out, I drove to the farmhouse and parked. Holt and I walked up the stairs to join Hob on the porch.

"*Guten abend*, please have a seat," he said in his German accent. "If I had known you were coming, I would have a plate ready for you. Tonight, we have *Zwiebelkuchen*, an old recipe from the *Vaterland*. I have grown the onions myself. Would you like some?"

"Thanks, but we just came to drop off some demons," I said.

"I'll take a piece," Holt said, sitting down at the table.

"Excellent," Hob said, standing up and disappearing into the house.

"You couldn't help yourself, could you?" I asked.

Holt shrugged. "You must not be smelling the same zwedible-whatever that I am."

Hob returned a second later with a spare plate and served Holt a large piece of the pie.

"You had many demons today," Hob said, returning to his seat. "It has been a rough day, *Ja?*"

"You don't even know the half of it," Holt said in the middle of chewing his first bite. "Obie, you should try this, it's really good."

"We had two run-ins," I said. "That load was from the first one. Innocents. They'd been in the truck most of the day. I'm afraid they're starting to turn. After I got that cleaned up, the Southern Outpost was attacked by a horde of demons."

Hob put his fork down and wiped his mouth, giving us his full attention. Holt on the other hand, was more focused on the food than the conversation.

I continued. "It was an organized attack, not like anything I've seen before. Someone was controlling the demons and targeted the outpost strategically. We think Patsy was the target, but the Queen had two daughters killed in the attack."

"I feel sorry for my brethren under the Queen's rule," he said. "I have no doubt her response will be harsh."

"We're definitely concerned about how it's all going to play out," I said.

Hob folded his hands in his lap. "Who would do such a thing?"

"We were hoping you could tell us," Holt said through a mouthful of pie.

Hob was sharp as a tack and the subtlety of the statement wasn't lost on him. "Surely you don't think I am the mastermind, hmm? Do we not know each other better than this?"

"I don't know you from Adam," Holt said.

I suddenly became aware of figures out in the cornfield around the house. I couldn't pinpoint exactly how many there were, but enough to surround us. Although I couldn't see them, I knew they were corn demons. Some of the many creatures Hob had helping out around the farm. They were demons in the sense that they were from another place, but unlike the demons I had fought this morning, they were more of sentient plants. Not really a threat, as far as I knew, but there were a bunch of them out there. They blended in with the stalks perfectly and the only hint they were around was that prickly feeling on the back of my neck.

I not so subtly bumped into Holt, knocking his next bite of pie off his fork and onto the plate.

"Of course we do," I said. "We didn't come to accuse you of anything, we're just trying to figure this out. Do you know anyone who has the skill and access to enough dust to pull something like that off?"

The tingly feeling subsided somewhat as he answered. "*Ja*, I know someone. It's me," he said without the least bit of concern in his voice.

"You aren't worried about implicating yourself with two Keepers right in front of you?" Holt asked.

"I do not see two Keepers here, there are only two friends," he said.

I leaned on the porch railing. "Can you think of anyone else that could do it?"

"I know of some, but they are not here. I know of no one with the dust, but with enough time it could be collected. All that is necessary is by buying a little now *und* again *und* saving it."

"It could be a group effort," Holt added. "A few people could put it together pretty fast."

If there was a group working together, it could be very difficult to find them. I was already behind the curve and not feeling any closer to finding our culprit, especially if that culprit was the guerrilla resistance group I had just become aware of.

"Have you ever heard of a magical resistance group inside the Elven Nation?" I asked. "Apparently they're some kind of terrorist group."

"*Ja*, I know of them. They are not the terrorist group," Hob said.

Holt dropped his fork on the empty plate and leaned back in his chair. "Yeah? Well what are they, then?"

"They protect those gifted with magic from the Elven Nation by taking them away to safety. If the Queen wants to do away with magic, then she should love these people," Hob said.

"So, kind of like a magical underground railroad?" I asked.

Hob looked confused. "*Nein*, Obie, they do not use a railroad."

"Right," I said, deciding not to explain the underground railroad. "Anyway, Harlan thinks the Queen is going to go after them first. If there is anything you can tell me about them, I would appreciate it."

"It is a waste of time," Hob said.

"We need to find somebody that could collect a lotta dust and is good with magic. Those people fit the bill," Holt said.

"Regardless of where the dust has come from, there has to be a circle for the portal to function. Find the circle *und* it will lead you to the one that has used it," Hob said.

"The Queen closed the outpost, so I'm not going to be getting in to look around anytime soon," I said. "Since you brought up dust, I have to ask . . . What do you do with your share of the dust?"

Hob sighed. "Let us take a walk. I will show you."

We followed Hob to the barn closest to the farmhouse. He opened the door and we walked inside. He flipped a light switch and the overhead fluorescents came to life. He had a couple tractors, some farm equipment, and toolboxes inside. We followed him to the far side of the barn where stairs tucked away behind the toolboxes went to an upper story. We followed Hob up the stairs and through a door at the top. Inside I found a nice, albeit modest, looking apartment. We stepped into the living room. A group of elves were sitting around the coffee table. Two women, a man, and a couple of kids lounged on a couch and loveseat playing cards. When we came in, one of the women got up and came over to us. Her hair was dyed a peach color and she wore a sweatshirt that almost perfectly matched it.

"This is the Corwin family *und* my assistant, Tiffany. We are helping to relocate them away from the Queen," Hob said.

"What did they do," Holt asked.

"They had the nerve to exist," Tiffany answered before turning to Hob. "Is everything okay?"

"*Ja, ganz gut.* These are friends," Hob said. "I am just checking, are they comfortable?"

"They're nervous, which is to be expected, but overall, yes," she said.

"We will not disturb them any longer," Hob said, ushering us out the door. "We remove those in danger, *und* if necessary protect ourselves. That is where my dust has gone."

CHAPTER·9

WE SPENT MOST OF the next week looking for leads and coming up with nothing. There weren't any more attacks and things seemed to be settling down. At least there weren't attacks that I heard about. The Queen might be keeping an incident secret—it wouldn't surprise me. Regardless, I didn't believe for a second someone had gone to all that trouble only to kill a couple of the Queen's daughters. It was a matter of time before more demons showed up. Having exhausted all other options, I was grasping at straws. I had one straw left, but I didn't want to go anywhere near it.

I pulled up to the house and honked the horn. The blinds on his window raised a moment later and Holt held a finger up in the international symbol of "give me a minute." I put the truck in park and waited. A few minutes later he came out wearing a Hawaiian shirt. It had a black base with leaves all over it. Blue and red flowers dotted the foliage, with multicolored parrots facing every direction filling in the gaps. It almost hurt to look at. He jogged up to the truck and hopped in.

"What are you wearing, and more importantly, why?" I asked.

He looked hopeful. "You like it?"

I put the truck in reverse and backed out onto the road. "I didn't say that."

"I was watching this documentary and it was talking about ornamentation with birds. They glued decorations on birds and the ones that were fancy attracted more mates. This one bird got just a plain stick on a plastic circle glued to its head and boom, mating advantage. I figured a little something extra to get noticed wouldn't hurt."

"Martina's still not talking to you?" I asked.

He shook his head. "Not a word since the incident."

"You did claw her right in the face."

"Under demon mind control! It's healed up, you can't even tell it happened," he protested.

"It doesn't mean it didn't leave a scar," I said. "Maybe you should just give her a little time."

"Like you're doing with Naylet?" he asked.

"That's different. The two of you just started talking. Naylet and I were together for over 150 years. Then her memory was wiped and now she apparently just found out I exist."

He smirked. "That's your own fault."

"She needed security and stability while she recovered. I did what I thought was right," I said.

"She could use your support or something," he said. "Chicks love that stuff."

He could have been right. The truth was, I didn't know how to handle it. There wasn't an amnesia expert in my back pocket I could talk to about it. I must have been lost in thought for a while because Holt started talking again.

"So where are we going?" he asked.

"Bear Book Market," I said. "It's a long shot."

He scoffed. "You think the guy in the bookstore is summoning demons?"

"No, I think he might be able to give me a lead."

"Oh yeah, why's that?" he asked.

I sighed, turned on my blinker and pulled into the turn lane for 400 North. "Have you been in the bookstore?"

"Just once, when you abandoned me in town last week," he said. "I stopped in to ask when you left."

"And what could you tell about the guy running the store?" I asked.

"Clay? He's all right, I guess," Holt said. "A little weird, maybe. We talked for a few minutes and got on the subject of blood somehow. He said he would give me five hundred dollars for a pint of blood. Who jokes like that?"

I rested an elbow on the door and rubbed my forehead. "He wasn't joking."

"What? He'd really give me five hundred for a pint?"

"I'm sure he would, but you'd be getting ripped off."

"Really? What do you think he would pay?" Holt asked.

I shrugged. "I can't say for certain, but I would expect at least five grand."

"Five thousand dollars for a pint of blood," Holt mumbled, looking out the window. "Huh."

"Don't get any ideas. Did you notice how he smelled?"

"Under the cologne?" Holt asked. "I noticed it, but I'm not familiar with it."

"He's a werebat," I said, throwing him a quick glance. "Remember the scent and don't ever turn your back on them."

"Is Clay really all that scary?" Holt asked.

"He may not look it, but he's dangerous. What do you know about the bats?"

"Not much. I don't think I've ever seen one before," he said.

"You probably have and didn't know it," I said. "They hardly change out of their human form. There's some speculation about it, but I think it's because they have wings in krasis. I don't see wings being as useful if there's trouble, unless you're trying to escape. The end result is that they blend in better with humans than anyone else."

"Do they really drink blood?" Holt asked.

"They don't live off it," I said. "They eat the same as anyone else, but they have the ability to pull power from the blood. The stronger the host, the stronger they get from it. The effect's temporary, but if you ever find yourself fighting a bat and they get their teeth into you just run. That's why you never turn your back on them."

Holt chuckled. "Come on, they can't be that bad."

"You can take my word for it, they are," I said. "If a werebat bites you, run, wait about twelve hours, and then find it and cut its head off, first thing."

We made it to Dahlonega just before sundown. I parked around the corner from the Bear Book Market, and Holt and I walked over. We found Clay standing outside, smoking a cigarette.

He smiled when he saw me. "Look who it is. Returning to the scene of the crime?"

"What's he talking about?" Holt asked.

"Your buddy's a shoplifter," Clay said, taking a puff from his cigarette. "Maybe I should call the cops."

"Shoplifter, huh?" Holt beamed. "And here I thought you didn't have any hobbies."

I had forgotten about the book in my glovebox. I didn't mean to steal it, and I didn't have a problem paying for it, but I would rather Holt not found out about it. Something told me he wasn't going to let me forget about it anytime soon.

"We both know you ain't callin' the cops," I said. "Don't be overdramatic."

Clay took a long drag from his cigarette and tossed the butt into the gutter. "If it was just me, I'd let it go, but I'm part of a community and it's my civic duty to report criminals."

"Look, I'll pay for the book."

"Oh, that we agree on. Come inside, gentlemen," Clay said, crossing the sidewalk and pulling the door open.

He held it for us as Holt and I walked inside. Clay took a seat behind the desk. I took a sawbuck out of my pocket and tossed it on the desk in front of him.

He eyed the twenty-dollar bill, but didn't pick it up. "That's not enough."

"The sticker on the book said eight dollars," I said.

"Sure, that was the price to buy it," Clay said. "You took it. We have to consider fair compensation. We have rental fees for the week you've kept it plus purchase price, plus damages both to my business and mental health."

"Mental health?" I questioned.

"I moved here under the impression that Dahlonega was a quiet mountain town, a safe place to do business. Here I haven't been in business but a few weeks before I'm robbed. I've been up nights, not sleeping. I'm thinking of getting a security system. I've experienced a great deal of mental anguish," he said calmly.

"I have no doubt you've been up nights, not that it has anything to do with me," I said. "I know what you are, and I know you don't really care about these books. They're just a cover for what you've really got going on. So let's cut the crap."

"Right to the point . . . a good trait for Keepers to have," he said.

"You know who we are?" Holt asked.

Clay gave him a smile. "You think you're the only one with a nose? Or that I would set up shop here without doing my research? An otter and a dog sticking their nose in everyone's business, who else could it be? I'm honestly surprised it took you this long to come by."

"Tell me what you're really doing here," I said. "Behind the books."

"Last time you were in the shop, I believe you were inquiring about Ichor? I may be able to get you some," Clay said. "Honestly, I thought Keepers would prefer something a little more natural . . . Weed maybe?"

"You can get us weed?" Holt asked.

I shot him a look.

"Not that I want any," Holt clarified.

"Sure, I can get all kind of things for my friends," Clay said. "And we are going to be friends, aren't we?"

I scratched my chin, thinking how to steer the conversation in the direction I wanted it to go. "What about information?"

"Everything's for sale. Except the heater. My landlord still hasn't turned the heat on in the building," Clay said, pointing to a rickety old heater a few feet away.

"What about dust?" I asked.

Clay tapped his fingers on the desk. "If you need dust, I may be able to locate some for you."

"Did you hear about the attack on the Southern Outpost?" I asked.

"I heard you got shot up," he said. "That's the day you decided to walk off with my merchandise, if I'm not mistaken."

"I've got bigger problems that anything you got going on here. I'm trying to figure out who orchestrated the attack. I'm looking for an elf that's been buying dust. Have you had any customers that fit that description?"

Clay gave me a smile. "Oh no, we've established you're the kind to run off. You're going to have to prepay."

"How much?" I asked.

He opened the drawer in his desk and pulled out an empty vial. "I'll tell you everything I know for one vial."

I shook my head. "Cash. I'm not giving you blood."

"That's the price of information," he said, waving the vial.

"Come on," I said. "You can take cash."

"You think you're some kinda Jedi, with the mind tricks?" Clay asked. "If you want the info, it costs blood."

I sighed. "Have you ever had Keeper blood?"

Clay leaned forward over his desk, with hunger in his eyes. "No, but I'm dying to try it."

I stared at him for a minute, thinking it over. Giving a werebat my blood wasn't something I planned to do, and definitely not an entire vial of it. It was too dangerous. If Clay drank it all at once, he'd be more trouble than Holt and I could handle. If he didn't hoard it all for himself he could sell it off a little here and there. Any werebat that got their hands on it would be hard to handle. There's no telling who would be hurt by it. Even though the effects only last for a short time it's still more risk than I was willing to take.

"Come on," he said, breaking the silence. "I'll even forget about that misunderstanding with the book."

"I'll give you one drop," I said. "I can't let you have enough to keep laying around."

Clay squinted at me, considering my offer. "Deal."

He opened the drawer again and brought out the kind of finger stick used in diabetes tests. He placed it on the desk in front of me.

I picked it up. "Where am I putting the drop?"

"Right in the pie hole," Clay said, pointing toward his mouth. "I want my first taste fresh."

"Open up, buttercup," I said, giving my finger a flurry of sticks, just to make sure I could get a drop out before I healed.

Clay tilted his head back as I raised my finger over his mouth, squeezing the end of it with my other hand to push the blood out. A drop formed on the end of my finger. The anticipation began to show in Clay's eyes. They widened and bulged to unnatural dimensions. As the drop formed his face began to elongate. Fangs grew out of his teeth and thick dark hair sprouted from his cheeks and chin.

"Jesus," Holt whispered under his breath.

His mouth opened wider and wider, much farther than seemed possible. His tongue grew slender and forked, swirling around in his mouth in anticipation. The blood fell from my finger. His jaws slammed shut around it, the momentum bowing him over and knocking the hat from his head onto the floor. I withdrew my hand and wiped my finger on the inside of my pocket. Clay rubbed the top of his head and began to shake it from side to side. He slammed his hands down on his desk and lifted his head to look at me. His face had returned to normal, mostly. I could see the veins in his neck bulging and his eyes had changed from hazel to a deep, almost blood red. Sweat dotted his forehead.

"You feel that," he said. "It's got a kick."

He stood up from the desk, walking over and leaning against a bookcase. He knocked a few books on the floor and didn't seem to notice.

I gave Holt my "get ready" look. He nodded and took a step away from me to put some distance between us.

"Well?" I asked. "What can you tell me?"

"I had an elf come in that wanted some dust. She lives right here in town," he said.

Finally, we were making some progress. This could be the only solid lead I'd had all week.

"Great," I said. "Who is it and where can I find her."

"I'd love to tell you more, but I just can't remember," he said. "Maybe if I had a little more of that finger candy?"

"We had a deal," I said. "I paid and you owe me."

Clay turned back to me with his tongue over his top teeth, sucking them. His eyes were still deep red. "A drop gets you a drop."

"That's it then?" I asked.

Clay stood breathing slow and heavy. He just smiled.

"Come on, Holt," I said, backing toward the door.

Holt followed my lead. He moved over to the desk, grabbed my twenty, and we left.

CHAPTER • 10

"SO, WHAT NOW?" Holt asked. "We heading to the party?"

I tapped my fingers on the steering wheel of my truck. If Clay was telling the truth and the elf lived in town, I had one other option, but it was a last resort.

"There's one more thing we can try. I know someone who lives in town that would probably know where this elf is," I said. "Assuming Clay was telling the truth."

"Who's that?" Holt asked.

"Her name's Slagtooth. She comes out some nights and prowls around town. If there's an elf around, she'll know it."

"Well then, let's go talk to her," Holt said.

I shook my head. "It's not that simple. We're going to need a lotta meat first."

We drove over to Walmart to pick up some meat. We ended up with just over fifty pounds of pork shoulder. By the time we made it back to downtown Dahlonega, the shops were just closing. The town began to clear as the tourists and locals headed to their cars. I pulled off the square and parked on the southeast side of Hancock Park. This time of night the back streets were deserted and poorly lit, just what I was looking for. The diving bell sat on the edge of the park, ahead of us on the left. It was a large metal box with a point on one end and what looked like a chimney coming out of the top. Back in the gold mining days it was attached to a barge and floated around the Chestatee. They lowered it into the river and pumped all the water out so they could pan the previously inaccessible riverbed.

"So, where's this contact at?" Holt asked.

"She lives in the diving bell," I said, pointing at the large metal box.

"Anything I need to know before we go?"

"Don't show fear, and don't run," I said, opening the door. "And don't get bit."

I grabbed the bags of meat, and we got out of the truck.

We walked up the sidewalk and under the pavilion that had been built to cover the artifact. It had a triangular roof with stone pillars that turned into large wood beams. A few large mechanical pieces of the contraption were mounted close by for inspection along with a few signs explaining the history of the bell. The bell itself was mounted about three feet off the ground on a wooden frame.

I sat down on the stone bench running in a half circle on the opposite side of the pavilion.

"Well? Where is she?" Holt asked.

"Go pound on the bell a few times," I said, starting to open the meat. The plastic covering the meat was thick and tough, and I wished I had a knife, but I managed to get a few of them ripped open.

Holt walked up to the bell, raised a fist, and paused. "What's going to happen?"

"Well, Slagtooth will know we're here," I said.

"And then?"

"And then she'll come out," I answered.

He started to hit the bell again and paused a second time. "What kind of lady is Slagtooth?"

"Oh, she's no lady," I said. "You'll be fine. I'm right over here."

Holt looked from me, sitting fifteen feet away on the bench, to the diving bell and back to me. "You knock and I'll sit over there," he said, moving to take my spot on the bench and jabbing a thumb at the bell.

"Suit yourself," I said, putting the bags of meat on the bench. "Finish opening these up. When she comes out, I want you to give one to her. Only one."

I gave the bell a solid knock. The metal reverberated, rumbling deeply like a drum. The long pipe sticking from the top of the bell had a small porthole, a few inches in diameter, about twelve feet off the ground. I stepped back to get a look at it and after a couple seconds I could hear shuffling from inside the bell. A reptilian eye appeared in the porthole. I gave it a wave. The eye disappeared and a door, disguised as part of the frame the bell sat on, burst open.

A lizard, roughly fifteen feet in length, shot out of the bell. Her body was covered in bony gray scales. She slithered on all fours in between a five-foot-long tubular hatch and an axle with a large gear in the middle. She stopped and eyeballed us with her head poking out from around the hatch. A slender forked tongue over a foot long popped in and out of her mouth. She stood up, stretching about ten feet with her tail trailing behind her and her front claws resting on the hatch. She looked pissed off to me, but I couldn't be sure, I've never known a lizard with a cheerful expression.

"What does the Keeper want?" she asked in a deep rumbling whisper of a voice.

"I need some information," I said, looking up at her. "But before we get into that, I brought you something."

I motioned at Holt to toss her some meat. Slagtooth whipped her head in his direction and with the sight of meat and the smell of blood her base instincts took over. She charged a few steps in his direction. Holt tossed the meat in the air and fell back over the stone bench. Slagtooth snatched the meat out of the air and swallowed it in a single gulp. Holt took off through the bushes, at least he tried to. The movement caught Slagtooth's attention and she pounced.

Holt grabbed her throat with one hand to keep her from biting him and changed to krasis. With the Doberman features and the horrendous shirt he looked like one of the old Egyptian gods on a Hawaiian vacation. He bit her neck, sinking his long teeth in between her scales. While he had her distracted, I grabbed the bags of meat. Holt was able to keep her from biting him. She had him pinned and resorted to the claws on her hind legs. She brought them up and tore them into Holt's belly.

"That's enough," I shouted, pulling her off him by the tail.

Hissing, she reeled around on me. I dropped her tail and punched her in the face. She fell against the stone bench before getting back to her feet and scurried behind one of the pillars.

"Stop," I commanded, holding up a finger.

Holt groaned, and got up, clutching his abdomen. Blood soaked through his tattered shirt. I could see traces of his intestines poking from around his fingers. She had torn him up good and he was going to need a few minutes to recover.

"We just came for some information, not to fight," I said.

"Why would Slagtooth tell you anything?"

"I brought you a snack," I said, shaking the bags of pork.

She peeked from around the pillar, but didn't come out.

"How about if I bring you some more at the beginning of spring when you wake up from hibernation?" I asked.

She eased her way out from behind the pillar. I pulled the meat out of the bags and stacked it on the ground in a big pile. I stepped to the side and held a hand, offering it to her. She charged and attacked them, cramming all fifty pounds into her mouth at once. While she was able to hold it in her mouth at once, she wasn't able to swallow it. She tried to stretch and wiggle her neck to work the meat down. When that didn't work, she moved over to the bench and slammed her mouth onto the corner of the stone, forcing the meat deeper and deeper until large lumps visibly moved down her throat. I noticed blood on her neck where Holt had bitten her.

I waited patiently as this circus of mastication played out. With a hand over his stomach, Holt watched from the safety of bushes. After swallowing the meat, the lizard creature crawled on all fours to the bushes and wiped her mouth on the leaves, pausing for a second for a closer look at Holt. The area looked like something out of a slasher film. Blood was everywhere.

"I was told there's an elf living in town," I said. "I need to find her. Have you smelled any elves around?"

She lowered her head in a posture that reminded me of a cat about to pounce. "Slagtooth didn't eat the elf."

I shook my head. "I'm not accusing you of anything. I just want to know where to find her."

"House on the edge of town," she said, pointing her nose toward the west.

"Okay, that's all I wanted," I said. "Hey, did he hurt you? Let me take a look."

She showed me the place on her neck where Holt had bitten her. She was bleeding, but didn't appear to be seriously injured. I moved my hand slowly, as not to appear threatening, over her injury. When it was in place, I healed her injury. She started making a guttural ticking sound. When her injuries were closed, I ran my hand over her scales. They were smooth and I could feel the power underneath as she moved. She circled around and rubbed up against me. I petted her.

"I'll bring you another snack in spring, okay?" I said softly.

She walked back to the diving bell, pausing for a second to send Holt an icy glare before she disappeared inside, closing the door behind her. I could hear the shuffling as she settled.

"You okay?" I asked when it was quiet.

He groaned. "Is this town full of monsters or what?"

"I wouldn't say *full*," I said. "Need help?"

Holt limped out of the bushes, easing his way to me with one hand on his gut. "I'm all right. She scratched the hell out of me and ruined my shirt."

"She did you a favor."

"But what about Martina?" he asked.

"I think you'd have more luck with a plunger glued to your head," I said. "Seriously though, you don't need gimmicks to get her attention. You did that already when you tried to claw her face off. You just need to let her come around."

He sighed. "And what if she doesn't come around?"

"Then you move on," I replied. "Either way, you can't walk around with bloody clothes. When you're up to it, we'll head to the truck and get you a fresh set."

"I never put new clothes in the car after the last time," he said.

"I'll give you some of mine," I said. "Always make sure to have spare clothes handy."

We went back to the truck and I gave Holt a change of clothes. He was still bloody, but it was dark, and I wasn't planning to be spending time around a lot of people. We walked a few blocks to the edge of town. There were only a couple rows of houses in that direction that the elf could live in. The street bordered woods.

"Let's use our animal forms to sniff around. We can use the woods for cover," I said. "I'll take Hawkins Street and you take Church Street."

We walked into the woods out of sight of the houses. I took the form of an otter and Holt changed into a Doberman. Holt took off down Church Street, zigzagging with his nose to the ground. I headed down the sidewalk of Hawkins, going into yards and onto porches to find our elf. I caught the scent of a number of humans, dogs, cats, squirrels, and even a chipmunk, but no elves.

Holt barked and I abandoned my search to see what he had found. He was sitting in front of a white house on top of a grassy hill. The house looked like it had been built about a hundred years ago. A cozy place that looked like a poster for reminiscing about America's past. The lights were off. I sniffed around a bit and confirmed that there had definitely been an elf here recently. We went back into the woods. I changed back to my human form, and started getting dressed.

"It doesn't look like anyone's home," I said. "Stay in that form and head down to the other end of the street. Find somewhere to keep out of sight. We'll hang out a bit and see if our elf comes back."

Holt barked in recognition and bounded off. I sat on an old brick wall off the edge of the road to wait. It was covered in vines and moss, slowly being reclaimed by the forest. The Tortured Occult's party was probably getting underway. I didn't mind missing it. The T.O. hadn't been the same since Otis's death. They were more crude and vulgar, definitely rougher around the edges. I hadn't realized how tame Otis had kept them. It wasn't the same wholesome bunch of ruffians I was used to. It was an important relationship, however, and Holt was looking forward to the party, so we would go. It would be good for him to blow off some steam.

After waiting close to an hour, a car pulled up to the house. Holt and I closed in. I got there first just as a woman was getting out. She closed the door and turned to see who was walking up her driveway. She reached a hand in a bag she had slung over her shoulder. I didn't know if she was reaching for a gun or dust.

She moved her hand deeper into her bag. Holt came up beside me and growled. She froze. If I hadn't recognized her, I would have charged her. It was the elven woman working with Hob.

"Tiffany?"

She took a step back in a defensive posture. "Are you following me?"

"I'm following a lead that led me to you," I said. "Did you try to buy dust from Clay over at the Bear Book Market?"

"How I spend my time's none of your business," she said.

Holt growled a little louder and took a step toward her.

I put my hands out to look as unthreatening as possible. "We're all friends here."

"No, you're friends with Hob," she corrected. "I don't know you."

"Fair enough. If you don't wanna be friends that's fine with me. I don't have to be friendly. Now answer the question."

I could see her wheels turning as she weighed her options. "Yeah, I talked to him about dust," she said.

"Was that so hard?" I asked. "Let's go."

I took a few steps back. Holt followed. She didn't take her hand out of the bag as we walked backward out of the driveway.

CHAPTER · 11

THE PROPERTY OF Morrison Salvage was fenced, but the gates were rarely closed. We pulled up to find the gate not only closed, but guarded by a bored looking man. He was Latino, a little round around the edges, with a scraggly beard. He wore the black leather kutte common to the Tortured Occult, but this one didn't have any patches on the front. It had a single rocker on the back, reading PROSPECT. I had seen him around, but hadn't spoken to him before. He walked over to the open window of the truck.

"Hey, I'm Obie, this is Holt. We were invited," I said.

He sighed. "I been waitin' forever on you two. Lemme get the gate."

He rolled open the chain link fence blocking the road. He stood by while I pulled through.

"It must suck to be a prospect," Holt mused as we passed. "Always having to do the shit jobs."

I shrugged. "It's like any other initiation. Proving your worth to be part of the group can be a powerful thing. Besides, it's not permanent."

"I'm glad the Keepers don't have something like that," Holt said.

"Don't we?" I asked. "You're kinda like my prospect, if you think about it."

"I think partners is more accurate. Hulk and Thor, you know?"

"Batman and Robin?" I suggested.

"Sure, if I'm Batman," he said. "I'm nobody's sidekick."

The prospect swung the gate closed behind us and started walking to the clubhouse.

I threw a thumb toward the bed of the truck out the window. "Jump in the back, I'll give you a ride."

He did and we pulled up the dirt path to the clubhouse. I parked beside a larger row of motorcycles than I had ever seen at the clubhouse. When we got out, the prospect had already changed to krasis. He had the catlike features and tawny yellow fur with black spots of a jaguar. He jumped out of the back of the truck, carrying the work boots he'd been wearing that wouldn't fit his paws.

The lights on the property were off, including the streetlight. The moon was a waxing crescent, not giving enough light to make walking in krasis an issue, even though we were only three hundred feet from the road. Holt and I kicked off our shoes and left them in the truck after making the change to krasis. We followed the prospect to the back of the building.

I found the party in full swing. There were more people there than I'd expected. Everyone was in krasis. All of the Tortured Occult were in attendance along with the people closest to the club. Holt, Adan, and me as well as a few others. What I didn't expect was an entire other motorcycle club. They looked to be all wolves and coyotes and the back of their kuttes had a dog's head engulfed in flames with a caption: WRETCHED DOGS MC, CHARLOTTE SC.

The only light came from a bonfire in the center of the event. There was a slight chill in the air, not anything that warranted an eight-foot-tall pyre, but I got the impression it was more for ambiance than function. There was a table with an assortment of liquor as well as beer coolers spread out around the party. You could stand anywhere and never be more than a few steps away from booze. Many of the partiers were smoking. Irregular puffs rose up from all around and the air hung heavy with the smell of weed. Empty bottles and cans littered the ground. Whole animals on spits spun on large rotisseries. Bikers would bite pieces directly off the carcasses. Many of the shifters, men and women, weren't wearing clothes, others just wore their kuttes and nothing else. There were a lot of women I didn't recognize. They were all drunk.

"I didn't think you were coming," Tico said.

He was sitting on an overturned five-gallon bucket, with a beer in his hand.

"You would miss me if I weren't here," I replied. "Who are the Wretched Dogs?"

"MC from South Carolina," he said. "They're a bunch of assholes, if you ask me."

He was much too relaxed and downright cheerful to be acting in his official capacity as a bartender. He must have made the list of friends of the club invited, which made sense since he spent so much time with them.

"Do you like anybody?" I asked.

He paused with the bottle in front of his mouth. "I like Naylet. She's a good person, much too good for you," he said, and threw his head back and finished off the beer and tossed the bottle on the ground. "I'm going to get another. You want one?"

I didn't really want one, but this was the best we had gotten along in as long as I could remember. So if he wanted to make a peace offering, I would take it.

"Sure," I said.

He walked toward a cooler. "Then get it yourself."

"What'd you do to him?" Holt asked.

"Why the hell is it that I had to do something to him? Did it ever occur to you, the guy's just a jerk?"

"Nah," Holt answered. "You probably did something. I'm going to get a drink."

Holt walked off toward the table of liquor. A sudden burst of laughter from behind me caught my attention. I turned around to find Cotton, Lug Nut, and Ginsu who were standing with some of the Wretched Dogs. Ginsu, a red wolf, and one of the most colorful members of the T.O., noticed me. He was called Ginsu because he had a thing for knives and was guaranteed to have at least three on him at any given time. The only one I could see was a large Bowie on his belt.

"Obie," Ginsu said. "You gotta hear this. What do you call an elf from France?"

I grinned and shook my head.

"A tree frog." He cackled. "Get it? Tree frog!"

It wasn't the best joke I had ever heard and I was sure the Queen wouldn't find the humor in it. I give him a polite smile and nod.

"What? You think you can do better?" Ginsu asked, the smell of alcohol heavy on his breath.

"No, it's pretty good," I answered.

He didn't seem satisfied and stumbled as he took a step forward. "Let's hear it then. Quiet everybody, the comedian here is going to tell us a joke."

The group looked at me, armed with smirks and judgment. I wasn't going to let him show me up.

"Two guys are walking through the woods and come up on a dog licking his balls. The first guy says, 'I wish I could do that.' The second guy says, 'That dog will bite *youuu*!'"

A hearty round of chuckles ran through the group. Lug Nut, Hank's oldest son, who was always quick to laugh, was in the middle of a swig from his beer and proceeded to spit it out all over Ginsu as he erupted in a fit. That set off the rest of the group into hearty fits of laughter. Lug Nut bent forward, slapping his leg as the remainder of the beer ran freely out of his mouth and nose and onto the ground. Ginsu wiped his face with his hands, removing the beer as well as he could from his fur. He didn't find it as funny as the rest of us, who burst out with even louder howls when they saw how sour he was about it. After a few seconds Ginsu started chuckling along with the rest of us.

"All right, pretty good, Obie," he said, shaking the beer off his hands and wiping them on his pants.

As the laughter died down, another sound from the other side of the bonfire overpowered our joviality—pain. Across the yard a fight was taking place. Close to a third of everyone at the party was gathered around watching. Whenever the T.O. had a party they always had a circle for some friendly competition. The rules were simple. A large circle was spray painted on the ground. Two people agree to terms, enter the circle, and fight. It doesn't end until one person leaves the circle, intentionally or not, or is unable to continue. I say the circle was for friendly competition and that's true enough, but things had a way of devolving. Egos get in the way, people start taking liberties with the agreed upon rules, and next thing you know, you end up with exactly what I was looking at now.

Through the legs of the crowd I could see a wolverine had a coyote pinned. I knew the wolverine was Big Ticket; I didn't recognize the coyote, they all look alike to me. B.T. was sinking his teeth into the coyote's soft belly. The coyote yelped in pain before wiggling free and dragging itself away as quickly as it could. B.T. pounced on the defenseless animal again. The coyote was trying to leave and end the fight—that was clear for anyone to see. Unfortunately, it had been maimed and couldn't move well. If its muzzle reached the edge of the orange circle painted on the ground, Big Ticket would stop attacking it. The coyote was learning the hard way what getting into the circle with B.T. meant. He never ran and he didn't accept it from anyone else either. The coyote succumbed to blood loss before it made it to the edge of the circle. Big Ticket changed to krasis, and walked out of the ring, leaving the coyote motionless behind him. It wasn't a huge deal; as a shifter the coyote would heal pretty quickly. I doubted it would forget his run-in with Big Ticket any time soon.

Cotton stepped in close to not be overheard. "B.T.'s been working his way through the Wretched Dogs all night. They haven't given him any real challenge so far."

Cotton was an artic wolf; one of the oldest members of the Tortured Occult. The light of the bonfire dancing on his thick white fur made him look like some kind of werewolf ghost.

"Maybe you should show 'em how it's done."

Cotton shook his head. "I'd rather stay in one piece tonight, besides we both know you're the one he really wants to fight."

"Yeah, I'll pass," I said.

"What's the matter?" one of the Wretched Dogs said. "You scared?"

Ginsu laughed. "Obie ain't scared. He won last time they got in the circle."

"Bullshit," the biker said.

"I saw it with my own eyes," Ginsu said. "Ever since, B.T.'s been wanting a rematch, but Obie hasn't given it to 'im."

The Wretched Dog chugged the rest of his beer, let out a loud belch, and tossed the bottle over his shoulder out into the junkyard. "That's just bad manners."

It was probably nice for Big Ticket to have some fresh competition. He thrived on fighting and dedicated himself to its perfection, making him possibly the most dangerous member of the T.O. He had long black and tan fur in a distinctive pattern. If you knew B.T., you wouldn't mistake him for any other wolverine you had the misfortune to cross paths with. I spotted Hank sitting at a table at the edge of the party. I excused myself and went over, pulling an empty chair beside him. I saw Holt take a bite out of one of the animals on the spits. I didn't think much of it until I noticed that the animal looked . . . different . . . than the others. It had no head or feet. It was just an abdomen and legs. I recognized it as human or maybe an elf.

"What kind of meat is that Holt's eating?" I asked.

"Something the Dogs brought," Hank said.

"I'm just curious."

Hank sighed. "Look, Obie, you're doing that thing again where you ask questions you don't really want the answers to. I made sure that everything we got here was sustainably sourced."

His answer confirmed it was some kind of humanoid. I didn't know if sustainably sourced meant they were someone bad or just that no one would miss them. Either way, I decided not to push it.

"Nice party. It smells like a music festival," I said. "I'm surprised to see another club here. You aren't thinking of taking them on the run tomorrow, are you?"

Hank drank straight from a bottle of Jack Daniels. "So what if I am?"

"We both know she wouldn't like it," I said. "If you're asking me, I don't think any of you should go."

"It doesn't matter what she likes, she agreed to it." Hank wiped his mouth on his forearm. "You think she's gonna try something?"

"You know how the Queen is. With the attack on the Southern Outpost, you should probably keep your distance till things cool off."

He ran a hand over the tuft of black fur on the end of his chin that resembled a goatee. "You're probably right, but it's too late to back out now. The club wants to go, so we'll go."

"What's it going to take to change your mind?"

"It's not just my mind you have to change." Hank held a hand out to the club enjoying the party. "You have to change enough of their minds to win a vote."

A rather curvy wereraccoon sat in Hank's lap under his outstretched arm. She, like many of the other ladies at the party, wasn't wearing any clothes and her eyes were glazed from alcohol or possibly something stronger. He rested his hand on her hip and took another swig from the bottle. I had never seen her before. She may have come with the Wretched Dogs. I looked from the girl to Hank and back to the girl.

Hank suddenly looked as if he had offended me. "Sorry, Obie, did you want one? You can have this one."

"No no," I said.

Hank took the girl's hand and directed her to my lap. She wrapped one arm around my neck and began to nuzzle my neck. Her other hand rested on my chest.

"I don't—" I said before Hank interrupted me.

"Okay, I get it," he said. "She's made a couple rounds already. I can get you a fresh one."

I shook my head. "It's not that. I didn't come here looking for companionship."

My body didn't get the memo that my mind was sending. I was suddenly aware of how long it had been since I had had some kind of intimate contact. My heart pumped a little faster with a familiar tingle welling up in my groin from her touch.

"Why the hell didn't you tell me?" Holt asked, walking up to where we were sitting.

"Tell you what?"

"That you beat Big Ticket," Holt said. "Everybody's talking about it."

I shrugged. "It never came up."

"I'm going to fight him. You got some advice? Weaknesses or anything like that?" Holt asked.

"Yeah, I got some advice for you," I said. "Don't fight B.T."

Holt chuckled. "Aw, come on, we're Keepers. He can't be that tough."

Hank leaned forward. "How about a bet? If he can beat B.T. in the circle, I'll try to get the run canceled."

"Hold on," Holt said. "Why do you want to cancel the run?"

I sighed. "I just don't think it's safe."

"No bet then?" Hank asked with a smirk. "It's the only way you have a chance to get the run canceled."

I looked up at Holt. "You shouldn't fight B.T."

He looked a little hurt. "You don't think I can win, do you?"

"I didn't say that."

"You got a bet, Hank," Holt said, turning and walking toward the circle.

I jumped from my seat, put the girl down as quickly and gently as I could, and went after him. "You don't have to do this."

"I'm going to show you I can win." Holt spotted Big Ticket, pointed a finger at him, and shouted, "I got next."

B.T. gave us a nod and walked over to the circle. He still had bites and scratches from his last fight that weren't fully healed, but they didn't seem to bother him.

I grabbed Holt's arm to get his attention. "Listen, I believe you can win, but you're going to have the fight of your life. He doesn't play and he isn't going to go easy on you. You have to go in hard, get the upper hand, and don't let up until he's unconscious. If you give him an inch or make a mistake, you lose."

He pulled free of my grip. "Relax, I got it under control."

I didn't get the impression he was taking what I was telling him seriously. I could see Big Ticket in the circle. As Holt continued to back toward it, Big

Ticket moved forward. The match would start as soon as they were both in the circle.

I pointed behind Holt and shouted, "Pay attention."

Holt held up his hands and unknowingly backed into the circle. "Don't worry so—"

Big Ticket popped up behind him and sank his teeth into Holt's right shoulder. Holt was pulled to the ground and the crowd cheered and closed in, blocking my view.

I put my hands on my hips and lowered my head. I knew Holt wasn't going to be able to recover from a start that bad. I walked back to my seat beside Hank.

Hank took a swig from the bottle. "Are you and Holt still joining us tomorrow?"

"We'll be there. In spite of Holt taking your stupid bet, he is looking forward to the run. I think it will be good for him to get out and experience some pack life. I'm not planning on running with you, my legs are too short for me to keep up with a bunch of bears and wolves. If you have a pack swim give me a call."

"You could always run in krasis," he offered. "That's what Skinny Pete does. He wouldn't be able to keep up with us as a rat either."

I looked around the yard at the Tortured Occult and Wretched Dogs drinking, laughing, and cheering on Big Ticket as he mangled Holt, all with a feeling of real comradery. Maybe Holt wasn't the only one who could benefit from some community. I had been lonely without Naylet around; being a Keeper can be isolating, even with a partner.

"What the hell," I said.

After a minute, Big Ticket came out through the crowd. His fur was stained with fresh blood that ran from his mouth to his knees. He must have really done a number on Holt. He walked over to where we were sitting.

"That was fun," he said. "You feeling up to a match?"

I shook my head. "Not tonight."

B.T. leaned forward and looked me in the eye to emphasize his words. "I'm going to get my rematch."

The party wound down, with bikers disappearing or passing out in random places around the yard. I eventually found myself not really feeling like dealing with drunken bikers so I went to my truck. I opened the windows, pulled a book out of the glovebox, and lay down with my feet sticking out the passenger side. I made it through a few chapters of *Henderson the Rain King* before I was interrupted.

"Where'd you get off to?"

I lowered my book and parted my feet to see Holt through the window, wearing a Tortured Occult T-shirt. "I got a little tired of the party. What are you wearing?"

He ran a hand over the shirt. "Yeah, Big Ticket was hard on your other one. I didn't want to take another change of clothes from you after Slagtooth. I'm going to have to keep more clothes on hand."

"Probably a good idea," I said, sitting up and sliding over into the driver's seat. "Is the party over?"

"I don't know if this run's going to happen. There's still a couple that haven't passed out yet, but most of them are unconscious. I don't see them getting up for more partying anytime soon."

I started the truck. "They'll be there. Hop in, we'll stop on the way and get you some new clothes. I don't want to show up with you wearing that shirt."

"Where are we going?" Holt asked.

"The Elven Nation. I want to get there early and check things out. I got a bad feeling."

CHAPTER 12

ABOUT THIRTY MINUTES before the run was scheduled to start, we pulled into a camping area deep inside the Elven Nation. It was just a dirt circle in the middle of the woods with no houses for miles. It spanned roughly fifty feet in diameter and still had the blackened remains of a campfire in the center. Here, the Tortured Occult could party to their hearts' content without worrying about being disturbed. The Queen's SUV and two escort trucks were parked to the right. There was a gray van I hadn't seen before. There was a slight slant of the land here and the Queen has opted to park on the high side. No surprise she took the high ground. I pulled in beside the closest truck and turned the engine off. Harlan got out of the front seat of the SUV and slung a satchel over his shoulder before opening the back door. I expected the Queen, but Isabelle slid out instead and shouldered her rifle.

"That's a good sign. The Queen wouldn't bring Isabelle if she was going to start trouble," Holt said.

I rolled down my window as the pair came to greet us. "You don't know that."

"Mother would like to speak to you," Isabelle said with authority.

"I'll be right there."

The princess was possibly the only person in the Elven Nation that would, or could, speak so informally about the Queen. The two of them walked back to the SUV.

I rolled up the window so Holt and I could have some privacy. "While I'm talking to the Queen, do me a favor and look around the area a little."

"What am I looking for?"

I shrugged. "Elves hiding in the bushes? Anything out of place. I don't want any surprises."

"Do you really think she's gonna try something?" he asked.

I opened my door. "Do you really think she isn't?"

We got out of the truck. Holt stripped down and changed into a Doberman; I walked over to the SUV. Four elves armed with rifles got out of the vehicles. The closest stepped forward and held a hand out to stop me. I heard the crunching of leaves and looked back to see Holt bounding off into the woods. The Queen got out of her SUV.

"Where's he going?" she asked.

She was dressed as usual: Black combat boots, jeans, a flannel shirt, and two chrome revolvers hanging from a leather belt that sagged from one hip.

"Just stretching his legs," I said. "He's excited about the run."

She crossed her arms. "I wasn't aware you would be joining them."

"I wasn't going to, but I got talked into it last minute."

She motioned for me to join her as she stepped away from her guards. "What have you found out about the attack?"

"I've been working on it, but haven't come up with anything."

She didn't look pleased. "You don't have a lead?"

I shook my head. "Well, no. I've been trying to track the dust. It would take a lot for an attack like that, but I haven't been able to find anyone able to pull it off."

She scowled at me. "Then how are you getting closer?"

"I ruled out some people. I've got a growing list of who it isn't."

"Your attention should be focused on the Tortured Occult. You will find all the connections you need there, if you bother to look."

"I was with them last night and spoke to Hank," I replied.

"As a friend or a suspect?"

I sighed. "Whatever's going on, I am confident Hank isn't part of it."

"You will do a thorough investigation of all members of the Tortured Occult," she commanded.

I was afraid she might try to pull something like this. I don't answer or take orders from her. I was hoping I didn't have to remind her.

"I will find whoever is responsible," I said. "These things take time; they aren't always what they seem on the surface. It's only been a week."

"Exactly, it's been a week. I expect faster results," she said.

I shrugged. "Well, I don't work for you."

I was a little concerned how she would take that and I wasn't alone. The elves within earshot exchanged some sideways glances. I caught the slightest raise of her lip. Expressed completely it would have been a scowl. She was very good at hiding her emotions normally. I wondered if she wasn't trying to hide it or if she was so pissed it slipped through.

"You refuse to take my orders, but you take my help when it suits you," she said. "Have you forgotten that you're in my debt?"

"I have tried to work that out and you refuse anything reasonable," I said. "I think you just want something to hold over my head."

I could hear the rumble of motorcycles coming down the road. They would be here in less than a minute.

"This is your last chance."

"Nothing has changed in the past three seconds."

She walked back to the SUV. "So be it."

Holt came bounding out of the woods and changed to krasis as the motorcycles rolled in. Hank was leading with the Wretched Dogs and the Tortured Occult in two rows behind him. They pulled in. With a precision that comes from practice they arranged the bikes in a neat row opposite the elves. The procession was followed by a large moving truck that parked off to the side. No doubt the truck carried everything they would need for three days of debauchery. They killed the engines, got off the bikes, and started congregating in the center. Their excitement was evident. Almost everyone was smiling, except for Chisel, and even he seemed less sour than usual.

"Well?" I asked Holt.

"It's all clear."

I was about to join Hank when the Queen stepped behind her SUV and addressed the group. "The attack on the Southern Outpost last week was unlike anything we have seen before. It was a personal attack on my family, taking the lives of two of my daughters. Despite that, we made an agreement and I keep my word," she said, giving me a sour glance. "However, before the run can begin, I need to know what you can tell me about the attack. Who perpetrated it, where they are hiding, and who the accomplices were. If you volunteer this information freely, I will not consider you all accomplices in the attack."

I gave Harlan, who was standing beside the SUV with Isabelle, a questioning glance. He met my gaze, but didn't give any hint at what was happening. I didn't like where this was going. I didn't need Harlan to tell me it was bad, everyone knew it. A mumble rose from the bikers. Chisel walked a few paces off to the right of the group, putting some space between himself and the rest of the pack, his normal scowl returning to his face.

"There's nothing to tell," Hank said. "We didn't have anything to do with the attack and we don't know anything about it."

The Queen's right hand drifted to the butt of her pistol. "You claim to be a friend that wants to work for mutual benefit. Yet, now that we've been attacked, you keep your mouth shut. Let me put this plainly: Someone here knows something about the attack and they are going to come forward."

The only thing I could tell her that might satiate her paranoia was that I had learned Hob was helping sneak magical adepts and dissenters out of the Nation. Since he worked with us, she would probably blame everyone for it and may do more harm than good. I didn't believe her when she said she wouldn't hold it against the group. Besides, I didn't believe Hob had anything to do with the attack. I wasn't going to be responsible for the Queen sending an assault team over to the farm, assuming she knew where it was. I walked over to put myself between the T.O. and the elves, a place I seemed to be in more and more lately.

"There's no reason for this to get out of hand. We're all friends here."

"Ah yes, Obie, friend to all. Do you think they would still consider you a friend if they knew the truth?" the Queen said with a sneer. "This is your last chance. Anyone with information about the attack, come forward now."

Razor stepped up beside me. "Listen, lady. Hank already told you we don't know nothin' and Obie proved himself repeatedly as a friend of the club. I don't care what you think you know."

"What if I told you I had Otis killed at the bridge and your good friend, Obie, not only knew about it, but kept it from you? I wouldn't think that's a very friendly thing to do, would you?"

"Obie?" Hank said.

I could feel all the eyes of the T.O. on me. There was no way I could explain this here, or maybe at all, tensions were too high. I didn't have the chance to try.

"Since you refuse to cooperate, our alliance is over. Hank, as the leader of this . . . club," she said waving a hand dismissively, "I hold you personally responsible."

With lightning fast reflexes, she drew and fanned the hammer of her revolver, firing a number of shots faster than I could count. The bullets screamed past me to my right. She spun the revolver and returned it to its holster like some gunslinger in a spaghetti Western.

I turned to see Hank collapsing to the ground. The club instantly surrounded him. I couldn't see where he was shot or how bad it was.

"Clean up the rabble," the Queen said with a wave of her hand.

The back doors of the van swung open, revealing one of the M134s. A large gun with six rotating barrels and an insane fire rate. This time it was pointed at me and the T.O.

"*Run!*" I shouted as the barrels began to spin.

A four-foot plume of flame burst from the barrel of the gun. Bullets buzzed all around me as the Queen's guard joined in firing their rifles into the crowd. The bullets slammed into the T.O. with the *thwack* of a hammer on a side of beef. The few lucky enough not to be immediately cut down, scattered. Dust and smoke filled the air, blocking my vision. The acidic smell of gunpowder hung heavy. As quickly as it started, the shooting stopped. Everything was silent for a few seconds. A few moans rose from the scattered bodies. Holt and I were the only ones left untouched. Hank lay on his back with Big Ticket and Lug Nut laying on top of him. Holt and I pulled them off. His kutte had fallen open, revealing his blood-soaked shirt. He had two bullet holes in his upper chest and a half moon across his abdomen. The blood seeping out into his white T-shirt made a gruesome looking smiley face. His chest heaved erratically. It didn't look like he was healing on his own and that meant she had used silver bullets. I put a hand over him and began to channel energy into his wounds.

"Wait, what about the silver?" Holt asked.

"He'll bleed to death before silver toxicity kills him," I said.

I didn't heal him all the way, just enough to stop the bleeding and give him a chance to get help. The blood soaking into the shirt stopped and his breathing eased.

"Start healing people," I said. "Big Ticket first."

I stood up and turned to the Queen. "What the hell?"

She smiled at me. "Relax, we didn't use silver, well, not on everyone. This is just a message."

"This is too much," I said, holding my hand out to the carnage. "You crossed the line."

"No, Obie, this is crossing the line." She motioned to the gun and again the barrels started spinning. "Hit the motorcycles."

Holt and I dove to the ground as the gun opened fire a second time. The ground had become muddy from the blood. I looked back to make sure Holt was alright, but found a dismembered hand instead. It had been shredded about halfway up the forearm. I tossed it away. The bikes were hit by what seemed like a solid stream of lead screaming over my head. They exploded from hundreds of impacts that compounded into complete destruction. Pieces of the motorcycles were scattered, tires exploded, and some burst into flames when the gas tanks were ruptured. After the line of bikes had been demolished the firing stopped.

I stood. Blood and mud clung to my clothes and skin. "You know it's war now," I said. "They aren't going to let this go."

The Queen motioned the air with her index finger. The elves broke ranks and began climbing into the trucks and van. "Obie, when did you become so tedious?"

Harlan had taken Isabelle behind the truck and was peeking out around the side. The Queen started walking for her SUV. I decided enough was enough. Everything I had done with the T.O. and the Elven Nation had been to keep the peace. I could see now there wasn't any peace and wouldn't be with a tyrant in charge. I couldn't look the other way any longer—I wasn't going to let her get away with this.

The elves weren't paying me any mind. Harlan and Isabelle were still behind the truck. I didn't expect any trouble from them. Deciding to take the guards out first before moving on to the Queen. It would be risky. I would probably have to use one of them as a shield to get close enough to kill the Queen. I was about to make my move when a blast of warm air and a familiar sulfuric stench hit me from behind. I looked over my shoulder to see a large portal roughly eight feet in diameter and five feet behind me. I could see the red landscape of the demon world with a large group of demons moving to come through.

CHAPTER·13

I DOVE TO THE GROUND, landing in the blood-soaked ash of the campfire. The elves opened fire as demons poured from the portal. Hounds hit the ground running with athol and winged snakes filling the skies. They seemed to be ignoring me, even though I was the closest; the movement and noise from the elves must have distracted them. I was showered with thick, black demon blood before the first one fell just to my left. The elves, the Queen included, fired as fast as they could. The doors to the van had been closed; it took a few seconds for them to get the doors open and the M134 spun back up before they could start firing. When they managed it, the demons coming through the portal were torn apart, raining down in pieces on top of me and the T.O.

I started my change into krasis as a number of athol landed on top of the gray van that held the M134. The demons grabbed hold of the van wherever they could and flapped their wings, lifting the van off the ground. The M134 kept firing as the van was raised, sending bullets into the ground with dirt and mud exploding into the air. The shooting stopped and a couple of the Queen's guards bailed out. They hit the ground running, heading for the Queen's SUV, but were quickly swarmed. The van fell back to the ground. It landed grill first, accordioning in on itself, before falling onto its side.

The portal slammed shut behind me. The elves were fighting a losing battle to keep the demons away as they closed in on the Queen's SUV. Harlan and Isabelle were cut off and ran into the woods. One of the Queen's guards followed them, shooting approaching demons. There was only one guard left covering the Queen as she climbed into the SUV. The SUV roared to life. The Queen either didn't know or didn't care that the guard was standing directly behind her vehicle. The SUV lurched backward, plowing over the guard. It skidded to a stop as the driver shifted gears. A hellhound bit the bumper and tugged at the vehicle. The tires began spinning, throwing waves of dirt up as the tires struggled to gain traction. After a quick tug of war the bumper broke free of the vehicle. The Queen sped off with a trail of demons chasing after her. One of the survivors hung out the back window, firing at their pursuers. They disappeared down the dirt road into a giant dust cloud with the sounds of gunfire fading into the distance.

When the dust settled, I surveyed the area. Harlan and Isabelle were gone. The air was heavy with the smell of smoke and blood. There were still demons around that hadn't chased the Queen. A few hounds sniffed around the trucks or chewed on the corpses of the Queen's Guard. An athol swooped out of the sky and grabbed the lifeless body of one of the bikers off the ground. It happened so quickly I couldn't tell who it was, but if he were still alive there was no saving him now. I would have expected the demons to attack right away. After all, the Tortured Occult were easy pickin's. Some of the T.O. were starting to wake up, but it would take time before they would be able to defend themselves. Unarmed and in the open, I wouldn't be able to protect them, even with Holt's help. I had a feeling it was just a matter of time before the demons that chased the Queen returned and then we'd really be in trouble.

Holt had finished healing B.T. and Lug Nut, and was moving on to two more. The two bikers changed to krasis and stood up slowly beside me.

"What are they doing?" Lug Nut whispered.

I raised a hand over my mouth to mute the sound of my voice. "Eating. When they realize we're here, they'll come after us."

"What do we do?" Big Ticket asked.

"Hank's been shot with silver," I said. We needed to get him to a doctor quick. The problem was, we couldn't get him into the truck or start it without attracting their attention. "We're gonna have to fight 'em."

Holt had just finished healing Ginsu and a Wretched Dog I didn't know. That gave us six people to three hounds. That would work, assuming the athol flying around didn't join in.

"Groups of two," I whispered.

I moved as quietly as I could, taking care to step over the recovering bikers and demon bodies the elves had shot down. It was much easier to walk once we were clear of the bodies, not just because of the obstacles, but because the ground wasn't a soppy mess. Everyone paired off and we charged the demons. We hadn't made it a few steps before the closest hound was aware of us. It turned and screeched, alerting the others to our presence. They charged us back, meeting somewhere in the middle. I was the first to a hellhound. It lurched at me and I dodged to the left, moving past it, and grabbing one of its back legs. I pulled, making it twist around to try to bite me. That gave Holt the opportunity to jump on its back and wrap his arms around its neck. It wasn't too difficult for the two of us to flip it on its back. With the softer underbelly exposed, I made quick work of the beast. While Holt held it in place as it bled out, I looked over to see Big Ticket wrestling with the second demon. He had bit it on the side of the throat and the hound screeched in pain as he literally tore it to pieces bit by bit. It would take him a minute to finish it off, but the hound seemed more interested in escaping than fighting. Lug Nut stood watching, clear of the melee, but ready to engage if needed. Behind him Ginsu and the Wretched Dog didn't have it so well.

The hellhound had Ginsu pinned with his arm in the demon's mouth. I knew from firsthand experience that Ginsu's arm would be broken. If we didn't get the hound off of him soon, he might lose it all together. The Wretched Dog punched at the hound as it shook Ginsu. The beast didn't seem to notice. I spotted Ginsu's Bowie knife on the ground. I ran over, picked up the knife and drove it into the neck of the hound. It stopped moving. I twisted the knife. The demon fell dead on top of Ginsu.

"Get Hank loaded in that cargo truck. We need to get him help ASAP," I said, pulling Ginsu from under the hound.

Ginsu pulled his Bowie from the neck of the hound while Lug Nut headed for the van. The rest of the bikers went to get Hank.

Holt started to go with them, but I grabbed his arm. "I'm going to go after Harlan and Isabelle. Help anyone whose life depends on it, but don't heal everybody. Some of them might be pissed at us and we're already outnumbered. We need things to calm down."

"Pissed at you, you mean," Holt said.

"Same thing."

Holt smiled. "Be careful."

I walked to the place Harlan had been standing with Isabelle during the attack. I easily located their trail leading off into the woods and followed it as fast as I could. Harlan's tracks led in a straight direction through the woods, never turning or shuffling steps, a man with a purpose. Isabelle's tracks weren't as certain. I found multiple places where she stopped and looked back toward the battle. Each time Harlan had pulled her along, leaving lines in the leaves and scuffs in the dirt where he had dragged her. I caught up to them about half a mile into the woods. The guard following them was more erratic in her movements. She moved ahead quickly, then turned back and waited before moving again. I heard shots ahead to my right and took off at a full sprint.

I spotted the elves through the trees. One athol lay motionless on the ground. A second demon wrestled with the guard. She held it back with the rifle, holding it between them to keep enough distance to keep from getting bit. Using it as a shield meant she was unable to bring it to bear on the demon. Isabelle stood between Harlan and an oak tree. Not much protection for her, but the best to be found in the forest.

I charged, grabbed the demon by the head, and pulled it back to the point where it was facing the sky. That left its neck exposed. With my free hand I sank my claws into its throat and squeezed. Thick dark blood ran around my fingers as the beast began to choke on its own blood. I gave it a quick jerk, ripping a handful of flesh away. I pushed the demon, still clinging to life, to my left and tossed the bit of neck to my right. The guard stood up and brought her rifle up in my direction. With a fluid motion I grabbed the barrel and redirected it to my right; she fired two shots that left my ears ringing. I gave the rifle a quick tug. The elf stumbled toward me and I sent a right cross to her face. She collapsed, leaving me holding her rifle by the barrel.

I heard a loud pop followed by a pressure in my gut and pain. I looked up to see Isabelle pointing her rifle at me. Whips of smoke drifted from the barrel. She started to work the bolt to chamber another round when Harlan grabbed the gun and pulled it out of her hands. He put himself between us and held a hand up to me in a defensive posture. The bullet had passed through the soft tissue in my abdomen. I was glad it hadn't hit any bones; those small calibers tended to bounce around inside if they contact bone.

"Relax," I said. "Just a flesh wound. Come on, we need to get you guys out of here."

"Don't shoot him again," Harlan said, handing the rifle back to Isabelle. He pulled me aside for a private word. "I can't go back. I won't."

I shook my head. "I didn't say go back. I said get out of here. There's a bunch of demons that are probably going to find their way back here in a few minutes, not to mention about twenty-five bikers that would love to get their hands on some elves right about now. It's not safe here for any of us."

"I'm going to be straight with you, Obie. I intend to take Isabelle away from the Queen. I won't let her grow up being indoctrinated into her beliefs," Harlan said. "If you aren't going to help us get away, then just leave us alone."

"After this, I'm done with the Queen," I said. "If you don't want to go back I'm not going to make you. I got a friend that doesn't live too far from here. We can stay there while things calm down."

"Okay," Harlan agreed.

I slung the guard over one shoulder and we started walking back toward the campsite.

CHAPTER·14

THE VAN, ALONG with Hank, Lug Nut, and Big Ticket, was gone when we made it back. Ginsu and Martina were sorting the victims of the Queen's attack into rows. No doubt Holt couldn't help himself and had healed her. A number of the bikers had regained consciousness, but not function. A few lay where they had fallen, ignored. They must be the ones that didn't make it. I hustled to my truck to get Isabelle and Harlan inside. I didn't want them exposed to the after-math of their mother's work. It had been parked to the side out of the way of the gunfire and with no one around it to attract the demon's attention it had made it through the attack without taking any damage. Holt and Ginsu came over when they saw us come out of the woods. Martina stayed behind and tended to the injured.

"You just couldn't help yourself, could ya?" I asked.

Holt shrugged. "We needed one more."

I opened the door for Isabelle and helped her into the back of the truck. "How is everyone?"

"Razor and a couple others are dead. The guns ripped 'em apart," Ginsu said. "Did you set us up?"

"I had nothing to do with this."

"You're a damn liar," Chisel yelled from the line of wounded. "I'm going to gut you like the traitor you are."

He tried to get up, but couldn't make it to his feet. The gaping wounds in his belly hadn't healed. I didn't think he would be gutting anyone in the immediate future. It wouldn't take him too long to heal, though, and I preferred to be gone by then. I'm sure many of the bikers were none too happy with me, but I still had the problem of stray demons running around. If Holt and I left, the club wouldn't be able to defend themselves from that many with only two in fighting shape.

"Here's a peace offering," I said, tossing the guard onto the ground.

Chisel rolled onto his back and grunted, "Shove it up your ass."

I heard the thumping of paws on the ground and turned to see a mass of hellhounds running in our direction. There were maybe nine or ten of them, enough to be a real problem. Considering we had four people able to fight and many more to defend. I found myself wishing for a weapon. I was still holding the guard's rifle, which was better than nothing. I didn't know how many rounds were left. I decided to wait to shoot until they were closer, since I wasn't any kind of crack shot. Ginsu pulled his Bowie knife and gave another blade, pulled from concealment on his belt, to Holt. Martina had her own knife in her boot.

"Get in the truck and stay quiet until this is over," I yelled to Harlan.

I raised the rifle and waited for the pack to come close enough so I wouldn't miss. It took everything I had not to start shooting. I moved my finger to the trigger. The pack slowed and then stopped fifty yards away. I lowered my rifle and exchanged confused looks with everyone. A portal formed beside them on the road. The demons slowed and milled around in front of the portal before going through it one by one. The last gave us a screech before disappearing though.

"That's good news," I said.

"What's good news?" Martina asked.

I tossed the rifle into the ground. "Whoever's doing this isn't interested in us. It's not much, but I'll take it. Tell Hank I'll come see him later to explain everything. We need to go for now."

"What if he doesn't make it?" Ginsu asked.

I shrugged and started walking toward the truck. "Let's not worry about that until we have to."

Holt jogged up beside me. "What if the elves come back? They aren't in any condition to defend themselves."

"If the Queen wanted to kill them, they'd all be dead right now. All she had to do was load those guns with silver bullets. You better believe she has a stockpile of them."

"If she didn't want to kill them, then why do all this?" he asked.

"Who knows why she does what she does? Maybe she just likes hurting people," I said. "If you kill all your enemies, you won't have anyone left to fight."

Martina jabbed a finger on my chest. "Hold on, we need help. The bikes are destroyed and we don't even have the van. We need to get everyone out of here."

I looked around at the injured. She was right, they did need help. I told Harlan to get in the truck and took Holt over to the wounded. Cotton and Fisheye seemed to be the best choice for healing based on injuries and how levelheaded they were. Holt and I each healed one.

Cotton opened his eyes. "Well, that was fucked up."

"We gotta go," I said holding a hand out. "We need to get the injured loaded and get them to safety."

Cotton took my hand and got to his feet.

"Loaded in what?" Fisheye asked, rubbing his face.

I pointed to the trucks the elves had left behind. "The Queen left two trucks that don't look damaged. I'll take some in the back of my truck and drop them at the clubhouse. That should be enough room to get everyone out of here."

I kept my distance from Chisel while we loaded everyone in the trucks. By the time we were finished Chisel was recovered enough to start trouble. Instead of doing so, he grumbled to himself. I dropped the bikers at the clubhouse. When we arrived, they were all able to get out of the trucks under their own power, although some were definitely the worse for wear. I didn't want to stick around any longer than I had to with Harlan and Isabelle in the truck. I had to get them somewhere they could lay low. If it were anyone but the Queen's descendants, I would have gone to Hank for help. That wasn't an option now. There was really only one safe place that came to mind.

THE ELVEN NATION was spider-webbed with not only paved roads but a lot of well-maintained forest service roads. Livy lived off one in the same house she had been living in for over 150 years. I turned onto a small trail leading downhill into the woods. After about thirty feet we passed through the magical barrier that kept her home hidden from the outside world.

The house was built into the hillside, using large, jutting boulders as a roof and walls. The gaps were filled with logs with a dirt mixture to seal it all together. My old truck, a '41 Ford, had been smashed into the side of it. Rather than have it towed and crushed, Livy decided to keep it where it was and used it as a garden shed and a raised bed to grow some vegetables and medicinal herbs. I was happy to see the truck get a new life. I pulled up beside it and we all piled out.

"Where are we?" Isabelle asked, slinging her rifle over her right shoulder.

"An old friend of mine lives here. You are going to stay with her for a while."

Her face scrunched up. "I want to go home."

"It's not safe for us to go home right now," Harlan said.

I did my best to look reassuring. "Once things calm down a bit."

"Trust me, you'll love it here," Holt chimed in.

She crossed her arms and pouted. "It looks like a dump."

Livy appeared in the doorway, wearing a light blue dress with long sleeves, the kind that went out of fashion at the turn of the last century.

"Spirits alive," Livy said. "I wasn't expecting company. Y'all come on in out of the chill. I'll make you a little something to eat."

"I'll be in in a sec," I said. "Y'all go ahead."

Holt, Isabelle, and Harlan went inside. I walked around to the side of the house to where Livy kept her firewood stacked. It looked like she was in good shape for the winter, but that's not what I went there for. I wanted some privacy.

"Thera," I said. "I need to talk to you."

Thera appeared, sitting on the woodpile. Her look changed with the seasons, or maybe it was the other way around. Now in autumn, her skin was the smooth gray of a beech tree with fiery red leaves cascading down around her shoulders all the way to the ground. She never wore clothes, but the leaves did a good job of maintaining her modesty.

"You called?"

"I have a problem," I said. "I am hunting someone who is summoning many demons at a time. Today I think there were around twenty in all, so many it was hard to count."

Thera tilted her head to the left. "That is a problem."

"I need a weapon," I continued. "Teeth and claws are great, but don't do much good if we're that outnumbered."

"What did you have in mind?" Thera asked.

I shrugged. "I hadn't thought about it much, to be honest. I liked my old blade, but that was destroyed a few months ago. Something that I can keep concealed, at least in forms besides krasis."

Thera nodded. "This can be done, but there's a cost."

"That's fine," I said. "Can we make something for Holt at the same time?"

"Will you pay the cost for him?" she asked.

"Sure. What do we need?"

"A metalworker," she said. "Call me when you've found one."

She vanished. I couldn't help but feel a little lucky since I had run across a blacksmith a week ago. I wanted to get a jump on this right away. Harlan and Isabelle should be safe here, I just needed to tell them I was leaving. Inside the house I found Livy washing her hands. A trough diverted a stream through the west wall of the kitchen to supply the house with water. Isabelle stood by the door with the rifle still slung over her shoulder. Holt and Harlan sat at the table. Livy dried her hands on a towel she'd knitted and went to sit in her rocking chair.

"It's time for my medicinal," she said, easing onto the chair. She reached for a jug resting on the floor. She took a long swig and, with a puckered mouth, recorked it and held the jug in her lap. She pointed at Isabelle. "Who's this?"

"This is Princess Isabelle," I said.

"Well, I'll be. I've never been visited by a princess before. Come over and let me get a look at you," Livy said, waving a hand.

Isabelle stepped over. "What were you drinking?"

"It's a concoction I made. It's some herbs I foraged from the forest, mixed with some alcohol, and a touch of magic. It's what keeps me young."

With a questioning look, Isabelle put her hands on her hips. "I don't think it's working."

Livy threw her head back and laughed deeply. "Isabelle, do you like to cook?"

"Mother says cooking is servant's work."

"Well, I've never had any servants and I need some help, so set your rifle down and come give us a hand," Livy said.

She set the jug on the floor and rose from the chair, walking slowly to the kitchen. Isabelle looked at Harlan for some kind of reassurance.

"Go on, it will be fun," Harlan said.

She seemed wary as she set the rifle by the door. Livy started a fire in the stove and set the pot of water on top to boil. She reached for a paper bag on a high shelf, barely able to put a finger on it. I got up and pulled it down, handing it to her.

"I had it," she said, taking the bag.

"I never said you didn't."

She gave me a wry smile and passed the bag to Isabelle. "Fill up the pot with these dried apples and keep an eye on them. We need them to be soft. It will take about ten minutes."

Isabelle added a generous amount of the dried apples to the water. Livy and I sat down at the table and watched Isabelle stir and poke at the boiling apples with a wooden spoon.

Eventually Livy broke the silence. "Something serious must have happened if you brought a royal over for a visit. I don't mind the company, of course, but I'm worried what it means. Is there anything I need to know?"

"They just need a safe place to stay. There's nowhere else for them to go," I said.

I filled her in about everything that happened between the Queen, the Tortured Occult, and Harlan. She listened intently. Isabelle could hear us, but didn't show any reaction. She kept her mouth shut and her attention on the pot of simmering apples.

"I'm going to have Holt stay with you just in case there's trouble. There shouldn't be any, though. The Queen doesn't know where they are and the Tortured Occult will be too busy with the elves to worry about her."

Isabelle jabbed the wet spoon in my direction. "Mother will find me, and when she does, you won't be able to keep me here."

I held up my hands defensively. "Isabelle, I don't want you to think or feel like you're a prisoner. That's not it at all. You're here because there's about to be a war and it's not safe for you anywhere else right now. I promise, as soon as it's safe, we will get you home. In the meantime, think of it like a vacation."

She didn't seem to like that answer, but she would come around. There's something magical about living simply and close to the earth, with dirt under your fingernails, in tune with the seasons. I hoped to get Isabelle back to some kind of regular life soon, but with so much uncertainty and instability there's no telling how long it would take.

I turned back to Livy and leaned forward. "I need to run an errand. I'll be back soon."

I PULLED UP TO Yarwor's house a little after sunset. No one was home. A week ago we left Yarwor with his dead wife and child to bury. Looking around the property, I found only one thing to be different. There were two fresh graves on the edge of the yard under a large oak tree. They weren't marked, just mounds of freshly churned earth, roughly body sized.

If Yarwor had been gone a week, he could be anywhere by now. A lot of rumors were circulating about what had happened and what he'd done. Some people dismissed the idea of demon possession, concluding he was some kind of serial killer. Those same people also said the T.O. and I messed up for letting him go. I've never cared for the opinions of the underinformed.

The bad news was, he was gone. The good news was, I had a good chance of finding him. I needed some help. I went back to Livy's. Stepping into her house was like stepping back in time. She used to make apple pocket pies back in the old days, but hadn't in years. They'd been my favorite, before I gave up eating, and the smell of them really sent me back. Everyone sat around the table, with a plate of half eaten pies, playing cards.

"I'm glad you're back, Obie. We need some music for this party. Go get your banjo and play us a little ditty," Livy said, waving to the armoire beside the bed.

"Banjo?" Holt exclaimed.

I shook my head. "Livy, I haven't played in years. You know that."

"Obie, please get your banjo," Holt mocked.

Livy put her cards on the table and looked hard at Holt. "You really are an unlicked cub, ain't ya?"

"Umm . . . I don't know what that means," Holt said.

"At least have the decency to know when you're being insulted," Livy said, before turning back to me. "Do it for me."

I sighed and walked over to the armoire. I found my banjo behind some clothes. When I pulled it out, it had a layer of dust on it, and two of the strings had broken.

I held it up for Livy to see and tried not to sound too pleased when I said, "Couple of the strings broke. I'll have to get some new ones."

"That's too bad. It's your turn, sweetheart," Livy said to Isabelle.

Isabelle drew a card from the deck and looked over the cards in her hand.

"Livy, are you feeling up to a spirit walk?" I asked. "I need some help locating someone."

"Oh, I reckon we can work that out," she said. "Why don't you go build us a fire and I'll be out as soon as we finish this game."

I went outside, assembled a bunch of twigs and sticks, and lit it. I had some larger pieces set aside that I fed into the fire bit by bit. By the time Livy came out, I had a nice little fire popping and crackling away. She brought a foldable camp chair to sit on.

"Tell me who you're looking for," she said as she got settled.

I sat beside her and told her everything I knew about Yarwor.

When I finished, she said, "Why don't you come with me?"

"Come with you? You know I've never done a spirit walk before. I wouldn't even know where to start."

"I can take you," she said, holding a hand out. "Just close your eyes and calm your mind. Focus on your breathing."

I held her hand, closed my eyes, and paid attention to the air moving in and out of my lungs. I sat there for what seemed like twenty minutes, but was probably closer to four. I had concluded that, despite my best efforts, I just wasn't cut out for a spirit journey. A part of me didn't want to admit failure, but there wasn't any other way around it. Maybe if I had a few months to practice I could manage it. I opened my eyes.

It took a moment for my brain to understand what I was seeing. Everything looked the same except overcast with a gray tint, and kind of wavy around the edges as if nothing understood where it ended. Livy stood beside me. I didn't recognize her at first: She looked to be in her mid-twenties. I hadn't met her until she was in her thirties and that was hundreds of years ago.

"Ready?" she asked, flashing me a smile. "Make sure not to let go of my hand or I'll lose you."

She lead me into the woods. I looked back to see that our bodies were still sitting by the fire. We had our eyes closed as if we were meditating.

I pointed with a questioning finger, making sure not to let go of Livy's hand. "Umm . . . How are we here and there?"

"A spirit journey doesn't rely on a physical body, so we'll leave them here," she said. "Don't worry, they'll be fine without us for a few minutes."

I nodded. "But if we aren't in our bodies, why do I see physical forms?"

"You don't. You perceive physical forms because that's what makes sense to you," she said.

"Okay, but you look younger than you did when I met you, so how am I perceiving you in a way that I've never seen you before? Unless the perception is coming from you instead of me?"

She patted my cheek with her hand. "It's best not to use the logical mind to try to figure out the spirit world."

I looked around with new eyes, like I was seeing everything for the first time. In a sense I was. I looked up and noticed a number of black dots moving through the sky.

"What are those?"

"I'll take you up for a closer look," she said with a smile.

We lifted off the ground and took flight, the Earth falling away from under us. As we flew closer, the dots took shape. They were huge, fish-like animals with stubby leathery wings. We stopped, close enough to get a good look, but far enough away to be what I would consider a safe distance.

"What are they?" I asked.

A voice in my head said, "We are the masters of humanity," followed shortly by, "We are the masters of the Earth."

I swiveled my head and somehow knew which one was speaking to me. It was the closest and off to my right, flying through the blackness of space with a sea of stars behind it.

Livy saw my reaction. "What did they say to you?"

"That they are the masters of the Earth and humanity."

She nodded. "They're always sayin' things like that. You wanna see something really special?"

"More special than the masters of humanity?" I asked.

We turned back toward Earth and I saw just how far up we had come. I could see the curvature of Earth. We descended. I held Livy's hand tighter as North America rushed toward us. We flew back to the yard in front of Livy's house where we'd been two minutes before and touched down. I followed Livy into the house. Holt, Harlan, and Isabelle were still sitting at the table. Holt was shuffling the cards. I followed Livy over to the far side of the house where there was an eight-inch diameter hole dug into the floor. I knew she used it for something shaman related, but we'd never discussed it in detail.

"This is where I normally descend into the earth," she said.

I scratched my head. "I don't think we're going to fit."

"It's just right," she said.

Livy took a step forward. I couldn't tell if the hole grew, or we shrank, but suddenly we were moving into it. We descended into a dark tunnel with the occasional twist and turn. After a minute I saw a pinprick of shimmering light in the tunnel ahead. It grew in size and brightness as we approached. I could just start to see movement in the light when we stopped.

"This is the closest I've been," Livy said, staring absently ahead at the light.

"Closest you've been to what?" I asked. "I thought we were looking for Yarwor."

She barely seemed aware of my presence as she looked ahead at the light. "The Mother."

"Thera?" I asked. "That light is Thera?"

She gave my hand a squeeze. "Yes, come on."

Now we walked. The light grew more intense the closer we got to it. By the time we reached the end of the cave, the light was blinding and enormous. More than plain light, it was liquid and churning with formless shadows moving through it, like a ball of lava.

"Isn't it beautiful?" she asked.

I would have found it beautiful, if I was in the headspace to appreciate it. Instead I was overwhelmed by what I was seeing. I had a perception of Thera from the times she had visited me. I looked the same, aside from wearing different clothes, and her appearance looked . . . sort of human, but changing with the seasons. If Livy was correct, and I had no reason to doubt her, then was this Thera's true form? I saw Livy here differently than I usually did, but it wasn't her true form, or was it? Livy started moving forward. I balked, and she ended up pulling me along as we approached the orb. I had a personal relationship with Thera and I knew that while she was beautiful and powerful, she could also be vicious and cold. Not the kind of person you drop in on unannounced.

"I think we're close enough," I said. "We should go back."

Livy continued walking, pulling me along behind her. Her tone was distant when she spoke. "Just a little closer."

I stopped, or tried to, but floated along against my will. I pulled against her, trying to dig my feet into the ground, but it wasn't solid. In the physical world, I could easily overpower Livy, but in this place our roles seemed to be reversed. I was the feeble one.

Livy pulled me up to the ball of light. She reached out her hand and touched the edge. Black streams flowed from where her fingertips touched the light. I saw a shadowy figure with a roughly human outline appear. It moved toward us from inside the ball.

"Livy, let's go back," I said, pulling at her with everything I had.

As the figure approached, I decided I didn't want anything to do with this anymore. I let go of Livy's hand. I was instantly back in my body. I opened my eyes and looked over at Livy. The shimmering light from the fire danced on her face and pushed back the autumn chill. She looked fine. If there was any trouble, I couldn't tell. I lay on my back, peering up at the forest canopy and the numerous stars peeking through the gaps in the leaves that had fallen. We were only thirty feet from her house, but as far into the mountains as we were, there wasn't any light other than the campfire and a bit that spilled from between the boards of the front door of her house. The result was a sky that was filled to the brim with stars. After ten minutes, she spoke.

Her voice was monotone and distant. "The red-eyed orc languishes by goats in the ruins of the city."

The problem with messages from the spirit world was that they were seldom clear. You always got what you were looking for, but it was never as easy as an address or GPS coordinates. I got up and went inside the house, leaving Livy by the campfire alone. If she had found Yarwor, then I doubted I had anything to worry about with her spirit journey. It would take her a bit to come out of her trance.

"Holt, come here a sec," I said, sticking my head in the door.

He stepped outside and closed the door behind him. "Well?"

"We're looking for goats in the ruins of the city," I said. "Whatever that means."

He pulled out his phone and started typing. "Search results don't tell us much. Most promising lead looks like a place in the Yucatan Peninsula."

I scratched at the stubble on my face. "I don't think he got that far. What about Atlanta? Maybe that's the city she's talking about? I hope so anyway."

He went back to typing on his phone. "Atlanta . . . Goats . . . Hmm . . . Atlanta's not exactly in ruins, but let me see what I can find. Looks like we have a string of coffee shops and hello . . . The Goat Farm."

He showed me a picture of industrial-style brick buildings, some of which were in a clear state of disrepair.

"And there are goats there?" I asked.

"Looks that way."

I pulled the phone out of my pocket and called Adan.

"Obie," Adan said. "What did you do?"

I sighed. "It's a long story."

"The club's pissed. I'm on my way back to Atlanta. I don't want to be around when the shooting starts."

"Smart move," I said. "Keep your head down. In the meantime, I have a question. What can you tell me about a place in Atlanta called The Goat Farm?"

"There's not much to tell, really. It's an old industrial complex that worked everything from cotton to mortars over the years. It got taken over by artists. There's a lot of ultras in the area. It's kind of moving back to Thera, if you know what I mean."

"I'm looking for someone I think is there. Is there anything I need to know before I show up?"

"There's a coffee shop at the center of the property that makes a good chai latte," he said. "It's called the Warhorse. You might try asking someone there if you need help."

"All right, thanks Adan. I'll be in touch."

I put the phone back in my pocket and turned to Holt. "I want you to keep an eye on everyone here. I've got to get Yarwor. Thera needs him to make something. After that, we can swing by the clubhouse and try to smooth things out with the T.O. I shouldn't be gone too long."

Holt nodded. "What are the chances they'll just forgive and forget?"

I smiled. "Slim to none, I'd say. One problem at a time, though."

CHAPTER·16

HOLT HAD PUT directions in my phone. I was still skeptical about having a smartphone, but for navigation, at least, it seemed to be beneficial. I pulled off the interstate, and dutifully followed the directions through unfamiliar city streets. I took my last turn beside an apartment complex to discover a line of trees on the right side of the road. They stood in stark contrast to the concrete, steel, and glass I had been immersed in a moment before. I turned right onto a dirt road running through the trees. It led me to a place that seemed more suited to the mountains where I lived rather than a bustling metropolis.

A few abandoned cars lined the road, slowly being swallowed up by brush. Next, I passed a large fenced-in area. An enormous metal sculpture of a two-headed goat sat in a large pile of rubble. A number of goats stood lazily around the strange monument.

"This must be the place," I said to myself.

I pulled into a gravel parking lot in front of a few brick buildings, finding a spot in line with a few other cars. I got out, and surveyed the area. The buildings were run down. Everything looked like it could use a little attention from a handyman. The property had the old industrial vibe down pat. I pretended to tie my shoe, in case someone was watching, and sniffed around for a few seconds. I was met by the scents of goats, humans, dogs, and most interestingly an assortment of ultranaturals, but none of them Yarwor.

I followed a path that ran between the buildings. It led past a large piece of antique machinery—some sort of large press. Years of exposure had taken its toll with rust claiming more of the machine than paint. I continued on toward the center of the property and down some steps beside a small chicken coop. The coop was open and a few of the birds were outside pecking at insects in the grass. They didn't pay any attention to me. At the bottom of the stairs, a single lane road wove its way between the buildings. I took a right and came to a large courtyard.

The building on the left didn't have a roof. All the windows were missing with vines climbing the brick. It was encouraging to see something that I would consider ruins. Between that and the goats I might actually be in the right place. Tables and chairs were set up in front of a building with a sign that read THE WARHORSE. A row of planters lined the wall. All the greenery gave the area a very relaxed and natural vibe. It was reminiscent of what I imagined an Italian café would be like, minus all the Italians.

All the tables were empty, save one, with a woman and a black dog with tan patches on its legs, belly, and face. It looked to be a German Shepard mix. She had brown hair pulled back in a ponytail and wore overalls and a sleeveless shirt. She spared a glance in my direction before returning her full attention to a mug of coffee.

"I hope he doesn't come over here Bhalu," the woman said giving the dogs neck a scratch. "He looks like a real tool."

A human would have been out of earshot. Enhanced senses aren't always an advantage. I didn't want to bother her, but she was the only person I had seen since I arrived. I started to approach her when a man came down some stairs on the far side of the courtyard. He had rich ebony skin, a flat nose, and full lips. He wore jeans, a gray button-up shirt, and flip flops. He said hello to the woman and gave me a smile and a nod as he disappeared into the Warhorse. I gave the air a few quick sniffs and picked up his scent. I couldn't place it. I didn't know what he was, but it wasn't human. He didn't have the stench of demon, so that was good enough for me. Adan had said I could find help at the Warhorse; maybe this was who he was talking about.

I followed the man into an eclectic coffee shop. Antique chairs and sofas with leather and natural fur were arranged around tables made of wood and metal. The back wall was lined with bookshelves that overflowed with old tomes. A piano with an antique typewriter sat under a painting of a man in a North Korean army uniform. Across the room, a bright yellow vending machine with the words KICKAPOO JOY JUICE plastered across the front. A few other patrons sat typing away on laptops. The man I followed in took a seat behind a simple counter with a red door behind it.

"What can I get you?" the man asked.

I looked over the menu written on chalkboards behind the counter. "What I'd really like is a little information."

His nose flexed subtly as he sniffed the air.

"Turn left in fifty feet," the automated voice of my phone chimed from my pocket.

"Information on how to use maps?" he asked with a smirk.

"Sorry about that," I said, pulling my phone out. The map was still on the screen with a triangle spinning around in the center. I hit the button on the side and the screen turned off. I put it back in my pocket. "I'm looking for someone I heard was here. His name is Yarwor. He's a big guy with umm . . . gray skin," I said a little softer, looking around to make sure we were out of earshot of anyone who might hear.

He didn't look concerned with anyone overhearing his answer. "Yeah, I know who you're talking about, but you might be better off not finding him."

"Why's that?"

"He's getting into some bad things. He keeps to himself and we don't mess with him. A few tried to help him at first, but he didn't seem to want it. Now he's just turning into a problem. If you could get rid of him, you would be doing us a favor."

"So where can I find him?"

He took a sip of coffee. "There's a building by the goat pens with a tree growing out of the wall. He's been staying there."

I thanked him and headed back the way I had come. I looked for the building I was told about. All seemed intact, no noticeable vegetation grew on the brick, let alone a tree. Before I could continue my search something small hit me in the back. I turned around just as another pebble bounced off my chest.

There was a goat standing on the other side of the fence from me chewing on some grass and not seeming to pay me any attention. I spotted a slim face peeking out from behind the rubble pile. It had short curly brown hair, a flat nose ridge ending in a black triangular nose, and two horns sticking up out of the hair, angling away from each other.

A satyr stepped out from behind the rubble pile. The top half of a human with goat legs and hooves, the face being a mix of both. She didn't wear any clothes and wasn't the least bit self-conscious about it. If you had dealings with a satyr, it was best to tread lightly. They could be mischievous or even dangerous if you pissed them off. Best to be polite and get back to looking for Yarwor as quickly as possible. I gave her a wave. She jumped over the fence to join me in the grass.

"Well, hello, handsome," she said batting her eyes. "What's your name?"

"Obie," I said. "Hey, maybe you could help me. I'm looking for someone."

She put her hands on her hips. "Don't you want to know my name?"

I guess this wasn't going to be easy.

"Of course I do, I'm sorry," I said, wishing I hadn't gotten roped into this conversation. "What's your name?"

"Tasha."

"It's very nice to meet you, Tasha. Like I was saying, I am looking for someone. He's an orc—"

"Surely there's time for a little pleasure before business," she said, stepping up and wrapping her arm around mine.

The goat in the pen behind Tasha bleated and she waved her hand in its direction dismissively.

"It's actually really important that I find him so if you wouldn't mind telling me if any orcs have been around lately? The guy at the Warhorse said he was hanging around in a building with a tree in the wall."

"We'll get to that later," she said. "Let's get to know each other a little first."

My phone spoke: "Recalculating."

I grabbed it though the fabric of my pocket and pressed any button I could find.

"I'm with someone, sort of," I said, wishing I had left off the *sort of.*

"You don't sound too sure. A few minutes with me and you'll know exactly where you stand," she said.

She clearly wasn't going to help me find Yarwor, at least not on any kind of timeframe that would work for me. Maybe flattery would make things go a little smoother.

"Tasha, normally I would love to get to know such a pretty girl, but right now I'm on urgent business," I said, pulling my arm away.

She stepped in front of me. "What's more important than making new friends?"

"Unfortunately," I said, stepping past her, "a lot of the things I have to deal with."

I only made it a couple steps when something grabbed my feet. I looked down to see roots had grown up around my ankles.

Tasha's head popped under my arm. "Oh, come on. What could you be doing that's so important?"

"I'm a Keeper of Thera and I'm here on business," I said. "So I'm afraid I have to insist that you let me go."

The goat bleated from behind us.

"Nobody asked you, Deloris!" Tasha screamed. "Are you sure?" she said, returning her attention to me.

"Yes, let me go."

She moved back; the roots retreated from my feet. Tasha pouted, her arms crossed.

"Over there's the building with a tree growing out of the roof that you're looking for," she said, pointing behind the goat pen. "He's been staying there."

I backed away from her. "Thank you."

Once I was a little farther away an argument broke out between Tasha and Deloris. I was glad Tasha's attention was on someone else. Deloris was officially my favorite goat.

CHAPTER · 17

I CAME TO A BUILDING that seemed, at first glance, to be intact, but covered with plant life. The brick walls had vines drooping down over them; most of the leaves had turned shades of yellow and red. Walking around, I found some yellow caution tape that had been set up to block off the back of the building. A large portion of the back wall had collapsed. A tree that had to be at least twenty years old grew out of the corner of the building. It had pushed what was left of the adjacent wall out about six inches. It didn't look too stable.

Peering around as best I could without stepping over the tape I spotted an old safe that had been built into the wall. The safe was about six feet tall and seemed to be providing the structural support that prevented the building from falling down all together. A path led through the rubble and into the brush on the back side. After a quick look around to make sure no one was watching, I stepped over the tape. I followed the trail through the brush into the back side of the building. It led to a relatively intact room.

It had three standing walls and most of a ceiling with numerous vines hanging down like a natural chandelier. It stank of urine. The rubble had been pushed away to the edges, making a clearing in the center. Yarwor lay face down on the floor with his face on a pile of bricks. It didn't make sense that anyone, including an orc, would use bricks for a pillow. Maybe he had died. He didn't appear to be breathing. I waited for any sign of life. Just when I'd decided he'd kicked the bucket, his chest suddenly heaved and he took in a large wheezing breath. The brick pillow must not be doing his breathing any favors.

Multiple five-gallon buckets were placed around the room. I thought one, or more, of them might've been used as a toilet—it would explain the smell. Only one had anything in it. I gave it a whiff and it turned out to be half full of water. A beetle had fallen into it and kicked its legs in a vain attempt to make it to the edge of the bucket. I scooped it out and held my hand against the wall for it to crawl off. I spotted a small hookah in the corner.

"Oh no," I said, stepping around the bucket for a closer look.

I took a whiff of the hookah. I recognized it right away from the bitter metallic smell: Ichor. A quick look at Yarwor's neck confirmed my suspicions. He had a bitemark that looked to be a few days old. Whoever he was buying from was old school. Werebats like Clay took their victim's blood intravenously. The old bite and suck was an outdated method. Bitemarks were much more conspicuous than track marks. On top of that, taking the blood intravenously allowed it to be stored, to be drunk later or turned into Ichor. Whoever Yarwor had gotten tangled up with was more concerned with pleasure than business.

"Yarwor, what have you done?" I mumbled to myself.

Ichor was dangerous because it didn't just give you a feeling of euphoria. It made people strong, violent, and feeling no pain. Smoking it too much made people a little crazy to boot. It was slightly reassuring to see Yarwor had used a hookah. Passing it through the water filtered it a little, letting it maintain a lot of the euphoria, but taking the edge off the psycho rampage qualities. Now I knew what that fella in the coffee shop meant by "bad things." If Yarwor kept it up, eventually he would hurt someone or himself. He needed help and I was just the guy to give it to him.

"Come on, wake up," I said, giving him a cautious nudge with my foot.

Yarwor let out a low rumble, but didn't move.

I gave him another tap. "Yarwor, I need your help."

He groaned and rolled over on his side. His pillow left indentations on his face, making him look like he'd run face first into a brick wall. One eye opened, just a sliver, and he groaned again before he ran his hands over his arms and started scratching them.

"I'm thirsty," he mumbled absently.

I knelt. "I need your help."

"I can't help you," he said, waving me off and reaching for the bucket with water in it.

He lifted the whole thing and gulped it as fast as he could, only stopping once to take a breath. He only managed to drink about half of it, the rest pouring over him in an impromptu shower. He picked up the other buckets, looking for more water, tossing the empties away.

"I need a blacksmith and you're the only one I know," I said.

"I don't know if you've noticed, but I'm no good to anyone," he said, rechecking the buckets for any drop of water that he'd missed. "Where'd all my water go?"

He became more frantic as the same few buckets were tossed around like there was one hiding somewhere he just hadn't spotted yet. Then he found the hookah. Before I could stop him he grabbed it, pulled the top off, and drank the brown murky water inside it. He doubled over and screamed as if his insides were on fire.

"Yarwor? You okay?"

"Where's my damn water?" he yelled.

He grabbed the buckets again and when they turned up empty this time, he threw them against the wall, shattering them to pieces. I took a step back to get away from the plastic shrapnel flying around the room.

"Where is that rushing coming from?" he said. His chest heaved with rapid breaths and sweat broke out all over his neck and back. No doubt the rushing he was talking about was the blood in his ears. He grabbed bricks and handfuls of dirt and plants and hurled them in every direction.

"Make a U-turn," my pocket announced.

I slapped my hand over my pocket to muffle the sound. Too late. Yarwor stopped his frantic digging and turned his head slowly toward me. His eyes were beyond bloodshot, there didn't seem to be any white left in them. Suddenly what Livy said about the "red-eyed orc" made sense.

Drool ran out of his mouth. "It's coming from you. You're full of water."

The veins in his neck and arms popped as he took a deliberate step toward me.

"Yarwor," I said, taking a step back. "We can get you more water."

It was falling on deaf ears. He lunged at me. I jumped back, but was caught in the brush that had grown up around the room. There was no time to change to krasis. He plowed me into the brush and had me pinned with one hand on my head and another on my legs. I felt his teeth sink into my abdomen, followed by a slurping sound. I have had demons try to eat me many times before, this was the first time someone tried to drink me.

I freed my arms from the brush and punched him. It didn't seem to faze him. Feeling around, I grabbed a brick off the ground and slammed it into his head, shattering it in my hand. This he took note of, but didn't stop, instead biting down harder. If brute force wasn't going to work, I'd have to try something else. I crammed two fingers up his large orc nose. He started gagging and when I wiggled them inside his sinus cavity he let me go and stepped back, rubbing his face frantically with both hands. I took the opportunity to jump on his back. I wrapped one arm around his neck and locked it with my other arm on the back of his head.

With my biceps on one side of his neck and forearm on the other, I was able to squeeze and cut off the blood flow to his brain. No matter how drugged he was, he couldn't stay conscious without oxygen. He grabbed at my arm, but couldn't get a grip with it pressed so tightly into his neck. He started swaying slightly. In a last-ditch effort he charged the brick wall. He passed out just before impact, but the momentum carried us into it.

I WOKE UNDER A tremendous weight. The wall, or maybe the whole building for all I knew, had come down on top of us. I was still clinging to Yarwor's back with my arm around his neck. He felt cold, but had a pulse. He wasn't moving, which I thought was a considerable improvement. I pulled my arms free and pushed the bricks off until I was able to squeeze my legs out from under Yarwor. I instinctively held my hand out to heal him, but stopped. If I healed him, he would probably wake up. If he woke up he would still be in a drug-induced rage and we would be back to where we started. I didn't want to leave him hurt, especially since I didn't know the extent of the injuries, but I didn't have any choice. He would need time for the drugs to work their way out of his system.

Most of the building remained standing. We had collided with one of the interior walls which collapsed. The rest of the building seemed to be in decent shape except for one wall that had picked up a slight lean. I couldn't be sure how stable the structure was and didn't want to stick around to find out. I pulled bricks away from Yarwor's head and chest. I would have to carry him to the truck and that meant he needed a disguise. He would normally use an illusion pendant, but I didn't know if he had it or if it was buried under the rubble.

"Where's your necklace? Please don't tell me you lost it," I said, more to myself than him.

I saw the chain around his neck and pulled it out. I flipped the arrow down so that it crossed the eye and waited a few seconds for the illusion to turn this battered and dirty orc into an equally battered and dirty human. Once the illusion had taken hold, I grabbed his arm and hoisted him into a fireman's carry. It was slow going getting out of the brush and uneven ground. Twenty minutes later, I had him at the passenger side of the truck. I felt around for my keys. They weren't in their usual pocket. I patted down all my pockets but couldn't find them. I opened the tailgate and sat Yarwor on it who promptly fell backward into the bed of the truck with his legs dangling off the tailgate.

I tried my pockets for the second time and turned up nothing. If dropped them in the fight before the wall collapsed I could be looking for them all day. Yarwor didn't look as if he was going to run off while I searched. That was fine as long as he didn't wake up and hurt someone while I was gone. It's not like I had a lot of choices. I left him lying in the truck.

When I passed the goat pen, frantic bleating caught my attention. Deloris was standing by the fence, bobbing her head, and stamping at the ground. I hesitated, wondering if it was some kind of trick, but went over to check it out anyway. On the ground in front of her were my keys. I picked them up cautiously and bounced them in my hand. There's no way they should've fallen out there.

"Thanks," I said to the goat.

She bleated a reply I couldn't understand but I assumed it was "You're welcome."

Yarwor was still unconscious when I made it back to the truck. I got him loaded in the passenger seat as quickly as I could. I decided to stop at the first place I passed and buy about ten gallons of water, just in case he woke up on the way back. I drove down the dirt road beside the goat pen. Tasha was standing by the fence. She gave me a mischievous smile with a corresponding wave. I pushed the pedal a little harder.

"You have arrived at your destination," my phone chimed as the tires chirped on the pavement.

CHAPTER·18

I PULLED UP TO the cottage and parked off to the side. Yarwor was still asleep and had only made a few grumbles in the roughly three hours it took to make it back. I had mixed feelings about bringing him here. He'd run away for a reason. Ultimately, how either of us felt about it didn't matter. This was where the smithy was. I carried the water I had bought inside first, just in case, and returned for Yarwor. I pulled him out into a fireman's carry. I closed the truck door and hit the button to lock it, sliding the keys into my pocket as I walked toward the house.

I still had my reservations about healing Yarwor. I was no expert on Ichor, and didn't know how long it stayed in the system, but I wasn't going to take another detour to Dahlonega to ask my new friend Clay. I put Yarwor on the bed as gently as I could and arranged the gallons of water on the floor in front of the bed. I looked at the jugs, unconvinced that it would be enough to satisfy him if he woke up thirsty again. If it came down to it I could use the kitchen faucet while he worked his way through the jugs on the floor. Maybe the running water would be enough to keep him from attacking me again. Just to be safe, I filled a pitcher, too.

Holding the pitcher in my left hand, I put my right over his chest and channeled energy into him. I could feel it flow, healing his injuries. He groaned as the healing took hold, and opened his eyes. I stopped the flow and pulled my hand back. He wasn't fully healed yet and I was all right with that. Yarwor sat up in the bed and looked around. He spotted me with the water at the ready and reached out a hand. I handed him the pitcher and he promptly dumped it and vomited a black sludge into it. He placed the pitcher on the floor and leaned forward on the edge of the bed to put his head between his knees.

He waved his hand and grunted, "Water," in a hoarse voice.

I was happy to supply it, pulling the lid off one of the gallon jugs and placing it in his hand. I preemptively took the lid off a second jug. Sitting up, he sipped gingerly before tucking it under one arm, clutching the water to his chest like a teddy bear. A little water splashed out as the plastic was compressed but he didn't seem to notice.

"How did I get here?" he asked, looking around.

"I found you squatting in a half-collapsed building in Atlanta and brought you back. You don't remember any of that?"

"No." He rubbed his face with his free hand. "Why does my nose hurt?"

I shook my head. "I sure didn't stick my fingers up there, I'll tell you that much."

He took another sip of water. "I don't want to be here."

"I'm sorry if being here is causing you pain. I wouldn't have brought you back if it wasn't necessary," I said.

He shook his head. "It's not just what happened here, it's everything. You know what they call me now? The butcher. You should see the looks I got last time I went to the clubhouse. This isn't a place I want to be anymore. I didn't mean to hurt anybody."

"I've heard the name and you have to know that Holt and I don't use it. We were here that day. I know you aren't responsible for what you did. How about this, you help me and I'll help you find somewhere where you can have a real life again. Somewhere far away from here."

"I don't deserve a real life," he answered.

I leaned forward and put a hand on his shoulder. "Sometimes people get things they don't deserve. Would it be so bad if it worked out for you?"

He took another drink from the pitcher. "What do you want my help with?"

"I need a weapon. Hell's breaking loose and I'm seriously outgunned and outnumbered. I asked Thera for help and she said I needed to find a blacksmith. So here you are."

He was in the middle of another swig of water and choked at my answer, coughing, and wiping his mouth on his arm. "Thera sent you to get me?"

"Not you, specifically," I said. "You're the only blacksmith I know."

"You really know how to make a guy feel special," he said. "If I'm being real honest I'm not exactly sure how much I believe in the whole *Thera* thing."

I smiled. "That's okay. She doesn't require you to believe in her."

"What the hell am I supposed to do?"

"Let's head out to the smithy," I said, pointing a thumb toward the door. "I'll have to call her to figure out what we do after that."

He sighed. "I'll go, but I have to be honest with you. You got the wrong guy."

He got to his feet and I followed him as he made his way slowly out of the house to the smithy. We went inside. Yarwor leaned against the anvil, still clutching the jug of water.

"Well?" he asked. "What now?"

I held up a finger. "Thera. I have the blacksmith."

Yarwor looked around the smithy. After a few seconds, he said, "Well?"

Thera appeared next to a workbench on the left side of the smithy.

"She's here," I said.

"I don't see anything," Yarwor said.

"If you could see her, you wouldn't have any problem believing, would you?"

"Put your hand on his head," Thera said.

"Hold still a second," I said, walking over to him.

"What are you doing?"

"Hold still," I said, resting a hand on the top of his head.

Yarwor crossed his arms. "This is stupid."

I felt an electric charge run up from the ground through my right leg, around my back, and down my left arm into Yarwor's head. He spasmed from the burst of energy and sprawled on the ground, dropping the jug of water. I lowered my arm, shaking my hand. It tingled from the burst of electricity and felt numb. Yarwor set up. He looked dazed, a distant kind of look in his eyes.

"I know what I have to do," he said, getting to his feet. "The first thing is the metal to make the blade from. I think I have something that'll work."

He walked over to a pile of scrap in the corner. He dug through it, tossing bent blades and rusted bars onto the floor behind him, before pulling out what looked like a rock. He turned it over in his hands before returning to the table and setting it down with a loud thud.

"It's a meteor I chanced across years ago," he said. "I've been waiting for something special to do with it. This definitely fits the bill."

He walked over to the hammer on the floor of the smithy. The depression where he had smashed Grubby into the dirt was still black from the demon's blood. He stared at it for a few seconds before sighing and picking it up.

"You're sure about this?" he asked, turning the hammer over in his hands. "It's not too late to call it off."

"Don't get cold feet on me now," I said.

He looked at me with sorrow on his face. "I need you to change to krasis."

I pulled the Velcro on my shorts to make room for my tail and made the change. As soon as I was done I looked up to see the hammer coming down on my head.

I BECAME AWARE OF myself, not of my surroundings, or what had happened to me, only that I again recognized I existed. It was like waking up from a deep sleep when you still linger halfway between dream and reality. The first thing I noticed was a sound. A rhythmic scraping, somewhere off in the distance, that seemed to get closer the more awake I became. The steady tempo seemed to come up from out of the darkness itself. Then another sensation, cold. Dull at first, but growing as I came out of my slumber. Finally, the pain started. Throbbing in my head and a burning sensation all over my body like I was on fire.

I opened my eyes to find myself laid out on the table in the smithy. My body was glossy and red, and the pain intensified through my neck and back from the movement. I couldn't make sense of what was on me, some kind of goo, like an acidic slime. That would account for the burning. Yarwor was seated with his back to me. He had a log resting on a couple of sawhorses with a hide draped over it. He was using a long blade to scrape the flesh and fat from the skin. I had seen the old timers do this with deer skins. As the fog cleared from my head, I realized it wasn't that there was something on me, but that something wasn't— my skin had been removed.

I wasn't going to lie here and be subjected to whatever else was in the works. I went to sit up and only managed to pull myself up on my elbows. The movement sent pain shooting through my body; that didn't subside, but it gave me the vantage point to see the full extent of what had been done. Besides being skinned, my legs had been removed just below the knee. I stared at the stumps where my legs should be, trying to make sense of what I was seeing. The realization sank in slowly that they weren't misplaced or hiding, but just gone.

"You aren't whole. Lie back," Thera said. She stood beside me.

I lay back on the table, sending fresh waves of pain shooting through my body when it made contact. I tried to speak, but couldn't get out anything more than grunts and groans. Thera waved a hand over me and the pain left my body. While I knew it was just the absence of suffering, it felt like bliss and I breathed a sigh of relief to be free of it.

"Your blade is being made," Thera said.

"When you said it would cost me, I didn't know this is what you had in mind," I said.

Now pain-free, I raised my head. Through the back door of the smithy I saw a large dirt oven with wisps of smoke coming out of the top. The heat distorted the air above it. A trashcan full of charcoal sat close by. Yarwor stopped his scraping and bent over to puke into a bucket on the ground beside him. He took a swig of water from a jug, and after swishing it around in his mouth, spit it into the bucket. He looked at me. Our eyes met, and he walked over to where I was lying. He stood there with a long face, wringing his hands for a moment.

"I don't know if you can hear me, but I'm sorry, Obie," he said before going back to his seat and continued scraping my hide.

"I have Holt coming here to watch over you while you heal," Thera said.

My thoughts drifted to my mentor, Cearbhall, and how he'd lost an eye long ago. He had worked with only one for as long as I knew him, but it never grew back. My skin would grow back, I was sure about that. I would probably be horrible scarred for a while. My legs on the other hand, I couldn't work without them.

"Will I get my legs back?" I asked.

"You will, but it will take time to regrow them. You will sleep," she said.

As soon as the words left her lips, my eyelids grew heavy and I fought to stay awake while vines appeared over the edge of the table. They grew up close to my body, weaving together into a dome over me. I was overcome with a warm peaceful feeling as the light of the smithy disappeared between the leaves.

"Holt . . ." I mumbled, trying to remember what I was going to say.

As the vines closed in around me I fell into the first sleep I had had in over two hundred years, since the day I became a Keeper.

CHAPTER·19

I LAY STILL, NOT wanting to move. I felt warm, comfortable, and protected in a way that I'd never experienced before. I don't know how long it took me to actually open my eyes. I saw the tangled branches that sheltered me from the world. It should have been dark inside my cocoon, but it wasn't. The light was dim and without a distinguishable source, it seemed to come from everything and nothing at the same time. I lay there, not wanting to move, and doing a good job with it, until I heard Thera's voice.

"You're healed," she said. "Get up."

It seemed to me to be as good an idea as anything else, and remembering what had happened last time she pushed me to get up, I decided sooner would be better than later. There wasn't a lot of room to move in the cocoon. I shifted around to make enough space to get my arms above me. I ran my hands along the tangled vines. They were twisted tightly together with barely enough room to wiggle my fingers in between them. They grew thick and tight and didn't want to budge as I began pulling them apart. After a few minutes of pulling and breaking the vines, I was able to make an opening large enough to fit through.

I crawled out enough so I could rest my arms on top of the cocoon. I was alone in the smithy. The doors were closed. It had been cleaned up since the last time I saw it. Everything sat neatly in its place, including the hammer, which rested on the anvil in front of the forge. I pulled myself out onto the floor. My clothes were gone, no surprise there. I ran a hand over my fur. It was softer than normal, not unexpected, considering it was new. I gave my legs a few steps to test them out and my toes a few wiggles; it was as if they had never been gone. There were no scars. A few stomps, kicks, and shakes, and I felt confident they were good to go. The table where I had seen Yarwor at work had been cleaned. On it I found some of my clothes folded beside a cloth with something lumpy under it. I knew Holt had brought them, but I doubted he would have folded them so neatly. Livy had been here as well.

The clothes were gray shorts and a yellow shirt that said BE KIND on the front. I had picked it up at a local school fundraiser a couple of years ago without any real intention of wearing it. Maybe someone wanted to send me a message. I flipped the cloth back. Underneath I found a large blade and a set of knuckle dusters. The blade had a beautiful swirling pattern and an off-white handle. The blade itself was fifteen inches long with a slight curve that came to a dangerous looking point.

I picked it up, feeling the balance. It felt lighter than I thought it would and reacted well when I gave it some test swings. Satisfied, I put it back on the table and picked up the knuckle dusters. I slid my fingers into them. They were shiny steel with aggressive points on the end of each knuckle, nice but not really my thing. I got dressed and went to the door. I undid the latch, pushing it open wide. The sun was shining. No sooner had I swung the door open than a cool breeze blew across my fur. Something strange about the trees caught my attention before I stepped out; they were bare. When I got here they still had leaves, albeit leaves that were about to fall.

I spotted Holt's Honda parked beside my truck as I walked out into the yard. I could tell they had both been parked there for a while from the leaves that had gathered around the windshield wipers. I could hear talking coming from inside the house. I opened the door and stepped in to find Holt, Livy, Harlan, Isabelle, and Yarwor sitting around the kitchen table. Isabelle was sitting in Yarwor's lap. They were in the middle of a game of cards with Isabelle and Yarwor playing together.

"Obie!" Isabelle shouted when I stepped in.

She jumped out of Yarwor's lap in her excitement. I didn't know why she was so thrilled to see me, but the rest of the room had more mixed reactions. Livy looked relieved, like when she'd been worrying about how a batch of cornbread muffins was going to turn out, even though they always came out perfect.

"You're awake," Holt said with a grin and a nod. "Glad to have you back."

Yarwor stood and walked over to me. "Obie, I'm really sorry. I can explain," he said. "I wasn't myself."

I probably should have been mad. It would be understandable to be angry at anyone who skinned you and cut your legs off, regardless of their good intentions. Maybe it was the time I spent in the cocoon, but I felt at peace.

"You don't have to tell me what can happen when Thera gets in your head," I said.

Yarwor breathed a sigh of relief. "I'm glad to hear you say that. I thought for sure you would be pissed."

I held out my hand and he shook it. "I saw the blade. How could I be mad? It looks awesome. Is it finished?"

"It still has to be bound. Other than that, yes," Yarwor replied.

I nodded. "How do we bind it?"

"That wasn't zapped into my cranium." He shrugged. "You'll have to ask Thera."

"Sounds like someone's a believer," I said.

Yarwor shrugged. "I wouldn't go that far. Something happened that I can't explain. Let's just say, I'm open to the possibility."

I nodded. "I'll take it. You look a lot better than last time I saw you."

"I'm doing my best," he said, looking at the ground. "I was lucky Holt showed up when he did. Livy helped me though the withdrawal with some concoction she made. It tasted like ass but really took the edge off. And Isabelle—let's just say, it's nice having people to care about again."

"I'm glad you're doing better," I said.

"You want to get your blade fitted?"

"I can't wait," I said. "Holt, let's go."

"What do you need me for?" Holt asked.

I looked at Yarwor. "Didn't you tell him?"

Yarwor shook his head. "Didn't seem like my place."

"We have something for you, too," I said.

The three of us walked to the smithy. Yarwor went over to the cloth the weapons were under and flipped the cloth back. He fished around under the table and came up with a belt and sheath for the blade. They were plain leather with only a few runes stamped in them.

Yarwor ran a hand over the smooth leather. "I had to make the buckle out of the same metal as the knife for it to work. It should work the same way as the knife once it's bound. Want to try it on?"

"Before I do, could you explain to me why I was skinned and had my legs cut off?" I asked. "I was surprised by it, to say the least."

"He cut your legs off?" Holt asked.

"The meteorite I used was mostly iron, but to make steel we had to add carbon. The . . . message . . . I got told me the carbon had to come from you. I needed bones." Yarwor shrugged.

"What about the skin?" I asked.

Yarwor looked at the sheath and belt he held. "I had to make leather."

I was hesitant to see how it fit, mostly because the idea of wearing something made from my skin skeeved me out. All I could think about were Nazis making lamp shades out of human skin. What's done was done. I had to have some way to hold the blade. There were no other options, so I was really just delaying the inevitable.

"Yeah, let's try it out," I said, ignoring the chill that ran down my back. I picked up the belt and placed it around my body to find a way to wear it.

I tried to orient the knife, so it rested horizontally across my hips between my shirt and shorts, but it wasn't comfortable. In order for it to change with my body it had to be worn under my clothes. I took my shirt off to find a more comfortable position. I slung it over my left shoulder with the handle down by my right hip. It was the only placement I could think of that would give me access to it without clothing getting in the way. I slid the knife into the sheath, giving it a little adjustment to find a comfortable position.

While I worked getting it in place, Yarwor gave the knuckledusters to Holt. "And these are for you."

"Sweet," Holt said, sliding them onto his fingers. "Thanks, Yarwor."

"Don't thank me," Yarwor said shaking his head. "Thank Obie, he's the one that paid for them."

"They feel great," Holt said. "I could really bust some skulls with these."

"That's the idea," I said.

Holt took a few practice swings to get a feel for them. "What now?"

"That's between you guys and Thera," Yarwor said. "I've had enough close encounters. I'll be in the house."

After Yarwor left, Holt asked, "He cut your legs off?"

"I was surprised as anybody," I said. "Probably more so. How long was I out?"

"Three weeks, two days," Holt said, peering into the cocoon on the table. "But who's counting?"

I wasn't sure I wanted an answer to the next question, but I had to ask. "What'd I miss?"

"Hank's in the hospital," he said. "And Lug Nut's in jail."

"What the hell are they doing there?"

"Well, after we put him in the truck, Lug Nut headed south to take him to Atlanta. He was speeding, of course, and got pulled over. Long story short, when they heard a biker was shot a lot of cops showed up. They ended up getting in a little tussle with Lug Nut. From what I heard he had four of them on him before he remembered he had to let them win. He got arrested and went to jail. The cops found a number of illegal recreational substances in the back of the truck, so I don't see him getting out anytime soon. They took Hank to the hospital.

That was bad news. Normal injuries for shifters didn't require medical attention. Injuries caused by silver wouldn't heal, or they wouldn't heal quickly I should say. The closest place to go for treatment was the wererats hospital in Atlanta. Normal hospitals were great for humans, but not the best place for an injured werebear. What was more concerning was that if he'd spent three weeks in the hospital that meant he had probably been poisoned by the silver the whole time. Otherwise he would have healed up and be out by now. I was surprised to hear he wasn't dead, to be honest.

"So who's leading the T.O.?" I asked.

He paused, knowing I wouldn't like the answer. "Chisel."

I sighed. "We need to get Hank back."

"I don't know if Chisel will give up the reins willingly. It's not the same Tortured Occult as it was when you . . . were indisposed. I think he saw an opportunity to take over the club. They haven't tried to save Hank and haven't posted bail for Lug Nut. A few of the T.O. left the club and are laying low. Chisel recruited some of the Wretched Dogs to fill in the ranks and declared war on the Elven Nation. I haven't had contact with anyone in a couple weeks, but things were heating up then," Holt said. "There's probably been bloodshed by now."

"Okay," I said. "What about everyone here? Harlan and Isabelle holdin' up all right?"

Holt shrugged. "Isabelle's having fun, but I can tell she wants to go home. She's really hit it off with Yarwor. He's become very protective of her in the past month."

"Good," I said. "And Harlan?"

"He disappears a lot. Goes on these long walks by himself for an hour or more at a time. I don't get the impression he wants to be here either, but he definitely don't want to go back to the Queen."

"We'll get 'em both where they need to go, but first things first," I said. "Let's get these weapons done. Then we can worry about Hank and Chisel."

Holt nodded. "Thera," he said, "we need you."

She appeared in the smithy. "Yes?"

"Our weapons are ready," I said, holding up my blade. "What's next?"

"Now we bind them. Fill a large container with the cleanest water you can find. Warming the water to your body temperature will ease the transition," she said. "Call me when it's done."

She vanished again.

"Easy enough," Holt said. "Yarwor's got a bathtub."

We walked back into the house, passing everyone in the living room without answering any of their questioning glances. The house itself was small and the bathroom was no exception. Just a tub, toilet, and sink with enough standing room for one person. Holt turned the hot water all the way and held his hand under it, waiting for it to get warm. When it started to heat up he plugged the tub and made adjustments to keep the water at the right temperature.

"That should just about do it," he said.

"You going first or should I?" I asked.

"I will," he said. "Thera, we're ready."

She appeared in the tub, standing not in the water, but on it. "Holt, in your human form wear your weapon and submerge your hands."

Holt made the change to his human form, put on his knuckledusters, and put his hands under the water. He screamed as the water started to bubble, steam rising from the tub. I waited and watched. Isabelle, Harlan, and Yarwor rushed over to find out what the commotion was. The water continued to boil and steam around Holt's hands for a few seconds and then abruptly stopped. Holt pulled his hands out of the water. The knuckledusters were gone. His hands shook as he held them up. He had scars around his fingers where the metal had been. He turned his hands over to reveal similar scars on his palms. They looked like burns. He flexed his hands.

"Now change to your other forms," Thera said.

He changed to a Doberman first. His front paws had been solid black but now they had brown rings around each of his toes. Then he changed to krasis and the knuckledusters came out of his flesh and into his hands.

"Okay, that's pretty cool," Holt said.

"Obie," Thera said.

I changed to my human form and lowered myself into the tepid water.

Livy poked her head around the corner. "What's all the fuss about?"

"Thera's about to burn a blade into Obie's back," Holt said.

I was going to say, "Let's not be overdramatic," when I was hit with an intense heat. The water in contact with the blade began to boil. Searing pain shot through my body. It focused on the areas the belt and blade touched, but spilled over to the rest of my body. It felt like I was being branded. I didn't scream the way Holt had. I would have liked to, but couldn't get it out. I could feel the blade bending from the center, coming in contact with my back as it burned into my flesh. When the blade had worked its way in and the pain subsided, I stood up. Water poured from my clothes as I raised my shirt to look. Like Holt, scars were left from the binding. Mine ran around my chest. I could see singed parts on my clothes where they had come into contact with the belt and blade. I changed into an otter to find a khaki discoloration in my normally light brown fur. Finally, I changed to krasis and the blade came out of my body.

I drew the blade and looked at my reflection in it. "All right. Let's get to work."

"What's the plan?" Holt asked.

"We're going to get Hank."

Holt and I changed into our human forms and I put on some dry clothes. We said our goodbyes and went out to my truck. I opened the door and was hit in the face with the scent of rotten fish.

"What the hell is that?" Holt said, with a hand over his nose.

I searched the truck and found something wrapped in paper under the driver's seat. The paper had soaked up some brown liquid and when I unfolded it a fish fell onto the ground.

"Looks like a trout. At least, it was a trout," I said.

There was some writing on the paper that I could barely make out through the fish juice. I pinched the paper between two fingers so I could read it.

Obie,

I didn't realize you were such a cold fish. Hopefully, this will provide companionship more in line with your tastes.

XOXO,
Tasha

CHAPTER 20

I'VE NEVER CARED for the smell of hospitals. Don't get me wrong, there are much worse things to smell, but the smell of a hospital has a quality all its own. I've always found it strange that the smell is uniform across the handful of hospitals I have been in. I shouldn't complain. For most of my life they didn't always have such a sterile, if unnatural, smell to them. They used to smell like death, but that's progress for ya.

I stepped into a normal looking hospital room. Machines with a few too many wires and cables coming off of them were positioned beside the bed in the center of the room. A loveseat sat under a window with a view of roof and sky, not the best view, but it's not as if patients in critical care gaze out for hours on end. There was a TV mounted to the wall opposite the bed. It was off. An I.V., that was almost empty, dripped steadily into Hank's hand.

He didn't look good. His normal java tone was a little more yellow and pallid. His eyes were sunken in and his cheek bones were poking out. He had lost weight, a lotta weight. A good portion of it looked to be muscle. He seemed to be shriveling up right in front of me.

"Hank?" I said, touching his hand.

It was cold. He didn't respond to my voice or touch. I pulled open an eye to find a sickly yellow ball with a dark brown pupil. It was what I was afraid of. The slow wasting away and jaundice, I had seen it before with silver poisoning. It didn't look like he had much time left.

I took a seat, pulled my phone out of my pocket, and dialed a number. It rang a few times before a familiar voice answered.

"This is Rebecca Lin," she said.

"Hey, Doc, it's Obie. Are you in the hospital?"

"I'm in administration. Are *you* in the hospital?" she asked warily.

"Yeah, I'm in 826," I said. "I need to see you when you got a minute."

There was a moment of silence before she spoke again. "Should I be worried?"

"No more than usual."

"Oh no," she said. "I'll be right there."

As I waited for her arrival, I looked at Hank again. This time not as a concerned friend but through a practical lens. My objective from Thera wasn't only to hunt demons, it was to protect life. Granted, there's a lot of interpretation there. That leeway is what caused issues between my mentor Cearbhall and me. A war between the Tortured Occult and the Elven Nation would cost a lot of lives. Not just between the club and the elves, it would spill over to everyone in the area. If there was any hope of restoring peace, I needed Hank to get back to his rightful position as head of the T.O. Between Chisel and the Queen, it would be a war of attrition. With Hank in charge, there might be hope for a solution with minimal loss of life.

Even if we were able to get him back on his feet today, I wasn't sure he would be up to it. Hank always had a presence about him, but now it seemed to be gone. He looked weak and shriveled and fragile. In a perfect world, he would show up and be accepted back with open arms. Chisel clearly made a power play for control of the club. Otherwise Hank would have been out of the hospital already. I wasn't sure Hank was going to be able to do what was necessary to take leadership back. If he wasn't up to it physically, we would have to take a grassroots approach. I sat, pondering the possibilities and alternative scenarios, when Doc Lin walked in and brought me back to reality. She was carrying an assortment of papers and X-rays under her arm and a clipboard in her hand.

"I pulled everything we have on Hank Morrison," she said, putting the documentation on the rolling table at the foot of the bed. "Why's he so important?"

"Kinda jumping the gun a little, aren't you? What if I just picked a room with some guy in a coma so we could talk privately?"

She put a hand on her hip and gave me a look that said she wasn't buying it. "I don't know hardly anything about you, except that you're kind and nothing is ever a coincidence with you."

"It was a coincidence I was there to pull you out of that car wreck," I shot back. "I was just passing by."

"It may have been a coincidence you were passing by, but it wasn't a coincidence you stopped. That's the kind of person you are. So why don't you cut the crap and tell me who this is?"

She had me there and I wasn't going to argue with her. "He's an old friend. I want to help him get better, but I'll need your help."

"Oh, you need help fixing the records? When you healed Ms. Heck a few months ago it was a big deal. They were floating all kinds of theories around. There was even an article in the paper. I see what you were saying about drawing attention. You're right that you can't go around healing everyone without exposing yourself."

"It's not so much about the records, I have another problem. He's being poisoned and until we remove it, he won't get better. I can't do anything about it until the poison's out," I said.

"Let's see," she said, rifling through papers. "Toxicology came back clear."

I shrugged. "I guess it would be closer to an allergy than a poison. I don't really know how to describe it medically."

"It says here he has hemolytic anemia. His red blood cells are being destroyed faster than they can be made. Doesn't look like they've been able to find the cause. He's been kept alive with multiple blood transfusions, but he's continuing to deteriorate."

"What about the gunshots?" I asked.

She returned to the documentation. "He was admitted with six gunshot wounds. Three of the bullets were removed."

"Why only three?" I asked.

"They were the only ones that were life threatening," she said. "We don't remove bullets when they aren't dangerous or if there is a risk of doing more damage getting them out than leaving them in."

"These are dangerous. They're causing his condition. We need to have them taken out."

She looked skeptical. "So, you're saying that the bullets are made out of a toxic metal?"

"Toxic to him," I said. "They're silver."

"Silver bullets?" she questioned.

I nodded.

"Is he a werewolf?" She laughed.

I wasn't sure how to answer. Obviously, Hank wasn't a werewolf, but he wasn't far off. What could I really tell her that wouldn't disclose more of my world than she should be aware of? On the other hand, she had to have an open mind since she knew I could heal people and seemed okay with it. But she didn't know what I was or what else was out there. It was risky to tell her because if she found out and wanted to tell people then I would have to keep her quiet, whatever it took. I liked her and didn't want to do something I would regret.

"Obie," she said after I hadn't answered. "He's not a werewolf . . . is he?"

"Well no, He's not a were*wolf*," I said. "It's complicated."

She dropped the papers on the table and crossed her arms. "Then uncomplicate it. If you want my help, I need to know what's going on."

"What's going on is dangerous and it could get you killed," I said. "The less you know the safer you are. We need to have the bullets removed."

"That's going to be a problem," she said.

"And why's that?"

"Well . . . besides the fact that he might be too weak to survive the surgery, and no one is going to want to perform the operation, take a look at this." She pulled out some X-rays and held them up to the light.

I moved over to get a closer look.

"You see these darker pieces?" she asked, pointing them out with her pinky.

I could see what looked like a leg bone with three darker spots on the X-ray.

"That's all foreign material. One of them is the bullet you're worried about, but which one?"

"How many times was he shot?" I asked.

Doc Lin checked the documentation. "Seven."

The Queen only had six rounds in her revolver. Hank must have picked up another bullet in all the commotion.

"And look at this," she said, pulling up another X-ray.

This one showed ribs and more dark spots. She swapped it for another that showed more.

"See? He's full of metal. I don't even know how he's survived all this. The only option we would have is to remove all the pieces in the areas he was shot to make sure we get the right ones and any fragments they may have broken into. All that's beside the point, because no surgeon is going to operate on him in this condition. He would die on the table and mess up their stats."

I pulled out my phone and called Holt. He had been waiting in the car. We'd come to the hospital in his Civic since my truck had a lingering unpleasant odor.

"I need the dust we stashed in your car," I said.

"That bad, huh?" he said. "I'll be right up."

If surgery wasn't an option, then maybe a little magic would do the trick. We kept a little dust hidden away in case of emergencies. This qualified. Holt walked in a few minutes later and slapped a bag in my hand. I would need his help. What I didn't need was spectators. Doc Lin would have to go.

"What's that?" she asked.

"The answer to my problem," I said. "Thanks for coming by. I appreciate the help, but I can take it from here."

"Unless you packed a surgeon and operating room in that little bag, I don't see how anything has changed," she said.

"I'm just going to do what I do, nothing to worry about," I said. "I have help now, so if you don't mind, a little privacy would be nice."

"You told me you couldn't *do what you do* as long as he had the silver in him." She put her hands on her hips. "I understand why you can't make what you do public, but I expect the truth. If you want to do whatever it is you're planning, then I'm going to be right here for it."

"And you are willing to accept any risks that come from what you will see and learn?" I asked.

"I am."

"Maybe you shouldn't agree too readily to things you don't understand," I offered. "I work pretty hard to keep people in the dark about things going on. There are people that would come after you, if they found out you knew about this stuff."

"Seems to me like there would only be three people that know," she countered. "If I don't tell anyone and you two don't tell anyone . . ."

I wasn't going to stand around and argue with her. Hank didn't have time. Doc Lin's a grown woman. If she's willing to take the risk, who am I to question.

"All right. In that case, there are some things I've got to tell you. All you need to know right now is that magic is real and I'm going to try to use it to pull the silver out of Hank's body. Holt's here to heal Hank and minimize the damage while I work."

"Holt's going to heal him?" Doc Lin asked. "How many of you are out there?"

"Just the two of us close by," I said.

She pointed at the bag in my hand. "What does the bag have to do with it?"

"The thing about magic is anyone can do it, but it has to have a power source," I said. "The fuel for what I'm going to do is in the bag."

She looked skeptical but open. "And where does the fuel come from?"

"If you want to learn more about this kind of stuff, we may be able to make it happen, but for now, baby steps, okay?"

"Hey, Doc," Holt said. "Can you get the door?"

Holt and I took positions on either side of the bed. I put the bag of dust on the table so as to not inadvertently set it off. I don't do magic a lot. I wasn't very comfortable with it, but I knew the process and figured I could make it work. I just needed a couple dry runs to get ready. I held my fists over Hank and visualized all the metal in his body being drawn out as if my hands were magnets pulling it. I ran through this process a few times in my mind before deciding I was ready. I retrieved the bag from the table.

"Okay, let's get started," I said.

Holt held out his hands and began channeling healing energy into Hank. I opened the bag, divided the dust as evenly as I could between my hands, and dropped the bag on the floor, out of the way. I held my fists over Hank the way I had practiced, focusing on the metal in his body being drawn out. I began to feel my hands warm from the dust, and figuring it was now or never, I opened my hands. I was startled when something wet splashed across my face. I didn't have time to worry about it because pain shot through my hands. I pulled them back and looked to find pieces of metal embedded in my palms. Holt was still healing Hank. The holes in Hank's body where the metal had exited were closing up quickly.

The metal came out with enough force to not only imbed itself in my hands, but to splatter Hank's blood all over Holt and me and a good portion of the room around the bed. It looked like Hank had exploded, which I suppose wasn't too far off. Doc Lin had been standing far enough back to avoid the blood spatter. I walked into the bathroom and got a look at myself in the mirror. The blood made me look like a victim in a horror flick. I turned on the sink and held my hands under the cool water. I would need to get the metal out quick, I didn't want it to heal in place.

"Doc, I need your help," I said.

She came in the bathroom. "What the hell was that?"

I gave her a sheepish grin. "Sometimes magic gets a little messy."

"That's a little messy?" she yelled.

"Keep your voice down. If you could pull these out for me I would appreciate it," I said holding my hands over the sink. "Quickly."

She left the room and returned a moment later with what were essentially a fancy looking pair of pliers. She pulled out the shrapnel piece by piece and dropped them into the sink.

She had only gotten one of them out, before I could start to feel the tug created from my flesh healing around the metal. She pulled another piece out and noticed the resistance.

"These things are really in there," she said. "Hold on . . ." She moved my hand under the water to clean off the blood. "Obie, these wounds closed up already, I can even see the one I just pulled closing. How is that even possible?"

"It's a long story," I said. "Just pull harder, they'll come out."

"I can't do that, they're really in there," she said, giving my palm a closer look. "We can take you down to the emergency room. They can take these out cleanly."

"We don't have time for that," I said, pulling my hand away from her.

I looked at my right hand, there were still three pieces of metal embedded in it. The one sticking out the most looked like the tip of a knife. I bit it and yanked it out of my palm, spitting it into the sink. The last two pieces were on the side of my palm and wouldn't get in the way of finishing up on my own.

I took the tool from Rebecca. "Why don't you check on Hank."

I was generally unsatisfied with the way this had gone. I was covered in blood, my hands hurt, and the hospital room was a mess. That was really what was frustrating me. There was always a mess. Whenever there was a mess, it causes more problems that lead to more messes. It would be nice, if for once, something, anything, would go as planned. I pulled the shrapnel out of my hands, one by one, dropping them into the sink. When I was done I took a couple minutes to relocate my center. I stood and breathed, holding my hands under the water as they healed. When they were done, I washed the blood off my face as best I could. The shirt was a lost cause until I could get to a washing machine.

I left the bathroom to find Holt using a wet towel to spot clean blood off the walls and medical equipment. He was almost finished when I came out. What he couldn't clean was the bed. The sheets covering Hank had bloody holes where the metal had been pulled through. I didn't see Rebecca in the room.

"Where did she go?" I asked.

Holt stopped scrubbing. "She's getting fresh sheets and a new gown for Hank. Think if you gave me a boost I could reach that?" he asked pointing at the ceiling.

There were spots on the ceiling where blood had made it past my hands. It wasn't a lot, just a few specks here and there.

"Don't worry about it," I said. "No one ever looks up and by the time someone does we'll be long gone. How's Hank?"

Holt leaned against the railing of the bed. "Well, he's not awake, but he ain't dead either."

Rebecca returned with an armload of linens. "I brought you both a scrub top to wear. As long as you don't hang out in the hallways, it should get you out of the building without any trouble. Give me a hand changing the sheets."

We changed Hank's bloody gown and sheets. In few minutes the room was back to normal—as long as no one looked at the ceiling.

"We're going to get out of here," I said. "Can you keep an eye on him and let me know when he wakes up, please?"

"You'll be my first call," Doc Lin said, shoving the bloody sheets into the hazardous waste bin.

Holt and I donned scrubs and headed for the car.

CHAPTER · 21

HOLT PULLED OFF the road onto the dirt path leading to the clubhouse. He stopped the car before passing through the open gate. "I'm not so sure about this."

"We've got to talk to the T.O. sooner or later," I said. "And if Hank's on the mend some of 'em might like to know."

It's hard to explain how the clubhouse could be empty. Sitting in the middle of a junkyard there were always plenty of cars around, even if most of them had seen better days. It wasn't that the clubhouse looked vacant, after all there seemed to be more motorcycles than normal parked out front. It's more that it felt isolated and empty.

Holt took great care driving his Civic up the dirt road. I knew he was proud of his car, but I'd been trying to get him to get something more practical ever since we started working together. There wasn't any room to transport slain demons, or anything else for that matter. It wasn't suited for the dirt roads we often had to travel. It just didn't make much sense, considering the needs of a Keeper. At the same time, Holt put a lot of work into the Civic. You'd never know it by looking at it; the only thing that hinted that it wasn't a regular car were the wider than normal tires and exhaust. The car crawled up the dirt path, the small bumps that I wouldn't have noticed in my truck were accentuated by the lack of speed and stiff suspension. I was sure I could walk it just as fast as Holt was driving.

"I know you're nervous about seeing the T.O., but this is ridiculous," I said. "Just drive up there already."

Holt shot me a look out the side of his eye. "It's not built for dirt. I don't want to mess anything up."

When we finally made it, we found Cotton standing outside with a biker I didn't recognize. They had been watching us crawl up the dirt path for what felt like the better part of twenty minutes. Holt backed the car up in front of the building to park it. I would have thought he was preparing for a speedy getaway if I didn't just live through the drive from the road to the clubhouse.

"You said you haven't talked to anyone in a couple weeks?" I asked.

"I wasn't sure who to talk to with Hank and Lug Nut out of the picture. I got a text message that said to stay away, but I didn't recognize the number. Might be good advice to take."

Cotton said something to the other biker and motioned toward the clubhouse. The second biker walked inside.

"You don't think you should have told me about that before now?" I asked, rolling down my window. "Keep the engine running."

Cotton walked over to the car, leaning forward to rest an elbow on the door. "You shouldn't be here."

"Yeah, that seems to be the consensus," I said.

"Look, I don't know where you've been, but you need to get out of here," Cotton said.

"I healed Hank," I said. "I expect him to be awake soon."

Cotton looked at me for a second before pulling a Sharpie out of his pocket. "Give me your hand."

I held out my hand and he scribbled something on it.

"If you've saved Hank, there may be some hope for us," Cotton said. "There's a number of us that aren't too pleased about the direction Chisel is taking the club, not to mention how he left Hank for dead and Lug Nut in jail."

"If you have a problem about it, why don't you do something?" I asked.

"The club voted," he said. "Some of us don't like it, but we won't go against the club."

"Even if it means the club's destruction?"

Cotton nodded. "Even if."

He put the cap on the Sharpie and stuck it in his pocket. The door to the clubhouse burst open and the Tortured Occult poured out.

"Make it look good," Cotton said.

I was about to ask, "Make what look good," when Cotton reached through the window and grabbed my shirt with one hand. With the other he punched me. I grabbed the hand holding my shirt and twisted, forcing his body to turn awkwardly to the right. I pulled his arm further into the car positioning my shoulder on his elbow. A quick jerk down on his wrist resulted in an audible pop. I pushed Cotton back. He fell to the ground out of sight.

"I'll give you a head start," Chisel shouted. "Then we're gonna hunt you down."

I gave the dash a few quick slaps. "Get us out of here!"

Holt threw it in drive and pulled forward. He drove down the dirt path barely faster than he had come in. Again the car jostled over the bumps. He leaned forward, gripping the wheel like an old woman trying to merge onto the interstate. I looked back to see the T.O. wasn't even bothering to run for their bikes. They looked at the Honda inching its way toward the road in disbelief. Cotton stood up with his harm hanging limply. The other bikers walked to their bikes, put their helmets on, and cranked the bikes at leisure.

I watched the bikers starting to pull out behind us and gaining fast. "If you don't pick up the pace, we're not going to make it out of the parking lot."

"We just have to get to the road," Holt said, white knuckling the wheel.

The scrap cars parked on either side of the road prevented us from being swarmed. One biker pulled up beside the car and started kicking the Honda. Holt swerved in his direction, but the snail's pace we were traveling gave him plenty of time to hit the brakes and avoid being driven into a blue Oldsmobile. The rear window shattered. I turned to see Ginsu on the right side swinging a tire iron. He swung again, this time breaking the right rear window.

"Let's hope they don't get off and run after us, then we would be in real trouble," I said.

"We made it," Holt said, pulling onto the pavement.

The bikes poured out after us as Holt turned to look at me. "You should buckle up."

He pushed the pedal to the floor and the car surged forward with a sudden acceleration that threw me back in my seat and made me scramble for the belt. I looked behind us to see the T.O. falling behind before they realized we were quickly becoming a speck on the horizon, and hit the gas.

"They're sticking with us," I said as I clicked the seatbelt.

"Yeah, bikes are fast," he said. "We can lose them in the curves."

"How?" I asked. "They're outrunning us."

"I put a V6 in my Civic here with a number of other upgrades. Power to weight ratios aren't that far off from a motorcycle. In the curves we have an advantage, another set of wheels. They'll have to slow down or crash," he said. "We have more stability."

"And if you're wrong?" I asked.

"I'm not," Holt said. "Where's the closest curvy road with no stop signs or traffic lights?"

I thought about where we were and said, "About a mile ahead, take a right at the gas station."

Between the traffic in the opposite lane and Holt's driving he was able to keep the T.O. behind us. When we got to the gas station he hit the brakes. The car lurched to the left, tires squealing as Holt made the turn. As soon as we were pointed in the right direction he floored it. I looked back to see the T.O. approaching the turn and slowing way down to make it without crashing. There was a lot less traffic on this road and if the T.O. caught up we might be in serious trouble. They started gaining on us again. The bikers directly behind us drew pistols and began shooting at the car. A few crashed through the already shattered rear window with more thudding into the trunk.

The car's tires screeched around the first turn and I could see what Holt was talking about. Every turn they fell behind, but gained on the straightaways.

"We need to slow them down," I said, looking through the side mirror at bikers gaining on us.

"We got no dust," Holt said.

I did a quick search through the car for anything that I could use. The only thing I came up with were the equipment bags in the back seat.

I grabbed them both. "Anything in here you mind losing?"

"What are you gonna do?"

I opened the bags and pulled everything out, so it was loose and bundled it up in my arms. When I saw a sharp turn ahead I unfastened my seatbelt and rolled down the window.

"Let them catch up for this turn," I said.

Holt let off the gas and the T.O. came up on us quickly. Bullets ricocheted off the car as we entered the turn. The bikers leaned their motorcycles over to make the turn. I hung halfway out the window and dumped our equipment in the road. The harder stuff, like the flashlights, bounced off the road and up into our pursuers. The clothing and bags spread out on the road. Chisel, leading the procession, swerved to avoid the debris and went off the far side of the road. The bikers behind him either hit the clothes or swerved to dodge the obstacles. The result was the same. The club broke ranks into a cluster of screeching tires, crashing bikes, and curses.

We lost sight of them after that. Holt kept our speed up, skillfully winding the car down the two-lane country road. We drove that way for about fifteen minutes without seeing the T.O. before turning off a side road and returning to normal speed. If they were still pursuing us, they never caught back up.

"Where to now?" he asked.

I looked at the writing on my hand. It was a phone number. I pulled the phone out of my pocket. "Let's find out."

A woman's voice answered. "Hello?"

"Hey, Cotton gave me this number," I said. "This is Obie."

"Where the hell have you been?"

"Who am I talking to?' I asked.

"It's Martina."

CHAPTER • 22

"THIS IS IT," I said.

We pulled up to a two-story, gray house in the middle of a subdivision. It was a nice-looking place in a quiet neighborhood. A blue Acura was parked in front of the garage.

"I don't like this," Holt said, glancing into the rearview.

"It'll be fine. We need to know what's going on," I said.

"What if it's a trap?"

"If they were going to set a trap then why bother to chase us from the club-house?" I asked.

"Realism."

I gave him a smile. "Come on, we get to see Martina."

The garage door began to open. When it was three-fourths of the way up it revealed Martina standing in the doorway leading into the house. Hob's truck and two black Harleys were parked in the garage. She was wearing green pajama pants and a loose gray shirt that fell down over one shoulder. Her silver hair was pulled back in a ponytail. I hardly recognized her, and it occurred to me I had never seen her not wearing the T.O.'s colors. She smiled and motioned for us to park in an open spot in front of the motorcycles. Holt pulled the car in and killed the engine. The garage door closed behind us as we got out of the car.

"It's good to see you, I'm glad you came," Martina said. "We're in the living room."

We followed her inside and down a hallway.

"Whose house is this?" I asked.

"It's mine. You didn't think I lived at the clubhouse did you? It smells funny."

"Of course not. It's a nice house," I said. "One question though, if you can afford a place like this, what were you doing hanging around a bunch of dirty bikers?"

"A girl's gotta have hobbies," she said as we rounded the corner into the living room.

Fisheye and Hob were sitting on the couch, each with a beer in their hand. They both stood up when we came in. Fisheye gave us a big hug.

"By the Earth Mother, I've missed you," he said. "Where have you been?"

"Down, boy," I said.

He jumped back, blushing, embarrassed by his show of affection. I shook Hob's hand and we took a seat . Holt and I changed to krasis. It was a strange sensation to feel the blade pull out of my back. I drew it from its sheath and put it in front of me on the coffee table, taking a second to stretch my lower back before sitting down.

"Considering the number of demons we've been seeing lately and the trouble between the T.O. and the Elven Nation . . . We needed some weapons. I spoke to Thera and we had these made. It was more of an ordeal than I intended," I said. "If I could have been here sooner, I would have."

"That's a mean lookin' blade," Fisheye said. "Mind if I check it out?"

I turned it around to hand it to Fisheye by the handle. He took it, turning it over in his hands, inspecting the craftsmanship. I could feel him touching it. I couldn't put a finger exactly where I felt it, everywhere and nowhere at the same time, like a stranger's hands that were a little too comfortable. Chills ran down my back and I could feel my left eye start to twitch involuntarily.

"Sorry, this is a look with your eyes and not your hands kind of thing. I didn't know it until just now," I said, taking the blade from him.

The anxiety that was welling up inside subsided as soon as I had the blade back in my hands. I let out a sigh of relief and sat down.

"You got a blade, too?" Fisheye asked turning to Holt.

Holt held up his hands with his knuckledusters. "I got these."

"You think I could get something like that made?" Fisheye asked.

I shook my head. "I wouldn't recommend it. Let's just say, it was too expensive. Tell me what's been happening while I was away."

"The world's gone to hell," Fisheye said. "With Hank gone, Chisel took over the T.O. He declared war on the Elven Nation. They've been hunting inside the Nation, picking up any elf they run across."

I shot a questioning look at Hob. "Any elf?"

"*Ja*," Hob confirmed. "I am no longer working with the Tortured Occult. They came to the farm making demands. I took the dust *und* left."

Martina leaned back putting her feet on the coffee table. "I had already left the club by then, but the farm was burned down. I don't know if it was the T.O. or the Queen."

"I wouldn't put it past either one of 'em," Fisheye agreed.

Holt took a seat on the couch beside Martina. "Did a lot of the T.O. leave?"

"Hank's sons and us. Some that stayed aren't happy with the direction of things, but aren't willing to leave," Martina said. "Chisel's new recruitment policy seems to focus on hating elves almost exclusively. With Otis, the club was always focused on positive things. Now it's negative and toxic."

"I think the Queen is going to roll up to the clubhouse and open fire with those big guns," Fisheye said. "But then again, the T.O. salvaged one of them from the wreckage when the demons attacked, so that might make her think twice."

I shook my head. "I think the Queen would sacrifice everyone in her kingdom if she thought it would get her what she wanted. She's cruel and reckless enough to attack the Tortured Occult in the open. I have no doubt of that. Something else must be keeping her away."

"*Ja*, she heard rumors the princess is alive," Hob added. "She will not attack if it could hurt the princess."

I shook my head. "That didn't come from any of us. The Tortured Occult were the only ones who knew. Someone's been talking."

Fisheye leaned forward in his chair. "I think Chisel did that on purpose. The idea was the Queen wouldn't attack if she thought they had the princess."

"But he doesn't," Holt said.

"The Queen does not know that," Hob said. "How are Isabelle *und* Harlan?"

"Still safe and bored, like I promised," I said. "They're going to stay that way until I get all this sorted out."

Hob nodded. "I need to know how you will handle Chisel *und* the Queen."

"It's simple, really," I said, leaning back in my chair. "I'm going to get Hank running the T.O. again."

Everyone stared at me silently. I could see the disbelief on their faces, no one wanted to state the obvious. Finally, Fisheye spoke with pain in his voice. "Obie, Hank's not going to make it. The club has been keeping an eye on him. I was at the hospital a couple days ago myself. He's going to check out any day now. I'm surprised he made it this long."

"We went to see him earlier today. We took the silver out and should have him on the mend," I said. "Right, Holt?"

Holt chimed in with a level of eloquence I had come to expect from him: "He looks like ass."

"Assuming he wakes up, that will give us another problem," Martina said. "Chisel isn't going to give up being club president willingly. If he gets word Hank is waking up, he might go finish the job," Martina said. "Even if he doesn't, Hank might be too weak to actually lead."

"The charter says to be in the club, much less run it, you have to ride. If he can't ride, he can't rule," Fisheye said.

"Let me worry about that," I said. "Do we know what Chisel's planning next?"

"Just hunting elves," Fisheye said. "There's not a lot of strategy going on."

The conversation was cut short by the sound of motorcycles on the street. Martina disappeared to the front door to check it out.

"They're here," she said. "Stay quiet and I'll get rid of them."

I gave Holt a nod and we got our weapons ready. I was anxious to see how my new blade performed. We went to the end of the hallway, as close as we could get to the front door without being seen.

The door hinges squeaked as Martina opened it. "What do you want?"

"This guy, Obie, came by the clubhouse earlier today. Chisel wants him and says you know him," the biker said.

"Yeah, I know him, but I haven't seen him in months," she said.

"We're checking around with everyone that knows him," the second biker said.

"I'm here alone," Martina said.

I could hear the bikers sniffing the air. We hadn't had any direct contact with Martina or been by the front door so they probably wouldn't pick up our scent.

"We're going to have to come in and check," the first biker said.

"You're not coming in my house," Martina said.

The second biker spoke up: "While we're checking things, we should make sure she inked over her T.O. tats. Strip search should do it."

"Chisel would want us to be thorough." The first one chuckled.

Holt took a step toward the door and I put a hand on his chest and signaled him to be quiet. We moved up to the edge of the hallway, my hand tightening around my blade. I wanted to see how it cut, but I wasn't going to make a move unless Martina needed me to.

"Before you get any ideas," Martina said, walking down the hall and opening the door to the coat closet beside where I was positioned. She pulled a shotgun out of the closet and pumped it before pointing it in their direction, aiming from the hip. "You're not coming in my house or putting your hands on me."

"Whoa, this is getting interesting," the second biker said. "I bet she doesn't even know how to use it."

"You willing to bet your life on that?" she asked.

"You know that ain't gonna stop us," the first one said.

"That's where you're wrong. See, I loaded these shells with sixteen Mercury dimes, which, in case you dimwits didn't know, are made of silver," Martina said. "So, the real question is: Would I spend twenty dollars to send your sorry asses straight to hell? If either of you want to find out, take a step forward."

It was quiet as the bikers made up their minds. The second biker chimed in, "There's nobody here. This is a waste of time."

"We'll see you later," the first one said as their footsteps retreated off the porch.

"Looking forward to it," Martina yelled after them and slammed the door.

We stayed quiet until we heard the bikes crank up and drive away.

"I can't believe guys in the T.O. are acting like that," Holt said. "There's no excuse for it."

"The club isn't what it used to be," Fisheye said.

I nodded. "Come on, let's finish our talk."

We all went back to the living room and sat down. Martina brought her shotgun.

"What are you thinking?" Hob asked.

I sighed. "As much as I hate the idea of regime change, I don't think the Queen should be running the Nation anymore. She's paranoid and ruthless. The problem is, Isabelle is her only heir. Hob, do you know any other royalty that the people might accept that we could bring in?"

"In my experience, elves are very reluctant to accept outsiders," he answered. "Especially these elves. The Queen has isolated them; they are mistrustful of nearly everyone."

"Could you do it?" I asked.

"Me? Be a king? *Nein*, Obie, you need the royal bloodline," he said.

"Okay, let's come back to that. We'll start with the T.O. That's easier and will give us some time to figure out how to handle the elves. Maybe that's enough, if the Queen will go back to isolating the kingdom. It's not a solution, but it's close," I said.

"So what do we have to do, just kill Chisel?" Holt asked.

"When he took over the club, he changed its dynamic. It's not enough just to take him out, if whoever takes over is the same," Fisheye said. "We need to make sure Hank is back in charge. For that we need enough members that support him. There are some that support him in the Tortured Occult, but I don't know if a majority do. Chisel's recruited a lot and we can't expect any of the new patches to support Hank."

"We can get back anyone that left," Martina said.

"Membership is voted on," Fisheye replied. "Even if we have enough members to vote everyone back in, there's not enough time to go through that process."

"So, we just have to make sure we take out anyone that doesn't support Hank," Martina said, resting the shotgun on her right shoulder.

Martina's phone rang.

She answered it. I turned to Fisheye and said, "Get everyone that you can. When we have everyone together, we'll figure out the best plan of attack."

"We have a problem," Martina said, hanging up the phone. "That was Cotton. Chisel has the princess."

Holt and I looked at each other with the same thought.

"We gotta go," I said. "Friends could be hurt."

"Okay, those guys are probably watching the house. I'll go first and lead them away. Give me five minutes," Martina said, returning the shotgun to the closet and grabbing her keys out of a bowl of change in the hallway.

"I'll start making calls," Fisheye said. "I'll let you know."

After Martina left, we watched the clock for what seemed like an hour until the five minutes passed and we pulled out.

"Holt," I said as we backed out of the garage.

"Yeah?"

"Show me how fast this car can go."

He shifted into first and said, "Hold on."

TO SAY WE MADE it to Yarwor's house in record time would be an understatement. Though I was in the car and witnessed the trip, it still didn't seem possible. One thing was clear, Holt was going to drive from then on out. He had offered to drive a few times before, but I hadn't let him. I could see he put a lot of time into driving and he could handle a vehicle better than I could. With that in mind, it only made sense that he should be the one behind the wheel. I hadn't taken him that seriously, to be honest, at least at first. The more I got to know him, the more I could see the untapped potential in him. Why Cedric had chosen him to be a Keeper was making more and more sense.

We skidded to a stop in front of the house. I had the door open and was stepping out before the car had come to rest. I ran inside, going from room to room, throwing the doors open and shouting names only to come up empty handed. The house was empty.

"Obie," Holt called from outside. "You'll want to see this."

I ran out of the house to find him standing in the doorway of the smithy. Inside was the body of a werecoyote wearing the T.O.'s colors sprawled out on the floor. I stepped into the building to see he had been beheaded. The dead body aside, I could tell from the footprints and scuff marks on the dirt floor that there had been a group of people engaged in a fight in the room. Multiple tracks surrounded the body, but I couldn't tell exactly how many had been here.

"Do you recognize him?" Holt asked, holding up the severed head.

I looked. Its eyes were rolled back and the tongue hung out limply. All I could think was: *This is why you don't mess with orcs.*

"Never seen him before," I said.

Holt dropped the head back to the ground with a melon-esque *thump* and wiped his hand on his pants. I found some tracks from the fight and a blood trail leading out the back door.

"Looks like they went that way," I said, pointing to the back door. "The area's trampled pretty well, but there were at least five or six of them, maybe more."

By the time I finished my sentence, Holt had taken the form of a Doberman and dashed past me into the woods behind the building. He had his nose to the ground, moving back and forth in a zigzag pattern. He disappeared into the underbrush and I set out after him.

By the time I made it through the bushes, I had lost him. I peered through the woods looking for any sign of him. I had decided to go back and follow the scent myself when barking erupted from off to my right. I took off like a shot.

The barking stopped for a few seconds and was replaced by Holt's yelling, "I found them! They're over here."

I crashed through a patch of blackberries, the thorns catching my clothes and scratching my flesh. Livy and Yarwor lay near the center of a small clearing surrounded on a couple of sides by the thorny bushes. Yarwor lay on his back with his head resting on Livy's lap. His body was covered in bites, scratches, and tears. He looked as if a pack of wild dogs had had their way with him. I slid on my knees in the leaves beside them.

"He's still alive, but barely," Holt said, holding his hands over his battered body. His eyes and hands glowed green as he began healing Yarwor's injuries.

I saw claw marks on Livy's face and neck. Tear tracks that hadn't quite dried ran down her face and over the cuts on her cheek. I turned her head to the side to see her injury. Four deep gashes ran down her cheek and neck, cutting deep. The blood that had spilled out had soaked into her shirt and started to dry around the edges. I began channeling energy to heal her wounds. The claw marks promptly closed up and when I felt the energy pouring over her, I stopped. She didn't open her eyes.

I gave her a little shake. "Livy?"

Yarwor groaned, slowly regaining consciousness. Yarwor looked dazed at first then sat straight up and grimaced in pain.

"Go easy," Holt said. "You aren't completely healed yet. They really did a number on you."

"Where's Isabelle?" he asked.

"I was going to ask you," I said, pulling Livy up into a sitting position. "We haven't found her yet,"

"They took her," he growled.

"What about Harlan?" I asked.

"He wasn't here," Yarwor said. "He was out on one of his walks."

"How long has he been gone?" I asked.

Yarwor shook his head. "I don't know exactly. I don't know how long he was gone before we were attacked. I was unconscious for a while, too. We have to get Isabelle back."

I motioned for him to relax. "We'll get her back."

"You're damn right we will," he said, pushing Holt away and getting slowly to his feet with a grunt.

"She's not waking up," I said, scooping Livy up in my arms. "I'm taking her back to the house."

I moved as gently and quickly as I could back to the house. I took her to Yarwor's bed and laid her down. I adjusted the pillow under her head and pulled the sheet over her. I rested a hand against her cheek and forehead. She didn't feel warm. I decided there really wasn't anything else I could do for her at the moment. My energy would be better spent coming up with a game plan to get Isabelle back. I wasn't doing any good for anyone standing around. I walked to the bedroom door, looking out into the kitchen. It was empty. I wasn't sure what was holding Holt and Yarwor up, but they should have been back by now.

"Obie?" a fragile voice said from behind me.

I turned to see Livy with her eyes barely opened.

I knelt beside her. "Hey, you're awake. I was starting to get worried."

"How's Yarwor?" she asked.

"He's fine, Holt's healing him up."

"And Isabelle?"

"They took her," I said.

"It's all my fault. I slowed them down. Yarwor could have gotten away with Isabelle, but he wouldn't leave me behind. He fought them the whole way, keeping them away from us until we got trapped by the briars and got surrounded. I tried to stop them. After they got her they turned on Yarwor. They said they were going to teach him a lesson. They were hurting him just to do it. They thought it was fun," she said with tears flowing down her cheeks. "When they were done, I went over to try to help him and that's when one of them hit me. I tried to take him back to the house, but I couldn't even move him an inch. I passed out right after that. I'm too old and useless to be any good to anybody."

"What did the one that hit you look like?" I asked.

"He had a red shirt and a mohawk," she said.

"Listen to me," I said, taking her hand. "It's not your fault, it's my fault. I shouldn't have put you in a dangerous situation to begin with. I'm going to get you squared away, and I'm going to get Isabelle back. This is all going to be okay."

She turned her head away and didn't say anything else.

"I'll make you some tea," I said.

I went to the kitchen and put a pot of water on to boil. Yarwor came storming in the house a minute later with Holt right behind him.

"What's going on?" I asked.

Holt shrugged. "He said he needed to get something."

Yarwor headed into the bedroom. I heard something heavy being dragged across the floor. Holt and I went into the bedroom to find Yarwor had pulled the dresser away from the wall. A large sword was attached to the back of the dresser. Yarwor pulled a dusty scimitar in a leather scabbard off some hooks. The sword reached to his chest with the tip on the ground. He slid it out a few inches and looked at the blade. The metal was red; not rusted, but the color of Georgia clay.

"What kind of blade is that?" I asked.

Yarwor looked down at the blade in his hands. "I don't know exactly. I was told my great-grandfather brought it through the portal with him from the homeland. They say it's a weapon of honor among my people, not that it means anything here. Just an heirloom without a family. Whatever it's made of, it's a different metal than anything I've seen on Earth."

He stepped past us and headed outside.

"Where's he going?" I asked.

Holt shrugged. We followed him outside. Yarwor walked to Holt's Honda. He opened the passenger side door, flipped up the seat, and crawled into the back. He was so large, he sat knees to chest, leaving less than a foot on either side of the back seat clear. The tip of his scimitar rested on the floor to his right with the pommel touching the ceiling to his left. He cradled it in his arms and sat quietly waiting for Holt and me to get in the car. I opened the passenger door and leaned in to speak to him.

"I need you to stay here," I said, giving it a second to sink in before continuing. "Livy's hurt. We can't leave her here alone. Harlan's still out there somewhere. I know you want to help. The way you can do that is to keep Livy safe while Holt and I get Isabelle."

He looked away as he thought about it. I knew he wasn't going to refuse, he was just that kind of orc, but he needed a minute to remember that about himself.

He climbed out of the car. Standing inches in front of my face he said, "I can't lose any more kids."

He wasn't speaking from a place of anger so much as desperation.

"We'll get her back," I said. "I swear by Thera."

He went back toward the house. Holt and I got in the car, but he didn't crank it.

"Something wrong?" I asked.

"Obie, I don't know if I can do this."

I fastened my seatbelt. "What are we talking about?"

"We're about to go to war with a bunch of people who a month ago were friends. It just doesn't seem right," he said.

"There's a lot of new members in the Tortured Occult. We aren't friends with them and from what I've seen, I don't want to be. The guys that were our friends in the club still are," I said. "Plus some of the people you're thinking about left the club. They'll either not be there or be on our side."

He put his hands on the wheel and looked out the window. "I don't want to hurt my friends."

I knew the uncertainty he was wrestling with. I had felt it, too. "Look," I said. "You're going to do fine. Try not to think too far ahead. All we have to do now is go to the clubhouse and get the princess back. Just do what you need to do. One step at a time."

He nodded and started the car.

CHAPTER·24

RIVER PARK WAS little more than a parking lot, a couple of picnic tables, and some steps leading down into the Etowah River. It was used by kayakers in Dawsonville to put in or take out, depending on what section of the river they were boating that day. Sometimes families would come there to swim in the river. Today it was the meeting place for our clandestine mission. I had chosen it because it was only about a mile away from the clubhouse, but in a place where we wouldn't attract a lot of attention. Holt drove us in a lap around the parking lot before parking out of sight of the road. There were a few cars in the lot but no people. It's true it was fall and the water would be cold, but diehard kayakers were still out on the rivers; they just wore wetsuits.

"Looks like they're not here yet," Holt said, rolling down the windows before killing the engine. "You want to get out."

"Sure," I said, opening the door.

We got out and leaned against the back of the Civic in silence. After a few minutes, Hob's old pickup pulled in. He parked beside us and Hob and Martina got out of the truck. Hob had a satchel slung over one shoulder. It looked like it had some bulk to it, but didn't seem to be too heavy. No doubt the dust he had brought for our raid.

"How far behind you is everyone else?" I asked.

Martina shrugged. "We're it."

"There's no one else from the Tortured Occult coming?" Holt asked. "Like, no one?"

"There are people that will support Hank, but Hank's not here," she said. "For the time being, what you see is what you get."

"What about Fisheye?" I asked.

Martina shrugged. "He's looking for Torch. Last I heard, he hadn't found him. It'll be fine though. Big Ticket called and said they were headed to the Elven Nation."

"What're they doing there?" Holt asked.

"Probably going to let the Queen know they have Isabelle and make some demands," I postulated. "At least, we won't have everyone to contend with."

"As long as we stick together we will be fine," Hob said.

Martina pulled a box of shotgun shells from the truck and shoved them into her pockets. "Let's get this over with."

Holt went to the Civic and opened the door.

I intercepted him before he could get in. "We should take the truck. We can't get everyone in and out quick with only two doors."

"We're going to leave my car here?" he asked.

I nodded "Yeah, it'll be fine. We'll be back in twenty minutes."

Hob and Martina got in the cab of the truck while Holt and I jumped in the back. Hob drove us about a mile over to the clubhouse and up the dirt path, parking in front of the door. I was sure they would hear the truck engine. A single engine in the middle of the day might not attract any suspicion, it would probably be construed as a customer headed to the shop. We all piled out of the truck. Martina pulled her shotgun from behind the seat. Hob slung the bag of dust over his shoulder. We stood so the truck was between us and the road to keep us out of sight of passersby and made the change to krasis.

"Ready?" I whispered.

Everyone nodded. I drew my new blade and led the group in. We moved in fast, going straight through the changing room into the bar. Inside I found a prospect mopping a bloody spot on the floor. When he saw us, he dropped the mop and moved away, holding his hands up. I ignored him, opting to confront the bikers sitting at the bar. I recognized Skinny Pete, a wererat. He was one of the original members of the Tortured Occult before the mess with Chisel started. He was sitting with Ginsu and a werewolf I didn't recognize. Must be a new patch. The werewolf jumped up and came toward me, baring teeth for the attack. I sidestepped him, slashing with my blade. I felt little resistance in the blade as I passed him. What I did feel was a sensation like dipping my hand in warm water, although not in my hand. It was a similar sensation to when Fisheye had handled my blade. It was going to take some getting used to, but the middle of a fight wasn't the time to figure it out.

I assumed from the ease of the swing the blade had only grazed the werewolf. I spun, expecting to see fangs chomping at my neck, but he wasn't there. I looked down to see the wolf had been cut in half cleanly at the belly. The sword passed through so smoothly I didn't think it possible to have done that kind of damage. He dragged himself away with trembling hands, leaving a bloody streak behind him. Martina stepped forward and smashed his head with the butt of her shotgun, rendering him unconscious. He wouldn't wake up.

My phone buzzed in my pocket. I looked down by reflex, distracted by the vibration, not really intending to answer it. Martina shouted my name in warning and a shooting pain exploded in my back. I could feel something foreign and pointy had found itself a home in my belly. I looked down to see the tip of a knife sticking through the front of my shirt. Blood began soaking into my shirt, making a ring around the tip of the blade. I could tell from the color that the knife was silver, which could have been a deadly injury if I had been a normal shifter. Being a Keeper, I lacked the vulnerability to silver. I tuned to find Ginsu with his hand on the blade. He let go of the knife as I turned to face him, the look of certainty draining from his face. I raised my blade to his neck. He didn't move back, but raised his head away from it.

I could feel it scratch him. "You can go sit down with Skinny Pete or you can die."

"Sure, Obie," he said, backing slowly, sheepishly scratching his neck. "Hey, you can't blame a fella for trying, right?"

"Sit," I commanded, pointing to the bar with my blade. "Hob, give me a hand with this."

He inspected the blade running through my back. He opened his bag and pulled out a hockey puck–sized piece of dust. He had pressed the dust with a binder into a mold. It was much easier to use these pucks over powder that could spill, or get blown away. Hob prepared to use magic to remove it.

"Just yank it," I said.

He put the dust puck back in his bag. Placing one hand on my back for support, with the other he took the handle of the knife, giving it a quick tug. I cringed at the feeling of the metal sliding out of my body. I would need a couple minutes to recover. Not a huge deal with three people backing me up.

"I don't want no trouble," the prospect said.

"You can drop the kutte and go, or you can stay and take your chances," I said.

It was a little dramatic, I'll admit, but it would be a good indication of how dedicated he was to the club.

He peeled off the kutte like it was made of lava before throwing it on the floor. He moved toward the door slowly, at first, giving us a wide berth. When he got halfway there, he broke into a run. He disappeared through the door never to be seen again.

"Where's the princess?" I asked, turning back to the bikers at the bar.

"In the conference room," Skinny Pete said. "But you don't wanna go back there."

"Why's that?" I asked.

Ginsu smiled. "Big Ticket's watching her."

"Yeah, yeah." I waved a hand dismissively in his direction as I walked toward the door leading to the princess. "Keep an eye on them, I'll be right back."

I stepped through the door into the back hallway. The kitchen was to my right with the conference room the first door on my left. I caught the smell of meat coming from the kitchen. I stuck my head in and saw a patch I didn't recognize. A werewolf with headphones, bobbing his head to some heavy metal. He had an apron tied around his waist that was smeared with a red sauce. He wore a red shirt under his kutte and his hair was trimmed into a mohawk. This was the guy that hurt Livy. If he knew I was there, he didn't turn around. Instead he put a hand on the door of a large, restaurant-style smoker normally reserved for whole pigs, goats, and the occasional slab of beef. He opened the door revealing an elf. I didn't know her. That didn't mean much, her skin had darkened and distorted from the cooking. She had been gutted with her arms and legs tied close to her body. The cook dabbed a sauce mop in a bucket. He basted the elf, dabbing the red liquid around her body. He put the mop down in the bucket and reached in the smoker to pull off a bit of meat. He blew on it a few times to cool it off before putting it in his mouth and closing the door.

"It's coming along real nice," he said, becoming aware someone was standing behind him. He wiped his hands on the apron and turned around. "When everyone gets back tonight—"

He stopped short when he saw I wasn't there to check on dinner. He pulled the headphones down around his neck.

"Earlier today you hurt a friend of mine," I said.

He smirked. "You come here to rough me up or somethin'?"

"Or something," I said, stabbing my blade into his belly.

He grunted and grabbed the blade. I twisted it and drew it back quickly. I pushed him. He fell back, leaning against the smoker and holding his stomach. I gave him a slash above his left knee, severing his leg. He screamed and fell to the floor, catching himself with his hands. He looked up as I brought the blade down on his neck. His body fell to the floor and his head rolled out in the hallway. I wiped my blade off on his clothes before going after his head. Kicking it back into the kitchen, I closed the door. I moved back down the hallway to the door of the conference room. I waited outside the door and listened.

"This time I'm going to get what I want. I'm not putting up with any more of your tricks," Big Ticket said.

I took a deep breath, testing how my injury had come along. I was almost healed; now I just had a dull ache in my lower back. I paused, not because I was injured, but because I really didn't want to have a go at B.T. one on one, even with my new blade. It wasn't that I was afraid to fight him, or that I thought I would lose, so much as that I considered him a friend. I don't like slicing up my friends. I could get Holt, but that would leave Hob and Martina outnumbered. I would have to do this alone. I could imagine myself charging in and getting drop kicked right back into the hallway. Big Ticket was capable in that way. I decided to open the door and stay in the hall, so I wasn't taken by surprise.

"Do you have," Big Ticket said, as I turned the handle and pushed the door open. "Any fours?"

The door swung wide, revealing B.T. and Isabelle sitting at the table opposite each other, with cards in their hands. There was a large pile of snacks on the table. Open bags of chips and candy spilled out onto the table for easy access.

"Obie," Isabelle shouted when she saw me.

I stepped into the room. "I have to take—"

"Hold on a second," Big Ticket said, holding up a finger. "Fours," he said turning back to Isabelle.

She looked down at her cards and then back up at him with a grin from ear to ear. "Go fish."

He took a card from the deck, added it to his hand, and placed his cards on the table before turning back to me. "Nice blade. Is that why you went M.I.A.?"

I looked down at the blade and turned it to the side, so he could see it. "Yeah, it's a little something from Thera that kept me . . . busy."

"I didn't expect to see you here," B.T. said.

"I came for Isabelle."

"And that scream a minute ago means my brothers are dead?" he asked.

"Two of the new guys," I said. "The first one attacked me. The second almost killed Livy, so he had it coming."

Big Ticket nodded. "Okay. What about the rest of us? Do we have it coming, too?"

"Ginsu put a knife through my back and I didn't hurt him so I'm showing restraint. I've got Holt, Martina, and Hob keeping an eye on them in the bar," I said. "We're putting an end to this war and getting things back to normal. We could really use you on our side."

"You want me to betray my club?" he asked, squinting suspiciously at me.

"Not at all. I want you to stay true to your club," I said. "From what I hear the club abandoned Hank and left Lugnut in jail . . . sounds like the club isn't taking care of its members."

"I don't like leaving Lugnut in jail, but that's what the club decided to do," B.T. said. "And Hank, there's no reason to think he would survive."

I grinned. "I wouldn't be so sure. I paid a visit to the hospital earlier today. Hank was in bad shape, I'll admit, but I was able to get the silver out."

This got his interest. His ears, that had been droopy, perked up a little. "He's okay?"

"He's still unconscious, but I think he'll be all right," I said.

"So, you think he'll be all right, but he could be too far gone to recover," he said.

Isabelle picked up a handful of gummy bears from the table as she quietly watched the exchange.

I leaned against the door frame and shrugged. "Don't be so negative. Everybody looks up to you. I need you on my side."

"You don't have a side," Big Ticket said. "The problems between us and the elves are between us. It's none of your concern, really."

"That may have been true before someone started bringing demon armies through to attack the elves," I said. "That's not good for anyone."

B.T. gave Isabelle a sideways glance and I knew what he was thinking, but not saying. He was thinking that demons eating elves worked out for the Tortured Occult. With the war going on, he was right. The most likely suspect was someone in the T.O. I didn't really think any of them was doing it though. Let's just say, they lacked interest in magic. The Tortured Occult wasn't the kind of group that would outsource its dirty work either.

Big Ticket leaned back in his chair. "You busted in here with your fancy knife to get Isabelle, so go ahead."

"Come on," I sighed. "I'm not gonna cut you up."

"You don't have a choice," Big Ticket said. "If Hank was awake, it might be different, but as it stands, you want Isabelle and I can't let you take her."

I scratched my chin. "How about this . . . I'll give you that fight you've been asking for. If I win, you hand over Isabelle and help us get rid of Chisel."

"And if you don't win?" he asked.

"Then I lose."

It was a vague answer to be sure. The worst-case scenario was that I lost the fight. If I did, Holt, Martina, and Hob would be right there to take care of B.T. Aside from taking the time for the fight, there wasn't really a downside to it.

"In the circle?" he asked.

"Yeah," I said. "No weapons, standard rules."

B.T. nodded. "All right, you got a deal."

The princess followed us out to the bar where Holt and Martina stood guard over the members of the Tortured Occult we had rounded up.

"We're taking this party outside," I said, walking to the door and holding it open for everyone.

Big Ticket walked through first, followed by the rest of the T.O., Martina, and Hob. Holt was last and stopped beside me before going outside.

"What's happening here?" Holt asked.

"B.T. and I are going into the circle," I answered. "If I win, he's going to help us out."

"And what happens if you don't win?" Holt asked.

I shrugged. "Tell Martina to shoot him first."

Holt put his hands on his hips and shook his head. "This is crazy. There has to be a better option."

"Well, we could kill 'em all," I offered.

He looked over at Big Ticket who was stretching his neck and back, getting loosened up for the fight. The bikers took a seat on a picnic table.

"Okay, good luck," he said. "And, Obie?"

"Yeah?"

"For the Mother's sake, bob and weave," he said. "That guy's no joke."

I walked over to a different picnic table with Holt. "Watch this stuff for me," I said putting my phone on the table.

I stabbed my blade into the wood, so it was standing on its own, and moved to the edge of the circle across from Big Ticket. "You ready?"

Big Ticket nodded and motioned toward the circle with his hand in a kind of half-salute, half-invitation. As if on cue, we both charged, colliding in the center. Our claws dug into the ground as we grappled on our feet, struggling to gain the advantage, neither one claiming any territory. I sank my claws into the tender flesh of his lower back. My fingers broke the skin. He screamed as his leg buckled. He pushed me back and tried to bite my neck, but I moved an arm in the way.

I clenched my jaw from the pain of his teeth sinking into my forearm and landed two elbow strikes into the side of his head before he brought his arm up to block. He countered with a few shots to my ribs that lifted me off my feet and made a popping sound that sent pain shooting through my side. I pushed him back to get some space and spun, delivering a tail whip that struck his face. I used the momentum from the spin to deliver a right cross that I was sure would put him back on his heels. He must have known it was coming; at the last second he dropped his head. Instead of landing in his face, my fist contacted with the front of his skull. Pain shot through my hand and I was sure it was broken as well. We paused for a second, I gave my hand a little shake and he did the same with his head. With less than a minute in, I had two broken bones and, aside from being a little dazed, it didn't appear B.T. was slowing down. It was becoming a real possibility that I wasn't going to win this fight if I continued breaking bones. I needed to get myself a little time to heal.

Big Ticket came in swinging his claws. I dodged the first few, but the pain in my side slowed me down. When it was clear I wasn't going to dodge the next one, I ducked, putting my arms around my head to protect myself. I could feel my back being torn to shreds from his claws. I charged in and wrapped my arms around his waist, lifting him off the ground. I could have thrown him out of the circle, but that was winning on a technicality. I respected B.T. too much to do that to him, so I slammed him on the ground instead. The back of his head hit the ground with a *thump*. He wasn't knocked unconscious from the impact, but he clearly was going to need a minute to recover.

I took a step back and put a hand on my ribs. I could feel the warm tingling as they healed. The pain eased. I was about to go over and stomp Big Ticket's head into the ground until I had officially won the fight when Holt entered the circle.

"Two on one?" Big Ticket asked, his eyes hazy.

Holt held my phone out to me. "You need to take this. It's Doc Lin. She says she's been calling you."

"I'm kind of in the middle of something."

"It's Hank," Holt said. "He's awake."

CHAPTER · 25

I LOOKED AT BIG Ticket, still laying on his back. Our eyes met, and I asked, "We done?"

"For now," he said, holding out a hand.

I pulled him to his feet. I took the phone from Holt and stepped away from everyone for some privacy.

"This is Obie," I said into the phone.

"He's awake," Doc Lin said. "He woke up about twenty minutes ago."

"How is he?"

"Weak, grumpy, and refusing treatment," she answered. "Someone needs to come get him."

"I'll be there soon," I said.

I hung up and walked back to the group. "Hank's awake. We need to go get him. It's decision time. Are you going to support Hank or Chisel?"

"We're going to need a minute," Skinny Pete said. "As a club."

I nodded. "No problem."

The bikers huddled and we moved away to respect their privacy.

"Do you think it is wise to let them speak alone?" Hob asked.

I grabbed my blade out of the picnic table. "I think it will be fine. If they want to try something, we still have them outnumbered and outgunned."

After speaking for a few minutes, Ginsu looked over and said, "Martina, come talk to us a sec."

Martina, with her shotgun, joined the conversation. They talked for a few minutes more before breaking the huddle.

"We're in," Skinny Pete said. "But I don't know how we're going to pull this off. Chisel has one of the new guys watching the hospital. There's no way we are going to get him out of there without being seen. He probably already saw you the other day and told Chisel something's up."

I smiled. "Don't be so paranoid. The new members probably wouldn't recognize us. Besides, we have Hob," I said, putting a hand on Hob's shoulder for emphasis. "When we get to the hospital, let's do a lap around the parking lot and find this lookout. We'll figure out a plan from there."

"If you say so," he mumbled. "Whatever voodoo he's going to do, he needs to do it fast. We're supposed to be bringing Isabelle up to meet Chisel. He called right before you showed up. I'm not sure what he has planned."

"One of you tell him there was a problem with the van to give us a little time."

"I'll do it," Big Ticket said.

B.T. made the call. Big Ticket and Ginsu rode their motorcycles while Skinny Pete drove the van. The rest of us piled in the back for the trip to the hospital. I didn't blame them for having doubts; anyone in their position would. Going against Chisel was a high stakes gamble. I had complete faith in Hob's abilities and he had enough dust on hand to work some serious magic. Once they saw what he could do, they wouldn't be concerned anymore.

We drove in silence and I found my thoughts drifting to my own doubts. Doc Lin had said Hank was weak. The last time I saw him he looked close to death. I wasn't sure how the club would feel if they saw him lying in the hospital bed the way Holt and I had. His condition didn't inspire confidence. I wasn't even sure he would be strong enough to assert his authority if it came down to it. We could cross that bridge when we got to it. For now, we just needed to get Hank and get him to where the T.O. was meeting. The plan was to get Hank and catch them by surprise. It's the only way we could get him in a position to talk to the club without Chisel interfering. I didn't believe Chisel would risk losing control of the club under any circumstances, even if it meant murdering club members.

Big Ticket and Ginsu pulled into a shopping center close to the hospital. Their bikes would be too high profile for what we were going for. We pulled into the hospital parking lot and Skinny Pete did a lap while we scanned the cars for the lookout. We spotted him parked up front. I recognized him right away; one of the Dogs that was at the clubhouse when Ginsu told his tree frog joke. I was afraid he was going to spot us, but his attention was focused on his phone instead of anything going on outside of the car he was in.

"Drive to the back on the lot," I said, pulling my phone out of my pocket. "I'll give Doc Lin a call."

I found her number in my contacts and called. She picked up on the second ring. "We're here. Is he ready?"

"Thank God," she said. "I'll have him right out."

We waited for a few minutes before Doc Lin came out the front of the hospital, rolling Hank in a wheelchair.

"Let's go," I said, turning to look at Hob. "Can you keep an eye on the look-out and if he spots us, break his phone?"

"*Ja*," Hob said, retrieving one of the pucks from the box. "It will not be a problem."

Skinny Pete drove the van around, pulling up in front of Hank. I got out of the passenger seat and held the door open for him. Hank looked like hell; his face was still sunken in and his color was off. He was wearing scrubs Doc Lin must have given him, and held a clear plastic bag with his belongings in it. He still looked better than he did when I saw him in the hospital bed.

"Good to see you awake," I said.

He gave me an angry-looking side-eye. I didn't know how much of it was him being upset with me, versus recovering from almost dying and still being on the mend. He put his hands on the arms of the wheelchair and grunted as he pushed himself into a standing position. He climbed into the passenger seat of the van and dropped the bag onto the floorboard. I closed the door.

"Really appreciate it," I said to Doc Lin.

She rolled the wheelchair out of the way and stepped closer to me. "I have some more questions that I want to have answered."

"After I get this sorted, I'll give you a call."

I climbed into the back and closed the door. Hob was holding the dust puck in his hand and staring out the tinted back windows. The puck was slowly dissolving into smoke as he concentrated, consuming the latent power in it. I noticed some powder falling from the puck unconsumed onto the leg of his pants. It must be whatever he used to bind the dust together into shape. I looked through the window to where the lookout was sitting in his car. He was fiddling with his phone in a way that told me he was having trouble with it.

Hob tossed what was left of the puck back in the box. "He will not be making any calls."

"Shouldn't we take care of him?" Holt asked. "What if he goes inside and makes a call? Just magic him to death."

"A dead body in the parking lot will draw too much attention," Hank said. "Pull out and see if he follows. If he does, we can take care of him somewhere more private."

"And if he doesn't?" I asked.

Hank looked back at us. "Then we'll have to draw some attention."

Hank's voice was gruffer than usual and he sounded tired, but I was glad to see he was thinking clearly and in the mood to take charge. Both would be critical if he was going to win confidence from the club. Skinny Pete pulled out of the hospital and we watched to see how the lookout would react. Sure enough, he pulled out behind us, keeping what he thought was a safe distance. The Tortured Occult was meeting in the Chattahoochee National Forest, inside the Queen's territory. It was over an hour drive. At some point along the way we had to take care of our tail. We were followed deep into the mountains where we came to an area secluded enough to deal with him. We still hadn't talked about how we were going to handle our tail.

"Do we have a plan for our shadow?" I asked.

"Hob, do you have enough dust to take care of him quickly?" Hank asked.

Hob lifted the bag of dust. "*Ja*, there is plenty."

"Pull over up here by the cliff," Hank said. "Hob, when he comes around the corner take care of him."

"When you say, 'take care of him,' how do you mean?" Hob asked.

"Just get rid of him quickly and don't leave a mess to draw attention," Hank answered.

I knew the cliff he was talking about. It was the largest pull-off on the winding mountain road between Dahlonega and Suches. A rock face fifty or sixty feet long and forty feet high bordered the right side of the road. It was one of the only places in the area where there was graffiti. Sometimes people used the rockface to climb or rappel, but when we got there it was empty. The other side of the road had a railing to keep cars from plummeting off the mountain side. I heard a rumor that a woman was driving with her granddaughter when she saw a black bear in the pull-off. She wanted to get a picture of it with her daughter so she put some honey on the girl's hand to draw the bear close. The bear ended up taking the girl's arm off. I understand people are going to do stupid things from time to time; I would just prefer innocent people not get hurt by it. Skinny Pete pulled the van over and put it in park. Hob grabbed a few pucks in each hand and jumped out of the back of the van.

A few seconds later the car came around the bend. Hob raised his left hand and the pucks began to disintegrate. The car lifted off the road, tires screamed and then were quiet as they lost their connection with the pavement. The car drifted through the air toward the railing. The biker behind the wheel saw what was coming and tried to open the door. It wouldn't budge. He became more frantic as the car floated over the railing. The biker slammed his body into the driver's door, trying in vain to force it open. As the car drifted out into the open air, the biker changed tactics and kicked the window. It took him a few kicks to clear the window from the passenger side. He stuck his head out and looked down into the landscape dropping away below him. Hob threw the pucks in his right hand. They ignited in midair. A massive fireball slammed into the side of the car with enough force to crush it. The car burned and spun from the impact as it dropped out of view.

For a second there was silence, then the car crashed far below. I jumped out of the van and jogged over to the railing. The only sign of the car was a smoke trail working its way up through the trees around 150 feet below. Hob wiped some sweat from his forehead with his shirtsleeve. It was one of the most impressive displays of magic I had ever seen, and it clearly took some serious effort on his part to pull it off.

I jogged back to the van. "I thought you said it was better to be more subtle with magic?"

"*Ja*, it is," Hob said. "But we are in a hurry *und* this is more fun."

We climbed back into the van and continued on to meet the Tortured Occult.

CHAPTER·26

DURING THE DRIVE, Skinny Pete filled Hank in about what he had missed while he was in the hospital. Hank took particular interest in why no one had bailed Lugnut out of jail or gone through the normal channels to get him a lawyer. Hank's other son, Torch, had disappeared. No one knew what had happened to him, but it was assumed he went into hiding.

"We're getting close," Skinny Pete said.

I stuck my head between the seats. "When we get there, position the van so the back doors are facing everyone. I don't want anyone getting hung up trying to go out one door or running around the van. Hank, you should probably climb in the back with the rest of us."

Hank undid his seatbelt. He grabbed the bag at his feet and moved between the seats to the back of the van. He sat down behind Skinny Pete with Hob in the middle and Holt by the door. I moved to the back across from Holt with Martina between Isabelle and me.

"How long till we get there?" I asked.

"A few minutes, just around the corner up here," Skinny Pete said.

"Let's get ready," I said, sitting down.

We all made the change to krasis. When we had finished, Isabelle sat wide-eyed and quiet.

"What's the matter?" I asked.

"I knew you could do that, but I had never seen it before," she answered.

"Really? Not even at the clubhouse?" I asked. "I thought for sure you would have."

She shook her head. "This is my first time out of the Nation. I've never been around shifters before."

"And? What do you think?" Martina asked.

"Some of you seem nice," Isabelle said. "Some not so nice."

Martina nodded in agreement. "Are we what you expected?"

"Not really. Mother says that shifters are savages and that Hank is the biggest savage of them all," she said.

"Hank's a good man," I said.

Her face scrunched up as she replied. "Mother says there's no such thing."

"You got to spend some time with us, what do you say?" Holt asked.

"I don't know," she said. "Can I ask you a question?"

I nodded. "Sure."

"Does it hurt? When you do that?" she asked, rolling her index fingers around each other.

"I can't speak for anyone else," I said, "but for me the first time was the worst pain I have ever experienced. It was like getting ripped apart and someone used salt to glue you back together with everything out of place. That was over two hundred years ago now. It hurt a little less every time and now I actually like it. It feels like a good stretch to me. It might be a different experience, though, since I was born human."

"That's pretty much the way it was for me," Hank said. "For those of us born into it, the first change happens around puberty and it's hell, but it gets better with time."

"I have another question," Isabelle said.

"Shoot," I said, no elf pun intended.

Isabelle looked up into my eyes. "Are you going to hurt my mother?"

I try not to lie, if I can help it, especially to kids, so this was a difficult answer. "I don't want to hurt her, but she is hurting a lot of other people right now and we have to stop her. If I can stop her without hurting her, I will."

I could see the answer didn't reassure her, but it's all I had. No one else in the van could step up with a more comforting answer. Isabelle turned her head toward the front of the van. She couldn't see out any windows from where she was sitting, but I think it was only important that she was looking away from us. I looked at Martina and she shrugged; she didn't have a better answer than I did.

After a minute Isabelle put her arms on her knees and put her head down to hide her face.

"All right, let's get our plan straight," I said.

Hank let out a heavy sigh. "Ginsu and Big Ticket will pull in with the club. They can get some of our people out of the way. Skinny Pete will get us into position. Y'all'll rush out and catch them by surprise. We need everybody to stay put long enough for me to get out of the van and sort things out. You shouldn't have to subdue everyone, but keep an eye on the new folks especially. There's a chance it could get a little hairy."

"And if things go sideways?" I asked. "What do we do then?"

"Do what you have to, and we'll figure it out later," Hank said.

It surprised me to hear him say that. I would have expected him to advise us against hurting the club if possible. Then again, the club hadn't exactly been living up to expectations lately.

"We're here," Skinny Pete said.

We had Isabelle hide in the footwell of the passenger seat. She could stay there unseen. I debated having Holt or Martina stay in the van with her, but I decided we needed everyone to keep things from getting out of hand. I pulled my blade and put a hand on the door handle as Skinny Pete circled around to get in position. I looked back at everyone as the van stopped. The group exchanged nods, we pushed the doors open, and rushed out.

I was out of the van first with Martina right behind me. Big Ticket grabbed Cotton and Fisheye and backed them away, keeping them out of the conflict. The startled expressions of the rest of the bikers as we poured out of the van confirmed we had caught them by surprise. The first biker I came to had his back to me. He spun around to see what the commotion was. I didn't have time to explain myself, so I crouched, and body-checked him over his motorcycle. The patch next to him reached for a knife he had strapped to his leg. I stepped forward with my right and pivoted, sending my blade up to his throat, stopping short of a fatal blow. I shook my head to impress upon him the urgency that he stayed still. He raised his chin away from the blade and I saw a trickle of blood roll down his neck. I didn't mean to cut him, but the blade and I were still new to each other and I lacked finesse. Either way, the message was sent.

A biker in the back started drawing a pistol from under his kutte. Ginsu grabbed his arm to stop him. Martina stepped up beside me, firing her shotgun. Both of them were hit and fell to the ground.

I looked over at Hob, standing on the other side of Martina. He was holding his hands up, reminiscent of a boxing stance. His hands were on fire. I'm not ashamed to say it, but Hob scared me a little. With enough dust that guy could probably blow up the world.

Chisel was in the center of the group and didn't look happy to see us. "What the hell is this?" he screamed.

Hank climbed out of the van slowly, grunting as he stepped gingerly to the ground. He looked much better in krasis than he did in human form. His fur covered his pale complexion. He looked a little thinner than normal and had droopy eyes, other than that, he looked all right. He had put his kutte on over the scrubs. The scrubs were stretched to their limit, barely able to accommodate the additional fur and bulk that came with krasis. It was a strange sight, but his kutte was a symbol of his authority—it didn't matter what he wore under it.

To say the situation was tense would be an understatement. When Hank stepped out of the van, his presence seemed to chill the vibe, if only a little. The original members of the Tortured Occult swapped glances as if they were children busted by a parent. The newer members seemed more confused than anything.

Hank put his hands on his hips, looking around the group. "Somebody want to tell me what's going on?"

"I'm glad you're back on your feet," Chisel said. "But you're not up to this. I got it under control, so why don't you go back to the clubhouse and I'll catch you up when we're done here."

"You're going to catch me up on how I have one son missing and another in jail you aren't helping?" Hank asked. "Or how when I got shot up you left me to die, so you could take over the club?"

Chisel shrugged. "It's complicated."

Hank took a step forward. "It's not complicated at all. Lugnut and Torch are part of this club, so besides being my sons, they're also your brothers. You turned your back on them. If we aren't looking out for each other, then none of this means anything. I'm calling a meeting. Everybody get to the clubhouse. We're going to sort this shit out."

Chisel took a step up to Hank. "We're in the middle of something. You need to go, and I'll deal with you when we get back."

Hank tapped a finger on the President patch sewn to the front of his kutte. "I give the orders in this club.

"You *did* give the orders," Chisel said putting a thumb under the President patch on his kutte and pushing it forward. "Not anymore."

Hank looked down at the patch and pulled a loose thread from it. He held it up. "Let's let the club decide. Most of you know me and how I lead. From what I hear, there's been nothing but trouble under Chisel's leadership. Not surprising, since he's new enough to still have loose threads on his patch."

"They're not going to decide." Chisel sneered. "This is my club now. They do what I tell 'em to do."

"The club has always been bigger than one person. You should of learned that by now," Hank said, stepping back. "Martina."

On cue, Martina fired her shotgun into Chisel's chest. He collapsed but he wasn't dead. His chest rose and fell with labored breathing.

"Everyone here has a choice," Hank said. "You can drop your kuttes and you can go, or you can head back to the clubhouse and we can sort this thing out. If you go, I don't want to see you around anymore. Otherwise, mandatory meeting now."

Three of the new members took off their leather vests, dropped them on the ground, and picked up their friend that had been shot. Stopping only long enough to remove his kutte and add it to the pile. They got on their bikes and drove away.

"Do you think it was smart to let them go?" Cotton asked.

Hank avoided the question completely. "Let's check out Ginsu," he said.

He was still alive and writhing in pain on the ground, which I didn't expect, knowing that the shotgun was loaded with silver.

"Lay still," I said.

He hadn't taken the brunt of the blast the way Chisel had. I put my blade back in its sheath and ripped his shirt open, exposing his injuries. I could see numerous entry points where the coins had slammed into his body.

"Turns out, coins aren't a very good shotgun load," Martina said, walking up behind me and eyeballing the injuries. "They don't penetrate deep enough to kill, at least not quickly, so they hurt like hell."

"What the hell did you shoot me for?" Ginsu groaned.

"Friendly fire," Martina answered.

"Next time I think about helpin' somebody, remind me not to," he said.

Martina shrugged. "Why don't you grow a pair and stop whining."

"He needs a doctor," I said.

"What now?" Fisheye asked.

"We get Ginsu some help, then figure out a plan of attack for the Queen," Hank answered.

"She's on the way now," Cotton said. "Chisel set this meeting to discuss terms for Isabelle's return. We could just put an end to all this now."

"No," Hank replied. "We're likely to get attacked by demons again or the Queen will just shoot us up as soon as she sees us."

"What about him?" Cotton asked, motioning toward Chisel.

"He went to a lotta trouble to set a meeting with the Queen. I'd hate for him to miss it. Let's leave him here."

"I know a doctor we can go to," I said.

"All right. Load Ginsu in the van and grab the bikes. We'll follow you," Hank said.

Ginsu was loaded in the back of the van with Isabelle and Hob. Martina and Skinny Pete jumped on the two open bikes.

"You're driving the van," I said to Holt.

I got in the back with Ginsu, pulled out my phone, and dialed. The phone rang a few times before a woman answered.

"Hey, Doc, it's Obie. If you still want to learn more, I need your help."

CHAPTER•27

MARTINA WAS RIGHT that the coins hadn't penetrated deeply. Ginsu's injuries didn't appear life threatening in the short term, but I kept a close eye on him just the same. We made it back to the clubhouse, and pulled Ginsu out of the van. Doc Lin pulled in. Her Mercedes, clean and freshly waxed, looked out of place, crawling its way up the dirt road surrounded by the rusted and broken vehicles in the junkyard. By the time she made it to the clubhouse, everyone else had gone inside, carrying Ginsu with them. She parked beside the van, popped the trunk, and got out.

"Where is he?" she asked.

I jabbed a thumb at the door. "They just took him inside."

"I've got a box of supplies in the back," she said. "Can you grab it please?"

I went to the back of the car and pulled out a box with all kinds of medical equipment in it. Some I recognized; most I didn't.

"I'll show you in," I said, holding the box in one hand and closing the trunk with the other.

She followed me to the door where I stopped. She hadn't officially been introduced to the world of ultranaturals. It could be rough the first time. I felt a warning was in order.

"Before we go in, you should know this is a safe place for them. They don't keep up their disguises inside and when I get in there, I am going to change as well," I said. "There aren't a lot of humans that come in here, so when we go in you need to take charge. Don't get hung up on appearances. You're here to do a job and they're just people, when it comes down to it. That being said, they can be a rough bunch and if you show fear or weakness, they're going to notice."

"Would they hurt me?" she asked.

"No," I said. "They would think you were weak, and they wouldn't respect you. If you want to learn more about this world, your best bet is to get on their good side."

Her face scrunched, and she walked past me with stubborn determination. I followed her into the changing room and set the box of equipment on a bench, adjusted my clothing, and made the change to krasis. I became aware that she had moved a couple steps back.

"Are you some kinda ferret?" she asked.

I sighed. "Otter."

"I have so many questions."

"I'll have to answer them later," I said, picking up the box. "You have a life to save, Doctor."

I retrieved the box, pushed the door to the bar open, and held it for her and she walked though.

"Where the hell's the prospect?" Skinny Pete said as we walked through the door. "He should be doing this, not me."

The bodies had been cleaned up, but the blood remained. Skinny Pete was standing by the blood pool in front of the bar with a mop and bucket. He sloshed the mop up and down in the soapy water. Isabelle was sitting at the bar with Holt. Fisheye was behind the bar, putting a glass of something in front of her. The rest of the T.O. were scattered around the room. Everyone stopped what they were doing to stare at Doc Lin and me. She looked around the room, from the bikers staring at her, to the blood pools, to Isabelle, to me, and back to the blood pools. I was more than a little worried she wasn't going to be able to handle it. It was a lot to take in all at once. I was about to lean in to quietly ask if she was all right when she spoke up.

"Well?" she commanded, putting her fists on her hips in a Supergirl-esque pose. "I didn't come here to get stared at. Where the hell is he?"

Everyone turned back to what they were doing. Smirks and chuckles ran through the room. Fisheye dropped a straw into Isabelle's drink and walked from behind the bar.

"He's back here," he said, holding the door to the back open for us. "I'll show you."

We followed him to the back hallway. The door to the kitchen was open and I glanced in as we walked by. I spotted the feet of the shifter I had killed on our raid sticking out from around the corner. The oven had been closed; no doubt the elf was still inside. I don't think Doc Lin noticed; or if she did, she didn't say anything.

She looked back at me with a questioning glance. I gave her a smile and a thumbs-up. We followed Fisheye past the conference room to a bedroom in the back. Ginsu was laid out on the bed with Hank sitting beside him in a chair. Hank stood when we came in and moved the chair out of the way.

"He passed out a few minutes ago," Hank said. "Probably a kindness for the doctor, knowing Ginsu."

Doc Lin retrieved a pair of scissors and cut Ginsu's shirt open to inspect the wounds. He promptly woke up and looked around the room through hazy eyes.

"Who the hell is this?" he mumbled.

"She's a doctor," Hank said. "She's going to fix you up."

Ginsu looked at her and gave the air a couple sniffs. "She's human."

"I am," Doc Lin said.

Ginsu laid his head back on the bed. "Tell me, doc, you a Chink?"

"I'm Chinese-American," she said.

"Good. If I'm stuck with a human doctor, Chinks are the best."

"I'll need some warm water, towels, and an extra pair of hands," she said. "Obie, can you move the chair over here and put my tools on it, please?"

I did as she asked. Hank and Fisheye exchanged a couple of nods, working out that Fisheye would help her with what she needed. Fisheye left the room to get the supplies she asked for.

Hank stepped up to me and whispered, "I need to talk to you."

No more putting it off, I guess. I wasn't looking forward to this conversation, but it would be good to get everything out in the open. I followed him into the conference room. I closed the door behind me. I was just opening my mouth to start my apology when Hank interrupted me.

"We need to come up with a plan for how to handle the Queen," he said. "I'm about to have to tell my plan to the club when we meet in a few minutes. That means I need to have one."

"What about Chisel's plan?" I asked. "Use some bait to lure her out and take care of her?"

Hank scratched his chin. "It's not very original."

"Doesn't have to be original, if it'll work," I said.

"So, we lure the Queen out, ambush, and kill her. Simple, to the point, I like it," Hank said.

"Almost," I said, rubbing my hands together nervously. "The thing is, we can't kill her."

He stared at me blankly before his face contorted with anger. "Maybe you can't kill her, considering how close you are, but I can."

"What's that supposed to mean?"

"It means you turned into the Queen's lapdog," Hank said.

I crossed my arms. "You know that's not true."

"Seems that way," he said. "If it's not true, then why'd I have to hear from the Queen that she had my father killed, right before she tried to kill me, too?"

"I was trying to avoid, well, all this," I said, waving my arms around at everything and nothing. "The confrontation, hurt feelings, not to mention war . . . What did you want me to do?"

"Tell me the truth, maybe? We're supposed to be friends," Hank said.

"If I told you the Queen had your father killed right there on the bridge, you would have killed all the elves there, they would have killed you, or somewhere in between. They brought silver with them. They could have killed the whole T.O. right there," I said. "So, I thought it would be best to wait until things calmed down before I told you. That's all."

He raised a clawed hand, stabbing an index finger into my chest emphasizing each word as he spoke. "It's. Not. Your. Decision. To. Make."

Each poke of his finger left a sharp pain in my chest. I looked down to see small dabs of blood soaking into my shirt. I'm sure he didn't mean to make me bleed; sometimes when you're pointy on the ends, stuff like that happens. Regardless of that understanding, when someone makes me bleed, it gets me a little worked up.

"It's not a chance I could take," I said, giving him a hard shove.

He took a step back. His face contorted in anger, baring his teeth, and he charged. He picked me up with his momentum and slammed me into the wall. The whole building seemed to shake with the impact and I yelped as the air was pushed from my lungs.

He definitely didn't have his usual level of strength, being that he was still healing from his injuries. I was glad about that or I might have been hurt. I managed to catch my breath, even with Hank grinding me into the wall with all his might. In his condition, I was pretty sure I could overpower him. I didn't want to. He needed to get some frustration out—and honestly, I had it coming. I braced myself. Not pushing him off, but not letting him pancake me against the wall, either. I could see the realization dawning that he really wasn't crushing me the way he had intended. Hank spun and threw me against the far wall.

I hit hard, but didn't react, opting instead to lean casually against the wall. "Feel better?"

"A little," he said. "You should have told me."

I nodded. "I had worked with Otis for years and we were close, but you're my best friend. I couldn't lose you both on the same night. I should have told you, I meant to, I wanted to, but I just didn't and I'm sorry."

The door to the conference room burst open. I looked over to see Fisheye, Cotton, and Big Ticket standing in the doorway. They must have heard the commotion and come to help. We looked at each other for a few seconds.

Hank asked, "You guys need something?"

"We heard, uh . . ." Cotton said, a little confused. "Just seeing when you're going to be ready for the meeting. Everybody's anxious to hear what you have to say."

"Just a few minutes," Hank answered. "Just wrapping things up here."

They clearly didn't understand, but backed out of the room and closed the door.

Once the sound of their footsteps had retreated down the hall, Hank asked, "So why can't we kill the Queen?"

"Because Isabelle loves her. She can't stay in power, that's clear, but who's going to replace her?" I said. "Isabelle hasn't been corrupted yet. We've got a shot at real lasting peace with her in charge. If we kill her mother, she'll hold it against us and eventually it will come back to haunt us. Maybe not right away, but one day."

Hank nodded. "You're probably right, but that's just not an option. She killed Razor and she shot up our bikes. I can't forgive that. Even if I could, the club won't. There's no getting around it."

"Then when it comes back to bite us, we'll handle it together."

"So, we agree then?" Hank asked. "We use Isabelle as bait, draw out the Queen and kill her?"

"That's the plan," I said. "Except with one correction. We use bait, but not Isabelle."

CHAPTER · 28

"HELLO?" I SAID, knocking on the door as I swung it open. "Anybody home?"

While I was sure it would be fine to just walk in, it was an orc's home, and I couldn't help but think of that large, red scimitar Yarwor had and the damage he could do with it. He came from the bedroom, with the scimitar in hand. Isabelle ran past me into the house and he knelt to give her a hug. Holt and I went in, and I closed the door behind us.

"Thank you for bringing her back," Yarwor said.

"How's Livy?

Yarwor stood. "She's in the bedroom. I think she's starting to feel better."

I went to the bedroom and peered in. She was lying in bed with Harlan sitting at the foot. They were talking. Harlan stood when I walked in.

"Hey, Harlan, I need to talk to you, but I want to check on Livy first, if you can give me a few minutes."

He nodded. "Sure, Obie, no problem. I'll wait outside. Come out whenever you're ready."

Harlan left, and I took his seat at the foot of the bed.

"How you feelin'?" I asked.

"Useless," Livy said. "Everybody's acting like I'm some kind of invalid."

I shook my head. "We're acting like you were attacked by a werewolf, which you were."

"I'm fine." She pouted. "You healed me up. I'm good as new."

"Then why are you still in bed?" I asked.

She wagged a finger in the direction of the door. "That orc won't let me up!"

"He's just lookin' after you," I said.

"Well, he can stop. I'm fine," she said, throwing off the covers and scooching over to the side of the bed. "I'll show you."

I held my hand out and she took it. I helped her to her feet.

She stretched her back. "I've been sittin' too long. I get stiff if I don't move around a little."

"I'm glad to hear you say that," I said. "I was hoping I could get you to take Isabelle and Yarwor up to see Walasi while we take care of the Queen. It would be a big help."

She headed for the kitchen, noticeably happier to be on her feet. "If that's what you need me to do, but first I'm going to have some tea."

"It would," I said. "And you're the only one that can do it."

"All right, all right, no one likes a suck up," she said, waving me off.

I followed her into the kitchen. She fetched a teapot and put water in it. I was concerned she would need help but she seemed to be doing just fine. Yarwor, Isabelle, and Holt were sitting at the table to help her if she needed it. I needed to talk to Harlan. Our whole plan relied on his cooperation. I found him outside, sitting on the tailgate of my truck. The weather was starting to cool. I could tell it was going to be a crisp night. I sat down beside him, but didn't say anything. I wanted him to speak first. I wanted to know where his mind was at, what he was thinking. I didn't have to wait long.

"A few months ago, you had the chance to let me run away. I understand why you didn't, but lately I've been thinking about something," he said. "Do you ever wonder what would have happened if you had?"

I paused for a second before shaking my head. "I'm going to be honest with you, I hadn't considered it."

"I think about it a lot." He sighed. "If you hadn't brought me back, there's no telling what I would be doing right now. I could've had a chance at a life. I could've been somebody."

"You are somebody," I said.

"Somebody else then."

"What's wrong with the person you are?" I asked.

Harlan stood and moved over to lean against the side of Holt's car. "I'm sorry I wasn't here when the Tortured Occult came."

"It's probably best you weren't," I said. "They might have killed you."

"I think I would've been all right," he said.

I didn't want to be contrary, but if the T.O. had Isabelle they probably wouldn't have taken him, too; they wouldn't have needed him. He didn't have a gun, claws, or teeth. He was largely defenseless. He was resourceful, though, maybe he would have come up with something. Either way, it was best not to contradict him. I might have been quiet too long.

When he spoke again, he got right to the point. "So, what did you want to talk to me about?"

"The Queen," I said. "Something has to be done."

He stuck his thumbs in his pockets. "That's what I've been saying."

"I don't want to make any assumptions, but there's a plan in the works to get rid of the Queen," I said. "We could use your help."

Harlan looked down at his foot and shuffled it in the gravel. "Get rid of the Queen could mean a couple things. What sort of 'get rid of' are we talking about?"

"The permanent kind," I said.

"You're going to kill the Queen?" he asked.

"Now I know you got a strained relationship with her, to say the least, but if you don't want to—"

"I'll help," he said before I could get my sentence out. "As long as we keep Isabelle safe, then just let me know what you need me to do."

"I wouldn't risk Isabelle," I said. "The plan's pretty simple, use you as bait to draw her into an ambush."

Harlan tilted his head. "You think she'll stick her head out for me?"

"Wouldn't she?"

Harlan shook his head. "She has to think Isabelle will be there or she won't come."

"Do you feel good about taking Isabelle with us?"

"Not even a little," he said.

I ran a hand through my hair. "So, what do we do?"

"We make her think Isabelle will be there." Harlan smiled.

I shifted around on the tailgate. "Right, okay. I'll just have to plan out what I'm going say when I talk to her."

Harlan laughed. "You talk to her? No offence, Obie, but you aren't that good of a liar. I'll set it up. Besides, I don't think she trusts you that much right now."

"Fair enough," I said.

"Who's watching Isabelle while it's going down?" Harlan asked.

"I'm going to have Yarwor take Isabelle and Livy to Walasi. He's an old Keeper in the mountains. If anyone can protect them, he can."

"The mountains inside the Elven Nation?" Harlan asked.

I shrugged. "Technically. But what are the chances the Queen will be looking for Isabelle inside the Nation?"

"It wouldn't surprise me at all," Harlan said.

"It's either that or we can send her away . . . far away," I said.

"Okay, it'll work." Harlan agreed. "What time should I set the meeting for?"

"Tomorrow morning?" I said. "The sooner the better. I don't want it to drag out."

Harlan held out his hand. "Let me use your phone."

"What good's that going to do?" I asked. "You can't get the Queen on the phone."

"*You* can't get the Queen on the phone, maybe, but I can," he said. "Go get Isabelle real quick, we'll need her."

I slapped my phone into his hand and jogged over to the house. I stuck my head in the door and called Isabelle. When we made it back to the cars, Harlan dialed a number and put it on speakerphone. It rang once before it was answered, but no one spoke on the other end of the line.

"Four . . . delta . . . one . . . India . . . hotel . . . five . . . golf . . . three . . . X-Ray," Harlan said into the phone. He hit the mute button. "Stay quiet. I'll let you know if I need you to say something."

I put Isabelle on the tailgate. There was a click on the phone.

"I need to speak to the Queen immediately," Harlan said.

We waited about thirty seconds. I was starting to wonder if it was going to work at all. The phone clicked again.

"I thought you were dead," the Queen said dispassionately. "What happened to Isabelle?"

"I have her here," Harlan said.

Harlan held the phone for Isabelle and gave her a nod.

"Hello, Mother," she said.

"Are you safe?" the Queen asked.

Isabelle answered. "Yes, Obie saved me from the shifters."

"Did he," the Queen stated. "Don't worry, Isabelle. I'm going to come get you."

Isabelle sniffled a little when she said, "Okay, I'm ready to come home."

"Stop sniveling," the Queen scolded. "I expect you to conduct yourself properly, regardless of the situation."

Isabelle looked as if she'd been struck. Her lip quivered, but she didn't make a sound. Harlan motioned for Isabelle to go inside and she didn't hesitate.

"Obie did save us," Harlan said. "When he heard the Tortured Occult had captured us, he busted into the clubhouse and freed us. He killed a few of them in the process."

"Why would he attack his friends to help me?"

I could hear the skepticism in the Queen's voice.

"You said it yourself, he's weak," Harlan said. "He still thinks he can restore the peace and prevent a war."

"He is rather simple," the Queen said. "Steal his car and bring Isabelle back."

"That's going to be tough," Harlan said. "He's got the keys in his pocket and you know he doesn't sleep."

"So, shoot him in the face and take them," the Queen suggested.

"I don't have a gun and Holt is here, too."

"I forgot about the sidekick," the Queen said.

"He's willing to bring us back. Can I have him drop us off at the southern outpost?" Harlan asked. "Or somewhere else in the Nation?"

There was silence on the other end as the Queen contemplated. She said, "Have him drop you at the Wolf Pen Gap store tomorrow at eight in the morning," the Queen said.

The Queen ended the call. Harlan handed the phone back to me.

"That was easy," I said.

Harlan shook his head. "Not as much as you think. Setting it up, yeah, but you can put money down that she's sending people out right now to watch the roads. The store's at a three-way intersection. We don't know which direction she's coming from, or where she'll go after she leaves. If you think the T.O. is going to ride up on their bikes and surprise her . . . It's just not going to happen."

"I agree," I said. "They aren't going to get the jump on anyone riding around on loud ass hogs. Don't underestimate the T.O., though, they'll surprise you. I'm more worried about the demon aspect."

"What demon aspect?" Harlan asked.

"There's been two large demon attacks recently—"

"That we know about," Harlan interrupted.

"That we know about," I agreed. "I still don't know who's doing it or even how they're doing it."

"So, what do you know?" he asked.

I sighed and rubbed a hand across my forehead. "The demons seem to be after the elves, specifically the Royal Family. It makes me a little worried about bringing you and Isabelle out into the open. Other than that . . . Nothing. I know nothing."

CHAPTER·29

IF I DID SLEEP, I wouldn't have that night. There was too much on my mind. I called Hank to tell him about the meeting and the concerns Harlan had with the Queen surveilling the area. He wasn't sleeping either but assured me that he had it under control. We agreed to meet in the parking lot of a church about a mile and a half away from the store. I sent Livy, Yarwor, and Isabelle to Desoto Falls to stay with Walasi. Holt, Harlan, and I piled into my truck. I'd cleaned it out as best I could. The fish smell still lingered a little, but with the windows cracked it was barely noticeable. That made for a chilly ride in the cool Autumn air. It was hardest on Harlan but he wore extra layers. He came prepared with his satchel.

It was still dark when we pulled into the church around seven in the morning. The parking lot was empty. The church was a two-story brick building with a modest paved lot in the front.

Holt stopped the truck horizontal to the lines, taking up a few parking spaces. "I thought they'd be here. You don't think they ran into trouble do you?"

I spotted a small road running to the side of the church. "Let's see where that goes," I said, pointing toward the road. "Maybe they're back there."

Harlan pulled the truck around the building. There was a second smaller parking lot with a large moving van parked behind the church. When the truck's headlights crossed the cab, Hank's head popped up. He must have been lying down in the seat. We parked beside the van and I got out. I met Hank in the headlights.

"Were you followed?" Hank asked.

I shook my head. "Nah, there's no one out right now. Is it just you?"

"We've got a lot of the hogs in the back," Hank said, throwing a thumb toward the moving van. "The club's out in the woods. They couldn't stay cooped up in the truck all night."

"Isn't that a little . . . obvious?" I asked.

"If there were elves around, we'd know it," he said. "And in the middle of the night no one else would even know they're there."

"Fair enough," I said. "So, what's the plan?"

"We have two other trucks watching the other roads. We let her come in and talk to you. On the way out, we use the vehicles to make a roadblock. We just have to stop her long enough for us to get there, four minutes tops," Hank said. "Then we finish her off."

It seemed like a good plan. I had one question. "Once she figures out we don't have Isabelle, what's to keep her from shooting us up?"

Hank thought about it. "You still have thirty minutes. I'm sure you'll come up with something."

Even if the Queen did shoot me, the plan still might work. Harlan would be killed, and I wouldn't be conscious to help out. They could still catch the Queen and kill her on the way out.

"One more thing. Wear this," Hank said, pulling an earbud out of his pocket and handing it to me. "I have one, as well as the other trucks. It's got a two-way mic. If you want to mute it, just press that little button on the outside. Hold the button to turn it on."

I took the device, slid it into my ear, and held down the button. After a few seconds there was a beep.

"Can you hear me?" Hank asked.

I could hear him, both in person and through the earpiece. It made a strange echo with the earpiece being a fraction of a second behind.

"I gotcha," I said, hearing my voice through the mic as well.

I pressed the button on the earpiece, and said, "We're going to head over."

"We'll be ready and let you know when we see anything," Hank said.

This time there wasn't an echo in my ear, confirming that I had my mic muted.

"You got one of these I can give Holt?" I asked, tapping a finger to the earpiece.

Hank went back to the truck and returned with another earbud. I gave him a nod, and climbed back into the truck. I gave Holt the earpiece and told him how to use it. When he had it working and muted we pulled out to meet the Queen. I had Holt park on the side of the Wolf Pen Gap Country Store. It was a plain looking, brick building with a brown roof over-hanging about a third of the building on the front and back. It reminded me of a barn. I checked the clock. We still had a few minutes.

"We should have brought Hob," Holt said, staring out the window. "He could have just blown her up."

"Maybe," I said. "I'll be happy as long as we get through this without getting shot or eaten by demons."

Holt chuckled. "There's no way we get out of this without getting shot."

"You're probably right," I conceded. "This is a big moment. We're a couple minutes away from changing the world."

"Only if our plan works," Holt said. "If we don't kill the Queen today, then nothing really changes."

"Things will change, all right," I said. "She'll come after us. There's been some little altercations but if we don't get her today, it's going to get ugly. We're talkin' Chicago in the late '20s kind of stuff."

"What does that mean?" Holt asked.

"A lotta violence."

"She's late," Harlan said from the seat behind me.

He had been so quiet, I had almost forgotten he was there. I could tell from the look on his face that he was worried.

"She's coming," I said.

"Maybe she's got someone watching," Harlan said. "She might already know Isabelle isn't here."

"You're here," Holt said. "You don't think she'd come for you?"

Harlan's silence was answer enough.

A voice that sounded like Skinny Pete spoke though the mic. "I see her. She's headed your way down Wolf Pen Gap. It's her SUV with a guard truck on either side."

Holt and I shared a look.

"Here we go," I said.

The Queen's SUV, flanked by her guard trucks, pulled into the parking lot slowly and idled on the far side.

I pressed the button on my earpiece. "She's here."

"You have eyes on her?" Hank asked.

"On her caravan," I answered.

"We need to make sure," Hank said.

He was right, of course. I got out of the truck. "Harlan, stand by the door. When we look over at you motion toward the backseat like Isabelle's in it."

I left my mic unmuted and started walking over to the SUV. Harlan got out and made himself visible. The three vehicles idled. The windows of the Queen's car were tinted, preventing me from seeing inside. I stood outside the window and waited. I looked at my reflection in the glass. The scruff on my face was getting long. I would have to remember to shave when I made it back to the house. The window rolled down, pulling me out of my thoughts, to reveal the Queen. She sat with a scowl, anger oozing out the window.

"Your Highness. A pleasure to see you again," I said.

It wasn't, of course, but I wanted Hank to know I had spotted her.

"We're on the way," Hank said.

"Where is she?" the Queen asked.

I motioned toward the truck. Harlan moved from where he was standing to fiddle around in the backseat.

"Bring me Isabelle," the Queen demanded.

"Right away," I said. "Should I bring Harlan as well or did you not want him back?"

If the Queen's eyes were guns, I would have been shot dead on the spot. I held up my hands and began walking backward toward the truck. Just as I was turning around I heard her driver announce that the Tortured Occult had been spotted. The pretense of our meeting would only last a few more seconds. I didn't want to get shot in the back, so I took off running. I waved at Harlan to let him know the jig was up. He climbed back in the truck as tires squealed and an engine roared behind me. I looked over my shoulder to see the lead truck bearing down on me. I dove to the side, avoiding getting run over as the caravan tore out of the parking lot.

"The caravan's headed sixty north," I said, pulling myself up off the ground.

A man stuck his head out of the door of the store. "You all right? They just about ran you down!"

"I'm fine," I assured him, getting to my feet.

"You want I should call the poh-lice?" The man asked.

I jogged to the truck and shouted back, "No thanks."

I got in and closed the truck door. A line of bikes appeared to our left. We pulled out ahead of them, quickly accelerating to close the distance with the Queen's caravan. There were a few miles of road ahead through the mountain-side. It was too steep to build houses directly on the sides of the road which gave us some privacy. It was a perfect place for the attack.

"Just keep some pressure on and we'll follow them into the trap," I said.

We gained steadily on the caravan until we were right behind them. The elf on the passenger side of the rear truck rolled down the window. She leaned halfway out the window with her rifle and opened fire on my truck. The bullets ricocheted off the armored hood and fenders and slammed into the bulletproof windshield I'd had Hank put in.

"Hang on," Holt said.

He floored the accelerator, closing in on the guard truck. He slammed into the rear. It jolted forward. The elf hanging out the window of the truck lost her balance and dropped the rifle to keep from falling onto the road. The rifle disappeared under my tires with a *thump-thump*.

A large pickup roared down a side road in front of the caravan. The lead truck had to have seen it coming, but instead of slowing down, the trucks collided at full speed. The Queen's SUV made an evasive maneuver to avoid the crash. The SUV clipped the truck's bumper, ripping it off, and sending it sliding into the ditch. Holt whipped the truck into the other lane, following the guard truck around the wreck.

I watched the line of bikes weave around the crash. "The Queen made it by the roadblock."

"We've got to stop her quick," Hank said. "She's got to have more troops on the way."

I turned to Holt, opening my mouth to speak, but he beat me to it.

"I heard," he said. "I don't know if I'm going to be able to stop both of them."

I was suddenly aware of the scent of something burning. I turned around to check on Harlan. He had his left hand gripping his right wrist. His hands shook as smoke rose from the palm of his right hand, filling the cab with the stench of burning flesh.

"Obie!" Holt shouted.

I turned around to see the largest portal I had ever seen snap open in the road in front of us. The Queen's SUV had no choice but to go through. Holt hit the brakes as the guard truck swerved to avoid the portal. The truck fishtailed, sliding through the portal sideways. It was cut in half. The back of the truck slid off the road while the cab went through the portal. We began to slide. I put a hand on the ceiling to brace myself, praying to Thera when the truck hit the portal, I wasn't cut in half. Holt let go of the brake and hit the gas, straightening the truck to drive cleanly through.

CHAPTER·30

IT FELT LIKE WE drove over a speedbump as we transitioned from our world into the demon landscape. I didn't get much of a look at it. The cab of the guard truck rolled when it hit the ground, throwing a cloud of rust-colored dust that obscured the windshield. Holt hit the brakes, sending the truck sliding to a stop in the soft earth. Through the back window I could see the blue circle of the portal through the dust shrinking and disappearing completely. Harlan sat in the back seat, still holding his hand. He grimaced in pain, but I had a hard time summoning up any sympathy.

"What the fuck, Harlan," I said. "You're the one doing this?"

Harlan grimaced, his hand still smoking. "I guess my secret's out."

"How?" I asked. "Why?"

"After I was lashed by the Queen, and you stood by and let it happen, I decided that running away wasn't an option any more. If I just left, she'd continue her reign of oppression and tyranny. The Queen had to be stopped. When you fought that demon on the bridge, I found an opportunity. You and Cearbhall went over the side with the demon into the water, so I drove down to see if you were okay. In the center of the bridge was a leather satchel with a book in it. I had just taken the book out to look at when an athol flew down and grabbed the book with one foot and the satchel with the other. I wrestled to hold onto it and the demon only got away with a few pages and the satchel. I intended to give you the book, at first, but after Otis's assassination we didn't end up sticking around to chat. When I got back, I looked at it and I had an idea— maybe there was something in it I could use to put the Queen in her place."

"I'm going to need that book," I said.

Harlan nodded. "Of course, Obie. I have no problem giving it to you. You see, what I found in the book changed everything. It turns out that I am a magical adept. I'm one of few that can do small bits of magic without dust. I think people like me don't even realize they're performing magic most of the time. Things just work out for them. It really makes me question why things haven't worked out better for me, but that's neither here nor there. When I found the book, I learned how to use that ability to open a portal. Just a sliver of a portal, barely even a pinprick. I had a plan to get my hands on some dust and summon enough demons to kill the Queen. That, in itself, wasn't enough though. I had to ensure the throne would pass to someone . . . different."

"Isabelle," I said.

"She hasn't been corrupted like my other sisters were. She was the only option," Harlan said.

"Where'd you get all the dust from?" Holt asked. "And where are you keeping it."

"There's no dust," Harlan said, a little pleased with himself. "I would open those tiny portals as practice for when I got my hands on enough dust. One day someone spoke to me. He said he could help me. I was skeptical at first, but we talked and over time I agreed to let him. He taught me how to create a link that lets me pull power directly from this world. I can use it to open portals and summon creatures. Pretty impressive, if I do say so myself."

I put my arm on the back of the seat and twisted around to look at Harlan directly. "Harlan, please tell me you don't think anything from this place is going to help you out of the kindness of its sludge-pumping heart."

"Oh, there's a price," Harlan said. "Lord Belial isn't kind, gentle, or understanding, which makes him similar to the Queen. They are very different in one aspect, though."

"What's that?" Holt asked.

"He respects me, which is more than I can say for anyone back on Earth," Harlan said.

"You know that's not true."

A breeze picked up, moving the dust, and giving us a clear view of the landscape for the first time. The terrain was mountainous and barren with two suns beating down. We looked to be in a holler; the ground here was mostly flat. I wasn't sure if Harlan put us here on purpose or if it was just a happy accident. Either way, I was glad we hadn't come out on the top of one of the mountains, we'd probably still be crashing down the side of it. The Queen's black SUV stood in stark contrast to the orange terrain. It had stopped thirty yards in front of us. The cab of the guard truck was much closer, only five yards. It rested upside down in the dirt. I could see the driver hanging motionless, strapped in with her seatbelt. The elf that had been shooting at us right before we went through the portal was missing. We had driven by the truck before we stopped, and I was glad we hadn't hit it. A car wreck my first time off Earth was the last thing I needed.

"We better get some weapons," Harlan said, opening the rear door and getting out.

Dust, heat, and the sulfuric stick of the demon world rushed in. He walked over to the disconnected cab and bent to look through the window.

"What are we going to do now?" Holt asked.

"Let's change to krasis," I said. "Harlan's right, we need weapons."

I started my change, but nothing happened. I remained in my human form. I looked over at Holt who hadn't changed either and now had a confused look on his face.

"Obie," he said. "We got a problem."

"We're not in Kansas anymore." I agreed. "We're cut off from Thera here."

"So, we can't change?" Holt asked.

"I'd be willing to bet we can't heal either," I said. "Here, we're human."

"By the Mother," Holt gasped. "What are we gonna do? How are we going to get home?"

"One step at a time," I said. "If we can't change to krasis, I might be able to get us some guns from that wreck."

"What about Harlan?" Holt shouted. "We should be ripping his throat out!"

I shrugged. "Hard to do without claws or teeth."

"To hell with him and the Queen," Holt shouted. "We need to get home."

I looked at Holt freaking out in the driver's seat. "Harlan got us here, so he should be able to get us home. Stay calm and think. We're in a bad spot, but we ain't dead yet," I said, opening my door. "Stay in the truck."

I got out and walked over to Harlan. As soon as my foot hit the ground, I broke into a sweat from the intense heat. I squinted involuntarily to keep my eyes from shriveling up in my head. The heat didn't seem to bother Harlan. I didn't know why he wasn't affected the same way I was.

"I got no problem with you handling the Queen, but how are we going to get home?" I asked.

"We?" he asked. "Are you including me in that?"

I put an arm over my eyes to give them some shade. "Sure, why wouldn't I?"

"You haven't been paying attention for the past few minutes, have you?" Harlan asked. "Do you believe in forgiveness, Obie? Do you think I can come back from the horrible things I've done? Forgive and forget, just like that?"

"I'm saying, I understand why you did it. What's done is done, though, right?" I asked. "You can come back and start over."

"Don't be naïve," Harlan said, smirking. "You couldn't let me come back to a normal life."

"If you're not summoning demons, then we don't have a problem," I said.

"How would you know what I'm doing?" he asked. "I could do whatever I want. I guess that means I'd have to stay where you could keep an eye on me, right? So, I wouldn't really be free. That's beside the point, though, because if I need to summon a demon, for whatever reason, then I will. I'm not going to give up my power. I'm not going back to being Harlan the servant, ignored doormat extraordinaire. I won't be ruled anymore."

What was I supposed to do with that? He might as well wear a T-shirt that says, *Kill me as soon as it's convenient*. I had tried to give Harlan the benefit of the doubt. It didn't sound like I could work with him. He was still my ticket home, though, so for the time being I wasn't going to piss him off.

"You didn't answer the question," I said. "Can you get us home?"

Harlan gave me a gentle smile. "Yes, Obie, I can get us home."

"Great, can you send me and Holt home now?"

"Don't worry, I'm going to make sure you get home," he said. "But I'm not going to open a portal until the Queen is dead. The sooner we finish up that loose end, the sooner you get home."

I sighed. "Fine."

I walked around to the driver's side of the cab and tried to open the door. The frame had been warped when the cab rolled. The door wouldn't budge. The window had broken out in the crash. I knelt and stuck my head in, avoiding the few shards of broken glass that remained in the cab. Harlan was pulling a rifle out the opposite window. The elf driver was suspended by her seatbelt and wheezed as she struggled to breathe. She had a pistol on her belt, but I didn't think I could get it without unbuckling her seatbelt. I slid in under her, supporting her neck with one hand, and with the other reached up to the buckle. When I undid the latch, she fell into my lap. I did my best to slide her out without killing her.

"You can't save everyone," Harlan said, from the other window.

"Isabelle's going to need guards," I said.

Once I got her outside the cab, I picked her up and took her to my truck.

Holt got out when he saw me coming and put down the tailgate. "It's hot as balls here. How the hell are we gonna get home?"

"Harlan says he will send us home once the Queen's dead," I said.

"You think he will?" Holt asked.

"We'll see, I guess," I said, laying the injured elf in the back of the truck as gently as I could.

I slid her up into the truck bed and put a rolled-up shirt from my clothes stash under her head. I took the gun belt from around her waist. She might not make it, but if she could hang on until we got home I could heal her.

I handed her gun belt to Harlan. "You take this, I'll find another one."

I went back to the cab and looked inside. I didn't see any other weapons. I could probably find another pistol on the guard that had been thrown from the cab—if I knew where she ended up. I looked around. I spotted the black uniform through the heat haze rising from the ground. As I was looking, a hellhound seemed to come up out of the ground and move over to the elf.

"They live under the ground," Harlan said, stepping up beside me. "The whole place is full of caves, like Swiss cheese."

"How do you know that?" I asked.

He met my gaze. "It's not my first time here," he said. "Stay here, I'll check her for a gun."

The hellhound started chewing on the elf as Harlan handed me the rifle and walked toward the beast. He looked like he was strolling through a park instead of walking on the roasting surface of the demon world. He walked right up to the demon and scratched it on its back. The hellhound gave him a sniff as Harlan bent down and pulled a belt off the body.

"You seeing this?" Holt asked. "How is that even possible?"

"I have no idea, but it's not a good sign," I said.

The demon went back to chewing on the guard as Harlan walked back to where we were standing.

"Harlan, assuming we get back, I'm going to need the grimoire," I said.

"What's a grimoire?" Harlan asked.

"The book you got from the demon on the bridge," Holt said.

Harlan smiled. "Oh, it's right here," he said.

Harlan opened the back door of the truck and fished around in his satchel.

He pulled out a leather-bound book. He held it out to me and I took it. I felt reassured that he was willing to hand it over. Then again, he didn't appear to need it anymore.

Harlan looked genuinely happy for the first time in a long time. "All right, let's kill the Queen."

CHAPTER·31

HARLAN SOUNDED DOWNRIGHT chipper when he suggested we kill his mother. Holt gave me a look I took as *How can you be okay with this?* I wasn't okay with it, of course. Harlan was on a dark path. I just didn't have any way to stop him. I gave Holt a shrug and we got in the truck. I wedged the grimoire between the seat and center console.

My relationship with Thera was tedious at times, and I wouldn't really consider her evil, so much as self-absorbed. I knew next to nothing about this Belial. If a deity can be judged by its creation, I had all the information I needed. This place was harsh and unforgiving, damn near inhospitable. Harlan was right in that he couldn't come back to a normal life. His admission that he intended to summon demons in the future put us at odds. I didn't want a conflict with Harlan, but it seemed inevitable. That problem could wait until later. It didn't make sense to get into it now; as long as we weren't even on Earth, it didn't really make a difference. I was off the clock, so to speak. My entire focus was living long enough to get home. If that meant working with a demon-summoner then so be it.

Holt drove us to where the Queen's SUV had stopped. The Queen and two guards got out as we pulled up. When we got out of the truck, the two guards raised their rifles and opened fire. We dove to the ground as, for the second time today, elven bullets slammed into my truck. They weren't actually trying to shoot us; if they had, we would have been shot. Just the Queen sending a message in her less than subtle way.

"Do I have your attention?" the Queen asked, stepping out from behind the SUV.

I sighed, pulling myself to my feet as the gunfire echoed off the mountains.

"If you want someone's attention, did it ever occur to you that you could just talk to them?" I asked, brushing the red dust off my clothes. "The answer to everything doesn't have to be to 'Open fire.'"

"Watch how you speak to me, Obie. I'm still the Queen, despite our situation," she said.

"That's where you're wrong," Harlan said, getting to his feet. "The second you went through the portal you stopped being Queen. Not that you ever deserved to be in the first place."

"You're lucky I haven't given you what you've deserved," the Queen spat.

"I'd be lucky if you did," Harlan said. "A child deserves, at the very least, to be safe. Forget attention, or even love. The best thing you've even done for me was ignore me. At least when you did, I didn't have to worry that you were going to hurt me."

"Harlan, if I didn't know better, I'd think you weren't grateful for what I've done for you," the Queen said coldly.

"That is all you've ever given me," Harlan said, pulling his shirt down to show a scar from when she had him lashed. "Pain."

"You don't want to feel pain anymore?" the Queen asked.

With a flash of her hand, she drew her revolver, fanned it with her left hand, firing a single shot, and spun it back into her holster. Harlan's body went rigid as if he were hit by lightning and fell backward with a *thud*. I looked down at him. He had a bullet hole in the center of his forehead. His eyes were still open, staring off into nothing with a blank expression.

"Maybe he's happy now," the Queen said. "And if not, who cares. At least I don't have to listen to him whine."

"You just killed our ride home," I said.

Holt bent over, putting his hands on his knees. He appeared to be having trouble breathing. His chest heaved. I couldn't tell if he was having a panic attack or if the heat was getting to him. He complained about the summers in Georgia. They were hot, but nothing like this place.

"You all right?" I said under my breath.

Holt nodded and waved a hand.

The Queen gave me a suspicious glance. "What do you mean?"

"Harlan's the one that's been opening portals and attacking the Nation," I said.

"Impossible," the Queen said.

"I realize you've never thought much of him, but you were wrong to underestimate and abuse him," I said.

"Don't lecture me," the Queen ordered, her hand sliding back to her revolver. "I'm not in the mood."

I started figuring what the odds were that I could shoot her without getting shot by either the Queen or her guards. It only took a quarter of a second to determine it was impossible. That didn't mean it wasn't a risk worth taking. We had gone to a lot of trouble to remove the Queen from the picture and while things didn't go according to plan, the objective was achieved. Harlan was right; we couldn't let the Queen get back to Earth. Until she was dead we weren't going anywhere—not that we had a way back in the first place. A shootout with the Queen and two of her guards was suicide, but it was better than roasting to death in this stink of a world or being torn apart by demons. I looked over at Holt. He seemed to know what I was thinking. He stood up straight and gave me a nod. I didn't see that we had any other choice.

I was preparing myself for what would most likely be my last minute when I noticed an orange light coming from the hole in Harlan's forehead. Then he sat up. Holt and I moved a few steps away. Harlan sat still with a blank expression. I wasn't surprised by that, considering bits of his brain were cooking on the ground behind him. He still had the hole in his head where he had been shot. I wouldn't say it healed so much as filled in . . . with fire. I could see into his head through the hole and it looked like coals glowing orange. What looked like burning veins began to spread from the hole over his bald head and down his cheeks. Harlan got to his feet and turned toward the Queen, taking a few steps forward.

"Harlan?" I said, coming up behind him and touching him on the shoulder.

It was as if I touched a hot stove. I jerked my hand back and shook it in a vain attempt to cool it. He turned to face me. Not his body, mind you, just his head, turning slowly around past normal limits until it was facing backward. His eyes looked strange and they bulged. I moved back to put some distance between us. His eyes popped, splattering and burning on his cheeks. His sockets now showed the same embers as the hole in his forehead, making the corners of a triangle. Smoke began to pour upward from his body as his flesh burned. His head continued around, still going in the wrong direction, until it was oriented correctly again. His attention was back on the Queen and I was glad for it. This was devolving into an every-man-for-himself kind of situation and I think everyone knew it.

"Let's get in the truck," I said.

Holt didn't waste time and sprinted for the driver's seat.

The Queen unloaded the remaining five shots in her revolver into Harlan's chest. His body jostled slightly from the impact. The holes seemed to let more heat out. His shirt caught fire from the impact points and began to burn.

"Shoot it!" the Queen shouted.

Harlan walked past her two guards.

They looked at each and then over in my direction, but didn't start shooting.

"If you want a ride, we're leaving now," I said.

They climbed into the back of the truck.

"Traitors!" the Queen shouted, pulling her other revolver. "Treasonous, backstabbing, disloyal—"

The Queen was still talking, but her words were drowned out by the roar of her revolver as she unloaded it into Harlan. The new volley didn't affect him any more than the last, and with a sudden burst of speed, he lurched and grabbed her arm. I could hear her flesh searing from Harlan's touch as he pulled her to the ground and bit into her. I got in the passenger seat.

"Get us out of here," I said.

"Three problems," Holt said. "The truck's overheating, we have nowhere to go, and the gunfire's attracting demons."

I looked out the window to see a few demons here and there coming up out of the ground. We were surrounded. A few athol had taken off from the mountains and were headed in our direction. Hellhounds popped up from the ground all around. I saw one demon that looked to be half-person, half-snake. The snake demon hung back and watched as the others headed toward us. It was a sign of intelligence not to run blindly in our direction and if it was intelligent, I was glad it was staying away from us.

Harlan rose from his attack on the Queen, and then she stood with a blank expression and bulging eyes.

"If the truck'll drive, put some distance between us and them," I said, pointing a finger at Harlan and the Queen.

Holt threw it into reverse, executing a J-turn to get us facing the other direction, and hit the gas. He sat up on the edge of his seat, getting as high a view as he could at the terrain to avoid holes. While we left Harlan and the Queen behind pretty quickly, the demons were another matter. The truck suddenly jolted as if the back wheels fell into a ditch. An athol had landed in the back. It grabbed the elf I had laid there and took off, carrying her away.

"Can you keep them off of us?" I asked the guards in the back.

"Until we're out of bullets," one of them responded.

They rolled down the back windows and hung out each side. Sporadic gunfire rang out as they opened fire on demons that approached the truck. I grabbed the pistol off Holt's belt, tossing it and the rifle I had in the back seat for the elves to use. I pulled my gear bag from the back floorboard.

"We're going to blow a gasket soon," Holt said. "Truck's getting real hot."

"I got an idea," I said. "Just keep us going for a few minutes."

"We may not have a few minutes."

I rummaged through my bag, grabbing my stash of emergency dust.

I took the grimoire I'd wedged beside the seat and flipped through it. If Harlan had been here before, like he said, and I believed he had, then he had to get home. When he opened the portal that brought us here, he did it without the normal chanting. There's no way the first time he came here and went home he did it that way. It's an advanced technique to *think* the incantation and have it work. A few pages in I saw notes someone had made in the book. I stopped flipping when the notes at the top of the page said, "to Earth."

There was a picture of a circle. It looked a lot like the circles I has seen before, but some of the symbols were different. There was a language I didn't recognize as well as a phonetic reference scribbled beside it. I pulled a utility knife from my gear bag, and started carving the circle from the book onto the dash of my truck.

"Try to hold it steady," I said.

"Oh sure, avoid giant holes in the ground and dodge incoming demons with a truck that's about to burst into flames, but do it gently." Holt scoffed.

"I'd appreciate it," I said, concentrating on the circle I was carving.

I finished it up and it looked all right, considering. I dropped the knife into the floorboard, opened the dust, and read the incantation in the book. When I finished, the circle started to glow on the dash. I could feel a tingle in my brain as the magic worked; I held onto that feeling to keep the circle growing.

"It's working," I shouted, feeling hope for the first time since we got here.

I saw a portal opening ahead of us. It was still too small for us to fit through by the time we passed it, but it was still growing.

"We'll have to turn around," I said.

I could hear the panic in Holt's voice as he spoke. "Turn around into the demon's chasing us?"

"It's either that or look for timeshares."

"Hold on!" Holt shouted, pulling the wheel to the right.

The truck turned. I could see a number of demons flying and running toward us. Hounds and athol, as well as some other demons that reminded me of snake and dragons. The portal continued to grow. The elves fired on the demons, sending many crashing to the ground. Holt swerved to avoid a hound that made it through the gunfire. It bit at the truck. Its teeth scraped the side of the truck, ripping the bumper off, and jolting the truck hard to the right. Holt maintained control and steered us back toward the portal.

"Uh, Obie?" Holt questioned. "There's no sky."

I looked through the portal and he was right. The portal had opened inside a building. I had no idea which building it was, but at this point in time it just didn't matter as long as it wasn't *here*.

"Buckle up!" I shouted.

The elves stopped shooting, dropped into their seats, and fastened their seatbelts. We didn't have time to put up the windows before driving through the portal.

CHAPTER · 32

I BRACED MY HAND against the dash as we exited the portal into a living room, through the wall into a bathroom, then through another wall to the outside. Holt slammed the brakes, bringing the truck to a stop. A bumpy ride, to say the least. We weren't moving, but the truck was shaking. A demon thrashed around in the bed of the truck. I threw the door open and was hit by a cold that felt as if I jumped into an ice bath. It was normal fall temperatures, of course, but the sudden transition from the heat of the other world to this was a shock to my system. As I stepped out of the truck the second thing I noticed was the familiar tingle of healing. I made the change to krasis and drew my blade just as something that reminded me of a pterodactyl with two sets of wings like a dragonfly popped out from under the building debris that had collected in the truck bed. I gave it a swift strike to the head and it collapsed lifeless.

I breathed a huge sigh of relief. Holt and the two guards got out of the truck.

"Hey, Holt," I said.

"Yeah?"

I smiled at him. "You owe somebody a house."

"It was your portal," he countered.

He and the elves laughed. It was surprising and nice to see. I hadn't ever seen one of the Queen's guards so much as smile before.

"Great job, you two. It was nice to be working together for a change," I said.

"I'm Tori and this is Meghan," Tori said. "I can't believe we made it back."

"How's the truck?" I asked.

Holt stuck his head in to look at the temperature gauge in the dash. "Still hot. It'll cool down pretty quick. There might be some damage, but it should get us where we need to go."

I tucked the wings of the demon that were hanging over the side of the truck back in the bed and threw debris from the house on top of it. "Can you all check the house, make sure we didn't run over anyone?"

Holt, Tori, and Meghan went into the wreckage, calling out for survivors and looking under collapsed walls. They finished their search by the time I got the demon covered.

"Looks like no one was home," Meghan said.

"Let's hope they have good insurance then."

We climbed into the truck and left. I flipped through the grimoire as we drove. It wasn't a very big book to have caused so many problems.

"What are you going to do with that?" Tori asked.

"Thera has ordered it be destroyed," I said, closing the book and putting it back between the seat and the center console. "Let me ask you, with the Queen gone, what will you do now?"

"We have a Queen," Meghan said. "It's just not the same one it was twenty minutes ago."

"You'll both stay with the Guard and work for Isabelle?" Holt asked.

Tori leaned forward. "We're soldiers of the Elven Nation. If there's a Queen to protect, then that's what we'll do."

"We're going to drop you at the Southern Outpost and then go get Isabelle," I said. "Can you get it ready for her?"

Tori nodded. "Leave it to us."

I PICKED UP ISABELLE from Desoto Falls. I didn't enjoy telling her that the Queen and Harlan were both dead. She took the news with the muted emotionality that the Queen would have expected from her. She nodded and we didn't say anything else about it. I wanted her to have a stable, caring figure, so I asked Livy to stay with her for a bit. I hadn't planned on taking Yarwor, but Isabelle wanted him to go and he wouldn't have taken no for an answer, so we piled into the truck and headed to the Southern Outpost.

Tori and Meghan were true to their word. When we arrived I didn't even have to stop at the checkpoint. They had a new guard detail and staff for the outpost. Holt and I hung out for a bit, just to make sure everything was kosher and there wasn't anything to worry about. All the angst with the Nation had come from the Queen's leadership and that was gone. For the first time, in as long as I could remember, we had a chance for a real lasting peace.

I reported to Thera that I had the grimoire that caused so much trouble and would be destroying it. She was as pleased as I had ever seen her—which is to say, no discernable amount. I took the book out to a burn barrel in my back yard, with a little gas and some matches. Standing in front of the barrel, I flipped through the book for one last time.

A COUPLE WEEKS HAD passed since the Queen was killed; things were slowly returning to normal. I had Morrison Salvage replace the bumper and windshield on my truck, as well as give the engine an overhaul. Livy had stayed with Isabelle while the management of the Elven Nation was put in order. Now she was ready to go home, and I was giving her a ride. I pulled into the little road winding its way up the mountain to the checkpoint. When I got there Meghan came outside. I rolled down the window as she crossed over to the driver's side.

"Hey, Obie," Meghan said. "One sec, we'll get you through."

"Thanks," I said with a smile.

Meghan rolled a finger in the air as she walked back to the checkpoint. The barricade rose, and I gave them a wave as I pulled through. I had never gotten through the checkpoint so easily. No metal detectors, cavity searches, or bomb sniffing dogs. I wasn't sure if it was because of policy changes since Isabelle took over the Nation, or because I knew Meghan and she was making exceptions. Whatever the cause, I hope it continued. I pulled up to the Southern Outpost and didn't have to wait long. Tori escorted Livy outside, opened the passenger door and helped her inside.

I put my arm on the seat and ducked my head, so I could see Tori. "I hope she wasn't too much trouble."

"Oh, stop it, Obie," Livy said.

"You're welcome here any time," Tori said, leaning in and giving Livy a hug.

Tori closed the door and waved as we turned around to leave.

"Did you have a good time?" I asked.

"They're good people, Obie," Livy said. "They're on a hard road, but they'll get there."

I put the truck in drive and headed down the mountain. "Seems like they're doing pretty well to me. I haven't seen them this happy in . . . well, never."

"Isabelle and the elves will be fine," Livy said. "How's everyone else doing?"

"The Tortured Occult's still figuring things out and Holt's the same old Holt," I said.

Livy looked out the window. "What about Naylet?"

I sighed, but didn't say anything. Livy caught on right away.

"What's the matter, hon?" she asked.

"We have a meeting at the clubhouse after I drop you off," I said. "I haven't seen Naylet in a couple weeks, but I arranged to meet her there. It's going to be tough."

"Ah, to be young and in love," she said with a smile.

"We're the same age!"

"So, what's the problem? You never had a problem talking to her before," she said.

"She's my first love. She found my heart and we broke it in together," I said. "I guess I'm afraid of the outcome."

Livy sighed and cocked her head. "Listen, Obie . . . people come and go in our lives. Sometimes they go and come back, sometimes they don't. I don't know what's gonna happen. Whatever happens don't change what you meant to each other. The best you can do is appreciate the time you had together. If you're meant to come back together, then you will when the time's right."

"You're right, of course," I said. "Doesn't make it easier."

"There's only one thing that does that," she said. "Time."

"I just have one question," I said.

"What's that, hon?"

I couldn't help but smirk as I spoke. "Is it a burden being so wise?"

"You're mean as a snake."

I dropped Livy off at her house and made sure she was settled before heading to the clubhouse.

People were starting to hang out there again, although it wasn't as busy as it had been before Chisel had taken over. Arriving early, I parked the truck out front and found myself sitting outside, dreading going inside. I showed up early to speak to Adin. I'd asked him to find someone for me. Laying my head back on the seat, I closed my eyes, and took a few deep breaths.

I was jarred by the sound of slurping and squeaking glass. I opened my eyes to find Holt standing outside the door. He had pressed his mouth against the driver's side window and was blowing to inflate his cheeks. His tongue flickered around on the glass. I thought about putting my fist through it, but I would just have to fix it if I did. Not worth it. Instead I turned the ignition and rolled down the window.

"What are you doing out here?" he asked, wiping his mouth on his sleeve.

"Just sitting. I'm about to come in," I said, getting a whiff of alcohol off him. "Are you drunk?"

He staggered back toward the clubhouse and shouted, "I'm not *not* drunk!"

I rolled up the window and followed him inside. I made the change to krasis and went to the bar. Adan was sitting at his normal table and came to greet me when he saw me.

"Were you able to find someone for the job I asked you about?"

"It took some looking but I found someone that I think will be a great match," he said, pointing to a honey badger sitting at a table alone. "There she is. Her name's Awiti. I wouldn't keep her waiting."

Even at its busiest, a honey badger in the clubhouse would have been an unusual sight. She had black fur, head to toe, with a wide silver stripe starting at her forehead and running all the way down her back. She wore plain comfortable clothes: khaki pants and a blue T-shirt that reminded me of someone hiking the Appalachian Trail. Her expression was the epitome of resting bitch face.

I thanked Adan and walked over. On the way, I passed a table with Holt, Skinny Pete, and Ginsu having a nice time, judging from the number of empty bottles and glasses on the table.

"You're over thinkin' this whole Martina thing," Ginsu said. "If you want to know how she feels about you, all you gotta do is bite her on the neck and growl a little. If she likes you, you'll know it pretty quick."

"And what if she doesn't like me?" Holt asked.

"You'll know that pretty quick, too," Skinny Pete said.

"You might want to wear a cup," Ginsu conceded. "Either way, your junk's going to get some attention."

I opted to ignore their conversation and went to meet Awiti.

"Hey, Awiti, I'm Obie. I appreciate you coming. Mind if I sit down?"

She waved a hand at the empty chair across from her.

"Did Adan explain the situation to you?" I asked, taking a seat.

"He said you wanted to hire me for a job. I came as a courtesy, but I'm not the type that stays in one place for too long, so this is probably a waste of time," she said.

"That's why you'll be perfect for the job," I said. "Why don't I get you a drink and you can tell me about yourself?"

"You can get me a drink, but if you think there's going to be something between us, I'll go ahead and tell you that you're a little too pretty for my taste," she said.

I smiled. "I'll take that as a compliment."

"You do that."

I signaled Tico for a drink. "So tell me about yourself. Where have you been? Where are you going? How many languages do you speak? All that kind of stuff."

"I've been to every continent, but only to Antarctica once. There's not a lot down there. I don't know where I'm going next. Sometimes I just start walking and see where I end up. I speak eight languages fluently and know bits and pieces of a few more."

Tico placed a couple of beers on the table and headed back behind the bar. Awiti took a glass and sniffed it before taking a long gulp.

"I suppose you've seen a fair share of trouble then?" I asked.

"Nothing I couldn't handle," she replied. "Why don't you tell me what you are looking for?"

"Basically, I need a tour guide. I'm looking for someone to take . . . a friend around," I said. "Her name is Naylet. She has amnesia and has had some trouble settling back into a life here. I want someone to travel with her, let her rediscover the world, and herself, and keep her safe."

"You want a babysitter," she said, not sounding excited by the prospect. "What are the terms?"

"I can give you a salary and I will cover all the expenses for your travels. You keep her safe and take her wherever she wants to go. Simple as that," I said.

"Is she prissy?" Awiti asked. "I don't do prissy. I travel cheap, sleep outside, and eat whatever I can find or hunt."

"That may be fine some of the time, but this is about Naylet. She needs to be exposed to a variety of experiences. If she wants to do that for a while, that's fine, but she needs to be exposed to art and culture as well."

Awiti looked down at her beer and slid it around in a circle on the table, swirling the beer inside the bottle. "I don't do culture. Doesn't sound like a good fit."

"You say you've been all over and travel cheap," I said. "Have you ever stayed in a nice hotel, taken a cruise or a train ride? Things that cost money."

"I stowed away on the top of a train in India once," she said.

I smiled. "It sounds to me like there's a bunch of things around the world you haven't done yet. If you take this job, it will open up a whole new world of experiences to you, as well. You can try another kind of life on for a while."

"How long would this arrangement be for?" Awiti asked.

"As long as she wants to travel. Whenever she wants to stop, or you want to quit just make sure she gets back here safe and sound. I've asked her to meet us here and she should be here soon. The two of you can get acquainted and see what you think. You can have this, too," I said, pushing my beer across the table to her. "If you accept, Adan has a package for you to get started. Anything else you want while you wait is on me."

She nodded. She leaned back in her chair and drank her beer. I saw Naylet walk in.

"Actually, there she is now," I said, getting up from the table.

I moved across the room and passed Holt's table again.

"Bullshit," Skinny Pete said.

Holt raised his right hand. "I swear by the Mother, lava zombies. Came back to life full of fire. Where's Obie? He can tell ya."

I walked a little faster toward Naylet. I wanted to be involved in that conversation even less than the last one. Naylet saw me coming and gave me a sheepish smile.

"Hey," she said.

"Hey, I'm glad you could make it," I said. "No Zaria this evening?"

"I didn't tell her I was coming," Naylet said. "She gave me my diary . . . I'm sorry I don't remember you. I wish I did."

"It's okay," I said. "I asked you to come because there's someone I want you to meet. She's sitting over there."

"Who is it?"

I pointed the table out. "Her name is Awiti and she is a traveler."

"Do I know her?" Naylet asked.

"No, you've never met her before. I was thinking about what you told me about how everyone knows more about you than you do. I figured the best way to fix that would be to take a trip. To go where no one knows you, get out and have some adventures, see the sights, try a bunch of stuff. Really get to know yourself."

She stuck her hands in the back pockets of her jeans and looked at the floor. "I don't know."

I knew this pose. I'd seen her make it many times before, but I wasn't going to tell her that.

"Why don't you meet her and see what you think. If you don't feel good about it, then don't go. Simple as that," I said. "There's no pressure."

"I like the idea," Naylet said. She looked up into my eyes. "If I was going to go with someone shouldn't it be—"

I interrupted her. "You can't ask me to go. If you ask me I won't be able to say no. The thing is, Thera won't stand for it. I have a job to do and that job's here."

She took my hand, stood on her tiptoes, and kissed me. "Okay, why don't you introduce me."

Naylet followed me to the table where Awiti was just starting on the second beer. She glanced up, put the glass down, and licked the foam away that had stuck to the fur above her mouth.

I started to choke up and had to clear my throat before I spoke. "Naylet, this is Awiti. I'll let you two get acquainted."

Naylet sat down and I went to join Adan at his table. I sure as hell didn't want to talk about lava zombies or Holt's love life. Turning the chair around, I took a seat without waiting to be invited. He was busy scribbling some notes on a scrap of paper the way he always did. I sat quietly, taking the opportunity to compose myself as I waited for him to finish. With the council meeting coming up as soon as Isabelle arrived, he had to wrap it up soon. He scribbled a bit more, raised the pen, and brought it down with a decisive tap on the paper.

"That's it for today," he said.

He closed his binder and put it, along with the rest of his papers, into the filing cabinet.

"Do you have everything ready for Naylet?" I asked.

"Assuming she decides to go you mean? Yes, right here," he said pulling a manila envelope out of the filing cabinet.

He returned it and locked everything with a key from his pocket before sitting back down.

"Identification, passport, cash, a credit card, it's all sorted out. Do you think she'll go?" he asked.

I didn't answer.

CHAPTER·33

THE CLUBHOUSE WENT quiet. Everyone turned to see Isabelle walk in. While she hadn't been crowned yet, she would be the first queen to ever set foot in the clubhouse. The grandiose nature of the event hadn't been lost on anyone, except for Naylet and Awiti. While Naylet didn't know the significance and Awiti didn't care, they both paused their conversation, aware that something unusual was happening.

Isabelle looked a little different than I was used to. She was dressed reminiscent of the Queen with combat boots and jeans. Where the Queen wore flannels, Isabelle opted for a spaghetti strap tank top. She wore a gray, short-brimmed, military-style cap. Instead of a pair of six shooters, Isabelle carried a nasty looking SMG on a two-point harness. Yarwor stood to her right. He wore plain clothes and had his scimitar on his belt. Tori stood to her left, wearing the uniform and carrying the accompanying weaponry of the Queen's Guard. I was surprised to see Hob walk in with them. I hadn't seen or spoken to him in the past couple weeks. Isabelle looked around the room and when she spotted me, I gave her a smile and motioned for her to join us.

The room was still silent with all eyes following as they crossed the room. When Isabelle got to the table, she took a deep breath before turning around to face the crowd. Everyone immediately went back to their own business. With the gentle rustle of conversation restored, she took a seat. Tori, Yarwor, and Hob remained standing.

"Your coronation's tomorrow," I said. "Are you nervous?"

Isabelle shrugged. "A little."

"No six-shooters?" I asked.

"I was advised to get something a little more modern," Isabelle said, presenting her gun. "It's a Sig MPX."

The submachine gun was compact and fit her better than a rifle would have, although not as well as a smaller pistol. A small pistol may not have been *royal* enough to be considered, though.

I motioned a hand across the table. "Let me introduce you to Adan. He's the emissary for the rats of Atlanta," I said.

"A pleasure," Adan said. "Should we get back there?"

"Yes. I'm getting more attention than I am comfortable with," Isabelle replied. "I need to bring Tori and Hob with me to the meeting. Is that all right?"

"If you want them there, then it will be fine," I said.

We went into the back room. Hank and Hambone were already seated when we walked in. Hambone had a small pile of candy bars on the table in front of him.

"Well! The new Queen," Hambone said. "Come sit by me, Your Majesty."

"I'm not the Queen until tomorrow," Isabelle said, moving around the table to the vacant chair beside Hambone.

"A technicality. Feel free to help yourself to some of my candy," he offered.

"Thanks," she said. "I might have one."

As we took our usual seats around the table, Hambone eyeballed the candy bars. He subtly picked one from the pile and moved it to the other side of the table, away from Isabelle. Then he moved another one.

"You wouldn't like this one, it has peanuts," he said, taking a third candy bar.

"Let's get this meeting started," Hank said. "Isabelle, I don't want to put you on the spot at your first meeting, but I think we need to clear the air. I assure you the Tortured Occult has no ill will for the Elven Nation. Otis, my father, along with members of my club have been killed in this conflict as well as your mother, sisters, and brother. I think enough is enough and I hope you feel the same way."

Isabelle sat her cap farther back on her head, showing more of her face. "I want to make it clear that I don't blame the Tortured Occult for any of the deaths in my family. My understanding is that my brother killed my sisters, and then my mother and brother killed each other. I should be apologizing to you. It was my family that was responsible for the trouble."

"If you don't want trouble, then there won't be any. We've seen enough blood over the years," Hank said.

"I'm glad to hear that," Isabelle said. "Actually, that's something else I wanted to talk about. In the past two weeks, I've named advisors. It's customary for the Queen to have a council. My mother disbanded hers before I was born, but I think it's a good idea. Hob is one of those advisors. I've asked him to be my magical council and he agreed. He wanted to come earlier to speak to you about it, but he hasn't been able to get away. I thought I should tell you. He will be living in the Elven Nation, and for the foreseeable future, won't be available to resume your dust operation."

"If we can't make dust, it's gonna get dangerous for a lot of people around here," Hank said.

"I agree," Hambone said, snagging another two candy bars. "If the dust runs out, it's going to be a big problem. Stores are already low."

"How long would it take to rebuild the facility?" I asked.

"Hob?" Hank asked.

"Three months, give or take," Hob said. "But you would need someone to oversee it."

"What about Wilix?" I asked. "Could he set up and run a dust operation?"

"*Ja*, it is possible," Hob said. "If he is willing, I could give assistance. With Isabelle's permission of course."

"It doesn't appear we have much of a choice," Hank said. "Does anyone know what happened to Wilix?"

"We'll have to track him down," I said.

"If it's going to take three months or more to get a facility up and running, what are we going to do with the bodies that we should be dusting in the meantime?" Adan asked.

"I took the demons I had to the copper mines," I said. "It's fenced off and cold enough in there to mute the stink. It's a fine place to store them in the short term."

"Does it even make sense to have this meeting if we can't make dust?" Hank asked.

Hambone grabbed his chest like he was struck by a heart attack. "Disband?"

Adan leaned forward. "Good point. If we're all at peace and can't make dust, then what are we really doing?"

"I don't like this one bit," Hambone said, standing up in his chair for emphasis. "I think you're forgetting people that would be perpetually damaged by the dissolution of this organization. We protect numerous ultranaturals all over North Georgia. We shouldn't forget them." Hambone sat down and then stood right back up. "And what about me? I'm a politician. If I lose this job, what will I do? I don't have any skills. It's like you're all just thinking of yourselves."

"There he is," I mumbled to myself as Hambone sat back down. "If we can get Wilix on board, we can get another operation up and running, or we may be able to find another duster. They're out there."

"All right," Hank said. "We'll give it a few months and see how it plays out. Isabelle, do you have anything to bring up?"

"Yes," Isabelle replied. "You had an agreement with Mother to do pack runs inside the Elven Nation. I wanted you to know that I intend to honor that agreement, but I will need time. I am already planning changes that may take a while to gain acceptance. Too much change at once will cause problems. I hope you can be patient."

"How much time are we talking about?" Hank asked.

"Can we revisit it in six months?" she replied. "I really would like to make it sooner, but I feel that's already moving quickly."

Hank leaned back in his chair and tapped the fingers of his right hand on the table. "Speaking of revisiting, who will be representing the Elven Nation at our meetings?"

"I'll attend them myself, with a couple of my council," Isabelle replied, holding a hand toward Tori and Hob. "I believe the relations with our neighbors are essential for our security and deserve my attention."

"You're shaping up to be a competent Queen already," Adan said. "There's a lot of business that we can do, now that we are going to be good friends."

"Speaking of friends," Isabelle said. "I hope that you will all come to the coronation tomorrow. It would be nice for people to see us getting along with the Tortured Occult."

"And maybe make your enemies think twice about crossing you, hmm?" Hambone said, swapping candy bars between piles.

"Closer to showing we don't have any enemies anymore," she said.

Our meeting lasted about thirty more minutes. By the time it was over the pile of candy bars Isabelle had to choose from was a Snickers with a bite out of it. It didn't seem to bother her, or if it did, she didn't show it, but she also didn't take the candy bar.

CHAPTER·34

I HAD NEVER SEEN so many elves in one place. Not only soldiers, of which there were many, but regular looking folks. Elves that could have been farmers or accountants. Children ran through the trees and the crowd. What looked like teenagers, but were probably closer to centenarians, hung out in groups, doing their best to look uninterested in the proceedings. I caught them, and many of the other elves, giving us sideways glances. No doubt we were the first shifters many of them had ever seen. Only the oldest elves here had a chance of remembering a time when the borders weren't closed, and shifters were allowed into the Elven Nation.

There was a stage with a podium in the center, a shooting bench beside it, and tables on either side. A long row of tables with green tablecloths ran out in front of the stage, looking like the elvish version of the Hogwarts dining hall. Tucked away in the woods were multiple trucks catering the event. They loaded tables along the sides with a selection of food and drinks. Holt and I were shown to the table to the right of the podium. We watched the crowd grow and waited for the ceremony to start.

Holt eyeballed the tables of food. "You think they have anything to drink?"

"Don't you think you had enough last night?" I asked.

Our natural healing ability prevented the more unpleasant effects of alcohol, namely hangovers.

"Oh yeah, I had way too much last night," he answered. "But it's a new day."

"Maybe we should just sit here, show our support, and not attract too much attention to ourselves?"

"All right. Fine," he said, bobbing his knee up and down. "I'm going to look at the food and get some water. I'm feeling parched."

I didn't want to argue with him in front of a few hundred elves. If I thought it would do any good, I might have. Hank, Adan, and Hambone walked up to the table as he was leaving.

Holt shook their hands as he passed them and said, "Obie's grumpy again."
They took their seats beside me at the table.

"Are you grumpy, Obie?" Hank asked.

I shook my head. "Don't listen to him, he's an idiot."

"Sounds pretty grumpy, to me," Adan mumbled.

Hambone nodded in agreement, but froze like a deer in headlights, when he realized I saw him.

"There is something I wanted to talk to you about," Hank said, leaning in for what little privacy we could get. "My son's missing."

"Wasn't Lugnut locked up?" I asked.

Hank shook his head. "Not Lugnut, he should be getting out soon. Torch. He stepped away from the club when he saw what Chisel was doing with it. The last time anyone talked to him was right before we ambushed the Queen. We don't know where he was staying exactly, but it shouldn't have been too far away. He was just laying low."

"Any idea what happened to him?"

Hank sighed. "I think the most likely thing is the elves got him."

That hadn't occurred to me and the line of thinking worried me a little. "You don't think Isabelle—"

"I don't," he said. "But she wasn't in charge then."

"Have you asked her? That seems like something she would know, or be able to find out," I said.

Hank shook his head. "Not yet. It's too early for any kind of tension with the elves. If he hasn't shown up by the next meeting, I'll ask."

"If you need me to help look just say the word," I said. "I'll keep an eye open in the meantime."

Holt sat down on the bench beside me with a turkey leg in one hand. He put a stein on the table in front of him. I could smell it wasn't water.

"Did you find any water?" I asked.

"Forgot to look," he said. "They do have a ton of wine, though. It was like pulling teeth to get anything besides those tiny wine glasses they're passing out. Once it was brought to their attention I was sitting at the Queen's table, they shut up pretty quick."

"You couldn't just stick to water for the ceremony?"

"How bad could a little wine be?" he asked. "Jesus turned water to wine. If it's good enough for him, it's good enough for me."

"So, get some water and if Jesus turns it to wine for you, I won't argue," I said.

"Nah, I'll just skip the middleman."

"There's turkey legs?" Hambone asked, lust dripping from his words.

"Oh, yeah," Holt said. "They still have turkeys attached to them, but they just pull right off."

"Gentlemen, if you will excuse me," Hambone said, disappearing under the table.

He popped out the far side and made a beeline for the food.

"I don't think I've ever seen him move that fast before," Adan said.

Hank nodded. "Something tells me we won't see him again today."

The guests continued to pile in. Hob showed two wererats we didn't recognize to our table. They sat on the end.

"Thank you all for coming," Hob said. "We're going to be getting started soon, so if you would not mind changing to krasis? We have a private area if you wish."

We all looked at each other, no one willing to hide their abilities. We made the change to krasis. Gasps rose from the assembled elves. It was one thing to know about shifters, it was something else entirely to witness a change for the first time. I wasn't concerned about their shock. We were building a new world and they'd have to get acclimated to people different from them.

"I will have to go up to be introduced, but after I will come back to explain the ceremony to you," Hob said.

A forest green, four-door Jeep Wrangler with a matching escort truck on either side parked in the back. A group of elves got out of the truck; had to be Royal Guard. They still had the weaponry and surly disposition of the Guard, but no longer wore the black uniforms. Now they wore khaki tops and dark green pants. It took me a minute to figure out where I had seen the color scheme before; it matched the forestry service uniform.

Three elves took positions on either side of the Jeep. The door opened, and Isabelle jumped out, landing between them. She wore matching colors, but with shorts and a tank top and a khaki cap.

Yarwor, with his scimitar, got out of the Jeep behind her. He was dressed similarly, except wearing all green and no khaki. They formed a procession with Isabelle in the center and made their way through the crowd. The crowd parted for them. The movement of the crowd combined with Yarwor's bald gray head bobbing up and down through the crowd like a buoy in the ocean gave away their position. When they made it to the stage, the guards stood in front at ground level while Isabelle and Yarwor came up onto the stage. Isabelle stood beside the podium with Yarwor standing behind her to her right.

A woman in a flowing robe the color of fresh pine needles stood up from the table on the other side of the stage and walked to the podium. She held up her hands to quiet the murmur of the crowd.

"Who is this?" I asked Hob.

"She is the sharpshooter. A kind of priest. For an elf, the highest ideal is one who never misses. This is true in both word and action. The sharpshooter is said to never miss."

The sharpshooter addressed the crowd. "Before we begin the ceremony, Isabelle would like to say something."

The sharpshooter stepped aside, and Isabelle took a step stool from inside the podium and placed it to grant her the clearance to be seen by the crowd. She stepped onto it and paused for a moment, inspecting the crowd.

"It's customary for a family member to hold the target during the ceremony. As you all know, my family has been killed. The right of revenge is mine, and mine alone, to claim."

I could feel everyone on the bench tense up at this statement and I couldn't blame them. If Isabelle had been holding a grudge this whole time, this would be the perfect opportunity to execute us in a very public way. If it were the Queen, I would be diving for cover right now, but we sat still, exchanged some nervous glances, and I made a note to ask Hob about what the *right of revenge* meant to elves. Isabelle looked at us and I felt my feet digging into the ground, ready to propel myself away as soon as the signal was given.

"I choose to reject that right," she said, turning back to face the crowd. "There is another right I will claim though. The right of the blood bond."

The table gave a coordinated sigh of relief as a new wave of murmurs rose from the audience. Isabelle gave Yarwor a nod. He drew his scimitar and held it between them, blade up. Isabelle went first, running her hand over the blade. Aside from a slight clenching of her mouth, she gave no indication that it hurt.

Yarwor did the same and they clasped hands, symbolically mixing their blood as it flowed from their hands and dripped onto the stage. They held up their hands to the crowd, showing the cuts. Then she motioned to our bench.

"She needs you now," Hob whispered in my ear.

I didn't know I was going to be part of the ceremony. I stood and joined them on the stage.

"Could you heal us?" Isabelle asked.

I nodded, and they held out their hands. I made quick work of the cuts. They wiped the blood from their hands and again held them up for the crowd. I returned to my seat.

"Yarwor is now my family and I choose him to be my target bearer," she said.

Hob whispered to us, "Now she will introduce us and tell everyone her plans for the Nation."

She introduced everyone at the tables. The only elves I knew were Hob and Tori. There were two others I didn't know. She then introduced us, giving explanations of who we were. The two wererats that joined us were representatives of Charlotte and Knoxville. Rat populations bordering the north side of the Elven Nation. Everyone went through a customary stand and wave as we were introduced. When the introductions were finished, Isabelle began to speak in a tongue I hadn't heard in hundreds of years. I knew it as elvish, but I hadn't known they still used it or taught it to the younger generations.

"Hob," I whispered. "you want to translate for us?"

"*Ja*, Obie," he said.

"My grandmother founded the Elven Nation in 1753 as a place for elves to find peace and protection away from the persecutions of the Old World. It's in this nation that many elves, some of you included, found refuge in isolation. Far removed from our enemies, the Nation grew strong, building new friendships and conducting trade for the good of elven kind. And so, when treachery ended my grandmother's rule, my mother stepped up to take her place. My mother was a great Queen. She fought relentlessly for the good of the Nation. She made controversial, difficult decisions, but she always did what she believed was right. She pushed the Nation forward into a new area of firearms and military superiority. But for the second time, our nation was isolated. As new challenges arose we had no friends, no support, to help us. The result was destruction.

"Now, as the last living descendant of the royal bloodline, it is my duty to take the throne. It is a great responsibility, one that cannot be taken lightly. With much consideration and council, I have decided to take the Nation in a new direction. We move forward, no longer isolated, relying only on ourselves. The Nation was made strong by the actions of my foremothers. We will honor them with continued strength in a new age of cooperation. One with few enemies and many friends, where we don't face every obstacle alone. It will be a challenging transition. One that will test us in ways we have never been tested before. The Nation will not only survive, it will prosper. The Nation is strong, and we are strong through it."

The crowd repeated the last line.

Isabelle said, "So I speak the truth, so shall I shoot true."

Isabelle stepped down from the podium and to the shooting bench. The sharpshooter produced a rifle from a chest behind the stage. It was a pristine Sharps rifle—I hadn't seen one in a long time—and after holding it up to the crowd for inspection, the sharpshooter presented the rifle to Isabelle. A Sharps was a hunting rifle from the 1800s that was known to be accurate at long ranges. As Isabelle loaded the rifle, Yarwor took a circular target attached to a piece of plywood and followed the sharpshooter through the crowd. We all stood as they walked through the woods into the distance. By the time they stopped, and Yarwor held the target up over his head, the orange circle in the center was barely visible.

Isabelle positioned the rifle on the bench and readied herself for the shot. It was much too large a gun for someone her size, but the only option she had was to shoot it. She cocked the hammer and sat perfectly still, taking aim down the barrel. The slow rise and fall of her breathing was the only sign of movement, and then that stopped. Hob stuck his hand discreetly in his pocket. I could see a faint light coming from it and the wisps of burning dust coming out. The gun fired. The recoil nearly pushed Isabelle off the bench altogether. Everyone was perfectly silent as Yarwor lowered the target and presented it to the sharpshooter. They walked back to the crowd, anticipation growing.

The sharpshooter held up the target. "Bull's-eye!" she shouted.

The crowd erupted with cheering.

Isabelle picked up the rifle and carried it behind the podium. She used the podium to shield her from the eyes of the crowd. I could tell her shoulder hurt, but she seemed all right. She breathed a sigh of relief.

I caught Hob's eye and he knew I had seen what he'd done. He gave me a wink. I was sure I was the only one that knew he had used magic to aid Isabelle's shot. I wasn't about to tell anyone about it.

Isabelle waited patiently as Yarwor and the sharpshooter made their way back through the crowd. They moved slowly, showing off the target as proof of Isabelle's right to the throne. When they made it back onto the stage she waved to the crowd, presenting herself for the first time as the Queen of the Elven Nation.

Torch's Fate

I WOKE FEELING LIKE I'd spent a good night drinking. My head pounded. I kept my eyes shut tight. I could see the light through my eyelids alternating between light and dark. It was coming back to me now. I was a member of the Tortured Occult Motorcycle Club, an outlaw motorcycle gang made up of any kind of shifter big enough to ride a hog. The nice thing about being a werebear was that I was bigger and stronger than most of the other shifters. It came in handy. I groaned in misery. Did the club have a party? That would explain how I was feeling. Last time, I woke up passed out in a ditch on the side of the road. My miserable nostalgia was suddenly interrupted by the gruff voice of a nearby man.

"You don't think it's waking up, do you?" the man asked.

"You new guys are so jumpy," another man chided. "They always make noise like that. We have it drugged and strapped down. There's nothing to worry about."

"It looks like a regular guy. Are you sure it's one of them?"

"The tests were conclusive," a third man said from in front of me.

I pretended to be asleep, trying to remember how I got here. My head was slowly clearing. The last thing I remembered, I was heading up Interstate 75. I was close to Dalton when I found a crappy hotel to stay at. I was laying low, waiting for some heat to die down. I got a pizza and a six pack. I was just sitting down for a nice night of watching reruns on a fuzzy TV, drinking, and jacking off. Then I woke up wherever the hell *here* was.

I could feel restraints on my arms and legs. They were tight enough that I knew I couldn't slip out of them. At the same time, I had no intention of just going along with whatever they had planned. They had to unstrap me at some point and, when they did, I'd make my move. I peeked an eye open—just a sliver. I was being wheeled down a hallway. Three people were pushing the gurney I was on, but I could see only the one in front of me clearly. He looked like a doctor with a white coat and a clipboard.

They didn't speak again, and I didn't move. They wheeled me into an operating room and put the gurney beside a table. I could feel them loosening the restraints on my left arm and leg. I was hoping they would undo all four, but I felt them starting to put restraints back on my free arm. I reasoned that the gurney was lighter and more movable than the table, so I knew I had to make my move. It was now or never.

My eyes popped open. The man trying to put a restraint around my left foot gasped with surprise and jumped back out of reach. The fear in his eyes told me he was the new guy.

"Hold him down, you fool!" the doctor bellowed from somewhere behind me.

One of the men, who I realized was an orderly, latched onto my arm. He couldn't match my strength, so I launched him over me and onto the floor. New guy came forward, and I kicked him hard in the stomach. Clutching his abdomen, he rolled backward and out of sight. Another of the men, dressed in a lab coat, pulled a syringe from his pocket. He yanked the cap off with his teeth and lunged at me.

I had no intention of letting him stick me with whatever the hell *that* was. I pushed off the operating table in his direction. The gurney shot across the room, plowing into him and dumping me onto the floor. I took the opportunity to unstrap myself before making the change into my werebear form. My body added bulk, black fur sprouted all over my body. Razor-sharp claws emerged from my fingertips, and my feet turned to paws. My head became that of a fierce black bear.

The orderly I had thrown pulled himself to his feet and took out a stun baton. The end crackled with electricity as he pushed the button on the shaft. He thrust it forward at my chest. I jumped to the side, dodging the baton. Grabbing his baton hand, I yanked him towards me. With my other hand, I grabbed him by the back of the neck and slammed him face first into the glass door they had wheeled me in through. He dropped the baton on the first hit. The second left a blood splatter on the splintered glass. He went limp on the third. His body fell to the floor in a heap when I let go.

"Is that the best you pig fucks got?" I shouted.

I shouldn't have stopped to talk. Electric pain shot through my back. The new guy had found some courage and a baton of his own. I convulsed involuntarily until he let go of the button. My legs gave out and I crumpled to the ground next to the gurney, which I pulled over my head to use as a shield.

"What do we do?" the new guy shouted.

"Keep shocking him," the doctor commanded.

I had a good view of the new guy's legs from under the gurney. I swung at his ankles and knocked him to the ground. Grabbing his shirt, I pulled him in and bit his head. He started to scream and thrash around on the floor as I increased the pressure from my jaws. The baton snapped like a bug zapper as he flailed around. His skull began to snap, crackle, and pop like a bowl of Rice Krispies and then gave way. My jaws clamped shut; his body went limp. My mouth filled with blood and brain matter that felt silky on my tongue. I spit out what I could and tossed the gurney to the side.

I stood up to find the doctor picking up a corded phone mounted on the wall in the corner. I took two steps towards him and raked my claws across his face. He collapsed face down, a puddle of blood running onto the floor around him.

They had taken everything I had. Wallet, phone, the buck knife I kept strapped to my boot, even my clothes. All I had on was a bloody hospital gown. I ripped it off, hit the door release, and stepped into the hallway. Outside the operating room, doors lined the hallway. They reminded me of the kind of doors they had in solitary the last time I got locked up. Beside each door was a control panel with lots of buttons and gauges. The hallway continued to the right. I didn't feel them turn the gurney when they rolled me in, so the exit must be straight ahead. I stopped by the first door on the way out for a closer look. I recognized only some of what all the gauges were measuring. Temperature, humidity, O2, and PSI.

I stepped up to the small window in the door and looked inside. The room resembled a plain metal box. No bed, no toilet. It had recessed lighting protected by grates. A woman lay beside a drain in the middle of the floor. She looked Middle Eastern and wore a hospital gown that had fallen open. She didn't seem to care or even notice. Her black hair was tangled and matted. She'd clearly been locked up a while. My last prison cell looked like the MGM Grand compared to this place.

She lifted her head and our eyes met. I could tell she'd given up already. I'd seen the look before. As she turned away and laid her head back on the floor, I heard a thumping coming from behind me. I turned to see a werewolf pounding on the glass in the cell across the hall. I didn't recognize him; he definitely hadn't spent any time at the clubhouse.

Get me out, he mouthed through the glass.

I had a feeling I'd run into more trouble before I made it out. A little help wouldn't hurt. I went over, gave him a nod, and noticed the sprinklers in his cell were on. They covered the entire inside of the cell with constant rain. He looked like he'd never been dry. I scratched my head and looked at the panel beside his cell.

Temperature: 37° Celsius
Humidity: 100%
PSI: 12.5
O2: 12%

I turned the humidity dial all the way to the right and pushed a button, causing all the lights in the cell to go off. I pushed it again, the lights came back on. I looked back in the cell. The sprinklers had stopped.

Pull the lever. He made a motion with his arm as if he was trying to get a truck driver to blow their horn.

I did see one big lever on the right side of the panel. I gave it a tug and could feel the metal flexing from the pressure, but it didn't move. Surely there was a release. I started pushing buttons all over the panel. The gauges changed, but the lever wouldn't move.

Temperature: 43° Celsius
Humidity: 100%
PSI: 14
O2: 20%

A wall-mounted alarm complete with red flashing lights sounded. I looked back into the cell to find him still standing by the door, but now steam seemed to be rising from his body. Back at the panel, I found a red button on the bottom by the lever. I pushed it and felt the lever release. The door swung open and the werewolf stepped out. The hallway filled with hot, humid air.

"How do we get outta here?" I asked.

The wolf shrugged. "How the hell should I know? I'm Atticus, by the way."

Two guards ran around the corner. The first collided with Atticus, sending them both tumbling to the floor. The second stepped back and raised a gun in my direction. I grabbed his wrist as he pulled the trigger. Bullets slammed into the wall and ceiling while I twisted his wrist until it popped. I grabbed him by the shirt, slamming him into the wall with as much force as I could muster. His ribs cracked upon impact, and I let him go. His body slid down the wall, coming to rest in a crumpled heap on the floor.

I turned to find Atticus wiping blood from his mouth. He had bitten and ripped out the guard's throat. I turned back to the first. He was still alive and holding onto his gun. I stepped on his hand and ground my foot with my full weight. He screamed as the bones in his hand were crushed. I picked up the gun from his mangled hand. He clutched his hand to his chest and coughed, blood trickling from his mouth. I pulled the magazine from the gun to find it loaded with silver bullets.

I knelt beside the injured man. "This ain't lookin' good for you. Tell me what I want to know, and I'll think about letting you live. How do we get outta here?"

The guard grimaced in pain. "There are three exits. Your best bet is the tunnel. Go up one floor and turn left. Follow it to the end. You'll find some stairs that will take you out."

"What about guards?" Atticus asked.

"Procedures are to contain the building and wait for help. Everyone will exit and call a team to retake the building. We were trying to get out when we ran into you."

"I believe you," I said.

I stood and kicked him in the chest. The impact forced the air from his lungs, sending blood splattering over my leg. He collapsed onto his side and struggled to breathe. I thought about kicking him again, but I was sure it would kill him. He was barely hanging on as it was and would probably be dead in a couple minutes. No reason he shouldn't spend his last minutes thinking about the mistake of fucking with me.

"What happened to 'thinking about letting him go'?" Atticus asked.

"I thought better of it," I said. "Let's get outta here."

"Hold on," Atticus said. "Let's let everybody out. If they're bringing in backup, we'll need some of our own."

I didn't think we were going to organize this group into some kind of militia, but the more of them there were to shoot at, the better the chance I had to get away. I went to the cell with the woman in it.

"They open like this," I said, pressing the button and pulling the lever.

The door swung open. The woman looked up at me again and laid her head down just like before. I wasn't surprised. I wasn't going to waste my time trying to help a corpse that didn't have the decency to die. I moved down one side of the hallway opening cells while Atticus opened the other side.

What came out of the cells was the sorriest excuse for backup I'd ever seen. There were a bunch of shifters, a goblin, and even a few humans. Most of them were emaciated. They looked sickly and pale. If any one of them had tried to join the Tortured Occult, they would've been laughed out of the clubhouse. But, since all I needed were meat shields, they would do.

What's weirder were their cells. They were all different. Atticus's cell was pouring water, others had bright lights, some were cold. There didn't seem to be any rhyme or reason to it. I saw only a few that seemed normal. Maybe it was some kind of experiment to see how people dealt with prolonged exposure to different conditions. It didn't matter, and I didn't care.

"Anybody that wants to get outta here, follow me," I said, holding up the gun I'd filched off the guard.

We moved quickly and quietly, following the guard's directions up the stairs and down the left hallway. It looked like he'd been telling the truth because the halls were empty. We rounded a corner and came to stairs leading up to a storm cellar door. I grabbed Atticus's arm to put some space between us and the others. I let go as soon as I did when I felt how hot he was. It was as if I had grabbed a radiator.

"Listen, if this whole thing goes sideways and I don't make it out, find a friend of mine named Obie," I said, shaking my hand. "He can help you. He's kind of a big shot in North Georgia. He'll find this place and shut it down. One of those do-gooder types that really annoy me." I whispered. "You hold the left door, I'll get the right. Let them go first."

He gave me a side-eyed glance then nodded. He knew what time it was: save your own skin time.

"When we get outside, spread out and move fast. Just get away for now, and we'll figure out what to do next when we're safe. Alright, let's go," I said, pushing the door open.

The door opened into the woods. Atticus and I got a chance to look around while the group shuffled past us. I could see the lights of a large house behind us through the trees, in the same direction as the tunnel. I figured that was where these people had been held. I could hear the rushing of a river off to my right.

The wind changed, and I caught the scent of humans. I couldn't tell exactly how many. I could hear rustling coming from all around us in the trees. As the last of the prisoners moved out past us, I caught Atticus's eye. I gave him a subtle nod in a different direction than the group was moving. We let go of the doors. Flood lights illuminated the area.

"Go back to your cells and you won't be hurt," a voice said over a megaphone. "If you attempt to escape, you'll be shot."

The spotlights were arranged in front of us in a half moon shape. It looked like I had a shot of escaping off to my right. Before I could make my move, the goblin with the group made a run for it. The guards had no intention of giving another warning. Guns burst to life, muzzle flashes giving away the positions of the guards. Atticus and I crouched instinctively. Then, Atticus started screaming.

I thought he'd been hit and looked over. Smoke rose from his body before he suddenly burst into flame. It wasn't like he was doused in gas; it was as if he was made of gas. He burned so hot he scorched some of my fur. The air filled with the sickening smells of burning hair and flesh. Atticus took off behind me in the direction of the river, leaving burning footprints on the ground.

I soon realized that most of the prisoners were having bizarre reactions. I didn't see any of them run off, but some had just disappeared. A couple of them dove to the ground and gave up. I moved up and used one of the prostrate shifters as a shield and returned fire. The guards fired back at me. I could feel the bits of rock coming off him hitting my fur. I managed to shoot out one of the spotlights on my side before my magazine ran out.

Staying there was suicide. I ran into the woods to my right. A stone coyote collapsed. I could see Atticus flailing around in front of me, catching brush and trees on fire. I took two bullets through the gut and fell to the ground. Atticus kept running, screaming and bouncing off trees, stumbling his way through the woods. I crawled through some brush for cover until I was clear, then got up and moved as fast I could.

I knew I'd been hit with silver. There's a special burn to it you just don't get from lead. When I'd put some distance between myself and the shooting, I leaned up against a tree and inspected my injuries. One bullet had passed clean through while the other was still in my belly. I'd die if I didn't get it out soon. Not knowing where I was, my best bet was to go to a human hospital. If I could find a road, I could get someone to call an ambulance. The club could sort out the rest.

I couldn't very well show up to a human hospital as a werebear. I'd have to change to my human form. Shifting with a silver injury was bad enough, but a silver bullet stuck in my body would do a lot of extra damage. I clenched my jaw and made the change. I could feel my flesh tearing around the bullet. I felt dizzy, but I had to keep moving. I wasn't sure exactly how long I stumbled through the woods before I found a road. I walked into approaching headlights with one hand up and the other holding where I'd been shot. The car slammed on its brakes and came to a stop a few feet away. I stepped forward, put a bloody hand on the hood, and passed out.

"DOCTOR, HE'S WAKING up," a woman said.

I could hear the steady beep of a heart rate monitor and smell disinfectant. I opened my eyes to see a young nurse standing over me.

"Try not to move," she said with a smile. "You were shot and have been unconscious for just over two weeks. I'm glad you're finally awake."

As my head cleared, I saw a man turn around. He was wearing a white coat and holding a chart. He had a bandage over one eye and four claw marks running down his face. I recognized him. My claws had given him those gashes.

"You caused quite a problem," he said as he absently flipped through the pages of the chart. "Yes, you should do nicely."

"What do you want with me?" I asked. "What is this place?"

"A research facility," the man answered. "We study your kind here and conduct experiments."

"What kind of experiments?" I asked.

"My specialty is bioengineering . . . genetics," he said. "There are numerous experts taking part in the experiments, though."

I tried to move but found my arms and legs in restraints. I pulled against them, shook, and screamed but couldn't break free.

"We upgraded our security measures after the trouble you caused. I should really thank you. While you cost us months of work in some cases, we'll be better off for it in the long run. Are we ready?" the man asked the nurse.

"Yes, doctor."

"Okay then . . . we'll just take a bit today," he said. He tied a tourniquet around my left arm, just below the shoulder. "We'll use the Gigli saw today."

The nurse handed him a wire with a handle on either end. He leaned over, inspecting my arm as I struggled. I knew I wasn't going to get loose this time.

"Do try to be still," he said. "I prefer to have a clean cut."

He looped the wire around my arm just below the elbow and gripped the handles firmly. The wire sliced down to the bone on the first pull. Blood, my blood, spilled out on the table. I could feel the wire bite into the bone with the next pull and then the pain hit.

TAKEN

SWEAT ROLLED OFF my forehead and into my eyes. I wiped it away and refocused on the task at hand. I held up the diagram, getting a closer look at my next step. I had been working on the assembly for the better part of an hour. Now I was at a critical juncture. If I didn't get this connection right, then I would have a disaster on my hands. I pushed the diagram away and picked up a bottle of cyanoacrylate. Once the adhesive was applied, I would be on the clock. I applied a thin strip and put the bottle back on the table. I exhaled half my breath and held the rest to steady my hands like a sniper preparing for a shot. I only had a few seconds to make the connection. As carefully as I could I brought the pieces together.

Just as they touched, I was startled by a buzzing in my pocket. I'd been so focused I nearly jumped out of my skin. I exhaled and looked at my work, it was a mess. I sighed out the breath I'd been holding as my phone buzzed again. I took it out and checked the screen, the caller ID said Restricted.

I put the phone to my ear. "Hello?"

The voice on the other end sounded like it was being put through one of those scramblers you see on television. "A demon is on its way to Dave Hutchinson. He'll be dead by midnight. If you hurry you can help him."

"Who is this?" I asked.

"A friend," the voice said. "I'll send you the address."

The call ended. I sat back in my chair, pondering the brief conversation. I'd never heard of Dave Hutchinson. I'd thought I'd put an end to the summoning, at least for the time being, when I'd gotten the Grimoire from Harlan. My phone buzzed again. I'd received a text from a restricted number with an address. I wasn't sure if the lead was credible, but it was less than an hour away. Seemed worth checking out.

"Holt," I shouted.

I could hear the thumping of his footsteps leave his room and walk down the hallway to where I was. He walked as if he had lead soled shoes. The footsteps stopped and the door opened.

Holt stuck in his head. "By the mother, why's it so hot in here?"

"I got a te—"

"I mean, even though winter's over, it's still been chilly but you keep tellin' me not to turn the thermostat over sixty-six, and I do it, 'cause I'm a pleasure to live with, but I'm walkin' around here freezin' my ass off and you got a space heater keeping your room a toasty fifteen hundred degrees. I'm just curious—" He stopped talking long enough to see what I was doing. "Oh no, not this again."

I scratched my chin and ran a hand over my face.

"Obie…this ain't healthy. We're supposed to be Keepers of the Earth Mother for fucks sake. Name takers and demon slayers," he said. "She's been gone what four or five months already and you hadn't done nothin' but sit around and mope and build these dump planes."

It had been four months and seventeen days since Naylet left on her trip of self-discovery, not that I was counting, I just hadn't been able to get the running tally out of my head. It seemed like since Naylet had left I couldn't stop thinking about her. Wondering where she was and what she was doing. I could probably find out if I wanted to; the wererats information network was vast, to say the least. I had no doubt Adan could, and would, use it to keep tabs on her if I asked him. I promised myself I wouldn't and I hadn't needed to, the postcards I'd been getting gave me a good idea of what she was up to.

"There's nothing wrong with assembling transportation collectibles," I said.

He put his hands on his hips and shook his head. "Do you hear yourself right now? Transportation collectibles? You know they do therapy online . . . It'll be real easy to find someone to talk to."

I was losing my patience with him. "Why. Are. You. Here?"

"How the hell should I know, you called me," Holt said.

"Right," I sighed. "I just got an anonymous lead that says a guy is going to be attacked by a demon. I figured we'd check it out."

"Hell yeah," Holt said. "It'll be good for you to get back to work."

"Give me five minutes and we'll go. And close the door behind you."

I looked back at the P-51 Mustang I had been working on. I'd been trying to glue the fuselage together. The pieces weren't on straight. I could pull it off and try it again but not without leaving marks on the plastic. Maybe I could add some bullet holes to cover up the imperfections. Or maybe Holt was right. I wouldn't tell him that, of course, but it might do me some good to get out of my head a little. I put the plane down on my worktable, turned off the heater, and rubbed my eyes. I wasn't sure how solid the lead was, but it would do me good to get out of the house.

When I made it outside, I found Holt behind the wheel of his Honda. After I'd discovered how good he was behind the wheel I always let him drive.

"You think Adan could find out who sent you that message?" Holt asked a few minutes down the road. "The wererats are good at finding out stuff like that."

"They're great if you're not in a hurry. It could take them a month to get back to us with something like that. By then we will have either figured it out ourselves or it won't matter anymore."

Holt shrugged. "Suit yourself. I don't see what it would hurt to get the ball rolling on it."

"When you're out on your own you'll have the luxury and responsibility of making the decision. As long as you're my apprentice just enjoy not having to make the hard decisions."

We rode in silence until we were close to our destination. I could see the blue and red lights flashing from the road before we pulled into the subdivision.

"Looks like we're too late," Holt said.

"Let's go in for a look anyway."

A couple firetrucks, an ambulance, and more than a few police cars were parked in front of the house.

"What now?" Holt asked.

"Just pull through," I said. "Let's see what we can see."

Holt drove slowly down the center of the street toward the lights. An officer waved us through. I couldn't see anything from the street and getting inside right now wasn't going to be an option. I was starting to think we'd have to come back the next day when things had calmed down when I spotted Detective Farwell standing in the yard. We'd met the day Naylet was turned to stone. I'd saved him from the same fate and in the process exposed him to our world. He wasn't my biggest fan . . . what an ingrate.

"Pull over up here," I said waving a finger at the road ahead. "I got an idea."

Holt took the next right beside a two-story brick house and parked up the street. I got out and walked to the corner in view of the house. Farwell talked to a woman wearing dark blue coveralls with a laminated badge hanging from her right chest pocket. Probably the medical examiner. I pulled my phone out of my pocket and gave him a call. I watched him fish the phone out of his pocket and stared at the screen as it rang. He looked at it for three rings before he shoved it back in his pocket and returned his attention to the woman.

I typed out a text message. *Brick house on the corner. Need to talk to you.*

Farwell glanced at his phone again, mouthed the word *Shit,* and looked down the street in my direction. When he spotted me, I put two fingers to my forehead and gave him a casual salute. He ducked the police tape and walked over to meet me on the corner.

"What the hell are you doing here?" he asked.

"I got a call that there was something going on here in my area of expertise. What happened?"

Farwell crossed his arms. "It's an ongoing investigation."

"Look, if you tell me this has nothing to do with the kinds of things I handle then I'll be more than happy to head home and leave you to it. If you think this might be . . . something else, then you know better than anyone the kind of danger you and your officers could be in without my help. Your call."

Farwell wrapped his tongue over his top teeth and sucked on them as he turned back to look at the house. "Alright. We found a man and woman handcuffed to chairs in the bedroom. The coroner said they were missing organs but she wouldn't know exactly how bad it was until she got them back for an autopsy."

"So, they had some organs harvested? Like black market, leave you in a bathtub full of ice, kind of thing?" I asked.

"Well, that's the kicker, there weren't any incisions. The bodies were in great shape, besides the missing organs," Farwell said. "The bodies are just . . . empty. What about you? What brought you out here?"

"I got an anonymous call that said there was demon stuff happening here. I guess I was too late to save Dave and his wife but I'll look into it."

"That's the thing. Mr. Hutchinson isn't here," Farwell said with a smirk. "The man we have is his business partner. It looks like he was giving it to Dave's wife on the side and they got caught. I was about to send a couple marked units to his construction site, see if we can pick him up."

"How about you give me the address and an hour head start?" I asked.

"Why would I do that?"

"I'm assuming the officers you send like their organs."

CHAPTER · 2

I BECAME AWARE I hadn't been paying attention. I glanced at the clock: 11:47. Holt was talking, which wasn't unusual for him. Assuming he'd been going the whole ride it meant he'd been droning on for over thirty minutes and I had been lost in thought the whole time.

"You see, it's a problem because it was unnecessary to begin with and it completely changed Han's character," Holt said. "He was a dangerous rogue and now he looks passive and weak, like he has a moral code that wasn't there in the original version."

"Mm hmm," I said absently. "I can see you feel strongly about this."

"Strong enough to give you a tee shirt about it when we first met." Holt waved a hand in the air to accentuate his point. "And what about Greedo? He went from a competent bounty hunter who Han got the drop on to a chump that couldn't hit someone three feet in front of him. Since he's the only Rodian we see in any of the movies, even one through three, which I try not to think about, it makes the whole species look incompetent."

"It's really not fair," I said and pointed ahead on the left. "It should be right up here."

Holt slowed as we came up to a construction site. The land had been cleared, leaving a wasteland of red clay. Heavy machinery sat quietly around a muddy square of barren earth. Holt pulled the truck into the site and killed the lights. Being close to midnight, all the workers were long gone, or they should have been.

"Looks like we found him," Holt said, motioning toward the foreman's trailer on the edge of the property.

Slivers of light escaped around the curtains hanging in the window. We pulled around and found a white truck parked in front. Holt and I got out and walked up on either side of the truck. In the back was a toolbox mounted behind the cab, some five-gallon buckets, and a couple suitcases. The cab had an assortment of trash filling up the passenger floorboard. Everything from fast food wrappers to beer cans. A little movement and extra light from the trailer got my attention. Blinds collapsed back together. We had lost the element of surprise. We walked up a ramp to the front door.

I knocked. "Dave Hutchinson, can you open the door please?"

"You sound like a cop," Holt chuckled.

I held up a finger over my lips.

Dave replied, "The site's closed. Make an appointment with my secretary."

"I need to talk to you about your wife," I said.

It was quiet for a second before Dave said, "What about her?"

"I'd rather speak face to face."

We waited. There was no reply, no footsteps, just silence.

"He's ignoring us," Holt said, sounding genuinely surprised.

"Yeah, it happens more than you think," I said. "I've found the best thing to do—"

Holt punched the door leaving a fist imprint. "Open the damn door, numb nuts!"

". . . is not that," I sighed.

That's when the chanting started and I realized that Dave wasn't a hapless victim, he was our villain with two murders under his belt. The time for talk had passed. If we didn't get in fast, we'd have another demon on our hands.

I opened the Velcro I added to all my pants to make room for my large muscular tail, kicked off my shoes, and made the change to krasis, my half animal half human form. I grew fur over my body with the head of an otter, paws instead of feet, clawed fingers on my hands, and of course the tail. The shifter blade that resided in my body in my other forms came out. It was in a leather sheath that held it to my back, the handle by my waist with the tip by my left shoulder. It was the only configuration I had found that was comfortable to wear and didn't destroy my clothes through the change.

Holt followed my lead and made the change to krasis, taking on the aspect of a Doberman. He stood seven feet tall, with the head, fur, and paws of a dog. He clenched his hands around the knuckledusters in his hands, his weapon of choice.

Holt tried the door. "It's locked."

"Watch out."

He moved to the side. I stepped back and delivered a kick that should have popped the door right open. Instead, it only moved about an inch and left me with a twinge in my ankle.

"He barricaded the door," I said.

I shook my foot out as Holt threw his body against the door. It opened a little more each time he collided with it. By the third hit the door was open a few inches and the chanting inside stopped. I could suddenly smell rotting meat wafting from inside the trailer. A second later it sounded like the foreman was choking.

"What do you see?" I asked.

Holt moved his head around trying to get a look inside. "Nothing, too much shit in the way."

I stepped up beside Holt. "Together this time."

The door shifted in a couple more inches on the bottom and collapsed in on the top and the barricade crashed down. I gave the door a final push and got it open enough to slide inside. I drew my blade and climbed over the pile of furniture into the trailer with Holt right behind me.

The foreman lay on the floor with blood running out of his mouth, nose, and ears. I couldn't tell what killed him but judging from the amount of blood, it wasn't an easy way to go. A cloth with a summoning circle drawn on it was spread out on the floor beside the body. A small cardboard box had been knocked over spilling gray powder onto the carpet.

I knew what it was right away, dust. The processed remains of ultranatural creatures like me. It was the power source for magic. Holt pulled a crumpled bag out of the box and scooped as much of the dust into it as he could. Since the processing facility Hob ran had been destroyed, dust was in high demand.

"Where is it?" He asked, shoving the bag into his pocket.

The desk chairs and filing cabinets had been pushed in front of the door to form the barricade with everything else from papers to a stapler to a houseplant thrown on top.

I scanned the pile. "Not sure. Stay alert."

The last thing I wanted was to get jumped by a demon trying to suck my brain out . . . again. I kept my blade in front of me and backed against the wall. I looked around the room. I didn't see anything in the furniture pile and the rest of the room was empty except for some strewn papers and the dead foreman. No bloodthirsty demons.

I scratched my head. "There's nothing here."

"You don't think it went back through the portal do you?" Holt asked.

"If it did, then who opened it?"

He shrugged. "Maybe it's a smart demon? It opened its own portal?"

It was a possibility. It wouldn't be the first time a demon took advantage of some poor sap and skipped town, leaving us to clean up the mess. No demon meant there wasn't anything for us to do but gather up any evidence of the occult. I'd give Farwell a heads-up once we were out of the way.

"There's a piece of paper under the body," Holt said.

I put my blade back in its sheath. "What is it?"

Holt took the corner of the paper, pulled it out, and passed it to me. It was stained with the foreman's blood. I didn't bother trying to keep the blood off my hands, it was a little late for that. It was a letter with a summoning ritual on it. Unlike most rituals I run across, it was a print-out, rather than handwritten, complete with step-by-step instructions and phonetic notations for the incantation.

"Let me see that box," I said.

Holt passed it to me. The return address was from a P.O. box in Oklahoma. I ripped off the address label and shoved it in my pocket with the letter.

"There's something weird with the body," Holt said. "There's a bulge in his belly, some kind of swelling or something."

He poked the body. The body shifted from the pressure. The swelling in the abdomen rippled.

"Obie . . ."

"I see it," I said, dropping the box and drawing my blade.

The rippling turned into a wave that rushed up the throat. A monster resembling a giant centipede shot out of the mouth at Holt. Holt fell back, grabbing the demon with both hands. The demon's jaws snapped as its body began to wrap around Holt's arm. I was able to get a swing in before the two of them became intertwined. My blade cut cleanly through it. It screeched, the top part of its body lashing wildly as its bottom part fell to the floor, still running down the corpse's throat.

"You got it?" I asked.

Holt held the thrashing beast at arm's length. "Yeah, what do we do with it now?"

"There's some buckets in the back of that truck," I said. "Hang onto it."

I climbed over the barricade and went outside. I grabbed a half full bucket of joint compound out of the back of the truck and dashed back inside. I ripped the lid off and used my hand to scoop what I could onto the floor.

I put the bucket in front of Holt and grabbed the lid. "Toss it in!"

"It's holding onto my arm," he said. "Hang on."

He slammed it down on the desk with a crunch. The demon shuddered, stunned from the impact. Holt threw the demon into the bucket as if spiking a football. I slammed the lid on top. No sooner had I snapped it into place than the bucket began to shake. I could see the shadow of the demon as it thrashed around inside the bucket.

"Uh . . . Obie," Holt said. "Where'd the rest of it go?"

I looked at the body. There had been two feet of demon centipede sticking out of Dave's mouth. His head had fallen to the side, his mouth open wide in a silent scream. The demon was missing.

"Stay quiet," I said.

I listened, but all I could hear was the thumping coming from the bucket. Holt moved around to the desk. A second centipede, presumably made from cutting the first, shot out and scurried up Holt's leg. He screamed and spun, trying to grab it, but it was too quick. It had already bit him on the neck before he could get a hand on it. He pulled it away with bits of his flesh in its jaws. Blood soaked into his shirt.

"Put it on the floor," I shouted.

He slammed it down on its back and held it in place. "You ain't going to cut it again are ya?"

"Nope."

I put a foot on top of the bucket to keep the other demon from getting out and stretched. It felt like a game of Twister. I held the demon still with one hand and with the other I lined the blade up with the center of its body. With a sudden stab, I drove the blade through its body and into the floor. It let out a high pitched squeal as it thrashed in pain. We had it pinned, it wasn't going anywhere for the time being.

"Hold this one," I said, pointing to the bucket.

Holt put a hand on it.

"Yell if they get loose," I said.

"You can count on it."

I climbed over the barricade and out the door. I grabbed another bucket from the back of the truck. When I made it back inside the trailer, I found Holt sitting on the bucket with the trapped demon. The second demon thrashed on the floor.

I pulled the top off the bucket and scooped it out as fast as I could. "Get that thing ready to move."

I put a foot on the bucket when Holt stood up. He knelt over the demon and flexed his right hand around the knuckleduster. He grabbed the demon with his left hand to hold it still and drove his weaponized fist down on its head. The first strike resulted in a stomach turning crunch. The second strike had less crunch and more splatter as the creature's head ruptured, spilling green ooze out onto the desk. The demon went limp.

"You think we killed it?" Holt asked.

I pulled my blade out of the floor. "Let's not risk it."

I grabbed it and tossed it in the bucket. I snapped the lid in place and put the buckets a few feet apart.

"Grab the desk," I said.

Holt cleared the desk and picked it up. "What are we doing with it?"

"Set it on top."

He flipped it over and placed it on the buckets. With the desk out of the way we were able to open the door and walk outside.

"Let's see that bag of dust," I said.

Holt pulled the bag out of his pocket. "What are we doin' with it?"

"We'll burn 'em."

Holt pulled the dust back from my outstretched hand. "Are you sure, this stuff's in short supply. It's worth a lotta money."

"Can you think of another option? Unless you got a full can of gas in your back pocket."

"Fair enough," he said. "Can I do it? I've never done it before."

"It's the only dust we have," I said. "Next time, okay?"

"Come on, how hard can it be? I've seen Livy light her fireplace a bunch a times. Same thing, right?"

I wasn't thrilled about the idea, but I was supposed to be teaching him and it would be good practice with minimal risk. "Alright, but be careful."

"Sweet," he said, moving in front of the door. "What do I do?"

"When you're ready, open the bag. Imagine fire in your mind. Throw the dust and ignite it."

He seemed hesitant. "How do I ignite it?"

"Imagine it catching fire. Livy says the word to help focus the intent. Folks like Hob don't have to do that anymore."

"Got it, he said.

He took the bag out, stood perfectly still for a second before tossing it in and shouting, "Fire!"

Flames erupted inside the trailer with enough force to send the window flying into the front of my truck. Flames roared through the open door and engulfed half of Holt. I dove to the ground.

"You alright?" I asked, picking myself up.

The air was heavy with the scent of burning hair.

"Yeah, just a little singed."

I headed for the truck. "Let's get out of here quick."

The flames were pouring out of the windows by the time Holt pulled onto the pavement.

"Where to?" Holt asked.

"We need to find out who's sending summoning rituals by mail."

"Kinda hard to do in the middle of the night," he said.

"We'll go home and take care of it after the sun comes up."

"I've got that job I've been looking into," Holt said. "You need me or can I work on my own thing."

Finding leads was a big part of being a Keeper. I'd had Holt start looking into some on his own. They had all turned into a dead-end, except one. That wasn't unusual, most leads turned out to be nothing. I was glad to see him getting involved in the work, taking a little initiative. I didn't want to discourage him and I didn't really need him to ask around about a letter.

"Sure," I said. "Don't engage anything without me, okay?"

"You got it."

CHAPTER · 3

THE PROBLEM I HAD was, anyone who knew about someone selling summoning rituals wouldn't be in my circles. If they were, they definitely wouldn't tell me about it. There was only one person I could think of that had an outside chance of knowing: a local hunter. *Wannabe hunter* might be more accurate. Travis was a nice guy, but wholly unsophisticated. To the best of my knowledge he had never actually caught or killed an ultranatural. That's probably why everyone tolerated him the way we did.

I would've liked to call him, but didn't have his number. Hell, I wasn't sure he even had a phone. I found his house, a run-down shack in the woods. It was well kept, but old and needed work that I got the impression Travis couldn't afford. A roughly thirty-year-old pickup was parked out front. I think it had been red when it was new but after decades in the rain and sun had faded into pink. I parked my truck beside it and got out. The sun was just coming up. I hated to show up so early but I needed answers.

I didn't make it onto the porch before Travis came out to greet me. "Well I'll be," he said, putting his hands on his hips. "Ain't this a surprise."

I smiled. "Hey, Travis, sorry to show up so early on a Sunday."

His black hair was buzzed short. He had a rather nice white button-up shirt under his usual dingy pair of overalls. He wasn't wearing any shoes.

I stuck my keys in my pocket. "You heading to church?"

"Naw, why do ya ask?"

"You're all dressed up. That's a nice shirt," I said.

Travis looked a little uncomfortable. "Oh, yeah, I found 'er at the Goodwill and was just tryin' her on."

"I didn't mean to interrupt. Is now a bad time?"

"Naw, not at all. Sit right here and I'll grab us a drink," he said. "I don't get visitors often. I got a couple beers, or some soda pop, what'll ya have."

"A little early for a beer ain't it?" I asked.

"It's five o'clock somewhere." He grinned. "You ain't gonna let me drink alone, is ya?"

I shrugged. "Just some water then."

Travis disappeared inside and returned a few minutes later wearing one of his normal ragged old tees under his overalls. He was carrying a dingy looking glass full of even dingier looking water in one hand and a Bud Light in the other. The water had a slight orange tint and smelled like rotten eggs. If I had smelled it under different circumstances I'd think I would have a demon to hunt. Here, it was just well water that needed a good filtration and softening system. We took a seat in rocking chairs at the end of the porch.

"Thanks," I said, taking the glass.

Even if I was thirsty, I wouldn't want to take a sip, but I decided to hold onto the glass long enough not to offend him.

"What can I do for ya, Obie?"

"I don't really know how to get into it, but you told me you were into cryptozoology . . . I have some questions."

He choked in the middle of a swig. He coughed, trying to catch his breath. Beer ran down his chin. "What'd ya see? A fairy? Werewolf? Were it Bigfoot?"

"Oh no, nothing like that," I said. "The truth is, I had a friend who's gotten into that occult stuff. I'm worried about him and thought with your experience you might be able to give me some direction."

"Let's be clear, Obie. The occult's 'nother can a worms," Travis said. "Take ya average sasquatch or leprechaun. They don't really mean no harm to nobody. They's just animals. You leave them alone and they leave you alone . . . for the most part. We ain't talking about them Wiccan's neither. They ain't Christian, don't get me wrong, but they ain't all bad. Occult is something different. Dark magic, sacrifices, baby killers and demon worshipers. People with evil in they's heart." Travis put his beer down on the porch and leaned forward for emphasis. "Obie, you get your friend away from that stuff. There ain't nothin' good that's gonna come from it."

"I'm trying," I said. "Do you have any idea where someone could get stuff like that? It came through the mail. Have you heard of anything like this before?" I pulled the shipping label out of my pocket and handed it to him.

Travis took the label, gave it a side eye, and passed it back. "I don't mess with the occult, except maybe with a scattergun, and I ain't too good on the internet neither."

I took out the letter and opened it. It was mostly dry. I was raised better than to hand people bloody letters, so I laid it out on a little table between the rocking chairs.

Travis leaned over for a closer look. "Is that blood?"

"I said I *had* a friend."

"Dagburn, Obie. What you got into?"

"It's a mess, I know," I said.

"I'll be right back."

When he went inside, I took the glass of water and dumped some over the side of the porch and then pressed my lip against the edge of the glass to make it look like I had taken a drink. I waited, holding it close to my mouth. When he came back outside, I put it back on the table.

"I was lookin' for a card I had. Some feller came by about a year ago. He said they was a place on the computer that I could go to order all kinds of stuff. Weapons, some kind of magic powder, even locations of monsters to hunt if I wanted. He said it was some special dark place on the internet and I could buy anything I wanted with some cryptic money. I ain't too good on the computer, and I ain't sitting too high on the hog, so I never done nothing with it. Could be that your friend got a card, too."

"How have I not heard of this?" I said more to myself than to Travis.

Travis sat back in the rocking chair. "Because you ain't a part of that world. I know you and Hank think I'm nuts, but I'm telling you, hand to God, they's some nasty things out there."

I HAD TO TALK to Travis for another twenty minutes before I was able to get away. My phone rang just as I got to the truck. It was Holt.

"Are you done?" Holt asked.

"Kind of hit a dead end. I should be home in about thirty minutes," I said.

"I'll be there as soon as I can. I'm about to finish up that job I was working on."

"Right now?" I asked.

I heard some leaves crunching through the phone.

"Yeah, I shouldn't be long."

"You were supposed to run it by me before you did anything," I said.

"Yeah, well, it's not what I thought, but something I need to handle," he said. "It's time sensitive."

"Alright, send me the address. And don't do anything until I get there."

"Can't promise that but I'll try," Holt said.

The address came through a moment later. I got there as fast as I could. Holt's car was parked on the side of the road. I pulled in behind him and followed his scent west into the woods. I hadn't gone far before Holt, in the form of a Doberman, came bounding up from my left. He stopped in front of me and motioned with his head in the direction he had come from. I followed him the rest of the way to a trailer. It was wholly unremarkable. Nothing about it stood out, the kind of place you forget two minutes after you see it. We stopped on the edge of the tree line and Holt made the change to krasis.

"You really didn't have to come," he said. "I can handle this one myself."

I changed to krasis and drew my blade. "Maybe, but I'm here and there's no reason to risk a fight alone."

Holt looked worried. He wasn't acting like his normal gung-ho self. "Alright, what do we do?"

"It's your hunt, I'll follow your lead," I said.

"Alright, there should only be one guy in the house we're worried about," he said. "We'll go in the back."

I followed Holt around to the back of the house and up a little porch to the door. He tried the handle. It wasn't locked. We stepped inside into a hallway. The house was quiet. The flicker of a screen in a room at the end of the hall caught my attention. Holt motioned for me to check the left side of the house while he went toward the light. I followed the hallway into a kitchen. The living room was beside it with a door on the far wall. I walked over to the door and listened. I didn't hear anything, so I opened it a crack. It looked like a spare bedroom. I heard a crash from the other side of the trailer.

I ran back to find Holt standing over a man. The man's forehead was dented from the impact of Holt's knuckledusters. Blood ran from his ears. He wasn't dead. His chest rose and fell lightly. I had no doubt he would die shortly without help.

"I'm not smelling any demons," I said. "I guess we got lucky. This one was easy. Let's find any magic stuff or dust he has and get outta here."

"He doesn't have anything like that," Holt said.

"What do you mean?"

Holt looked me in the eye. "He's not summoning demons."

The man's chest stopped moving.

"Okay. It seems to me like we just broke in and killed a guy for no reason," I said. "What am I missing?"

Holt turned the computer monitor the man had been looking at so I could see it. It was pornography . . . of young boys. I looked at the man lying on the floor. I didn't feel the need to try and revive him. I wasn't sure how to handle this. It wasn't really in our jurisdiction. It made no difference to Thera, so we weren't obligated to police it.

"How did you find out about this guy?" I asked.

"By accident," he said. "I've been looking for people doing hinky shit. I found one." He pointed to a closet with a padlock on it. "You want to do the honors?"

I stuck my blade between the lock and the door and pried it off. The closet stunk and was empty except for a five-gallon bucket and a boy that looked to be about six years old. He cowered in the corner. He had his head buried in his arms and wouldn't look up at us. That was alright with me, I didn't want him to see us. I grabbed Holt's arm and pulled him down the hallway.

Holt held up his hands. "I know what you're thinking. It's true he wasn't summoning demons or whatever but he was hurting people . . . kids, and that's just as bad. You told me I have to decide the kind of Keeper I want to be. I'm the kind that isn't going to let a kid get hurt if I can help it."

"What about him?" I asked pointing at the corpse with my chin.

"Look, a couple months ago that lizard thing Slagtooth just about disemboweled me. As far as I'm concerned that thing's a demon. If I was you, I'd head over to the diving bell and cut its head off. That tells me there's some discretion in the decision making. I'm not going to apologize for doing what's right."

"No," I said. "I mean what are you going to do with the body."

Holt shrugged. "There's nothing really to do is there? I don't really want the kid to see him. Could he be 'sustainably sourced'?"

"Even the Tortured Occult won't eat a pedophile," I said. "Just leave him for the cops. We don't want them to waste time looking for him."

I grabbed a blanket off the bed and tossed it over the body. I took out my phone and called Detective Farwell. He would no doubt be thrilled to hear from me again so soon. It rang a few times. I was beginning to think I would have to leave a message when he finally answered.

"What the hell do you want now?" he said.

"That's no way to answer the phone."

"You're lucky I answered at all," Farwell said. "Are you watching me again? Which finger am I holding up?"

"I have an anonymous tip for you."

"It's not really anonymous if I know who you are is it?" he said.

I ignored his comment and continued. "I'm looking at a little boy that needs some help and a dead pedophile. I'm sure his parents are missing him. The kid, not the pedophile. Well, I guess his parents could be missing him too. I can't be sure."

"Is he safe?" Farwell asked.

"He's dead."

Farwell sighed. "No, the boy."

"I'll stay with him," Holt said.

"Yeah, he's safe. We'll keep an eye on him until you get here," I said. "You got a pen to write the address down?"

"Alright," he said. "Let me have it."

I relayed the address to him.

"One other thing," Farwell said. "If I find evidence that you murdered him, I will arrest you. No one's above the law."

I hung up the phone and turned to Holt. "I'll catch you up on everything later. Just meet me at the house when you're done here," I said.

"Should we be worried about Farwell?"

I gave him a smile. "No."

Holt took the form of a Doberman. I was curious so I stayed back and out of sight. After a few minutes Holt led the boy out of the trailer. They walked into the front yard and lay down beside each other. Just a boy and a dog waiting for the police.

CHAPTER·4

I DIDN'T KNOW WHAT Travis was talking about, but something told me Holt would have a better idea. He was more savvy with technology than I was. Hell, I'd only had a smartphone for less than a year now. I made it onto the front porch with my hand on the doorknob when I stopped short. I got that prickly feeling on the back of my neck I had come to trust. I turned to my right facing the woods. Everything seemed normal. I didn't see anyone sneaking through the trees. A brown thrasher landed on the porch railing, took a couple hops, and flew away. A cool breeze blew in from the west. I took a whiff of the air. I could smell petroleum products. The closest neighbor I had was a stone's throw through the trees in that direction. He did a lot of work on cars, rebuilding engines and oil changes. There was always some stench wafting over to my place.

I went to my room and sat at my desk. Holt would be a bit, I had some time to waste. I picked up the mangled P-51. It wasn't as bad as I'd originally thought. I could fix it.

Holt's words popped in my mind. *This ain't healthy.*

He was probably right. I didn't really give him credit for it, but for a goofball, he was surprisingly insightful. I pulled out my trashcan and dropped the plane into it. I ran an arm across the table, pushing the instructions and loose pieces into the can and put it back under my desk. Leaning back in the chair I let out a heavy sigh. My thoughts returned to Naylet. I picked up the stack of postcards Naylet had sent me. There were six so far being held together with a rubber band. I ran a thumb across the edge with enough pressure to make them flex and thump together as my thumb moved from one to the next. I tossed the cards on the desk. The models were a good distraction. I wasn't sure what I would do now. Maybe I should just finish the P-51. I'd already paid for it. I was reaching for the trashcan when my phone buzzed. I fished it out and looked at the screen. It was a restricted number . . . again.

I put it on speaker but didn't say anything right away. I wasn't sure what to say. I didn't know anything about this person. Maybe it was paranoia but I couldn't escape the feeling that whoever it was had an ulterior motive.

Finally, I spoke. "Yeah."

The scrambled voice said, "You weren't able to save Dave?"

"I wasn't given the whole story."

I could hear the smile as the person spoke. "Want to try again?"

"I want you to cut the crap."

"I assume you're aware of the disappearances?"

There had been a number of disappearances lately. I didn't know exactly how many. It seemed like every couple weeks, I'd get a call that someone didn't come home or didn't show up to work. I'd checked it out but never turned up anything. It's like they just vanished. Dishes in the sink and clothes in the wash, it was strange for sure. Sometimes ultranaturals don't put down roots in an area and move on after a bit. It makes it hard to know if someone's disappeared or just left. It's rare for them to leave all their belongings in place when they go but it isn't unheard of. There isn't exactly a national phone directory I can look them up in.

"Eddie, a forest troll you know, is next on the list. You might be able to save him, if you hurry."

"Who the hell is this?"

He hung up. I couldn't help but feel like I was being sent on a wild goose chase. Eddie had been doing some work for Hank, remodeling part of the club-house. Maybe he could give me an idea if Eddie was all right.

When Hank answered the phone, I asked, "You seen Eddie today?"

"No, he was supposed to do some work for me, but he didn't show up. Everything alright?"

"Send me his address and I'll let you know," I said.

"Yep."

I sat there wondering if I was actually going to go as the address came through. I didn't like being jerked around but I didn't really have anything else to go on. If I didn't show and Eddie got hurt that would be on me. I had no choice when it came down to it. I made it outside to see Holt pulling up.

He opened door of his Civic and got halfway out. "You good?"

I tossed him the key to my truck which he caught in his left hand. "I got another anonymous tip. Sounds like Eddie's in trouble."

I got in the passenger seat of my truck and pulled up the directions.

"How far is it?" he asked.

"Fifteen minutes. Listen, I've got some questions for you."

Holt cranked the engine and backed out. "I know what you're going to say. I know it wasn't demon stuff, but I wasn't going to let some kid get . . . I wasn't going to let him get any more hurt than he already was."

"No, I don't have a problem with that at all." I plugged my phone into the truck to display the directions for him. "You have to figure out what kind of Keeper you're going to be. Most Keepers would have just called it into the police. Some would have ignored it. Looks like you're the kind that will help a kid if you find one in trouble. Not everyone's like that. The truth is, I'm proud of you."

"Let's not make a big deal about it. Just doing my job," Holt said.

"Fair enough," I said. "I wanted to ask you about some things Travis told me about. It doesn't make any sense to me but you're more up to speed on technology."

Holt chuckled. "Ya think."

I ignored him. "He mentioned a dark place on the internet. Does that mean anything to you?"

"He was probably talking about the dark web. I don't really know anything about it other than people do a lot of illegal shit there."

"Okay, what about *cryptic currency*?" I asked, making air quotes with my fingers.

"Cryptocurrency." Holt nodded. "It's digital currency. That makes sense, I've heard people use cryptocurrency to buy things on the dark web. I'm no expert though."

"Alright, first things first, we'll check on Eddie and then figure out this dark web stuff."

CHAPTER·5

WE DROVE TO THE address Hank supplied. It was a rundown trailer set back about thirty feet from the road. There wasn't a clearly defined yard, there wasn't even any grass. It was as if someone cleared the trees, put a trailer in, and forgot about it. The whole place looked like a dump. There was a pickup truck with flat tires parked beside the trailer with thirty or forty bags of trash in the back. A rusted-out Oldsmobile, that looked like it might still run, was parked beside it. Holt pulled the truck in behind the Olds and we got out. The trailer was surrounded by what I would consider trash. Rusted grills, a few lawn mowers, a filing cabinet toppled over on top of a koi pond that was half full of green algae. That was just the nicer stuff. It would take a couple dumpsters and a week of work to get this place cleaned up. The door to the trailer was open. That wasn't something to be concerned about. A lot of poorer folks around here would open the doors and windows when the weather was nice. Being a couple weeks out of winter the weather was still cold but trolls tended to like it that way.

"What do ya think?" I asked.

"Well," Holt said, looking around. "I'd say we should look for signs of a struggle but how would we know?"

A frog jumped into the koi pond from a patch of weeds. I walked toward the front door. "Let's check inside."

We followed a trail that wound its way through the debris in the yard to the front door. I leaned in and gave the air a couple sniffs. The house smelled like mildew and troll.

Eddie was a regular at the clubhouse, but he wasn't in the T.O. He liked to hang around and play pool. I'd played him a few times over the years and I lost every time. I'd never been to his house before but it was about what I'd expect from a troll.

"Eddie," I shouted, leaning in the doorway. "You home?"

"You ain't worried about alerting the abductors?" Holt asked.

"I've got you watching my back."

I stepped into the living room. There was a couch with a flower print that looked as if it had been pulled out of a catalog from the seventies. A well-worn coffee table and modest tv were the only other adornments in the room.

"You smell that?" Holt asked.

I could smell something that reminded me of road construction. It reminded me of what I'd smelled on my front porch. "Yeah, stay alert."

The kitchen was off to the right with a hallway to the left. I walked into the kitchen and stuck my head into what turned out to be a laundry room. The kitchen had a few dirty dishes in the sink with a trail of ants scavenging the food remnants.

Holt looked at the ants and shook his head. "I feel sorry for them, having to live in a dump like this."

"Let's check the back," I said.

We walked down the hallway and the smell grew stronger. I followed the scent past a bathroom before coming to the bedroom. The smell intensified in the bedroom. A large window on the back wall stood open. There wasn't a bed, or any other furniture in the room. Large vines grew in through the open window. They curled around, filling a corner of the room forming a kind of nest. Plenty of water had come in through the window over the years, leaving a mat of leaves and small plants growing on the floor. A bird took flight, rushing out the window. I could feel the floor flexing from our weight.

It may sound like a strange scene, and I suppose it would be for someone unfamiliar with forest trolls. What I found strange was a large black puddle around the nest. I knelt beside it and gave it a whiff. It was definitely the source of the smell. I didn't know how or why it was here.

I stuck the end of my finger in the puddle. It was viscous and sticky. "Got some tar."

"Shit," Holt said. "That's more than some. What the hell did that?"

I shrugged. "Your guess is as good as mine."

"I guess Eddie's gone," Holt said.

I understood why he felt that way. With as many people as we had seen disappear, I was almost getting used to it. None of the missing people had come back, there wasn't a ransom, or any demands. Up until now there weren't any clues.

"Let's not give up just yet," I said. "We're not going to pack up and go home because we found a puddle."

Holt sighed. "I wish we had some dust. We could track them pretty easy if we did."

"Yeah, well . . . if ifs and buts were pixie dust—"

"Take a look at this," he said.

Holt pointed at a mark on the wall. It was a troll's three fingered handprint smeared in tar on the wall beside the closet. The closet door was closed. The floor and walls surrounding the door were black but the door itself remained impossibly clean.

"What the hell?" I muttered.

I picked up a leaf and wiped my finger off on it before joining Holt in front of the closet.

"You don't think there's something in there?"

"Krasis," I said before making the change to my half human, half otter form.

When Holt completed his change I motioned toward the closet with my head.

Holt shook his head. "You open it," he whispered. "I don't want something jumping out to eat my face like last time. It's the diving bell all over again."

"I told you to knock on the bell and I would handle the meat but you didn't want to. If you had done as you were told you would've been fine."

He looked from me to the door and back. "This is different."

I pointed to him and then to the closet and mouthed the words *open it*.

He gave me a scowl before stepping up to the closet. I readied my blade when I felt something cold and wet on my foot. I looked down to see the tar covering my foot. It confused me a little since I shouldn't have stepped in it from where I was standing. It quickly made sense as the tar started to move up my leg.

"Holt," I said trying to pull my foot free.

The tar held onto my foot. I say *held on* because it wasn't just sticky, it had grip. This stuff was alive.

"What do we do?" he shouted.

I pulled my foot up leaving a string of tar and lifted my blade above my head. I hesitated for a second, imagining my blade getting stuck as well. Ultimately it was the only chance I had to get unstuck. I brought the blade down as hard as I could. It cut cleanly through the string. The pull on my leg suddenly released and I fell backward against the wall. The tar fell away onto the floor and moved back to join the larger puddle. I jumped to the right and Holt to the left as the puddle lunged in our direction. I moved back into the hallway as the puddle spread out in the floor. Holt was cut off by the closet.

"Jump over it," I said.

The tar puddle was only a couple feet wide by the wall, he could easily clear it. Holt nodded and leapt over the puddle. He cleared it, at least he would have, if the tar hadn't lurched up from the floor and grabbed his legs. Holt slammed down onto the floor in front of the door. I stuck my blade in the wall and grabbed him by the arm. I tried to pull him out of the tar. It seemed to be pulling him back into the puddle at the same time that it slowly moved up his body.

Holt grabbed the doorframe. "Get this shit off me!"

I took a few swings with my blade. The tar split from where I struck and then filled back in almost immediately. The tar engulfed his lower body and flowed slowly up his torso. I wasn't going to be able to cut it off him without taking pieces of him off with it. I'd have to find another solution.

"Don't let go," I said, turning and running down the hallway towards the kitchen. I needed to find something to stop the tar. How do you fight a liquid? If I could freeze it that would probably work. I picked up a roll of paper towels off the counter and wondered how many rolls it would take to soak up a tar monster.

"Obie!" Holt shouted. "Hurry up. It's—"

His cries for help were replaced with gagging followed by muffled screaming. I could imagine the black sludge covering his face and oozing down his throat. There wasn't another option, a last resort. I grabbed a bottle of vegetable oil and doused it over the paper towel. I turned the knob of the stove hoping there was some gas in the tank outside. The stove clicked a few times and fire jumped up from the eye. I lit my makeshift torch and ran back down the hallway.

Burning it wasn't an ideal option. It would mean a lot of pain for Holt, both now and during the healing process that would follow. There wasn't an alternative at this point. How I felt about it didn't matter, I couldn't let it take him. When I made it back, the room was clean. All traces of tar were gone, and Holt was gone with it.

CHAPTER · 6

I STARED AT THE room in disbelief. The tar around the closet was still there, and the handprint, but the rest was gone and Holt with it. The smoke detector's alarm brought me back to reality. I had all but forgotten that I was holding a burning roll of paper towels billowing black smoke. I went to the bathroom and doused the flames in the tub, leaving the charred roll behind. I grabbed a crumpled up towel from the floor and fanned the smoke detector until it went silent. I tossed the towel into the hallway and knelt in the doorway. I found claw marks Holt left in the doorframe and the cuts in the floor from where I had tried to cut the tar away from him. There wasn't any other sign that he had been there at all.

A bird flew in through the window, landing on one of the vines next to the nest. It chirped a couple times, jumped around the nest, and flew away. I walked over to look out the window. The forest was quiet. I could smell the leaves and trees and the faint scent of tar. After the screeching of the smoke detector, it seemed peaceful.

I heard a thump behind me. It sounded like it came from the closet. I moved, my blade ready. *Could Holt have made it into the closet?* I thought. *And if he did, what happened to all the tar?* I turned the door handle. I jumped back as the door swung open. The closet was full of roots and vines.

Forest trolls could manipulate vegetation. They used their magic to form nests like the one in the bedroom and stay hidden. In extreme circumstances, they used it to defend themselves. Trolls get a bad rap in pop culture but the truth is, I've never met a troll I didn't like. They're some of the most kind and gentle people you'll ever run across.

I leaned an arm against the doorframe. "Eddie . . . You in there?"

I didn't get a response, but an intact cocoon told me he was. I went to work with my blade. It took me a couple minutes to make a hole large enough to see inside. Eddie was in there all right. He was unconscious, collapsed on the floor.

"Eddie," I said. "Wake up."

He didn't respond so I went to work clearing the cocoon enough to get him out. After a little work I made the hole large enough to pull him through. It was then I discovered not all the tar had gone. He was covered in it head to toe. I laid him out on the floor. I got the towel from the hallway and wiped what I could off of his face. The tar that was on him didn't seem to be alive. Maybe if it got too far from the central mass it severed its connection with . . . whatever that was.

I sheathed my blade and knelt beside him. "Eddie, you alright?"

He didn't answer. I gave him a couple pats on the cheek. Still nothing. I held a hand over his chest and channeled healing energy into him. It flowed over him almost immediately, telling me he wasn't physically injured.

"Alright, let's go," I said.

I heaved him onto my shoulders in a fireman's carry and headed for the truck. Maybe Doc Lin could figure out what was wrong with him. I made it outside and halfway to the truck when I stopped in my tracks. I patted my pockets looking for my keys. They weren't there. Holt drove over and hadn't given them back to me before he was abducted. I didn't see them in the ignition or on the console. Holt must still have them. I took Eddie back inside and laid him down on the couch, pulled out my phone, and called Doc Lin.

She sounded half asleep and whispered when she answered. "Hello."

"Hey, Doc, I've got an emergency. I have someone here that needs your help, and we could use a ride to the clubhouse."

"Obie, I just got home. I had a late night at the uh . . . hospital." I could hear the agitation in her voice. "I'm not a taxi."

"I never said you were. I would've called Hank but like I said, I got someone here that needs your help, so I had to call you anyway." There was silence on the other end. After twenty seconds I was starting to think we got disconnected. "Doc? You there?"

"Send me the address," she whispered.

I hung up and texted her Eddie's address. Now all I had to do was wait. With nothing to do my thoughts turned to Holt and the tar. I couldn't wrap my head around where they had gone. I did a lap around the house, looked through every room inside and even opened the door to the crawlspace. I came up with nothing. Not a trace of tar on anything but Eddie and the closet. I was starting to understand what happened to all the folks that had gone missing lately. I figured someone or something had been taking them but until now I had no idea of *how* they were doing it.

There was a bright side. Thera should be able to direct me to where Holt was. With her help I could track him down in no time. He might even lead me to the other missing Ultras. I changed back to my human form and sat in the doorway of the trailer to wait for Doc Lin. I looked back to see Eddie was still passed out on the couch. He hadn't moved an inch.

"Thera," I said. "Holt's in trouble. I need your help."

There wasn't a response.

"Thera. I really need to talk to you," I said. "It's important."

Thera made sure all Keepers knew that we worked for her. At the same time, when we called, most of the time she came. If she would help or not was anyone's guess. This seemed to be one of the occasions she decided not to show. I'd get Eddie to the clubhouse and try again. I could always annoy her into showing if I had to. I'd avoid that strategy if I could, she wouldn't be in the best mood if I'd pestered her into paying attention to me. After twenty minutes Doc Lin's Mercedes pulled in behind my truck, Thera still hadn't responded. I went inside, picked up Eddie, and carried him out.

She opened the back door of the car and closed it when she saw us coming. "What's all over him?"

"Tar, I think."

"It's going to get all over the back seat . . . This is a Mercedes."

"He's hurt," I said.

"Hold on," she said.

She took a newspaper she had in the front and layered the pages to protect the seat. I laid Eddie down in the back. The paper stuck to him which helped in keeping the car clean but didn't do much for him personally.

I got in the passenger seat. "I really appreciate the ride. I hope I haven't put you out any."

The way her face crumpled up told me I had in fact. "What's wrong with him?"

I shrugged. "I was hoping you could tell me. He was attacked by something that left him like this. I healed him but he's not waking up."

She scowled. I'd never seen her in a foul mood before. There's a first time for everything, I guess.

"Umm . . . You okay?" I asked.

She sighed. "Yeah, sorry. Things are a little rough at home."

"Sorry to hear."

"How do you maintain a relationship when you have to keep so many secrets?" she asked.

"Was that a rhetorical question?" I asked.

"I'll take an answer if you have one."

"Well . . . I wish I did, but the truth is I don't really know," I said.

"But you've been in at least one serious relationship. I've heard people talk about it. How did you do it?"

"That was different. Naylet's a nymph. She was on the secret side of things so there really wasn't much I had to keep from her," I said.

"What happened to her?" she asked. "Did it not work out?"

I looked out the window. "It's a long story."

We rode in silence for a few minutes before Doc Lin spoke again. "You've never dated a human?"

"Nah, between the secrecy and lifespan difference . . . I just don't see it working out," I said. "Holt, well . . . I don't think I'd call what he does with human women *dating* but he has more experience with it than I do."

"Speaking of lifespan, How long does a Keeper live exactly?" she asked.

"Indefinitely."

"Is that the gift you get for working for Thera?"

"Being immortal doesn't mean we don't die. It just means we don't die naturally. There's no growing old and passing in your sleep. No chance for a peaceful end. I will die one day; I have no doubt of that. And when I do it will be through violence. It's going to be bad. Violent and painful most likely," I said. "That's not a gift."

"Where is Holt anyway? I thought he'd be your first call if you needed a ride."

I sighed. "That's another long story."

Doc Lin smiled. "Sounds like we're both having a rough day."

We pulled into the junkyard that surrounded Morrison Salvage and the clubhouse of the Tortured Occult Motorcycle Club. Driving up the dirt path through the rusted and parted out vehicles, we parked in front of the clubhouse. We took Eddie out of the back of the car. The newspaper had managed to cover him almost completely during the drive.

I hauled him inside. We got some looks from the patrons enjoying drinks and company around the bar. No one really gave us more than a passing glance. I wish I could say hauling a half-dead ultranatural into the clubhouse was unusual for me. It wasn't.

Adan, the wererat emissary from Atlanta, got up from his usual table in the corner and followed us into the back. We took Eddie to one of the bedrooms and laid him down on the bed. His breathing was slow and steady.

"What happened?" Adan asked.

"I'm not sure honestly." I shrugged.

Adan looked at his phone. "The meeting's in twenty minutes, we're supposed to head over to Ground Zero right after. I think the new doctor is over getting the medical facilities set up. Maybe we should take him?"

I had forgotten about the council meeting I was supposed to be attending today. The council was comprised of the rats, elves, Tortured Occult, myself, and a representative of the masses. It wasn't a perfect system but it was better than no system at all.

"If it resembles a real hospital, then it would be better than this," Doc Lin said.

"Alright," Adan said. "I'll give him a call and let him know you'll be bringing him over."

"Actually, can you give us a ride?" I asked. "I don't have my truck."

"Yeah, no problem." Adan said. "You need anything, Doc?"

"We'll do what we can for him," Doc Lin said. "Can you send someone in please."

"Sure, Doc, no problem," he said. "We'll head over after the meeting."

Adan left me alone with Eddie and Doc Lin. She was holding up one of the troll's eyelids and shining a light on and off his eye when Ginsu walked in.

"Well damn," Ginsu said. "Somebody traded out the feathers for newspaper. That's new. He's only half covered though."

"He's hurt," I said. "It's not the time to make fun of him."

"It ain't that, Obie," Ginsu said. "I just hate to see a job half done. I think we got some down pillows around here somewhere if you want to wrap this up real quick. Worse case I can get a box of napkins. Tarred and napkinned . . . Has a nice ring to it."

Doc Lin turned around and looked Ginsu in the eye. "Shut up and get me some towels, soap, and warm water."

"Must be on the rag," Ginsu mumbled as he left the room.

I didn't know if Doc Lin heard him. Sometimes when you have enhanced senses it's easy to forget that everyone doesn't. If she did hear him, she didn't show it. It might just be that she had gotten used to his uncouth ways in the past few months. Doc Lin had officially decided to study ultranatural biology. Whenever someone had an injury they needed help with, they called Doc Lin.

"Well? I asked.

She clicked the light off and put it in her pocket. "I don't know. Once he's cleaned up, I'll have a better idea. It's going to take a while."

Ginsu came back a minute later with what Doc requested. She used the soapy water to wipe the tar off his face and neck.

"Alright," I said. "Let me know if you need me."

"Obie, wait," Doc Lin said. "He's waking up."

Eddie groaned and opened his eyes just a sliver. He raised a hand to his head and started to sit up.

Doc Lin put a hand on his shoulder to stop him. "Take it easy. You've been through a lot."

"Where am I?" he asked.

"You're at the clubhouse," I said. "I found you in the closet at your house. What do you remember?"

His voice was hoarse. "Water."

"Hold tight," I said.

Tico, the wereraccoon, was tending bar today. I went out to the bar and stood at the end. Tico was wiping down a glass at the other end of the bar. He looked over at me. I gave him a nod. He went back to wiping the glass. I waited through a full minute of being ignored before I walked around the bar to where he was standing.

"I need a glass of water."

"Sounds like a personal problem," he said.

I'd like to think he didn't like me because I rarely ordered anything. That meant no tips for him. I found out the truth the last time the club had a run. He was hung up on my ex and he blamed me for what happened to her and the fact that she was gone now.

I reached behind the bar and grabbed a glass and the soda gun. He didn't try to stop me, probably because he knew if it turned into a fight, I'd trounce him. There were a bunch of buttons on it and I didn't know what any of them stood for. I pushed them, shooting random liquids on the counter until I found the one for water and filled up the cup. When the glass was full I headed to the back.

"You really are a first-class asshole, ain't ya?" Tico called after me.

I turned and pushed the door open with my back, raising the glass as if I was giving him a toast and headed back to Eddie. We sat Eddie up and he downed half the water in two gulps.

"How're you feeling?" Doc Lin asked.

Eddie held his arms out from his body. "Sticky."

Doc Lin passed him a bottle of dish soap. "Get a shower and scrub off all the tar you can. I'm sure you'll feel a lot better. We're going to take you over to Ground Zero to get checked out."

"If Doc clears it, come into the council meeting when you're done. I'd like to update everybody on what's going on and we need to hear your story."

Eddie disappeared into the bathroom and the shower came on.

"Is he going to be alright?" I asked.

Doc Lin sat on the edge of the bed. "We'll have to keep an eye on him, but if there's no other issues besides being covered in tar and exhausted, then he should make a full recovery."

CHAPTER · 7

I WAS NEXT TO last to walk in the conference room. Hank, the werebear leader of the Tortured Occult Motorcycle Club, looked at the clock. I never got the impression he cared for council meetings, but he was a good sport about them. He understood the importance of working together to maintain order. Adan sat beside him with Queen Isabelle across the table. She'd settled into her responsibilities as Queen well. She was young for a Queen, it's true, still a child really but many of us aren't afforded the luxury of choosing when we grow up. She seemed to have aged a few years, by human standards, in the past few months, making her seem like a mature human child of twelve or thirteen.

I slid the chair up to the table and took a seat.

"You're late," Hank said. "Anyone seen Hambone?"

"I'm here," Hambone said, walking through the door. "Apologies, it couldn't be avoided."

Kobolds resembled half human-half coyotes. Hambone's most distinguishing feature was his weight. Big boned would be a nice way to describe him, morbidly obese would be another. He was carrying a white box with a big birthday cake in it.

"Could you stick this on the table for me please?" He held the box out to me.

I looked through the plastic on the top of the box. It was decorated in white buttercream with blue detailing. It read, Happy Eighty Seven point five Hambone. Eighty-seven was a little over middle age for a kobold. Probably well over for Hambone considering how poorly he took care of himself.

"I didn't know it was your point five already," I said, sliding the box in front of the empty chair. "Happy point five!"

His chest puffed with pride and he flashed me a smile that ran from ear to ear. "Thanks, Obie! I've been looking forward to it for months."

"Probably about six," I said, pulling Hambone's chair away from the table for him.

"Roughly," he said.

We waited patiently, for the most part, as he hoisted himself into his chair. It took him a full minute of effort and three tries but he eventually made it. By the time he pulled it off he was panting and out of breath.

"What's a point five?" Isabelle asked.

Hambone took gasping breaths as he spoke. "Well Queen . . . Isabelle . . . I understand that . . . I may . . . not . . . be as long lived . . ." He held up a finger and took a moment to catch his breath. "Ahem . . . Long lived as a kobold without some of my health concerns. I decided to pack all the joy from those years I expect to lose into what I have left so I doubled the frequency of my birthdays. I celebrate my actual birthday and six months later, today, I have a point five."

"I'm sorry, I didn't know," Isabelle said. "I would have brought you a present. It was nice of you to bring cake for everyone though."

Hambone's coyote-like jaws flapped in shock. "Everyone? Well . . . I mean . . . Obie doesn't eat, especially cake," Hambone said, looking over at me. "It would be rude for everyone to eat in front of him . . . Wouldn't it?"

Isabelle smiled. "I'm just playing. Have a very merry point five."

"You really had me going there." Hambone chuckled. "All right then."

He opened the box with reverence. Drool pooled up on his tongue and dripped onto his considerable girth. He leaned in slowly, inhaling the delicate aromas. He gingerly licked a bit of frosting off a corner of the cake. He swirled it in his mouth, savoring the flavor and moaned in pleasure.

"I feel dirty," Adan said. "Can we start already?"

The door opened and Eddie walked in carrying a glass of water. He was a touch over seven feet tall. His skin looked more like bark, rough and light grey with touches of brown. His hair grew in short, thick, and green like moss. I could still see some black from the tar worked into the crevices in his skin.

"This is a private meeting," Hank said.

Eddie stopped in his tracks looking wide eyed at the group around the table.

"I asked him here," I said getting up from my chair. "Have a seat here, Eddie."

Eddie sat at the table looking generally uncomfortable. I stood behind him to address the council.

"We're all aware of the disappearances that have been happening over the past few months. We haven't had any real leads until today. Eddie was almost abducted. Holt and I got there in time to save him. Unfortunately, it took Holt instead. I wanted the council to hear Eddie's story." I turned to Eddie. "Can you tell us what happened?"

"I don't really know. I was at the house. I heard a noise from outside the bedroom window. It sounded like a deer. I went to get a look at it. Next thing I know I'm covered in this black sludge. It'd come through the window as a big mass and just hit me all of a sudden. I tried to get it off at first but then I realized it was alive. It tried to pull me out the window. I figured if it wanted me outside I should go the other way. I made it to the closet and put up roots to seal the door." He paused to finish the rest of the water in the glass. "The tar would come in through the cracks in the roots and suffocate me. I would wake up and the tar would seep in and suffocate me again. It went on like that until you found me. I don't know how long I was in there or how many times I passed out."

"You were in there about a day," I said.

I looked at Hambone. He hadn't seemed to pay attention at all while Eddie updated the council on the morning's adventure. He had made it though about a quarter of the birthday cake. The buttercream frosting and cake crumbs had gotten all over his hands, face, and chest. It was embedded in his fur and fell in clumps on the table.

"Thanks, Eddie," Isabelle said. "We need to talk about it privately, if you don't mind."

Eddie nodded, and left.

As soon as the door closed behind him, Adan said, "What the hell could do something like that?"

"I've never seen anything like it," I said. "There was a puddle of tar in the middle of the bedroom when Holt and I walked in. Like Eddie said, it was alive. We didn't realize it at first but before we knew what was happening it was on us. I figured I'd burn it off of him and went to get some fire. By the time I got back Holt was gone. The thing is, whatever it was moved fast. Once it got Holt it was just gone. It makes sense why we haven't been finding evidence left behind of the people that were taken."

Isabelle turned in her chair to look at Hob. "Do you have any idea what this creature could be?"

"*Nein*, my Queen. I will need more information to make the determination."

"Here's what I want to know." Adan leaned forward and rested an elbow on the table. "You said when this thing disappeared it took all the tar with it, right?"

"Yeah," I said.

"So why is Eddie still covered in the stuff?"

"Huh," I said, shifting back in my chair and looking at the door Eddie had just walked out of. "Maybe it was cut off. Eddie said he was closing himself in with the vines. What if the tar was left behind because he sealed it in with him?"

"It makes sense," Isabelle said. "Do you have a plan to find Holt?"

"Thera should be able to lead me to him but she's not answering me."

Hank sighed heavily and spoke for the first time. "I have been waiting to bring it up, but my son, Torch, is still missing. No one's heard from him for months. He was the first one that disappeared. Isabelle confirmed that the Queen, the old Queen, didn't get him." He paused and shook his head. "I know you've all been looking for him and I appreciate it. I need to find my son."

"Does anyone have any dust?" asked Adan. "We could do a tracking spell."

Everyone looked at each other around the table. After a few seconds it was clear no one was coming forward about a dust stash they had squirreled away. I wasn't going to mention I'd had some earlier.

"There's just not a lotta dust to go around right now," I said. "First Torch and now Holt. This is officially getting out of control. The good news is, when I can get Thera to answer me she can lead us to them, assuming it was the same thing that took them both."

"You think something else happened to Torch?" Isabelle asked.

I shrugged. "It's too soon to tell. I mean, it's our best lead."

Hambone spit masticated cake all over the table when he spoke. "It's a big problem! The longer we go without dust the more trouble it's going to be. It's going to be pandemonium! Murder in the streets! We have to do something, and we have to do it quick."

"I know you don't want to hear it but there's nothing we can do about it right now," Adan said. "The new facility will be completed as soon as possible."

"And after it's finished how long before it's up and running?" Hambone asked.

Adan ran a hand over his rat snout. "We still have to move the equipment in. Some of it's going to have to be made special. Willix estimates another couple months to get everything up and running before we can start dusting."

Hambone closed the lid of the cake box and sat. He had icing all over his face and his hands. I'd never seen him so upset that he stopped eating.

"And another three months to actually process some dust," Hambone said. "People are disappearing. There are rumors of hunters. We need to get this under control now."

Hank nodded but didn't say anything. He was used to keeping his emotions close to his chest, but I knew it was weighing heavy on his mind. The fact that we were at least five months out from having some dust didn't help.

"Hob, do we have to have all the equipment in place before we start dusting?" Isabelle asked.

Hob stepped up to the table. "*Nein*, the process has many stages. Some of these processes take weeks to complete. It is possible to have the equipment put in place as its needed."

"That'll shave some time off," I said. "We have bodies piling up in the Copper Mines ready to go."

"What about the people that are disappearing?" Hambone shouted, standing up in his chair and slamming his hands on the table. Buttercream icing splattered my shirt.

Hank sat up straight. "Look, no one wants to find out what's going on more than I do but we can only work with what we have. Without dust or a lead there's nothing we can do right now."

"I'll see if our network can round up some dust," Adan said. "If they can, it won't be cheap."

Hambone wiped a hand across his forehead smearing icing into his fur. "Do we know where that dust will come from? We could be buying the people we're trying to save."

"I'm not worried about the cost," Hank said. "And no matter who the dust was made from, if it prevents more folks going missing, it's worth it."

I looked Hank in the eye. "I'll keep trying to contact Thera. She has to respond eventually. We'll find them."

I didn't know if I was trying to reassure myself or him more. The truth was, Thera didn't have to do anything she didn't want to. She could go months without responding to a call; it wouldn't be the first time.

There was a knock at the door.

Hank called, "Yeah, it's open."

Big Ticket stuck his head in. "Sorry to interrupt but we got a problem."

CHAPTER · 8

"ABOUT HALFWAY BACK, behind the grey Crown Vic," Big Ticket said.

Hank stepped up to the window and spread the blinds with a couple fingers. "Hmm," he grunted as he peeked through the hole he made. "Who is it?"

"No idea," B.T. said. "I haven't seen him before."

"What's he doing?" I asked.

The bedroom's second-story window gave us a good vantage point for the west side of the junkyard. It wasn't uncommon for random folks to drive up to the junkyard and look around for a car that might have a part they needed. I wasn't sure why a single person in the junkyard would raise such suspicion.

After a few seconds Hank stepped back from the window. "Just watching."

I peeked through the window. I scanned the junkyard, my eyes going from car to car looking for the grey car Big Ticket said this mystery man was hiding behind. I felt as if I was playing a game of Where's Waldo, junkyard edition. I was beginning to think I would have to ask one of them to point him out when I saw a glint of light from behind a lime green Volkswagen Beetle. Someone was peeking up just behind the hood with a pair of binoculars. The window hadn't been cleaned in maybe ever and had a hazy film that prevented me from discerning much.

Hank sighed. "Do you know how long he's been there?"

Big Ticket shook his head. "I got you as soon as we found him. I told everybody to stay out of sight."

"Get everybody ready, human form with weapons," Hank said, walking toward the door. "I'll go see what he's doing."

I followed him. "I'm curious about this one. I'll come with you, okay?"

"Suit yourself."

I followed Hank down the stairs and out the back door of the clubhouse, opting for a stealthy approach. If he was going to act like he was up to no good, the least we could do was play along. We cut across the junkyard of Morrison Salvage, staying low to avoid being seen. We weaved our way through the cars to the fence and then turned west, following it around behind the intruder.

We worked our way quietly, being careful not to disclose our presence. We moved up a few cars behind the intruder. It was a man wearing brown penny loafers complete with pennies in them, khakis, and a navy polo. Whoever this guy was, he was dressed too nicely to be creeping around in a junkyard. I didn't get the impression we had to work so hard to sneak up on him. He was focused on the clubhouse, still looking though the binoculars.

"What do you think?" Hank whispered. "Should we jump him?"

I shrugged. "Let's see what he's doing here first."

Hank held up two fingers, motioning to move forward. We went around opposite sides of the car we were crouching behind. We positioned ourselves behind the intruder about five feet apart. When we were in position I gave Hank a nod.

"You must be lost?" Hank said.

The man spun around, dropping the binoculars. He was Asian, Japanese maybe. What concerned me more than his motivation was the revolver tucked into his pants.

"If you need a part you can talk to one of the mechanics at the shop," Hank said. "If not, you need to go."

He grabbed the piece, pointing it at me, then Hank, then back to me. "I'm not leaving until I get what I came for."

We were far enough apart that he couldn't cover both of us at the same time. His hands shook enough to give the gun's barrel a noticeable quiver. Sweat dotted his forehead and soaked into his shirt. His eyes were wide and strained, the eyes of a desperate man. He definitely wasn't a professional, this was personal for him. He looked like a guy in over his head and he knew it. That made him unpredictable, and unpredictable people were dangerous.

"You got some real stones, I'll give you that," Hank said, more amused than threatened. "Do you have any idea of the shit storm that's about to rain down on you?"

His eyes darted back and forth. "Shut up, I have the gun so I'm in charge." He jerked the gun in Hank's direction and pulled the hammer back. "No one's going to do anything as long as I have a gun on you."

"What do you want?" I asked.

He whipped the gun to point it at me. "You, I know you have Rebecca Lin inside. You're going to stay here with me and he's going to go bring her out. If you try anything funny your friend here's going to get it."

Hank smirked. "You think he practiced that line in the mirror?"

"He sounds like he's in a bad detective novel," I said.

He shouted, "Shut the hell up! I'm not going to tell you again."

I held my hands chest high. I wanted him to think I was surrendering. I took a step forward. "Hey buddy, I'm not sure what you think's going on—"

The gun went off. The man flinched from the sound as a percussive wave hit me. The bullet whizzed to my right shattering the window of the car behind me. I looked at Hank. He was running out of patience. The clubhouse was well outside the city and a single shot wasn't necessarily something that would draw a lot of attention. If he kept shooting and someone a little nosy happened to drive by and saw it, we would have a much bigger mess on our hands. Police weren't welcome or wanted at the clubhouse.

"Hurry up if you're going to do something," Hank said.

The man thought he was speaking to him. "I didn't mean to do that. I don't want to hurt anybody."

Being faster and stronger than the average bear often comes in handy. I rushed forward and grabbed the man's gun hand. Bending his wrist, I pointed the gun harmlessly to the side and delivered a right cross to his face. His head whipped from the impact. He let go of the gun and his body went limp and he fell face first in the dirt. He lay still.

I held the gun. Opening the cylinder of the revolver I found five bullets. I pulled one out and looked at it. Just a simple hollow point, not silver. It was the last bit of evidence to confirm my suspicion; he had no idea who he was messing with.

I tossed the gun to Hank. "Do you recognize him?"

"Nope," Hank said. "Let's get him inside quick."

Hank picked him up and heaved him over one shoulder. The road was visible from where we were standing but it was still early. Only one car passed in the time it took to us to carry him to the clubhouse. He was still unconscious when we took him inside. Doc Lin was sitting at the bar. Her face went pale when she saw Hank and the man over his shoulder.

She stood. "Hank, hold on a second," she said. "I know him."

Hank ignored Doc Lin but when he spotted Cotton he said, "We need a deadbolt put on the back bedroom."

I pulled Doc Lin aside as Hank disappeared into the back. "Who is he?"

She sighed. "My husband. What did you do to him?"

"He was sneaking around in the junkyard and pulled a gun on me and Hank," I said. "I defended myself."

"Did you kill him?"

I put a hand to my chest and feigned shock. "Rebecca! Don't you know me better than that?"

"Obie . . ."

I shrugged. "I punched him in the face. What'd ya want?"

"I want you to not beat up my husband."

"I want to not get shot at," I said.

Hank returned and joined us.

"It's Doc's husband," I said.

"What the hell's he doing here?" Hank asked.

Doc Lin looked mortified. "Well, I haven't been home much lately, the work I'm doing over here is taking up a lot of time, not to mention being on call all hours. He's been getting suspicious. I told him I've been working overtime at the hospital. He must have followed me here."

"He's staying until we figure out what to do with him," Hank said.

"What do you mean *what to do with him*?" Doc Lin asked, panic creeping into her voice.

We all knew what it meant. Besides the normal issue of risking the secrecy of our world, he had come to the club house with a gun. That alone was enough to at least get him a beating by the club.

Hank looked her in the eye before he turned to me. "You need a ride to Ground Zero?"

"Adan's got us," I said.

He walked away. "I'll see you over there."

When he had disappeared through the door Doc Lin turned to me. "Obie, you've got to help me."

"Hank's pissed and rightly so. He brought a gun with him," I said. "This is really club business so there may not be much I can do."

"They listen to you," Doc Lin said. "If you vouch for him they'll have to let him go."

"Vouching for someone I don't know and took a shot at me might be a problem," I said. "I'll try to help, but believe me, they don't *have* to do anything. Let's go check him out and then we have to get Eddie over to Ground Zero."

Doc got a rag and some water. We went to the bedroom Hank had put him in. Cotton stood guard in front of the door.

"Is he awake?" I asked.

Cotton shrugged. "Hell if I know."

We went in. He was sprawled on the bed, still unconscious.

Doc Lin rushed to the bed. "Will . . . ? Can you hear me?"

She repositioned him with his head on the pillow. He had a pretty serious bloody nose and his eyes had already turned black. I'd got him a little better than I'd realized. The blood had gotten smeared around his face in transport. He looked like hell.

Doc Lin turned back to me. "Obie, heal him."

I put a hand over his head channeling healing energy into him. He started to wake. I moved back to stand by the door.

Doc Lin sat over him on the bed. "Will? Can you hear me?"

Will opened his eyes. "Rebecca?"

She put a hand on the side of his face. "Are you okay?"

He sat up, touching a couple fingers to his nose. They came away bloody. He wiped the blood onto his pants. "My car's parked down the street," he whispered. "I packed a few essentials and have a couple plane tickets to Vancouver. We just have to get to the car."

Doc Lin didn't whisper when she replied. "Do you think I'm a hostage or something?"

"You're not?" Will asked. "Then what are you doing here?"

"I'm working."

"Working . . ." Will took the rag from her and cleaned blood on his own. "I called the hospital. They said you hadn't worked there in a couple months. You're telling me you left your job as Chief of Medicine to work in a biker bar?"

"It's complicated." She sighed. "You've caused a lot of problems by coming here."

"You've been distant, secretive . . . At first I thought you were having an affair. Now I don't know what's going on but I'm the one that's causing problems? It's time for you to tell me the truth."

Doc Lin looked over at me. I shook my head as subtly as possible.

"What are you looking at him for?" He asked.

"I told you I was working and that is true," she said.

"You told me you were working at the hospital," he said.

Doc Lin sighed. "I know, I'm sorry."

There was a knock at the door. I opened it a crack.

Adan was standing on the other side in krasis. "We need to hit the road. We're already gonna be late."

"We're coming," I said.

"So you're going then?" Will asked.

"We can talk more when I get back."

I opened the door a little more and Doc Lin slid out of the room. I was about to follow when Will stopped me.

"Hey." He paused to spit some blood out on the floor. "Nice right."

I gave him a nod and followed Doc Lin outside to Adan's car. Eddie and Adan were leaning against the truck, waiting for us.

When he saw us, Eddie came over. "Hey, Doc, look I'm just a little tired. I'm not hurt. What do you say we call off this whole checkup thing and I'll just get some rest?"

Doc Lin let out a heavy sigh. "Nothing would make me happier than to blow it off, but we need to get you checked out, just to be sure. We don't want any surprises, okay?"

Eddie nodded. "Alright."

CHAPTER·9

"SHOTGUN," HAMBONE SAID.

Eddie had just got into the back seat of Adan's car. I was standing with the passenger door open, about to claim my seat. Hambone was still covered in frosting and cake crumbs. Pretending I didn't hear him, I jumped in the seat. He would probably complain about it the entire ride but he was always going on about something.

When Adan saw Hambone, he said, "Hold up, you're not getting in the car like that."

"What?" Hambone was genuinely confused as to the problem. "I left the rest of the cake. What's the matter?"

"You're going to get icing everywhere."

Hambone shrugged. "Well, I don't have another ride so . . ."

"Go clean up. We'll wait," Adan said.

"Fine," Hambone said.

He sulked over to the spigot on the side of the clubhouse, complaining the entire way. After a couple minutes of scrubbing in cold water he looked eighty-five percent cleaner and one hundred percent miserable.

He climbed into the seat behind me, looking generally sour. "I don't see what all the fuss is about. It was just a few crumbs and a touch of frosting."

Adan started the car and drove down to the road. As we pulled onto the pavement I heard faint crunching coming from the back seat. Adan turned around to look at Hambone.

"Are you eating?" Adan asked.

Hambone held up his hands to show they were empty but kept his mouth shut. Adan turned back around. I watched Hambone in the side mirror. He sat still for a few seconds and then his jaw moved slowly down and back up. The same subtle crunch emerged from the back seat again. Adan sighed as Hambone discreetly munched. Queen Isabelle's motorcade, her SUV and two guard trucks, and Hank on his Harley, pulled out behind us.

With the old dusting facility destroyed and Hob working with Queen Isabelle, we had to find a new location and someone to run it. Willix was a no brainer to run the facility. He had been working with Hob ever since he lost the council election to Hambone in '84. He seemed happy to have the opportunity to continue his work. That was the easy part. Construction of a new facility with the required equipment was the bigger issue. For that we turned to the wererats. The rats had mini cities for ultranaturals called undergrounds set up in almost every major city across the world. You could find an underground from Atlanta to Beijing to Hamburg and everywhere in between. The T.O. was resistant at first to allow the rats a foothold so deep in their territory but in the end they relented.

We drove into Dawson Forest ten minutes away. It was an undeveloped area of land in North Georgia officially owned by the city of Atlanta. Unofficially, it belonged to the wererats. It had been a nuclear test site in the sixties. There were still a few concrete structures scattered around the property. We called the largest of them Ground Zero.

Adan made a couple turns on the dirt roads running through the forest and then veered off the road driving down a hillside to a creek at the bottom. Instead of crossing the creek he turned and drove downstream. I expected a rough ride from the rocks that inevitably lined the bottom. To my surprise, it was smooth. We followed the creek around a hundred yards through a slight turn to a giant concrete culvert disappearing into the hillside. It looked like a drainpipe. A small steady stream of water ran out from the bottom. Adan drove into the pipe.

"Where's the water coming from?" I asked.

"While we were excavating the area we hit a spring. We're using it as a water source. The excess is diverted out the pipe and to the creek," Adan said.

"Is the site off grid then?"

"It'll be completely self sufficient and concealed. Many streams and one large river flow through the forest. We've set up hydropower generators to provide all the electricity the facility will need," Adan said. "When it's all done, someone could stand by the front door and never know we're here."

The culvert dead-ended into a concrete wall. Water flowed from a smaller pipe coming out of the side wall. Adan pulled up a small ramp and stopped in front of the wall. There was a loud ka-chunk, and the wall swung open. Adan drove forward into a parking deck that looked like it belonged in an airport or train station. The parking deck was empty except for a few work trucks parked in the far corner. It looked new with pristine yellow lines painted on the pavement. Lights hung from the ceiling with arrows directing the flow of traffic. Adan pulled forward, ignoring the arrows, to a spot up front with Queen Isabelle and Hank close behind. We got out and congregated around the vehicles. Isabelle, Yarwor, and the guards from two trucks joined us.

"Yarwor will escort me. The rest of you stay with the vehicles please," Isabelle instructed as Doc Lin and Eddie climbed out of the car.

When Adan had our attention, he began, "Welcome to the new Ground Zero. This is the parking deck, we have sixty spaces. The first floor is complete and we're about seventy percent through the second floor. If you'll follow me . . ."

Adan led us to a security booth built into the back wall. It had a door on either side. The door on the left looked plain, except it had two doorknobs. One in the normal position and one about a foot lower. The door on the right only had one doorknob but it had a red cross in a circle designating it as a hospital entrance. A wererat sat at a console in the booth, sipping a cup of coffee and monitoring multiple screens. He was dressed in a plain gray uniform with UPD embroidered above the left chest pocket.

"This is our first point of security. This booth monitors all incoming and outgoing traffic. The booth is always manned by at least one member of the Underground Police Department." Adan pointed as he spoke as if he was a flight attendant. "There are multiple entrances around Dawson Forest that converge into the east and west tunnels." Adan pointed to hallways on either side of the parking deck. "All of those entrances are hidden and locked. This booth monitors them. There is a separate booth for internal security which I will show you in a moment. The door to your right is the emergency entrance to the hospital. The door to your left leads into Ground Zero. Doc, you want to take Eddie through there and we'll catch up to you."

"Sure," Doc Lin said.

She walked with Eddie to the hospital door. The guard pushed a button, a buzzer sounded and the door released, opening a crack.

Adan asked, "Does anyone have any questions before we continue?"

"Tell me about the Underground Police," Hank said. "What's going on there?"

"The wererats have a single government with uniform laws. You can walk in Underground London to Underground Tokyo and the laws are the same. The UPD enforces those laws."

"Think of the bureaucracy," Hambone said. His eyes glazed over as if he were dreaming of cheesecake. "Red tape for miles!"

"What happens if they arrest you?" Hank asked. "Is the Tortured Occult expected to be held accountable to these laws."

"This is a wererat facility. Anyone that sets foot inside will be expected to conduct themselves in accordance with rat law. This facility isn't completed so things are a little more lax for our tour. For example, most weapons are prohibited inside the Collective Underground. Today though we won't worry about it. Which takes us to our next part of the tour. If you'll follow me please."

We walked through the two-handled door leading into Ground Zero. The bottom handle opened the bottom half of the door for people closer to Hambone's size and the top door handle opened the full door. We entered into a hallway with a door on the end and a row of lockers built into the right wall. The left wall was a second security desk, much larger than the previous one. The glass spanned the entire hallway with multiple officers manning multiple counters.

"All cities in the Collective Underground have a place to keep prohibited items during your stay," Adan said. "You're free to carry your weapons today but after Ground Zero is officially open you will need to either get a permit or stow them in these lockers. This is the main security office. If you are interested in applying for a weapons permit you can do that here. In fact, we'll go ahead and get you what you need." Adan turned to the officer manning the counter and said, "Can we get five welcome pamphlets and weapon permit applications please?"

The officer retrieved some papers from a filing cabinet. He placed them in an electric drawer like you would see in a bank drive through and hit the button to slide the drawer out to us. Adan passed out papers.

I looked at the pamphlet. WELCOME TO THE UNDERGROUND! HERE'S WHAT YOU NEED TO KNOW.

Adan moved to the door on the far side of the room. A sign affixed to the door read YOU ARE NOW ENTERING GROUND ZERO. We stepped through into an upscale looking shopping plaza. It had generous lighting which almost made it feel like we were outside. The center of the plaza was planted with bushes and grass. Pillars ran down either side, floor to ceiling. Shops were built into the walls.

"We have space for twenty-two businesses, not including the hospital and bank. We're still reviewing vendor applications. You can expect restaurants and night life, as well as clothing and grocery stores that cater to the wants and needs specific to the ultranatural community."

Tables with red-and-white checkered tablecloths were outside one of the stores. "What's that place?" I asked.

We followed Adan down the left side of the plaza. "Whisker's Café. It's pretty good. They aren't officially open, of course, but they have been serving the workers and staff getting Ground Zero ready. You're all welcome to stop for a bite when we're finished. At the end of the plaza will be the Department of Records which I'm sure you'll all be using from time to time."

"What's the Department of Records?" Hambone asked.

"The DoR handles driver's licenses, birth certificates, deeds, permits . . . Any documentation necessary for the human world can be acquired for a nominal fee and a short wait," Adan said. "If you'll follow me downstairs, I'll show you the part of the complex most people don't get to see."

CHAPTER·10

ADAN LED US to a door beside the Department of Records. He pulled a key-card from his pocket and swiped it on a black pad mounted beside the door. Locks released with an audible *click*. He opened the door and held it for us. We walked down a flight of concrete stairs and exited through another door into a hallway. This was much plainer than the plaza. It was just gray concrete walls and floors without any decoration. Doors with keypads lined the hallway. I could hear construction noise from multiple directions.

Adan moved ahead of me. "These rooms will be used for the management of the facility. They house the machinery needed to run the facility. They are finishing construction on office space right now. Nothing we need to get into. The dusting facility is this way."

We followed Adan through a door at the end of the hall. We stepped into a large empty room. It had tile floors with drains and an industrial sink on the wall beside us. It looked like a laboratory without any equipment. Three doors lined the far wall. Adan opened one of the doors revealing a walk-in freezer. It was reminiscent of a meat packing plant, but instead of hunks of beef, an assortment of demon carcasses were suspended by hooks.

"It was built to the specifications Hob provided. Willix has been overseeing the construction, but I'm not sure if he's here now," Adan said. "This is the space for dust production and storage. Not much to see at the moment. We've already moved the corpses that were being stored in the copper mines. Going forward you should bring all bodies here."

I stepped into the freezer for a closer look at the frozen-solid carcasses. The copper mines were chilly but weren't cold enough to keep them from rotting, however slowly. Their time in the mines hadn't been kind to them. The oldest of them had decomposed quite a bit. It didn't instill a lot of confidence in me that we were going to get the dust we needed in three months. The degradation had to have an effect on the quality, quantity, or both.

"Let me show you where you'll drop off the fresh ones," Adan said.

He opened a door that lead to another parking deck. This one was much smaller than the first. There looked to be only one way in, a cargo elevator on the far side of the room. There were clearly marked arrows leading from the elevator, around the parking deck, and back to the other side of the elevator. An automatic carwash was on the right side of the parking deck.

"When you bring a body for dusting you will drive onto the service elevator. Pull up in front of this door," Adan said motioning toward the freezer. "The bodies will be unloaded and weighed. After that, if your truck is dirty you can clean it up quick with our automated carwash. You don't have to spray your truck down with a garden hose anymore. There are also restrooms with showers behind the carwash where you can get cleaned up, if needed. Once you're ready, drive back on the elevator and be on your way.

"Seems simple enough," I said.

"If you'll accompany me onto the elevator we'll get you back to your vehicles," Adan said.

Adan pulled up a gate and we stepped onto the elevator. It was a large industrial style model with plenty of room to move around in, even if there was a truck inside. Adan pulled the gate closed. He hit the button marked ONE and it brought us back up to the parking deck where we started. "Does anyone have any questions?"

"What would you recommend at the Whisker's Café?" Hambone asked.

Adan smiled. "Ask for the stout pie."

"Stout . . . pie . . . It really was a lovely tour," Hambone said, backing away from us. "Isabelle, Obie, etcetera, it's always good—" He jogged toward the café without finishing his sentence.

The rest of the group started walking toward their vehicles. It occurred to me Hank had been unusually quiet. The Tortured Occult had been through a lot of changes in the past six months. The change in leadership after Otis was killed would be enough to cause some serious turmoil. Along with a new identity came a new kutte. The old kutte had a bear's head made of oak leaves, now it was just a bear skull with a pentacle surrounding it. It was a much more aggressive design. The change in leadership was only part of the trouble the T.O. had been through. The trouble with Chisel had caused some internal strife and Torch's disappearance hadn't helped either.

I caught up to Hank. "You hardly said anything the whole time. You doing okay?"

"I've got my mind on other things," he said.

"Torch?"

Hank nodded.

I tried to sound reassuring. "I'll get Thera to lead me to Holt and the people that took Torch. I'm sure we're going to find your boy."

Hank stopped and looked me in the eyes. "If they have him there's no way he's still alive. They've had him over four months already."

"We'll find him. We won't stop until we do," I said.

"Thanks, Obie, I appreciate it." He didn't sound reassured. "I sent a prospect for your keys. He should be here soon. He'll give you a ride to your truck."

Movement out of the corner of my eye caught my attention. Adan was waving for me.

"Thanks, Hank. I'll let you know what I find out."

I went to see what Adan wanted. He held out a card. It was a black card with a red stripe down the middle. It read PINES across the top and Chestatee Reginal Library System in white lettering. There was a barcode with a letter and number combination on the bottom of the card.

"A library card?" I asked. "It doesn't look right."

"That's because it's not a library card," Adan said. "It's your Underground Passport. You use it for everything you need in any Underground worldwide. It will open doors at your access level or below. It's linked to your bank account so you can use it to pay at all the shops or take cash out of the ATM. I took care of your weapons permit as well. If the UPD hassles you about your blade, just give them this card. Oh, and if you *did* want to go to the library it works there too."

I became aware of a rumbling sound coming from the direction of the entrance to the parking deck. As it grew louder, I recognized it as a motorcycle of the hog variety. Something the T.O. would be proud to deafen random strangers with. The rumble dropped to an idle and the concrete door slid open. The engine thumped to life and the biker rode slowly in. I didn't recognize him; he must be new. He looked over at Hank who pointed in our direction.

He pulled up beside us. "You Obie?"

I nodded. "Have something for me?"

He reached into the pocket on his kutte and produced the spare keys to my truck. "I'll take you to your truck when you're ready."

"I'm ready now." I slid the card and keys into my pocket and got on the back of the bike. "Thanks, Adan."

"Good luck finding Holt," Adan said.

"What's your name?" I asked when we pulled up to the exit.

"Officially, prospect," he said, throwing a thumb to the kutte he was wearing.

"How about unofficially?"

The door swung open and he drove down the tunnel.

"Jim," he said. "Hey, next time maybe let the folks at your house know someone's coming over, it almost got ugly."

"Who's at my house?" I asked.

"Some cougar and . . . well, hell, I don't know what he was. Looked like a hairless dog covered in burn scars with an anxiety disorder."

CHAPTER · 11

I SPENT THE RIDE home wondering who Prospect Jim had seen in my house. Could it be possible that Holt escaped the tar? If he managed to set it on fire it would explain the description of a "scarred up dog." Holt wasn't the anxious type though, but I suppose being lit on fire would put anyone on edge.

I had Jim drop me at the end of the driveway. I wanted to know who I was dealing with before they knew I was there. I didn't think they were hostile. If they were waiting to ambush me then they would have killed Jim rather than lose the element of surprise. Then again, if I didn't have keys to get home they'd be waiting around a long time. Maybe they were planning a more up-front attack rather than an ambush . . . or maybe I was just being paranoid. It wouldn't be the first time.

I gave Jim a wave as he drove away. The ultras in my house had no doubt heard the motorcycle. I wanted to wait a few minutes before I went inside. I could walk up through the woods and get an idea who had made themselves at home before they knew I was there. While I waited for the noise from the hog to die off, I decided to give Thera another try.

I closed my eyes and concentrated on Thera. I didn't know how she experienced it when we called her or if the focus would make the "signal" stronger but it was worth a shot.

"I really need to talk to you. Things have gone to shit here and I need some help."

I waited with my eyes closed hoping to hear her ill-tempered voice. I opened one eye and looked around. Nothing. I sighed and opened the mailbox. I had some bills, some junk mail, and a postcard.

The postcard had a picture of buildings I didn't recognize with NEW ORLEANS LOUISIANA plastered across the front. It had a matching postmark on the back with a hand written note.

Heading to Poverty Point and then on to Dallas. Thinking of you and wishing you were here. —N

"Me too." I sighed and put the postcard in my pocket.

The bills and junk mail went back in the mailbox. I walked up the driveway, then around the last turn before the house came into view, and slipped into the woods. I used the trees for cover until I had a good view of the front of the house. An orange Subaru I didn't recognize was parked out front. Lights were on in the house. Whoever was in there wasn't hiding. I watched for a while, catching bits of movement through the living room window.

Waiting wasn't getting me anywhere. Whoever it was had been there for hours already. I could wait for them to come out, but there's no telling how long that would take. I needed to find Holt, this was just getting in the way. No more beating around the bush. I changed to krasis, drew my blade, and walked to the front door.

No sooner had I set foot inside than a woman's voice I recognized called my name from the direction of the living room. "Obie? Is that you?"

I walked toward the living room and ran into Mila. She was a Keeper who worked around Tennessee. She was bound to the mountain lion but when we met in the hallway she was in her human form. She had blond hair buzzed short around the sides and longer and spiked on the top. She wore faded jeans and a red tank top. She was all muscle and curves. She gave me a hug. Her body felt hard and soft at the same time, like steel wrapped in cotton.

"What are you doing here?" I asked.

She pulled away, putting her hands on my cheeks. She squished my face a little and looked deep into my eyes. Her eyes were a light brown, almost matching her hair. "I heard about Naylet . . . Are you okay?"

"Oh yeah," I said, my words distorted the same amount as my mouth. "I'm fine."

She gave me a sad smile. "Obie . . . It's me. Come on."

I put my blade back in its sheath and took her hands. I held them against my chest. "I'm fine, I promise. Even if I wasn't, I have more important things going on. I hear you brought someone with you. I'm guessing this isn't a social visit?"

"Afraid not. This werewolf named Atticus found me and said he had a message for you. It's better if you hear it from him." She turned to the living room but stopped in her tracks. "Oh, and whatever you do don't agitate him. He's been through a lot."

I followed her into the living room. I found a shifter sitting on the mantle of the fireplace. He had a blanket draped around his body with only his muzzle sticking out as if he were doing an impression of Darth Sidious. I couldn't see his eyes, but the blanket shifted slightly, indicating he was looking at me. Mila and I sat on the couch across from him. A couple of fire extinguishers were on the floor in front of the couch. I waited for him to speak but he just sat there breathing deeply.

"I hear you have a message for me?" I said.

"Yes," Atticus said. "You're going to have to bear with me. This is a difficult subject and I have to stay calm. Bad things happen when I get too excited."

"What, you Hulk out or something?"

Mila leaned in and whispered, "He catches on fire."

"What do you mean?"

"He bursts into flames, with all the flailing and screaming you would expect of someone burning alive. If he doesn't keep it together, he'll probably burn your house down."

"Thanks for bringing him inside," I whispered before picking up a fire extinguisher. "Take your time, Atticus, no pressure."

"I had a job with a cable company. I was out on a service call and everything seemed routine. Next thing I know, I'm getting electrocuted. I think it was a trap. Somebody put current where it shouldn't have been. I was taken to a kind of prison. They did some kind of surgery on me and kept me in a special cell where there was water coming out of sprinklers constantly. I was always wet and cold and miserable. I know now it was to keep me from igniting." Atticus paused to take a few deep breaths. "They have a lot of ultras there. They're constantly taking old ones away and bringing new ones in. One day they brought in someone new, a biker by the name of Torch. Long story short, we escaped. I didn't think it was possible, but we actually made it outside. When the shooting started, I burst into flame for the first time. I ran into the river to put myself out. I passed out when I hit the water and woke up washed up against the bank downstream. I don't know what happened to Torch or the other prisoners, but he told me to find a guy named Obie, that he would help me. When I made it back, I asked around and found Mila and here we are."

"Do you know where the prison is?" I asked. "Can you find it again?"

"I don't know the exact location, but we should be able to find it. But if I help you, I want something in return," Atticus said.

"What's that?"

"I want you to take me back."

"You want us to return you to the people that took you?" Mila asked.

Atticus took a deep breath. "My cell was the only place where I don't have to worry about catching fire. By all means, get rid of those bastards, but once you do, I'm going back in that cell until somebody can find a way to fix me."

"You got a deal," I said. "Let me just talk to Mila for a minute."

I took Mila outside on the front porch. "Do you trust this guy?"

Mila nodded. "He's at least telling the truth about the fire. I've seen him do it and it's not pretty. There have been people disappearing from my territory for the past few months and this is the first real lead I've had."

"It's been the same here," I said. "I'm not sure exactly how many, more than ten disappeared without a trace . . . Today it was Holt."

Mila looked shocked by the revelation. "Holt was taken?"

"Yeah." I nodded. "It was some kind of living tar. If Atticus can lead us to the abductors, then we might be able to get them back before anything bad happens to them."

"If they took a Keeper we don't need Atticus, Thera can lead us to him. It's bad for Holt but if he can hold out until we can get there then it's the break we need to find them quick."

"You would think so but Thera isn't answering my call. I've tried twice already."

Mila almost shouted when she spoke. "Thera." After a few seconds of no reply she tried again. "We need to speak to you now. We need your help. You need to answer us."

It was a more direct approach than Thera would appreciate. Mila might have taken that tone out of frustration or she could be using a strategy that hadn't oc-curred to me: Piss Thera off. It was risky but if it got her to reply . . .

Mila threw her hands up in frustration. "How can she not answer? If one of us is in trouble she should show up and help."

"You don't gotta tell me," I said. "We can't make her do anything, so until she decides to talk to us, it is what it is. Atticus is our best bet right now."

"Let's get on the road then," Mila said. "We don't have time to waste."

"You're driving. I don't like the idea of my truck getting blown up."

Mila shot me a smile. "Fair enough."

We got Atticus loaded in the back seat and headed northwest.

"Tell me everything you know about the place," I said.

"Like I said, it's on a river. I saw two bridges when I was brought in. An old one and a new one right beside each other. The old bridge is really old, made of stone. The house is big, three . . . maybe four stories. It was hard to tell. I only got a glimpse of the lights through the woods before the shooting started."

"Anything else?"

Atticus thought for a moment. "I can't be sure, but I think there's a waterfall close by. I heard rushing water, a lot of it. More than just a river."

I pulled up a map on my phone and did a search for bridges in north Geor-gia. I got a lot of results for covered bridges and not much else.

"Were either of the bridges covered?" I asked.

"No, just normal," Atticus said.

I searched for waterfalls. I scrolled through the results. Ruby Falls, nope, DeSoto falls, definitely not. Hemlock falls, Holcomb Creek, Cascade falls. I knew most of them and could rule them out right away. Of the ones I didn't, one by one I checked them off the list.

When I had run out of options, I dropped my phone in my lap. "Nothing. We need to get some help finding this place."

"I know someone that lives around there," Mila said. "She helps me some-times when I need information."

CHAPTER·12

ATTICUS DIDN'T SPEAK for the entire car ride. Mila and I just made small talk. For Keepers, small talk usually centered around what monsters we had fought. There seemed to always be something new and nasty coming through portals and it was good to get a heads-up on what we might run into. When the conversation lulled, my thoughts drifted to Naylet. *Wish you were here . . .* I wondered how serious she was. There was a part of me that wanted to get in the truck and go see her. It was nothing more than a pipedream. I was a Keeper of Thera. The job didn't come with vacation time. I found myself wishing for freedom, that Thera would just stay gone. I knew it wasn't going to happen though. Maybe one day Naylet would come back. Then, maybe, we could see about rekindling our relationship.

"We're here," Mila said, snapping me out of my daydream.

I looked up to see a single-story white house by the river. A simple country home, modest by modern standards, it looked to be from the late forties or early fifties. It had a rustically constructed outbuilding that looked older than the house. An old pickup and a newer sedan were parked inside.

Mila parked behind the pickup. "Atticus, wait here for me. We won't be long."

The blanket he was wrapped in nodded a little.

Mila and I headed to the front door.

Mila rang the doorbell. "Let me do the talking. She takes a bit to open up to people."

As soon as the doorbell rang a small dog started raising hell inside the house. The barking got louder as the door opened a crack. A young woman peeked through the crack. At least she looked like a young woman. She seemed more interested in me than Mila.

She eyeballed me up and down. "Who's this?"

Mila spoke softly. "This is Obie. He's a Keeper like me and a good friend. We need your help."

The door closed, muffling the yapping. I was starting to think that was her way of telling us to fuck off when the door opened again to reveal a gray werefox holding a black-and-white shih tzu. The dog growled and barked as we stepped inside the house.

"Obie, this is Jessie and Oreo," Mila said.

The dog growled in my direction. Jessie looked at me before turning to Mila. "You should've called."

"Sorry," Mila said. "It's a last minute emergency kind of thing."

Jessie shrugged. "So, what did you need?"

"We need to find a house," Mila said.

"You can look realtors up online."

"Not to buy," I said. "If we're right it's full of hunters that have been abducting people. We think it's close by."

She looked at me blankly before turning back to Mila. "Let's make it fast, I'm in the middle of a *Vampire Diaries* marathon." Jessie walked down a hallway.

"Haven't you seen it a hundred times already?" Mila asked.

"What's your point?" Jessie asked.

We followed her into an office. She put Oreo down and sat at a desk with four monitors and a computer with lights casting a blue tint on the room. I didn't know much about computers but even I could tell this was a serious setup. The computer's tower had a clear side, showing off the components inside. It looked like a piece of alien technology to me. It wasn't the only computer in the room either. The walls had numerous computers and components piled around. The room was kind of a mess, but the desk was neat and clean and looked like some kind of shrine, a place to worship at the altar of technology. In a way, it reminded me of the clubhouse in the middle of the junkyard of Morrison Salvage.

Jessie grabbed the mouse and wiggled it back and forth on a mousepad. The monitors blinked to life. "Tell me what you know."

"We're looking for a house. It's old and big, there's three or four stories, and it's beside a waterfall," Mila said. "Oh, and there are two bridges beside each other. One is an old stone number and the other is newer."

Jessie stopped typing when Mila mentioned the bridges. She spun around in her chair to face us. "Looks like I'll be back to my show in a few minutes."

"You know it?" Mila asked.

"The place you're looking for is about five miles upriver from here. It's an old grist mill. The waterfall was manmade. They used it to turn the wheel originally but replaced it with a generator so it makes its own power."

"What can you tell us about the owner?"

Jessie sighed. I looked over her shoulder as she pulled the property up on the computer.

She stopped typing. "*Ocupado.*"

"Sorry," I said, taking a step back.

She resumed typing. "Let's see. It looks like it was sold a few years ago to . . . a dummy corporation. I might be able to find out some more for you but it will take time. I should be able to have something for you tomorrow morning."

"There was one more thing," I said. "This may not make any sense but if I needed to look at a dark place on the internet where would I go? Dark web something or other?"

Holt had already given me input on it, but Jessie was clearly an expert. I hoped she could help me figure out what Travis was talking about.

"Yeah, the dark web is a thing. You can't just look at it, it takes a special browser. It's basically the black market online. You can buy just about anything illegal there from drugs to weapons to people."

"What about 'cryptic currency'?"

"Cryptocurrency. It's digital money."

"Is there any way to trace purchases?" I asked.

Jessie nodded. "Most people think its untraceable, but there is a ledger of transactions called a blockchain. It takes some work, but transactions can be traced."

I pulled the address label and instructions we'd picked up from the foreman and handed it to Jessie. "A guy bought a summoning ritual at the dark web place and had it delivered. Could you look up who's selling this stuff, and if possible, who's purchased from them?"

Jessie handed me her notepad. "Write down everything you know about the buyer. I'll have to start there and work my way back."

I wrote down the foreman's name, the name of his construction company, and any other details that might come in handy outside of the address she already had on the return label.

Jessie eyed the notes I had written. "Eight."

"Eight what?" I asked.

Jessie crossed her arms and leaned back in her chair. "Eight thousand dollars. You think some stranger comes into my house, starts barking orders, and I'm going to drop everything I'm doing and work for free?"

"Well no . . . I just didn't know what you were talking about," I said.

"Check back in a couple days and be ready to pay," Jessie said. "Mila knows the way out."

"Umm . . . Is there a reason you couldn't do it now?" I asked.

"Let's say I was able to look it up for you in the next five minutes. What are you going to do with that information between now and two days from now?"

"I mean . . . Well . . . Nothing I guess," I said.

"I'm a few episodes away from Elena and Damon driving the car into the mystic grill. I'm not working on anything more complicated than a bag of popcorn before then."

I scratched my head. "I don't know what that means."

"It means it's time to go," Mila said. "Can you give us the address or directions to the house so we can check it out?"

Jessie flipped to a blank page of the notepad and scribbled on it. Ripping it free from the pad she flipped her wrist, presenting the paper to me held between two fingers. The gesture was a flashy way to present the paper and simultaneously say *get out*.

"Thanks," I said, taking the paper. "I'll check back in a few days."

"With cash," Jessie added.

I followed Mila outside, passing the paper to her halfway to the car. "With any luck we'll have Holt and be heading home before morning."

"Let's not count our Keepers before they're rescued," Mila said.

We headed north. In fifteen minutes, we came to a pair of bridges. One was modern, made of concrete and steel. The other was old, made of natural stone that I'd bet was pulled out of the river it crossed.

Mila slowed the car to a crawl as we crossed the bridge. She asked Atticus, "Is this it?"

Atticus studied a large three-story house built riverside, about two hundred yards downstream from the bridges. Even from this distance I could hear the water rushing.

"That's it," Atticus said. "I'm sure of it."

I caught the smell of something burning and felt heat coming from the back seat. Heat waves and little wisps of smoke rose from Atticus.

"Deep breaths, okay?" Mila said, looking in the rearview.

Atticus nodded, inhaling deeply. He held the breath for a few seconds and blew it out. The heat dissipated slightly.

"Let's find somewhere to park and get a closer look," I said.

Mila pulled off the road out of sight of the house. "Stay here and don't catch my car on fire."

We left Atticus in the back seat. Mila stepped into the woods, out of sight of the road, and pulled her shirt off.

"What are you doing?" I asked.

"We'll have an easier time staying hidden in our animal forms," she said.

I didn't need to remove my clothes to take the form of an otter. I made the change, crawling out through the neck hole of my shirt in time to get a view of Mila au natural. Her body was all powerful curves and silky definition. She looked as if she had been carved out of marble. Statuesque perfection in a living form.

It had been a while since I'd seen a naked woman. Yes, there were some at the T.O.'s run a few months ago but in krasis the fur tends to cover things up. I was suddenly aware not only that I was staring but that she was watching me watching her.

"Like what you see?" she asked doing a little spin.

I didn't know what to say other than a stammering apology that would only make this more awkward. Instead, I scampered deeper into the woods.

"So that's what an otter looks like blushing." She chuckled.

She appeared a moment later in the form of a mountain lion. We moved closer to the house, staying as quiet as we could in the crisp autumn leaves. It was easy to stay concealed in the darkness. I could smell cigarette smoke. A figure on the porch moved lazily, the faint red dot of a cigarette floating along with him at mouth level. The red dot turned into a glow, lighting up his face before fading back to an almost imperceptible speck.

While I didn't recognize his face, I knew the body language. The way he was holding his arms close to his chest told me he held a gun. It's not completely un-heard of for a guy to be hanging out on a porch with a gun in these parts. But Atticus identified the location, I doubted it was just some guy spending quality time with his rifle.

"What do you think?" Mila asked.

She was able to shift only her vocal chords, allowing her to speak as a moun-tain lion. I hadn't practiced that specifically, but I had worked on partial changes to be able to pull my blade out of my back in my human form. This would be the same thing only different. I concentrated on shifting my throat.

I could feel the movement of the shift as my neck changed. "It's worth a look," I said, sounding like I had just taken a hit from a helium balloon.

Mila put her head down and covered her face with her paws. She laughed. I would have told her it wasn't funny but speaking more would only encourage her. I could feel my brow furrow and the left side of my mouth raise as I waited for her to get herself under control. When she looked over at me and saw my face she started up all over again.

I made my way back to my clothes, changed into krasis, and started getting dressed. Mila followed right after.

"I'll call Hank and get the Tortured Occult up here to help out," I said, but-toning my pants.

Thera appeared beside us. "I have a job for you. Mila, since you're here you can go as well."

"Where have you been? I've been calling you," I said.

Thera looked at me with a blank expression. "I heard your calls."

"And?"

"I chose not to answer," she said.

"Can you locate Holt?" Mila asked. "Is he in that building over there?"

"I have a job for you," Thera repeated.

"My first priority is Holt," I said. "If I'm right, he's inside that house and in big trouble."

Thera ignored me and continued with her instructions. "Eirene spoke to me. There are humans hurting her children. You will go to her and stop them. Do not impose on her."

"I'll be sure not to, right after I get Holt back," I said. "That's the priority."

Electricity shot through me. My body convulsed and I fell to my knees. I looked up at Thera.

She looked down her nose at me. "I grow weary of your insolence. You have become too comfortable making demands of me. It's time you remembered your place."

I went to stand up when I was hit again. My body shot with pain and I fell, flopping like a fish as a second jolt hit me. Mila stood by and quietly watched. I couldn't blame her. Protesting would have only brought Thera's wrath on her. The pain ceased. I was able to move again. I knelt in front of Thera, holding back my anger.

"Do you have anything else to say?" Thera asked.

I didn't say anything but sat there with my head bowed.

Thera waved her arm and a portal opened in front of us. "Then go."

CHAPTER·13

WE STEPPED THROUGH the portal into a small clearing. We were surrounded by a jungle with dense vegetation and strange animal sounds emanating from all around us, it's what I imagined the Amazon rainforest would be like. The air felt heavy and smelled like rain. Movement in the foliage directly in front of us caught my attention. I put a hand on the handle of my blade as Mila moved a few feet to my right. A standard tactic. If something rushed us we would be ready.

A woman materialized out of the jungle. Her skin was stone gray with a mix of green foliage that matched the jungle for hair. I knew the look, it was the same way Thera appeared, when she chose to.

I dropped my hand from my blade. "Eirene?"

Mila moved toward me cautiously. She gave me a look that I recognized as anxious. I understood it, I was feeling the same way. We learned how Thera liked things done. Eirene was an unknown. How were we supposed to handle this meeting? Do we bow, kneel, or stand there looking stupid. Was there a way she wanted to be addressed and what were the consequences for breaking the rules? Was I going to say the wrong thing and end up flailing in pain again?

Eirene smiled and stepped up to me. She looked kind enough but I didn't trust her. She raised her hands to my face. I took half a step back. She saw my trepidation and paused. I relaxed a little and she placed a middle finger on each temple. A warm tingle ran from her fingers into my head; my right eye twitched involuntarily from the energy flow. When she finished with me she went to Mila. I didn't know what she had done but it didn't hurt. I gave Mila a nod. She let Eirene put her hands to her temples.

When Eirene had finished she stepped back. "Now you are as my children. Thank you for coming. I hope you will be able to put an end to the violence quickly. Your guide will be here soon."

Eirene disappeared.

"What'd ya think that meant?" Mila asked. "You are as my children."

I shrugged. "Has to be a good thing, right?"

We were left standing alone in the jungle surrounded by strange noises. There was chirping, screeching, and howling but the most alarming sound was a deep guttural thumping. *Kuh, kuh, kuh.*

Mila looked around at the jungle. "What now?"

"She said there's a guide. Maybe just wait here?"

Mila took a step closer to the jungle. "You hear that? What do you think's making all that racket?"

"Probably a lot of creatures we've never seen before. I don't want to piss off Eirene. I think it'd be smart to avoid killing as much as we can while we're here."

"Except the humans," Mila interjected.

I smiled. "Of course."

I felt a tap on my whiskers that made me wiggle my mouth. It began to rain, the pitter pat of the raindrops hitting the leaves grew into a shushing drone as if the jungle was telling us to be quiet.

I didn't mind the water. It soaked my clothes but my fur offered excellent protection. Mila, on the other hand, wasn't as comfortable. The rain soaked into her fur, weighing it down against her skin. She looked like a drowned cat, which wasn't far from the reality.

"You look miserable," I said.

"Where's that guide already?" She asked, taking shelter under one of the larger leaves.

There was a rustling in the brush. Mila and I turned to face the noise. "Finally," Mila said.

I waited for the guide we had heard about. There wasn't any movement I could see but the jungle was thick with vegetation. This guide sure was taking their sweet time. Somewhere in the brush the same low thump sounded much closer than it had been. *Kuh kuh kuh kuh.*

Something large rushed us from behind, knocking me to the ground. I landed face down in the dirt. Something large and heavy stood on my back, pinning me to the ground. The pressure made it hard to breathe. A sharp pain stabbed into my back in multiple places. A lizard-like foot with razor sharp claws dug into the ground beside my head.

I reached back, trying to pull my blade from its sheath. The creature had it pinned to my body. I could feel the claws digging into my back and realized there wasn't much I could do about it. Mila came to the rescue. She raked her claws across the beast's face. It roared and charged her. She dodged its lunge but it spun slamming its tail into her, sending her flying into the brush. I wasn't one to lay around when there's work to be done. I got to my feet and drew my blade.

In front of me was a creature that looked like a cat with feathers and spikes on the end of its tail. While I'd intended to leave no trace, I had no intention of being disemboweled. I lunged, stabbing my blade into the beast's side. It spun, snapping at me. I jumped back, avoiding the bite. It took a few steps toward the jungle and collapsed. A second beast jumped out of the jungle, putting itself between me and the injured one. Its throat lurched like a bullfrog, making a guttural thump. *Kuh . . . kuh.* It waved its spiked tail threateningly back and forth.

As long as I could avoid its tail, I felt confident I could take it. I was used to fighting things with sharp claws and teeth. There was a rustling in the brush to my right. I took a step away. I'd have a hard time fighting off two of them at the same time. I hadn't seen Mila since she took that tail hit. If she could heal enough to give me some backup, we might have a chance.

It surprised me when an orc crashed through the brush. He stood five and a half feet tall with gray skin and a couple of large teeth sticking out from his bottom jaw. He was stocky with the thick muscular build common to orcs. He was dressed in a tunic and kilt made of some kind of woven material and carried a staff covered with intricate carvings.

He looked from me to the monsters and back to me. He jumped between us pointing his staff at my face in a threatening gesture. The staff had objects tied to the end of it with ropes that matched his clothing. A small skull, a bouquet of plants, a shiny rock, and a feather that looked like it came from one of these creatures bounced around on the end of the staff.

"Back, demon!" The orc shouted. "You shall not hurt Eirene's children."

Taken off my guard, I stepped back. It wasn't what he said, but how he said it. He wasn't speaking English, I didn't know the language, but I understood. Eirene must have given me the language when she touched me. If I could understand the language, I might be able to speak it.

I concentrated on what I wanted to say and gave it a shot. "If they don't hurt me, I won't hurt them."

The sounds that came out of my mouth were made up of long vowels and staccato grunting. I could tell by his change in expression that the orc understood me. What was weird was that I could understand what I said as well. It was mildly disorienting to fluently speak a language I didn't even know the name of.

He lowered the staff slightly. "If you know my language then you must be who I'm here to meet. I was told there were two of you."

Mila stumbled out of the brush. Her clothes were blood stained. "There is," she snarled. "Not if those beasts had their way about it."

The orc lowered his guard. He stabbed the butt of his staff into the ground. "They are leeree and one is injured. I must help her before we can continue our mission."

"Don't worry about me, I'm fine. By all means let's help the vicious predators," Mila scoffed.

She spoke in English but since she responded to what the orc had said I knew she understood and could speak his language. It also meant we had a way to speak privately. I doubted Eirene knew English, or that she planted it into his mind.

The orc knelt beside the injured leeree. The second leeree stood over him as he looked at the animal's injuries. It regarded us threateningly but didn't mind the orc's presence in the least. It was as if it was guarding both of them.

I kept my blade out and stood at a safe distance. "What's your name?"

"Krom," he said. "This injury is severe. You have a sharp claw."

"It was made by an orc like you," I said.

"Oorug."

"No, his name was Yarwor."

Krom stopped tending to the leeree and looked at me. "We are oorug, not orc."

"Sounds similar enough to me," Mila said in his language.

Krom grunted his disapproval and turned back to the wounded animal. "I'll need to gather some plants for the healing ritual."

"How long's that going to take?" I asked.

"I have to gather everything and prepare the ritual," Krom said. "It will take some time, impossible to tell."

Mila was particularly pissed off after being punted into the jungle. "Just leave it and let's go. There are more important things to handle right now."

"If this one loses its mate she will become sad. A sad leeree is a dangerous leeree," Krom said. "Oorug are stewards of Eirene. It is my duty to heal this gentle creature."

I put my blade in its sheath. "We don't have time for that. Can you keep this fuckin' thing from attacking me?"

"I won't let you harm it more than you have," Krom said.

"I'm not going to hurt it. Can you just do as I ask?"

Krom stood and led the uninjured leeree to the side of the clearing. I looked over at Mila. She gave me a nod affirming she had my back. I moved forward slowly, wary the leeree would attack. I knelt beside the animal, holding my hand out over it, and began channeling energy into it. I wasn't sure it would work since I hadn't tried any of my normal abilities. The energy began to flow through my body and into the leeree. I could see pink of the animal's wound begin to disappear as the injury closed.

When the energy spilled over the animal, the healing was complete. I stood and backed away slowly. The leeree got to its feet. It turned and lurched its head at me. *Kuh*. With that, the two leeree disappeared into the jungle.

Krom looked at the blood on Mila's clothes. "How badly are you injured? Can you walk?"

"I'm fine," she said.

"Remarkable. Eirene was wise to obtain the help of such powerful demons."

"How far do we need to go?" I asked.

"Half Kuu," Krom said, walking in the direction he had come from.

"What's a Kuu?" Mila asked.

"It's the seed of a goroo tree," Krom said.

"How are we half a seed away?" I asked. "That doesn't make any sense."

Krom turned around, holding his hands about a meter apart. "A Kuu is about this big. It has a thick fibrous husk that we use to weave into clothing, ropes, nets. After the husk is removed the seed is cooked in a pit filled with coals covered in goroo leaves and buried. One Kuu is the time it takes for the Kuu seed to cook."

"So the time it will take us to get there is half the time it takes a Kuu seed to cook?" Mila asked.

Krom started walking again. "Yes."

"That clears it up," I said.

CHAPTER • 14

IT RAINED FOR close to an hour. After the first fifteen minutes, Mila was so soaked it looked like she'd never be dry again. We both seemed to get considerably more sour as we walked. It wasn't the rain for me, it was that I had time to think. It didn't sit right with me that Thera forced us to come here and leave Holt in trouble.

"Relax," Mila said. "You're too distracted. Just focus on the job at hand."

We had been speaking in English while we walked, mostly because I had been complaining most of the way and I didn't want Krom to hear what a whiner I was being.

"I don't get what we're doing here. Why couldn't we just come through the portal close to the folks we're supposed to handle?" I asked. "We're out here wandering through the jungle wasting time when Holt's in real trouble."

Mila put a hand on a branch in front of her and bent it out of our way. "All I'm saying is, focusing on that isn't going to get us out of here any sooner."

I stopped. "Yeah yeah . . . I know. It's just that we were right outside. We could have gone in, got him back, and put an end to people getting snatched on our own planet. It wouldn't have taken more than an hour. Instead, we had to come here to solve other peoples' problems."

"These oorug seem pretty peaceful," Mila said. "I'm not sure they could take care of themselves."

"Maybe they should learn."

"You don't mean that," she said. "You're just upset."

"Yeah, I am upset."

Mila must have been tired of my bitching because she changed the subject. "Why do you think they measure time in kuu?"

"Well, I'm sure they have days, the sun has to go down sometime doesn't it?"

She thought about it. "Maybe it's like Alaska where it's light and dark for months at a time?"

"Maybe, this thick canopy would block out sunlight either way. A sundial wouldn't work. I guess it makes sense, they would all know how long it takes kuu to cook."

"We should keep moving," Krom said. "It is dangerous here for you."

I stepped past Mila and the branch she was holding. "How much farther?"

"It's not far now," he said. "It's just ahead."

"Good, someone back home needs my help. We need to get this over with quick."

Krom looked confused. "You're showing concern for another."

"So?" I scoffed.

"You're not what I expected. Demons are notorious for viciousness. It's strange to hear one showing concern."

"We have names," I said. "I'm Obie, this is Mila."

"I am curious about your species. May I ask you some questions?" Krom asked.

"Anything to pass the time," Mila said.

"Have you killed many creatures."

"What do you consider many?" Mila asked.

Krom pondered the question. "I am unsure."

"Yes, we've both killed many," I added. "More than could be counted."

That wasn't exactly true, but it got the point across.

Krom walked quietly for a moment before posing his next question. "Are you a mated pair?"

I looked back at Mila. She had a grin running from ear to ear.

"Are you going to start blushing again?" she asked in English.

I rolled my eyes. "We aren't a mated pair."

"Do you have mates?"

Mila spoke up after I didn't answer. "Obie had one until recently. I have a few."

"Private," I said in English.

"What?" Mila smirked. "When we're done here you'll never see him again. Who do you think he's going to tell?"

"That's not really the point is it?"

Krom turned around to me. He put a hand on my shoulder. "Demon Obie, you've lost a mate. You're sad and grumpy like the leeree. It takes countless kuu for a leeree to return to itself after losing a mate as well as care from the oorug. I will show you the care of a mateless leeree."

I wanted to be mad at him but how could I when he was expressing genuine concern for me. The truth was, I was just annoyed with the whole situation.

"This is your fault," I said to Mila before turning back to Krom. "Thanks . . . I think. How much farther?"

Krom gave me a smile and a shoulder squeeze before he disappeared through the brush in front of us. "We have arrived."

I drew my blade and went in after him. I emerged through the brush expecting explosions, screaming, or gunfire. What I found was a tree branch as wide as a road. It stretched from the distance into the ground in front of us and shot back up into what looked like a new tree. A small group of oorug were gathered around. Some were braiding cords, others were cooking. Children played in the clearing around a group of adults that looked to be sitting and talking around a small fire.

Panic erupted when they saw us. They dropped whatever they were doing. Some bolted up the limb while others ran after children.

Krom waved his hands. "Don't be concerned by their hideous appearance. They were brought to us by Eirene, no need to panic."

Some of the oorug didn't slow down and continued their ascent up the branch. Others waited cautiously, unsure about Krom's claim. The children clung close to adults or peeked around their legs. They seemed to ease a little when I put my blade back in its sheath.

"Krom, where are the humans?" I asked.

He looked confused. "What are *hoomans*?"

"The demons . . . we thought you were taking us to them," Mila said.

"Come," he said, walking toward the branch. "I will show you."

The crowd of oorug moved aside leaving a path. We followed Krom up the branch. The bark of the tree was thick and knotted but the top of the branch had smooth trails worn into it from the traffic. As we cleared the tree line I could see where we were headed, a massive tree, one whose trunk stretched at least fifty yards in diameter. The trunk was straight with a few branches like the one we were standing on reaching out in different directions into the jungle. Its canopy was enormous and as we got closer I could see huts constructed onto the branches or built into the side of the trunk. We walked for twenty minutes before we got to the trunk.

Krom disappeared inside an oorug-sized hole in the trunk. Mila and I ducked to get in and found the oorug utilized the inside of the tree as well. The tree was hollow nearly to the top. Huts were built into the trunk above us. Multiple rope bridges spanned the interior. There were a lot of openings in the trunk that light came through, but it wasn't enough to light the inside of the tree. There was light from scattered candles or lamps. The closest was on a platform suspended by ropes in the middle of the tree. We followed Krom to the platform. He picked up a large shell resembling a conch shell. The end of the shell had been hollowed out and held a small flame.

Krom handed it to Mila. "If it tips the oil will spill. Stand here." He indicated the platform.

We got on and Krom pulled a rope that ran to the top of the tree. The platform started to ascend. A net full of red rocks acted as a counterweight coming down beside us. The rocks looked familiar. It took me a second to figure out why—they reminded me of Yarwor's scimitar. His blade was made out of a red metal I hadn't seen anywhere else. It made sense it came from here but metalworking seemed beyond the skills of the oorug people, at least the ones I had seen so far. Krom calling my blade a claw instead of a sword told me they didn't engage in metalworking.

"Krom, do the oorug people travel through portals to other worlds?" I asked.

Krom pulled another rope. The platform stopped with a jolt in front of a hut. Mila was caught off guard by the jolt and the lamp tipped spilling a little oil.

He tied off the rope and stepped off the platform into the hut. "It is said that long ago our people did travel. It led to great suffering so now it is forbidden."

The hut seemed to be used for storage. There were a number of what I guessed to be kuu seeds as well as ropes, shells, and other things that I didn't recognize. The hut was well organized with everything stacked neatly or held in baskets. A door on the other side of the hut led to one of the large lower limbs. The limb was about fifteen feet across with a well-worn path in the middle. Large clumps of seeds, that reminded me of grapes, hung from the branches above us.

Krom pointed off into the distance. "The demons are there."

I stepped past him and squinted. There seemed to be a hole in the jungle. The white tops of tents were visible near the center of the void.

"Looks like they made themselves at home," Mila said.

"They brought strange animals with them. The animals sleep most of the time but when they wake they roar."

"What do they do with these animals?" I asked.

"Some they ride, others they use to chew through trees. They are killing the trees to make room for their cloud huts," Krom said.

"What are they doing here?" Mila asked.

"They are capturing Eirene's children. I do not know the purpose."

"Okay, Let's get over there and put a stop to it," I said.

"It will be dark soon. We should wait until light . . . you smell wrong," Krom said. "Follow me."

He took us back to the storage hut and picked up a gourd, liquid sloshed inside it. He took the lamp from Mila and put it on a stack of seeds behind him.

He took a stopper out of the top of the gourd and began slinging the liquid on Mila and me. "It is oil of the goroo leaf. It should mask your scent."

I wiped oil out of my face. "What's the point of this again?"

"Eirene's children hunt by scent. Now you will smell like oorug and be safe. You should rub it in."

CHAPTER·15

WHEN I WAS A kid in the orphanage one of my favorite things to do when I snuck out at night was to stargaze. That was back before smartphones and TVs and you could see stars all the way down to the horizon. Now, with nothing to do but wait, I lay on one of the enormous limbs of the kuu tree and looked up through the branches. Krom snored lightly, leaning against the trunk. There were two moons on this world, both were close to full which were doing a good job illuminating the jungle below. The only other light came from the camp in the distance. I could barely make out the steady rumble of a generator providing power to light up the camp like Christmas.

I could see why Krom wanted to wait until morning. The jungle was alive with howls and screeches. If I'd had my druthers I would have headed straight to the camp. I had no idea, however, what other dangerous creatures were out there. Even covered in goroo oil, I wouldn't feel good about moving through the jungle at night.

I was worried about what was happening to Holt right now. Hunters only had two motivations, hate and dust, neither of which required their victims to be alive. They were normally a shoot first kind of bunch. I couldn't figure out why this group changed strategies to capture rather than kill. Then there was the tar, that meant magic. This wasn't just a couple hunters working on their own. They were organized. Professional. That worried me as much as anything. One thing I was sure about, any harm that came to him would be on Thera. I just wanted to be home to handle it. Instead, I had all night to lay around doing nothing. Having nothing to focus on besides my thoughts wasn't making the situation any better.

I didn't even have Mila to talk to. She had gotten bored and decided to look around. The oorug were a peaceful people, stewards of Eirene. They posed no threat to us or anything higher on the food chain than a kuu seed from what I could see. It made sense to me now why Thera ordered us to come here—not that I was happy about it. These people were wholly unequipped to handle violence. The threat on this world was from the animals that lived here. Firearms alone would make conquering this entire planet a cake walk.

My thoughts turned to Naylet. She would normally have been my confidant in times like this but she was gone, too. I stuck my hand into my pocket and pulled out the postcard. It had gotten a little frayed around the edges at some point, probably in the fight with the leeree. I looked at the picture on the front and flipped it over. *Wish you were here.* I ran a finger over the words, feeling the indentations in the paper. It may sound strange, but lying there with just a postcard and the stars I felt closer to her than I had in a long time even though we'd never been farther apart.

Her handwriting looked different than it had before the attack. I couldn't put my finger on what was different about it, it was just a little off, as if it were a good forgery. They say you can tell things about a person's personality in their handwriting. If there was actually anything to that I wondered what it said about Naylet. Was she mostly the same or was it just muscle memory? That's when I made the decision. I had to find out. When I put an end to these hunters, got back to Earth, and rescued Holt, I'd track down Naylet. Maybe go for a cup of coffee.

"What's that?" Mila asked.

I tilted my head back. She walked out of the tree onto the branch past Krom.

"A postcard," I said, wondering exactly how much I wanted to tell her. "It's from Naylet."

Mila sat beside me. "Oh, she's sending you postcards?"

"A few here and there. Just to let me know where she's going kind of thing."

"Can I see it?" She asked, holding out her hand.

I hesitated before handing the card to her. She read it and with a light *hum* she passed it back.

"What?"

She shrugged. "Nothing, It's not my place."

"No. What?" I asked. "If you got something to say spit it out."

"Well, it's just . . . Have you considered she's just telling you what you want to hear?"

I gave her a squinted glare. "What do you mean?"

"You're paying all the bills for her trip, right? What happens to her if you decide to stop?"

"You think she's using me."

"I think it's a possibility. How much have you actually talked to her since she . . . got better? Does she know you well enough to actually miss you?"

I didn't have a good answer, but Naylet wasn't using me as Mila was suggesting. You can't steal what's freely given. I put no conditions on the money. There was no reason for Naylet to think she had to manipulate me into paying. I suppose it's possible she could be hedging her bets. It wasn't something the old Naylet would do, but it accentuated the question I already had. How different was she?

"Look," she said, "I'm saying you should see what's out there. Stop focusing so much on the past. Have some fun."

"I think it's going to work out in the long run," I said, shoving the postcard back in my pocket. "It sounds cheesy but I really believe we're soulmates. It's fate or something."

Mila tilted her head and pursed her lips. A pitying expression I didn't much care for. "In my experience fate is wholly unreliable."

I changed the subject. "You've been gone a while. Anything interesting out there?"

Mila shrugged. "I explored the tree. You can get almost to the very top. It's like standing on a skyscraper."

"I'll have to check that out," I lied.

"The sun will be up soon," Mila said.

I propped myself on my elbows. "And how do you know that?"

She pointed to the horizon. "You can see it."

She was right, the sky was beginning to lighten.

"What d'ya think? About one sixteenth kuu until the sun's up?"

She laughed. "Let's just say *soon*."

"Fair enough," I said. "I don't think measuring time in vegetables is going to catch on."

Mila got to her feet. "Technically, it's a fruit I think."

"Same difference."

She walked over to Krom, giving him a nudge with her paw. He snorted in surprise and opened his eyes.

He ran a hand over his face. "What's the matter?"

"The sun's coming up," I said. "It's time to go."

He grunted and got to his feet. "Almost."

"I've been thinking," Mila said. "You told us that they capture Eirene's children. How do they do that?"

"Magic. They have long sticks. When they point the sticks at something it falls asleep," Krom said.

"Do the sticks make noise?" I asked.

Krom shook his head. "Not those sticks. They do have thunder sticks but those bring death."

I could see the sorrow in his face. I wondered if some of the oorug had been killed but I wasn't going to ask.

"How many demons are there?" Mila asked.

"About fifteen," Krom said. "A big group goes out to hunt with a few staying behind with the cloud huts."

"How long will it take to get to the demons?" I asked.

"Two *kuu*," Krom said.

Mila bent over, picked up my blade, and handed it to me. "We better get started."

I could feel her hands on the blade, and I expected to be skeeved out by it but I wasn't. It didn't bother me at all and that caught me off guard. She must have realized something was up when she caught me looking at her.

"What's that face mean?" she asked.

I didn't know what it meant. She was the first person to touch my blade without making my skin crawl. I didn't know what it meant or how I felt about it.

I shook my head and looked away. "Nothing. It's just . . . nothing."

CHAPTER · 16

KROM MOVED THROUGH the jungle in a carefree stroll as if he were walking through a park. It was clear the oorug were outside the food chain, at peace with all life on this world. I didn't share his jovial attitude. Something about watching Mila getting clubbed into the jungle yesterday gave me a little more apprehension about our jungle stroll. The oil Krom threw on us smelled like a mix of coconut and sage. I was skeptical that it would actually work, but after walking for hours we weren't attacked once so it must be doing something. We saw a number of strange creatures on the way, some of which looked predatory, but none gave us more than a sniff and a passing glance.

After about four hours of walking we came to a river roughly thirty feet across. The water was deep enough that I couldn't see the bottom even though the water would have looked pristine except for some cans and plastic that had found its way into the water.

"The cloud huts are close," Krom said.

I knelt on the riverbank and splashed cool water on my face. It felt great after the trek through the jungle. "I can see their—" The oorug word for trash or litter wasn't coming to me. I thought I was just having a hard time thinking of it but then I realized the words didn't exist. The closest thing was a phrase I wasn't sure applied but it was the best I could do. "Discarded seeds."

Krom shook his head. "Those are not seeds."

"They're not," I agreed. "We'll clean it up after we get rid of the demons."

"Why don't you head back to the tree," Mila said. "This could get dangerous and . . . Let's just say your people don't seem suited to violence."

"I'm your guide," he said. "I need to protect Eirene's children from you and you from them."

"Suit yourself," I said. "I'm gonna look around a little, get a feel for things."

"I'll look around this side of the river," Mila said.

I took the form of an otter, shrinking to a fraction of my size in krasis. Since I didn't undress first, I ended up inside a pile of clothes. I felt something poking me through my shirt. Climbing out through the neck hole of my shirt I looked up to see Krom poking at my clothes with his staff. It was clear he had never seen a shifter before.

"Eirene's blessings," Krom exclaimed. "Do you have this power?" he asked, turning to Mila.

"Yes, but I'm a much scarier creature," she said, peeling off her clothes.

She took the form of a mountain lion and headed for the trees. I gave them a squeak, and walked to the river bank. The water was about eight feet deep and thirty feet across with a swift but manageable current. I headed downstream first, I felt like taking it easy after the hike. I could rest up on the way down and fight the current on the way up or get out and walk if it came to it. I hadn't gone far when I found the first sign of people. A beer can was trapped between a rock and the shore. Next, I spotted some brown plastic stuck on a root a little farther downstream. I swam to it and picked it up. It had MRE stamped across the front.

"Meal, Ready to Eat," I squeaked. "Menu one, chili with beans."

I gave the open end of the package a sniff. Any trace of the chili had been washed out of the bag; it had been here a while. Swimming farther downstream, I found a few more pieces of garbage. I didn't see any sign of the camp besides trash, and considering the direction the water was flowing, it would put camp upstream. I turned around. It took a lot more work to get back to where I had left Krom. When I got to the spot, I saw him disappearing into the jungle. He carried our clothes. I figured his plan was to stay hidden to make sure we weren't discovered. Smart.

I swam farther upstream, the litter growing more dense as I went. Around the next bend I heard people talking. I climbed out of the river and followed the voices into the jungle. I found a man standing beside a woman kneeling over something. I couldn't see the woman clearly through the vegetation. The man had a light auburn beard, a black baseball cap with a four leaf clover, and gray coveralls. He had a rifle that looked to fire darts as well as a pistol on his hip.

"Heather, I really think we should go back," the man said. "We're not supposed to be out here alone."

She fished around in her pocket for something. "Relax, Jarod, this area's clear, and address me as Professor or Professor Bennett."

"Sorry, Professor, but if that was true then the trap wouldn't have been sprung," Jarod said.

"Cleared of anything dangerous," the woman corrected. She held a recorder to her mouth. "Subject is one half meter long. Body is gray in color with a dark green tail. Four light green stripes run from head to tail, resembling a five lined skink from the southeastern United States." She stopped the recorder. "Alright, let's bag it."

Jarod hesitated. "Should I . . . I don't know. Shoot it or something?"

"I don't want the specimen more damaged than it already is," the professor said.

Jarod stood. "The trap's crushed it pretty good. It's going to suffer being put in a bag and carried back to camp like that," he said.

She stood and faced him. "You're not being paid to think or care about these creatures. I'm the one with the doctorate in zoological medicine and you're just an overpaid porter. While I'm sure your GED is really paying off, if I tell you to carry something try not to think too much and just do as you're told."

Jarod pursed his lips and nodded.

I snuck forward to get a better look. The woman wore coveralls that matched Jarod's. It must be a uniform. She had blonde hair pulled back in a ponytail. She didn't look like a professor to me. Maybe that's why she made such a point about Jarod using the title.

She was hunched over a large lizard caught in what looked like a giant rat trap. It had snapped across the lizard's hindquarters. I was sure the trap had broken the animal's back and crushed its organs. It would die for sure if I didn't help. I wasn't going to let them take the animal back to their camp in any condition. I'd wait for them to open the trap, then I could move in, heal it, and deal with these humans. Not necessarily in that order. I backed away slowly, changed to krasis, and drew my blade. When Jarod opened the trap, I charged forward. He stood up with a writhing lizard in one hand just as I got to him. I ran my sword through his stomach and threw a shoulder into his chest. The impact made him fly off into the brush, dropping the lizard.

I knelt, holding a hand over the injured lizard and channeled healing energy into it. In a few seconds it fully recovered. A gunshot rang out. The bullet whizzed just to my right. The lizard took off into the jungle and I dove to my left. The second shot missed high as I scurried on all fours into the bushes. The gun kept firing and I kept moving, getting glimpses of the professor through the leaves. She didn't seem to be very comfortable with a pistol. She wasn't holding it correctly, exaggerating the recoil. She was more throwing bullets in my direction than shooting at me. When I got as close as I could, I charged her. I came out of the brush swinging my blade at the hand holding the gun. The blade cut through cleanly, sending a severed hand and pistol falling to the ground. I changed the momentum of the blade, bringing it low to hit her legs. I cut through one and nicked the other. She fell forward with a gasp. I drove the blade into her back and twisted it to finish her off.

It happened so fast I didn't realize what had happened until it was over. I hadn't intended to kill both of them. I wanted one alive for questioning. Krom was a fine guide but didn't understand the technology well enough to be of much help. I needed to know exactly what I was up against. I wiped my blade on the professor's shirt to clean off the blood.

Something crashed through the brush, headed in my direction. I turned to face the noise and flexed my hand around the handle of my blade, ready for whatever was about to arrive.

Mila exploded through the vegetation, skidding to a stop in front of me. "You alright? I heard the shooting."

I relaxed the grip on my blade. "Nothing I couldn't handle."

"Looks like I missed all the fun," Mila said, looking at the professor's body.

A wheezing sound drifted from the bushes. I pulled branches aside to discover Jarod wasn't dead after all. He had one hand on his belly where I had run him through. Blood trickled from his mouth. His chest heaved irregularly. He didn't have long, without help he would die. I knelt over him, tossed his pistol away, and put a hand over his wound, channeling energy into him.

"Aren't we here to stop them?" Mila asked.

I nodded. "We need information on the camp. You're not scared are ya?"

"We can always kill him later I guess."

His breathing eased as the energy healed his injuries. When the energy flowed over him I took my hand back. He opened his eyes and jumped with surprise. He looked over at the professor's body, then to his rifle lying a few feet away, then back to me.

"We need your help. You can come with us and live, or I'll make it as quick and painless as I can," I said, placing my blade against his neck. "Your call."

CHAPTER·17

"WHY DID YOU bring a demon here?" Krom asked. "I thought you were supposed to get rid of them."

"We will get rid of him and all the others," I said. "I need information and he's going to give it to me."

Jarod sat against a tree. Of course, he couldn't understand a word of what we were saying and I liked it that way. He sat perfectly still. It was probably because Mila was standing over him, giving him the stink eye. We hadn't said more than a few words to him since we captured him. I'm sure he was wrestling with the uncertainty of the situation. I didn't care.

Krom crossed his arms. "I don't see why the demon would help."

I gave him a smile. "You don't understand the demons like I do. Did you forget, I'm a demon, too. Oh, since I need him alive, can you douse him with the goroo oil?"

Krom pulled a gourd from his belt and scowled as he unceremoniously doused Jarod. "I feel I should voice my displeasure. This is against our mission and a waste of oil."

Jarod jumped when the first shot of oil hit his face. "What the hell? This an exorcism or something?"

"It'll keep animals from biting your face off," I said. "You might want to rub it in."

He hesitated at first but must have figured it was worth a shot because he started rubbing the oil into his hair and skin. "I'll do it but I won't like it."

"Nobody cares what you like," Mila said.

When Krom had finished, he backed away from Jarod, pulled out some kuu pieces, and ate. With both of my companions thoroughly displeased, I could turn my attention back to the mission.

I sat beside Jarod. "Let's get down to it."

"How is it you speak my language?" Jarod asked.

"Because I'm from Earth, you idiot," I said. "Now it's your turn to answer some questions. You can start with who you work for."

"Doctor Tsukimora," he said.

"Details."

"I really don't know much. I was barely scraping by as a truck driver when I found out about this job. It was a friend of a friend kinda thing. It sounded good, too good to be honest, but I have a daughter to take care of so I was open to it." Jarod held out his right arm. There was a tattoo that said HAILEY in large letters with a date underneath. I did some rough math in my head, his daughter would be about six years old. "It seemed a little strange to be honest, but the pay was too good to pass up. Three months away would make me more than I could make five years driving a truck so I signed up. Things got weird after that. I've only met doctor Tsukimora once when I was hired and seen him in passing a couple times."

"What's he look like?" Mila asked.

Jarod waggled his head a little to shake recollection free. "Short hair, he's always wearing suits, he's . . . Just a guy. He looks like a Wall Street type."

"Where's this facility at?" I asked.

"I really don't know exactly. Northwest Georgia somewhere. There's a giant old house by a river. It's not really a house anymore though. They're powering the place with hydropower from the river. The house itself is normal enough but there's a whole underground complex they added on underneath. I don't have access to most of it."

That sounded like the house Mila and I had been staking out. Further proof that if Thera had just let me do my job this would all have been over with already. It was frustrating to say the least.

"What about the team here?" I asked. "Tell me everything you know."

"There were twenty-five of us when we got here. Setting up camp was hell. We lost six the first day before we could get the fence set up. The animals here . . . hey, they're no joke. Our mission was to capture them alive and get them ready to take back to Earth. Don't ask me what for. The first time they left camp to try and catch something they lost another three. They changed tactics. Now, if it looks dangerous, they shoot first. The traps turned out to be more reliable so they focused on those. They set the traps and wait in camp until the sensors indicate one has been triggered. Then they go out and see what they caught."

"You said there's a fence?"

Jerod nodded. "You've seen *Jurassic Park*? You know those big electric fences they keep around the dino pens? It's like that."

Mila asked, "How's it powered?"

"Solar and batteries with a generator backup," he said. "There's a gate that's electrified that has to be shut off before it's opened or closed."

"What kind of contact is there with Earth?" I asked.

"None. They're supposed to open a portal to Earth in two days to move the things we catch. They do it on a schedule. We are supposed to be able to open one for an emergency but that won't happen now."

"Why's that?"

"You killed the person who knew how to do it. There's an instruction manual but most of the people left . . . Let's just say I don't feel good about our chances of relying on them to get home."

"Have you sent any animals to Earth already?" Mila asked.

"We sent six or seven a couple days ago. They were moved into pens right on the other side of the portal."

Mila crossed her arms. "Which is it, six or seven?"

Jarod shrugged. "My job is equipment, not livestock."

I nodded. "So here's where we're at. We were sent here to put an end to your expedition. We're going to do that first. Then we're going to get all the animals you stole back. I just have one more question for you . . . What are you willing to do to see Hailey again?"

Jarod looked away from me into the jungle and pursed his lips. "All we've got is each other. I'm here so she can have a better life than I did. I'll do whatever it takes."

"I like you, Jarod. I'm not going to lie, I can't guarantee you'll make it but I am your best chance. I can open a portal to Earth. We can help each other get home."

"I'm not stupid," he said. "You're not going to just let me go."

I knelt before him. "On this world, you're right, but on Earth you're just another guy."

Jarod nodded. "What choice do I have really?"

"What choice do you have," I agreed.

"A word," Mila said.

We walked away as not to be overheard, which turned out to be unnecessary.

"What are you doing?" she said in Oorug.

"What do you mean?"

"Well, you got this guy for information and now you're planning to take him back to Earth? Just let him go?"

"He could be useful, and if he helps us are we supposed to just turn on him?"

"We aren't turning on anyone," she said, crossing her arms. "He's one of the bad guys, remember?"

"He seems like a normal guy to me. It could be anybody sitting there. It just happened to be Jarod this time."

Mila furrowed her brow. "Where's your head at?"

"Right here, getting this job done as quick as possible so we can get home."

CHAPTER·18

THE TREES AND brush had been cleared thirty feet around the camp, leaving vegetation in place to rot. It served its purpose of providing a clear view of the surrounding area. Jarod was right when he said it was something out of *Jurassic Park*. The camp had cables running the perimeter, an enormous electric fence. The wires appeared to be about two feet apart, enough for Mila and me to slide under safely. The only clear path inside was the gate. A guard tower was erected by a front gate. In the tower, a single person armed with a rifle watched the jungle around the camp. I wouldn't want to try to charge into that camp. The electric fence aside, I'd bet dollars to doughnuts the shooting would start before we made it halfway across the clearing. Even without the camp's security, I didn't want to attack fifteen armed people. I was good, Mila would say she's better, but that's a lotta guns. The first thing to do was split them up.

"Jarod, how long does it take them to get to the farthest trap from camp?" I asked.

"Between loading the vehicles and drive time, about thirty minutes," he said. "They found some game trails they've been using as roads. Its about a mile up river."

I cocked my head to the side. "By upriver you mean the trap is beside the water?"

"Yeah, they found a place where the trail crosses the river. It's a natural bottleneck so a great place for a trap."

"That'll do." I mumbled to myself.

"You're planning a jungle ambush then?" he asked.

"No, I'm going to draw them out. When they're gone you'll kill the power to the fence and Mila and I'll clear the camp."

Jarod shifted uncomfortably. "How am I going to do that from out here?"

"Obviously you're not," I said. "When they leave, you walk up to the front gate and get them to let you in. As soon as you can you turn off the power to the fence. We'll handle the rest."

I looked over at Mila. She was sitting with Krom listening to our conversation. I could tell she was as excited about the plan as Jarod was.

Jarod was talking but I hadn't been listening. ". . . and where do I tell them I've been this whole time?"

"You have an hour to figure it out. Just remember, the best lies have a touch of truth to them." I went and sat beside Mila leaving Jarod out of earshot.

"You don't think we should have come up with a plan together?" she asked.

I shot her a smile. "That's not the plan. When he get's their attention focused on the gate we'll go in under the fence around back. Unless you have a better idea?"

"Why not just tell him that?"

"Let's call it plan B. If we can't get in then maybe he can kill the power and we have another shot. That way I don't have to go over what he should do in every scenario."

She crossed her arms. "What if they catch him?"

"What do you care? You're team 'kill Jarod' remember? He's not growing on you is he?"

"No," she scoffed. "Let's just get this done."

I took off my clothes and hung my shirt on a stick on the riverbank. I slipped out through the jungle alone and found the trail they had been using. The tires had ripped up the ground leaving a trail that was impossible to miss. I followed it ignoring any path that looked like it would take me away from the river. Eventually I found the trap just off the side of the trail by the riverbank. It wasn't complicated, just a bear trap with a transmitter. I found a branch sturdy enough to do the job. Once I tripped it the clock started ticking. I was sure I could make it back before they did but I needed to get there with enough time to spare. I knew from experience that I could swim about nine miles an hour. It should take me about six minutes to swim it. That was the best case scenario. Rivers weren't straight.

I stabbed the branch into the trap. Its jaws snapped shut biting into the wood. I ran for the river. I jumped from the bank in krasis and made the change in mid air hitting the water as an otter. I wove my way around the rock and branches swimming as fast as I could downstream following the twists and turns of the river. I was aware of the occasional creature in the water. Vibrations in my whiskers gave away their position. I didn't know if they were a threat or not, I didn't stop to check. I swam until I saw my shirt on the bank and got out hoping I had some time to catch my breath. I changed to krasis and got dressed. Mila, Krom, and Jarod were right where I left them watching as the camp, huddled on the edge of the clearing.

"How're we looking?" I asked.

They should be leaving any minute now," Jarod said.

I sat beside Mila to wait.

"Have any trouble?" she asked.

I shook my head. "Nah, it was a nice swim."

The gates swung open. Two vehicles loaded with people and equipment rolled out. I counted the people on the vehicles as they passed. I wasn't sure on the exact number—it was either nine or ten—leaving four or five minding the camp. That should be easy enough to deal with.

"You clear on what to do?" I asked.

"I got it," Jarod said. "Relax."

Jarod backed away slowly, disappearing into the jungle.

Mila had a sour look on her face. I was pretty sure I knew what she was going to say. "What? What's the face?"

"I've said it before," she said without taking her eyes off the camp. "It's a bad idea to trust this guy. I don't think this is going to work out the way you think."

"I agree with Mila. We can't trust a demon," Krom butted in.

"We're demons, remember?" I said.

"You're not like those though," he said with a flick of his fingers in the direction of the camp.

"Look, if he believes that we are going to kill everyone before the portal opens again then he'll help us."

"But if he thinks his chances are better with them then he'll tell them all about us and this'll get a lot harder," Mila said.

I shook my head. "Nah, then we'll just go to plan C."

Mila and Krom both looked at me and said in unison, "What's plan C?"

"In five minutes we're going to know where Jarod's loyalty lies. If things don't come up in our favor we go after the group that went to check the trap. It will be harder but doable," I said. "Then we use the cars to crash through the gate and finish off the camp."

Mila nodded slowly, considering. "Alright, that could work."

"Will you be able to control their animals?" Krom asked. "Those *cars* look like nasty beasts."

I considered how to explain machines to him. There wasn't vocabulary to do it justice in the oorug language. "It's false life," I said. "They don't have a mind of their own and only do what someone tells them."

He looked confused but let it go.

Jarod ran out of the jungle, looking panicked. Shouting rose from the camp.

He made it to the gate and bent forward resting his hands on his knees. "Let me in," he wheezed.

"We thought you were dead," the man in the tower shouted. "We found the professor out there cut to pieces. What the hell happened?"

Jarod sounded panicky. "Damn it, Arvidson, there's something after me. Open the fucking gate!"

Jarod looked around the jungle nervously while they shut off the fence and swung the gate open. I had to give it to him, he was a good actor—*if* he was acting.

"You ready?" Mila asked.

"Yep," I said, "Let's do it."

We worked our way around to the backside of the camp opposite the tower. Mila and I changed into our animal forms. All Jarod had to do was keep the guards distracted as we made our approach. It shouldn't be hard as they all would want to hear about what happened to him.

While the trees they cut down made for open viewing, they also gave us a way to sneak up to the camp. We worked our way through the debris, staying low to avoid detection. When we got to the wire I could hear the light buzz of power running through it. I pressed my body against the dirt and slid forward until I was clear. Mila followed my lead. When we had both made it through safely we changed to krasis.

A tent gave us concealment and a chance to devise a plan of attack. I peeked around the edge of the tent. Jarod stood with four people with their backs to us; Arvidson in the tower split his attention between what was going on inside the camp and his responsibility to watch outside.

"When the guy in the tower looks away we'll charge," I whispered. "I'll go for the tower."

I drew my blade. I looked around the tent again. Arvidson was watching the discussion. As soon as he turned away I charged. I ran to the left of the group toward the tower. They must have heard our footsteps thumping on the ground because they turned just before we got to them.

Panic erupted in the group and they fumbled with weapons. I gave the one closest to me a blade in the gut. I didn't stop running. Arvidson turned to see me charging the tower. He raised his rifle and fired and I jumped to the left. The bullets slammed into the ground. I threw my blade at him. He used his rifle as a shield, deflecting it.

I leapt onto the ladder, got my footing, and jumped to the platform, landing with my arms on the edge and feet dangling off. It only had enough space for one person to stand comfortably. I steadied myself with a foot on the ladder. He brought the rifle to bear. I grabbed the barrel and shoved it to the side. He fired again. The noise turned my hearing into little more than a loud ringing. I pulled the rifle free and tossed it off the tower.

He wasn't ready to lay down and die just yet. He started kicking me in the head. I climbed onto the platform. I gave him a shot to the gut that stunned him. I got a handful of shirt with one hand and a leg with the other. I tossed him onto the electric fence. Sparks erupted. He landed with a thud and didn't move.

I looked back to see Mila, claws buried deep in a man's throat. A quick tug and he collapsed, holding the gaping wound while his life slipped away. Jarod stayed out of the fight.

"You alright?" I called down.

Mila nodded. "Took one in the arm. I've had worse."

Jarod stepped forward. "We need to hurry. They'll be back soon."

CHAPTER·19

WE SABOTAGED THE generator and destroyed the batteries. I didn't want the fence up and running when we came back to finish the job. Krom and Jarod helped Mila and me carry the bodies and all the ammunition we could find into the jungle. We moved out of sight and waited by the equipment we had stolen.

While we waited, Jarod looked through the crates. "Maybe we should use some of this, it could come in handy."

"Keepers don't use guns all that much," Mila said, flashing the razor sharp claws on the ends of her fingers. "We have weapons built in."

"What the hell's a Keeper?" Jarod asked.

I kept my eyes on the camp when I answered. "Don't worry about it."

"I'm going to grab some food and stuff," Jarod said.

It hadn't occurred to me that he hadn't eaten since we captured him. He was probably starving. I gave him a dismissive wave.

We only had a few minutes to spare before I heard the rumble of engines.

The two vehicles stopped in front of the open gate, unsure what had happened. I watched them drive forward with their guns pointing in all directions, ready for anything. Anything wouldn't be coming for them for a bit though.

A couple hours more and the sun went down, shrouding the jungle in darkness. It was different being in the jungle at night. The noises we heard from the top of the kuu tree were now surrounding us and we didn't have the luxury of elevation.

"Are you sure it's safe out here?" Jarod asked, taking the last bite of a power bar he had looted from the supplies.

He had filled up a knapsack and was smart enough to put the wrapper back into it when he was finished.

"He's asking if it's safe," Mila translated to Krom.

Krom shrugged. It may not be safe but this had gone on long enough. We were ending this tonight. I had things to tend to at home.

We waited and watched. We had all night. Without power the camp was relying on flashlights and a few lanterns positioned by the gate so they could see a threat coming. They must have decided to take shifts rather than keep everyone up until the portal was opened. After a few hours I heard snoring.

"Ready?" Mila asked.

"It's now or never," I replied. "The two of you stay here, we'll be back."

Again we took animal forms and worked our way to the edge of the fence. We slipped under the now dead wires and changed to krasis behind some crates behind the tents. Mila and I swapped some hand gestures to work out that she would take the right tent and I would take the left one.

I peeked inside. There were ten cots set up in two neat rows. Most were empty, a few had equipment stowed on them. I counted six people sleeping or at least laying down. A couple snored lightly, one was gobbling air like a chainsaw. They all either had guns draped across their chest or propped beside their cots. With so many in here I doubted there was anyone in Mila's tent.

I moved up to the closest cot and looked down at the man sleeping there. I realized I hadn't thought through how I was actually going to dispatch them without waking anyone up or alerting the guards. I thought about holding him down and cutting his throat. This wasn't some fiction novel, it was the real world. When you cut a throat they do die quickly but not immediately the way you see in the movies. They have ten or fifteen seconds to fight for life. In my experience, they fight hard. That meant thrashing and gurgling as they choked on their blood before they blacked out.

I may be able to get through a couple of them before they woke someone up but there was no way to get through all six without someone figuring out something was up. On the other hand, I couldn't just stand there all night. I got tired of thinking and worrying. Instead of trying to be quiet, I moved to the front of the tent and drew my blade.

I struck the first cot and moved toward the back, taking one swing to each cot as I went. I was on the third before the first two start making noise. The last one woke up and managed to prop himself up on his elbows before he got his.

I went out the back of the tent and ducked behind a crate. Mila was waiting there for me.

"What the hell was that?" she whispered. "I thought you were going to do it quietly."

"What about me makes you think I'm a ninja?" I jerked my head at the other tent. "Have any trouble?"

"Empty."

"Let's split up," I whispered. "I'll take this way."

"Jesus, they're all dead!" Someone shouted from inside the tent.

There wasn't much light so I wasn't worried about being silhouetted against the canvas. What I hadn't counted on was how trashy the camp was. I suppose I shouldn't be surprised considering how much garbage was in the river. I had unwittingly stumbled into the dump. Clanking from cans and swooshing from MRE bags gave away my position.

"There's something back here!" The man shouted before spraying rounds through the tent in my direction.

"Damn it, cease fire!" Another man shouted. "We don't have rounds to waste. Don't shoot until you have a clear shot."

"It's right there, behind the tent," the first man said.

Another man barked an order: "Get back behind the barricade!"

Barricade . . . I didn't like the sound of that. I'd rather get this guy before he was under cover. I stepped around the trash as quietly as I could and moved up beside the tent. I peeked around the side to see the vehicles pulled beside each other with the gaps between them blocked with crates and equipment. The one who had shot at me was backing away from the front of the tent. He was only about eight feet away but hadn't spotted me. After a few steps he turned to run.

I charged, grabbing him by the back of the neck and driving my blade into his back. I guess they weren't concerned about their comrade, or maybe they figured he was already a goner, because a fraction of a second after I stepped out they opened fire.

It turns out people make inconsistent shields. Unless the bullets hit bone they go right through and sometimes the bone doesn't stop them either. The bullets tore through the man's body as I pulled him back to the tent. Some were stopped when they hit my blade but others made it through. Pain shot through my body.

I jumped into the tent, pulling the man in with me. We fell to the ground inside with a thud. I pushed him off of me. He'd gotten the worst of it and was already dead. As soon as we disappeared through the tent flaps the shooting stopped. I could see the flashlights bathing the front of the tent as they searched for any sign of what happened to me. I'd been shot in my left arm, both legs, and more to the body than I cared to count. I coughed up some blood and I knew one of my lungs was hit. It was hard to breathe, and I hurt all over. I hoped I had a few minutes to rest. I laid down in the dirt and closed my eyes. Warmth tingled as my body began to push out the bullets and repair the damage.

"The fuck was that?' someone said from the direction of the lights.

Someone else chimed in. "You think we got it?"

"Nothing could've lived through that," the first one replied.

I lay still and healed. I figured if I didn't move then maybe they would come see if they got me. That would give Mila an opportunity to attack.

Fortunately, or unfortunately depending how you look at it, they stayed behind cover. It gave me plenty of time to heal but it meant we would have to go to them. Whoever went first wasn't going to make it, maybe neither one would. We would heal of course but it would hurt. Not exactly something to volunteer for. What other option did we have though? Stay behind cover for the next day and hope they all fell asleep or the jungle killed them? I had the time to wait but Holt didn't. I needed to find Mila.

When my body had healed enough, I stayed low and crawled out the back. I found Mila sitting behind the other tent. She was laid back in a casual pose, looking as if she was at a park on a Sunday afternoon rather than in an alien world full of things that wanted to kill us.

I sat beside her. "Got any bright ideas?"

"I think our best bet is to wait them out."

I was afraid she would say that. "We don't have time to wait."

"Then we need some way to stop bullets," Mila said.

"Maybe we could get the generator and use it as a shield?"

Rustling on the other side of the electric fence got our attention. Mila crouched, going from *a day at the park* to *what's about to jump out and eat my face*. Jarod crawled under the fence, dragging a knapsack behind him.

"What the hell are you doing here?" I asked.

He looked confused. "What? I thought we were doing this?"

"I told you to wait."

"No, you said a bunch of stuff in whatever the hell language that is and then left."

I guess we'd forgotten to switch to English. He'd just have to crawl back. We didn't have time to babysit in the middle of a gun fight.

"What's going on?" he asked.

"They're holed up behind the cars. Can't get to them," Mila said.

Jarod fished around in the knapsack and pulled out a grenade. "Will this help?"

I was a little dumbstruck. "Where'd you get that?"

"From the supplies," he said innocently.

"I thought you were getting food," I said.

Jarod nodded. "Food and stuff. Grenades are in the 'and stuff' category."

"That'll work," Mila said. "Obie and I will move to the sides. Give us thirty seconds to get in position and throw it. Just don't miss."

"I have two," he said, pulling out a second grenade. "Should I use both?"

"I was skeptical at first but you're really growing on me," Mila said with a smile. "As a person."

"Okay, whatever," I said. "Thirty seconds and throw them both."

I counted in my head as I got into position. I had counted to twenty-seven when I heard metal on metal of a grenade hitting a car followed a second later by a *thunk* of a grenade on dirt. I couldn't tell exactly where they had landed but I wasn't going to step out to look.

After the first explosion the screaming started. I saw people run from behind cover. I took off after them. The second grenade exploded. It turns out that grenade had landed on my side of the car. The two people that had come out had taken the brunt of the blast but I still caught a lot of shrapnel.

I fell, getting a face fill of dirt. Everything was quiet for a second before a shadow crossed my vision. I could feel someone standing over me. I rolled over and opened my eyes expecting Mila but found a stranger instead. He pointed his rifle at me, I closed my eyes tight as gunfire erupted. I expected to black out almost immediately. Instead, I didn't feel anything but warm blood sprinkling onto my fur and whiskers. I opened my eyes to see a hole in the man's chest. He collapsed on top of me. Mila stood behind him with a shotgun.

CHAPTER·20

"HAS THE DEMON not served its purpose?" Krom asked. "Should he not be eliminated?"

I sighed. "I still need his help to dismantle the demon structures. The things here are still dangerous. I need to get them back to our world."

Krom sat and crossed his legs. "Don't expect me to like it."

Jarod was working on taking down the camp but must have noticed Krom's tone and body language. "What's his problem?"

I smiled. "He thinks we should kill you."

Jarod paused, not finding the humor in it, and went about his task.

We found garbage bags in the camp's equipment, not that they appeared to know how to use them. I spent hours pulling litter out of the river. It was actually the most fun I'd had since I'd gotten here. I hauled the trash back to camp. Jarod and Mila had made good progress on packing up the camp. I helped dismantle the electric fence and put all the equipment and bodies in a big pile.

When we had everything ready, I used a clawed finger to draw a circle in the dirt. It was the same one I had scratched into the dash of my truck when we followed the Queen through the portal to the demon world. I would subconsciously trace my finger over it sometimes when being taxied around by Holt. The end result was that I could draw it blindfolded with both hands tied behind my back. The incantation had been harder to memorize but with a little practice I'd managed it. I decided I never wanted to be in the situation again where I was trapped on another world with no way to get home. Call it off-world insurance.

With two of the three components settled, all I needed was some dust to power it. Of course, I didn't have any dust. Even if there wasn't a shortage back home, I wasn't given time to get anything before Thera forced me through.

"Eirene, I need your help," I said to the jungle.

She appeared beside me.

"I've taken care of the demons. I need to borrow energy to open a portal to get rid of the bodies and equipment," I said.

She looked at Jarod sitting by the pile of gear. "You didn't get rid of them all."

"I need him to get your children back," I said. "I assumed that was the most important thing."

"When will my children return?"

"They should be back in . . . two kuu."

"Very well. You already have the power you need. Channel the energy into your circle when you're ready." She disappeared.

I knelt in front of the circle. I wasn't exactly sure how this was going to work. I'd just *heal* the circle? I held a hand out over it and let the energy flow. The circle began to glow with a deep blue light. I whispered the incantation and a portal opened. It started as a speck of light and grew to roughly eight feet in diameter. I could see the inside of the barn behind my house, the location I had been focusing on.

"Alright, move everything through," I said.

Jarod looked at the giant pile in front of us. "Are you going to help?"

"I have to keep the portal open," I said. "Hurry up."

I was hoping I could get a cell signal with the portal open. I hadn't looked at my phone since we left Earth. I pulled it out of my pocket to find it busted. It looked black and charred, as if it had short circuited or something. I guess the electricity Thera had hit me with had fried it. I tossed it through the portal with the growing pile of equipment. It took the three of them about thirty-five minutes to move the gear and bodies through and dump them into a big pile. They came back through the portal. Jarod picked up the last duffle bag of gear and tossed it through. I stopped channeling the energy and the portal slammed shut.

"What the hell?" Jarod shouted. "I thought we were going home?"

"We are but not yet," Mila said. "We have to get the animals back that your team took."

Jarod sighed. "Fine. Do your little magic trick and let's get it done."

I shook my head. "I can't do that. I've never been to the place before. You have to concentrate on the place you want to go. I can get us close, but you said they open the portal from where the animals are kept. So we wait for them."

The area had been quiet since the animals fled the humans, but now they started to return. The jungle slowly but surely came alive around us. I was confident by this time tomorrow everything would be back to normal for Eirene. I didn't *think* the animals would pose any threat to us at this point, but I was grateful for the goroo oil and the cleared trees supplying us with a buffer.

Most of the time the work I do seems temporary. Yes, I may stop some evil and save some lives but there's always something around the corner to start over with. I looked forward to the day humans got some sense and demons lost interest in our world, not that I believed I'd still be around to see it.

Jarod had been stewing in the now vacant campsite for close to twenty minutes before he spoke. "Why haven't you killed me already? What are you waiting for?"

Mila chuckled. "He's so dramatic."

"How long until your people open the portal?" I asked.

"That's it then? You'll kill me when the portal opens?"

I sighed. "If I intended to kill you, I'd have done it already. How long?"

Jarod fidgeted uncomfortably and looked at his watch. "If they're on schedule, six minutes."

"Here's what's gonna happen. When the portal opens, you're gonna go through in front of me. Mila and I are gonna kill everybody there, except for you, and send the missing animals back through. If we get separated, make your way southeast to Morrison Salvage in Dawsonville. Tell them that Obie sent you and they will keep you safe until I get there. Then I'll take you home."

"Can't I just take a bus?" Jarod asked.

"You can do whatever you want," Mila said. "Out of those choices, listening is probably the smartest."

I stood and shook out my arms and legs. "After I get the animals back, I'm getting a team together and clearing the house. Until I take those bastards out you need to stay out of sight. I don't want you getting caught in the middle."

"Alright, fair enough," Jarod said.

"How long?"

Jarod looked at his watch. "Two minutes."

The portal opened exactly on time. I took Jarod by the back of his collar and as soon as the portal was large enough pushed him through in front of me with Mila right on our tail. We came out into a barn with a number of stalls and cages. The man who had opened the portal stood in front of us. I pushed Jarod to the side and with a single strike cut the man down. With the portal's power severed it slammed shut behind us. There were two other men in the barn. They were wholly unprepared for an attack.

One man ran for the door. I was on him in an instant. I slammed into him, the momentum of my charge sandwiching him between a beam and my body. He let out a wheeze as the air was pushed from his lungs. I bit into his neck. Blood poured into my mouth. Struggling to breathe, he began to gurgle while blood filled his lungs. I threw him to the ground. The other man stuck a long cattle prod into my belly and pulled the trigger. Pain exploded through my abdomen. I grabbed the rod and pulled it out of my stomach. The man let go and turned to run out a side door. I threw my blade at his back.

I'd like to tell you it spun through the air and embedded itself deep between his shoulders, but the truth is, I was still new to blade throwing. It spun and it hit him, but didn't stick. He screamed and fell. The blade bounced off to the left. Blood soaked through his shirt. He started to get up. I pinned him to the ground with a foot on his back. He squirmed from the pain of having my paw pressed into his fresh wound. I gave his head a couple stomps. He didn't move anymore.

I rubbed the still tingling spot on my belly where the cattle prod had got me. "You couldn't have helped?" I said to Mila.

"There were only two." She shrugged. "You had it handled."

I suddenly felt a nauseous anxiety, the feeling I got when someone touched my blade. I turned to see Jarod had picked it up.

"We still have a deal, right?" he asked. "You won't kill me?"

"We have a deal but pulling a weapon on me is breach of contract."

Looking uncertain he turned the weapon around to hold it by the blade. He held the handle out to me. I exhaled a heavy breath as the uneasy feeling subsided. I put the blade back in its sheath and gave the barn a quick once over. The cages looked to be about half full with an assortment of Eirene's children. I didn't recognize any of them. It occurred to me I hadn't actually seen much wildlife during my stay with Eirene.

I found the keys on the body of the man that had opened the portal. "Is this doctor Tsukimora?"

"No," Jarod said. "That's Dean, or was Dean, I guess. Doctor Tsukimora rarely leaves the house."

"I'm going to make sure no one's coming."

I peeked out the main door at the house. It was definitely the same house Mila and I had been looking at when I was forced though the portal. I saw a figure on the front porch. I thought I was seeing things are first. It was Torch. Hank's youngest son was standing on the porch by the front door, appearing to be standing guard. He was wearing jeans and a tee shirt with his Tortured Occult kutte.

I motioned Jarod over. "What do you know about that guy?"

"Nothing much," Jarod said. "He's a machine. Never smiles and is always working. I don't think he sleeps."

"Start opening the cages," I said, tossing the keys to Jarod. "Thera, I have Eirene's children. They're ready to go back."

Thera appeared on the far side of the barn. A portal opened beside her with Eirene standing on the other side. We began to shepherd the animals out of the pens and through the portal. They were hesitant at first but as soon as they saw their home world they moved with a purpose.

"Some are missing," Eirene said from the other side of the portal.

"They aren't here. I'll keep looking," I said.

Thera disappeared and the portal closed.

"Who were you talking to?" Jarod asked.

"Don't worry about it," I said. "Listen, I appreciate your help. You've held up your end of the deal and I'll hold up mine. I need to check something. Go with Mila, I'll catch up."

"Hopefully, my car's still close by," Mila said.

If I hadn't spotted Torch, I would call this a job well done and move on to hunting down Holt and doctor Tsukimora. Yes, there were some missing animals, but if they weren't in the pens, they were most likely already victims of whatever they were brought here for. We would find answers in the house.

Hank had been looking for Torch for months. If I had a chance to bring him home, I had to take it. Still, it didn't look as if he was a prisoner. There were a lot of unanswered questions, lucky for me the person with all the answers was in front of me. I slid the door open a little more to get a view of the area. It looked clear but the people I killed would be missed soon. I had a short window to act before the alarm was raised. I moved across the yard. Torch saw me coming and took a few steps toward me. He had a blank expression. I didn't see any indication that he recognized me.

"Torch, we've been looking for you everywhere," I said. "We gotta go."

Torch jumped off the porch. I could feel the shockwave run through the earth when he landed. His feet sank into the earth a couple inches. The ground wasn't particularly soft, so the only conclusion was that he was heavy . . . *too* heavy. He lunged for me. I avoided him. He was slower than normal; we'd sparred many times over the years so I knew his moves. He threw punches. I maneuvered, easily avoiding his strikes.

"Snap out of it," I said. "Something's happened to you. Let me help."

I ducked a punch that contacted the railing of the porch steps. The railing ripped off the stairs. Everyone in the house must have heard it. A few figures appeared in the windows. Torch took advantage of my momentary distraction. He grabbed me by the throat, lifting me off the ground. I tried to pry his hand open but I couldn't budge it. It didn't feel normal. It was cold and there wasn't any of the normal give of flesh to it.

I punched a pressure point behind his elbow. It felt like I was punching stone. Pain shot through my hand. He started squeezing my throat. I grabbed my blade from its sheath and stabbed him in the chest. The blade barely bit in and there wasn't any blood. I began to gag from the pressure. I had to get loose soon or I wouldn't get free at all. I started to panic. I brought the blade down on his head, chest, and shoulders. It cut through his clothes but didn't seem to hurt him at all. My vision started to go dark around the edges. I was suddenly free, landing awkwardly on my back.

I looked up to see a severed arm flopping down the bank to the river. Torch began to disintegrate in front of me, crumbling into a pile of earth. I got to my knees gasping for breath. Three dark figures came around the side of the house. They weren't human. They looked like large cats, tigers or panthers, made of tar. They sort of oozed as they moved. These must have been what took Holt. I had no intention of letting them get me too. I grabbed Torch's kutte out of the dirt and ran for the river. The tar monsters charged after me. I dove into the water, disappearing under the surface.

CHAPTER · 21

I SURFACED. THE tar cats prowled back and forth along the water's edge. It didn't look as if they would come in and that was fine with me. I sheathed my blade and put on Torch's kutte to free my hands to swim. Upriver, the old bridge was three hundred yards away. I could try to flag down a car. I'd have to figure out how to lose the tar cats before I could get out of the water. Downstream, the water poured over the dam that ran parallel to the house. Below that the river disappeared into the woods.

Footsteps and shouting from the house told me I was out of time to decide. Two men with rifles ran out onto the top floor balcony. I dove underwater and swam downstream. The two men opened fire. The water was only five or six feet deep but it was enough to protect me from the bullets. Their supersonic rounds broke up on contact with the water, only penetrating a few inches. I jumped over the dam and pressed my back against the natural stone wall. The water pouring over the dam left me with enough room to keep my head out of the water between the wall and the wave.

Dark figures moved on the bank. I was out manned here, I'd need to get some backup. I didn't know if they knew where I was. If not, I didn't want to give my position away. I took a deep breath and slid into the water below the wave. This didn't go as smoothly as I'd hoped. The water churned there in a circle pulling everything back toward the damn. After getting tossed around in it I was able to swim down below the current and escape.

I could hold my breath for close to ten minutes. I swam, weaving my way through the rocks lining the river bottom. When I felt the need for air, I came up slowly, just sticking my nose out of the water. I took a few breaths, inhaled deeply, and slipped under the surface leaving barely a ripple on the surface.

I swam as far as I could for another breath. When my air gave out, I stuck my head out of the water for a look around. All I heard was the flow of the water and the rhythmic chirp of cicadas. It looked clear but I wasn't ready to get out of the water just yet. It occurred to me Mila's friend Jessie lived just off the river. I could keep swimming downstream until I found the house. Maybe I could lay low there until Mila could get me. Hopefully she and Jarod had gotten away.

I swam several miles before I saw lights off the house in the distance. I came up behind the house through the woods. The flicker of a television came through the windows. I crept up slowly, pausing every so often to listen for the tar monsters. Peeking in, I saw Jessie on a sofa, wrapped in a blanket, eating popcorn. In her human form, she was young and thin with blonde hair. Oreo lay on the couch beside her. The little dog lifted its head and started barking in my direction. I ducked to avoid being seen. I needed her help and being caught peeking in her windows wasn't the way to get it.

I went around to the front of the house. If I were lucky Mila would have stopped here first. A blue sedan was in the carport, but no sign of Mila. I absent mindedly reached for my phone only to remember it wasn't in my pocket. Oreo was still losing her mind inside the house. Jessie would be looking out any second to see what was responsible for the ruckus.

As if on cue the door opened and Oreo came bounding out, barking viciously. If she was a bigger dog I might have been worried, as it was, she wasn't a threat.

Jessie looked annoyed. "You couldn't have called ahead?"

"I really couldn't."

"Well, I haven't looked into the address yet. I've been busy." Jessie crossed her arms and cocked her head to one side. "I told you I'd call when I had something."

Oreo added growling into the barking. The incessant yapping of little dogs always annoyed me. Why can't they just accept that a small stature isn't a reflection on their worth as dogs?

"I need to make a call. Can I come in?"

Jessie scoffed. "And drip all over the carpet?"

That's when I realized, Oreo wasn't barking at me anymore. Something in the woods had her attention. It was too dark for me to see what she was barking at. I sniffed the air and caught the chemical scent I had smelled in Eddie's trailer. I took a step into the house bumping into Jessie.

"Hey!" she shouted, trying to shove me out the door.

A tar cat came out from around the edge of the carport.

It lowered its head and made a low-pitched whistling sound. I could see air pushing through the tar on its back. The same sound came from somewhere off in the woods to my left. It went quiet and prowled into the yard toward us. I put my hand on my blade but didn't draw it. I didn't think it would be an effective weapon in this situation. This cat was more liquid than solid, so cutting it probably wouldn't do much damage, and from what I've seen, they engulfed their victims. Close combat was a losing proposition.

Jessie gasped when she spotted the thing from the doorway. "Oreo, get back inside!"

Oreo ignored her. Barking wildly, she charged the tar monster and took the cat's attention away from me. Leaves crunched behind me; a second cat was on its way. The first cat lunged at Oreo. The little dog leapt back to avoid it. I charged into the house, picking up Jessie, and slammed the door.

She screamed in my ear loud enough to make it start ringing. She hit me. I tossed her on the floor of the hallway.

"Got a setta pipes on you, don't you?" I asked, rubbing my ear. "Where are your car keys?"

"Go get my dog!" she screamed.

"You need to worry about how we're gonna get outta here more than what's going on outside."

The barking stopped.

"Keys!" I shouted.

Jessie got to her feet. "Right there," she said, pointing to a table by the front door.

I spotted a keychain clump about the size of a baseball. I grabbed it just as a tar cat slammed against the door, splattering tar across the window. I took a step back, glad to see the structural integrity of the door was holding . . . for now.

"What are those things?" Jessie asked.

"Trouble. We need to get outta here now."

The tar on the window flowed out of sight. There was a second collision. The impact ripped the bottom hinge from the wall, leaving a crack between the door and the frame. While it would have still blocked the entry of a more solid being, the tar began to flow in around the door.

"Let's go," I said, pushing Jessie down the hall. "Do you have a back door?"

"This way!"

The back door had a large window in the middle that gave a clear view of the yard outside. I ran into Jessie when she suddenly stopped.

"There's another one out there," she said.

We ran back into the hallway. A large puddle of tar was starting to take shape by the front door. I ran into the living room, looking for a way out. I grabbed a recliner and tossed it through the double windows on the back wall. I jumped out the window, landed on the recliner, and toppled over. I looked up to see if Jessie was going to follow me. She appeared in the window with a phone in her hand.

I held a hand out for her. "We gotta go!"

She put a foot on the window ledge and the hand with the phone in mine. Black sludge exploded over her and the window. I jerked my hand back, bringing the phone with it. Our eyes met, I could see the fear and silent pleading for help on her face. She grabbed the window sill, struggling to pull herself free from the tar. I reached to pull her free, but stopped short when the tar covered her face. It gave her another tug and she disappeared into the house.

"Sorry, Jessie," I said.

I ran for the carport, flipping through an unnecessary amount of flair on the keychain until I found the key I was looking for. I jumped into the sedan, tossed the phone into the passenger seat, and cranked the engine. I didn't see any movement in the house when I headed down the driveway. I would figure out how to get to the interstate after I put some distance between me and these monsters. I watched the house in the rearview. I was sure the two back there wouldn't be able to catch up to me. They were quick, sure, but not interstate speeds.

The third tar cat appeared in the road in front of me. It charged toward the car. If it wanted a game of chicken that was alright with me. I hit the gas. The monster never turned away. It collided with the front of the car and splattered. I turned on the wipers and hit the fluid to clear what had made it into the windshield. I changed into my human form as the smell of burning tar filled the car. I rolled down the window for some fresh air and checked the gas. Half a tank, enough to get me home.

CHAPTER · 22

THE CAR WAS TRASHED, and not because I had run over a tar cat with it. The floorboards were full of fast food wrappers, mail that had been opened, some that hadn't, and other assorted trash. The cupholders were packed with makeup, bobby pins, hair ties, lighters, and more smaller bits of trash.

"By the Mother, Jessie's a slob," I said.

It was hard to see through the windshield with tar splattered all over it. The wipers hadn't done much more than smear it around the glass. I kept at it with the wipers until the fluid ran dry. By the time I made it to the interstate there was little more than hazy streaks. It wasn't ideal but it was good enough to get me home. The headlights on the car were dim, no doubt covered with sludge. I looked in the rearview mirror. There were plenty of cars behind me but none seemed to be following me. I took a deep breath, confident I'd made my escape.

I grabbed the phone from the passenger seat and dialed the only number I had memorized.

I recognized Tico's nonchalant, "Yep," when he answered.

"Tico, it's Obie. I need to talk to Hank."

His voice was muffled as if he were holding the phone below his chin. "He's busy. I'll have him call you when I see him."

"Alright," I said, fishing a pen out of the debris in the cupholder. "I need to talk to Hob, can you give me the number for the Southern Outpost?"

Tico let out a heavy sigh. "Don't you have it already?"

"I did, but not anymore so I need it."

"Hang on," he said.

I waited, listening to the sounds of clinking glasses and murmuring conversation. Tico came back on and rattled off ten digits that I scribbled onto my hand. I tossed the pen over my shoulder into the back seat and dialed the number on my hand.

I waited impatiently as it rang. A woman answered after the second ring. "Hey, Obie, It's Meghan. What can I do for you?"

After our little excursion into the demon world and Harlan's fall she had been put in charge of the Southern Outpost. I was happy about it. Since I'm the one who brought her back from the demon world, we got along like peaches and cream and that meant everyone at the outpost treated me with a modicum of respect.

"Hey, Meg, I need to talk to Hob. It's kind of urgent."

"Okay, hang on."

The line went silent. Since Hob worked with Queen Isabelle getting in touch with him meant jumping through hoops.

Finally, I was routed to Hob. "*Ja, hello.*"

I put the phone on speaker and placed it on the dash. "Hey, Hob, sorry to bug you. I wanted to ask you about some magic I ran into."

"*Gute Nacht,* Obie, there is no bugging me. It is good to hear from you," Hob said. "Tell me about this magic."

"It was a man made out of dirt, well . . . mostly dirt. As far as I could tell it was a real arm on a dirt body."

"*Ja,* it sounds like the golem," Hob said.

"What, that guy from *Lord of the Rings*?"

There was a moment of silence before Hob answered. "*Nein,* the golem is made of earth. Let me ask you, Obie, did the creature speak?"

"No, I don't think it could. I tried talking to it, but it didn't say anything back."

"You say it had an arm from a living person?" Hob asked. "Was there a paper in its mouth?"

"It kept its mouth closed, so I don't know about the paper, but I hit it with my blade a few times. It didn't do anything until I severed the arm, then the body fell apart into a pile of dirt."

"A golem is a formidable creature. They are a *Jüdish* creation *und* very strong," Hob said. "It is pure magic. The golem you speak of, however, uses a piece of a real person as the base ingredient. It is sloppy magic."

"So, the mage that did it is an amateur?" I asked.

"Oh, *Nein,* do not make the mistake of thinking this is unskilled," Hob said. "Whoever did this is powerful if not a little lazy perhaps."

That's when I noticed I could see through the windshield a little better. I'd given up on the wipers when the fluid ran out, so I couldn't think of any reason the windshield would have cleared. The headlights seemed brighter as well. I sped up to get beside a car and compared how bright the headlights were. No question, the tar had definitely cleared. It's possible the tar dripped off. Who knows what happened to those things when they were killed. Then again, if it wasn't dead . . .

"Obie? Have I lost you?"

"Hob, I'll have to call you back." I rolled up the window.

If that thing was still alive I didn't want to be stuck in a confined space when it had congealed enough to come after me. Even if it didn't attack me in the car, I couldn't risk taking it back to the clubhouse. If we didn't manage to eliminate the facility, I didn't want to let them know about the T.O.

"Shit," I said. "What do I do now?"

"Everything alright?" Hob asked.

Apparently he hadn't hung up.

"Yep, talk soon," I said and hung up.

I held my feet off the floor while picturing tar pouring from under the dash. Before I knew it, I'd be up to my knees and that would be it for me. I'd get hauled off to that facility never to be heard from again. It was hard to keep the gas pressed while holding my feet off the floor. The car began to lurch.

Sludge oozed from the vents and ran down the dashboard. I unbuckled the seatbelt and crouched on the driver's seat. The car coasted down from eighty miles per hour. I was going to have to jump. I reached for a lighter from the cup holder. I ended up with a gum wrapper and a zip tie as well. I put the zip tie in my mouth and grabbed some of the mail from the passenger seat. I lit the paper with the lighter. Flame licked my fingers.

I held the flame to the tar. It began to burn and retreated into the vents. I tossed the burning paper into the floorboard and reached for more. I lit everything I could find that would burn and tossed it around the car. The cab began to fill with smoke, not just smoke from burning paper, but harsh chemical smoke that burned thick and black and hurt my lungs.

Fire burst from the vents. Tar poured out and ran down the dash. It seemed to move by a force other than gravity telling me it wasn't dead, at least not yet. That left me without any real options. Getting swallowed by one of these things would be bad enough, with it on fire . . . let's just say a lava bath wasn't on my to-do list.

I waved a hand in front of the speedometer to clear the smoke enough to get an idea how fast I was going. I'd coasted down to fifty-five. The smoke burned my lungs. I coughed. I looked in the rearview mirror and didn't see any headlights directly behind me. It was going to be bad enough to jump out of a moving car, I didn't want to get run over in the process. I opened the door and rolled out.

I WOKE UP, ACHING all over, lying against the barrier at the center of the interstate. A man stood over me. He wore work boots, jeans, and a tee shirt. I had an excellent view of the boots. They had traces of paint, different colors in irregular patterns, clearly a painter by trade. A baseball cap was pushed far back on his head. He scratched his forehead with one hand and held a phone to his ear with the other.

"It's real bad," he said. "A bunch of the lanes are blocked, one car's on fire."

I groaned, pulling myself into a sitting position and realized the zip tie was still in my mouth. I leaned against the concrete barrier, pulling the zip tie out, and looked at it. There were teeth marks in the plastic. I shoved it in my pocket.

The man knelt in front of me. "Jesus, I thought you were dead."

"Not yet," I grunted. "Help me up."

"I really think you should stay put. There's an ambulance on the way."

"I'm getting up with or without you."

The man looked around nervously before taking my hand. "Just take it easy, okay?"

"Don't worry about me. I'll be fine." I got to my feet.

As I tried to stretch out the aches I could see the burning car sixty feet ahead. I couldn't tell how many cars were involved in the pile up. I thought the car would coast off the road and come to a stop. I guess that didn't work out as planned. It looked like the far left lane was still open and some cars were moving around the wreck on the right shoulder.

I'd need to find a car to make it back to the clubhouse. I'd walk to the next off ramp, find a car to rent or *borrow,* and get back on the road. The cars around me were moving at a snail's pace so getting to the other side wouldn't be a problem. I limped into traffic, giving the cars I walked in front of a courteous wave as I went. I could see the lights of emergency vehicles working their way though the traffic. Two lanes over I used the hood of an old pickup to brace myself. I raised my hand in an apologetic wave and stopped in my tracks when I saw the driver. It was Jarod. I limped over to the passenger seat, opened the door, and eased in.

"Uh . . . This isn't the ambulance buddy." Jarod said.

I put my head back and closed my eyes. "Yeah, I need a ride and we're going to the same place. It's me, Obie."

CHAPTER · 23

"IT WAS JUST A big charred spot with some melted plastic and broken glass," Jarod said. "It burned hot, too. The branches above where the car was parked were wilted."

"How did Mila take her car getting burned up?" I asked.

"She just stared for a few minutes and then we left. She, uh, *found* this truck for me and told me to head to Morrison Salvage. She said she had to find the guy that did it. I'm glad I'm not him. He's going to get it."

I shook my head. "Nah. She won't hurt him, she's helping him."

"Why would she help someone who lit her car on fire?"

I sighed. "Its complicated. We're Keepers, it's what we do."

"I saw how you helped the guys at the camp," Jarod mumbled under his breath.

He probably thought I couldn't hear it, and if I was human I wouldn't have. "Sometimes helping people means hurting other people. I don't like it but that's the way it is."

We drove the rest of the ride in silence. I was feeling a little paranoid after my adventure in the car so the first thing I did when we got to the clubhouse was check the truck for traces of tar. I didn't see any. I crammed Torch's kutte into the pocket of my cargo shorts. It stuck out of the top a bit but it was good enough.

"You're about to see a world you've never seen before," I said, walking with Jarod to the clubhouse. "You've dealt with people like this before but you didn't know it. They like to stay outta sight. Most of the folks in here can hear very well, so just keep your mouth shut and you'll be fine."

I shifted to krasis in the changing room and took Jarod into the bar. As soon as we entered he stopped in his tracks. His eyes grew wide. Trolls, goblins, orcs, not to mention a number of shifters filled the room.

I took him by the arm and pulled him toward the bar. "Be cool," I whispered. I waved Tico over.

Tico gave the air a couple sniffs. "Human?"

"This is Jarod," I said. "He'll be hanging out here for a while. Put him on my tab."

"Humpf," Tico scoffed. "What can I get ya?"

"You have Johnny Walker?" Jarod asked.

"How's blue label sound?" Tico asked.

Jarod shrugged. "I mean . . . yeah, if Obie's good with it."

I leaned an elbow against the bar. "Why wouldn't I be good with it?"

"It's about fifty dollars a shot," Jarod said.

"Fifty-five," Tico corrected. "That's nothin' for a big shot like you right?"

"Sure, whatever," I said.

Tico went to get Jarod's drink.

"He's kind of a douche but he's a good bartender," I said.

"So, you want me to hang out at a bar full of . . . Whatever these folks are, and drink for free?" he asked.

"That sums it up," I said.

"Cool."

Tico placed a glass on the table in front of Jarod. "Obie, why are you such an ass?"

Jarod picked up the glass. "They do have good hearing," he mumbled.

I flashed Tico an insincere smile. "Where's Hank?"

"Conference room," Tico said motioning with his head.

I walked around the bar toward the back hallway.

"Listen, don't worry about the cost of drinks," Tico said. "Obie has more money than God. Did you know he's footing the bill to send his ex traveling all over the world on an indefinite trip? She's probably out banging her way across the country right now. The point is, we're going to have some fun on Obie's dime. I've got some Lewis XIII cognac you need to try next."

I opened the door to the back and looked back at the bar. Tico gave me the same smile I'd given him a moment before.

I sighed. I gave Cotton a nod in the kitchen and went to the conference room. I knocked on the door as I opened it. Hank was sitting at the table, looking through a stack of papers.

"Have a second?"

"Yeah, just club business." He put the paper in his hand down on the stack. "I'm glad to have a break honestly."

The most important thing I needed to talk to him about was Torch but I wasn't sure how to broach that subject so I started off with something a little lighter. "How's Doc Lin's husband?"

"William . . . He's still alive if that's what you're asking," Hank said. "And he's still locked up. If it weren't for Doc we would've had this wrapped up already. Given him a beating, convinced him to stay away . . . Doc's been a good friend to the club but I can't have him comin' around causing trouble."

"If you are sure he won't talk or come back causing trouble you'll let him go?"

Hank shifted in his seat. "It's not that simple. We have rules. Folks don't get to come to our house with a gun and just walk away. I want this whole fucking mess to go away. It gives me a headache."

"And if the club had more important things to worry about?" I asked. "William apologizes and slips out the back?"

Hank's expression hardened. "What aren't you telling me?"

I pulled Torch's kutte from my pocket and draped it on the table in front of him.

His voice took an urgent tone. "Where'd you get this from?"

"Is it Torch's?" I asked. "It's not a knockoff or something?"

Hank took the kutte and looked it over closely inside and out, sticking his fingers through the cuts I had made with my blade. "It's Torch's . . . I'm sure. After so long I knew he was probably dead. I'd hoped to find him alive, but I think I knew deep down I was fooling myself."

"We don't know he's dead, not for sure."

"If he wasn't dead he'd still be wearing this," he said. "Where'd you get it."

"I'd tracked Holt to an old house a couple hours northwest of here. I was about to go in and get him when Thera shows up and sent me on a job. When I get back I see what I thought was Torch standing in front of this house. I tried to talk to him but he attacked me. Turns out it wasn't him at all. I talked to Hob about it and he thinks it was a golem. When I got away from it, it collapsed into a pile of dirt. I grabbed the kutte and made a run for it. I almost didn't get away. There were armed guards that started shooting as well as the same tar things that took Holt. Besides the kutte, I have someone that spotted him alive and well two weeks ago."

"Who?"

"A wolf named Atticus," I said. "He says Torch told him to find me. He's the one that led us to the facility."

"I want to talk to him," Hank said. "Where is he?"

"Heh heh, well . . . We lost him." I scratched the back of my neck. "But Mila's tracking him down right now. I'm not waiting on her though. I'm heading to the facility and I'm getting them both back."

Hank leaned forward. "Do I need to tell you the T.O.'s coming along on this?"

"And here I was gonna ask you for help." I chuckled.

"Do you have a plan?"

"The house is a fortress. I think I saw a back entrance on the river. They won't expect an attack from there. I'll go in the back and we'll meet in the middle."

"I'll get the club together," Hank said. "We'll be ready in about an hour."

"And the William situation?" I asked.

"Get him to apologize and he can go."

CHAPTER · 24

THERE WASN'T A guard in front of William's room. Even if he got out somehow, he couldn't get out of the building. Without a silver weapon he posed absolutely no threat to the T.O. beyond being able to reveal what they were. The key to the deadbolt hung on a nail in the doorframe. I changed to my human form, used the key, and went inside. William lay on the bed with his eyes buried in the crook of his elbow. The room was plain with just the bed, a small desk, and a chair.

Will looked out from under his elbow. He sat up, sitting on the edge of the bed. "Well?"

"I'm Obie."

"You can't keep me here," he said. "Eventually someone will figure out where I am and come looking for me."

I pulled a chair from the desk in the corner, placed it in front of the bed, and sat down. "Will, you seem like a smart guy. I'm surprised you haven't figured out that that's not a good thing for you." He didn't respond so I continued. "I don't think you understand what kind of trouble you're in. I know you don't understand the trouble you made for Rebecca. I am going to do my best to be truthful with you. I'll answer any questions you have, if I can."

He turned his head to the side and squinted at me. "How do you know my wife?"

"About three years ago Rebecca was in a car wreck. Collision at a red light," I said. "You remember that?"

Will nodded. "The drunk driver? It was a miracle she wasn't killed. The car was totaled, cops never found the guy."

"It wasn't a miracle." I sighed. "I was chasing someone. They drove their car through the light and plowed into the side of her car. They ran off. I probably could have caught him right there, but I checked on the car he hit rather than chase him. I try to prevent collateral damage like that if I can. Some in my line of work don't bother but I think it's the right thing to do. Anyway, I found Rebecca in bad shape. I healed her."

"What do you mean you *healed* her?" he asked.

"You've heard of laying on hands? Faith healing?" I asked. "That's the closest thing to what I do. She woke up, almost good as new."

"Yeah, you really think I'm going to believe that?"

"She wouldn't have believed it either if she hadn't seen it," I said. "You said yourself it was a miracle."

I could see him thinking, wondering if what I was telling him could be true. "That's bullshit."

I shot him a smile. "We'll see."

"So what is this like Stockholm Syndrome or something?" he asked.

"I already told you, It's not like that."

He leaned forward, putting his elbows on his knees and wrung his hands. "Then how do you explain the lying and late nights? Disappearing at all hours, saying there's an emergency at the hospital? I went by the hospital and they told me she hadn't worked there in over a month."

"I don't know what she was telling you. It never occurred to me, to be honest, but she's still practicing medicine, just in a different way."

"Then explain to me what's so special about this place that she leaves her job as chief of medicine to work in a biker bar."

"I can't tell you that," I said.

Will smirked. "You can but you won't."

"That's fair," I said, "but it doesn't change anything. We both want the same thing, to get you outta here."

"I don't even know why they're keeping me," Will said. "I'd understand if they beat me up and tossed me out or something but kidnapping?"

"Rebecca's been a big help around here and they don't want to damage that relationship by damaging you. At the same time, coming here with a gun causing trouble requires a response. No one does that and leaves untouched." I leaned back in the chair. "You happened to come here at the worst time. There's a lot going on which is going to work in your favor. You need to apologize for intruding and make Hank believe you won't cause anymore trouble. Do that and you walk away."

Will sneered. "Yeah, that's going to be a no from me."

"What's the hold up here, Will? You can't enjoy being here."

He looked me straight in the eye. "It's that I don't believe a word you're saying."

"Okay, I guess a demonstration is in order." I stood and turned, showing him my back flattening my tee shirt against my skin. "Nothing here right?"

I turned back, putting my arm behind me so he couldn't see it, took a deep breath, and focused on changing my blade hand to krasis. I didn't want to make a full change; Will didn't need that much convincing. When I could feel the claws on my fingertips I reached into krasis on my back and pulled out my blade. I changed my hand back to its human orientation. His eyes went wide as the two-foot blade appeared seemingly out of nowhere.

"Do you believe this is real?" I asked, holding the blade out for him to inspect.

He reached forward hesitantly and gave it a little pinch. "Yes."

I sat and lined the tip of the blade up with my forearm. I gritted my teeth and with a quick thrust I put it all the way through. I let go of the handle and held the impaled arm out to him. Blood ran from the injury, dripping on the floor.

I held the arm out to him. "Is this real, Will? Do I have a piece of metal going though my arm?"

He had slid back on the bed against the wall and didn't look like he wanted to give it a close inspection.

I stood and took a step toward him. "Don't be shy, Will, its not like anyone's bleeding to death here."

He held his hands up and looked away. "Fine, yes . . . I believe you!"

"Alright," I said, sitting back down. "Pay attention now, this is where it gets good."

He cringed when I pulled the blade free and stuck it into the floor. I held a hand over the injury and began channeling energy. My eyes and hands emitted a blue aura and I gave my hand a little shake for good measure. It's not that I could heal myself any faster than I already did but I could put on a little show.

When the injury had closed, I wiped the blood from my arm on my pants and held it out to him. He slid forward for a better look.

"So, you can believe what you've seen and that I'm telling you the truth. That I saved Rebecca's life, that she is working in medicine here, and that anything you aren't being told is for your safety. You can accept that I'm trying to help you and that the only way out of this is for you is to apologize. Or I can give you a more *personal* demonstration."

"What about all the lying?" he asked.

I shrugged. "That's between you and her."

"I'll apologize."

I headed out the door. "Don't touch that," I said, pointing to my blade. "I'll know if you do."

I found Hank in the bar talking to Mila.

"Will needs to talk to you," I told Hank.

"What's he gonna say?"

"I think he's ready to leave."

Hank nodded. "You coming?"

"I'll be right in."

Hank went to talk to Will, leaving me with Mila.

"Did you find Atticus?"

"Yeah," Mila said. "He's outside."

"Give me a sec to wrap this up and we'll ride together," I said.

I went back to see how things were going with Will and Hank.

Will had his head down in mid-sentence when I walked in. ". . . wrong of me to come here and I'm sorry for the trouble I've caused. If you're willing, I'd like to pretend this never happened. I won't say anything to anyone. I've been in bed with the flu for the past few days."

"Alright," Hank said. "I'll have Rebecca take you home. Don't come back."

CHAPTER · 25

"I DON'T SEE WHY I need this," I said. "I'm not even interested."

Mila gave me a pitying smile. "I don't know how you've stayed so innocent all this time. It's not 1875 anymore. Nowadays, people use apps."

Mila and I sat on my truck's tailgate, waiting for the Tortured Occult. I couldn't tell why she was so interested in finding me a date and I wasn't sure how I felt about using an app to do it. I hadn't told her I planned to track down Naylet. I was sure she would just tell me all the things wrong with my plan. Thera wouldn't let me run off; things might not go as I want with Naylet . . . I knew all that. I would just have to figure it out.

A rattling car passed in front of the gas station where we were parked. It looked to be patched together parts from many junkyard trips, leaving it with mismatched paint. A frankencar. I watched it disappear down the remote country road before looking back at the screen Mila held out to me.

"Alright, it's easy," Mila said. "A picture comes up and if you like what you see you put your finger on the screen and push the picture to the right. If you aren't interested then you push it to the left. Swipe right and swipe left, get it?"

I sighed. "What I'm not getting is, how could I know if I want to court any of these women from a picture and a few sentences?"

"By the Mother! *Court*? Do ya hear yourself? Who talks like that?"

"I haven't been single for a very long time." I raised an eyebrow with annoyance. "And I've heard you speak the same way."

"I quit saying court for anything outside of legal proceedings by 1950. Just touch their profile to get more info," she said. "We haven't finished your profile yet, so you haven't got that far."

The screen showed a young blonde woman with the user name Ashleigh. She had some pictures with a cat and some with friends. She had a couple paragraphs that didn't really tell me anything about her. Content without substance. I suddenly felt much more out of touch than I ever had before.

"This isn't really telling me much," I said. "How do I know if I want to swipe her?"

"You're overthinking it," Mila said. "This is less with your head and more with your . . . you know."

"Heart?"

Mila grinned. "Think a little lower."

"Gut?"

"Keep going. You'll get there eventually."

I heard the rumble of motorcycles in the distance. Mila turned the phone off and slid it into her pocket. The Tortured Occult rode up in two rows and pulled into the parking lot. They backed their motorcycles into a neat row and killed the engines. Hank, Big Ticket, and Cotton got off their bikes and joined us at the car.

I opened the back door of the truck. Atticus climbed out, his muzzle sticking out slightly from under his hoodie. I didn't really want to bring him but it was what it was.

"This the guy?" Hank asked.

"This is Atticus, he escaped the facility with Torch's help." I turned to Atticus. "Tell them what you told me."

"There's a tunnel that goes into the lower levels of the facility. It looks like a storm cellar in the middle of the woods. If you can get in there, follow the hallway and go down the stairs, it will take you to the cells. If they have Torch, you'll find him there."

"Atticus told me you can see the house from the cellar door," I said. "I did some research. A real estate site with some pictures. The facility used to be a grist mill in the 1800s. It's been converted to hydropower, so I was thinking I'll kill the power and then you can get in quick and get to the cells before they figure out what's going on. The generator is on the back of the house by the river. From the pictures it looks like I can swim up to the generator and take out the power for you. I'll get in and meet you at the cells." I pointed west. "The house is about three miles up the road. We can leave the bikes here and take a shortcut through the woods."

"Alright, let's get it done," Hank said. "Remember, we want to take some alive if we can manage it. If Torch isn't there, I want to know what happened to him."

"We can expect to find other hostages besides Torch and Holt," I said. "Eddy was taken a couple days ago, as well as Jessie last night. There's no telling how many hostages they could have or what they're doing to them."

The T.O. left some prospects behind to watch the bikes. We headed off through the woods as a group. When we got within sight of the house I turned north, leaving the group behind. I needed to come in from upriver. I made my way to the river's edge. I looked around before I made the change to krasis. I wasn't really worried about being spotted, the area was remote and I had the cover of night. I slid into the cool water and swam lazily downstream, I wanted to make sure they had time to find the hatch and get into position.

I stopped under the old bridge and held onto the stone. I could see shadows moving around inside the house and one person strolling around the exterior. I didn't see any weapons on him. That didn't mean a whole lot. He could be a golem. There's no telling how many of them could be on the property—not to mention the tar cats. They seemed to be used to catch people, a kind of mobile trap. Still, if they were ordered to kill, or decided to, they could suffocate someone without any trouble.

I took a breath and dove under water. I swam into an alcove in the house's foundation. I found a ladder mounted to the concrete and climbed up. Peeking over the edge, I saw a large generator in the corner. There was a door to my right with a ladder and some tools on the back wall. I put my ear against the door but didn't hear anything. I tried the handle. Locked. The door looked to be made of cast iron, probably original to the house. Getting in this way might be a problem.

I realized I hadn't thought through how to actually disable the generator. I didn't really know what I was looking at. It reminded me of an engine, except without all the engine parts I was used to seeing. It had an on and off switch, but I had something more permanent in mind. I found some conduit running from the generator into a fuse box mounted to the wall. I found some tools and took the cover off the circuit breaker, revealing the wiring and switches. I hit the off switch on the generator, flipped the main breaker off, and pulled switches from the box and tossed them into the river behind me.

I pulled six of them before I heard the door lock click. I moved to the wall beside the door and pulled my blade. A man swung the door open and stepped out. I plunged my blade into his side, pushing him toward the railing. He screamed. I sank the claws of my left hand into his back enough to get a grip. My new-found handle and the weapon buried in his body gave me holds to pick him up and throw him into the river. The momentum pulled him off the blade. He belly flopped into the water below.

I stepped through the door into a hallway. It looked like a normal house, carpeted floors, a nice paint job with artwork on the walls. Not what I was expecting, not that I really knew what to expect. I could see the beam of a flashlight waving around past the hallway. I followed the hall, passing a couple bedrooms and a bathroom, to a living room where a man was using a flashlight to look for something under the couch. I'd been moving quietly but my first step into the room made a floorboard release a long groaning squeak.

"Will you get the lights on already? I dropped my card, I thought it went under the couch but I don't see it," the man said.

I stuck my blade into his back before he had time to realize I wasn't who he thought I was. He grunted in surprise. I gave the blade a twist as I pulled it back. He collapsed with shallow erratic breaths that ended a moment later. He dropped a phone he had been using as a flashlight.

It came to rest with the light pointing up. It reflected off the walls, resulting in a dim lighting that would have been romantic in a nice restaurant with some flowers and candles. The fresh corpse bleeding into the carpet would have killed the vibe.

The card he had mentioned was on the floor beside the couch. If he'd looked a few feet to the side he would have easily found it. I picked it up and gave it a quick once over. It had his picture on the front and was attached to a retractable lanyard. I tossed it over my shoulder. With the power out, I didn't have to worry about key cards. There was a door on the far side of the room with a card scanner. I tried the handle, the door swung open revealing a flight of stairs with a different look than the house I had seen so far.

The passageway was cold concrete and steel. I moved down the stairs and peeked around the corner. Emergency lights mounted to the ceiling thirty feet apart spun in their housings, throwing red light up and down the hallway. The light wasn't enough to illuminate the corridor completely, leaving long shadows that shifted with the moving lights making the corridor seem to churn with life.

CHAPTER · 26

I CAUGHT MOVEMENT IN the distance and heard the steady *clack* of footsteps echoing through the corridor. I flattened myself against the wall and waited as they approached. Peeking around the corner, I saw two men with guns coming in my direction. When they reached the corner, I spun out and hit the closest one, my blade easily cutting through him. He fell to the floor with a surprised wheeze as his last breath left his body.

The second man grabbed his pistol and brought it to bear. I swung at his weapon hand. Our weapons collided as he fired. I cringed from the muzzle blast, my ears screaming in protest. I was stunned momentarily. I looked over to see the man holding his right hand against his body. The gun and a thumb lay on the floor beside him. He bent to retrieve the weapon.

I leapt for him. He fell face first to the ground with me on his back. I bit the back of his head, my teeth scraping across his skull, filling my mouth with flesh and hair. I'd scalped him. He writhed underneath me. I spit out his scalp, gagging on the hair. A loud percussive *thump* hit my ears followed a moment later by pain shooting through my abdomen. I knew the sensation, I'd been shot. The gun pointed at my guts just before it went off for a second time. He had managed to get hold of it with his left hand, pointing it at me from under his body.

The gun flashed with a *thump*. The bullet tore into me a few inches away from the first. I pinned his hand to the floor. He pulled the trigger for the third time. The bullet slammed into the wall beside my head, sending concrete shards into my face. Keeping him pinned, I bit at his face and neck, tearing off bits and pieces until he didn't have any fight left in him.

I rolled off him and propped myself against the wall. I needed a couple minutes to recover after taking two to the gut. I used a claw to get the hair that was stuck in between my teeth and spit it out onto the floor. When the pain receded to a dull ache I got to my feet and continued down the hallway.

I caught movement in the distance, a lot of movement. Large figures were headed in my direction. At first I thought I might be in trouble, but then I recognized the group as the Tortured Occult. Hank led the group. We met in front of stairs going down to another level.

"What happened to you?" Hank asked.

I looked down to see the blood, some mine some not, covering my fur and clothes. "Just another day at the office. Have any trouble?"

"Nothing we couldn't handle."

Hank looked past me. He looked more confused than alarmed. He put a hand to my chest and moved me out of the way. Torch, or more likely a Torch golem, came up behind me.

Hank walked over slowly. "Torch?"

This Torch was wearing jeans, a grey tee shirt, and a canvas jacket. He wasn't wearing a kutte, which wasn't surprising since I'd taken the real one back with me. Torch and Hank walked up to each other. Torch sucker punched him. Hank took a hard shot to the face and fell limply to the ground. Ginsu charged Torch, taking a shot to the gut. Ginsu fell, holding one hand where he'd been hit.

The T.O. tackled the golem, taking it to the ground buried under a pile of bikers. If this Torch was like the last one, part was from the real Torch. If I found what part of this abomination was original hardware, I could remove it and destroy the creature. I knew it wasn't the left arm.

I stepped over Hank to the churning pile of bikers. "Hold him down," I said, drawing my blade.

Ginsu grabbed my arm holding the weapon from behind. "Don't," was all he could get out before hacking up blood that he wiped away with his arm.

"Relax," I said. "It's not Torch."

The club pinned the golem, giving me time to find what the real piece was. I could smell the sourness of meat starting to turn. I sniffed the right arm first, then the left leg. As soon as I gave the right leg a sniff, I knew I had found it. I cut the pant leg away and felt for the connection point. My stomach turned as I ran my hand over the cold flesh I knew was Torch's leg. Just below the knee I found the transition from flesh to stone. I swung. My first strike hit high putting a notch into the creature. The second swing hit the mark and cut through, the blade biting into the floor. The T.O. fell forward onto a pile as the golem lost its shape and melted into earth. I pulled my blade free from the floor and stuck it back into its sheath.

Big Ticket picked himself up off the floor. He spit out a mouthful of dirt. "What the fuck was that?"

"A golem," I said. "Anybody hurt?"

"Here," Ginsu said from behind me.

He sat against the wall breathing heavily, with strings of blood and saliva dripping onto his shirt. I held a hand over his chest and let the energy flow. His breathing smoothed out immediately.

He wiped his mouth on his arm and got to his feet before I had finished. "I'm good, check Hank."

I looked over to see Hank still lying face down on the floor. I knelt and flipped him over. A trickle of blood ran from his nose and ears. The club gathered around.

"He gonna be alright?" Lug Nut asked.

I put a hand on either side of his head to heal him. I could feel the energy flowing into him. "Yeah, he'll be fine."

After half a minute Hank came to. Cotton and Big Ticket each took and arm and pulled him to his feet.

"What happened?" Hank asked.

"A golem sucker punched you," Cotton said. "I thought we lost you."

Hank walked over to the pile of dirt and looked down at the leg. The dark skin had taken on a gray tint.

Hank nudged it with his foot. "What's this?"

"Hob said to make this type of golem it uses a body part from the person the golem is imitating," I said.

"Why didn't you tell me that earlier?" he asked.

"I didn't want you to lose hope that we'd find him alive."

Hank ran his tongue over his teeth. "You said you fought a golem of Torch earlier . . . What part did they use for it?"

"Left arm."

Hank nodded and turned to the club. "We're gonna kill every one of the motherfuckers. No mercy, rip 'em to pieces." He whispered in my ear, "You should have told me."

CHAPTER · 27

THE REVELATION THAT someone here had been cutting Torch into pieces sent the Tortured Occult into a rage. They abandoned me and caution, rushing through the hallways like a wave, crashing over anyone they came into contact with. I was left behind listening to the erratic growls, screams, and gunfire echoing through the building.

I followed the T.O. at a more leisurely pace. The last place I wanted to be was in the middle of an enraged shifter mosh pit. Around the first corner I found the remains of some guards that looked like they had been dragged behind a truck. They'd been ripped apart to the point dental records might not be enough to identify them. Blood was splattered floor to ceiling with body parts and bits of flesh scattered down the hallway. There wasn't a way to move down the hallway without stepping in blood so I didn't try. I stepped over the worst of the mess making my way down the hallway.

A number of steel doors lined the hallway. Each door had a corresponding control panel full of levers, gauges, and buttons. At the end of the corridor was a pair of glass doors. The T.O. were piled up in front of the doors, pounding on them, trying to break them down. I couldn't see what had them so riled up.

I approached slowly. They would either break down the door and kill whoever was inside, or they would lose steam and calm down. Either one meant I didn't need to be in a hurry. I looked through a small window in the metal door. They were cells, the kind used for solitary confinement. Where you would expect to see at least a bed and a toilet, these were empty. They were concrete walls with drains in the floor. The most intricate part of the cell was the ceiling. It had recessed lighting with a number of pipes, conduit, and a sprinkler system all protected behind a heavy duty cage that ran wall to wall.

The muffled yapping of a small dog caught my attention. I followed the sound down two cells and looked inside. Jessie and Oreo were covered head to toe in tar. It took me a second to recognize them. I was glad to see they were safe . . . miserable from the looks of it, but safe. She saw me, got to her feet and came over to the window.

"Are you okay? I asked.

She gave me a death stare and the finger.

"I'll get you out, hang on."

I looked at the control panel beside the cell. I couldn't make much sense of it. There wasn't a clearly labeled *let your friends out* button. I tried hitting a button and flipped a switch. The door didn't open. I heard something from the cell; the sprinkler had come on. Jessie looked even more pissed. I decided it would be better to find someone who knew how to work the controls—if there were any still alive. The way the Tortured Occult was trying to break down the glass doors it was a safe bet there was someone in there.

I headed over to them. My curiosity got the better of me and I found myself pausing at each window to take a peek inside. In one cell, a woman huddled in the corner. The sprinkler system had a constant rain falling inside the cell. The woman looked damp and miserable. She shivered. I thought about turning off the sprinkler since it was the one control I knew how to operate. Then I thought of Atticus. He had been kept in a cell with the sprinklers on and was eager to get back. Could they have done the same thing to her as they did to him?

A person on the ground in the next cell made me do a doubletake. It was Torch. He sat propped up against the wall, missing an arm and both legs. I'd seen a golem made from an arm and a leg so far. There must be third running around somewhere. I knocked on the cell door to get his attention, but he didn't look up. Judging from the way Oreo's bark had been muffled the cells seemed to have some level of soundproofing. I gave the door three solid hits but he still didn't respond.

"Hank!" I shouted, moving from cell to cell, looking through the windows.

Most of the cells were empty; only a few had people in them. Besides Torch and the woman there was a werewolf sitting with his back to the door. There was no sign of Holt, maybe they had another cell block I hadn't seen yet? We hadn't searched the upstairs either. It's possible he could be held somewhere else on the property.

"Hank," I said again.

He was standing at the back of the ruckus watching the progress. Turning around he said, "There you are."

"Have you found Holt?"

"We haven't found anybody," he said. "Just clearing the facility."

I pointed to the cell with Torch. "We need someone alive to open these cells and tell me where they took Holt."

"There's three holed up in there," Fisheye said, emerging from the pack, wiping blood from his mouth to his arm. "Give me a blowtorch and I can get in there."

"We can't get in, but they can't get out either," I said. "We should secure the facility. That will give us time to get the gear we need and get some answers."

"Alright!" Hank shouted to the club. "Half of you get outside and keep watch. The rest of us will clear upstairs." He turned to Fisheye. "Call the prospects and have them bring up something to get that door open . . . and get the Tennessee chapter down here."

I pointed my chin in the direction of the door. "I'll watch them."

The Tortured Occult split up for their assignments. I approached the doors the T.O. had been trying to break down. It looked like plain sliding glass doors. The kind you would see at any supermarket. I could tell there was more to them from the pounding the club had given them. The glass was scratched all over with so much blood and spit smeared over them that it was hard to see inside. Using the heel of my hand I wiped a circle large enough to look through. There were three people inside, standing against the back wall. They were wearing scrubs, standing in what looked like an operating room any hospital would be proud to have.

The tallest woman walked over to a phone on the wall, picked it up, and dialed a few buttons. Her voice was muffled enough that I couldn't make out what she said. She hung up and went back to her place behind the table.

I took my blade and tried to stick it between the doors to pry them open. It didn't work. They seemed to have some kind of locking mechanism that kept them firmly in place. I thought about trying to break in but if the T.O. couldn't break it down it would probably take me a week to chop a hole big enough to get through.

They didn't appear to have any weapons, or fighting spirit, so I doubted they were anything to worry about. Still, I needed answers and they were the only ones that could give them to me.

I knocked on the glass. They looked at each other, exchanging words before one of the women came over to the glass.

"What's your name?"

"Suzette," the woman answered.

"Well, Suzette, if you open the door, I can get you outta here alive," I said.

She looked skeptical. "You can't expect me to believe that."

"If you aren't the one that's been cutting up folks then I can," I said. "You help me and I'll help you."

She motioned toward the other two with her head. "What about them?"

I looked past her at the two standing in the back of the room. "The real question is how bad do you want to live?"

"Nice try," she said.

There was a loud click and the doors shuddered in their tracks. They opened, leaving me standing face to face with Suzette. She jumped back so fast she tripped, falling in the middle of the room, but scrambling to her feet in a fraction of a second.

"I want to live," the other woman said, her hand on the door release.

"You fucking idiot," Suzette sneered. "He's going to kill us all."

CHAPTER·28

"COOL YOUR TITS, Suzette," I said, stepping into the room.

She stood with the man against the wall.

I asked the woman who'd opened the door, "What's your name?"

"Jill." Her eyes went wide moving to something behind me. "Don't!"

Stabbing pain shot through my shoulder. The man who'd been standing behind the surgical table had buried a scalpel into my left shoulder. I spun in time to take another scalpel to the gut. I grabbed his wrist and twisted until his fingers were pointing toward the ceiling. The scalpel clattered to the floor. I jerked his hand down, sending him toppling to the floor with a pop from his wrist and a scream from his lips. He held his wrist to his chest. He looked up in time to catch my fist colliding with his face. He collapsed unconscious.

Suzette bolted out the open door, barreling down the hallway. Jill watched Suzette go, looked at me, and then back to Suzette. I could see her calculating her chances.

"Are you going to make a run for it, cause I could use some help with this," I said, holding a hand out to the scalpel buried in my shoulder.

I didn't really need help, but I needed Jill alive. If she followed Suzette she would be killed by the first member of the T.O. that found her.

"Did you mean what you said? You'll make sure we make it out alive?"

"No," I said. "I'll get *you* out alive. Suzette and Mr. Stabby are on their own."

Jill looked back down the corridor. Suzette made it to the end of the corridor just as Skinny Pete came around the corner. Jill turned away, putting a hand to her stomach, as Skinny Pete pounced.

She didn't look sure about hitching her horse to my wagon but must have decided I was her best chance.

"Sit on the table. I'll need sutures, antiseptic—"

"Just pull it," I said, turning to give her access.

She was hesitant but gave the scalpel a quick tug. "Did I hurt you?"

I rolled my shoulder a few times. "I'm fine. Stay close to me. If they catch you alone, I won't be able to protect you." I got a little of the blood from my shoulder and wiped it on her forehead. "It'll smell like me, might help."

She didn't look particularly happy, but didn't argue either. Skinny Pete came down the hallway dripping Suzette's blood from his mouth. He had a bit of flesh stuck in the hair on his chin. He looked at Jill the way a wolf looks at a sheep.

"She's with me," I said. I put a finger to my chin. "You've got a little something right there."

He swiped a couple fingers over his fur knocking the bit of Suzette free. "Did I get it?"

"Yep."

"I'm going to be sick." Jill moved her hand from her stomach to her mouth.

Skinny Pete looked down at the man just starting to stir on the ground. "And this one?"

I shrugged.

"Excellent," he grinned. "We've got company. Hank needs you upstairs. I'll be right behind you." Skinny Pete stood over the man on the ground.

I took Jill by the arm and directed her out of the room. "Come on, we gotta move."

We barely made it out of the room before Skinny Pete tore into the man on the floor. Jill went from a brisk walk to a jog and then slowed down at the other side of the hallway when we came to Suzette's body. She tiptoed around the bloody body before we moved around the corner and up the stairs.

She stopped again at the bodies of the guards, staying out of the carnage lining the hallway. I could hear gunfire that sounded like it was coming from somewhere in the house above us. I almost passed the guards by, but with the sounds of gunfire I thought it might be good to have a little more range. I took two pistols and handed them to Jill. I scrounged a fresh magazine from the belt of one of the guards.

"You aren't afraid I'll shoot you?" Jill asked from behind me.

I moved to the other guard to see what he had on him. "I've found people act in their own interests. If you shoot me you'll be stuck with a bunch of pissed off shifters to deal with by yourself." I found a second magazine on the man's belt. I took it and turned around to face her. "Not to mention that you can't kill me with those. No matter how many times you shoot me I'll wake up. Needless to say, our deal will be off."

I reloaded the pistols before continuing down the hallway. I stopped when I realized Jill wasn't behind me anymore. When I looked I'd found she hadn't followed me past the guards bodies. She moved from one side of the hallway to the other looking for a way to get through without stepping in the gore. A futile exercise to say the least. I walked back through the mess, handed her the pistols, and crouched in front of her.

"Hop on," I said. "I'll carry you."

She climbed on my back and I stepped through the blood. When I cleared, it rather than putting her down, I took off at a run down the hallway. I needed her but she was slowing me down and the T.O. needed my help.

I followed the sounds of fighting. I went up the flight of stairs into the house proper, stopping short of opening the door. I put Jill down and took the pistols.

"Stay safe but close," I said.

I cracked the door open and peered out. Through the kitchen, I saw the front door being covered by five people with guns and two standing on either side of the door. One was Torch, or another copy of him. I'd already taken one with his right arm and left leg. From what I saw in the cell this one had to be from a right leg. I didn't recognize the other man, but from his blank stare and lack of concern about the bullets flying back and forth, I had to assume he was a golem too. The T.O. couldn't get in without getting shot up. I could hear the Tortured Occult on the porch. I didn't think the guards had silver bullets, the guards I took the guns from didn't. Either way I was in a better position to even the playing field and get the T.O. in the house. I raised a pistol in each hand, holding them by my head and took a deep breath. This was gonna hurt.

I jumped into the kitchen, leveling the pistols at the guards. I charged, firing off as many rounds as I could. I wasn't aiming so much as just pointing and shooting. Spray and pray, that was the name of the game. I hit a few of them before they realized what was happening. The golems moved to intercept me. My bullets slammed into them, tearing gashes into their bodies, exposing the earth they were made of. Dirt sprayed back on me as I closed in on them. The guards that hadn't been hit opened fire. It was lucky for me the golems had moved between us. They stopped most of the bullets intended for me. The ones they didn't stop went wide and missed me entirely.

The slides on the pistols locked open as I reached the kitchen counter. I ducked below the counter for cover, dropped the pistols, and drew my blade. The Torch-golem came around the corner first. That was lucky for me because I knew what to target. I swung at its right leg as soon as it came around the corner. The blade cut through cleanly. The golem's leg was severed and it dissolved into a pile of dirt. I expected the other golem to come around the corner behind the first. I could easily get at least two swings and maybe kill it before it became a problem.

I held the blade at the ready, waiting for it to come around the corner, when hard cold hands grabbed me from above. The golem had reached over the counter. I didn't expect it to have that kind of foresight and I was about to pay for it. It grabbed my arm holding the blade with one hand. Its other hand held firmly against the back of my neck. I tried to kick free as it dragged me over the counter into the living room. The T.O. poured through the door. If they had taken a few seconds longer I'd be getting shot up about then. They made quick work of the remaining guards before turning their attention to the golem. Unfortunately, it wasn't going to stand still waiting to be destroyed. It slammed me down into the counter, my head contacting hard and the room went dark, sounds muffled. I could tell I was lying flat and something was off with my body but I couldn't tell what. Everything was numb.

I started to come out of the haze only to realize I was being stepped on and kicked. The T.O. were wrestling with the golem on top of me. I needed to crawl away, I didn't know what direction to go but anywhere had to be better than being trampled. I became aware my left arm wasn't working when I tried to move. I rolled.

The tunnel vision receded. The T.O. piled on the golem, pinning it against the counter. With two members on each arm and leg it looked like they were still having trouble keeping it under control. I could hear muffled shouting but couldn't make out what they were saying. It looked like they were having trouble finding the piece the golem was made from. Ginsu jumped up on the counter behind the golem and sunk his claws into its head under the jaw. He pulled as if he were doing a deadlift. The head ripped free. The body disintegrated into dust, leaving Ginsu holding a head. He tossed it into the living room. It rolled to a stop a few feet from me.

Mila knelt in front of me. "You alright? You gotta nose bleed."

"Yeah," I said, running an arm across my nose to wipe the blood away. "I got my bell rung. I'll be fine."

Big Ticket dragged Jill by the arm and threw her to the floor. She rolled to a stop, realized she was lying on a dismembered head, and scooted away like a crab only to discover she was surrounded by bikers with nowhere to go.

CHAPTER · 29

"SHE'S WITH ME," I said, getting to my feet.

My head hadn't quite cleared and I stumbled a little from the dizziness.

"You can't save everybody," Hank said.

I helped Jill up by the arm and pulled her behind me. "I'm not trying to save everybody. Just this one."

"You better have a good reason after what they did to Torch," Hank sneered.

"Because we haven't found Holt. I need to figure out what happened to him and she's going to tell me."

Hank's expression softened a bit. "Alright, but she comes back to the clubhouse and if she doesn't come through, she's ours."

"Agreed."

Hank turned to the club. "Secure this fucking place and find out what happened to the group that should have cleared the house."

"Up here," Cotton shouted from the top of the stairs. "They're shot up."

Mila headed for the stairs. "I got it."

"Obie, take her to the cells and get Torch out," Hank said. "Get 'em both to the clubhouse."

I took Jill by the arm and headed for the stairs.

"What the hell was that?" She said when we'd made it into the hallway. "We had a deal now you're going to hand me over to them?"

We reached the massacre in the hallway. I bent down so Jill could get on my back. "We still have a deal. If you come through you'll be fine."

She climbed on to avoid the gore. "There's a lot of them and one of you. If they decide they want to hurt me you can't stop them. You're just handing me over to them."

I put her down when we passed the blood. "Hank gave us his word. That may not mean much for most folks but his word is good."

"You'll have to forgive me if I'm skeptical," Jill said.

We made it to the cells.

I looked at the prisoners through the glass. "We aren't going to be able to fit everyone in the truck. Do they have a van or something we can move everyone in?"

Jill pointed down the hallway. "There's an elevator that goes up to a separate garage. They have an ambulance parked there. We'll need a gurney to move thirty-sev— uh, Torch . . . We have one in storage."

"Alright, show me how to open these doors."

Jill pressed a button on the bottom of the panel. "The release is here then pull this," she said, pulling a large lever down.

I could hear the discharge of air of the room's pressure being equalized followed by a heavy locking mechanism being disengaged. She pulled the handle and the door swung open freely.

"Listen . . . Taking Torch is fine but you should probably leave everyone else where they are. They're dangerous."

"We can't just leave them," Mila said.

She had followed us down the stairs.

"Everyone okay up there?" I asked.

"Just some cuts and bullet wounds," Mila said. "They'll be fine."

"If no one is going to be here to take care of them then we should kill them," Jill said. "A number of the experiments escaped with Torch when he broke out. It's not good for them, or anyone else, to have them running around."

Mila crossed her arms. "We're taking everyone with us."

"Hold on . . ." I said holding up a hand. "Atticus wants to come back, under different management of course. She's right, we can't take 'em all with us. Let's get Torch now. We'll have to figure out what to do with the rest later."

Mila crossed her arms. "Fine, but I don't like it."

"Noted," I said. "Let's get that gurney."

Jill led me to a storage room. It contained metal shelves stacked with neatly labeled medical supplies. A clipboard with an inventory sheet was hanging off the closest shelf. Say what you will, they were organized.

Jill fetched a gurney. "Who is that?"

"A friend of mine. She's cool."

"Is she like . . . them?" Jill asked.

"She's like me."

I was sure she didn't know what that meant but she didn't ask any more questions. We rolled the gurney back to Torch's cell. Mila was standing by the open door.

"He told me to leave him alone."

"Alright, hang on." I stepped past her into the cell. "Hey, buddy, We're here to take you home."

He looked up at me for the first time. It was as if someone had taken all the fight out of him. His eyelids and mouth drooped, making him look sickly, which he probably was.

"Obie, we've been friends my whole life. I'd like to think we're close."

"Yeah, of course we are," I said. "Where are you going with this?"

"I need you to do something for me, no questions asked."

I walked over and knelt in front of him. "What?"

"Kill me."

I was afraid he was going to ask something like that. I'm a firm believer in a person's right to choose how they live, or not live as they case may be, but this wasn't the time for him to make that decision.

"I'll make you a deal. Come to the clubhouse and learn what life will be like for you. In six months if you still don't believe you have a future then I'll help you."

"What kind of future could I have? They didn't just take my limbs, they took my life. I can't ride anymore."

"You're still part of the club," I said. "I know the T.O. isn't going to turn its back on you."

"I'm not going to be a charity-case hang-around that everyone feels sorry for. I'd rather die."

"And if you still feel that way in six months then we'll talk," I said. "It's the best offer you're going to get."

"Fine." He looked at the floor. "It's not like I have a choice."

I brought in the gurney and placed him on it. We wheeled him into the hallway.

I walked over to Jessie's cell. Oreo started yapping.

"Did they do anything to your newest addition here?" I asked.

Jull shook her head. "She just got here."

I opened the door to her cell. The sprinklers were still on. She and Oreo came out of the cell dripping wet. While the water hadn't improved her spirits it had whittled away at some of the tar.

"Let's get you outta here," I said.

She sneered at me as she walked past. We wheeled Torch down the hall to the elevator. We took it up to the garage. Mila found the keys to the ambulance while we loaded Torch in the back. Jill, Jessie, and Oreo climbed in with Torch.

I got in the passenger seat. "Alright, let's roll. Drop me at my truck. Hopefully it's still in one piece."

When we got to the gas station we found everything was quiet. The prospects were lounging lazily around the bikes. My truck wasn't burned to a crisp. That was a good sign. Mila pulled the ambulance in beside my truck. The back of the ambulance opened. I thought it was Jill making a run for it. I jumped out and went around to find Jessie standing by the back door.

"What're you doing?" I asked.

"Take me home."

"It may not be safe for you there. They know where your house is."

She jabbed a finger into my chest. "And who's fault is that?"

"I'm not gonna be able to protect you if something happens."

"'Cause you're doing a bang up job of that already?" she asked.

I held a hand out directing her to my truck. "We'll meet you at the clubhouse," I said to Mila before closing the ambulance door.

The truck looked to be in good shape. The windows were down but Atticus wasn't in it.

He walked out of the shadows beside the gas station. "How'd it go?"

"Pretty good," I said. "Get in, we need to get back."

He got in the back. "Who's this?"

I started the truck. "A friend, we're taking her home."

"We're not friends," Jessie said.

"Where's my car?" she said when we pulled up to her house.

It was the first thing she noticed.

"Last time I saw it, it was on fire on the side of seventy five," I said.

She got out of the truck, sat Oreo down, and turned to me. "Obie, in the future, should you find yourself in trouble, don't come to me."

I nodded. "That's fair."

CHAPTER·30

"WE'RE HEADED SOUTH," Atticus said.

"We are."

"The facility's north."

"It is," I agreed.

"So where are we going?"

I could feel the temperature in the truck start to rise with his anxiety. "You promised me you would take me back and put me in a cell."

"And I will," I said. "I'm trying to look out for you. The Tortured Occult is watching the facility but we don't know if they are going to try to take it back and we need to get some more people over there to help out. On top of that I saw one of the staff making a phone call. There could be a team coming to retake the facility right now. If you want to go back before we feel we can protect you, then I'll take you. You could end up right back where you started."

"How long will I have to wait?" he asked.

"A day, two tops."

He took a deep breath. "Let's hope for a day."

I caught up to the ambulance twenty minutes before we got to Morrison Salvage. Doc Lin was waiting for us at the clubhouse. Looking sour, she leaned against her Mercedes. Mila backed the ambulance up to the back door. I parked the truck and went to talk to Doc Lin.

"Thanks for coming," I said.

She crossed her arms. "Did I have a choice?"

"If you'll accept the consequences you can make any choice you want." I said, opening the ambulance doors.

Her attitude changed when she saw the condition Torch was in. We pulled him out of the ambulance and took him to one of the bedrooms. We put him on the bed and I left Doc Lin and Jill alone with him as I took the gurney back to the ambulance. Hank, Big Ticket, and Cotton rolled up as I was loading it.

Hank pulled up beside me. "Where is he?"

"In the back. Doc Lin and Jill are checking him out."

I followed him to Torch's room.

"Well?" Hank asked. "What d'ya think?"

Doc Lin finished inspecting Torch. "He's got a fever. From what I know of ultranatural physiology he should have healed by now. He's really not doing well. He should be in a hospital."

"Unfortunately, that's not an option," I said. "Just do your best."

She snapped the latex gloves off her hands and tossed them into the trash. "I don't need you to tell me how to do my job."

It's the first time she'd snapped at me. I wasn't going to make a big deal about it. She was probably upset about everything that happened with her husband. I wasn't sure she made up her mind if she was still going to pursue working with the ultranatural community. We needed her and she came, that was enough for now.

"Fair enough," I said. "Do you need Jill for anything?"

"I'm fine."

I opened the door and held it. "Jill," I said. "It's time we had a chat."

I led her into another room and closed the door. She stood on the far side of the room while I stood in front of the door.

"Listen, I'm not gonna lie to you, you're in a bad spot. I'm sure you don't know anything about number thirty-seven but he's a member of the Tortured Occult Motorcycle Club. The leader's son. I go back with Hank and the club a long time, since its inception. All this is to say, I have some pull. I'm sure Hank will want to talk to you and if you get out of here in one piece or not depends on how you speak to him so keep that in mind. I'll do what I can for you and in return, I need to know only one thing. Where is Holt?"

Jill shrugged. "I don't know who Holt is. They have numbers, not names. What did he look like?"

I hadn't taken any pictures of Holt. We weren't the kind of guys that stood around taking selfies. Hell, I just learned what a selfie was.

"He's a Doberman. Seven feet tall with black fur."

"Ah," Jill said. "I saw him. He wasn't like the others. I don't know what but there was something special about him. He was only at the facility for about a day. Dr. Tsukimora took him from the facility about an hour before you showed up."

"Took him where?"

"I heard him mention the Nacoochee Mound to his guards. I don't know what it is though."

I headed for the door. "I do."

A crash and yelling erupted from the bar.

"Come on, something's up," I said.

Jill followed me into the hallway. We ran into Mila and Atticus.

"What's she doing here?" Atticus asked.

I could feel the temperature start to rise.

Jill backed down the hallway away from him.

"What was the noise?" I asked, moving to the bar.

Just as I put my hand on the door it crashed in on me, throwing me against the wall and knocking me to the ground. A tar cat stood in the hallway. It was the size of a Saint Bernard. Its body glistened and churned. Jill ran out the back when she saw it.

If it had jumped on me there would have been nothing I could've done to defend myself. It was looking at Mila and Atticus. It charged them before I could get to my feet. Mila pushed Atticus down the hall. There was no chance they could outrun it and, in the confines of the hallway, Mila couldn't outmaneuver it either. The tar cat charged. It leapt for Mila. She dropped to the floor avoiding it. It collided with Atticus instead.

Flames erupted, engulfing the end of the hallway. I raised a hand to shield my eyes from the heat. I couldn't see any trace of Atticus or Mila. I got to my feet.

I burst through the first door on my right and almost ran into Doc Lin.

"What's happening?" she asked.

"The clubhouse is on fire, I'll get Torch, you get out now."

She disappeared into the hallway.

Torch tried to push me away as I bent down to pick him up. "Just leave me here," he said. "Save yourself."

"We're not going over this again," I said, pushing his hand out of the way and hoisting him up.

The flames had already made it halfway down the hall by the time I got Torch out of the room. In the bar one of the Tortured Occult, I couldn't tell who, writhed on the floor, covered in tar. Most of the patrons had already made a beeline for the exit. Hank and Big Ticket were standing by helplessly watching the tar suffocate their brother.

Hank yelled, "What the fuck's going on?"

"Fire," I said. "Get Torch out."

Hank took him from me and headed for the exit. No sooner had I spoken than the tar assumed the shape of a cat, revealing Cotton gasping for breath on the floor. The cat prowled toward me. Big Ticket scooped Cotton off the floor.

"Fire extinguishers?" I shouted.

Big Ticket pulled Cotton's arm over his shoulder. "Behind the bar."

"Get out," I shouted. "I'm right behind you."

I backed away from the tar cat. I didn't know if a fire extinguisher would do any good against it, I doubted it. I didn't bother to draw my blade. It wasn't going to do any good. I was back to the problem I had at Eddy's trailer; How do you fight a liquid?

I was surprised the tar cat hadn't attacked. It prowled towards me as if it was trying to back me into a corner. I'd decided to make a run for it when the door to the back burst open, dumping flames into the bar. The tar cat was immediately engulfed. It writhed in on itself as it caught fire. The new fuel source made the bar catch that much faster. I could feel my whiskers singeing from the heat. I jumped over the bar, landing hard on the floor.

While it only took a few seconds to find the fire extinguishers, I realized that there was an exorbitant amount of high proof alcohol lining the wall behind me. With the amount of heat coming over the top of the bar, it wouldn't be long before the booze went up as well. I'd jumped out of the frying pan and into the fire.

"Obie," a voice said from the flames.

I didn't recognize it. I peeked over the bar. I had to squint to see Atticus standing in the middle of the room. It wasn't that he was on fire, it's as if he was fire itself.

He took a step toward me. "You should've taken me back."

I pulled the pin on a fire extinguisher. I gave him a blast. He roared like an inferno and fell back, disappearing into a white cloud. I emptied the entire can into the room. It didn't put out the flames, but did push them back. I coughed from the smoke. I put my head to the floor and took a deep breath. I could hold my breath for about ten minutes. It should be more than enough to get out, if the fire didn't get me first.

Big Ticket came through the door to the changing room. "Come on, Obie, this place is coming down."

He didn't realize there was a werewolf made of fire standing in the room until Atticus turned toward him. He strode forward leaving flaming footprints on the wood floor. The fire department would be here soon. If they found Atticus, a lot of fire fighters would die. Then again they were probably better equipped to fight him than I was. Either way, the survivors would become aware that the world is a little more diverse than they thought. I had to take care of him quick.

I pulled my blade and jumped over the bar. Atticus's flaming figure was standing in the doorway to the changing room which was now engulfed. It was my only way out. I charged into the heat, slashing into his back. My blade passed through the center of his body with little resistance. It didn't seem to slow him down one bit. He spun around swinging a flaming arm at me. I ducked under it, barely avoiding the strike. The smell of singed fur filled my nose. I dove away and rolled to a table. There were some unfinished drinks on top. I picked them up one by one and hurled them at Atticus. I didn't hit with all of them but the ones that did just evaporated like a drop of water on a hot skillet. I threw a chair at him and it went through his body, crashing to the floor, engulfed in flames.

Atticus raised his arms over his head and brought them crashing down on me. I dove under the table. As he hit the table flames poured over the sides. I closed my eyes tight to protect them from the heat. It seemed like the whole world was on fire. I dove out from under the table and got to my feet in time to see Atticus spinning with an arm extended. The result was a wave of flame sweeping in my direction. I rolled over the bar, falling onto the floor as the wave crashed into it sending flames and broken glasses raining down on me.

I pulled a zip tie from my pocket. Grabbing the other extinguisher, I pulled the pin and zip tied the handle. I was granted an immediate reprieve from the heat and I was grateful to have it. I didn't have long before it would run out but it gave me a few seconds to come up with another plan. I tossed the extinguisher over the bar like an anti-fire grenade, knocking the soda gun off its hook.

The nozzle of the soda gun fell from the bar into my lap. Atticus said that water had put the flame out the first time he ignited. If I could get him back into his normal physical form, he would be easy to deal with.

I jumped up, pointed the soda gun at Atticus, and pushed a button. I expected the kind of powered stream from a carbonated water dispenser you see on The Three Stooges. What I got was a flaccid stream that went about a foot forward on the bar.

Atticus sent a wave of flame, engulfing the arm holding the soda gun. I dropped it and fell back behind the bar clutching my charred appendage to my chest. It hurt too much to scream and if I had I would have lost all my air. I figured that was it for me. If it was just me in a burning building, I could make it out. With Atticus between me and the door there was nothing I could do.

If I'd had my druthers, I would have died of smoke inhalation. Burning alive was gonna be a bitch, and considering how fast I healed, it would take much longer than a human. That was a bad way to go, but that's the life of a Keeper. We don't get happy endings.

Bottles of liquor exploded, raining down glass and fire. I couldn't avoid it, I had nowhere to go. I thought about exhaling and getting a big breath of smoke. I could put my blade through my chest and at least be unconscious for the inevitable. I pulled my blade and lined it up with the tip over my heart. Just one strong pull, and it would all be over.

A new commotion in the room. The roar of the fire transitioned into a scream of agony. Water splashed over the bar, accompanied by the sound of a fire being quenched. Steam clouds rolled. I peeked out. Fire fighters stood in the doorway to the changing room. They held a large hose that sprayed a steady stream of water into Atticus. I couldn't let them see me in krasis so I changed back to my human form, but kept my blade handy.

It wasn't enough to put him out, but where the water hit he phased back into physical form. He reignited when the stream moved away. I waited until the water hit him again and swung for the fences. I couldn't tell where I hit him but the blade bit into something solid. By the third hit there was no trace of him. I ran through the steam and smoke to make my escape.

CHAPTER · 31

OUTSIDE THE CLUBHOUSE, I exhaled the breath I had been holding and took in fresh air through clenched teeth. My left arm was missing skin in some places, was black in others. It was a mess and hurt like hell to boot.

A fireman carrying an oxygen tank ran up to me. He stopped in his tracks when he saw my arm. Then he looked at my blade and up to my grimacing face.

"Thanks," I said. "I'm alright."

The fireman held his hands up, making it clear he wasn't going to argue. The fire chief was talking to Hank by one of the fire trucks on the scene.

The chief cut the conversation short. "Get everybody out," he yelled. "We've got ammunition inside. Get everybody down to the road."

I slid into the ambulance's driver seat. I tossed my blade on the passenger seat, rested my charred left arm in my lap, and cranked the engine. I moved the ambulance to a safe distance, put it in park, and closed my eyes. I sat and breathed, needing a few minutes for the pain to subside. A tap on my window. I opened my eyes to see Hank. I reached over with my right hand to lower the window.

"Jill ran off."

I sighed. "Just let her go. It's not like she can expose the clubhouse now."

"You alright?" Hank asked.

I nodded. "I will be. Just need to sit for a few minutes and then I'm going after Holt. Jill gave me a lead before everything went to shit."

"Where's Mila?" He asked.

I shook my head. "She was in the hallway where the fire started. I don't think she made it out."

"You need help with Holt?"

I shifted to try and find a position that didn't hurt. "You should stay here and deal with the clubhouse. I'll handle it."

"Alright," he said patting a hand on the door. "Go get him."

It still hurt like hell, but I needed to get on the road. I threw the ambulance in drive and headed north to the Nacoochee Indian Mound.

I arrived just after sundown. The mound was in the middle of a field flanked on two sides by roads with forest in the back. A wire fence around the field and another at the base of the mound kept out the public. It was little more than a large earthen mound constructed by indigenous people long before my time. A gazebo had been built on the top. I couldn't make out anyone on top of the mound or in the gazebo, it was too dark, but that didn't mean they weren't there. I needed a stealthy approach and an ambulance wasn't the most discreet vehicle.

I drove past the mound and pulled off on the side of the road where the ambulance would be obscured by the forest. I checked out my arm. It still looked like hell but I could move it again. I grabbed my blade from the passenger seat and walked into the woods to make the change to krasis. Securing the blade in its sheath, I crept up close enough to the tree line to get a look at the mound. I sat for a few minutes and watched. I didn't see any movement or hear any noise coming from the mound. I took off my clothes, took the form of an otter, and headed for the mound.

I had to maneuver a field of cows and cowpies. Halfway through the field the wind shifted and I got a whiff of humans. There were a few dark figures on the top of the mound silhouetted against the night sky. Getting under the fence was easy. Getting to the top would prove more difficult.

"There's something down there," a woman said.

I crouched low and still.

It was quiet for a few seconds before a man answered. "I don't see anything."

"Something small, it ducked into the grass at the bottom of the hill."

"We're almost done," the man said. "Shoot anything that moves."

I poked my head up until I could see through the grass. Two figures were looking down in my direction. Rifle barrels stuck out from their sides. The little bit of light from passing cars reflected off something on their faces—night vision goggles. This was going to get hairy. I heard a *pfft pfft*. Something whizzed past me. It took me a second to realize what was happening. They were using silencers. I ducked back into the grass. Cows behind me trotted farther away.

There was no way up without taking fire, not after I was spotted. Maybe I should have taken Hank up on his offer for help. I would just have to make a run for it.

Someone started reciting an incantation in the gazebo. I didn't know the spell but I recognized the voice, I just couldn't place it.

"Obie." Thera was suddenly standing beside me. "Stop this now. I won't be contained again."

"What do you mean again?" I said in otter squeaks.

"What the fuck is that?" the man on top of the mound asked.

"It's like before, when I was trapped in Holt," she said. "Stop it now."

"I have to find a way to get up there safely," I said. "If you could give me a lightning strike just over there it would blind them and I—"

"You're out of favors and time. Take your real form and go now," Thera commanded.

"Look, if I go now I'll—"

Thera put a finger to my forehead and forced my body into krasis. The shooting started almost immediately. I took a bullet in the leg and one in the shoulder before I could get moving. I did my best to be hard to hit but there was no cover available and moving uphill slowed me down. Not as much as the bullets, mind you, but it was all working against me. I made it halfway up the hill before I took a shot to the gut then another to the chest before everything went black.

I woke with a face full of grass. My body ached in the many places I'd been shot. I picked my head up and looked around. I had been carried up to the top of the mound, just outside the gazebo.

"He's waking up," the man said.

"If he makes any sudden moves, shoot him again," the familiar voice said. "Obie, please just stay still. This is only going to take a few minutes more."

Inside the gazebo Holt was laid out on the floor in a circle, just like the time when Petra had captured him in the apartment building. A man knelt over him, a man I knew. I couldn't believe what I was seeing.

"Travis? Is that you?"

He smiled at me. "You don't recognize me? I can't say I blame you. I'm not wearing rags and speaking like some backwoods hick. Let me introduce myself again, Travis Tsukimora. Nice to meet you for real."

"You're a real son of a bitch."

"Don't be like that," Travis said. "You're not really mad at me, you're mad at yourself for not figuring it out."

"No, I'm mad at you."

"I have to admit, I like you, Obie. I thought I was going to have to use you for this, but you got a new apprentice. I have to say I'm glad."

I got slowly on my knees. "Use me anyway. Let Holt go."

"I'm not going to do that."

"Why the hell not? Why do you care?"

Travis put a small box on the ground beside Holt and opened it. "You pretended to drink the water."

"What the hell are you talking about?"

Travis laughed and ran a hand over his head. "When you came to see me a couple days ago. I thought you figured it out! You actually caught me alone. I thought I was in real trouble but I threw on the overalls and donned the hick talk and you were clueless. You even said something about how the shirt didn't match." Travis shook his head and walked around to the other side of the circle. "I brought you water in the first glass I could find. I don't even use that one, I have clean ones downstairs. That came with the house."

"Is there a point to all this?"

"I have cameras all over the property. I saw you pour out some of the water and press it to your lip. You did that to protect my feelings, Obie. My fucking feelings! Jesus! Who acts like that?"

"So, you didn't use me because I was nice to you?"

Travis shrugged. "Long and short of it, yes. The world's in short supply of good people and you're good people. I'd feel bad doing this to you. Don't get me wrong, I'd still do it if I didn't have another option, but I do, so no problem."

I looked over my shoulder. The two guards pointed rifles at me. "Yes, problem. What's the point of all this anyway, to kill Thera?"

"I don't think it's possible to kill Thera." Travis chuckled. "It's nothing so devious. I'm part of an organization whose purpose is to find a way to practice magic without dust."

I sighed. "You can't practice magic without dust. It's impossible. People have tried."

"Harlan found a way to do it, although it didn't end well for him."

"How do you even know about that?" I asked.

"I know a lot of things," he said. "He made a deal with the devil, so to speak, not what I had in mind. Have you heard of ley lines?" He didn't wait for me to answer. "They're veins of magical energy running through the earth. The problem is, they are inaccessible. If we can tap into those lines, we can practice magic without dust. Do you realize what that means? No more hunting. Your friends won't have to look over their shoulders anymore."

"Don't pretend you're doing this as a kindness," I spat. "How many of my friends have you killed trying to make this happen?"

"Many I'm afraid and I'm sorry about that. Let's cut the bullshit, Obie. People like to pretend that the ends don't justify the means, but they do. The winners write history and when it's all said and done, no one cares how progress is made. Sure, people will piss and moan for a bit and then they forget."

"I won't forget," I said.

Travis pulled a knife in the shape of a talon out of the box. "I know you won't, Obie. When this is all over, if you want to come after me . . . Well, let's just say I expect it. You'll have a hard time finding me though. I don't plan to stick around when this is done."

"Time's on my side," I said. "I can invest as many years as it takes to find you."

"That's true, you can. But I think you won't. I'm putting money down that when this is all over you won't come after me at all."

"I'll take that bet," I said.

Travis held up the knife and knelt beside Holt. "I suspect when this is all said and done you won't be a Keeper anymore, just a normal shifter. If I'm right, that means you won't be silver immune. I told you I like you and I meant it. I don't expect you to sit there and watch but if they shoot you with those silver bullets it will probably kill you in a few minutes." He reached inside his jacket and pulled out a revolver. "These are just lead." He pointed the gun at me and pulled the trigger.

WHEN I WOKE, IT was still dark. The ground was soft from blood. Headshots were the worst. My head felt like a smashed watermelon. I put a hand to my temple. It was just Holt and I alone on the mount. Travis and his lackies had split while I was unconscious.

I rubbed my eyes and got to my feet. "Holt, you awake yet?"

He was lying on his back in the middle of a circle drawn on the ground. Half empty crates of dust had been left around him. His forearms had long cuts running from his wrists to the crook of his elbow. I didn't know how long I had been out, but Holt should have healed by now. I held my hand over his arm and channeled energy into him—at least I tried to. The energy flowed over him instead of healing his cuts. I touched his arm. He was cold. I watched the cuts on his arm for any sign they were healing.

After a couple minutes I fell back into a seated position. "I'm sorry, Holt."

CHAPTER·32

I LOADED HOLT'S BODY in the ambulance and took him home. I made some calls and got to work building a funeral pyre. I dug a pit and collected all the firewood I had on hand. I'd never built a funeral pyre before and I wasn't sure exactly how large it should be. I figured too large was better than too small and piled the wood wide and high. It took me all morning. I kept checking periodically throughout the day to see if he had miraculously started healing. He hadn't. I put his body on the pyre, placing his arms by his sides to hide the cuts.

When I was done I sat in front of the pyre, staring at my failure. Mila had lived through the fire but wasn't in good shape. When Atticus ignited, it killed the tar cat almost instantly. Unfortunately, Mila had been covered in burning tar. She made it out the back and collapsed between some cars in the junkyard. The T.O. had found her in the morning.

I'd arranged for her to stay with my friend Livy while she healed. I'd known Livy most of my life. It was a different kind of magic that had kept her alive. Her home was secluded in the woods. A perfect spot for a recovering Keeper to stay out of sight.

I heard a car pull up to the house. A few minutes later someone walked up behind me. I didn't want to talk to anyone. I knew I was about to be on the receiving end of a steady stream of pity.

"You're gonna have to help me sit," Livy said. "I don't get up and down as easy as I used to."

I held out a hand. She eased down beside me. She was my oldest friend and the only person that I could tolerate right now.

We sat quietly for a few minutes before she spoke. "What's the matter, hun?"

"Maybe it's my dead friend up there," I said, holding a hand out to the pyre. "That's a stupid question."

Livy shifted her weight from side to side. "I swannie," she mumbled to herself.

That may not seem like a lot but for Livy that was as close to cursing as she got. I'd hurt her feelings and now I felt like a dick.

I sighed. "Look, I'm sorry. This has been rough on me."

"I've buried all my family and most of my friends," she said, putting a hand on my knee. "It will be my turn soon and if I'm being honest, I'm ready. It's hard being old. You hurt all the time. I know that you've lost a lot of people, too, and I know that you're taking this one hard but you still have people that care about you. You don't have to do this alone."

"For the last time, we're the same age," I said.

Livy patted my knee with her wrinkled hand. "We're the same age, but you aren't old."

She was right of course. I hadn't experienced the past two hundred years the same way she had. I'd never know what it was to grow old, at least I thought. Travis's words stuck in my mind: *just a normal shifter*. If he was right, the clock could have just started for me. I'd watched Livy grow old and feeble. Gray hair, wrinkled face, arthritic hands . . . could that be me? I found the idea strangely comforting.

"What I was saying was that you've got a lot of people here for you," she continued. "I expect you to be upset, I just don't want you to think you have to go through this alone."

I sighed. "I hear you and I appreciate it. This really got to me because it didn't have to happen. I could have saved him but I was prevented from doing it . . . twice."

"I'm not one to tell someone how to feel. Go ahead and be angry if you need to," she said. "Just keep lookin' forward."

Our friends began showing up in the evening. Mila decided to wait in the house until everyone had left, I didn't blame her. The T.O. was first to arrive. They rolled in on their motorcycles followed by the van. I went up to greet them as they were taking a wheelchair out of the back of the van. They took it to the passenger side and helped Torch into it. He looked like hell.

Hank was the first to greet me. "Can we do anything to help?"

"There's some chairs in the barn if you could set them out for folks," I said. "And . . . don't mind the bodies and junk. I haven't had a chance to pick up."

I hadn't had a chance to dispose of the bodies and equipment we'd brought back from Eirene.

He grinned. "Sure."

I tipped my head toward Torch. "How's he doing?"

"His body's healing fast, faster than I expected to be honest, but he's not doing well," Hank said. "We'll get those chairs for you."

Queen Isabelle came next with Yarwor, Hob, and a procession of elves. I thanked them one by one but noticed Hob had stayed back waiting to talk to me last. I shook hands and gave them all sad smiles. When the procession had finally passed, Hob came up to me.

"Something is different," he said.

"What are we talking about?"

He raised a hand and snapped his fingers leaving his thumb pointing up. On the tip of his thumb a flame the size of a candle burned. He didn't have any dust, at least none I could see. Travis had said his mission was to have magic without the restriction of dust . . . Could his plan have worked?

I cocked my head. "How'd you do that?"

"It is the same process but without dust. I can feel an energy move through *mine* body," he said.

I wondered if it was the same way I felt the energy move when I healed people. I had no way to know.

"I have a lot to tell you. I'll come up tomorrow and we'll see if we can't figure it out," I said.

Holt had only been in north Georgia for about six months but he had a good turnout; the Tortured Occult, Hambone, and more ultras than I could shake a stick at. When everyone had paid their respects, I lit the pyre. We all stood around watching it burn and listening to stories about Holt. He'd made friends with more of these people than I'd realized. He was a goofball and kind of a screw up, but he was kind and loyal and brave. They all loved him for it, and so did I. He'd made a big impact in such a short time and found a home and a family here.

By the time the pyre had burned down to embers the only ones left were Keepers. Mila came out of the house and joined us. Even in the dim light of the fire I could see the damage that had been done to her body. It was gruesome.

Cearbhall had come up from Jekyll. They were the only two Keepers I knew well but all Keepers shared a bond of brotherhood that made them instant family. I'd filled them in on what happened earlier. We sat quietly for a while, no one wanting to break the silence. The orange glow of the embers lit our faces, accentuating our connectedness to Holt and each other.

Babatunde, a hyena from Africa who'd moved to Virginia a few years back, was the first to speak. "So, what are we going to do about Thera?"

"What's there to do?" Cearbhall asked. "We don't even know what happened to her."

Drool drizzled out of a hole in Mila's cheek and onto some exposed bone in her arm as she spoke. "Obie, what do you think happened."

I tapped my fingers on my leg. "Well, I'm no expert. Travis said he linked or connected Holt to Thera. I think that when he . . . cut Holt that it sort of cut Thera as well. He wanted to open the ley lines, flood the world with magic. He said the ley lines were like magical veins running through the earth. He opened Holt's veins and spilled his blood, by extension he cut Thera and spilled hers. I think it worked. Hob can do at least basic magic without dust now. He showed me earlier."

"So, Thera's injured then," Roscoe said. He was a werewolf from Louisiana.

"It stands to reason," Cearbhall said. "But again, what are we going to do about it? How do you heal the Earth Mother?"

"Travis said he was part of an organization that had been working on opening the ley lines," I said.

Roscoe sounded excited. "Then they would know best how to reverse what he did."

"Sure," I said. "If we can find them. I may not have his real name. It turns out I didn't know him at all."

"It might be worth looking into," Babatunde said.

"We need to talk about if we want to put things back the way they were," Mila said.

"Why the hell wouldn't we?" Roscoe said.

Mila eased back in the wheelchair she was using while her body recovered. "Thera doesn't care about us. I didn't realize the extent of it until I met Eirene. We're tools to Thera. Expendable. I used to think that's the way her kind was but it's not true. She's cold and self-absorbed."

Roscoe looked angry. "You shouldn't talk about her like that."

"No, I haven't been *able* to talk about her like that," Mila said. "It was a crime to even think things like that before now. I'm free for the first time and I'm not feeling motivated to go back. We should be asking ourselves if Thera deserves our loyalty."

"She has mine," Roscoe said. "And you might want to think about what she'll do when she comes back. What if we don't do anything and she wakes up in a month. Where will you be then?"

Babatunde nodded. "That's a good point. We don't even know how permanent this is."

Cearbhall sighed. "How long have you been doing this, Roscoe?"

"I became a Keeper in 1934."

Cearbhall nodded. "You're still a puppy. I've been doing this longer than anyone here. I remember the Roman invasion in Ireland. I've dedicated over two millennium to Thera's service. I've lost countless friends and an eye in the process. I'm tired."

"I can't believe what I'm hearing!" Roscoe shouted. "We owe our lives to her. I don't care what any of you say. I'm going to do everything in my power to restore Thera. I feel sorry for any of you that are on the wrong side of things when she's back. I guess it's just me and Obie. Right, Obie?"

Everyone looked at me. "Holt should still be alive. When I tried to save him the other night Thera intervened, sent me on another job. Then when I had found him she forced a change on me that got me shot and captured. I don't know if I would have been able to save him . . . I do know I would have at least had a chance. Cearbhall was a better father to me than I deserved. He taught me everything I know. I've seen the toll first hand being a Keeper's taken on him. I also think of Walasi buried in a hillside alone like trash thrown out on the side of the road. There's no future in service to Thera, only pain and misery." I took a deep breath. "I've been giving this a lot of thought. No one can tell another what to do. If you want to try and save Thera then good luck to you. I won't be helping."

Roscoe stood. "You're all a bunch of cowards. If you aren't going to do the right thing then there's nothing else to discuss."

He stormed away into the night. I didn't blame him for his reaction. I'd been gung-ho in my younger days too. It was easier back then, everything was black and white. Whatever Thera said was right. Do what you're told and don't ask questions. I hadn't felt that way in a long time.

"What about Travis?" Babatunde asked.

"We can do something about Travis, if we can find him," I said. "I'll put feelers out. He's out there somewhere, it's a matter of time before he turns up. When he does, I'll handle it."

CHAPTER·33

HANK'S HOUSE WAS a single-story brick ranch tucked away in the woods. I pulled up a little before noon. I got out to find Hank's cupita, Marge, working in her garden. She stood when she heard the truck coming. I gave her a wave as I got out of the truck and got one back. On the way to the front door I saw two young black bears peeking out at me from behind a pickup. They were Hank's two youngest, Joel and Adaline. I pretended not to notice them as I walked to the door.

When I had just gotten past them they charged. Joel, the younger of the two, went for my legs while Adaline jumped on my back. Joel wrapped around my right leg, which let me brace enough to not be knocked over.

I thrashed around in feigned panic and shouted, "Oh no! I'm being attacked by vicious bears!"

Hank came out of the house. "Get off him. You're supposed to be helping your mother in the garden."

Adaline jumped off my back and ran off in the opposite direction of the garden. I looked down at Joel who still had my leg in his mouth. He looked up at me.

Hank said, "Spit him out already. You've got to stop doing this to every person that comes over."

Joel ran off after his sister.

"Those kids'll be the death of me. Just about gave the mailman a heart attack last week. I told Marge to have her Amazon orders sent to the shop from now on," Hank said, shaking his head. "So, what can I do for ya?"

"I came for Torch. I thought of a way we might be able to get him some legs. I don't know if it will work, but I was on the phone with Hob this morning and he thinks it's worth a shot."

"You can talk to him . . . see if you can convince him," Hank said.

"You don't think he'd go for it?"

Hank put his hands on his hips. "If I'm being honest, I barely recognize him. Torch didn't come back. We got a shell of the person he was. But go try."

I walked past him into the house. I found Torch in the living room, staring at a blank television.

"Hey, Torch, I'm gonna cut to the chase here. I think I found a way to get you a new arm and legs. I came over to see if it's something you're interested in."

He was quiet for a few seconds. "Like prosthetics? Hunks of plastic that don't do anything but make me look more normal?"

I sat on a chair across from him. "Kinda, but fully functional limbs, and no plastic."

"How?"

"Magic," I said. "Hob thinks we can do it."

"There's no dust, or at least not enough."

"We don't need it anymore." I leaned forward to emphasize the point. "After everything that's happened I think we could both use a win. I don't want to see you like this and I know you don't want to be like this. What d'ya say?"

He looked at me for the first time. "Fully functional?"

"That's the plan."

"Then get that damn chair and let's go." He pointed to the wheelchair folded up in the corner.

For the first time since I found him, I saw the old fighting spark in his eye.

TO MEET HOB, I first had to go to the Southern Outpost. I pulled up the small winding road to the checkpoint and was waved through. I didn't have time to park before Meghan met us. She was wearing her green and khaki uniform and had her blond hair pulled back. I rolled down the window as she approached.

"We have a little drive ahead of us," she said, eyeballing Torch in the passenger seat. "Just follow me."

I gave her a nod and turned the truck around. She got in one of the black trucks parked by the checkpoint. I followed her deep into the Elven Nation. After many twists and turns we finally turned onto a well maintained gravel road with a checkpoint at the end of it. It reminded me of the checkpoint at the southern outpost except this one had two buildings and an unknown number of guards protecting it. The barricade was lowered as soon as our trucks were in sight. We didn't even have to slow down; Meg just gave them a little wave out the window as we passed.

We pulled up to an enormous house. It was constructed with large wood beams and windows. I'd never been big on architecture, but I can honestly say this building was beautiful. There was a fountain out front that wasn't on. The grass looked freshly mowed. I could see a few other buildings around the property. The forest had grown up close, giving them heavy shade and obscuring my view. The whole place had an air of reclamation.

We pulled around the fountain and parked. In the center of the fountain an elven woman poured water out of a large jug, at least she would have been pouring if the fountain was working. She had the typical delicate and slender elven features. She wore a long flowing robe and had flowers in her hair. Moss had grown over parts of the fountain. A few inches of stagnant water sat inside.

"This way," Queen Isabelle called.

I realized I had been lost in a kind of daydream. I smiled and got out of the truck. I grabbed the wheelchair out of the back and helped Torch into it. There wasn't a ramp up the stairs to where Isabelle was standing so I hauled Torch up backward. I tried not to jar him too much as the chair rolled from step to step.

When we made it to the top, Isabelle was standing with a servant by the front door. He was around five feet tall, wearing a gray suit and tie. He looked like a butler.

"Obie, this is Bertram," Isabelle said, holding a hand out to the man. "Bertram, this is Obie and Torch. They're friends."

Bertram bowed slightly and gave us a nod. "A pleasure, gentlemen."

"Bertram is in charge of the palace and grounds," Isabelle said. "Hob is waiting for you in the east wing; Bertram will take you to him. If you'll excuse me, I have some business to attend to."

"Thanks," I said.

Bertram bowed as Isabelle passed. When she had disappeared, he turned to us. "This way please."

We followed Bertram down a hallway with double doors at the end. Each door had a carving of an oak tree inside a circle. He opened one of the doors and stood aside for us to enter. On the other side was another hallway. I assumed this was the east wing. We followed him to the library. The walls were lined with bookshelves, neatly filled with old books. There was one section of the library where the shelves were bare. Crates sat on the floor in front of the empty shelves. A fireplace was built into the wall. There was a table and a pair of plush chairs in front of it.

Hob sat on the floor with the crates. I could see they were full of books, but couldn't tell if he was boxing them up or putting them on the shelves.

He stood to greet us. "It is good to see you both. *Willkommen.*"

"What is this place?" I asked, looking around the room.

"It is a library," Hob said without a hint of sarcasm.

"No, I mean the whole palace," I said, waving my hands around in the air. "Where did it come from?"

"It was built by the first Queen," Hob said. "This is the palace of the Elven Nation. It was not used for many years. Bertram did an excellent job maintaining it, although it was too much work for one person."

I nodded. "He must be happy to see it being used again."

"We all are," Hob said.

"Is everything ready?" I asked.

"Please follow," Hob said.

He led us down the hall into a room that was empty except for a sheet-covered table. The sheet had three lumps under it. Hob pulled back the sheet to reveal an arm and two legs molded out of clay. The day before, I had delivered the clay the golems had been made out of to the Southern Outpost. Hob had an elven ceramist mold it into limbs for Torch. I could see magical circles carved into molds.

"Let's get this done already," Torch said, looking at his spare parts on the table.

Hob held up a hand. "Before we start I must say that once the limbs have been connected if you make the change it will break the spell and they will crumble. You must not change from your human form."

"I'd rather have one form than be a cripple in three," he said.

"Then onto the table please," Hob said.

I helped Torch onto the table. He lay on his back.

Hob lined up the arm and legs where they should go. "You must stay very still. Obie, I will need your help. I tested some magic. While it is true we do not need dust, channeling the energy is strenuous. I feel something on this level is more than I can handle on my own. I need you to heal me while I am casting the spell. My hope is that it will be enough."

"Okay," I said. "I'm ready when you are."

Hob held out his hand over Torch. "Begin."

I poured energy into Hob. I could feel it flowing into him and then be directed away like a leaf being washed downstream. Sweat broke out on Hob's forehead and his hands shook from the strain. The limbs attached to Torch and slowly took on the appearance of flesh. It was easy to see where the limbs connected because while they looked like real flesh, they didn't match his dark pigmentation.

Hob's knees started to buckle from the strain. I thought about stopping but didn't know what would happen to him if I did. When Hob finished the spell, he fell forward, catching himself on the edge of the table. He panted trying to catch his breath.

"You okay?"

Hob nodded. "*Ja,* I need a moment."

Torch raised his arm—his new arm. He flexed his hand and turned it, looking at it.

"Well?" I asked. "What d'ya think?"

"It feels weird." He sat up and moved his feet. "Let's try them out."

He eased off the table. He tested his weight on the legs and then took a step. He instantly lost his balance, falling forward but catching himself with his hands.

I grabbed his arm and helped him up. "Everything okay?"

He grinned at me. "Yeah, just figuring out how they handle."

He practiced walking around the room and by the time Hob caught his breath he was walking on his own without too many balance issues.

CHAPTER 34

"SO THAT'S IT?" Jarod asked. "Torch got his legs, and all the Keepers just went their separate ways?"

I nodded. "Cearbhall's going to visit his homeland. He's never said anything but I know he's missed it. Mila's taking some time to recover. I don't know what she'll do after that."

The last thing on my to-do list was to take Jarod back to Texas. I'd been filling him in along the way. It's not something I'd normally have done but it didn't seem like keeping it all a secret was that important and he knew half the story anyway. Besides, it was a long drive.

"What about you?" I asked. "What's next in Jarod's story?"

"I'm going to focus on my daughter, Hailey. I took that job to try and give her a better life but I've come to realize that being there for her is the best thing I can do. I'm swearing off questionable high paying jobs. I'll probably go back to truck driving until I can save enough to start a business. I think I want to be my own boss. Maybe a vape shop?"

I didn't know what a vape shop was. It would be one of those things I'd normally ask Holt about. He really kept me up to date.

Jarod pointed ahead. "Second house on the right. The blue one."

I pulled up to a nice looking, two-story.

"Thanks for the ride and not, you know, killing me," Jarod said.

"No problem." I chuckled. "One more thing, open the glovebox. There's an envelope for you."

He took out a manila envelope. "What's this?"

"Open it."

He found a stack of cash. "Holy shit, how much money is this?"

"Enough to start a vape shop . . . I think."

"I can't take your money," Jarod said.

"Sure you can, you just hold onto it and get out of the truck. Don't overthink it."

He was about to protest again when an older couple and a young girl walked out of the house.

"Is that Hailey?" I motioned toward the group.

"Yeah," he said.

"What are you sitting here for? Go."

He got out of the truck. Hailey ran and jumped into his arms. I reached into my pocket and pulled out the stack of postcards. *I would like to see you.* I typed a new address in my phone. When the map came up I backed out of the driveway and gave Jarod a wave as I pulled out. I was already halfway to Vegas. In sixteen hours I'd be there. I was looking forward to a fresh start.

www.authorbenmeeks.com/thank-you

Ben is a North Georgia native, and world traveler, who prides himself on using real world experiences to add realism to his fiction. He was a medal winner in a martial arts competition, been in a high speed car chase, had a late night phone call from the Secret Service, who he hung up on, and been shot. When not writing about himself in the third person he is hard at work writing Contemporary Fantasy and Science Fiction.

Made in the USA
Columbia, SC
22 February 2023

12755683R00272